She turned to her friend. God, he was handsome.

His green eyes brooding and intense. His medium-brown hair living in that space between perfectly groomed and purposely messy. The ever-present five-o'clock shadow crawling over his clenched jaw.

"Thank you, Ryan." She needed to quell the thoughts in her head. "This is all so amazing and incredibly thoughtful. I know this fantasy date isn't real, but you went out of your way to make it feel that way, and I appreciate it."

Tessa leaned in to give her friend a kiss on his stubbled cheek, something she'd done a hundred times before over the years. But Ryan turned his head and her lips met his.

It was an accidental kiss.

So why did she lean in? And why didn't Ryan pull back, either?

She parted her lips and Ryan accepted the unspoken invitation. The kiss moved from a sweet, inadvertent, closed-mouth affair to an intense meshing of lips, teeth and tongues. Ryan moved his hands to her back, tugging her closer.

And she wanted more.

They'd gone this far. Had let down the invisible wall between them. There was nothing holding them back now.

* * *

His Until Midnight by Reese Ryan is part of the Texas Cattleman's Club: Bachelor Auction series.

Dear Reader,

His Until Midnight is my first contribution to Harlequin Desire's ongoing Texas Cattleman's Club series, and I'm thrilled to be a part of this beloved fan favorite.

Friends to lovers is one of my favorite romance tropes. So I enjoyed writing about longtime best friends Ryan Bateman and Tessa Noble. The banter between these two crackles with warmth, affection and humor. And when they are finally forced to acknowledge the attraction that's been simmering just below the surface of their friendship for the past ten years, things heat up.

Bring your fan and an icy glass of your favorite beverage, because things are gonna get *hot*.

If you've read the previous installments of Texas Cattleman's Club: Bachelor Auction, in this story we get to the highly anticipated bachelor auction where surprises are in store. And we'll catch up on the plot hatched by sworn enemies Gus Slade and Rose Clayton to keep their grandchildren apart.

After you've read *His Until Midnight*, visit me online at reeseryan.com/desirereaders to discover my Bourbon Brothers and Pleasure Cove series. For news, reader giveaways and more, be sure to join my VIP Readers list.

Until the next adventure,

Reese Ryan

REESE RYAN

———

HIS UNTIL MIDNIGHT

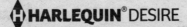
HARLEQUIN® DESIRE

Special thanks and acknowledgment are given to Reese Ryan for her contribution to the Texas Cattleman's Club: Bachelor Auction miniseries.

Recycling programs for this product may not exist in your area.

ISBN-13: 978-1-335-97189-0

His Until Midnight

Copyright © 2018 by Harlequin Books S.A.

Printed in U.S.A.

HARLEQUIN®

™ www.Harlequin.com

Reese Ryan writes sexy, deeply emotional romances full of family drama, surprising secrets and unexpected twists.

Born and raised in the Midwest, Reese has deep Tennessee roots. Every summer, she endured long, hot car trips to family reunions in Memphis via a tiny clown car loaded with cousins.

Connect with Reese at ReeseRyanWrites on Instagram, Twitter and Facebook or at reeseryan.com/desireaders.

Books by Reese Ryan

Harlequin Desire

The Bourbon Brothers
Savannah's Secret
The Billionaire's Legacy

Texas Cattleman's Club: Bachelor Auction
His Until Midnight

Harlequin Kimani Romance

Playing with Desire
Playing with Temptation
Playing with Seduction

To Johnathan Royal, Stephanie Perkins, Jennifer Copeland, Denise Stokes, Sharon Blount, Stephanie Douglas-Quick and all of the amazing readers in the Reese Ryan VIP Readers Lounge on Facebook. Seriously, y'all rock! I appreciate your readership, engagement, enthusiasm and continued support. Thank you to each and every one of you!

To my infinitely patient and ever-insightful editor, Charles Griemsman, thank you for all you do.

* * *

Don't miss a single book in the Texas Cattleman's Club: Bachelor Auction series!

Runaway Temptation
by *USA TODAY* bestselling author Maureen Child

Most Eligible Texan
by *USA TODAY* bestselling author Jules Bennett

Million Dollar Baby
by *USA TODAY* bestselling author Janice Maynard

His Until Midnight
by Reese Ryan

The Rancher's Bargain
by Joanne Rock (available January 2019)

Lone Star Reunion
by Joss Wood (available February 2019)

One

Tessa Noble stared at the configuration of high and low balls scattered on the billiard table.

"I'm completely screwed," she muttered, sizing up her next move. After a particularly bad break and distracted play, she was losing badly.

But how on earth could she be expected to concentrate on billiards when her best friend Ryan Bateman was wearing a fitted performance T-shirt that highlighted every single pectoral muscle and his impressive biceps. He could have, at the very least, worn a shirt that fit, instead of one that was a size too small, as a way to purposely enhance his muscles. And the view when he bent over the table in a pair of broken-in jeans that hugged his firm ass like they were made for it…

How in the hell was she expected to play her best?

"You're not screwed," Ryan said in a deep, husky voice that was as soothing as a warm bath. Three parts sex-in-a-glass and one part confidence out the wazoo.

Tessa's cheeks heated, inexplicably. Like she was a middle schooler giggling over double entendres and sexual innuendo.

"Maybe not, but you'd sure as hell like to be screwed by your best friend over there," Gail Walker whispered in her ear before taking another sip of her beer.

Tessa elbowed her friend in the ribs, and the woman giggled, nearly shooting beer out of her nose.

Gail, always a little too direct, lacked a filter after a second drink.

Tessa walked around the billiard table, pool cue in hand, assessing her options again while her opponent huffed restlessly. Finally, she shook her head and sighed. "You obviously see something I don't, because I don't see a single makeable shot."

Ryan sidled closer, his movements reminiscent of a powerful jungle cat stalking prey. His green eyes gleamed even in the dim light of the bar.

"You're underestimating yourself, Tess," Ryan murmured. "Just shut out all the noise, all the doubts, and focus."

She studied the table again, tugging her lower lip between her teeth, before turning back to him. "Ryan, I clearly don't have a shot."

"Go for the four ball." He nodded toward the purple ball wedged between two of her opponent's balls.

Tessa sucked in a deep breath and gripped the pool cue with one hand. She pressed her other hand to the table, formed a bridge and positioned the stick between her thumb and forefinger, gliding it back and forth.

But the shot just wasn't there.

"I can't make this shot." She turned to look at him. "Maybe you could, but I can't."

"That's because you're too tight, and your stance is all wrong." Ryan studied her for a moment, then placed his hands on either side of her waist and shifted her a few inches. "Now you're lined up with the ball. That should give you a better sight line."

Tessa's eyes drifted closed momentarily as she tried to focus on the four ball, rather than the lingering heat from Ryan's hands. Or his nearness as he hovered over her.

She opened them again and slid the cue back and forth between her fingers, deliberating the position and pace of her shot.

"Wait." Ryan leaned over beside her. He slipped an arm around her waist and gripped the stick a few inches above where she clenched it. He stared straight ahead at the ball, his face inches from hers. "Loosen your grip on the cue. This is a finesse shot, so don't try to muscle it. Just take it easy and smack the cue ball right in the center, and you've got this. Okay?"

"Okay." Tessa nodded, staring at the center of the white ball. She released a long breath, pulled back the cue and hit the cue ball dead in the center, nice and easy.

The cue ball connected with the four ball with a smack. The purple ball rolled toward the corner pocket and slowed, teetering on the edge. But it had just enough momentum to carry it over into the pocket.

"Yes!" Tessa squealed, smacking Ryan's raised palm to give him a high five. "You're amazing. You actually talked me through it."

"You did all the work. I was just your cheering section." He winked in that way that made her tummy flutter.

"Well, thank you." She smiled. "I appreciate it."

"What are best friends for?" He shrugged, picking up his beer and taking a sip from the bottle.

"Thought I was playing Tess," Roy Jensen grumbled. "Nobody said anything about y'all tagteaming me."

"Oh, quit complaining, you old coot." Tessa stared down her opponent. "I always turn a blind eye when you ask for spelling help when we're playing Scrabble."

Roy's cheeks tinged pink, and he mumbled under his breath as Tessa moved around the table, deciding which shot to take next. She moved toward the blue two ball.

"Hey, Ryan." Lana, the way-too-friendly barmaid, sidled up next to him, her chest thrust forward and a smile as wide as the Rio Grande spread across her face. "Thought you might want another beer."

"Why thank you, kindly." Ryan tipped an imaginary hat and returned the grin as he accepted the bottle.

Tessa clenched her jaw, a burning sensation in her chest. She turned to her friend, whispering so neither Lana nor Ryan could hear her.

"Why doesn't she just take his head and smash it between the surgically enhanced boobs her ex-boyfriend gave her as a consolation prize? It'd be a lot easier for both of them."

"Watch it there, girl. You're beginning to sound an awful lot like a jealous girlfriend." Gail could barely contain her grin.

"There's nothing to be jealous of. Ryan and I are just friends. You know that."

"*Best* friends," her friend pointed out, as she studied Ryan flirting with Lana. "But let's face it. You're two insanely attractive people. Are you really going to try and convince me that neither of you has ever considered—"

"We haven't." Tessa took her shot, missing badly. It was a shot she should've hit, even without Ryan's help. But she was too busy eavesdropping on his conversation with Lana.

"Well, for a person who doesn't have any romantic interest in her best friend, you seem particularly interested in whether or not he's flirting with the

big-boobed barmaid." Gail shrugged when Tessa
gave her the stink eye. "What? You know it's true."

Tessa scowled at her friend's words and the fact
that Roy was taking advantage of her distraction.
He easily sank one ball, then another. With no more
striped balls left on the table, Roy had a clear shot
at the eight ball.

He should be able to make that shot blindfolded.

"Well?" Gail prodded her.

"I'm not jealous of Lana. I just think Ryan could
do better. That he *should* do better than to fall for
the calculated ploy of a woman who has dollar signs
in her eyes. Probably angling for butt implants this
time."

Gail giggled. "And why would he want a fake ass
when he was mere inches from the real deal?" She
nodded toward Tessa's behind, a smirk on her face.

Tessa was fully aware that she'd inherited her
generous curves from her mother. She was just as
clear about Ryan Bateman's obliviousness to them.
To him, she was simply one of the guys. But then
again, the comfy jeans and plaid button-down shirts
that filled her closet didn't do much to highlight her
assets.

Hadn't that been the reason she'd chosen such a
utilitarian wardrobe in the first place?

"Dammit!" Roy banged his pool cue on the
wooden floor, drawing their attention to him. He'd
scratched on the eight ball.

Tessa grinned. "I won."

"Because I scratched." Roy's tone made it clear that he felt winning by default was nothing to be proud of.

"A win's a win, Jensen." She wriggled her fingers, her palm open. "Pay up."

"You won? Way to go, Tess. I told you that you had this game in the bag." Ryan, suddenly beside her, wrapped a big, muscular arm around her shoulder and pulled her into a half hug.

"Well, at least one of us believed in me." Tessa counted the four wrinkled five-dollar bills Roy stuffed in her palm begrudgingly.

"Always have, always will." He beamed at her and took another swig of his beer.

Tessa tried to ignore the warmth in her chest that filtered down her spine and fanned into areas she didn't want to acknowledge.

Because they were friends. And friends didn't get all…whatever it was she was feeling…over one another. Not even when they looked and smelled good enough to eat.

Tessa Noble always smelled like citrus and sunshine. Reminded him of warm summer picnics at the lake. Ryan couldn't peel an orange or slice a lemon without thinking of her and smiling.

There was no reason for his arm to still be wrapped around her shoulder other than the sense of comfort he derived from being this close to her.

"Take your hands off my sister, Bateman." Tessa's

brother Tripp's expression was stony as he entered the bar. As if he was about five minutes away from kicking Ryan's ass.

"Tessa just beat your man, Roy, here." Ryan didn't move. Nor did he acknowledge Tripp's veiled threat.

The three of them had been friends forever, though it was Tessa who was his best friend. According to their parents, their friendship was born the moment they first met. Their bond had only gotten stronger over the years. Still, he'd had to assure Tripp on more than one occasion that his relationship with Tess was purely platonic.

Relationships weren't his gift. He'd made peace with that, particularly since the dissolution of his engagement to Sabrina Calhoun little more than a year ago. Tripp had made it clear, in a joking-not-joking manner, that despite their longtime friendship, he'd punch his lights out if Ryan ever hurt his sister.

He couldn't blame the guy. Tess definitely deserved better.

"Way to go, Tess." A wide grin spread across Tripp's face. He gave his sister a fist bump, followed by a simulated explosion.

The Nobles' signature celebratory handshake.

"Thanks, Tripp." Tessa casually stepped away from him.

Ryan drank his beer, captivated by her delectable scent which still lingered in the air around him.

"You look particularly proud of yourself today,

big brother." Tessa raised an eyebrow, her arms folded.

The move inadvertently framed and lifted Tessa's rather impressive breasts. Another feature he tried hard, as her best friend, to not notice. But then again, he was a guy, with guy parts and a guy brain.

Ryan quickly shifted his gaze to Tripp's. "You still pumped about being a bachelor in the Texas Cattleman's Club charity auction?"

Tripp grinned like a prize hog in the county fair, his light brown eyes—identical to his sister's—twinkling merrily. "Alexis Slade says I'll fetch a mint."

"Hmm…" Ryan grinned. "Tess, what do you think your brother here will command on the auction block?"

"Oh, I'd say four maybe even five…dollars." Tessa, Ryan, Gail and Roy laughed hysterically, much to Tripp's chagrin.

Tripp folded his arms over his chest. "I see you all have jokes tonight."

"You know we're just kidding." Ryan, who had called next, picked up a pool cue as Roy gathered the balls and racked them. "After all, I'm the one who suggested you to Alexis."

"And I may never forgive you for creating this monster." Tessa scowled at Ryan playfully.

"My bad, I wasn't thinking." He chuckled.

"What I want to know is why on earth you didn't volunteer yourself?" Gail asked. "You're a moderately good-looking guy, if you like that sort of thing." She laughed.

She was teasing him, not flirting. Though with Gail it was often hard to tell.

Ryan shrugged. "I'm not interested in parading across the stage for a bunch of desperate women to bid on, like I'm a side of beef." He glanced apologetically at his friend, Tripp. "No offense, man."

"None taken." Tripp grinned proudly, poking a thumb into his chest. "This 'side of beef' is chomping at the bit to be taken for a spin by one of the lovely ladies."

Tessa elbowed Ryan in the gut, and an involuntary "oomph" sound escaped. "Watch it, Bateman. We aren't *desperate*. We're civic-minded women whose only interest is the betterment of our community."

There was silence for a beat before Tessa and Gail dissolved into laughter.

Tessa was utterly adorable, giggling like a schoolgirl. The sound—rooted in his earliest memories of her—instantly conjured a smile that began deep down in his gut.

He studied her briefly. Her curly, dark brown hair was pulled into a low ponytail and her smooth, golden brown skin practically glowed. She was wearing her typical winter attire: a long-sleeved plaid shirt, jeans which hid her curvy frame rather than highlighting it, and the newest addition to her ever-growing sneaker collection.

"You're a brave man." Ryan shifted his attention to Tripp as he leaned down and lined his stick up with the cue ball. He drew it back and forth between his forefinger and thumb. "If these two are any indication—" he nodded toward Tess and Gail "—those women at the auction are gonna eat you alive."

"One can only hope." Tripp wriggled his brows and held up his beer, one corner of his mouth curled in a smirk.

Ryan shook his head, then struck the white cue ball hard. He relished the loud cracking sound that indicated a solid break. The cue ball smashed through the triangular formation of colorful balls, and they rolled or spun across the table. A high and a low ball dropped into the pockets.

"Your choice." Ryan nodded toward Tessa.

"Low." Hardly a surprise. Tessa always chose low balls whenever she had first choice. She walked around the table, her sneakers squeaking against the floor, as she sized up her first shot.

"You know I'm only teasing you, Tripp. I think it's pretty brave of you to put yourself out there like that. I'd be mortified by the thought of anyone bidding on me." She leaned over the table, her sights on the blue two ball before glancing up at her brother momentarily. "In fact, I'm proud of you. The money you'll help raise for the Pancreatic Cancer Research Foundation will do a world of good."

She made her shot and sank the ball before lining up for the next one.

"Would you bid on a bachelor?" Ryan leaned against his stick, awaiting his turn.

He realized that Tess was attending the bachelor auction, but the possibility that she'd be bidding on one of them hadn't occurred to him until just now. And the prospect of his best friend going on a date with some guy whose company she'd paid for didn't sit well with him.

The protective instinct that had his hackles up was perfectly natural. He, Tripp and Tessa had had each others' backs since they were kids. They weren't just friends, they were family. Though Tess was less like a little sister and more like a really hot distant cousin, three times removed.

"Of course, I'm bidding on a bachelor." She sank another ball, then paced around the table and shrugged. "That's kind of the point of the entire evening."

"Doesn't mean you have to. After all, not every woman attending will be bidding on a bachelor," Ryan reminded her.

"They will be if they aren't married or engaged," Gail said resolutely, folding her arms and cocking an eyebrow his way. "Why, Ryan Bateman, sounds to me like you're jealous."

"Don't be ridiculous." His cheeks heated as he returned his gaze to the table. "I'm just looking out for my best friend. She shouldn't be pressured to participate in something that makes her feel uncomfortable."

Tessa was sweet, smart, funny, and a hell of a lot of fun to hang out with. But she wasn't the kind of woman he envisioned with a paddle in her hand, bidding on men as if she were purchasing steers at auction.

"Doesn't sound like Tess, to me. That's all I'm saying." He realized he sounded defensive.

"*Good.* It's about time I do something unexpected. I'm too predictable...too boring." Tessa cursed under her breath when she missed her shot.

"Also known as consistent and reliable," Ryan interjected.

Things were good the way they were. He liked that Tessa followed a routine he could count on. His best friend's need for order balanced out his spontaneity.

"I know, but lately I've been feeling... I don't know...stifled. Like I need to take some risks in my personal life. Stop playing it so safe all the time." She sighed in response to his wide-eyed, slack-jawed stare. "Relax, Rye. It's not like I'm paying for a male escort."

"I believe they prefer the term *gigolo*," Gail, always helpful, interjected, then took another sip of her drink.

Ryan narrowed his gaze at Gail, which only made the woman laugh hysterically. He shifted his attention back to Tessa, who'd just missed her shot.

"Who will you be bidding on?"

Tessa shrugged. "I don't know. No one in particular in mind, just yet. The programs go out in a few days. Maybe I'll decide then. Or… I don't know… maybe I'll wait and see who tickles my fancy when I get there."

"Who *tickles your fancy*?" Ryan repeated the words incredulously. His grip on the pool cue tightened.

He didn't like the sound of that at all.

Two

Tessa followed the sound of moaning down the hall and around the corner to her brother's room.

"Tripp? Are you all right?" She tapped lightly on his partially opened bedroom door.

"No!" The word was punctuated by another moan, followed by, "I feel like I'm dying."

Tessa hurried inside his room, her senses quickly assailed by a pungent scent which she followed to his bathroom. He was hugging the porcelain throne and looking a little green.

"Did you go out drinking last night?"

"No. I think it's the tuna sandwich I got from the gas station late last night on my way back in from Dallas."

"How many times have I told you? Gas station food after midnight? No *bueno*." She stood with her hands on her hips, looking down at her brother who looked like he might erupt again at any minute.

Austin Charles Noble III loved food almost as much as he loved his family. And usually he had a stomach like a tank. Impervious to just about anything. So whatever he'd eaten had to have been pretty bad.

"I'm taking you to Urgent Care."

"No, I just want to go to bed. If I can sleep it off for a few hours, I'm sure I'll be fine." He forced a smile, then immediately clutched his belly and cringed. "I'll be good as new for the bachelor auction."

"Shit. The bachelor auction." Tess repeated the words. It was the next night. And as green at the gills as Tripp looked, there was little chance he'd be ready to be paraded on stage in front of a crowd of eager women by then. The way he looked now, he probably wouldn't fetch more than five dollars and a bottle of ipecac at auction.

"Here, let me help you back to bed." She leaned down, allowing her brother to drape his arm around her and get enough leverage to climb to his feet on unsteady legs. Once he was safely in bed again, she gathered the remains of the tainted tuna sandwich, an empty bottle of beer, and a few other items.

She set an empty garbage can with a squirt of soap and about an inch of water beside his bed.

"Use this, if you need to." She indicated the garbage can. "I'm going to get you some ginger ale and some Gatorade. But if you get worse, I'm taking you to the doctor. Mom and Dad wouldn't be too happy with me if I let their baby boy die of food poisoning while they were away on vacation."

"Well, I am Mom's favorite, so..." He offered a weak smile as he invoked the argument they often teased each other about. "And don't worry about the auction, I'll be fine. I'm a warrior, sis. Nothing is going to come between me and—" Suddenly he bolted out of bed, ran to the bathroom and slammed the door behind him.

Tessa shook her head. "You're staying right here in bed today and tomorrow, 'warrior.' I'll get Roy and the guys to take care of the projects that were on your list today. And I'll find a replacement for you in the auction. Alexis will understand."

Tripp mumbled his thanks through the bathroom door, and she set off to take care of everything she had promised him.

Tessa had been nursing her brother back to health and handling her duties at the ranch, as well as some of his. And she'd been trying all day to get in touch with Ryan.

Despite his reluctance to get involved in the auction, he was the most logical choice as Tripp's replacement. She was sure she could convince him it was a worthy cause. Maybe stroke his ego and tell him there would be a feeding frenzy for a hot stud like him.

A statement she planned to make in jest, but that she feared also had a bit of truth to it. Tessa gritted her teeth imagining Lana, and a whole host of other women in town who often flirted with Ryan, bidding on him like he was a prize steer.

Maybe getting Ryan to step in as Tripp's replacement in the auction wasn't such a good idea after all. She paced the floor, scrolling through a list of names of other possible options in her head.

Most of the eligible men that came to mind were already participating, or they'd already turned Alexis and Rachel down, from what Tessa had heard.

She stopped abruptly mid-stride, an idea brewing in her head that made her both excited and feel like she was going to toss her lunch at the same time.

"Do something that scares you every single day." She repeated the words under her breath that she'd recently posted on the wall of her office. It was a quote from Eleanor Roosevelt. Advice she'd promised herself that she would take to heart from here on out.

Tessa glanced at herself in the mirror. Her thick hair was divided into two plaits, and a Stetson was pushed down on her head, her eyes barely visible. She was the textbook definition of Plain Jane. Not because she wasn't attractive, but because she put zero effort into looking like a desirable woman rather than one of the ranch hands.

She sighed, her fingers trembling slightly. There was a good chance that Alexis and Rachel would veto her idea for Tripp's replacement. But at least she would ask.

Tessa pulled her cell phone out of her back pocket and scrolled through her contacts for Alexis Slade's number. Her palms were damp as she initiated the call. Pressing the phone to her ear, she counted the rings, a small part of her hoping that Alexis didn't answer. That would give her time to rethink her rash decision. Maybe save herself some embarrassment when Alexis rejected the idea.

"Hey, Tess. How are you?" Alexis's warm, cheerful voice rang through the line.

"I'm good. Tripp? Not so much. I think he has food poisoning." The words stumbled out of her mouth.

"Oh my God! That's terrible. Poor Tripp. Is he going to be okay?"

"I'm keeping an eye on him, but I'm sure he'll be fine in a few days. I just don't think he's going to recover in time to do the bachelor auction."

"We'll miss having him in the lineup, but of course we understand. His health is the most important thing." The concern was evident in Alexis's voice. "Tell him that we hope he's feeling better soon. And if the auction goes well, maybe we'll do this again next year. I'll save a spot in the lineup for him then."

"Do you have anyone in mind for a replacement?" Tessa paced the floor.

"Not really. We've pretty much tapped out our list of possibilities. Unless you can get Ryan to change his mind?" She sounded hopeful.

"I considered that, and I've been trying to reach him all day. But just now, I came up with another idea." She paused, hoping that Alexis would stop her. Tell her that they didn't need anyone else. When the woman didn't respond, she continued. "I was thinking that I might replace my brother in the lineup." She rushed the words out before she could chicken out. "I know that this is a bachelor auction, not a bachelorette—"

"Yes!" Alexis squealed, as if it were the best idea she'd heard all day. "OMG, I think that's an absolutely fabulous idea. We'll provide something for the fellas, too. Oh, Tessa, this is brilliant. I love it."

"Are you sure? I mean, I like the idea of doing something completely unexpected, but maybe we should see what Rachel thinks." Her heart hammered in her chest.

She'd done something bold, something different, by offering to take Tripp's place. But now, the thought of actually walking that stage and praying to God that someone…anyone…would bid on her was giving her heart palpitations.

"That's a good idea, but I know she's going to agree with me. Hold on."

"Oh, you're calling her now?" Tessa said to the empty room as she paced the floor.

Rachel Kincaid was a marketing genius and an old college friend of Alexis's. She'd come to Royal as a young widow and the mother to an adorable little girl named Ellie. And she'd fallen in love with one of the most eligible bachelors in all of Texas, oil tycoon Matt Galloway.

"Okay, Rachel's on the line," Alexis announced a moment later. "And I brought her up to speed."

"You weren't kidding about doing something unexpected." There was a hint of awe in Rachel's voice. "Good for you, Tess."

"Thanks, Rachel." She swallowed hard. "But do you think it's a good idea? I mean, the programs have already been printed, and no one knows that there's going to be a bachelorette in the auction. What if no one bids on me? I don't want to cause any embarrassment to the club or create negative publicity for the event."

"Honey, the bachelors who aren't in the auction are going to go crazy when they discover there's a beautiful lady to bid on," Rachel said confidently.

"We'll put the word out that there's going to be a big surprise, just for the fellas. I can email everyone on our mailing list. It will only take me a few minutes to put the email together and send it out," Alexis said.

"Y'all are sure we can pull this off?" Tess asked one last time. "I swear I won't be offended if you think we can't. I rather you tell me now than to let me get up there and make a fool of myself."

"It's going to be awesome," Alexis reassured her. "But I'm sensing hesitation. Are you second-guessing your decision? Because you shouldn't. It's a good one."

Tessa grabbed a spoon and the pint of her favorite Neapolitan ice cream hidden in the back of the freezer. She sat at the kitchen island and sighed, rubbing her palm on her jeans again. She shook her head, casting another glance in the mirror. "It's just that… I'm not the glamorous type, that's for sure."

"You're gorgeous, girl. And if you're concerned… hey, why don't we give you a whole beauty make-over for the event?" Rachel said excitedly. "It'll be fun and it gives me another excuse to buy makeup."

"That's a fantastic idea, Rachel!" Alexis chimed in. "Not that you need it," she added. "But maybe it'll make you feel more comfortable."

"Okay, yeah. That sounds great. I'd like that." Tessa nodded, feeling slightly better. "I was gonna take tomorrow off anyway. Give myself plenty of time to get ready. But I'm sure you both have a million things to do. I don't want to distract you from preparing for the auction, just to babysit me."

"Alexis is the queen of organization. She's got everything under control. Plus, we have a terrific crew of volunteers," Rachel piped in. "They won't miss us for a few hours. I promise, everything will be fine."

"Have you considered what date you're offering?"

"Date?" Tessa hadn't thought that far in advance. "I'm not sure. I guess…let me think about that. I'll have an answer for you by tomorrow. Is that all right?"

"That's fine. Just let me know first thing in the morning," Alexis said.

"I'll make a few appointments for the makeover and I'll text you both all the details." Rachel's voice brimmed with excitement.

"Then I guess that's everything," Tessa said, more to herself than her friends. "I'll see you both tomorrow."

She hung up the phone, took a deep breath, and shoveled a spoonful of Neapolitan ice cream into her mouth.

There was no turning back now.

Three

Ryan patted the warm neck of his horse, Phantom, and dismounted, handing the majestic animal off to Ned, one of his ranch hands. He gave the horse's haunches one final pat as the older man led him away to a stall.

Ryan wiped his sweaty forehead with the back of his hand. He was tired, dirty and in desperate need of a shower.

He'd been out on the ranch and the surrounding area since the crack of dawn, looking for several steer that had made their great escape through a break in the fence. While his men repaired the fence, he and another hand tracked down the cattle and drove them back to the ranch.

He'd been in such a hurry to get after the cattle, he'd left his phone at home. Hopefully, his parents hadn't called, worried that he wasn't answering because he'd burned down the whole damn place.

He grumbled to himself, "You nearly burn the barn down as a kid, and they never let you forget it."

Then again, his parents and Tess and Tripp's seemed to be enjoying themselves on their cruise. Their calls had become far less frequent.

Who knows? Maybe both couples would decide it was finally time to retire, give up ranch life, and pass the torch to the next generation. Something he, Tessa and Tripp had been advocating for the past few years. They were ready to take on the responsibility.

When he'd been engaged to Sabrina, his parents had planned to retire to their beach house in Galveston and leave management of the ranch to him. Despite the fact that they hadn't much liked his intended. Not because Sabrina was a bad person. But he and Sabrina were like fire and ice. The moments that were good could be really good. But the moments that weren't had resulted in tense arguments and angry sex.

His mother, in particular, hadn't been convinced Sabrina was the girl for him. She'd been right.

A few months before their wedding, Sabrina had called it off. She just couldn't see herself as a ranch wife. Nor was she willing to sacrifice her well-earned figure to start "popping out babies" to carry on the Bateman name.

He appreciated that she'd had the decency to tell him to his face, well in advance, rather than abandoning him at the altar as Shelby Arthur had done when she'd decided she couldn't marry Jared Goodman.

At least she'd spared him *that* humiliation.

Besides, there was a part of him that realized the truth of what she'd said. Maybe some part of him had always understood that he'd asked her to marry him because it felt like the right thing to do.

He'd been with Sabrina longer than he'd stayed in any relationship. For over a year. So when she'd hinted that she didn't want to waste her time in a relationship that wasn't going anywhere, he'd popped the question.

Neither he nor Sabrina were the type who bought into the fairy tale of romance. They understood that relationships were an exchange. A series of transactions, sustained over time. Which was why he believed they were a good fit. But they'd both ignored an essential point. They were just too different.

He loved everything about ranch life, and Sabrina was a city girl, through and through.

The truth was that he'd been relieved when Sabrina had canceled the wedding. As if he could breathe, nice, deep, easy breaths, for the first time in months. Still, his parents called off their plans to retire.

Maybe this trip would convince them that he and the Bateman Ranch would be just fine without them.

Ryan stretched and groaned. His muscles, taut from riding in the saddle a good portion of the day, protested as he made his way across the yard toward the house.

Helene Dennis, their longtime house manager, threw open the door and greeted him. "There you are. You look an unholy mess. Take off those boots and don't get my kitchen floor all dirty. I just mopped."

Sometimes he wondered if Helene worked for him or if he worked for her. Still, he loved the older woman. She was family.

"All right, all right." He toed off his boots and kicked them in the corner, patting his arms and legs to dislodge any dust from his clothing before entering the house. "Just don't shoot."

Helene playfully punched his arm. "Were you able to round up all of the animals that got loose?"

"Every one of them." Yawning, he kneaded a stubborn kink in his back. "Fence is fixed, too."

"Good. Dinner will be ready in about a half an hour. Go ahead and hop in the shower. Oh, and call Tess when you get the chance."

"Why?" His chest tightened. "Everything okay over at the Noble Spur?"

"Don't worry." She gave him a knowing smile that made his cheeks fill with heat. "She's fine, but her brother is ill. Tess is pretty sure it's food poisoning. She's been trying to reach you all day."

"I was in such a hurry to get out of here this morning, I forgot my phone."

"I know." She chuckled softly "I found it in the covers when I made your bed this morning. It's on your nightstand."

Managing a tired smile for the woman he loved almost as much as his own mother, he leaned in and kissed her cheek. "Thanks, Helene. I'll be down for dinner as soon as I can."

Ryan dried his hair from the shower and wrapped the towel around his waist. The hot water had felt good sluicing over his tired, aching muscles. So he'd taken a longer shower than he'd intended. And though he was hungry, he was tempted to collapse into bed and forgo dinner.

Sighing wearily, he sat on the bed and picked up his phone to call Tess.

She answered in a couple of rings. "Hey, Rye. How'd it go? Were you able to find all the steer you lost?"

Helene had evidently told her where he was and why he hadn't been answering his cell phone.

"Yes, we got them all back and the fence is fixed." He groaned as he reached out to pick up his watch and put it back on. "How's Tripp? Helene said he got food poisoning."

"Wow, you sound like you've been ridden hard and put away wet." She laughed. "And yes, my brother's penchant for late night snacks from suspect eateries finally caught up with him. He looks and feels like hell, but otherwise he's recovering."

"Will he be okay for the auction tomorrow?"

"No." She said the word a little too quickly, then paused a little too long. "He thinks he'll be fine to go through with it, but I'm chalking that up to illness-induced delusion."

"Did you tell Alexis she's a man down?"

"I did." There was another unusual pause. Like there was something she wanted to say but was hesitant.

Ryan thought for a moment as he rummaged through his drawers for something to put on.

"Ahh…" He dragged his fingers through his damp hair. "Of course. She wants to know if I'll take Tripp's place."

Tessa didn't respond right away. "Actually, that's why I was trying so hard to reach you. I thought I might be able to convince you to take Tripp's place… since it's for such a good cause. But when I couldn't reach you, I came up with another option."

"Which is?" It was like pulling teeth to get Tess to just spit it out. He couldn't imagine why that would be…unless he wasn't going to like what she had to say. Uneasiness tightened his gut. "So this other option…are you going to tell me, or should I come over and you can act it out in charades?"

"Smart-ass." She huffed. "No charades necessary. *I'm* the other option. I decided to take Tripp's place in the auction."

"You do know that it's women who will be bidding in this auction, right?" Ryan switched to speakerphone, tossed his phone on the bed, then stepped into his briefs. "Anything you need to tell me, Tess?"

"I'm going to give you a pass because I know you're tired," she groused. "And we've already considered that. If you check your in-box, you'll see that Alexis sent out an email informing all attendees and everyone else on the mailing list that there is going to be a surprise at the end of the auction, just for the gents."

"Oh."

It was the only thing that Ryan could think to say as the realization struck him in the gut like a bull running at full speed. A few days ago, he'd been discomfited by the idea of his friend bidding on one man. Now, there would be who knows how many guys angling for a night with her.

"You sure about this?" He stepped into a pair of well-worn jeans and zipped and buttoned them. "This just doesn't seem much like you."

"That's exactly why I'm doing it." Her voice was shaky. "It'll be good for me to venture outside of my comfort zone."

He donned a long-sleeved T-shirt, neither of them speaking for a moment.

Ryan rubbed his chin and sank on to his mattress. He slipped on a pair of socks. "Look, I know I said I didn't want to do it, but with Tripp being sick and all, how about I make an exception?"

"You think this is a really bad idea, don't you?" She choked out the words, her feelings obviously hurt.

"No, that's not what I'm saying at all." The last thing he wanted to do was upset his best friend. He ran a hand through his hair. "I'm just saying that it's really last minute. And because of that, it might take people by surprise, that's all."

"I thought of that, too. Alexis and Rachel are positive they can drum up enough interest. But I thought that…just to be safe…it'd be good to have an ace up my sleeve."

"What kind of an ace?"

"I'm going to give you the money to bid on me, in case no one else does. I know it'll still look pretty pathetic if my best friend is the only person who bids on me, but that's a hell of a lot better than hearing crickets when they call my name."

"You want me to bid on you?" He repeated the words. Not that he hadn't heard or understood her the first time. He was just processing the idea. Him bidding on his best friend. The two of them going out on a date…

"Yes, but it'll be my money. And there's no need for us to actually go on the date. I mean, we can just hang out like usual or something, but it doesn't have to be a big deal."

"Sure, I'll do it. But you don't need to put up the money. I'm happy to make the donation myself."

His leg bounced. Despite what his friend believed, Ryan doubted that he'd be the only man there willing to bid on Tessa Noble during her bachelorette auction.

"Thanks, Ryan. I appreciate this." She sounded relieved. "And remember, you'll only need to bid on me if no one else does. If nothing else, your bid might prompt someone else to get into the spirit."

"Got it," he said gruffly. "You can count on me."

"I know. Thanks again, Rye." He could hear the smile in her sweet voice.

"Hey, since Tripp won't be able to make it…why don't we ride in together?"

"Actually, I'm going straight to the auction from…somewhere else. But I'll catch a ride with a friend, so we can ride home together. How's that?"

"Sounds good." He couldn't help the twinge of disappointment he felt at only getting to ride home with her. "I guess I'll see you there."

"I'll be the one with the price tag on her head." Tessa forced a laugh. "Get some rest, Rye. And take some pain meds. Otherwise, your arm'll be too sore to lift the auction paddle."

Her soft laughter was the last thing he heard before the line went dead. Before he could say goodnight.

Ryan released a long sigh and slid his feet into his slippers. He didn't like the idea of Tess putting herself on the auction block for every letch in town to leer at. But she was a grown woman who was capable of making her own decisions.

Regardless of how much he disagreed with them.

Besides, he wasn't quite sure what it was that made him feel more uneasy. Tess being bid on by other men, or the idea that he might be the man who won her at the end of the night.

Four

Tessa had never been plucked, primped and prodded this much in her entire life.

She'd been waxed in places she didn't even want to think about and had some kind of wrap that promised to tighten her curves. And the thick head of curls she adored had been straightened and hung in tousled waves around her shoulders. Now Milan Valez, a professional makeup artist, was applying her makeup.

"I thought we were going with a natural look," Tess objected when the woman opened yet another product and started to apply what had to be a third or fourth layer of goop to her face.

"This *is* the natural look." The woman rolled her

eyes. "If I had a dime for every client who doesn't realize that what they're calling the natural look is actually a full face." The woman sighed, but her expression softened as she directed Tess to turn her head. "You're a beautiful woman with gorgeous skin. If you're not a makeup wearer, I know it feels like a lot. But I'm just using a few tricks to enhance your natural beauty. We'll make those beautiful eyes pop, bring a little drama to these pouty lips, and highlight your incredible cheekbones. I promise you won't look too heavily made up. Just trust me."

Tessa released a quiet sigh and nodded. "I trust you."

"Good. Now just sit back and relax. Your friends should be here shortly. They're going to be very pleased, and I think you will, too." The woman smiled. "Now look up."

Tessa complied as Milan applied liner beneath her eyes. "You sure I can't have a little peek?"

"Your friends made me promise. No peeking. And you agreed." She lifted Tess's chin. "Don't worry, honey, you won't have to wait much longer."

"Tessa? Oh my God, you look...incredible." Rachel entered the salon a few minutes later and clapped a hand over her mouth. "I can hardly believe it's you."

Alexis nearly slammed into the back of Rachel, who'd made an abrupt stop. She started to complain, but when she saw Tessa, her mouth gaped open, too.

"Tess, you look…stunning. Not that you aren't always beautiful, but…wow. Just wow."

"You two are making me seriously self-conscious right now." Tessa kept her focus on Milan.

"Don't be," the woman said emphatically. "Remember what we talked about. I've only enhanced what was already there."

Tessa inhaled deeply and nodded. She ignored the butterflies in her stomach in response to the broad grins and looks of amazement on Alexis's and Rachel's faces.

"There, all done." Milan sat back proudly and grinned. "Honey, you look absolutely beautiful. Ready to see for yourself?"

"Please." Even as Tessa said it, her hands were trembling, and a knot tightened in her stomach. How could something as simple as looking in the mirror be so fraught with anxiety? It only proved she wasn't cut out for this whole glamour-girl thing.

Milan slowly turned the chair around and Alexis and Rachel came over to stand closer, both of them bouncing excitedly.

Tessa closed her eyes, took a deep breath and then opened them.

"Oh my God." She leaned closer to the mirror. "I can hardly believe that's me." She sifted her fingers through the dark, silky waves with toffee-colored highlights. "I mean, it looks like me, just…more glamourous."

"I know, isn't it incredible? You're going to be

the star of the evening. We need to keep you hidden until you walk across the stage. Really take everyone by surprise." Rachel grinned in the mirror from behind her.

"Oh, that's a brilliant idea, Rachel," Alexis agreed. "It'll have more impact."

"This is only the beginning." Rachel's grin widened. "Just wait until they get a load of your outfit tonight. Every man in that room's jaw will hit the floor."

Tessa took another deep breath, then exhaled as she stared at herself in the mirror. Between her makeover and the daring outfit she'd chosen, there was no way Ryan, or anyone else, would take her for one of the boys.

Her heart raced and her belly fluttered as she anticipated his reaction. She couldn't wait to see the look of surprise on Ryan's face.

Ryan entered the beautiful gardens where The Great Royal Bachelor Auction was being held. Alexis Slade, James Harris and the rest of the committee had gone out of their way to create a festive and beautiful setting for the event. Fragrant wreaths and sprigs of greenery were strung from the pergolas. Two towering trees decorated with gorgeous ornaments dominated the area. Poinsettias, elegant red bows and white lights decorated the space, giving it a glowing, ethereal feel. The garden managed to be both romantic and festive. The kind of setting that almost made you regret not having someone to share the night with.

He sipped his Jack and Coke and glanced around the vicinity. Everyone who was anyone was in attendance. He made his way through the room, mingling with Carter Mackenzie and Shelby Arthur, Matt Galloway and Rachel Kincaid, Austin and Brooke Bradshaw, and all of the other members of the club who'd turned out for the event. Several of the bachelors moved around the space, drumming up anticipation for the auction and doing their best to encourage a bidding frenzy.

But Tessa was nowhere to be found. Had she changed her mind? He was looking forward to hanging out with her tonight, but he'd understand if she'd gotten cold feet. Hell, there was a part of him that was relieved to think that maybe she'd bailed.

Then again, Tess had said she'd be coming from somewhere else. So maybe she was just running late.

He resisted the urge to pull out his cell phone and find out exactly where she was. For once in his life, he'd be patient. Even if it killed him.

"Ryan, it's good to see you." James Harris, president of the Texas Cattleman's Club, shook his hand. "I hate that we couldn't convince you to be one of our bachelor's tonight, but I'm glad you joined us just the same."

"Didn't see your name on the list of bachelors either." Ryan smirked, and both men laughed.

"Touché." James took a gulp of his drink and Ryan did the same.

"Looks like y'all are doing just fine without me." Ryan gestured to the space. "I wouldn't have ever imagined this place could look this good."

"Alexis Slade outdid herself with this whole romantic winter wonderland vibe." James's eyes trailed around the space. "To be honest, I wasn't sure exactly how her vision would come together, but she's delivered in spades. I'm glad we gave her free rein to execute it as she saw fit."

"Judging from everyone here's reaction, you've got a hit on your hands." Ryan raised his glass before finishing the last of his drink.

"Let's just hope it motivates everyone to dig deep in their pockets tonight." James patted Ryan on the back. "I'd better go chat with Rose Clayton." He nodded toward the older woman, who looked stunning in her gown. The touch of gray hair at her temples gleamed in the light. "But I'll see you around."

"You bet." Ryan nodded toward the man as he traversed the space and greeted Rose.

"Ryan, how are you?" Gail Walker took a sip of her drink and grinned. "You look particularly handsome tonight. But I see Alexis still wasn't able to talk you into joining the list of eligible bachelors."

"Not my thing, but looks like they've got plenty of studs on the schedule for you to choose from." Ryan sat his empty glass on a nearby tray. "And you clean up pretty well yourself."

"Thanks." She smoothed a hand over the skirt of her jewel-tone green dress. "But I've got my eye on one bachelor in particular." Her eyes shone with mischief. "And I'm prepared to do whatever it takes to get him."

"Well, I certainly wouldn't want to be the woman who has to run up against you." Ryan chuckled. "Good luck."

"Thanks, Ryan. See you around." Gail made her way through the crowd, mingling with other guests.

Ryan accepted a napkin and a few petite quiches from a server passing by. Ignoring the anticipation that made his heart beat a little faster as he considered the prospect of bidding on his friend.

Tessa paced the space that served as the bachelors' green room. Everyone else had spent most of the night mingling. They came to the green room once the start of the auction drew closer. But she'd been stuck here the entire evening, biding her time until she was scheduled to make her grand entrance.

"Tessa Noble? God, you look…incredible." Daniel Clayton shoved a hand in his pocket. "But what are you doing here? Wait…are you the surprise?"

"Guilty." Her cheeks warmed as she bit into another quiche.

She tried her best not to ruin the makeup that Milan had so painstakingly applied. The woman had assured her that she could eat and drink without the lipstick fading or feathering. But Tess still found herself being extra careful.

"Everyone will definitely be surprised," he said, then added, "Not that you don't look good normally."

"It's okay, Daniel. I get it." She mumbled around a mouthful of quiche. "It was a surprise to me, too."

He chuckled, running a hand through his jet-black hair. "You must be tired of people telling you how different you look. How did Tripp and Ryan react?"

"Neither of them has seen me yet." She balled up her napkin and tossed it in the trash. "I'm a little nervous about their reaction."

"Don't be," Daniel said assuredly. "I can't imagine a man alive could find fault with the way you look tonight." He smiled, then scrubbed a hand across his forehead. "Or any night...of course."

They both laughed.

"Well, thank you." She relaxed a little. "You already know why I feel like a fish out of water. But why do you look so out of sorts tonight?"

He exhaled heavily, the frown returning to his face. "For one thing, I'd rather not be in the lineup. I'm doing this at my grandmother's insistence."

"Ms. Rose seems like a perfectly reasonable woman to me. And she loves you like crazy. I'm pretty sure if you'd turned her down she would've gotten over it fairly quickly."

"Maybe." He shrugged. "But the truth is that I owe my grandmother so much. Don't know where

I would've ended up if it wasn't for her. Makes it hard to say no." A shadow of sadness passed over his handsome face, tugging at Tessa's heart.

Daniel had been raised by Rose Clayton after his own mother dumped him on her. It made Tessa's heart ache for him. She couldn't imagine the pain Daniel must feel at being abandoned by a woman who preferred drugs and booze to her own son.

"Of course." Tess nodded, regretting her earlier flippant words. She hadn't considered the special relationship that Daniel had with his grandmother and how grateful he must be to her. "I wasn't thinking."

They were both quiet for a moment, when she remembered his earlier words.

"You said 'for one thing.' What's the other reason you didn't want to do this?"

The pained look on Daniel's face carved deep lines in his forehead and between his brows. He drained the glass of whiskey in his hand.

"It's nothing," he said in a dismissive tone that made it clear that they wouldn't be discussing it any further.

She was digging herself deeper into a hole with every question she asked of Daniel tonight. Better for her to move on. She wished him luck and made her way over to the buffet table.

"Hey, Tessa." Lloyd Richardson put another slider on his small plate. "Wow, you look pretty amazing."

"Thanks, Lloyd." She decided against the slider

and put some carrots and a cherry tomato on her plate instead.

There wasn't much room to spare in her fitted pantsuit. She wore a jacket over the sleeveless garment to hide the large cutout that revealed most of her back. That had been one idea of Rachel's for which she'd been grateful.

"Hey, you must be plum sick of people saying that to you by now." Lloyd seemed to recognize the discomfort she felt at all of the additional attention she'd been getting.

Tess gave him a grateful smile. No wonder her friend Gail Walker had a crush on Lloyd. He was handsome, sweet and almost a little shy. Which was probably why he hadn't made a move on Gail, since he certainly seemed interested in her.

"Okay, bachelors and bachelorette." Alexis acknowledged Tess with a slight smile. "The proceedings will begin in about ten minutes. So finish eating, take a quick bathroom break, whatever you need to do so you'll be ready to go on when your number is called."

Alexis had her serious, drill sergeant face on. Something Tessa knew firsthand that a woman needed to adopt when she was responsible for managing a crew of men—be they ranchers or ranch hands.

Still, there was something in her eyes. Had she been crying?

Before she could approach Alexis and ask if she

was all right, she noticed the look Alexis and Daniel Clayton exchanged. It was brief, but meaningful. Chock full of pain.

Could Alexis be the other reason Daniel hadn't wanted to be in the bachelor auction? But from the look of things, whatever was going on between them certainly wasn't sunshine and roses.

Tessa caught up with Alexis as she grabbed the door handle.

"Alexis." Tessa lowered her voice as she studied her friend's face. "Is everything okay? You look like you've been—"

"I'm fine." Alexis swiped at the corner of one eye, her gaze cast downward. "I just… I'm fine." She forced a smile, finally raising her eyes to meet Tessa's. "You're going to kill them tonight. Just wait until you come out of that jacket. We're going to have to scrape everyone's jaws off the floor." She patted Tess's shoulder. "I'd tell you good luck, but something tells me that you aren't going to need it tonight."

With that, Alexis dipped out of the green room and was gone.

When Tess turned around, Daniel was standing there, staring after the other woman. He quickly turned away, busying himself with grabbing a bottle of water from the table.

There was definitely something going on with the two of them. And if there was, Tessa could understand why they wouldn't want to make their relationship public. Daniel's grandmother, Rose Clayton, and Alexis's grandfather, Gus Slade, once an item, had been feuding for years.

In recent months, they seemed to at least have found the civility to be decent toward one another. Most likely for the sake of everyone around them. Still, there was no love lost between those two families.

"Looks like Royal has its very own Romeo and Juliet," she muttered under her breath.

Tess took her seat, her hands trembling slightly and butterflies fluttering in her stomach. She closed her eyes, imagining how Ryan would react to seeing her out there on that stage.

Five

Ryan hung back at the bar as the bachelor auction wound down. There were just a couple more bachelors on the list, then Tess would be up.

He gulped the glass of water with lemon he was drinking. He'd talked to just about everyone here. But with neither Tripp nor Tess to hang out with, he'd been ready to leave nearly an hour ago.

Then again, his discomfort had little to do with him going stag for the night and everything to do with the fact that his best friend would be trotted out onto the stage and bid on. His gaze shifted around the garden at the unattached men in attendance. Most of them were members of the Texas Cattleman's Club. Some of them second, third or even fourth generation. All of them were good people, as far as he knew. So why was he assessing them all suspiciously? Wondering which of them would bid on his best friend.

The next bachelor, Lloyd Richardson, was called onto the stage and Alexis read his bio. Women were chomping at the bit to bid on the guy. Including Gail Walker. She'd started with a low, reasonable bid. But four or five other women were countering her bids as quickly as she was making them.

First the bid was in the hundreds, then the thousands. Suddenly, Steena Goodman, a wealthy older woman whose husband had been active in the club for many years before his death, stood and placed her final bid. Fifty-thousand dollars.

Ryan nearly coughed. What was it about this guy that had everyone up in arms?

Steena's bid was much higher than the previous bid of nine thousand dollars. The competing bidders pouted, acknowledging their defeat.

But not Gail. She looked angry and hurt. She stared Steena down, her arms folded and breathing heavily.

Alexis glanced back and forth at the two women for a moment. When Rachel nudged her, she cleared her throat and resumed her duties as auctioneer. "Going once, going twice—"

"One hundred thousand dollars." Gail stared at Steena, as if daring her to outbid her.

The older woman huffed and put her paddle down on the table, conceding the bid.

"Oh my God! One hundred thousand dollars." Alexis began the sentence nearly shrieking but ended with an implied question mark.

Probably because she was wondering the same thing he was.

Where in the hell did Gail Walker get that kind of cash?

Alexis declared Gail the winner of the bid at one hundred thousand dollars.

The woman squealed and ran up on stage. She wrapped her arms around Lloyd's neck and pulled him down for a hot, steamy kiss. Then she grabbed his hand and dragged him off the stage and through the doors that led from the garden back into the main building.

Ryan leaned against the bar, still shocked by Gail's outrageous bid. He sighed. Just one more bachelor, Daniel Clayton. Then Tess was up.

"That was certainly unexpected." Gus Slade ordered a beer from the bar. "Had no idea she was sitting on that kind of disposable cash."

"Neither did I, but I guess we all have our little secrets."

The older man grimaced, as if he'd taken exception to Ryan's words. Which only made Ryan wonder what secrets the old man might be hiding.

"Yes, well, I s'pose that's true." Gus nodded, then walked away.

Ryan turned his attention back to the stage just in time to see Daniel Clayton being whisked away excitedly by an overeager bidder.

There was a noticeable lull as Alexis watched the woman escort Daniel away. Rachel placed a hand on her cohost's back as she took the microphone from Alexis and thanked her for putting on a great event and being an incredible auctioneer.

Alexis seemed to recover from the momentarily stunned look she'd had seconds earlier. She nodded toward Rachel and then to the crowd which clapped appreciatively.

"This has been an amazing night, and thanks to your generosity, ladies, and to the generosity of our bachelors, we've already exceeded our fund-raising goal for tonight. So thank you all for that. Give yourselves a big hand."

Rachel clapped a hand against the inside of her wrist as the rest of the audience clapped, hooted and shouted.

"But we're not done yet. It's time for the surprise you gents have been waiting for this evening. Fellas, please welcome our lone bachelorette, Miss Tessa Noble."

Ryan pulled out his phone. He'd promised Tripp that he'd record his sister's big debut.

There was a collective gasp in the room as Tessa stepped out onto the stage. Ryan moved away from the bar, so he could get a better view of his friend.

His jaw dropped, and his phone nearly clattered to the ground.

"Tess?" Ryan choked out the word, then silently cursed himself, realizing his stunned reaction would end up on the video. He snapped his gaping mouth shut as he watched her strut across the stage in a glamorous red pantsuit that seemed to be designed for the express purpose of highlighting her killer curves.

Damn, she's fine.

He wasn't an idiot. Nor was he blind. So he wasn't oblivious to the fact that his best friend also happened to be an extremely beautiful woman. And despite her tomboy wardrobe, he was fully aware of the hot body buried beneath relaxed fit clothing. But today…those curves had come out to play.

As if she was a professional runway model, Tess pranced to the end of the stage in strappy, glittery heels, put one hand on her hip and cocked it to the side. She seemed buoyed by the crowd's raucous reaction.

First there was the collective gasp, followed by a chorus of Oh my Gods. Now the crowd was whooping and shouting.

A slow grin spread across her lips, painted a deep, flirtatious shade of red that made him desperate to taste them. She turned and walked back toward where Rachel stood, revealing a large, heart-shaped cutout that exposed the warm brown skin of her

open back. A large bow was tied behind her graceful neck.

Tessa Noble was one gift he'd give just about
anything to unwrap.

She was incredibly sexy with a fiercely confident
demeanor that only made him hunger for her more.

Ryan surveyed the crowd. He obviously wasn't
the only man in the room drooling over Tessa 2.0.
He stared at the large group of men who were wide-
eyed, slack-jawed and obviously titillated by the
woman on stage.

Tessa's concerns that no one would bid on her
were obviously misplaced. There were even a couple of women who seemed to be drooling over her.

Ryan's heart thudded. Suddenly, there wasn't
enough air in the tented, outdoor space. He grabbed
his auction paddle and crept closer to the stage.

Rachel read Tessa's bio aloud, as Alexis had done
with the bachelors who'd gone before her. Tessa
stood tall with her back arched and one hand on her
hip. She held her head high as she scanned the room.

Was she looking for him?

Ryan's cheeks flushed with heat. A dozen emotions percolated in his chest, like some strange,
volatile mixture, as he studied his friend on stage.
Initially, he wanted to rush the stage and drape his
jacket over her shoulders. Block the other men's
lurid stares. Then there was his own guttural reaction to seeing Tess this way. He wanted to devour
her. Kiss every inch of the warm, brown skin on

her back. Glide his hands over her luscious bottom. Taste those pouty lips.

He swallowed hard, conscious of his rapid breathing. He hoped the video wasn't picking that up, too.

Rachel had moved on from Tessa's bio to describing her date. "For the lucky gentleman with the winning bid, your very special outing with this most lovely lady will be every man's fantasy come true. Your football-themed date will begin with seats on the fifty-yard line to watch America's team play football against their division rivals. Plus, you'll enjoy a special tailgating meal before the game at a restaurant right there in the stadium. Afterward, you'll share an elegant steak dinner at a premium steak house."

"Shit." Ryan cringed, realizing that, too, would be captured on the video.

There was already a stampede of overly eager men ready to take Tessa up on her offer. Now she'd gone and raised the stakes.

Just great.

Ryan huffed, his free hand clenched in a fist at his side, as her words reverberated through him.

You're only supposed to bid if no one else does.

Suddenly, Tessa's gaze met his, and her entire face lit up in a broad smile that made her even more beautiful. A feat he wouldn't have thought possible.

His heart expanded in his chest as he returned her smile and gave her a little nod.

Tess stood taller. As if his smile had lifted her. Made her even more confident.

And why shouldn't she be? She'd commanded the attention of every man in the room, single or not. Had all the women in the crowd enviously whispering among themselves.

"All right, gentlemen, get your paddles ready, because it's your turn to bid on our lovely bachelorette." Rachel grinned proudly.

He'd bet anything she was behind Tessa's incredible makeover. Ryan didn't know if he wanted to thank her or blame her for messing up a good thing. Back when no one else in town realized what a diamond his Tess was.

He shook his head. *Get it together, Bateman. She doesn't belong to you.*

"Shall we open the bidding at five-hundred dollars?" Rachel asked the crowd.

"A thousand dollars." Clem Davidson, a man his father's age, said.

"Fifteen hundred," Bo Davis countered. He was younger than Clem, but still much older than Tess.

Ryan clenched the paddle in his hand so tightly he thought it might snap in two as several of the men bid furiously for Tess. His heart thumped. Beads of sweat formed over his brow and trickled down his back as his gaze and the camera's shifted from the crowd of enthusiastic bidders to Tessa's shocked expression and then back again.

"Ten thousand bucks." Clem held his paddle high

and looked around the room, as if daring anyone else to bid against him. He'd bid fifteen hundred dollars more than Bo's last bid.

Bo grimaced, but then nodded to Clem in concession.

"Twelve thousand dollars." It nearly came as a surprise to Ryan that the voice was his own.

Clem scowled. "Thirteen thousand."

"Fifteen thousand." Now Ryan's voice was the one that was indignant as he stared the older man down.

Clem narrowed his gaze at Ryan, his jaw clenched. He started to raise his paddle, but then his expression softened. Head cocked to the side, he furrowed his brows for a moment. Suddenly, he nodded to Ryan and put his paddle back down at his side.

"Fifteen thousand dollars going once. Fifteen thousand dollars going twice." Rachel looked around the room, excitedly. "Sold! Ryan Bateman, you may claim your bachelorette."

Ryan froze for a moment as everyone in the room looked at him, clapping and cheering. Many of them with knowing smiles. He cleared his throat, ended the recording and slowly made his way toward the stage and toward his friend who regarded him with utter confusion.

He stuffed his phone into his pocket, gave Tess an awkward hug and pressed a gentle kiss to her cheek for the sake of the crowd.

They all cheered, and he escorted Tess off the stage. Then Rachel and Alexis wrapped up the auction.

"Oh my God, what did you just do?" Tessa whispered loudly enough for him to hear her over all the noise.

"Can't rightly say I know," he responded, not looking at her, but fully aware of his hand on her waist, his thumb resting on the soft skin of her back. Electricity sparked in his fingertips. Trailed up his arm.

"I appreciate what you did, Rye. It was a very generous donation. But I thought we agreed you would only bid if no one else did." Tessa folded her arms as she stared at him, searching his face for an answer.

"I know, and I was following the plan, I was. But I just couldn't let you go home with a guy like Clem."

Tessa stared up into his green eyes, her own eyes widening in response. Ryan Bateman was her oldest and closest friend. She knew just about everything there was to know about him. But the man standing before her was a mystery.

He'd gone beyond his usual protectiveness of her and had landed squarely into possessive territory. To be honest, it was kind of a turn-on. Which was problematic. Because Rye was her best friend. Emphasis on *friend*.

She folded her arms over her chest, suddenly self-conscious about whether the tightening of her nipples was visible through the thin material.

"And what, exactly, is it that you have against Clem?"

Ryan shook his head. "Nothing really." He seemed dazed, maybe even a little confused himself. "I just didn't want you to go out with him. He's too old for you."

"That's ageist." She narrowed her gaze.

It was true that she'd certainly never considered Clem Davidson as anything other than a nice older man. Still, it wasn't right for Ryan to single him out because of his age. It was a football date. Plain and simple. There would be no sex. With anyone.

"Clem isn't that much older than us, you know. Ten or fifteen years, tops." She relaxed her arms and ran her fingers through the silky waves that she still hadn't gotten accustomed to.

Ryan seemed to tense at the movement. He clenched his hand at his side, then nodded. "You're right on both counts. But what's done is done." He shrugged.

"What if it had been Bo instead? Would you have outbid him, too?"

"Yes." He seemed to regret his response, or at least the conviction with which he'd uttered the word. "I mean…yes," he said again.

"You just laid down fifteen grand for me," Tess said as they approached the bar. "The least I can do is buy you a drink."

She patted her hips, then remembered that her money and credit cards were in her purse backstage.

"Never mind. I've got it. Besides, I'm already running a tab." Ryan ordered a Jack and Coke for himself and one for her, which she turned down, requesting club soda with lime instead. "You...uh... you look pretty incredible."

"Thanks." She tried to sound grateful for the compliment, but when everyone fawned over how good she looked tonight, all she heard was the implication that her everyday look was a hot mess.

Her tomboy wardrobe had been a conscious choice, beginning back in grade school. She'd developed early. Saw how it had changed the other kids' perception of her. With the exception of Ryan, the boys she'd been friends with were suddenly more fascinated with her budding breasts than anything she had to say. And they'd come up with countless ways to cop an "accidental" feel.

Several of the girls were jealous of her newfound figure and the resulting attention from the boys. They'd said hateful things to her and started blatantly false rumors about her, which only brought more unwanted attention from the boys.

Tess had recognized, even then, that the problem was theirs, not hers. That they were immature and stupid. Still, it didn't stop the things they'd said from hurting.

She'd been too embarrassed to tell Tripp or Ryan, who were a few grades ahead of her. And she was worried that Ryan's temper would get him in serious trouble. She hadn't told her parents, either. They would've come to her school, caused a scene and made her even more of a social pariah.

So she'd worn bulky sweaters, loose jeans and flannel shirts that masked her curves and made her feel invisible.

After a while, she'd gotten comfortable in her wardrobe. Made it her own. Until it felt like her daily armor.

Wearing a seductive red pantsuit, with her entire back exposed and every curve she owned on display, made her feel as vulnerable as if she'd traipsed across the stage naked.

But she was glad she'd done it. That she'd reclaimed a little of herself.

The bartender brought their drinks and Ryan stuffed a few dollars into the tip jar before taking a generous gulp of his drink.

"So, is this your new look?" An awkward smile lit Ryan's eyes. "'Cause it's gonna be mighty hard for you to rope a steer in that getup."

"Shut it, Rye." She pointed a finger at him, and they both laughed.

When they finally recovered from their laughter, she took his glass from his hand and took a sip of his drink. His eyes darkened as he watched her, his jaw tensing again.

"Not bad. Maybe I will have one." She handed it back to him.

Without taking his eyes off of her, Ryan signaled for the bartender to bring a Jack and Coke for her, too. There was something in his stare. A hunger she hadn't seen before.

She often longed for Ryan to see her as more than just "one of the boys." Now that it seemed he was finally seeing her that way, it was unsettling. His heated stare made her skin prickle with awareness.

The prospect of Ryan being as attracted to her as she was to him quickened her pulse and sent a shock of warmth through her body. But just as quickly, she thought of how her relationship with the boys in school had changed once they saw her differently.

That wasn't something she ever wanted to happen between her and Ryan. She could deal with her eternal, unrequited crush, but she couldn't deal with losing his friendship.

She cleared her throat, and it seemed to break them both from the spell they'd both fallen under.

They were just caught up in emotions induced by the incredibly romantic setting, the fact that she looked like someone wholly different than her everyday self, and the adrenaline they'd both felt during the auction. Assigning it meaning…that would be a grave mistake. One that would leave one or both of them sorely disappointed once the bubble of illusion burst.

"So…since it's just us, we don't need to go out on a date. Because that would be…you know…weird.

But, I'm totally down for hanging out. And seats on the fifty-yard line…so…yay."

"That's what I was really after." Ryan smirked, sipping his drink. "You could've been wearing a brown potato sack, and I still would've bid on those tickets. It's like the whole damned date had my name written all over it." His eyes widened with realization. "Wait…you did tailor it just for me, didn't you?"

Tessa's cheeks heated. She took a deep sip of her drink and returned it to the bar, waving a hand dismissively.

"Don't get ahead of yourself, partner. I simply used your tastes as a point of reference. After all, you, Tripp and my dad are the only men that I've been spending any significant time with these days. I figured if you'd like it, the bidders would, too."

"Hmm…" Ryan took another sip of his drink, almost sounding disappointed. "Makes sense, I guess."

"I'm glad you get it. Alexis and Rachel thought it was the least romantic thing they could imagine. They tried to talk me into something else. Something grander and more flowery."

"Which neither of us would've enjoyed." Ryan nodded. "And the makeover… I assume that was Rachel's idea, too."

"Both Alexis and Rachel came up with that one. Alexis got PURE to donate a spa day and the makeover, so it didn't cost me anything." Tessa tucked her hair behind her ear and studied her friend's face. "You don't like it?"

"No, of course I do. I love it. You look…incredible. You really do. Your parents are going to flip when they see this." He patted the phone in his pocket.

"You recorded it? Oh no." Part of her was eager to see the video. Another part of her cringed at the idea of watching herself prance across that stage using the catwalk techniques she'd studied online.

But no matter how silly she might feel right now, she was glad she'd successfully worked her magic on the crowd.

The opening chords of one of her favorite old boy band songs drew her attention to the stage where the band was playing.

"Oh my God, I love that song." Tessa laughed, sipping the last of her drink and then setting the glass on the bar. "Do you remember what a crush I had on these guys?"

Rye chuckled, regarding her warmly over the rim of his glass as he finished off his drink, too. "I remember you playing this song on repeat incessantly."

"That CD was my favorite possession. I still can't believe I lost it."

Ryan lowered his gaze, his chin dipping. He tapped a finger on the bar before raising his eyes to hers again and taking her hand. "I need to make a little confession."

"You rat!" She poked him in the chest. "You did something to my CD, didn't you?"

A guilty smirk curled the edges of his mouth. "Tripp and I couldn't take it anymore. We might've trampled the thing with a horse or two, then dumped it."

"You two are awful." She realized that she'd gone a little overboard in her obsession with the group. But trampling the album with a horse? That was harsh.

"If I'm being honest, I've always felt incredibly guilty about my role in the whole sordid affair." Ryan placed his large, warm hand on her shoulder. The tiny white lights that decorated the space were reflected in his green eyes. "Let me make it up to you."

"And just how do you plan to do that?" Tessa folded her arms, cocking a brow.

He pulled out his phone, swiped through a few screens. "First of all, I just ordered you another copy of that album—CD and digital."

She laughed. "You didn't need to do that, Rye."

"I did, and I feel much better now. Not just because it was wrong of us to take away something you loved so much. Because I hated having that secret between us all these years. You're the one person in the world I can tell just about anything. So it feels pretty damn good to finally clear my conscience." He dropped his hand from her shoulder.

"All right." She forced a smile, trying her best to hide her disappointment at the loss of his touch. "And what's the second thing?"

He held his large, open palm out to her. "It seems I've bought myself a date for the night. Care to dance?"

"You want to dance to this sappy, boy band song that you've always hated?"

He grabbed her hand and led her to the dance floor. "Then I guess there's one more confession I need to make... I've always kind of liked this song. I just didn't want your brother to think I'd gone soft."

Tessa laughed as she joined her best friend on the dance floor.

Six

Gus Slade watched as Tessa Noble and Ryan Bateman entered the dance floor, both of them laughing merrily. Gus shook his head. Ryan was one of the prospects he'd considered as a good match for his granddaughter Alexis. Only it was clear that Ryan and Tess were hung up on each other, even if the self-proclaimed "best friends" weren't prepared to admit it to themselves.

It was no wonder Ryan's brief engagement to that wannabe supermodel he'd met in the city didn't last long enough for the two of them to make it to the altar.

Encouraging Alexis to start something with the Bateman boy would only result in heartache for his granddaughter once Ryan and Tess finally recognized the attraction flickering between them.

He'd experienced that kind of hurt and pain in his life when the woman he'd once loved, whom he thought truly loved him, had suddenly turned against him, shutting him out of her life.

It was something he'd never truly gotten over. Despite a long and happy marriage that lasted until the death of his dear wife.

Gus glanced over at Rose Clayton, his chest tightening. Even after all these years, the woman was still gorgeous. Just a hint of gray was visible at her temples. The rest of her hair was the same dark brown it was when she was a girl. She wore it in a stylish, modern cut that befit a mature woman. Yet, anyone who didn't know her could easily mistake her for a much younger woman.

And after all these years, Rose Clayton still turned heads, including his. The woman managed to stay as slim now as she had been back when she was a young girl. Yet, there was nothing weak or frail about Rose Clayton.

Her every move, her every expression, exuded a quiet confidence that folks around Royal had always respected. And tonight, he had to admit that she looked simply magnificent.

Gus glanced around the tented garden area again. The space looked glorious. Better than he could ever have imagined when the club first decided to undertake a major renovation of this space and a few other areas of the club, which had been in operation since the 1920s.

Alexis had headed up the committee that put on the auction. And his granddaughter had truly outdone herself.

Gus searched the crowd for Alexis. Her duties as Mistress of Ceremony appeared to be over for the night. Still, he couldn't locate her anywhere.

Gus walked toward the main building. Perhaps she was in the office or one of the other interior spaces. But as he looked through the glass pane, he could see Alexis inside, hemmed up by Daniel Clayton. From the looks of it, they were arguing.

Fists clenched at his sides, Gus willed himself to stay where he was rather than rushing inside and demanding that Daniel leave his granddaughter alone. If he did that, then Alexis would defend the boy.

That would defeat the purpose of the elaborate plan he and Rose Clayton had concocted to keep their grandkids apart.

So he'd wait there. Monitor the situation without interfering. He didn't want his granddaughter marrying any kin to Rose Clayton. Especially a boy with a mother like Stephanie Clayton. A heavy drinker who'd been in and out of trouble her whole life. A woman who couldn't be bothered to raise her own boy. Instead, she'd dumped him off on Rose who'd raised Daniel as if he was her own son.

From where he stood, it appeared that Daniel was

pleading with Alexis. But she shoved his hand away when he tried to touch her arm.

Gus smirked, glad to see that someone besides him was getting the sharp end of that fierce stubborn streak she'd inherited from him.

Suddenly, his granddaughter threw her arms up and said something to Daniel that he obviously didn't like. Then she turned and headed his way.

Gus moved away from the door and around the corner to the bar as quickly and quietly as he could. He waited for her to pass by.

"Alexis!" Gus grabbed hold of her elbow as she hurried past him. He chuckled good-naturedly. "Where's the fire, darlin'?"

She didn't laugh. In fact, the poor thing looked dazed, like a wounded bird that had fallen out of the nest before it was time.

"Sorry, I didn't see you, Grandad." Her eyes didn't meet his. Instead, she looked toward the office where she was headed. "I'm sorry I don't have time to talk right now. I need to deal with a major problem."

"Alexis, honey, what is it? Is everything all right?"

"It will be, I'm sure. I just really need to take care of this now, okay?" Her voice trembled, seemed close to breaking.

"I wanted to tell you how proud I am of you. Tonight was magnificent and you've raised so much money for pancreatic cancer research. Your grandmother would be so very proud of you."

Alexis suddenly raised her gaze to his, the corners of her eyes wet with tears. Rather than the intended effect of comforting her, his words seemed to cause her distress.

"Alexis, what's wrong?" Gus pleaded with his darling girl. The pain in her blue eyes, rimmed with tears, tore at his heart. "Whatever it is, you can talk to me."

Before she could answer, Daniel Clayton passed by. He and Alexis exchanged a long, painful look. Then Daniel dropped his gaze and continued to the other side of the room.

"Alexis, darlin', what's going on?"

The tears spilled from her eyes. Alexis sucked in a deep breath and sniffled.

"It's nothing I can't handle, Grandad." She wiped away the tears with brusque swipes of her hand and shook her head. "Thank you for everything you said. I appreciate it. Really. But I need to take care of this issue. I'll see you back at home later, okay?"

Alexis pressed a soft kiss to his whiskered cheek. Then she hurried off toward the clubhouse offices.

Gus sighed, leaning against the bar. He dropped on to the stool, tapped the bar to get the bartender's attention, and ordered a glass of whiskey, neat. He gripped the hard, cold glass without moving it to his lips.

Their little plan was a partial success. Neither he nor Rose had been able to match their grandchildren up with an eligible mate. Yet, they'd done exactly what they'd set out to do. They'd driven a wedge between Daniel and Alexis.

So why didn't he feel good about what they'd done?

Because their grandkids were absolutely miserable.

What kind of grandfather could rejoice in the heartbreak of a beautiful girl like Alexis?

"Hello, Gus." Rose had sidled up beside him, and ordered a white wine spritzer. "The kids didn't look too happy with each other just now."

"That's an understatement, if ever I've heard one." He gripped his glass and gulped from it. "They're in downright misery."

"Is it that bad?" She glanced over at him momentarily, studying his pained look, before accepting her glass of wine and taking a sip.

"Honestly? I think it's even worse." He scrubbed a hand down his jaw. "I feel like a heel for causing baby girl so much pain. And despite all our machinations, neither of us has found a suitable mate for our respective grandchildren."

She nodded sagely. Pain dimmed the light in her gray eyes. And for a moment, the shadow that passed over her lovely face made her look closer to her actual years.

"I'm sorry that they're both hurting. But it's better that they have their hearts broken now than to have it happen down the road, when they're both more invested in the relationship." She glanced at him squarely. "We've both known that pain. It's a feeling that never leaves you. We're both living proof of that."

"I guess we are." Gus nodded, taking another sip of his whiskey. "But maybe there's something we hadn't considered." He turned around, his back to the bar.

"And what's that?" She turned on her bar stool, too, studying the crowd.

"Daniel and Alexis share our last names, but that doesn't make them us. And it doesn't mean they're doomed to our fates."

Rose didn't respond as she watched her grandson Daniel being fawned over by the woman who'd bought him at auction. He looked about as pleased by the woman's attentions as a man getting a root canal without anesthesia.

"We did what was in their best interests. The right thing isn't always the easiest thing. I know they're hurting now, but when they each find the person they were meant to be with, they'll be thankful this happened."

Rose paid for her drink and turned to walk away.

"Rose."

She halted, glancing over her shoulder without looking directly at him.

"What if the two of them were meant to be together? Will they be grateful we interfered then?"

A heavy sigh escaped her red lips, and she gathered her shawl around her before leaving.

His eyes trailed the woman as she walked away

in a glimmering green dress. The dress was long, but formfitting. And despite her age, Rose was as tantalizing in that dress as a cool drink of water on a hot summer day.

After all these years he still had a thing for Rose Clayton. What if it was the same for Daniel and Alexis?

He ordered another whiskey, neat, hoping to God that he and Rose hadn't made a grave mistake they'd both regret.

Seven

Ryan twirled Tessa on the dance floor and then drew her back into his arms as they danced to one of his favorite upbeat country songs. Everyone around them seemed to be singing along with the lyrics which were both funny and slightly irreverent.

Tessa turned her back to him, threw her hands up, and wiggled her full hips as she sang loudly.

His attention was drawn to the sway of those sexy hips keeping time to the music. Fortunately, her dancing was much more impressive than her singing. Something his anatomy responded to, even if he didn't want it to. Particularly not while they were in the middle of a crowded dance floor.

Ryan swallowed hard and tried to shove away

the rogue thoughts trying to commandeer his good sense. He and Tessa were just two friends enjoying their night together. Having a good time.

Nothing to see here, folks.

"Everything okay?" Tessa had turned around, her beautiful brown eyes focused on him and a frown tugging down the corners of her mouth.

"Yeah, of course." He forced a smile. "I was just…thinking…that's all." He started to dance again, his movements forced and rigid.

Tessa regarded him strangely, but before she could probe further, Alexis appeared beside them looking flustered. Her eyes were red, and it looked like she'd been crying.

"Alexis, is something wrong?" Tessa turned to her friend and squeezed her hand.

"I'm afraid so. I've been looking everywhere for you two. Would you mind meeting with James and me in the office as soon as possible?" Alexis leaned in, so they could both hear her over the blaring music.

"Of course, we will." Tessa gave the woman's hand another assuring squeeze. "Just lead the way."

Alexis made her way through the crowd with Tessa and Ryan following closely behind.

Ryan bit back his disappointment at the interruption. If the distress Alexis appeared to be experiencing was any indication, the situation was one level below the barn being on fire. Which triggered a burning in his gut.

Whatever Alexis and James wanted with the two of them, he was pretty sure neither of them was going to like it.

"Tessa, Ryan, please, have a seat." James Harris, president of the Texas Cattleman's Club, gestured to the chairs on the other side of the large mahogany desk in his office.

After such a successful night, he and Alexis looked incredibly grim. The knot that had already formed in her gut tightened.

She and Ryan sat in the chairs James indicated while Alexis sat on the sofa along one wall.

"Something is obviously wrong." Ryan crossed one ankle over his knee. "What is it, James?"

The other man hesitated a moment before speaking. When he did, the words he uttered came out in an anguished growl.

"There was a problem with one of the bids. A *big* problem."

"Gail." Tessa and Ryan said her name simultaneously.

"How does something like this happen?" Ryan asked after James had filled them both in. "Can anyone just walk in off the street and bid a bogus hundred K?"

James grimaced.

Tessa felt badly for him. James hadn't been president of the Texas Cattleman's Club for very long. She could only imagine how he must be feeling. He'd been riding high after putting on what was likely the most successful fund-raiser in the club's history. But now he was saddled with one of the biggest faux pas in the club's history.

"It's a charity auction. We take folks at their word when they make a bid," James replied calmly, then sighed. "Still, I don't like that this happened on my watch, and I'll do everything I can to remedy the situation."

Tessa's heart broke for the man. She didn't know James particularly well, but she'd heard the tragic story about what had happened to his brother and his sister-in-law. They'd died in an accident, leaving behind their orphaned son, who was little more than a year old, to be raised by James.

He was a nice enough guy, but he didn't seem the daddy type. Still, he was obviously doing the best he could to juggle all the balls he had in the air.

Tessa groaned, her hand pressed to her forehead. "I knew Gail had a thing for Lloyd Richardson, but I honestly never imagined she'd do something so reckless and impulsive."

"No one thinks you knew anything about it, Tess. That's not why we asked you here," Alexis assured her.

"Then why are we here?" Ryan's voice was cautious as he studied the other man.

"Because we have another dilemma that could compound the first problem." James heaved a sigh as he sat back in his chair, his hands steepled over his abdomen. "And we could really use your help to head it off."

"Was there another bid that someone can't make good on?" Ryan asked.

"No, but there is a reporter here, whom I invited." Alexis cringed as she stood. "He's intrigued by that one-hundred thousand dollar bid, and he wants to interview Gail and Lloyd."

"Damn. I see your dilemma." Ryan groaned sympathetically. "Instead of getting good press about all of the money the club did raise, all anyone will be talking about is Gail and her bogus bid."

"It gets even worse," Alexis said. She blew out a frustrated breath as she shook her head, her blond locks flipping over her shoulder. "We can't find hide nor hair of either Gail or Lloyd. It's like the two of them simply vanished."

Ryan shook his head. "Wow. That's pretty messed up."

"What is it that you want Ryan and me to do?" Tessa looked at James and then Alexis.

"The reporter was also very intrigued by everyone's reaction to you and all the drama of how Ryan beat out Clem and Bo's bids." A faint smile flickered on Alexis's mouth. "So we suggested that he follow the two of you on your little date."

"What?"

Panic suddenly seized Tessa's chest. It was one thing to play dress up and strut on the stage here at the club. Surrounded mostly by people she'd known her entire life. It was another to be followed by a reporter who was going to put the information out there for the entire world to see.

"We hadn't really intended to go on a date," Tessa said. "Ryan and I were just going to hang out together and have fun at the game. Grab a bite to eat at his favorite restaurant. Nothing worthy of reporting on."

"I know." There was an apology in Alexis's voice. "Which is why I need to ask another big favor..."

"You want us to go on a real date after all." Ryan looked from Alexis to James.

"Going out with a beautiful woman like Tess here, who also just happens to be your best friend... not the worst thing in the world that could happen to a guy." James forced a smile.

"Only...well, I know that the date you'd planned is the perfect kind of day for hanging with the guys." Alexis directed her attention toward Tess. "But this needs to feel like a big, romantic gesture. Something worthy of a big write-up for the event and for our club."

"I d-don't know, Alexis," Tessa stuttered, her heart racing. "I'm not sure how comfortable either of us would feel having a reporter follow us around all day."

"We'll do it," Ryan said suddenly. Decisively. "For the club, of course." He cleared his throat and gave Tess a reassuring nod. "And don't worry, I know exactly what to do. I'll make sure we give him the big, romantic fantasy he's looking for."

"I'm supposed to be the one who takes you out on a date," Tess objected. "That's how this whole thing works."

"Then it'll make for an even grander gesture when I surprise you by sweeping you off your feet."

He gave her that mischievous half smile that had enticed her into countless adventures. From searching for frogs when they were kids to parasailing in Mexico as an adult. After all these years, she still hadn't grown immune to its charm.

"Fine." Tessa sighed. "We'll do it. Just tell him we'll need a day or two to finalize the arrangements."

"Thank you!" Alexis hugged them both. "We're so grateful to you both for doing this."

"You're saving our asses here and the club's reputation." James looked noticeably relieved, though his eyebrows were still furrowed. "I can't thank you enough. And you won't be the only ones on the hot seat. Rose Clayton persuaded her grandson Daniel to give the reporter an additional positive feature related to the auction."

Alexis frowned at the mention of Daniel's name, but then she quickly recovered.

"And about that bid of Gail's…no one outside this room, besides Gail and Lloyd, of course, knows the situation." James frowned again. "We'd like to keep it that way until we figure out how we're going to resolve this. So please, don't whisper a word of this to anyone."

"Least of all the reporter," Alexis added, emphatically.

Tessa and Ryan agreed. Then Alexis introduced them to the reporter, Greg Halstead. After Greg gathered some preliminary information for the piece, Ryan insisted that he be the one to exchange contact information with Greg so they could coordinate him accompanying them on their date.

Every time Greg repeated the word *date*, shivers ran down Tessa's spine.

The only thing worse than having a thing for her best friend was being shanghaied into going on a fake date with him. But she was doing this for the club that meant so much to her, her family and the community of Royal.

Alexis had worked so hard to garner positive publicity for the club. And she'd raised awareness of the need to fund research for a cure for pancreatic cancer—the disease that had killed Alexis Slade's dear grandmother. Tess wouldn't allow all of her friend's hard work to be squandered because of Gail's selfish decision. Not if she could do something to prevent it.

Maybe she hadn't been aware of what Gail had planned to do tonight. But she'd been the one who'd invited Gail to tonight's affair. Tess couldn't help feeling obligated to do what she could to rectify the matter.

Even if it meant torturing herself by going on a pretend date that would feel very real to her. No matter how much she tried to deny it.

Eight

Ryan and Tessa finally headed home in his truck after what felt like an incredibly long night.

He couldn't remember the last time he and Tessa had danced together or laughed as much as they had that evening. But that was *before* James and Alexis had asked them to go on an actual date. Since then, things felt…different.

First, they'd politely endured the awkward interview with that reporter, Greg Halstead. Then they'd gone about the rest of the evening dancing and mingling with fellow club members and their guests. But there was a strange vibe between them. Obviously, Tessa felt it, too.

Why else would she be rambling on, as she often did when she was nervous.

Then again, lost in his own thoughts, he hadn't been very good company. Ryan drummed his fingers on the steering wheel during an awkward moment of silence.

"This date…it isn't going to make things weird between us, is it?" Tess asked finally, as if she'd been inside his head all along.

One of the hazards of a friendship with someone who knew him too well.

He forced a chuckle. "C'mon, Tess. We've been best buds too long to let a fake date shake us." His eyes searched hers briefly before returning to the road. "Our friendship could withstand anything."

Anything except getting romantically involved. Which is why they hadn't and wouldn't.

"Promise?" She seemed desperate for reassurance on the matter. Not surprising. A part of him needed it, too.

"On my life." This time, there was no hesitation. There were a lot of things in this world he could do without. Tessa Noble's friendship wasn't one of them.

Tessa nodded, releasing an audible sigh of relief. She turned to look out the window at the beautiful ranches that marked the road home.

His emphatic statement seemed to alleviate the anxiety they'd both been feeling. Still, his thoughts kept returning to their date the following weekend. The contemplative look on Tess's face, indicated that hers did, too.

He changed the subject, eager to talk about anything else. "What's up with your girl bidding a hundred K she didn't have?"

"I don't know." Tess seemed genuinely baffled by Gail's behavior.

Tessa and Gail certainly weren't as close as he and Tess were. But lately, at her mother's urging, Tessa had tried to build stronger friendships with other women in town.

She and Gail had met when Tessa had used the woman's fledgling grocery delivery business. They'd hit it off and started hanging out occasionally.

He understood why Tess liked Gail. She was bold and a little irreverent. All of the things that Tess was not. But Ryan hadn't cared much for her. There was something about that woman he didn't quite trust. But now wasn't the time for I told you so's. Tessa obviously felt badly enough about being the person who'd invited Gail to the charity auction.

"I knew she had a lightweight crush on Lloyd Richardson," Tessa continued. "Who doesn't? But I certainly didn't think her capable of doing something this crazy and impulsive."

"Seems there was a lot of that going around," Ryan muttered under his breath.

"Speaking of that impulsiveness that seemed to be going around…" Tessa laughed, and Ryan chuckled, too.

He'd obviously uttered the words more to himself than to her. Still, she'd heard them, and they provided the perfect opening for what she'd been struggling to say all night.

"Thank you again for doing this, Rye. You made a very generous donation. And though you did the complete opposite of what I asked you to do—" they both laughed again "—I was a little...no, I was a *lot* nervous about going out with either Clem or Bo in such a high pressure situation, so thank you."

"Anything for you, Tess Noble." His voice was deep and warm. The emotion behind his words genuine. Something she knew from their history, not just as theory.

When they were in college, Ryan had climbed into his battered truck, and driven nearly two thousand miles to her campus in Sacramento after a particularly bad breakup with a guy who'd been an all-around dick. He'd dumped her for someone else a few days before Valentine's Day, so Ryan made a point of taking her to the Valentine's Day party. Then he kissed her in front of everyone—including her ex.

The kiss had taken her breath away. And left her wanting another taste ever since.

Tessa shook off the memory and focused on the here and now. Ryan had been uncharacteristically quiet during the ride home. He'd let her chatter on, offering a grunt of agreement or dissension here or there. Otherwise, he seemed deep in thought.

"And you're sure I can't pay you back at least

some of what you bid on me?" Tessa asked as he slowed down before turning into the driveway of the Noble Spur, her family's ranch. "Especially since you're commandeering the planning of our date."

"Oh, we're still gonna use those tickets on the fifty-yard line, for sure," he clarified. "And there's no way I'm leaving Dallas without my favorite steak dinner. I'm just going to add some flourishes here and there. Nothing too fancy. But you'll enjoy the night. I promise." He winked.

Why did that small gesture send waves of electricity down her spine and make her acutely aware of her nipples prickling with heat beneath the jacket she'd put on to ward against the chilly night air?

"Well, thank you again," she said as he shifted his tricked out Ford Super Duty F-350 Platinum into Park. Ryan was a simple guy who didn't sweat the details—except when it came to his truck.

"You're welcome." Ryan lightly gripped her elbow when she reached for the door. "Allow me. Wouldn't want you to ruin that fancy outfit of yours."

He hopped out of the truck and came around to her side. He opened the door and took her hand.

It wasn't the first time Ryan had helped her out of his vehicle. But something about this time felt different. There was something in his intense green eyes. Something he wouldn't allow himself to say. Rare for a man who normally said just about anything that popped into his head.

When she stepped down onto the truck's side rail,

Ryan released her hand. He gripped her waist and lifted her to the ground in a single deft move.

Tessa gasped in surprise, bracing her hands on his strong shoulders. His eyes scanned her once more. As if he still couldn't believe it was really her in the sexiest, most feminine item of clothing she'd ever owned.

Heat radiated off his large body, shielding her from the chilliness of the night air and making her aware of how little space there was between them.

For a moment, the vision of Ryan's lips crashing down on hers as he pinned her body against the truck flashed through her brain. It wasn't an unfamiliar image. But, given their positions and the way he was looking at her right now, it felt a little too real.

Tessa took short, shallow breaths, her chest heaving. She needed to get away from Ryan Bateman before she did something stupid. Like lift on to her toes and press a hot, wet kiss to those sensual lips.

She needed to get inside and go to her room. The proper place to have ridiculously inappropriate thoughts about her best friend. With her battery-operated boyfriend buried in the nightstand drawer on standby, just in case she needed to take the edge off.

But walking away was a difficult thing to do when his mouth was mere inches from hers. And she trembled with the desire to touch him. To taste his mouth again. To trace the ridge behind the fly of his black dress pants.

"Good night." She tossed the words over her shoulder as she turned and headed toward the house as quickly as her feet would carry her in those high-heeled silver sandals.

"Tessa." His unusually gruff voice stopped her dead in her tracks.

She didn't turn back to look at him. Instead, she glanced just over her shoulder. A sign that he had her full attention, even if her eyes didn't meet his. "Yes?"

"I'm calling an audible on our date this weekend." Ryan invoked one of his favorite football terms.

"A last-minute change?" Tessa turned slightly, her curiosity piqued.

She'd planned the perfect weekend for Ryan Bateman. What could she possibly have missed?

"I'll pick you up on Friday afternoon, around 3:00 p.m. Pack a bag for the weekend. And don't forget that jumpsuit."

"We're spending the entire weekend in Dallas?" She turned to face him fully, stunned by the hungry look on his face. When he nodded his confirmation, Tessa focused on slowing her breath as she watched the cloud her warm breath made in the air. "Why? And since when do you care what I wear?"

"Because I promised Alexis I'd make this date a big, grand gesture that would keep the reporter preoccupied and off the topic of our missing bachelor and his hundred-thousand-dollar bidder." His words were matter of fact, signaling none of the raw, primal heat she'd seen in his eyes a moment ago.

He shut the passenger door and walked around to the driver's side. "It doesn't have to be that same outfit. It's just that you looked mighty pretty tonight. Neither of us gets much of a chance to dress up. Thought it'd be nice if we took advantage of this weekend to do that." He shrugged, as if it were the most normal request in the world.

This coming from a man who'd once stripped out of his tuxedo in the car on the way home from a mutual friend's out-of-town wedding. He'd insisted he couldn't stand to be in that tuxedo a moment longer.

"Fine." Tessa shrugged, too. If it was no big deal to Ryan, then it was no big deal to her either. "I'll pack a couple of dresses and skirts. Maybe I'll wear the dress I'd originally picked out for tonight. Before I volunteered to be in the auction."

After all that waxing, she should show her baby smooth legs off every chance she got. Who knew when she'd put herself through that kind of torture again?

"Sounds like you got some packing to do." A restrained smirk lit Ryan's eyes. He nodded toward the house. "Better get inside before you freeze out here."

"'Night, Ryan." Tessa turned up the path to the house, without waiting for his response, and let herself in, closing the door behind her. The slam of the heavy truck door, followed by the crunch of gravel, indicated that Ryan was turning his vehicle around in the drive and heading home to the Bateman Ranch next door.

Tessa released a long sigh, her back pressed to the door.

She'd just agreed to spend the weekend in Dallas with her best friend. Seventy-two hours of pretending she didn't secretly lust after Ryan Bateman. Several of which would be documented by a reporter known for going after gossip.

Piece of cake. Piece of pie.

Nine

"Tessa, your chariot is here," Tripp called to her upstairs. "Hurry up, you're not gonna believe this."

Tripp was definitely back to his old self. It was both a blessing and a curse, because he hadn't stopped needling her and Ryan about their date ever since.

She inhaled deeply, then slowly released the breath as she stared at herself in the mirror one last time.

It's just a weekend trip with a friend. Ryan and I have done this at least a dozen times before. No big deal.

Tessa lifted her bag on to her shoulder, then made her way downstairs and out front where Tripp was handing her overnight suitcase off to Ryan.

Her eyes widened as she walked closer, studying the sleek black sedan with expensive black rims.

"Is that a black on black Maybach?"

"It is." Ryan took the bag from her and loaded it into the trunk of the Mercedes Maybach before closing it and opening the passenger door. He gestured for her to get inside. "You've always said you wanted to know what it was like to ride in one of these things, so—"

"You didn't go out and buy this, did you?" Panic filled her chest. Ryan wasn't extravagant or impulsive. And he'd already laid out a substantial chunk of change as a favor to her.

"No, of course not. You know a mud-caked pickup truck is more my style." He leaned in and lowered his voice, so only she could hear his next words. "But I'm supposed to be going for the entire illusion here, remember? And Tess…"

"Yes?" She inhaled his clean, fresh scent, her heart racing slightly from his nearness and the intimacy of his tone.

"Smile for the camera." Ryan nodded toward Greg Halstead who waved and snapped photographs of the two of them in front of the vehicle.

Tess deepened her smile, and she and Ryan stood together, his arm wrapped around her as the man clicked photos for the paper.

When Greg had gotten enough images, he shook their hands and said he'd meet them at the hotel later and at the restaurant tomorrow night to get a few more photos.

"Which hotel? And which restaurant?" Tessa turned to Ryan.

A genuine smile lit his green eyes and they sparkled in the afternoon sunlight. "If I tell you, it won't be a surprise, now will it?"

"Smart-ass." She folded her arms and shook her head. Ryan knew she liked surprises about as much as she liked diamondback rattlesnakes. Maybe even a little less.

"There anything I should know about you two?" Tripp stepped closer after the reporter was gone. Arms folded over his chest, his gaze shifted from Ryan to her and then back again.

"You can take the protective big brother shtick down a notch," she teased. "I already explained everything to you. We're doing this for the club, and for Alexis."

She flashed her I'm-your-little-sister-and-you-love-me-no-matter-what smile. It broke him. As it had for as long as she could remember.

The edge of his mouth tugged upward in a reluctant grin. He opened his arms and hugged her goodbye before giving Ryan a one-arm bro hug and whispering something to him that she couldn't hear.

Ryan's expression remained neutral, but he nodded and patted her brother on the shoulder.

"We'd better get going." Ryan helped her into the

buttery, black leather seat that seemed to give her a warm hug. Then he closed her door and climbed into the driver's seat.

"God, this car is beautiful," she said as he pulled away from the house. "If you didn't buy it, whose is it?

"Borrowed it from a friend." He pulled on to the street more carefully than he did when he was driving his truck. "The guy collects cars the way other folks collect stamps or Depression-era glass. Most of the cars he wouldn't let anyone breathe on, let alone touch. But he owed me a favor."

Tessa sank back against the seat and ran her hand along the smooth, soft leather.

"Manners would dictate that I tell you that you shouldn't have, but if I'm being honest, all I can think is, Where have you been all my life?" They both chuckled. "You think I can have a saddle made out of this leather?"

"For the right price, you can get just about anything." A wide smile lit his face.

Tessa sighed. She was content. Relaxed. And Ryan seemed to be, too. There was no reason this weekend needed to be tense and awkward.

"So, what did my brother say to you when he gave you that weird bro hug goodbye?"

The muscles in Ryan's jaw tensed and his brows furrowed. He kept his gaze on the road ahead. "This thing has an incredible sound system. I already synced it to my phone. Go ahead and play something. Your choice. Just no more '80s boy bands. I heard enough of those at the charity auction last week."

Tessa smirked. "You could've just told me it was none of my business what Tripp said."

His wide smile returned, though he didn't look at her. "I thought I just did."

They both laughed, and Tessa smiled to herself. Their weekend was going to be fun. Just like every other road trip they'd ever taken together. Things would only be uncomfortable between them if she made them that way.

Ryan, Tessa and Greg Halstead headed up the stone stairs that led to the bungalow of a fancy, art-themed boutique hotel that he'd reserved. The place was an easy drive from the football stadium.

Tessa had marveled at the hotel's main building and mused about the expense. But she was as excited as a little kid in a candy store, eager to see what was on the other side of that door. Greg requested to go in first, so he could set up his shot of Tessa stepping inside the room.

When he signaled that he was ready, Ryan inserted the key card into the lock and removed it quickly. Once the green light flashed, he opened the door for her.

Tessa's jaw dropped, and she covered her mouth

with both hands, genuinely stunned by the elegant beauty of the contemporary bungalow.

"So…what do you think?" He couldn't shake the nervousness he felt. The genuine need to impress her was not his typical MO. So what was going on? Maybe it was the fact that her impression would be recorded for posterity.

"It's incredible, Ryan. I don't know what to say." Her voice trembled with emotion. When she glanced up at him, her eyes were shiny. She wiped quickly at the corners of her eyes. "I'm being silly, I know."

"No, you're not." He kissed her cheek. "That's exactly the reaction I was hoping for."

Ryan stepped closer and lowered his voice. "I want this to be a special weekend for you, Tess. What you did last week at the charity auction was brave, and I'm proud of you. I want this weekend to be everything the fearless woman who strutted across that stage last Saturday night deserves."

His eyes met hers for a moment and his chest filled with warmth.

"Thanks, Rye. This place is amazing. I really appreciate everything you've done." A soft smile curled the edges of her mouth, filling him with the overwhelming desire to lean down and kiss her the way he had at that Valentine's Day party in college.

He stepped back and cleared his throat, indicating that she should step inside.

Tessa went from room to room of the two-bedroom, two-bath hotel suite, complete with two balconies. One connected to each bedroom. There was even a small kitchen island, a full-size refrigerator and a stove. The open living room boasted a ridiculously large television mounted to the wall and a fireplace in both that space and the master bedroom, which he insisted that she take. But Tessa, who could be just as stubborn as he was, wouldn't hear of it. She directed the bellman to take her things to the slightly smaller bedroom, which was just as beautiful as its counterpart.

"I think I have all the pictures I need." Greg gathered up his camera bag and his laptop. "I'll work on the article tonight and select the best photos among the ones I've taken so far. I'll meet you guys at the restaurant tomorrow at six-thirty to capture a few more shots."

"Sounds good." Ryan said goodbye to Greg and closed the door behind him, glad the man was finally gone. Something about a reporter hanging around, angling for a juicy story, felt like a million ants crawling all over his skin.

He sank on to the sofa, shrugged his boots off, and put his feet up on the coffee table. It'd been a short drive from Royal to Dallas, but mentally, he was exhausted.

Partly from making last-minute arrangements for their trip. Partly from the effort of reminding himself that no matter how much it felt like it, this wasn't a real date. They were both just playing their parts. Making the TCC look good and diverting attention from the debacle of Gail's bid.

"Hey." Tess emerged from her bedroom where she'd gone to put her things away. "Is Greg gone?"

"He left a few minutes ago. Said to tell you goodbye."

"Thank goodness." She heaved a sigh and plopped down on the sofa beside him. "I mean, he's a nice guy and everything. It just feels so... I don't know..."

"Creepy? Invasive? Weird?" he offered. "Take your pick."

"All of the above." Tessa laughed, then leaned forward, her gaze locked on to the large bouquet of flowers in a glass vase on the table beside his feet.

"I thought these were just part of the room." She removed the small envelope with her name on it and slid her finger beneath the flap, prying it open. "These are for me?"

"I hope you like them. They're—"

"Peonies. My favorite flower." She leaned forward and inhaled the flowers that resembled clouds dyed shades of light and dark pink. "They're beautiful, Ryan. Thank you. You thought of everything, didn't you?" Her voice trailed and her gaze softened.

"I meant it when I said you deserve a really special weekend. I even asked them to stock the freezer with your favorite brand of Neapolitan ice cream."

"Seriously?" She was only wearing a hint of lip gloss in a nude shade of pink and a little eyeshadow and mascara. But she was as beautiful as he'd ever seen her. Even more so than the night of the auction when she'd worn a heavy layer of makeup that had covered her creamy brown skin. Sunlight filtered into the room, making her light brown eyes appear almost golden. "What more could I possibly ask for?"

His eyes were locked on her sensual lips. When he finally tore his gaze away from them, Tess seemed disappointed. As if she'd expected him to lean in and kiss her.

"I like the dress, by the way."

"Really?" She stood, looking down at the heather-gray dress and the tan calf-high boots topped by knee socks. The cuff of the socks hovered just above the top of the boot, drawing his eye there and leading it up the side of her thigh where her smooth skin disappeared beneath the hem of her dress.

His body stiffened in response to her curvy silhouette and her summery citrus scent.

Fucking knee socks. *Seriously*? Tess was *killing* him.

For a moment he wondered if she was teasing him on purpose. Reminding him of the things he couldn't have with her. The red-hot desires that would never be satisfied.

Tess seemed completely oblivious to her effect on him as she regarded the little gray dress.

Yet, all he could think of was how much he'd

like to see that gray fabric pooled on the floor beside his bed.

Ryan groaned inside. This was going to be the longest seventy-two hours of his life.

Ten

"Is that a bottle of champagne?" Tessa pointed to a bottle chilling in an ice bucket on the sideboard along the wall.

She could use something cold to tamp down the heat rising in her belly under Ryan's intense stare. It also wouldn't be a bad idea to create some space between them. Enough to get her head together and stop fantasizing about what it would feel like to kiss her best friend again.

"Even better." Ryan flashed a sexy, half grin. "It's imported Italian Moscato d'Asti. I asked them to chill a bottle for us."

Her favorite. Too bad this wasn't a real date, because Ryan had ticked every box of what her fantasy date would look like.

"Saving it for something special?"

"Just you." He winked, climbing to his feet. "Why don't we make a toast to kick our weekend off?"

Tessa relaxed a little as she followed him over to the ice bucket, still maintaining some distance between them.

Ryan opened the bottle with a loud pop and poured each of them a glass of the sparkling white wine. He handed her one.

She accepted, gratefully, and joined him in holding up her glass.

"To an unforgettable weekend." A soft smile curved the edges of his mouth.

"Cheers." Tessa ignored the beading of her nipples and the tingling that trailed down her spine and sparked a fire low in her belly. She took a deep sip.

"Very good." Tessa fought back her speculation about how much better it would taste on Ryan's lips.

Ryan returned to the sofa. He finished his glass of moscato in short order and set it on the table beside the sofa.

Tessa sat beside him, finishing the remainder of her drink and contemplating another. She decided against it, setting it on the table in front of them.

She turned to her friend. God, he was handsome. His green eyes brooding and intense. His shaggy brown hair living in that space between perfectly groomed and purposely messy. The ever-present five o'clock shadow crawling over his clenched jaw.

"Thanks, Rye." She needed to quell the thoughts

in her head. "This is all so amazing and incredibly thoughtful. I know this fantasy date isn't real, but you went out of your way to make it feel that way, and I appreciate it."

Tessa leaned in to kiss his stubbled cheek. Something she'd done a dozen times before. But Ryan turned his head, likely surprised by her sudden approach, and her lips met his.

She'd been right. The moscato did taste better enmeshed with the flavor of Ryan's firm, sensual lips.

It was an accidental kiss. So why had she leaned in and continued to kiss him, rather than withdrawing and apologizing? And why hadn't Ryan pulled back either?

Tessa's eyes slowly drifted closed, and she slipped her fingers into the short hair at the nape of Ryan's neck. Pulled his face closer to hers.

She parted her lips, and Ryan accepted the unspoken invitation, sliding his tongue between her lips and taking control. The kiss had gradually moved from a sweet, inadvertent, closed-mouth affair to an intense meshing of lips, teeth and tongues. Ryan moved his hands to her back, tugging her closer.

Tessa sighed softly in response to the hot, demanding kiss that obliterated the memory of that unexpected one nearly a decade ago. Truly kissing Ryan Bateman was everything she'd imagined it to be.

And she wanted more.

They'd gone this far. Had let down the invisible wall between them. There was nothing holding them back now.

Tessa inhaled deeply before shifting to her knees and straddling Ryan's lap. He groaned. A sexy sound that was an undeniable mixture of pain and pleasure. Of intense wanting. Evident from the ridge beneath his zipper.

As he deepened their kiss, his large hand splayed against her low back, his hardness met the soft, warm space between her thighs, sending a shiver up her spine. Her nipples ached with an intensity she hadn't experienced before. She wanted his hands and lips on her naked flesh. She wanted to shed the clothing that prevented skin-to-skin contact.

She wanted...sex. With Ryan. Right now.

Sex.

It wasn't as if she'd forgotten how the whole process worked. Obviously. But it'd been a while since she'd been with anyone. More than a few years. One of the hazards of living in a town small enough that there was three degrees or less of separation between any man she met and her father or brother.

Would Ryan be disappointed?

Tessa suddenly went stiff, her eyes blinking.

"Don't," he whispered between hungry kisses along her jaw and throat that left her wanting and breathless, despite the insecurities that had taken over her brain.

Tess frowned. "Don't do what?"

Maybe she didn't have Ryan Bateman's vast sexual experience, but she was pretty sure she knew how to kiss. At least she hadn't had any complaints.

Until now.

"Have you changed your mind about this?"

"No." She forced her eyes to meet his, regardless of how unnerved she was by his intense stare and his determination to make her own up to what she wanted. "Not even a little."

The edge of his mouth curved in a criminally sexy smirk. "Then for once in your life, Tess, stop overthinking everything. Stop compiling a list in your head of all the reasons we shouldn't do this." He kissed her again, his warm lips pressed to hers and his large hands gliding down her back and gripping her bottom as he pulled her firmly against him.

A soft gasp escaped her mouth at the sensation of his hard length pressed against her sensitive flesh. Ryan swept his tongue between her parted lips, tangling it with hers as he wrapped his arms around her.

Their kiss grew increasingly urgent. Hungry. Desperate. His kiss made her question whether she'd ever *really* been kissed before. Made her skin tingle with a desire so intense she physically ached with a need for him.

A need for Ryan's kiss. His touch. The warmth of his naked skin pressed against hers. The feel of him inside her.

Hands shaking and the sound of her own heartbeat filling her ears, Tessa pulled her mouth from his. She grabbed the hem of her dress and raised it. His eyes were locked with hers, both of them breathing heavily, as she lifted the fabric.

Ryan helped her tug the dress over her head and he tossed it on to the floor. He studied her lacy, gray bra and the cleavage spilling out of it.

Her cheeks flamed, and her heart raced. Ryan leaned in and planted slow, warm kisses on her shoulder. He swept her hair aside and trailed kisses up her neck.

"God, you're beautiful, Tess." His voice was a low growl that sent tremors through her. He glided a callused hand down her back and rested it on her hip. "I think it's pretty obvious how much I want you. But I need to know that you're sure about this."

"I am." She traced his rough jaw with her palm. Glided a thumb across his lips, naturally a deep shade of red that made them even more enticing. Then she crashed her lips against his as she held his face in her hands.

He claimed her mouth with a greedy, primal kiss that strung her body tight as a bow, desperate for the release that only he could provide.

She wanted him. More than she could ever remember wanting anything. The steely rod pressed against the slick, aching spot between her thighs indicated his genuine desire for her. Yet, he seemed hesitant. As if he were holding back. Something

Ryan Bateman, one of the most confident men she'd ever known, wasn't prone to do.

Tess reached behind her and did the thing Ryan seemed reluctant to. She released the hooks on her bra, slid the straps down her shoulders and tossed it away.

He splayed one hand against her back. The other glided up and down her side before his thumb grazed the side of her breast. Once, twice, then again. As if testing her.

Finally, he grazed her hardened nipple with his open palm, and she sucked in a sharp breath.

His eyes met hers with a look that fell somewhere between asking and pleading.

Tessa swallowed hard, her cheeks and chest flushed with heat. She nodded, her hands trembling as she braced them on his wide shoulders.

When Ryan's lips met her skin again, she didn't fight the overwhelming feelings that flooded her senses, like a long, hard rain causing the creek to exceed its banks. She leaned into them. Allowed them to wash over her. Enjoyed the thing she'd fantasized about for so long.

Tessa gasped as Ryan cupped her bottom and pulled her against his hardened length. As if he was as desperate for her as she was for him. He kissed her neck, her shoulders, her collarbone. Then he dropped tender, delicate kisses on her breasts.

Tessa ran her fingers through his soft hair. When

he raised his eyes to hers, she leaned down, whispering in his ear.

"Ryan, take me to bed. Now."

Before she lost her nerve. Before he lost his.

Ryan carried her to his bed, laid her down and settled between her thighs. He trailed slow, hot kisses down her neck and chest as he palmed her breast with his large, work-roughened hand. He sucked the beaded tip into his warm mouth. Grazed it with his teeth. Lathed it with his tongue.

She shuddered in response to the tantalizing sensation that shot from her nipple straight to her sex. Her skin flamed beneath Ryan's touch, and her breath came in quick little bursts. He nuzzled her neck, one large hand skimming down her thigh and hooking behind her knee. As he rocked against the space between her thighs, Tessa whimpered at the delicious torture of his steely length grinding against her needy clit.

"That's it, Tess." Ryan trailed kisses along her jaw. "Relax. Let go. You know I'd never do anything to hurt you." His stubble scraped the sensitive skin of her cheek as he whispered roughly in her ear.

She did know that. She trusted Ryan with her life. With her deepest secrets. With her body. Ryan was sweet and charming and well-meaning, but her friend could sometimes be a bull in the china shop.

Would he ride roughshod over her heart, even if he didn't mean to?

Tessa gazed up at him, her lips parting as she took

in his incredibly handsome form. She yanked his shirt from the back of his pants and slid her hands against his warm skin. Gently grazed his back with her nails. She had the fleeting desire to mark him as hers. So that any other woman who saw him would know he belonged to her and no one else.

Ryan moved beside her, and she immediately missed his weight and the feel of him pressed against her most sensitive flesh. He kissed her harder as he slid a hand up her thigh and then cupped the space between her legs that throbbed in anticipation of his touch.

Tessa tensed, sucking in a deep breath as he glided his fingertips back and forth over the drenched panel of fabric shielding her sex. He tugged the material aside and plunged two fingers inside her.

"God, you're wet, Tess." The words vibrated against her throat, where he branded her skin with scorching hot kisses that made her weak with want. He kissed his way down her chest and gently scraped her sensitive nipple with his teeth before swirling his tongue around the sensitive flesh.

Tessa quivered as the space between her thighs ached with need. She wanted to feel him inside her. To be with Ryan in the way she'd always imagined.

But this wasn't a dream; it was real. And their actions would have real-world consequences.

"You're doing it again. That head thing," he muttered in between little nips and licks. His eyes glinted in the light filtering through the bedroom window. "Cut it out."

God, he knew her too well. And after tonight, he would know every single inch of her body. If she had her way.

Eleven

Ryan couldn't get over how beautiful Tessa was as she lay beside him whimpering with pleasure. Lips parted, back arched and her eyelashes fluttering, she was everything he'd imagined and more.

He halted his action just long enough to encourage her to lift her hips, allowing him to drag the lacy material down her legs, over her boots, and off. Returning his attention to her full breasts, he sucked and licked one of the pebbled, brown peaks he'd occasionally glimpsed the outline of through the thin, tank tops she sometimes wore during summer. He'd spent more time than he dared admit speculating about what her breasts looked like and how her skin would taste.

Now he knew. And he desperately wanted to know everything about her body. What turned her on? What would send her spiraling over the edge, his name on her lips?

He eagerly anticipated solving those mysteries, too.

Ryan inserted his fingers inside her again, adding a third finger to her tight, slick channel. Allowed her body to stretch and accommodate the additional digit.

He and Tess had made it a point not to delve too deeply into each other's sex lives. Still, they'd shared enough for him to know he wouldn't be her first or even her second. She was just a little tense, and perhaps a lot nervous. And she needed to relax.

Her channel stretched and relaxed around his fingers as he moved to her other nipple and gave it the same treatment he'd given the first. He resumed the movement of his hand, his fingers gliding in and out of her. Then he stroked the slick bundle of nerves with his thumb.

Tessa's undeniable gasp of pleasure indicated her approval.

The slow, small circles he made with his thumb got wider, eliciting a growing chorus of curses and moans. Her grip on his hair tightened, and she moved her hips in rhythm with his hand.

She was slowly coming undone, and he was grateful to be the reason for it. Ryan wet his lips with a sweep of his tongue, eager to taste her there. But he wanted to take his time. Make this last for both of them.

He kissed Tessa's belly and slipped his other hand between her legs, massaging her clit as he curved the fingers inside her.

"Oh god, oh god, oh god, Ryan. Right there, right there," Tess pleaded when he hit the right spot.

He gladly obliged her request, both hands moving with precision until he'd taken Tess to the edge. She'd called his name, again and again, as she dug the heels of her boots into the mattress and her body stiffened.

Watching his best friend tumble into bliss was a thing of beauty. Being the one who'd brought her such intense ecstasy was an incredible gift. It was easily the most meaningful sexual experience he'd ever had, and he was still fully clothed.

Ryan lay down, gathering Tess to him and wrapping her in his arms, her head tucked under his chin. He flipped the cover over her, so she'd stay warm.

They were both silent. Tessa's chest heaved as she slowly came down from the orgasm he'd given her.

When the silence lingered on for seconds that turned to minutes, but felt like hours, Ryan couldn't take it.

"Tess, look, I—"

"You're still dressed." She raised her head, her eyes meeting his. Her playful smile eased the tension they'd both been feeling. "And I'm not quite sure why."

The laugh they shared felt good. A bit of normalcy in a situation that was anything but normal between them.

He planted a lingering kiss on her sweet lips.

"I can fix that." He sat up and tugged his shirt over his head and tossed it on to the floor unceremoniously.

"Keep going." She indicated his pants with a wave of her hand.

"Bold and bossy." He laughed. "Who is this woman and what did she do with my best friend?"

She frowned slightly, as if what he'd said had hurt her feelings.

"Hey." He cradled her face in one hand. "You know that's not a criticism, right? I like seeing this side of you."

"Usually when a man calls a woman bossy, it's code for bitchy." Her eyes didn't quite meet his.

Ryan wanted to kick himself. He'd only been teasing when he'd used the word bossy, but he hadn't been thinking. He understood how loaded that term was to Tess. She'd hated that her mother and grandmother had constantly warned her that no ranch man would want a bossy bride.

"I should've said assertive," he clarified. "Which is what I've always encouraged you to be."

She nodded, seemingly satisfied with his explanation. A warm smile slid across her gorgeous face and lit her light brown eyes. "Then I'd like to assert that you're still clothed, and I don't appreciate it, seeing as I'm not."

"Yes, ma'am." He winked as he stood and removed his pants.

Tessa gently sank her teeth into her lower lip as she studied the bulge in his boxer briefs. Which only made him harder.

He rubbed the back of his neck and chuckled. "Now I guess I know how the fellas felt on stage at the auction."

"Hmm…" The humming sound Tess made seemed to vibrate in his chest and other parts of his body. Specifically, the part she was staring at right now.

Tess removed her boots and kneeled on the bed in front of him, her brown eyes studying him. The levity had faded from her expression, replaced by a heated gaze that made his cock twitch.

She looped her arms around his neck and pulled his mouth down toward hers. Angling her head, she kissed him hard, her fingers slipping into his hair and her naked breasts smashed against his hard chest.

If this was a dream, he didn't want to wake up.

Ryan wrapped his arms around Tess, needing her body pressed firmly against his. He splayed one hand against the smooth, soft skin of her back. The other squeezed the generous bottom he'd always quietly admired. Hauling her tight against him, he grew painfully hard with the need to be inside her.

He claimed her mouth, his tongue gliding against

hers, his anticipation rising. He'd fantasized about making love to Tess long before that kiss they'd shared in college.

He'd wanted to make love to her that night. Or at the very least make out with her in his truck. But he'd promised Tripp he wouldn't ever look at Tess that way.

A promise he'd broken long before tonight, despite his best efforts.

Ryan pushed thoughts of his ill-advised pledge to Tripp and the consequences of breaking it from his mind.

Right now, it was just him and Tess. The only thing that mattered in this moment was what the two of them wanted. What they needed from each other.

Ryan pulled away, just long enough to rummage in his luggage for the condoms he kept in his bag.

He said a silent prayer, thankful there was one full strip left. He tossed it on the nightstand and stripped out of his underwear.

Suddenly she seemed shy again as his eyes roved every inch of her gorgeous body.

He placed his hands on her hips, pulling her close to him and pressing his forehead to hers.

"God, you're beautiful, Tess." He knew he sounded like a broken record. But he was struck by how breathtaking she was and by the fact that she'd trusted him with something as precious as her body.

"You're making me feel self-conscious." A deep

blush stained Tess's cheeks and spread through her chest.

"Don't be." He cradled her cheek, hoping to put her at ease. "That's not my intention. I just…" He sighed, giving up on trying to articulate what he was feeling.

One-night stands, even the occasional relationship…those were easy. But with Tess, everything felt weightier. More significant. Definitely more complicated. He couldn't afford to fuck this up. Because not having Tess as his friend wasn't an option. Still, he wanted her.

"Ryan, it's okay." She wrapped her arms around him. "I'm nervous about this, too. But I know that I want to be with you tonight. It's what I've wanted for a long time, and I don't want to fight it anymore."

He shifted his gaze to hers. A small sigh of relief escaped his mouth.

Tess understood exactly what he was feeling. They could do this. Be together like this. Satisfy their craving for each other without ruining their friendship.

He captured her mouth in a bruising kiss, and they both tumbled on to the mattress. Hands groping. Tongues searching. Hearts racing.

He grabbed one of the foil packets and ripped it open, sheathing himself as quickly as he could.

He guided himself to her slick entrance, circling his hips so his pelvis rubbed against her hardened clit. Tessa gasped, then whimpered with pleasure each time he ground his hips against her again. She writhed against him, increasing the delicious friction against the tight bundle of nerves.

Ryan gripped the base of his cock and pressed its head to her entrance. He inched inside, and Tess whimpered softly. She dug her fingers into his hips, her eyes meeting his as he slid the rest of the way home. Until he was nestled as deeply inside her as the laws of physics would allow.

When he was fully seated, her slick, heated flesh surrounding him, an involuntary growl escaped his mouth at the delicious feel of this woman who was all softness and curves. Sweetness and beauty. His friend and his lover.

His gaze met hers as he hovered above her and moved inside her. His voice rasping, he whispered to her. Told her how incredible she made him feel.

Then, lifting her legs, he hooked them over his shoulders as he leaned over her, his weight on his hands as he moved.

She gasped, her eyes widening at the sensation of him going deep and hitting bottom due to the sudden shift in position.

"Ryan… I…oh… God." Tessa squeezed her eyes shut.

"C'mon, Tess." He arched his back as he shifted his hips forward, beads of sweat forming on his brow and trickling down his back. "Just let go. Don't think. Just feel."

Her breath came in quick pants, and she dug her

nails in his biceps. Suddenly, her mouth formed a little *O* and her eyes opened wide. The unmistakable expression of pure satisfaction that overtook her as she called his name was one of the most beautiful things he'd ever seen. Something he wanted to see again and again.

Her flesh throbbed and pulsed around him, bringing him to his peak. He tensed, shuddering as he cursed and called her name.

Ryan collapsed on to the bed beside her, both of them breathing hard and staring at the ceiling overhead for a few moments.

Finally, she draped an arm over his abdomen and rested her head on his shoulder.

He kissed the top of her head, pulled the covers over them, and slipped an arm around her. He lay there, still and quiet, fighting his natural tendency to slip out into the night. His usual MO after a one-night stand. Only he couldn't do that. Partly because it was Tess. Partly because what he'd felt between them was something he couldn't quite name, and he wanted to feel it again.

Ryan propped an arm beneath his head and stared at the ceiling as Tessa's soft breathing indicated she'd fallen asleep.

Intimacy.

That was the elusive word he'd been searching for all night. The thing he'd felt when his eyes had met hers as he'd roared, buried deep inside her. He'd sounded ridiculous. Like a wounded animal, in pain. Needing someone to save him.

Ryan scrubbed a hand down his face, one arm still wrapped around his best friend. Whom he'd made love to. The woman who knew him better than anyone in the world.

And now they knew each other in a way they'd never allowed themselves to before. A way that made him feel raw and exposed, like a live wire.

While making love to Tess, he'd felt a surge of power as he'd teased her gorgeous body and coaxed her over the edge. Watched her free-fall into ecstasy, her body trembling.

But as her inner walls pulsed, pulling him over the cliff after her, he'd felt something completely foreign and yet vaguely familiar. It was a thing he couldn't name. Or maybe he hadn't wanted to.

Then when he'd startled awake, his arm slightly numb from being wedged beneath her, the answer was on his tongue.

Intimacy.

How was it that he'd managed to have gratifying sex with women without ever experiencing this heightened level of intimacy? Not even with his ex— the woman he'd planned to marry.

He and Sabrina had known each other. What the other wanted for breakfast. Each other's preferred drinks. They'd even known each other's bodies. *Well.* And yet he'd never experienced this depth of connection. Of truly being known by someone who could practically finish his sentences. Not because Tessa was so like him, but because she understood him in a way no one else did.

Ryan swallowed the hard lump clogging his throat and swiped the backs of his fingers over his damp brow.

Why is it suddenly so goddamned hot in here?

He blew out a long, slow breath. Tried to slow the rhythm of his heart, suddenly beating like a drum.

What the hell had he just done?

He'd satisfied the curiosity that had been simmering just below the surface of his friendship with Tessa. The desire to know her intimately. To know how it would feel to have her soft curves pressed against him as he'd surged inside her.

Now he knew what it was like for their bodies to move together. As if they were a single being. How it made his pulse race like a freight train as she called his name in a sweet, husky voice he'd never heard her use before. The delicious burn of her nails gently scraping his back as she wrapped her legs around him and pulled him in deeper.

And how it felt as she'd throbbed and pulsed around his heated flesh until he could no longer hold back his release.

Now, all he could think about was feeling all of those things again. Watching her shed the inhibitions that had held her back at first. Taking her a little further.

But Tessa was his best friend, and a very good friend's sister. He'd crossed the line. Broken a promise and taken them to a place they could never venture back from. After last night, he couldn't see her and not want her. Would never forget the taste and feel of her.

So what now?

Tess was sweet and sensitive. Warm and thoughtful. She deserved more than being friends with benefits. She deserved a man as kind and loving as she was.

Was he even capable of being that kind of man?

His family was nothing like the Nobles. Hank and Loretta Bateman weren't the doting parents that kissed injured knees and cheered effort. They believed in tough love, hard lessons and that failure wasn't to be tolerated by anyone with the last name Bateman.

Ryan knew unequivocally that his parents loved him, but he was twenty-nine years old and could never recall hearing either of them say the words explicitly.

He'd taken the same approach in his relationships. It was how he was built, all he'd ever known. But Tess could never be happy in a relationship like that.

Ryan sucked in another deep breath and released it quietly. He gently kissed the top of her head and screwed his eyes shut. Allowed himself to surrender to the sleep that had eluded him until now.

They'd figure it all out in the morning. After he'd gotten some much-needed sleep. He always thought better with a clear head and a full stomach.

Twelve

Tessa's eyes fluttered opened. She blinked against the rays of light peeking through the hotel room curtain and rubbed the sleep from her eyes with her fist. Her leg was entwined with Ryan's, and one of her arms was buried beneath him.

She groaned, pressing a hand to her mouth to prevent a curse from erupting from her lips. She'd made love with her best friend. Had fallen asleep with him. She peeked beneath the covers, her mouth falling open.

Naked. Both of them.

Tessa snapped her mouth shut and eased the cover back down. Though it didn't exactly lie flat. Not with Ryan Bateman sporting a textbook definition of morning wood.

She sank her teeth into her lower lip and groaned internally. Her nipples hardened, and the space between her thighs grew incredibly wet. Heat filled her cheeks.

She'd been with Ryan in the most intimate way imaginable. And it had been…incredible. Better than anything she'd imagined. And she'd imagined it more than she cared to admit.

Ryan had been intense, passionate and completely unselfish. He seemed to get off on pleasing her. Had evoked reactions from her body she hadn't believed it capable of. And the higher he'd taken her, the more desperate she became to shatter the mask of control that gripped his handsome face.

Tessa drew her knees to her chest and took slow, deep breaths. Willed her hands to stop shaking. Tried to tap into the brain cells that had taken a siesta the moment she'd pressed her lips to Ryan's.

Yes, sex between them had been phenomenal. But the friendship they shared for more than two decades—that was something she honestly couldn't do without.

She needed some space, so she could clear her head and make better decisions than she had last night. Last night she'd allowed her stupid crush on her best friend to run wild. She'd bought into the Cinderella fantasy. Lock, stock and barrel.

What did she think would happen next? That he'd suddenly realize she was in love with him? Maybe even realize he was in love with her, too?

Not in this lifetime or the next.

She simply wasn't that lucky. Ryan had always considered her a friend. His best friend, but nothing more. A few hours together naked between the sheets wouldn't change that.

Besides, as her mother often reminded her, tigers don't change their stripes.

How many times had Ryan said it? *Sex is just sex.* A way to have a little fun and let off a little steam. Why would she expect him to feel differently just because it was her?

Her pent-up feelings for Ryan were her issue, not his.

Tessa's face burned with an intense heat, as if she was standing too close to a fire. Waking up naked with her best friend was awkward, but they could laugh it off. Blame it on the alcohol, like Jamie Foxx. Chalk it up to them both getting too carried away in the moment. But if she told him how she really felt about him, and he rejected her...

Tessa sighed. The only thing worse than secretly lusting after her best friend was having had him, knowing just how good things could be, and then being patently rejected. She'd never recover from that. Would never be able to look him in the face and pretend everything was okay.

And if, by some chance, Ryan was open to trying to turn this into something more, he'd eventually get bored with their relationship. As he had with every relationship he'd been in before. They'd risk destroying their friendship.

It wasn't worth the risk.

Tessa wiped away tears that stung the corners of her eyes. She quietly climbed out of bed, in search of her clothing.

She cursed under her breath as she retrieved her panties—the only clothing she'd been wearing when they entered the bedroom. Tessa pulled them on and grabbed Ryan's shirt from the floor. She slipped it on and buttoned a few of the middle buttons. She glanced back at his handsome form as he slept soundly, hoping everything between them would be all right.

Tessa slowly turned the doorknob and the door creaked open.

Damn.

Wasn't oiling door hinges part of the planned maintenance for a place like this? Did they not realize the necessity of silent hinges in the event a hotel guest needed a quiet escape after making a questionable decision with her best friend the night before?

Still, as soundly as Ryan was sleeping, odds were, he hadn't heard it.

"Tess?" Ryan called from behind her in that sexy, sleep-roughened voice that made her squirm.

Every. Damn. Time.

She sucked in a deep breath, forced a nonchalant smile and turned around. "Yes?"

"Where are you going?"

He'd propped himself up in bed on one elbow as he rubbed his eyes and squinted against the light. His brown hair stood all over his head in the hottest damn case of bed head she'd ever witnessed. And his bottle-green eyes glinted in the sunlight.

Trying to escape before you woke up. Isn't it obvious?

Tessa jerked a thumb over her shoulder. "I was about to hop into the shower, and I didn't want to wake you."

"Perfect." He sat up and threw off the covers. "We can shower together." A devilish smile curled his red lips. "I know how you feel about conserving water."

"You want to shower…together? The two of us?" She pointed to herself and then to him.

"Why? Were you thinking of inviting someone else?"

"Smart-ass." Her cheeks burned with heat. Ryan was in rare form. "You know what I meant."

"Yes, I do." He stalked toward her naked, at more than half-mast now. Looking like walking, talking sex-on-a-stick promising unicorn orgasms.

Ryan looped his arms around her waist and pressed her back against the wall. He leaned down and nuzzled her neck.

Tessa's beaded nipples rubbed against his chest through the fabric of the shirt she was wearing. Her belly fluttered, and her knees trembled. Her chest rose and fell with heavy, labored breaths. As if Ryan was sucking all the oxygen from the room, making it harder for her to breathe.

"C'mon, Tess." He trailed kisses along her shoulder as he slipped the shirt from it. "Don't make this weird. It's just us."

She raised her eyes to his, her heart racing. "It's already weird *because* it's just us."

"Good point." He gave her a cocky half smile and a micro nod. "Then we definitely need to do something to alleviate the weirdness."

"And *how* exactly are we going to do—" Tess squealed as Ryan suddenly lifted her and heaved her over his shoulder. He carried her, kicking and wiggling, into the master bathroom and turned on the water.

"Ryan Bateman, don't you dare even think about it," Tessa called over her shoulder, kicking her feet and holding on to Ryan's back for dear life.

He wouldn't drop her. She had every confidence of that. Still...

"You're going to ruin my hair."

"I like your curls better. In fact, I felt a little cheated that I didn't get to run my fingers through them. I always wanted to do that."

Something about his statement stopped her objections cold. Made visions dance in her head of them together in the shower with Ryan doing just that.

"Okay. Just put me down."

Ryan smacked her bottom lightly before setting

her down, her body sliding down his. Seeming to rev them both up as steam surrounded them.

She slowly undid the three buttons of Ryan's shirt and made a show of sliding the fabric down one shoulder, then the other.

His green eyes darkened. His chest rose and fell heavily as his gaze met hers again after he'd followed the garment's descent to the floor.

Ryan hooked his thumbs into the sides of her panties and tugged her closer, dropping another kiss on her neck. He gently sank his teeth into her delicate flesh, nibbling the skin there as he glided her underwear over the swell of her bottom and down her hips.

She stepped out of them and into the shower. Pressed her back against the cool tiles. A striking contrast to the warm water. Ryan stepped into the shower, too, closing the glass door behind him and covering her mouth with his.

Tessa lay on her back, her hair wound in one of Ryan's clean, cotton T-shirts. He'd washed her hair and taken great delight in running a soapy loofah over every inch of her body.

Then he'd set her on the shower bench and dropped to his knees. He'd used the removable shower head as a makeshift sex toy. Had used it to bring her to climax twice. Then showed her just how amazing he could be with his tongue.

When he'd pressed the front of her body to the

wall, lifted one of her legs, and taken her from behind, Tessa honestly hadn't thought it would be possible for her to get there again.

She was wrong.

She came hard, her body tightening and convulsing, and his did the same soon afterward.

They'd gone through their morning routines, brushing their teeth side by side, wrapped in towels from their shower together. Ryan ordered room service, and they ate breakfast in bed, catching the last half of a holiday comedy that was admittedly a pretty crappy movie overall. Still, it never failed to make the two of them laugh hysterically.

When the movie ended, Ryan had clicked off the television and kissed her. A kiss that slowly stoked the fire low in her belly all over again. Made her nipples tingle and the space between her thighs ache for him.

She lay staring up at Ryan, his hair still damp from the shower. Clearly hell-bent on using every single condom in that strip before the morning ended, he'd sheathed himself and entered her again.

Her eyes had fluttered closed at the delicious fullness as Ryan eased inside her. His movements were slow, deliberate, controlled.

None of those words described the Ryan Bateman she knew. The man she'd been best friends with since they were both still in possession of their baby teeth.

Ryan was impatient. Tenacious. Persistent. He

wanted everything five minutes ago. But the man who hovered over her now, his piercing green eyes boring into her soul and grasping her heart, was in no hurry. He seemed to relish the torturously delicious pleasure he was giving her with his slow, languid movements.

He was laser-focused. His brows furrowed, and his forehead beaded with sweat. The sudden swivel of his hips took her by surprise, and she whimpered with pleasure, her lips parting.

Ryan leaned down and pressed his mouth to hers, slipping his tongue inside and caressing her tongue.

Tessa got lost in his kiss. Let him rock them both into a sweet bliss that left her feeling like she was floating on a cloud.

She held on to him as he arched his back, his muscles straining as his own orgasm overtook him. Allowed herself to savor the warmth that encircled her sated body.

Then, gathering her to his chest, he removed her makeshift T-shirt turban and ran his fingers through her damp, curly hair.

She'd never felt more cherished or been more satisfied in her life. Yet, when the weekend ended, it would be the equivalent of the clock striking twelve for Cinderella. The dream would be over, her carriage would turn back into a pumpkin, and she'd be the same old Tessa Noble whom Ryan only considered a friend.

She inhaled his scent. Leather and cedar with

a hint of patchouli. A scent she'd bought him for Christmas three years ago. Ryan had been wearing it ever since. Tess was never sure if he wore it because he truly liked it or because he'd wanted to make her happy.

Now she wondered the same thing about what'd happened between them this weekend. He'd tailored the entire weekend to her. Had seemed determined to see to it that she felt special, pampered.

Had she been the recipient of a pity fuck?

The possibility of Ryan sleeping with her out of a sense of charity made her heart ache.

She tried not to think of what would happen when the weekend ended. To simply enjoy the moment between them here and now.

Tessa was his until "midnight." Then the magic of their weekend together would be over, and it would be time for them to return to the real world.

Thirteen

Ryan studied Tessa as she gathered her beauty products and stowed them back into her travel bag in preparation for checkout. They'd had an incredible weekend together. With the exception of the time they spent politely posing for the reporter at dinner and waxing poetic about their friendship, they'd spent most of the weekend just a few feet away in Ryan's bed.

But this morning Tessa had seemed withdrawn. Before he'd even awakened, she'd gotten out of bed, packed her luggage, laid out what she planned to wear to the football game, and showered.

Tessa opened a tube of makeup.

"You're wearing makeup to the game?" He stepped behind her in the mirror.

"Photos before the game." She gave his reflection a cursory glance. "Otherwise, I'd just keep it simple. Lip gloss, a little eye shadow. Mascara."

She went back to silently pulling items out of her makeup bag and lining them up on the counter.

"Tess, did I do something wrong? You seem really... I don't know...distant this morning."

A pained look crimped her features, and she sank her teeth into her lower lip before turning to face him. She heaved a sigh, and though she looked in his direction, she was clearly looking past him.

"Look, Rye, this weekend has been amazing. But I think it's in the best interest of our friendship if we go back to the way things were. Forget this weekend ever happened." She shifted her gaze to his. "I honestly feel that it's the only way our friendship survives this."

"Why?"

His question reeked of quiet desperation, but he could care less. The past two days had been the best days of his life. He thought they had been for her, too. So her request hit him like a sucker punch to the gut, knocking the wind out of him.

She took the shower cap off her head, releasing the long, silky hair she'd straightened with a blow-dryer attachment before they'd met Greg at the restaurant for dinner the night before.

"Because the girl you were attracted to on that stage isn't who I am. I can't maintain all of this." She indicated the makeup on the counter and her straightened hair. "It's exhausting. More importantly, it isn't me. Not really."

"You think all of this is what I'm attracted to? That I can't see...that I haven't always seen you?"

"You never kissed me before, not seriously," she added before he could mention that kiss in college. "And we certainly never..." She gestured toward the bed, as if she was unable to bring herself to say the words or look at the place where he'd laid her bare and tasted every inch of her warm brown skin.

"To be fair, you kissed me." Ryan stepped closer.

She tensed, but then lifted her chin defiantly, meeting his gaze again. The rapid rise and fall of her chest, indicated that she was taking shallow breaths. But she didn't step away from him. For which he was grateful.

"You know what I mean," she said through a frustrated little pout. "You never showed any romantic interest in me before the auction. So why are you interested now? Is it because someone else showed interest in me?"

"Why would you think that?" His voice was low and gruff. Pained.

Her accusation struck him like an openhanded slap to the face. It was something his mother had often said to him as a child. That he was only interested in his old toys when she wanted to give them to someone else.

Was that what he was doing with Tess?

"Because if I had a relationship...a life of my

own, then I wouldn't be a phone call away whenever you needed me." Her voice broke slightly, and she swiped at the corners of her eyes. "Or maybe it's a competitive thing. I don't know. All I know is that you haven't made a move before now. So what changed?"

The hurt in her eyes and in the tremor of her voice felt like a jagged knife piercing his chest.

She was right. He was a selfish bastard. Too much of a coward to explore his attraction to her. Too afraid of how it might change their relationship.

"I… I…" His throat tightened, and his mouth felt dry as he sought the right words. But Tessa was his best friend, and they'd always shot straight with each other. "Sex, I could get anywhere." He forced his gaze to meet hers. Gauged her reaction. "But what we have… I don't have that with anyone else, Tess. I didn't want to take a chance on losing you. Couldn't risk screwing up our friendship like I've screwed up every relationship I've ever been in."

She dropped her gaze, absently dragging her fingers through her hair and tugging it over one shoulder. Tess was obviously processing his words. Weighing them on her internal bullshit meter.

"So why risk it now? What's changed?" She wrapped her arms around her middle. Something she did to comfort herself.

"I don't know." He whispered the words, his eyes not meeting hers.

It was a lie.

Tess was right. He'd been prompted to action by his fear of losing her. He'd been desperate to stake his claim on Tess. Wipe thoughts of any other man from her brain.

In the past, she had flirted with the occasional guy. Even dated a few. But none of them seemed to pose any real threat to what they shared. But when she'd stood on that stage as the sexiest goddamn woman in the entire room with men falling all over themselves to spend a few hours with her...suddenly everything was different. For the first time in his life, the threat of losing his best friend to someone else suddenly became very real. And he couldn't imagine his life without her in it.

Brain on autopilot, he'd gone into caveman mode. Determined to win the bid, short of putting up the whole damn ranch in order to win her.

Tessa stared at him, her pointed gaze demanding further explanation.

"It felt like the time was right. Like Fate stepped in and gave us a nudge."

"You're full of shit, Ryan Bateman." She smacked her lips and narrowed her gaze. Arms folded over her chest, she shifted to a defensive stance. "You don't believe in Fate. 'Our lives are what we make of them.' That's what you've always said."

"I'm man enough to admit when I'm wrong. Or at least open-minded enough to explore the possibility."

She turned to walk away, but he grasped her fingertips with his. A move that was more of a plea than a demand. Still, she halted and glanced over her shoulder in his direction.

"Tess, why are you so dead set against giving this a chance?"

"Because I'm afraid of losing you, too." Her voice was a guttural whisper.

He tightened his grip on her hand and tugged her closer, forcing her eyes to meet his. "You're not going to lose me, Tess. I swear, I'm not going anywhere."

"Maybe not, but we both know your MO when it comes to relationships. You rush into them, feverish and excited. But after a while you get bored, and you're ready to move on." She frowned, a pained look furrowing her brow. "What happens then, Ryan? What happens once you've pulled me in deep and then you decide you just want to go back to being friends?" She shook her head vehemently. "I honestly don't think I could handle that."

Ryan's jaw clenched. He wanted to object. Promise to never hurt her. But hadn't he hurt every woman he'd ever been with except the one woman who'd walked away from him?

It was the reason Tripp had made him promise to leave his sister alone. Because, though they were friends, he didn't deem him good enough for his sister. Didn't trust that he wouldn't hurt her.

Tessa obviously shared Tripp's concern.

Ryan wished he could promise Tess he wouldn't break her heart. But their polar opposite approaches to relationships made it seem inevitable.

He kept his relationships casual. A means of mutual satisfaction. Because he believed in fairy-tale love and romance about as much as he believed in Big Foot and the Loch Ness Monster.

Tess, on the other hand, was holding out for the man who would sweep her off her feet. For a relationship like the one her parents shared. She didn't understand that Chuck and Tina Noble were the exception, rather than the rule.

Yet, despite knowing all the reasons he and Tess should walk away from this, he couldn't let her go.

Tessa's frown deepened as his silent response to her objection echoed off the walls in the elegant, tiled bathroom.

"This weekend has been amazing. You made me feel like Cinderella at the ball. But we've got the game this afternoon, then we're heading back home. The clock is about to strike midnight, and it's time for me to turn back into a pumpkin."

"You realize that you've just taken the place of the Maybach in this scenario." He couldn't help the smirk that tightened the edges of his mouth.

Some of the tension drained from his shoulders as her sensual lips quirked in a rueful smile. She shook her head and playfully punched him in the gut.

"You know what I mean. It's time for me to go

back to being me. Trade my glass slippers in for a pair of Chuck Taylors."

He caught her wrist before she could walk away. Pulling her closer, he wrapped his arms around her and stared deep into those gorgeous brown eyes that had laid claim on him ever since he'd first gazed into them.

"Okay, Cinderella. If you insist that things go back to the way they were, there's not much I can do about that. But if you're mine until midnight, I won't be cheated. Let's forget the game, stay here and make love."

"But I've already got the tickets."

"I don't care." He slowly lowered his mouth toward hers. "I'll reimburse you."

"But they're on the fifty-yard line. At the stadium that's your absolute favorite place in the world."

"Not today it isn't." He feathered a gentle kiss along the edge of her mouth, then trailed his lips down her neck.

"Ryan, we can't just blow off the—" She dug her fingers into his bare back and a low moan escaped her lips as he kissed her collarbone. The sound drifted below his waist and made him painfully hard.

"We can do anything we damn well please." He pressed a kiss to her ear. One of the many erogenous zones he'd discovered on her body during their weekend together. Tessa's knees softened, and her head lolled slightly, giving him better access to her neck.

"But the article…they're expecting us to go to the game, and if we don't…well, everyone will think—"

"Doesn't matter what they think." He lifted her chin and studied her eyes, illuminated by the morning sunlight spilling through the windows. He dragged a thumb across her lower lip. "It only matters what you and I want."

He pressed another kiss to her lips, lingering for a moment before reluctantly pulling himself away again so he could meet her gaze. He waited for her to open her eyes again. "What do you want, Tess?"

She swallowed hard, her gaze on his lips. "I want both. To go to the game, as expected, and to spend the day in bed making love to you."

"Hmm…intriguing proposition." He kissed her again. Tess really was a woman after his own heart. "One that would require us to spend one more night here. Then we'll head back tomorrow. And if you still insist—"

"I will." There was no hesitation in her voice, only apology. She moved a hand to cradle his cheek, her gaze meeting his. "Because it's what's best for our friendship."

Ryan forced a smile and released an uneasy breath. Tried to pretend that his chest didn't feel like it was caving in. He gripped her tighter against him, lifting her as she wrapped her legs around him.

If he couldn't have her like this always, he'd take

every opportunity to have her now. In the way he'd always imagined. Even if that meant they'd be a little late for the game.

Fourteen

They'd eaten breakfast, their first meal in the kitchen since they'd arrived, neither of them speaking much. The only part of their conversation that felt normal was their recap of some of the highlights during their team's win the day before. But then the conversation had returned to the stilted awkwardness they'd felt before then.

Ryan had loaded their luggage into the Maybach, and they were on the road, headed back to Royal, barely two words spoken between them before Tessa finally broke their silence.

"This is for the best, Rye. After all, you were afraid to tell my brother about that fake kiss we had on Valentine's Day in college." Tessa grinned, her voice teasing.

Ryan practically snorted, poking out his thumb and holding it up. "A… I am *not* afraid of your brother."

Not physically, at least. Ryan was a good head taller than Tripp and easily outweighed him by twenty-five pounds of what was mostly muscle. But, in all honesty, he *was* afraid of how the weekend with Tessa would affect his friendship with Tripp. It could disrupt the connection between their families.

The Batemans and Nobles were as thick as thieves now. Had been since their fathers were young boys. But in the decades prior, the families had feuded over land boundaries, water rights and countless other ugly disputes. Some of which made Ryan ashamed of his ancestors. But everything had changed the day Tessa's grandfather had saved Ryan's father's life when he'd fallen into a well.

That fateful day, the two families had bonded. A bond which had grown more intricate over the years, creating a delicate ecosystem he dared not disturb.

Ryan continued, adding his index finger for effect. "B… Yes, I think it might be damaging to our friendship if Tripp tries to beat my ass and I'm forced to defend myself." He added a third finger, hesitant to make his final point. An admission that made him feel more vulnerable than he was comfortable being, even with Tess. "And C…it wasn't a fake kiss. It was a little too real. Which is why I've tried hard to never repeat it."

Ryan's pulse raced, and his throat suddenly felt

dry. He returned his other hand to the steering wheel and stared at the road ahead. He didn't need to turn his head to know Tessa was staring at him. The heat of her stare seared his skin and penetrated his chest.

"Are you saying that since that kiss—" Her voice was trembling, tentative.

"Since that kiss, I've recognized that the attraction between us went both ways." He rushed the words out, desperate to stop her from asking what he suspected she might.

Why hadn't he said anything all those years ago? Or in the years since that night?

He'd never allowed himself to entertain either question. Doing so was a recipe for disaster.

Why court disaster when they enjoyed an incomparable friendship? Shouldn't that be good enough?

"Oh." The disappointment in her voice stirred heaviness in his chest, rather than the ease and lightness he usually felt when they were together.

When Ryan finally glanced over at his friend, she was staring at him blankly, as if there was a question she was afraid to ask.

"Why haven't you ever said anything?"

Because he hadn't been ready to get serious about anyone back then. And Tessa Noble wasn't the kind of girl you passed the time with. She was the genuine deal. The kind of girl you took home to mama. And someone whose friendship meant everything to him.

"Bottom line? I promised your brother I'd treat you like an honorary little sister. That I'd never lay a hand on you." A knot tightened in his belly. "A promise I've obviously broken."

"Wait, you two just decided, without consulting me? Like I'm a little child and you two are my misfit parents? What kind of caveman behavior is that?"

Ryan winced. Tessa was angry, and he didn't blame her. "To be fair, we had this conversation when he and I were about fourteen. Long before you enlightened us on the error of our anti-feminist tendencies. Still, it's a promise I've always taken seriously. Especially since, at the time, I did see you as a little sister. Obviously, things have changed since then."

"When?" Her tone was soft, but demanding. As if she needed to know.

It wasn't a conversation he wanted to have, but if they were going to have it, she deserved his complete honesty.

"I first started to feel some attraction toward you when you were around sixteen." He cleared his throat, his eyes steadily on the road. "But when I left for college I realized how deep that attraction ran. I was miserable without you that first semester in college."

"You seemed to adapt pretty quickly by sleeping your way across campus," she huffed. She turned toward the window and sighed. "I shouldn't have said that. I'm sorry. I…" She didn't finish her statement.

"Forget it." Ryan released a long, slow breath.

"This is uncharted territory for us. We'll learn to deal with it. Everything'll be fine."

But even as he said the words, he couldn't convince himself of their truth.

After Ryan's revelations, the ride home was awkward and unusually quiet, even as they both tried much too hard to behave as if everything was fine.

Everything most certainly was *not* fine.

Strained and uncomfortable? *Yes*. Their forced conversation, feeble smiles and weak laughter were proof they'd both prefer to be anywhere else.

And it confirmed they'd made the right decision by not pursuing a relationship. It would only destroy their friendship in the end once Ryan had tired of her and was ready to move on to someone polished and gorgeous, like his ex.

This was all her fault. She'd kissed Ryan. Tessa clenched her hands in her lap, willing them to stop trembling.

She only hoped their relationship could survive this phase of awkwardness, so things could go back to the way they were.

Tessa's phone buzzed, and she checked her text messages.

Tripp had sent a message to say that he'd landed a meeting with a prospect that had the potential to become one of their largest customers. His flight to Iowa would leave in a few days, and she would be in charge at the Noble Spur.

She scrolled to the next text and read Bo's message reminding her that she'd agreed to attend a showing of *A Christmas Carol* with him at the town's outdoor, holiday theater.

Tessa gripped her phone and turned it over in her lap, looking over guiltily at Ryan. After what had happened between them this weekend, the thought of going out with someone else turned her stomach, but she'd already promised Bo.

And even though she and Bo were going to a movie together, it could hardly be considered a date. Half the town of Royal would be there.

Would it be so wrong for them to go on a friendly outing to the movies?

Besides, maybe seeing other people was just the thing to alleviate the awkwardness between them and prompt them to forget about the past three days.

Tessa worried her lower lip with her teeth. Deep down, she knew the truth. Things would never be the same between them.

Because she wanted Ryan now more than ever.

No matter how hard she tried, Tessa would never forget their weekend together and how he'd made her feel.

Fifteen

Gus sat in his favorite recliner and put his feet up to watch a little evening television. Reruns of some of his favorite old shows. Only he held the remote in his hand without ever actually turning the television on.

The house was quiet. Too quiet.

Alexis was in Houston on business, and her brother Justin was staying in Dallas overnight with a friend.

Normally, he appreciated the solitude. Enjoyed being able to watch whatever the hell he wanted on television without one of the kids scoffing about him watching an old black-and-white movie or an episode of one of his favorite shows that he'd seen half a dozen times before. But lately, it had been harder to cheerfully bear his solitude.

During the months he and Rose had worked together to split up Daniel and Alexis, he'd found himself enjoying her company. So much so that he preferred it mightily to being alone in this big old house.

Gus put down the remote and paced the floor. He hadn't seen Rose since the night of the bachelor auction at the Texas Cattleman's Club. They'd spoken by phone twice, but just to confirm that their plan had worked.

As far as they could tell, Alexis and Daniel were no longer seeing each other. And both of them seemed to be in complete misery.

Gus had done everything he could to try and cheer Alexis up. But the pain in her eyes persisted. As did the evidence that she'd still been crying from time to time.

He'd tried to get his granddaughter to talk about it, but she'd insisted that it wasn't anything she couldn't handle. And she said he wouldn't understand anyway.

That probably hurt the most. Especially since he really did understand how she was feeling. And worse, he and Rose had been the root cause of that pain.

The guilt gnawed at his gut and broke his heart.

Rose had reminded him of why they'd first hatched the plan to break up Daniel and Alexis.

Their families had been mortal enemies for decades. Gus and Rose had hated each other so much they were willing to work together in order to prevent their grandchildren from being involved with each other. Only, Gus hadn't reckoned on coming to enjoy the time he spent with Rose Clayton. And he most surely hadn't anticipated that he'd find himself getting sweet on her again after all these years.

He was still angry at Rose for how she'd treated him all those years ago, when he'd been so very in love with her. But now he understood that because of her cruel father, holding the welfare of her ill mother over Rose's head, she'd felt she had no choice but to break it off with him and marry someone Jedediah Clayton had deemed worthy.

He regretted not recognizing the distress Rose was in back then. That her actions had been a cry for help. Signs he and his late wife, Sarah, who had once been Rose's best friend, had missed.

Gus heaved a sigh and glanced over his shoulder at the television. His reruns could wait.

Gus left the Lone Wolf Ranch and headed over to Rose's place, The Silver C, one last time to say goodbye. Maybe share a toast to the success of their plan to look out for Alexis and Daniel in the long run, even if the separation was hurting them both now.

The property had once been much vaster than his. But over the years, he'd bought quite a bit of it. Rose had begrudgingly sold it to him in order to pay off the gambling debts of her late husband, Ed.

Rose's father must be rolling over in his grave because the ranch hand he'd judged unworthy of his daughter was now in possession of much of the precious land the man had sought to keep out of his hands. Gus didn't normally think ill of the dead. But in Jedediah's case, he was willing to make an exception.

When Gus arrived at The Silver C, all decked out in its holiday finest, Rose seemed as thrilled to see him as he was to see her.

"Gus, what on earth are you doing here?" A smile lighting her eyes, she pulled the pretty red sweater she was wearing around her more tightly as cold air rushed in from outside.

"After all these months working together, I thought it was only right that we had a proper good-bye." He held up a bottle of his favorite top-shelf whiskey.

Rose laughed, a joyful sound he still had fond memories of. "Well, by all means, come on in."

She stepped aside and let Gus inside. The place smelled of pine from the two fresh Christmas trees Rose had put up. One in the entry hall and another in the formal living room. And there was the unmistakable scent of fresh apple pie.

Rose directed Gus to have a seat on the sofa in the den where she'd been watching television. Then she brought two glasses and two slices of warm apple pie on a little silver tray.

"That homemade pie?" Gus inquired as she set the tray on the table.

"Wouldn't have it any other way." She grinned, handing him a slice and a fork. She opened the bottle of whiskey and poured each of them a glass, neat.

She sat beside him and watched him with interest as he took his first bite of pie.

"Hmm, hmm, hmm. Now that's a little slice of heaven right there." He grinned.

"I'm glad you like it. And since we're celebrating our successful plot to save the kids from a disastrous future, pie seems fitting." She smiled, but it seemed hollow. She took a sip of the whiskey and sighed. "Smooth."

"That's one of the reasons I like it so much." He nodded, shoveling another bite of pie into his mouth and chewing thoughtfully. He surveyed the space and leaned closer, lowering his voice. "Daniel around today?"

"No, he's gone to Austin to handle some ranch business." She raised an eyebrow, her head tilted. "Why?"

"No reason in particular." Gus shrugged, putting down his pie plate and sipping his whiskey. "Just wanted to ask how the boy is doing. He still as miserable as my Alexis?"

Pain and sadness were etched in Rose's face as she lowered her gaze and nodded. "I'm afraid so. He's trying not to show how hurt he is, but I honestly don't think I've ever seen him like this. He's already been through so much with his mother." She sighed, taking another sip of whiskey. Her hands were trembling slightly as she shook her head. "I hope we've done the right thing here. I guess I didn't realize how much they meant to each other." She sniffled and pulled a tissue out of her pocket, dabbing at her eyes.

Rose forced a laugh. "I'm sorry. You must think me so ridiculous sitting here all teary-eyed over having gotten the very thing we both wanted."

Gus put down his glass and took Rose's hand between his. It was delicate and much smaller than his own. Yet, they were the hands of a woman who had worked a ranch her entire life.

"I understand just what you're feeling." He stroked her wrist with his thumb. "Been feeling pretty guilty, too. And second-guessing our decision."

"Oh, Gus, we spent so many years heartbroken and angry. It changed us, and not for the better." Tears leaked from Rose's eyes, and her voice broke. "I just hope we haven't doomed Alexis and Daniel to the same pain and bitterness."

"It's going to be okay, Rose." He took her in his arms and hugged her to his chest. Tucked her head beneath his chin as he swayed slowly and stroked her hair. "We won't allow that to happen to Alexis and Daniel. I promise."

"God, I hope you're right. They deserve so much more than that. Both of them." She held on to him. One arm wrapped around him and the other was pressed to his chest.

He should be focused on Daniel and Alexis and the dilemma that he and Rose had created. Gus realized that. Yet, an awareness of Rose slowly spread throughout his body. Sparks of electricity danced along his spine.

He rubbed her back and laid a kiss atop her head. All of the feelings he'd once experienced when he'd held Rose in his arms as a wet-behind-the-ears ranch hand came flooding back to him. Overwhelmed his senses, making his heart race in a way he'd forgotten that it could.

After all these years, he still had a thing for Rose Clayton. Still wanted her.

Neither of them had moved or spoken for a while. They just held each other in silence, enjoying each other's comfort and warmth.

Finally, Rose pulled away a little and tipped her head, her gaze meeting his. She leaned in closer, her mouth hovering just below his, her eyes drifting closed.

Gus closed the space between them, his lips meeting hers in a kiss that was soft and sweet. Almost chaste.

He slipped his hands on either side of her face, angling it to give him better access to her mouth. Ran his tongue along her lips that tasted of smooth whiskey and homemade apple pie.

Rose sighed with satisfaction, parting her lips. She clutched at his shirt, pulling him as close as their position on the sofa would allow.

She murmured with pleasure when he slipped his tongue between her lips.

Time seemed to slow as they sat there, their mouths seeking each other's out in a kiss that grew hotter. Greedier. More intense.

There was a fire in his belly that he hadn't felt in ages. One that made him want things with Rose he hadn't wanted in so long.

Gus forced himself to pull away from Rose. He gripped her shoulders, his eyes searching hers for permission.

Rose stood up. She switched off the television with the remote, picked up their two empty whiskey glasses, then walked toward the stairs that led to the upper floor of The Silver C. Looking back at him, she flashed a wicked smile that did things to him.

"Are you coming or not?"

Gus nearly knocked over the silver tray on the table in front of him in his desperation to climb to his feet. He hurried toward her but was halted by her next words.

"Don't forget the bottle."

"Yes, ma'am." Grinning, he snatched it off the table before grabbing her hand and following her up the stairs.

Sixteen

When he heard his name called, Ryan looked up from where Andy, his farrier, was shoeing one of the horses.

It was Tripp.

The muscles in Ryan's back tensed. He hadn't talked to Tess or Tripp in the three days since they'd been back from their trip to Dallas. He could tell by his friend's expression that Tripp was concerned about something.

Maybe he had come to deliver a much-deserved ass-whipping. After all, Ryan had broken his promise by sleeping with Tess.

"What's up, Tripp?" Ryan walked over to his friend, still gauging the man's mood.

"I'm headed to the airport shortly, but I need to ask a favor."

"Sure. Anything."

"Keep an eye on Tess, will you?"

Ryan hadn't expected that. "Why, is something wrong?"

"Not exactly." Tripp removed his Stetson and adjusted it before placing it back on his head. "It's just that Mom and Dad are still gone, and I'm staying in Des Moines overnight. She'll be kicking around that big old house by herself mostly. We let a few hands off for the holidays. Plus… I don't like that Bo and Clem have been sniffing around the last few days. I'm beginning to think that letting Tessa participate in that bachelor auction was a mistake."

Ryan tugged his baseball cap down on his head, unsettled by the news of Bo and Clem coming around. He'd paid a hefty sum at the auction to ward those two off. Apparently, they hadn't gotten the hint.

"First, if you think you *let* your sister participate in that bachelor's auction, you don't know your sister very well. Tess has got a mind of her own. Always has. Always will."

"Guess you're right about that." Tripp rubbed the back of his neck. "And I'm not saying that Bo or Clem are bad guys. They're nice enough, I guess."

"Just not when they come calling on your sister." Ryan chuckled. He knew exactly how Tripp felt.

"Yeah, pretty much."

"Got a feeling the man you'll think is good enough for your little sister ain't been born yet."

"And probably never will be." Tripp chuckled. "But as her big brother, it's my job to give any guy who comes around a hard time. Make him prove he's worthy."

"Well, just hold your horses there, buddy. It's not like she's considering either of them." Ryan tried to appear nonchalant about the whole ordeal. Though on the inside he felt like David Banner in the midst of turning into the Incredible Hulk. He wanted to smash both Bo and Clem upside the head and tell them to go sniffing around someone else. "I think you're getting a little ahead of yourself."

"You haven't been around since you guys got back." The statement almost sounded accusatory. "Looks like the flower show threw up in our entry hall."

"Clem and Bo have been sending Tessa flowers?" Ryan tried to keep his tone and his facial expression neutral. He counted backward from ten in his head.

"Clem's apparently determined to empty out the local florist. Bo, on the other hand, has taken Tessa out to some play and this afternoon they're out riding."

Ryan hoped like hell that Tripp didn't notice the tick in his jaw or the way his fists clenched at his sides.

Tripp flipped his wrist, checking his watch. "Look,

I'd better get going. I'll be back tomorrow afternoon, but call me if you need anything."

"Will do." Ryan tipped the brim of his baseball hat. "Safe travels."

He watched his friend climb back into his truck and head toward the airport in Dallas.

Jaw clenched, Ryan uncurled his fists and reminded himself to calm down. Then he saddled up Phantom, his black quarter horse stallion, and went for a ride.

For the past few days, he hadn't been able to stop thinking about his weekend with Tess. The moments they'd shared replayed again and again in his head. Distracted him from his work. Kept him up staring at the ceiling in the middle of the night.

He knew Tess well. Knew she'd been as affected by their weekend together as he had. So how could she dismiss what they'd shared so easily and go out with Bo, or for God's sake, Clem?

Phantom's hooves thundered underneath him as the cold, brisk air slapped him in the face. He'd hoped that his ride would calm him down and help him arrive at the same conclusion Tess had. That it would be better for everyone if they remained friends.

But no matter how hard and fast he'd ridden, it didn't drive away his desire for Tess. Nor did it ease the fury that rose in his chest at the thought of another man touching her the way he had. The way he wanted to again.

He recognized the validity of Tessa's concerns that he wasn't serious and that he'd be chasing after some other skirt in a few months. He couldn't blame her for feeling that way. After all, as Helene was fond of saying, the proof was in the pudding.

He wouldn't apologize for his past. Because he'd never lied to or misled any of the women he'd dated. So he certainly wouldn't give his best friend any sense of false hope that he'd suddenly convert to the romantic suitor he'd been over the course of the weekend, for the sake of the Texas Cattleman's Club.

Ryan wasn't that guy any more than Tessa was the kind of woman who preferred a pair of expensive, red-bottomed heels to a hot new pair of sneakers.

So why couldn't he let go of the idea of the two of them being together?

He'd asked himself that question over and over the past few days, and the same answer kept rising above all the bullshit excuses he'd manufactured.

He craved the intimacy that they shared.

It was the thing that made his heart swell every time he thought of their weekend together. The thing that made it about so much more than just the sex.

He'd even enjoyed planning their weekend. And he'd derived a warm sense of satisfaction from seeing her reaction to each of his little surprises.

Ryan had always believed that people who made a big show of their relationships were desperate to make other people believe they were happy. But despite his romantic gestures being part of a ruse to keep the club from being mired in scandal, they had brought him and Tess closer. Shown her just how much he valued her.

Maybe he didn't believe that love was rainbows and sugarplums. Or that another person was the key to his happiness. But he knew unquestionably that he would be miserable if Tess got involved with someone else.

He couldn't promise her that he'd suddenly sweep her off her feet like some counterfeit Prince Charming. But he sure as hell wanted to try, before she walked into the arms of someone else.

Ryan and Phantom returned to the stables, and he handed him off to Andy. Then he hurried into the house to take a shower. He needed to see Tess right away.

Seventeen

Tessa checked her phone. The only messages were from Tripp, letting her know that his plane had landed safely, and from Clem asking if she'd received his flowers ahead of their casual dinner date later that night.

She tossed the phone on the counter. No messages from Ryan. They'd maintained radio silence since he'd set her luggage in the entry hall, said goodbye, and driven off.

Tessa realized that the blame wasn't all his. After all, the phone worked both ways. On a typical day, she would've called her best friend a couple of times by now. She was clearly avoiding him, as much as he was avoiding her.

She was still angry that Ryan and Tripp had made a pact about her. As if she were incapable of making her own decisions. Mostly, she was hurt that Ryan hadn't countered her accusation that he'd eventually tire of her and move on to someone else.

She wanted him to deny it. To fight for her. But Ryan hadn't raised the slightest objection. Which meant what he really wanted was a no-strings fuck buddy until something better came along.

For her, that would never be enough with Ryan. She was already in way too deep. But the truth was, she would probably never be enough for him. She was nothing like the lithe, glamorous women who usually caught Ryan's eye. Women like Sabrina Calhoun who was probably born wearing a pair of Louboutins and carrying an Hermès bag. Or women like Lana, the overly friendly barmaid. Women who exuded sex and femininity rather than looking like they shopped at Ranchers R Us.

Headlights shone in the kitchen window. Someone was in the driveway. As soon as the vehicle pulled up far enough, Tess could see it clearly.

It was Ryan's truck.

Her belly fluttered, and her muscles tensed. She waited for him to come to the kitchen door, but he didn't. Instead, he made a beeline for the stables.

Ryan had likely come to check on the stables at Tripp's request. He was obviously still avoiding her, and she was over it.

Nervousness coiled through her and knotted in

her belly. They both needed to be mature about this whole thing. Starting right now.

She wouldn't allow the fissure between them to crack open any wider. If that meant she had to be the one to break the ice, she would.

Tessa's hair, piled on top of her head in a curly bun, was still damp from the shower. She'd thrown on an old graphic T-shirt and a pair of jeans, so she could run out and double-check the stables.

Not her best look.

Tess slipped on a jacket and her boots and trudged out to the stables.

"Hey." She approached him quietly, her arms folded across her body.

"Hey." Ryan leaned against the wall. "Sorry, I haven't called. Been playing catch-up since we returned."

"I've been busy, too." She pulled the jacket tighter around her.

"I heard. Word is you've got a date tonight." The resentment in his voice was unmistakable. "You spent the weekend in my bed. A few days later and suddenly you and Bo are a thing and Clem is sending you a houseful of flowers?"

"Bo and I aren't *a thing.* We've just gone out a couple times. As friends." Her cheeks were hot. "And despite what happened this weekend, you and I *aren't* a thing. So you don't get a say in who I do or don't spend time with." The pitch of her voice was high, and the words were spilling out of her mouth. Tessa sucked in a deep breath, then continued. "Besides, are you going to tell me you've never done the same?"

Crimson spread across his cheeks. He stuffed his hands in his pockets. "That was different."

"Why? Because you're a guy?"

"Because it was casual, and neither of us had expectations for anything more."

"How is that different from what happened between us?"

Ryan was playing mind games with her, and she didn't appreciate it.

"Because I *do* expect more. That is, I want more. With you." He crept closer.

Tessa hadn't expected that. She shifted her weight from one foot to the other, her heart beating faster. "What are you saying?"

"I'm saying I want more of what we had this past weekend. That I want it to be me and you. No one else. And I'm willing to do whatever you need in order to make it happen."

"Whatever *I* need?" The joy that had been building in her chest suddenly slammed into a brick wall. "As in, you'd be doing it strictly for my benefit, not because it's what you want?"

"You make it sound as if I'm wrong for wanting you to be happy." His brows furrowed, and his mouth twisted in confusion. "How does that make me the bad guy?"

"It doesn't make you a bad person, Ryan. But I'm

not looking for a fuck buddy. Not even one who happens to be my best friend." She pressed a hand to her forehead and sighed.

"I wouldn't refer to it that way, but if it makes us happy, why not?" Ryan's voice was low, his gaze sincere. He took her hand in his. "Who cares what anyone else thinks as long as it's what we want?"

"But it isn't what *I* want." Tears stung Tessa's eyes, and her voice wavered.

Ryan lifted her chin, his green eyes pinning her in place. "What *do* you want, Tess?"

"I want the entire package, Ryan. Marriage. Kids, eventually." She pulled away, her back turned to him for a moment before turning to face him again. "And I'll never get any of that if I settle for being friends with benefits."

"How can you be so sure it wouldn't work between us?" he demanded.

"Because you can't even be honest about what you want in bed with me." She huffed, her hands shaking.

There, she'd said it.

"What the hell are you talking about, Tess?"

Her face and chest were suddenly hot, and the vast barn seemed too small a space for the two of them. She slipped off her jacket and hung it on a hook.

Though the remaining ranch staff had left for the day and Tripp was gone, she still lowered her voice. As if the horses would spread gossip to the folks in town.

"I know you like it…rough. You weren't like that with me."

"Really? You're complaining about my performance?" He folded his arms, his jaw clenched.

"No, of course not. It was amazing. *You* were amazing. But I overheard Sabrina talking to a friend of hers on the phone when you two were still together. She was saying that she liked rough sex, and there was no one better at it than you."

Tessa's heart thumped. Her pulse, thundering in her ears, seemed to echo throughout the space.

"You overheard her say that on the phone?"

Tessa nodded.

"You know that wasn't an accident, right? She got a kick out of rattling your cage."

Tess suspected as much. Sabrina had never much liked her.

"You didn't answer my question." She looked in his direction, but her eyes didn't quite meet his. "No judgment. I just want to know if it's true."

"Sometimes." He shrugged. "Depends on my mood, who I'm with. And we're not talking whips and chains, if that's what you're imagining." He was clearly uncomfortable having this discussion with her. Not that she was finding it to be a walk in the park either. "Why does it matter?"

"Because if that's what you like, but with me you were…"

"Not rough," he offered tersely. "And you're angry about that?"

"Not angry. Just realistic. If you can't be yourself with me in bed, you're not going to be happy. You'll get bored and you'll want out."

Ryan stared down at her, stepping closer. "I responded to you. Gave you what I thought you wanted."

"And you did." She took a step backward, her back hitting the wall. She swallowed hard. "But did it ever occur to you that I would've liked the chance to do the same for you?"

Sighing heavily, Ryan placed one hand on the wall behind her and cradled her cheek with the other. "It's not like that's the only way I like it, Tess. I don't regret anything about my weekend with you."

"But the point was you felt you *couldn't*. Because of our friendship or maybe because of your promise to Tripp. I don't know. All I know for sure is that pretending that everything will be okay is a fool's game." She forced herself to stand taller. Chin tipped, she met his gaze.

"So that's it? Just like that, you decide that's reason enough for us to not be together?" His face was red, and anger vibrated beneath his words, though his expression remained placid.

"Isn't that reason enough for you?"

"Sex isn't everything, Tess."

"For you, it always has been. Sex is just sex, right? It's not about love or a deeper connection."

The knot in Tessa's stomach tightened when Ryan dropped his gaze and didn't respond. She sighed. "Tigers can't change their stripes, Ryan. No matter how hard they might try."

She turned to dip under his arm, but he lowered it, blocking her escape from the heated look in his eyes. His closeness. His scent. Leather. Cedar. Patchouli. *Damn that patchouli.*

"Ryan, what else is there for us to say?"

"Nothing." He lowered his hands to her waist and stepped closer, his body pinning hers to the wall.

Time seemed to move in slow motion as Ryan dipped his head, his lips hovering just above hers. His gaze bored into hers. She didn't dare move an inch. Didn't dare blink.

When she didn't object, his lips crushed hers in a bruising, hungry kiss that made her heart race. He tasted of Helene's famous Irish stew—one of Ryan's favorite meals—and an Irish ale.

His hands were on her hips, pinning her in place against the wall behind her. Not with enough force to hurt her, but he'd asserted himself in such a way that it was crystal clear that he wanted her there, and that she shouldn't move.

She had no plans to.

As much as she'd enjoyed seeing a gentler side of Ryan during their weekend together, the commanding look in his eye and the assertiveness of his tone revved her up in a way she would never have imagined.

He trailed his hands up her sides so damned slowly she was sure she could count the milliseconds that passed. The backs of his hands grazed her hips, her waist, the undersides of her breasts.

The apex of her thighs pulsed and throbbed with such power she felt like he might bring her over the edge just from his kiss and his demanding touch.

Her knees quivered, and her breaths were quick and shallow. His kisses grew harder, hungrier as he placed his large hands around her throat. Not squeezing or applying pressure of any real measure. But conveying a heightened sense of control.

Ryan pulled back, his body still pinning hers, but his kiss gone. After a few seconds, her eyes shot open. He was staring at her with an intensity that she might have found scary in any other situation. But she knew Ryan. Knew that he'd never do anything to hurt her.

"You still with me, Tess?"

She couldn't pry her lips open to speak, so she did the only thing she could. Her impression of a bobblehead doll.

His eyes glinted, and he smirked. Ryan leaned in and sucked her bottom lip. Gently sank his teeth into it. Then he pushed his tongue between her lips and swept it inside the cavern of her mouth. Tipped her head back so that he could deepen the kiss. Claimed her mouth as if he owned every single inch of her body and could do with it as he pleased.

Her pebbled nipples throbbed in response, and

she made a small gasp as his hard chest grazed the painfully hard peaks.

His scorching, spine-tingling kiss coaxed her body into doing his bidding, and his strong hands felt as if they were everywhere at once.

Tessa sucked in a deep breath when Ryan squeezed her bottom hard, ramping up the steady throb between her thighs.

When she'd gasped, he sucked her tongue into his mouth. He lifted her higher on the wall, pinning her there with his body as he settled between her thighs.

She whimpered as his rock-hard shaft pressed against the junction of her thighs. He seemed to enjoy eliciting her soft moans as she strained her hips forward, desperate for more of the delicious friction that made her belly flutter and sent a shudder up her spine.

"Shirt and bra off," he muttered against her lips, giving her barely enough room to comply with his urgent request. But she managed eagerly enough and dropped the garments to the floor.

He lifted her higher against the wall until her breasts were level with his lips. She locked her legs around his waist, anchoring herself to the wall.

Ryan took one heavy mound in his large hand. Squeezed it, then savagely sucked at her beaded tip, upping the pain/pleasure quotient. He gently grazed the pebbled tip with his teeth, then swirled his tongue around the flesh, soothing it.

Then he moved to the other breast and did the

same. This time his green eyes were locked with hers. Gauging her reaction. A wicked grin curved the edge of his mouth as he tugged her down, so her lips crashed against his again.

Could he feel the pooling between her thighs through her soaked underwear and jeans? Her cheeks heated, momentarily, at the possibility. But her embarrassment was quickly forgotten as he nuzzled her ear and whispered his next command.

"When I set you down again I want you out of every single stitch of clothing you're wearing."

"Out here? In the stable? Where anyone could see us?" she stuttered, her heart thudding wildly in her chest.

"There's no one but us here," he said matter-of-factly. "But if you want me to stop…"

"No, don't." Tess was shocked by how quickly she'd objected to ending this little game. The equivalent of begging for more of him. For more of this.

At least he hadn't made her undress alone. Ryan tugged the beige plaid shirt over his head and on to the floor, giving her a prize view of his hard abdomen. She wanted to run the tip of her tongue along the chiseled lines that outlined the rippled muscles he'd earned by working as hard on the ranch as any of his hands. To kiss and suck her way along the deep V at his hips that disappeared below his waist. Trace the ridge on the underside of his shaft with her tongue.

Ryan toed off his work boots, unzipped his jeans

and shoved them and his boxers down his muscular thighs, stepping out of them.

Tess bit into her lower lip, unable to tear her gaze from the gentle bob of his shaft as he stalked toward her and lifted her on to the edge of the adjustable, standing desk where she sometimes worked.

He raised the desk, which was in a seated position, until it was at just the right height.

"I knew this table would come in handy one day." She laughed nervously, her hands trembling slightly.

He didn't laugh, didn't smile. "Is this why you came out here, Tess? Why you couldn't be patient and wait until I came to your door?"

Before she could respond, he slid into her and they both groaned at the delicious sensation of him filling her. His back stiffened and he trembled slightly, his eyes squeezed shut.

Then he cursed under his breath and pulled out, retrieving a folded strip of foil packets from the back pocket of his jeans.

They'd both lost control momentarily. Given into the heat raging between them. But he'd come prepared. Maybe he hadn't expected to take her here in the stable or that he'd do so with such ferocity. But he had expected that at some point he'd be inside of her.

And she'd caved. Fallen under the hypnotic spell of those green eyes which negated every objection she'd posed up till then.

Sheathed now, Ryan slid inside her, his jaw

tensed. He started to move slowly, but then he pulled out again.

"On your knees," he growled, before she could object.

Tessa shifted onto all fours, despite her self-consciousness about the view from behind as she arched her back and widened her stance, at his request.

Ryan adjusted the table again until it was at the perfect height. He grabbed his jeans and folded them, putting them under her knees to provide cushion.

Then suddenly he slammed into her, the sound of his skin slapping against hers filling the big, empty space. He pulled back slowly and rammed into her again. Then he slowly built a rhythm of rough and gentle strokes. Each time the head of his erection met the perfect spot deep inside her she whimpered at the pleasure building.

When he'd eased up on his movement, stopping just short of that spot, she'd slammed her hips back against him, desperate for the pleasure that the impact delivered.

Ryan reached up and slipped the tie from her hair, releasing the damp ringlets so that they fell to her shoulders and formed a curtain around her face.

He gathered her hair, winding it around his fist and tugging gently as he moved inside her. His rhythm was controlled and deliberate, even as his momentum slowly accelerated.

Suddenly, she was on her back again. Ryan had

pulled out, leaned forward, and adjusted the table as high as it would go.

"Tell me what you want, Tess," he growled, his gaze locked with hers and his eyes glinted.

"I… I…" She couldn't fix her mouth to say the words, especially here under the harsh, bright lights in the stable. She averted her gaze from his.

He leaned in closer. His nostrils flared and a subtle smirk barely turned one corner of his mouth. "Would it help if I told you I already know *exactly* what you want. I just need to hear you say it. For you to beg for it."

His eyes didn't leave hers.

"I want…" Tessa swallowed hard, her entire body trembling slightly. "Your tongue."

He leaned in closer, the smirk deepening. "Where?"

God, he was really going to make her say it.

"Here." She spread her thighs and guided his free hand between her legs, shuddering at his touch. Tess hoped that show-and-tell would do, because she was teetering on the edge, nearly ready to explode. "Please."

"That wasn't so hard, now, was it?" He leaned down and lapped at her slick flesh with his tongue.

She quivered from the pleasure that rippled through her with each stroke. He gripped her hips, holding her in place to keep her bottom at the edge of the table, so she couldn't squirm away. Despite the pleasure building to a crescendo.

Tess slid her fingers in his hair and tugged him

closer. Wanting more, even as she felt she couldn't possibly take another lash of his tongue against her sensitive flesh.

Ryan sucked on the little bundle of nerves and her body stiffened. She cursed and called his name, her inner walls pulsing.

Trailing kisses up her body, he kissed her neck. Then he guided her to her feet and turned her around, so her hands were pressed to the table and her bottom was nestled against his length.

He made another adjustment of the table, then lifted one of her knees on to it. He pressed her back down so her chest was against the table and her bottom was propped in the air.

He slid inside her with a groan of satisfaction, his hips moving against hers until finally he'd reached his own explosive release. As he gathered his breath, each pant whispered against her skin.

"Tess, I didn't mean to…" He sighed heavily. "Are you all right?"

She gave him a shaky nod, glancing back at him over her shoulder. "I'm fine."

He heaved a long sigh and placed a tender kiss on her shoulder. "Don't give up on this so easily, Tess. Or do something we'll both regret."

Ryan excused himself to find a trash can where he could discreetly discard the condom.

Tessa still hadn't moved. Her limbs quivered, and her heart raced. Slowly, she gathered her bra, her jeans and her underwear. Her legs wobbled, as if she were slightly dazed.

She put on the clothing she'd managed to gather, despite her trembling hands.

When he returned, Ryan stooped to pick up her discarded shirt. Glaring, he handed it to her.

She muttered her thanks, slipping the shirt on. "You're upset. Why? Because I brought up your sex life with Sabrina?"

"Maybe it never occurred to you that the reason Sabrina and I tended to have rough, angry sex is because we spent so much of our relationship pissed off with each other.

He put his own shirt on and buttoned it, still staring her down.

Tessa felt about two inches tall. "I hadn't considered that."

She retrieved the hair tie from the standing desk, that she'd never be able to look at again without blushing. She pulled her hair into a low ponytail, stepped into her boots, and slipped her jacket back on.

"It can be fun. Maybe even adventurous. But in the moments when you're not actually having sex, it makes for a pretty fucked-up relationship. That's not what I want for you, Tess. For us." He shook his head, his jaw still clenched. "And there's something else you failed to take into account."

"What?"

"Rough sex is what got Sabrina off. It was her

thing, not mine. What gets me off is getting you there. But I guess you were too busy making your little comparisons to notice." He stalked away, then turned back, pointing a finger at her for emphasis. "I want something more with you, Tess, because we're good together. We always have been. The sex is only a small component of what makes us fit so well together. I would think that our twenty plus years of friendship should be evidence enough of that."

Tessa wished she could take back everything she'd said. That she could turn back time and get a do-over.

"Rye, I'm sorry. I didn't mean to—"

"If you don't want to be with me, Tess, that's fine. But just be honest about it. Don't make up a bunch of bullshit excuses." He tucked his plaid shirt into his well-worn jeans, then pulled on his boots before heading toward the door. "Enjoy your date with Clem."

"It's not a date," she yelled after him, her eyes stinging with tears.

He didn't respond. Just left her standing there shaking. Feeling like a fool.

And she deserved it. Every angry stare. Every word uttered in resentment.

She'd been inventing reasons for them not to be together. Because she was terrified of the truth. That she wanted to be with Ryan more than anything. She honestly did want it all—marriage, a house of her own, kids. And she wanted them with her best friend. But she wouldn't settle for being in a relationship where she was the only one in love.

And she was in love with Ryan.

But as much as she loved him, she was terrified of the deafening silence she'd face if she confessed the truth to him. Because Ryan didn't believe in messy, emotional commitments.

He'd never admitted to being in love with a single one of his girlfriends. In fact, he'd never even said that he loved Sabrina. Just that there was a spark with her that kept things exciting between them. Something he hadn't felt with anyone else.

Tessa's sight blurred with tears and she sniffled, angrily swiping a finger beneath each eye. She'd done this, and she could fix it. Because she needed Ryan in her life. And he needed her, too. Even if all they'd ever be was friends.

Tessa's phone buzzed. She pulled it from her pocket.

Clem.

She squeezed her eyes shut, her jaw clenched. Tess hated to bail on him, but after what had happened between her and Ryan, the thought of going out with someone else made her physically ill.

She answered the phone, her fingers pressed to her throbbing temple.

"Hey, Clem, I was just about to call you. Suddenly, I'm not feeling very well."

Eighteen

Ryan hopped into his truck and pulled out of the Noble Spur like a bat out of hell. He was furious with Tess and even madder that he'd been so turned on by her when she was being completely unreasonable.

He pulled into the drive of the Bateman Ranch and parked beside an unfamiliar car. A shiny red BMW.

As Ryan approached the big house, Helene hurried to the door to meet him. By the way she was wringing that dish towel in her hand, he wasn't going to like what she had to say one bit.

He glanced at the car again, studying the license plate. Texas plates, but it could be a rental car. And only one person he knew would insist on renting a red BMW.

Hell.

This was the last thing he needed.

"Ryan, I am so sorry. I told her that you weren't home, but she insisted on waiting for you. No matter how long you were gone." She folded her arms, frowning.

"It's okay, Helene." Ryan patted the woman's shoulder and forced a smile.

"Well, well, well. Look who finally decided to come home." His ex-fiancée, Sabrina Calhoun, sashayed to the front door. "Surprised to see me, baby?"

The expression on Helene's face let him know she was fit to be tied. Never a fan of the woman, his house manager would probably sooner quit than be forced to deal with his ex's condescending attitude again.

Ryan gave Helene a low hand signal, begging her to be civil and assuring her that everything would be all right.

Sabrina was the kind of mistake he wouldn't make twice. No matter how slick and polished she looked. Outrageously expensive clothes and purse. A haircut that cost more than most folks around here made in a week. A heavy French perfume that costed a small mint.

His former fiancée could be the dictionary illustration for high maintenance. He groaned internally, still kicking himself for ever thinking the two of them could make a life together.

Sabrina wasn't a villain. They just weren't right for each other. A reality that became apparent once she'd moved to Texas and they'd actually lived together.

Suddenly, her cute little quirks weren't so cute anymore.

"What brings you to Royal, Sabrina?" Ryan folded his arms and reared back on his heels. He asked the question as politely as he could manage.

"I happened to be in Dallas visiting a friend, and I thought it would be rude not to come by and at least say hello." She slid her expensive sunglasses from her face and batted her eyelashes. "You think we can chat for a minute? Alone?"

She glanced briefly at Helene who looked as if she was ready to claw the woman's face off.

"Do you mind, Helene?" He squeezed her arm and gave her the same smile he'd been using to charm her out of an extra slice of pie since he was a kid.

She turned and hurried back into the house, her path littered with a string of not-so-complimentary Greek terms for Sabrina.

Ryan extended an arm toward the front door and followed Sabrina inside.

Whatever she was here for, it was better that he just let her get it out, so she could be on her merry way.

They sat down in the living room, a formal space she was well aware that his family rarely used. An indication that he didn't expect her visit to last long. And that he didn't consider her visit to be a friendly one.

"The place looks great." Sabrina glanced around.

He crossed his ankle over his knee and waited a beat before responding. "I don't mean to be rude, Brie, but we both know you're not the kind of person who'd drop by unannounced without a specific purpose in mind. I'm pressed for time today. So, it'd be great if we could just skip to the part where you ask whatever it is you came to ask."

"You know me well. Probably better than anyone." Sabrina moved from the sofa where she was seated to the opposite end of the sofa where he was situated.

Ryan watched her movement with the same suspicion with which he'd regard a rattlesnake sidling up to him. Turning slightly in his seat, so that he was facing her, he pressed a finger to his temple and waited.

He knew from experience that his silence would drive Sabrina nuts. She'd spill her guts just to fill the empty void.

"I have a little confession to make. I visited my friend in Dallas because she emailed that article about you."

He'd nearly forgotten about that article on the bachelor's auction featuring him and Tess. Helene had picked up a few copies for his parents, but he hadn't gotten around to reading the piece. Between issues on the ranch and everything that had been going on with Tess, the article hadn't seemed important.

"And that prompted you to come to Royal because…?"

Sabrina stood, walking over to the fireplace, her back to him for a moment. She turned to face him again.

"It made me think about you. About us. I know we didn't always get along, but when we did, things were really great between us. I miss that." She tucked her blond hair behind her ears as she stepped closer. "I miss you. And I wondered if maybe you missed me, too."

Ryan sighed heavily. Today obviously wasn't his day. The woman he wanted insisted they should just be friends, and the woman he didn't want had traveled halfway across the country hoping to pick up where they'd left off.

He couldn't catch a break.

Ryan leaned forward, both feet firmly on the floor. "Sabrina, we've been through all this. You and I, we're just too different."

"You know what they say." She forced a smile after her initial frown in response to his rejection. "Opposites attract."

"True." He had been intrigued by their differences and because she'd been such a challenge. It had made the chase more exciting. "But in our case, it wasn't enough to maintain a relationship that made either of us happy. In fact, in the end, we were both miserable. Why would you want to go back to that?"

"I'm a different person now. More mature." She joined him on the sofa. "It seems you are, too. The time we've spent away from each other has made me realize what we threw away."

"Sabrina, you're a beautiful woman and there are many things about you that I admire." Ryan sighed. "But you just can't force a square peg into a round hole. This ranch is my life. Always has been, always will be. That hasn't changed. And I doubt that you've suddenly acquired a taste for country living."

"They do build ranches outside of Texas, you know." She flashed her million-dollar smile. "Like in Upstate New York."

"This ranch has been in my family for generations. I have no interest in leaving it behind and starting over in Upstate New York." He inhaled deeply, released his breath slowly, then turned to face her. "And I'm certainly not looking to get involved."

"With me, you mean." Sabrina pushed to her feet and crossed her arms, the phony smile gone. She peered up at him angrily. "You sure seemed eager to 'get involved' with your precious Tess. You went all out for her."

"It was a charity thing. Something we did on behalf of the Texas Cattleman's Club."

"And I suppose you two are still *just* friends?" The question was accusatory, but she didn't pause long enough for him to respond either way. "Suddenly you're a romantic who rents her fantasy car, knows exactly which flowers she likes, and which wine she drinks?" She laughed bitterly. "I always suspected you two were an item. She's the real reason our relationship died. Not because we're so different or that we want different things."

"Wait. What do you mean Tess is the reason we broke up?"

Sabrina flopped down on the sofa and sighed, shaking her head. "It became painfully obvious that I was the third wheel in the relationship. That I'd never mean as much to you as she does. I deserve better."

Ryan frowned, thinking of his time with Sabrina. Especially the year they'd lived together in Royal before their planned wedding.

He hadn't considered how his relationship with Tessa might have contributed to Sabrina's feelings of isolation. At the time, he'd thought her jealousy of Tess was unwarranted. There certainly hadn't been anything going on between him and Tess back then. Still, in retrospect, he realized the validity of her feelings.

He sat beside Sabrina again. "Maybe I did allow my relationship with Tess to overshadow ours in some ways. For that, I'm sorry. But regardless of the reason for our breakup, the bottom line is, we're just not right for each other. In my book, finding that out before we got married is a good thing."

"What if I don't believe it. What if I believe…" She inhaled deeply, her stormy blue eyes rimmed with tears. "What if I think it was the biggest mistake I ever made, walking away from us?"

"We never could have made each other happy, Brie." He placed his hand over hers and squeezed it. "You would've been miserable living in Royal, even if we had been a perfect match. And God knows I'd be miserable anywhere else. Because this is where my family and friends are. Where my future lies."

"Your future with Tessa?" She pulled her hand from beneath his and used the back of her wrist to wipe away tears.

"My future with Tessa is the same now as it was back then." Regardless of what he wanted. "We're friends."

Sabrina's bitter laugh had turned caustic. She stalked across the floor again. "The sad thing is, I think you two actually believe that."

"What do you mean?"

"You've been in love with each other for as long as I've known you. From what I can tell, probably since the day you two met in diapers. What I don't understand is why, for the love of God, you two don't just admit it. If not to everyone else, at least to yourselves. Then maybe you'd stop hurting those of us insane enough to think we could ever be enough for either of you."

Ryan sat back against the sofa and dragged a hand across his forehead. He'd tried to curtail his feelings for Tess because of his promise to Tripp and because he hadn't wanted to ruin their friendship. But what lay at the root of his denial was his fear that he couldn't be the man Tess deserved. A man as strong as he was loving and unafraid to show his affection for the people he loved.

A man like her father.

In his family, affection was closely aligned with weakness and neediness. In hers, it was just the opposite. With their opposing philosophies on the matter, it was amazing that their parents had managed to become such good friends.

He'd been afraid that he could never measure up to her father and be the man she deserved. But what he hadn't realized was the time he'd spent with Tessa and her family had taught him little by little how to let go of his family's hang-ups and love a woman like Tess.

Sabrina was right. He *was* in love with Tess. Always had been. And he loved her as much more than just a friend. Tessa Noble was the one woman he couldn't imagine not having in his life. And now, he truly understood the depth of his feelings. He needed her to be his friend, his lover, his confidante. He wanted to make love to her every night and wake up to her gorgeous face every morning.

He'd asked Tess to give their relationship a chance, but he hadn't been honest with her or himself about *why* he wanted a relationship with her.

He loved and needed her. Without her in his life, he felt incomplete.

"It wasn't intentional, but I was unfair to you, Sabrina. Our relationship was doomed from the start, because I do love Tess that way. I'm sorry you've come all this way for nothing, but I need to thank you, too. For helping me to realize what I guess I've known on some level all along. That I love Tess, and I want to be with her."

"As long as one of us is happy, right?" Her bangs fluttered when she blew out an exasperated breath.

Ryan stood, offering her an apologetic smile. "C'mon, it's getting late. I'll walk you to your car."

Ryan gave Sabrina a final hug, grateful to her. He'd ask Tess again to give them a chance.

This time, he wouldn't screw it up.

Nineteen

Tessa had been going crazy, pacing in that big old house all alone. She hadn't been able to stop thinking about Ryan. Not just what had happened in the stables, but she'd replayed everything he'd said to her.

She hadn't been fair to him, and she needed to apologize for her part in this whole mess. But first, she thought it best to let him cool off.

Tessa got into her truck and drove into town to have breakfast at the Royal Diner. It was a popular spot in town, so at least she wouldn't be alone.

She ordered coffee and a short stack of pancakes, intending to eat at the counter of the retro diner owned by Sheriff Battle's wife, Amanda. The quaint establishment was frozen in the 1950s with its red, faux-leather booths and black-and-white checkerboard flooring. But Amanda made sure that every surface in the space was gleaming.

"Tessa?"

She turned on her stool toward the booth where someone had called her name.

It was the makeup artist from PURE. Milan Valez.

"Milan. Hey, it's good to see you. How are you this morning?"

"Great. I always pass by this place. Today, I thought I'd stop in and give it a try." Milan's dark eyes shone, and her pecan brown skin was flawless at barely eight in the morning. "I just ordered breakfast. Why don't you join me?"

Tessa let the waitress know she'd be moving, then she slid across from Milan in the corner booth where the woman sat, sipping a glass of orange juice.

When the waitress brought Milan's plate, she indicated that she'd be paying for Tess's meal, too.

"That's kind of you, really, but you're the one who is new in town. I should be treating you," Tess objected.

"I insist." Milan waved a hand. "It's the least I can do after you've brought me so much business. I'm booked up for weeks, thanks to you and that article on the frenzy you caused at the charity auction. Good for you." Milan pointed a finger at her. "I told you that you were a beautiful woman."

"I'm glad everything worked out for at least one

of us." Tess muttered the words under her breath, but they were loud enough for the other woman to hear.

"Speaking of which, how is it that you ended up going on this ultra-romantic weekend with your best friend?" Milan tilted her head and assessed Tessa. "And if you two are really 'just friends'—" she used air quotes "—why is it that you look like you are nursing a broken heart?"

Tessa's cheeks burned, and she stammered a bit before taking a long sip of her coffee.

"Don't worry, hon. I don't know enough folks in town to be part of the gossip chain." Milan smiled warmly. "But I've been doing this long enough to recognize a woman having some serious man troubles."

Tessa didn't bother denying it. She took another gulp of her coffee and set her cup on the table. She shook her head and sighed. "I really screwed up."

"By thinking you and your best friend could go on a romantic weekend and still remain just friends?" Milan asked before taking another sip of her orange juice.

"How did you—"

"I told you, been doing this a long time. Makeup artists are like bartenders or hairdressers. Folks sit there in that chair and use it as a confessional." Milan set her glass on the table and smiled. "Besides, I saw those pictures in the paper. That giddy look on your face? That's the look of a woman in love, if ever I've seen it."

"That obvious, huh?"

"Word around town is there's a pool on when you two finally get a clue." Milan laughed.

Tessa buried her face in her hands and moaned. "It's all my fault. He was being a perfect gentleman. I kissed him and then things kind of took off from there."

"And how do you feel about the shift in your relationship with…?"

"Ryan," Tess supplied. She thanked the waitress for her pancakes, poured a generous amount of maple syrup on the stack and cut into them. "I'm not quite sure how to feel about it."

"I'm pretty sure you are." Milan's voice was firm, but kind. "But whatever you're feeling right now, it scares the hell out of you. That's not necessarily a bad thing."

Milan was two for two.

"It's just that we've been best friends for so long. Now everything has changed, and yeah, it is scary. Part of me wants to explore what this could be. Another part of me is terrified of what will happen if everything falls apart. Besides, I'm worried that…" Tessa let the words die on her lips, taking a bite of her pancakes.

"You're worried that…what?" One of Milan's perfectly arched brows lifted.

"That he'll get bored with a Plain Jane like me. That eventually he'll want someone prettier or more glamorous than I could ever be." She shrugged.

"First, glammed up or not, you're nobody's Plain

Jane," Milan said pointedly, then offered Tess a warm smile. "Second, that look of love that I saw... it wasn't just in your eyes. It was there in his, too."

Tessa paused momentarily, contemplating Milan's observation. She was a makeup artist, not a mind reader, for goodness' sake. So it was best not to put too much stock in the woman's words. Still, it made her hopeful. Besides, there was so much more to the friendship she and Rye had built over the years.

They'd supported one another. Confided in each other. Been there for each other through the best and worst of times. She recalled Ryan's words when he'd stormed out of the stables the previous night.

They *were* good together. Compatible in all the ways that mattered. And she couldn't imagine her life without him.

"Only you can determine whether it's worth the risk to lean into your feelings for your friend, or if you're better off running as fast as you can in the opposite direction." Milan's words broke into her thoughts. The woman took a bite of her scrambled eggs. "What's your gut telling you?"

"To go for the safest option. But that's always been my approach to my love life, which is why I haven't had much of one." Tessa chewed another bite of her pancakes. "In a perfect world, sure I'd take a chance. See where this relationship might lead. But—"

"There's no such thing as a perfect world, darlin'." A smile lit Milan's eyes. "As my mama always said, nothing ventured, nothing gained. You can either allow fear to prevent you from going for what you really want, or you can grow a set of lady *cojones*, throw caution to the wind, and confess your feelings to your friend. You might discover that he feels the same way about you. Maybe he's afraid of risking his heart, too."

Milan pointed her fork at Tessa. "The question you have to ask yourself is—is what you two could have together worth risking any embarrassment or hurt feelings?"

"Yes." The word burst from her lips without a second of thought. Still, its implication left her stunned, her hands shaking.

A wide smile lit the other woman's face. "Then why are you still sitting here with me? Girl, you need to go and get your man, before someone else does. Someone who isn't afraid."

Tess grabbed two pieces of bacon and climbed to her feet, adrenaline pumping through her veins. "I'm sorry, Milan. Rain check?"

"You know where to find me." She nodded toward the door. "Now go, before you lose your nerve."

Tessa gave the woman an awkward hug, then she hurried out of the diner, determined to tell Ryan the truth.

She was in love with him.

Ryan was evidently even angrier with Tessa than she'd thought. She'd called him repeatedly with no answer. She'd even gone over to the Bateman Ranch, but Helene said he'd left first thing in the morning and she didn't expect him until evening. Then she mentioned that his ex, Sabrina, had been at the house the day before.

Tess's heart sank. Had her rejection driven Ryan back into the arms of his ex?

She asked Helene to give her a call the second Ryan's truck pulled into the driveway, and she begged her not to let Ryan know.

The woman smiled and promised she would, giving Tess a huge hug before she left.

Tessa tried to go about her day as normally as possible. She started by calling Bo and Clem and apologizing for any misunderstanding. Both men were disappointed, but gracious about it.

When Tripp arrived back home from the airport, he brought her up to speed on the potential client. He'd landed the account. She hugged her brother and congratulated him, standing with him when he video conferenced their parents and told them the good news.

Tripp wanted to celebrate, but she wasn't in the mood to go out, and he couldn't get a hold of Ryan, either. So he called up Lana, since it was her day off.

Tessa had done every ranch chore she could think of to keep her mind preoccupied, until finally Roy Jensen ran her off, tired of her being underfoot.

When Roy and the other stragglers had gone, she

was left with nothing but her thoughts about what she'd say to Ryan once she saw him.

Finally, when she'd stepped out of the shower, Helene called, whispering into the phone that Ryan had just pulled into the drive of the Bateman Ranch.

Tessa hung up the phone, dug out her makeup bag and got ready for the scariest moment of her life.

Ryan hopped out of the shower, threw on a clean shirt and a pair of jeans. He picked up the gray box and stuck it in his pocket, not caring that his hair was still wet. He needed to see Tess.

He hurried downstairs. The entire first floor of the ranch smelled like the brisket Helene had been slow-cooking all day. But as tempted as he was by Helene's heavenly cooking, his stomach wasn't his priority. It would have to wait a bit longer.

"I was beginning to think you'd dozed off up there. And this brisket smells so good. It took every ounce of my willpower not to nab a piece." Tessa stood in the kitchen wearing a burgundy, cowl-neck sweater dress that hit her mid-thigh. "I mean, it would be pretty rude to start eating your dinner before you've had any."

"Tessa." He'd been desperate to see her, but now that she was here, standing in front of him, his pulse raced and his heart hammered against his ribs. "What are you doing here?"

She frowned, wringing her hands before forcing

a smile. "I really needed to talk to you. Helene let me in before she left. Please don't be mad at her."

"No, of course I'm not mad at Helene."

"But you are still angry with me?" She stepped closer, peering up at him intensely.

"I'm not angry with you, Tess. I…" He sighed, running a hand through his wet hair.

He'd planned a perfect evening for them. Had gone over the words he wanted to say again and again. But seeing her now, none of that mattered. "But I do need to talk to you. And, despite the grand plans that I'd made, I just need to get this out."

"What is it, Rye?" Tessa worried her lower lip with her teeth. "What is it you need to tell me?" When he didn't answer right away, she added, "I know Sabrina was here yesterday. Did you two… are you back together?"

"Sabrina and me? God, no. What happened with us was for the best. She may not see it now, but one day she will."

Tessa heaved a sigh of relief. "Okay, so what do you need to tell me?"

Ryan reached for her hand and led her to the sofa in the family room just off the kitchen. Seated beside her, he turned his body toward hers and swallowed the huge lump in his throat.

"Tess, you've been my best friend since we were both knee-high to a grasshopper. The best moments of my life always involve you. You're always there with that big, bright smile and those warm, brown eyes, making me believe I can do anything. That I deserve everything. And I'm grateful that you've been my best friend all these years."

Tess cradled his cheek with her free hand. The corners of her eyes were wet with tears. She nodded. "Me, too. You've always been there for me, Ryan. I guess we've both been pretty lucky, huh?"

"We have been. But I've also been pretty foolish. Selfish even. Because I wanted you all to myself. Was jealous of any man who dared infringe on your time, or God forbid, command your attention. But I was afraid to step up and be the man you deserved."

"*Was* afraid?'" Now the tears flowed down her face more rapidly. She wiped them away with the hand that had cradled his face a moment ago. "As in past tense?"

"*Am* terrified would be more accurate." He forced a smile as he gently wiped the tears from her cheek with his thumb. "But just brave enough to tell you that I love you, Tessa Noble, and not just as a friend. I love you with all my heart. You're everything to me, and I couldn't imagine my life without you."

"I love you, too, Rye." Tessa beamed. "I mean, I'm in love with you. I have been for so long, I'm not really even sure when it shifted from you being my best friend to you being the guy I was head over heels in love with."

"Tess." He kissed her, then pulled her into his arms. "You have no idea how happy I am right now."

Relief flooded his chest and his heart felt full, as

if it might burst. He loved this woman, who also happened to be his best friend. He loved her more than anything in the world. And he wanted to be with her.

Always.

For the first time in his life, the thought of spending the rest of his days with the same woman didn't give him a moment's pause. Because Tessa Noble had laid claim to his heart long ago. She was the one woman whose absence from his life would make him feel incomplete. Like a man functioning with only half of his heart.

"Tessa, would you…" He froze for a moment. His tongue sticking to the roof of his mouth. Not because he was afraid. Nor was he having second thoughts. There were a few things he needed to do first.

"What is it, Ryan?" She looked up at him, her warm, brown eyes full of love and light. The same eyes he'd been enamored with for as long as he could remember.

"I'd planned to take you out to dinner. Maybe catch a movie. But since Helene has already made such an amazing meal…"

"It'd be a shame to waste it." A wicked smile lit her beautiful face. "So why don't we eat dinner here, and then afterward…" She kissed him, her delicate hands framing his face. "Let's just say that dinner isn't the only thing I'm hungry for."

"That makes two of us." He pulled her into the kitchen and made them plates of Helene's delicious meal before they ended up naked and starving.

After their quick meal, Ryan swept Tessa into his arms and kissed her. Then he took her up to his bedroom where he made love to his best friend.

This time there was no uncertainty. No hesitation. No regrets. His heart and his body belonged to Tessa Noble. Now and always.

Ryan woke at nearly two in the morning and patted the space beside him. The space where Tess had lain, her bottom cuddled against his length. Her spot was still warm.

He raised up on his elbows and looked around. She was in the corner of the room, wiggling back into her dress.

"Hey, beautiful." He scrubbed the sleep from his eye. "Where are you going?"

"Sorry, I didn't mean to wake you." She turned a lamp on beside the chair.

"You're leaving?" He sat up fully, drawing his knees up and resting his arms on them when she nodded in response. "Why?"

"Because until we talk to our families about this, I thought it best we be discreet."

"But it's not like you haven't spent the night here before," he groused, already missing the warmth of her soft body cuddled against his. It was something he'd missed every night since their return from Dallas.

"I know, but things are different now. I'm not

just sleeping in the guest room." She gave him a knowing look.

"You've slept in here before, too."

"When we fell asleep binge-watching all the Marvel movies. And we both fell asleep fully dressed." She slipped on one of her boots and zipped it. "Not when I can't stop smiling because we had the most amazing night together. Tripp would see through that in two seconds."

He was as elated by her statement as he was disappointed by her leaving. What she was saying made sense. Of course, it did. But he wanted her in his bed, in his life. Full stop.

Tessa deserved better than the two of them sneaking around. Besides, with that came the implication that the two of them were doing something wrong. They weren't. And he honestly couldn't wait to tell everyone in town just how much he loved Tessa Noble.

"I'll miss you, too, babe." She sat on the edge of the bed beside him and planted a soft kiss on his lips.

Perhaps she'd only intended for the kiss to placate him. But he'd slipped his hands beneath her skirt and glided them up to the scrap of fabric covering her sex.

She murmured her objection, but Ryan had swallowed it with his hungry kiss. Lips searching and tongues clashing. His needy groans countered her small whimpers of pleasure.

"Rye... I really need to go." Tess pulled away momentarily.

He resumed their kiss as he led her hand to his growing length.

"Guess it would be a shame to waste something that impressive." A wicked smile flashed across Tess's beautiful face. She encircled his warm flesh in her soft hand as she glided it up and down his straining shaft. "Maybe I could stay a little longer. Just let me turn off the light."

"No," he whispered against the soft, sweet lips he found irresistible. "Leave it on. I want to see you. All of you."

He pulled the dress over her head and tossed it aside. Then he showed Tess just how much he appreciated her staying a little while longer.

Twenty

Ryan waved Tripp to the booth he'd secured at the back of the Daily Grind.

Tripp was an uncomplicated guy who always ordered the same thing. At the Royal Diner, a stack of pancakes, two eggs over easy, crispy bacon and black coffee. Here at the Daily Grind, a bear claw that rivaled the size of one's head and a cup of black coffee, two sugars.

Ryan had placed their order as soon as he'd arrived, wanting to get right down to their conversation.

His friend slid into the booth and looked at the plate on the table and his cup of coffee. "You already ordered for me?"

"Don't worry. It's still hot. I picked up our order two minutes ago."

Tripp sipped his coffee. "Why do I have the feeling that I'm about to get some really bad news?"

"Depends on your point of view, I guess." Ryan shoved the still warm cinnamon bun aside, his hands pressed to the table.

"It must be really bad. Did something happen to our parents on the cruise?"

"It's nothing like that." Ryan swallowed hard, tapping the table lightly. He looked up squarely at his friend. "I just… I need to tell you that I broke my promise to you…about Tess." Ryan sat back in the booth. "Tripp, I love her. I think I always have."

"I see." Tripp's gaze hardened. "Since you're coming to me with this, it's probably safe to assume you're already sleeping with my little sister."

Ryan didn't respond either way. He owed Tripp this, but the details of their relationship, that was between him and Tess. They didn't owe anyone else an explanation.

"Of course." Tripp nodded, his fists clenched on the table in front of him. "That damn auction. The gift that keeps on giving."

Ryan half expected his friend to try to slug him, as he had when they were teenagers and the kids at school had started a rumor that Ryan was Tess's boyfriend. It was the last time the two of them had an honest-to-goodness fight.

That was when Tripp had made him promise he'd never lay a hand on Tess.

"Look, Tripp, I know you didn't think I was good

enough for your sister. Deep down, I think I believed that, too. But more than anything I was afraid to ruin my friendship with her or you. You and Tess… you're more than just friends to me. You're family."

"If you were so worried about wrecking our friendships, what's changed? Why are you suddenly willing to risk it?" Tripp folded his arms as he leaned on the table.

"I've changed. Or at least, my perspective has. I can't imagine watching your sister live a life with someone else. Marrying some other guy and raising their children. Wishing they were ours." Ryan shook his head. "That's a regret I can't take to my grave. And if it turns out I'm wrong, I honestly believe my friendship with you and Tess is strong enough to recover. But the thing is… I don't think I am wrong about us. I love her, Tripp, and I'm gonna ask her to marry me. But I wanted to come to you first and explain why I could no longer keep my promise."

"You're planning to propose? Already? God, what the hell happened with you guys in Dallas?" Tripp shut his eyes and shook his head. "Never mind. On second thought, don't *ever* tell me what happened in Dallas."

"Now that's a promise I'm pretty sure I can keep." Ryan chuckled.

"I guess it could be worse. She could be marrying some dude I hate instead of one of my best friends."

It was as close to a blessing as he was likely to get from Tripp. He'd gladly take it.

"Thanks, man. That means a lot. I promise, I won't let you or Tess down."

"You'd better not." Tripp picked up his bear claw and took a huge bite.

It was another promise he had every intention of keeping.

Ryan, Tessa, Tripp and both sets of their parents, had dinner at the Glass House restaurant at the exclusive five-star Bellamy resort to celebrate their parents' return and Tripp landing the Noble Spur's biggest customer account to date.

The restaurant was decked out in festive holiday decor. Two beautiful Douglas firs. Twinkling lights everywhere. Red velvet bows and poinsettias. Then there were gifts wrapped in shiny red, green, gold and silver foil wrapping paper.

Tessa couldn't be happier. She was surrounded by the people who meant the most to her. And both her parents and Ryan's had been thrilled that she and Ryan had finally acknowledged what both their mothers claimed to have known all along. That she and Ryan were hopelessly in love.

Ryan had surprised her with an early Christmas gift—the Maybach saddle she'd mused about on their drive to Dallas.

Even Tripp was impressed.

The food at the Glass House was amazing, as always. And a live act, consisting of a vocalist and an acoustic guitar player, set the mood by serenading the patrons with soft ballads.

When they started to play Christina Perri's "A Thousand Years," Ryan asked her to dance. Next, the duo performed Train's song, "Marry Me."

"I love that song. It's so perfect." Tessa swayed happily to the music as the vocalist sang the romantic lyrics.

"It is." He grinned. "And so are you. I'm so lucky that the woman I love is also my best friend. You, Tess, are the best Christmas gift I could ever hope for."

"That's so sweet of you to say, babe." Her cheeks flushed and her eyes shone with tears. She smiled. "Who says you're not romantic?"

"You make me want to be. Because you deserve it all. Romance, passion, friendship. A home of our own, marriage, kids. You deserve all of that and more. And I want to be the man who gives that to you."

Tessa blinked back tears. "Ryan, it sounds a lot like you're asking me to marry you."

"Guess that means I ain't doing it quite right." Ryan winked and pulled a gray velvet box from his pocket. He opened it and Tessa gasped, covering her mouth with both hands as he got down on one knee and took her left hand in his.

"Tessa Marie Noble, you're my best friend, my lover, my confidante. You've always been there for me, Tess. And I always want to be there for you, making an incredible life together right here in the town we both love. Would you please do me the great honor of being my wife?"

"Yes." Tessa nodded, tears rolling down her cheeks. "Nothing would make me happier than marrying my best friend."

Ryan slipped on the ring and kissed her hand.

He'd known the moment he'd seen the ring that it was the one for Tess. As unique and beautiful as the woman he loved. A chocolate diamond solitaire set in a strawberry gold band of intertwined ribbons sprinkled with vanilla and chocolate diamonds.

Tessa extended her hand and studied the ring, a wide grin spreading across her gorgeous face. "It's my Neapolitan engagement ring!"

"Anything for you, babe." Ryan took her in his arms and kissed her with their families and fellow diners cheering them on.

But for a few moments, everyone else disappeared, and there was only Tessa Noble. The woman who meant everything to him, and always would.

* * * * *

*How will Rose and Gus explain the new turn
in their relationship?
Will they continue to keep Alexis and Daniel apart?*

Find out in The Rancher's Bargain
*by Joanne Rock!
Available January 2019!*

*To pay her sister's debt, Lydia Walker agrees to a
temporary job as a live-in nanny for hot-as-sin
rancher, James Harris. There's no denying the
magnetic pull between them, but can they detangle
their white-hot desire and stubborn differences
before time runs out?*

*Don't miss a single installment of the six-book
Texas Cattleman's Club:
Bachelor Auction*

*Will the scandal of the century lead to love
for these rich ranchers?*

Runaway Temptation
by USA TODAY *bestselling author Maureen Child*
Most Eligible Texan
by USA TODAY *bestselling author Jules Bennett*
Million Dollar Baby
by USA TODAY *bestselling author Janice Maynard*
His Until Midnight
by Reese Ryan
The Rancher's Bargain
by Joanne Rock
Lone Star Reunion
by Joss Wood

COMING NEXT MONTH FROM

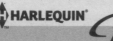 HARLEQUIN

 *Desire*

Available December 31, 2018

#2635 THE RANCHER'S BARGAIN

Texas Cattleman's Club: Bachelor Auction
by Joanne Rock

To pay her sister's debt, Lydia Walker agrees to a temporary job as a live-in nanny for hot-as-sin rancher James Harris. There's no denying the magnetic pull between them, but can they untangle their white-hot desire and stubborn differences before time runs out?

#2636 BOMBSHELL FOR THE BOSS

Billionaires and Babies • by Maureen Child

Secretary Sadie Matthews has wanted CEO Ethan Hart for five years—and quitting hasn't changed a thing! But when fate throws him a baby-sized curveball and forces them together again, all the rules are broken and neither can resist temptation any longer...

#2637 THE FORBIDDEN TEXAN

Texas Promises • by Sara Orwig

Despite a century-old family feud, billionaire Texas rancher Jake Ralston hires antiques dealer Emily Kincaid to fulfill a deathbed promise to his friend. But when they're isolated together on his ranch, these enemies' platonic intentions soon become a passion they can't deny...

#2638 THE BILLIONAIRE RENEGADE

Alaskan Oil Barons • by Catherine Mann

Wealthy cowboy Conrad Steele is a known flirt. He's pursued beautiful Felicity Hunt with charm and wit. The spark between them is enough to ignite white-hot desire, but if they're not careful it could burn them both...

#2639 INCONVENIENTLY WED

Marriage at First Sight • by Yvonne Lindsay

Their whirlwind marriage ended quickly, but now both Valentin and Imogene have been matched again—for a blind date at the altar! The passion is still there, but will this second chance mend old wounds, or drive them apart forever?

#2640 AT THE CEO'S PLEASURE

The Stewart Heirs • by Yahrah St. John

Ayden Stewart is a cunningly astute businessman, but ugly family history has him distrustful of love. His gorgeous assistant, Maya Richardson, might be the sole exception—if he can win her back after breaking her heart years ago!

**YOU CAN FIND MORE INFORMATION ON UPCOMING HARLEQUIN® TITLES,
FREE EXCERPTS AND MORE AT WWW.HARLEQUIN.COM.**

HDCNM1218

Get 4 FREE REWARDS!

We'll send you 2 FREE Books <u>plus</u> 2 FREE Mystery Gifts.

Harlequin® Desire books feature heroes who have it all: wealth, status, incredible good looks... everything but the right woman.

FREE
Value Over
$20

SPECIAL EXCERPT FROM

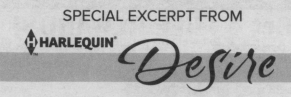

HARLEQUIN®

Desire

*Ayden Stewart is a cunningly astute businessman,
but ugly family history has him distrustful of love.
His gorgeous assistant, Maya Richardson, might be
the sole exception—if he can win her back after
breaking her heart years ago!*

Read on for a sneak peek of
At the CEO's Pleasure *by Yahrah St. John,
part of her Stewart Heirs series!*

He would never forget the day, ten years ago, when Maya
Richardson had walked through his door looking for a
job. She'd been a godsend, helping Ayden grow Stewart
Investments into the company it was today. Thinking
of her brought a smile to Ayden's face. How could it
not? Not only was she the best assistant he'd ever had,
Maya had fascinated him. Utterly and completely. Maya
had hidden an exceptional figure beneath professional
clothing and kept her hair in a tight bun. But Ayden had
often wondered what it would be like to throw her over
his desk and muss her up. Five years ago, he hadn't gone
quite that far, but he had crossed a boundary.

Maya had been devastated over her breakup with her
boyfriend. She'd come to him for comfort, and, instead,
Ayden had made love to her. Years of wondering what
it would be like to be with Maya had erupted into a

HDEXP1218

passionate encounter. Their one night together had been so explosive that the next morning Ayden had needed to take a step back to regain his perspective. He'd had to put up his guard; otherwise, he would have hurt her badly. He thought he'd been doing the right thing, but Maya hadn't thought so. In retrospect, Ayden wished he'd never given in to temptation. But he had, and he'd lost a damn good assistant. Maya had quit, and Ayden hadn't seen or heard from her since.

Shaking his head, Ayden strode to his desk and picked up the phone, dialing the recruiter who'd helped him find Carolyn. He wasn't looking forward to this process. It had taken a long time to find and train Carolyn. Before her, Ayden had dealt with several candidates walking into his office thinking they could ensnare him.

No, he had someone else in mind. A hardworking, dedicated professional who could read his mind without him saying a word and who knew how to handle a situation in his absence. Someone who knew about the big client he'd always wanted to capture but never could attain. She also had a penchant for numbers and research like no one he'd ever seen, not even Carolyn.

Ayden knew exactly who he wanted. He just needed to find out where she'd escaped to.

Don't miss what happens next!
At the CEO's Pleasure *by Yahrah St. John,*
part of her Stewart Heirs series!

Available January 2019 wherever
Harlequin® Desire books and ebooks are sold.

www.Harlequin.com

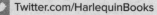

CRITICAL ACCLAIM FOR

ANNE MARIE WINSTON

"Anne Marie Winston deftly fashions a strong love story
with solid and distinctive characterization."
—*Romantic Times*

"Anne Marie Winston scorches each page
with intensity and passion."
—*Rendezvous*

"Anne Marie Winston writes the kind of wonderful book
that makes you feel like a million bucks
when the last delicious page is turned."
—*Romantic Times*

PRAISE FOR

TERESE RAMIN

Here's what critics have had to say
about *An Unexpected Addition*:

"A master of characterization,
Ms. Ramin knocks our socks off
with another unique, unforgettable love story."
—*Romantic Times*

"Ms. Ramin has a winner in
An Unexpected Addition—an emotionally stirring story
with outstanding characterizations."
—*Rendezvous*

"...a winner from beginning to end!"
—*Romance Forever Magazine*

ANNE MARIE WINSTON

RITA® Award finalist and bestselling author
Anne Marie Winston loves babies she can give back
when they cry, animals in all shapes and sizes and just
about anything that blooms. When she's not writing, she's
chauffeuring children to various activities, trying *not* to eat
chocolate, or reading anything she can find. She will dance
at the slightest provocation and weeds her gardens when
she can't see the sun for the weeds anymore. You can learn
more about Anne Marie's novels by visiting her Web site
at www.annemariewinston.com.

TERESE RAMIN

The granddaughter of an Irish Blarney Stone kisser (who,
lowered by her ankles to do so, kissed it last at the age of
ninety-six) and the oldest of eight, Terese Ramin has been
surrounded by kids, chaos and storytelling all her life. At the
request of her siblings she told outrageous stories late into the
night, which caused a great deal of giggling among the kids
and aggravation for her parents, who merely wanted them all
To Go To Sleep! Terese lives in Michigan with five dogs,
three cats, two kids and a husband who creates sawdust.

Baby Be Mine

ANNE MARIE WINSTON
TERESE RAMIN

Silhouette® Books

Published by Silhouette Books

America's Publisher of Contemporary Romance

SILHOUETTE BOOKS

ISBN 0-373-21731-5

by Request

BABY BE MINE

Copyright © 2002 by Harlequin Books S.A.

The publisher acknowledges the copyright holders
of the individual works as follows:

FIND HER, KEEP HER
Copyright © 1994 by Anne Marie Rodgers

AN UNEXPECTED ADDITION
Copyright © 1997 by Terese daly Ramin

Printed In U.S.A.

CONTENTS

Dear Reader,

As a child, I rescued abandoned cats and dogs. At age twelve, I slept with so many cats that at one point my father said either I could go or the cats could. As an adult, my penchant for helping our four-footed friends hasn't waned. Our home is filled with pets, most of whom are rejects from someone else who didn't want them. My first collie, Winston's Shining Fancy, and I went through obedience together and after a lot of mistakes (mostly on my part!) he got his first obedience title. I am fascinated by animal behavior and so it was only natural for me to write a book in which my hero and heroine were brought together by a dog!

On my Web site, there's a section called "The Critter Corner" devoted to all kinds of animal information. When you visit, be sure to check it out—and don't miss the story about the day my mother buried the wrong dog.

Dane Hamilton is my kind of hero, and when you read this story, you'll know why. I'm a sucker for a man who admits to loving a pet. Enjoy!

Anne Marie Winston

FIND HER, KEEP HER
Anne Marie Winston

For The Boop—
the finest Maw-in-law a gal could ever have

One

He would wring her beautiful neck when he caught her. Dane Hamilton sprinted down the tree-shaded block, cursing the August heat wave in Chicago and everything else in sight.

"Get back here, Miss—!"

But she just tossed a laughing glance over one shoulder and kept right on running.

Okay, fine. "I'm going home," he yelled after her. "I'm not chasing you one step farther. Do you hear me? *Not one step!* I don't care if you never come home!" Dane turned around and took several rapid strides back the way he'd come. He peeked over his shoulder.

She had stopped and was watching him. Little witch.

Dane kept on going. This was it. Absolutely it. He'd moved to River Forest, Illinois, only two weeks ago and he would bet all the neighbors thought he was crazy.

Come to think of it, he was. And undignified, to boot.

Here he was, the new vice president of a local bank, chasing down the street after her. For the third day in a row.

He should have followed his instincts and gotten rid of her before he left Peoria. The trouble was, she was so damned cute. She'd wormed her way into his heart despite his reservations. If anything happened to her, he'd never forgive himself. His steps slowed. Maybe he should go back and try to catch her one more time. Maybe—

A cold, wet nose thrust into his palm. "Miss Mess," Dane said with fond exasperation. He hunkered down to nuzzle his face into the neck of the black Doberman that was gazing up at him with innocent eyes. While he hugged her, his hand caressed her neck, easing down to get a death grip on her collar before she realized it. "You're going to drive me insane," he told the dog.

With his hand firmly on her collar, Dane headed for home. Missy, her youthful energies apparently expended in the wild chase, trotted docilely beside him, the stump of her tail wagging madly. By the time they'd traveled three blocks, Dane was furious again. He was too tall to be comfortable in this position. His back was killing him.

As he rounded the corner and turned onto his own street, he saw the couple who lived in the corner house taking in groceries. Damn. The fellow had smiled tolerantly at him just yesterday when Dane was towing Missy home. The man's grin had been amused. And the woman...

She was exactly what he was looking for in a wife.

He assessed the petite lines of her figure just before she disappeared into the house, mildly surprised at the instant physical response the unknown woman aroused in him. He hadn't wanted a woman in a long time, even though he knew it was past time he got back to the business of finding a wife. But now...

He wanted. Oh, yes indeed, he wanted. And nothing would please him more than coming home every night to a woman who looked like this one. She was perfect.

At least, physically she was, with the kind of full hour-glass curves that men loved and women constantly tried to diet away. She had a delicate little nose and sharply defined cheekbones. Her forehead was broad, her face heart-shaped.

He hadn't met her, so he didn't know if she possessed any of the qualities he'd come to realize were vital in a wife. But he could imagine himself coming home to this woman every night, tucking the children they'd have together into their beds before taking her to the larger bed in the room they'd share....

Too bad she was taken.

Nearly every day, he was conscious of his best years slipping away silently, uneventfully. He'd envisioned himself a father by the time he hit thirty-five, in love and happily married and raising the family of which he'd dreamed.

Well, it wasn't too late. He wouldn't let it be. Maybe the love part had turned out to be a royal joke, but he was determined to make the rest come true...on his terms. When he reentered the marriage sweepstakes, he would have his eyes wide open. He would marry for companionship and sexual compatibility.

And he would demand a sworn affidavit from his bride-to-be that she fully intended to present him with children as soon as possible after the wedding date.

Once again, the bitter taste of rage rose to taunt him. Maybe he wasn't ready to jump into another relationship yet.

Still, he thought, his eyes appreciatively scanning every curve as the woman made another trip from the house to the car, a man could enjoy. As she straightened up, the long, dark braid that started at the crown of her head slipped across her fanny, gently swishing back and forth with every step she took. As she disappeared into a side door with the man behind her, Dane let out his breath in a silent whistle. Yes, indeed, a man could enjoy.

Just as he drew even with their driveway, the man

bounced through the screen door, letting it slam behind him. His red hair was a flaming halo backlit in the early-evening sun.

"Hello," he said. "Got a runaway, have you?"

Dane nodded.

"Patrick Murphy." The redhead was striding down the driveway, extending a hand.

Dane halted. He couldn't help but notice the slogan scrawled above the silhouette of a skier on the front of Patrick Murphy's T-shirt: Skiers Do It With Poles. Nice, he thought with reluctant amusement, real nice. He was still bent over at an awkward angle, holding on to Missy's collar, but he extended his own hand. "Dane Hamilton."

When Patrick Murphy shook his hand, Dane winced. What kind of work did the guy do to have a grip like that? Unobtrusively, Dane flexed his mangled fingers.

"You moved in a few doors down, right?" Patrick said.

Dane nodded. "Yes, two weeks ago. I was fortunate to find a house in this neighborhood."

"Have you lived in the Chicago area long?" The redhead fairly radiated exuberant friendliness.

"No. I just moved from Peoria. I'm looking forward to getting to know my way around."

Patrick nodded. "I grew up in Chicago. It's a great town." He looked down at Missy. "Your dog?"

"Yeah. Miss Mess, meet Mr. Murphy."

"Mind if I pet her?"

When Dane indicated his assent, Patrick extended his fisted hand for Missy to sniff. She evidently took it as a sign of encouragement. Before Dane could stop her, she leaped at Patrick, her huge front paws planted firmly on his chest. Patrick didn't appear to mind, crooning ridiculous baby talk to her as she licked his face with great, sloppy swipes of her tongue. It occurred to Dane that he must sound exactly the same sometimes.

The screen door slammed again. Over Patrick's shoulder,

Dane saw the woman he'd been watching. She hesitated when she saw Patrick with him, then slowly she walked down the driveway.

"Hello," she said.

Up close, Dane could see that her eyes were big and blue, serious eyes that didn't match the half-hearted smile she was aiming his way. This close, he could see that her hair was a dark, coppery red. She wore it all pulled back in the braid except for some wispy bangs. Her mouth was wide and she had a hint of an overbite that only added to his overall impression of cute and cuddly. He wondered if she was Patrick's wife.

If she was, he got a ten in the Great Taste Ratings.

He cleared his throat, aware that he'd been staring. "Hello."

Patrick waved an arm at him, craning his neck away from the dog's incessant licking. "Annie, this is Dane Hamilton. He's our new neighbor." Missy licked Patrick right across the lips and he sputtered. "All right. That's enough kissing for me."

Annie. It suited her.

"Still a puppy, isn't she?" Annie said, eyeing Missy critically.

Dane nodded ruefully. "I'm afraid so. About ten months old."

"She's a real beauty. Is she registered?"

"Yes. She came from a line of champions bred at a kennel in Bolingbrook. She was a birthday present from my parents." Dane shook his head. "I doubt I'd have kept her if I'd known I would be moving to Chicago. My home in Peoria had a huge, fenced yard. I'm having a terrible time keeping tabs on her here. I've been trying to train her to come when I call, but so far I haven't had much success."

Patrick groaned. "Now you've done it."

Dane looked at him quizzically, then at Annie.

Patrick looked at her, too, and Dane envied them the unspoken communication in the wordless exchange. Then Patrick said, "Do you want to tell him or shall I?"

Annie gave a small shrug of her shoulders and turned back to Dane. "I'm a dog trainer. She's the perfect age for a Basic obedience course, if you're interested."

She was a *dog trainer?* Somehow, Dane couldn't envision this tiny, delicate woman handling big, bouncy dogs likes Missy. But still…dog obedience school might not be a bad idea. "Would she come when I called her then?"

"Eventually. How obedient your animal becomes is due, in large part, to how consistent you are with your training." Her eyes slid to Patrick. "My brother, for instance, can't bring himself to slip a training collar on a dog, let alone actually use it."

Patrick shrugged. "I'm softhearted. What can I say?"

Annie narrowed her eyes at him. "You could say that you know that dogs have very strong, muscular necks and the collars don't harm them."

"Wait a minute." Dane stared at them. "You two are brother and sister?" As he studied them, he could see a resemblance. Something about the eyes…

Annie nodded, distracted from what was apparently a familiar argument.

"Everyone says I'm better-looking." Patrick patted his own chin fondly.

His sister shook her head. "We allow him these little delusions," she said to Dane. Then her teasing manner faded and the serious expression returned. "Let me get you one of my business cards, in case you're interested in enrolling your dog in obedience classes." She turned to go back up the driveway.

Absently watching the twitch of her braid as she walked away, Dane said, "I thought you two were husband and wife." As she crawled into the passenger side, he could see the gently rounded curves beneath her white shorts, and he held his breath as the shorts inched higher, revealing smooth, tanned thighs.

Patrick cleared his throat loudly.

Dane jerked his gaze away from the view in time to note the amused sympathy in Patrick's green eyes. "Is your sister...involved...with anyone?"

"No." Patrick's eyes lost their humor. The single syllable sounded oddly flat. "Annie doesn't date."

Doesn't date? Dane considered the possible meaning behind the words. "Should I take that as a warning?"

Patrick shook his head and the friendliness returned, though a shadow still lingered in his eyes. "No. Just a fact. She's a widow."

She's a widow. Dane took the white card from his pocket and fingered the elegant gray lettering of the business card, which read: Evans' Canine Training School, A.E. Evans, Certified Instructor. All Levels of Puppy and Dog Obedience Classes Available.

It had been on the wide ledge above his kitchen window for three weeks. On the Wednesday evening after he'd met Patrick Murphy and his beautiful sister, he'd gone to a local department store and purchased a six-foot leash for Missy. Annie had suggested it, and he'd felt foolish after she'd explained that the only way to teach Missy not to run from him was to start from the beginning, to keep her on a leash all the time unless he tied her in the yard.

He'd called the number on the card and had gotten a recording asking him to leave his name and number if he was interested in the class schedule. As soon as he'd received the brochure in the mail, he'd enrolled Missy and himself in a beginners class that started the first week in September.

He hadn't even known Annie's last name until he'd seen it on her business card.

As he parked the car, he was conscious of a keen anticipation tightening his stomach muscles. He could attribute it to his desire to have his dog better trained, but he would be lying to himself.

He wanted to see Annie again. Tonight, at her fall orientation and open house, he would have the opportunity.

Every evening when he'd walked Missy, he'd watched for Annie when he came past her property, but he hadn't seen her since. He might not be looking for another wife yet, but he wasn't averse to some harmless flirtation, maybe a little dating that might lead to…well, what was the point in that kind of speculating? He would only drive himself crazy.

Maybe he'd imagined the sexual pull that had hit him deep in the gut the first time he'd seen her. Maybe she wasn't as great-looking as he remembered. Maybe—

Oh, hell. He hadn't imagined or exaggerated anything. Annie was waiting outside the door of her dog center, her hair braided in the same style it had been the first time he'd met her. She was tinier than he remembered, but every bit as appealing, with her lush curves and that indefinable something that told every male instinct he had to stand up and howl.

Too bad he didn't affect her the same way. Her blue, blue eyes were serious as she watched him approach, wary even. She didn't return his smile.

"Hi." Surely he could get her to relax her mouth from that straight, firm line. "You don't know how I'm looking forward to this."

"Don't expect miracles. Training a dog doesn't happen overnight, and it takes a lot of diligent work." She pointed to the fenced yard to the left of the training facility. "The grassy area is for the dogs to relieve themselves before and after class." As he moved toward the door, she added, "And over there's the shovel and the trash can for cleaning up."

So much for getting her to relax.

Once inside the building, he found a seat along the wall and waited. There was a large crowd, maybe seventy people, in the room. After a few more had come in, Annie entered and stepped to the middle of the floor.

"Good evening. Welcome to the Evans' Canine Training School. This is the orientation session for all seven of the upcoming Basic classes. I'm Annie Evans, and I'm a canine trainer certified by the National Association of Dog Obedience Instructors. For the next eight weeks, you and I will be working together to teach your dog basic obedience commands."

So that was why there were so many people here. He was relieved that there wouldn't be seventy-plus dogs all in one class. He listened carefully as she explained the history of the canine, offered an overview of the training program and gave the group information on preventing dogfights for the first few weeks while the dogs were still unsocialized.

She was impressive in her professional mode. He didn't know what he'd expected but he suddenly realized he'd been thinking of her as a small, helpless creature who needed protection. Seeing her in this setting where she shouldn't fit so comfortably but did, he acknowledged to himself just how badly he wanted to get to know her.

"Now," she said, "I know many of you think, 'My dog's never going to listen.' I'm here to tell you any dog can be trained. What it takes from you as a trainer is patience, persistence, consistency, and perhaps most important, love. I'm going to introduce you to several dogs and handlers who take classes here. Each will briefly demonstrate aspects of our obedience programs. As you watch these dogs, remember that they all started out with the same lack of skills that your dog has today. Obedience training and love are the combination that created the handler-dog relationship you see."

She turned and beckoned toward a far door and three

people came through it. Trotting at the left side of each was a dog.

"This is Jennifer. Her dog is an American Eskimo, commonly known as an Eskimo spitz...."

Dane was fascinated. The spitz was a midsize, fluffy white dog. The other two dogs were a German shepherd dog and a small black Skye terrier whose long hair was combed and tied at its ears with red ribbon. As Annie explained what the handlers were doing, all three dogs walked calmly on-lead at their handlers' sides and carried out the verbal commands they were given.

He couldn't believe Missy ever would be that well behaved. Even the little Skye terrier, whom Annie explained had just completed Basic, was a model of decorum compared to Dane's bouncy pet.

The dogs finished their demonstration. Even when the group applauded, not one of the dogs barked. As handlers and dogs filed off the floor, Dane was sorry to see the demonstration end. Not only had he genuinely enjoyed watching the dogs in action, he'd been able to observe Annie. Her eyes glowed as she spoke of the dogs, her body language was relaxed and confident and her piquant face radiated enthusiasm. It was quite a contrast to the reserved, wary woman he'd met three weeks ago.

"...now you can meet my dog."

With a start, Dane realized the demonstration wasn't over. Annie went to the far door, turned and faced the group, and, as if by magic, a large black dog appeared and sat at her side.

Dane couldn't take his gaze off the dog.

Sure, Missy was big. But floppy, ungainly and full of puppy friendliness. This creature had a squared-off, jowly face and a powerful, muscled body that would have done a prizefighter proud. This dog looked as if it could tear a person's face off without giving it a second thought.

"This is Evans' Ebony Rescuer, Ebony for short," Annie

said. "Ebony is a three-year-old female Rottweiler. Rotties are descended from the dogs that herded the cattle for the Roman army."

"Will you show us what she can do?" This was from a woman in the front row.

Annie smiled. "I'd love to."

As she turned and asked the handlers to assist her in moving some equipment into place, Dane shook his head slowly. Whoa. The impact of that smile had caught him squarely in the solar plexus. She was gorgeous.

Then she turned to the black dog, who was lying near the door where she'd left her.

"Ebony, heel."

Immediately the dog sprang up and crossed to her in quick, eager steps, taking a sitting position at her left side.

Dane was impressed. Ebony's eyes were on Annie's face, her entire attention focused on her. She started forward, and so did the dog, still watching her face.

How long had it taken to create that kind of harmony, that perfectly attuned awareness that was obvious between the woman and the dog? She'd said obedience training demanded a lot of time. Judging from the depths of devotion shining in the animal's eyes, Dane could see she was a person who was able to give her dog that time.... What would it take to get her to focus that kind of attention on a man?

As she began the demonstration, he forced himself to quit thinking about Annie Evans on a personal level, and turned his attention to the floor. As he did, the scene before him grew more and more amazing.

Annie ran the Rottweiler through a series of increasingly complex exercises that involved a number of types of equipment. In the course of the demonstration, Ebony responded to about thirty different verbal commands before ending by retrieving a specific glove that carried Annie's scent out of a group of several others.

The woman next to him murmured, ''Wow!'' and he nodded in agreement.

Annie was thanking them all for attending and giving them last-minute reminders to be sure their dogs were brought on six-foot leads next week. He badly wanted to talk to her, but the moment she finished speaking, at least half the people in the room descended on her with questions. Reluctantly, he went out to the parking lot, wondering whether she'd accept if he asked her out on a date.

God, he hated the thought of getting back into the dating scene. Did women realize how stressful dating was for a man? How much courage it took to ask a woman out?

He'd done very little real dating in the two years since his divorce was final. The few times he'd been with a woman had been more of the scratching-a-mutual-itch date than the meeting-of-the-minds variety. In fact, *date* was a strong word for the kind of encounters he'd had in recent years.

But now, he found himself wanting Annie in more ways than merely the physical, though he certainly didn't discount that. He wanted to hear her voice, to know her dreams, to learn what was important in her life.

Unfortunately, he wasn't at all sure she was interested in him the same way.

The next day was a Thursday. Dane had just finished a conference call with two other bankers who were participating in negotiating a multimillion-dollar loan package for a local school complex when his secretary buzzed him.

''Mr. Patrick Murphy is on the line for you.''

Dane's pulse speeded up a bit. Annie's brother. Picking up the line, he said, ''Patrick. What can I do for you?''

Patrick's hearty laugh boomed on the other end. ''How about a million or two? I've been thinking about this nice little trip to the Caribbean and I could probably manage it on that.''

"One would hope," Dane returned dryly. "I might be able to swing that if you have room to take along a banker who'd be out of work."

Patrick laughed again. "I guess I'd better forget it. I couldn't ask you to risk your job, but there's a request that I don't think will get you in trouble. Annie and I are having a little barbecue Saturday and we'd like you to join us."

"Sounds good. I'm free Saturday." He fought to keep the elation out of his voice. In two days, he'd have an opportunity to see her again.

"Great! We'll be getting started around seven."

"Seven it is. What can I bring?"

"Nothing. Just bring yourself."

Dane hung up the phone a moment later, erasing his wide grin just as his secretary walked into the room. He was going to see her again, and he hadn't even had to call her for a date!

The doorbell's imperious summons rang again and Annie pulled open the heavy door. She'd been greeting guests by the dozens as she plastered another social smile in place. As she registered the wall of broad masculine chest covered in a blue knit shirt standing on her doormat, she had to force the words from a suddenly dry throat. "Welcome to the party."

"Thank you."

"Please come in."

Her foyer was immediately too small, lacking in oxygen. She dragged her gaze upward, but the moment she met piercing blue eyes, she knew she'd made a mistake. Those eyes were compelling, far too beautiful and thickly lashed for any man to own. Dane. Her new neighbor. Her client. She'd been aware of him in the audience at orientation the other night, aware of every move he'd made around the big training room afterward.

Not that she'd wanted to be. But something about the man

pulled at her consciousness as if she were a metal filing and he the magnet. Suddenly, she realized she was blocking the hallway. Flushing, she stepped back, leaving plenty of room for him to pass.

Despite her care, he brushed by her as he stepped into the foyer, and she took in a deep gasp of air as the contact point where his thick arm brushed her shoulder sizzled. This close, she was even more acutely aware of how big the man was. Nick had been tall, and Patrick was over six feet, but Dane easily topped them both. His shoulders were broad, and even though the short sleeves of his shirt were loose, they didn't disguise the bulge of powerful muscle beneath.

He was smiling down at her, his eyes warm and his black curls straggling across his forehead. He extended a brown paper sack. "Patrick wouldn't let me contribute, but I brought a small token of my thanks. I haven't had much time to socialize yet, so this was a welcome invitation."

"Thank you." She felt tongue-tied and awkward as she took the bag from his and drew out the bottle. Her eyes widened as she took in the expensive label on the bottle of wine. Either the man knew his vintages or the clerk at the store had been awfully helpful. She glanced at him again, then away quickly, needing space more than she needed to breathe. "The party's out back. Follow me."

As she led the way down the hall, she was supremely aware of his large presence behind her. She should be making small talk, social patter to smooth over the awkward silence. But she'd never been good at that. It was one of the regrets she'd lived with since Nick's death.

Besides, with Dane there was some additional inhibitor catching at her tongue. She felt jumpy, as if she were in touch with a mild electrical field around him. Dane's eyes seemed to see too much, penetrating the indifference with which she'd cloaked herself in the past three years. When she looked at him, she felt an instant tug of attraction, the first time since Nick's death that a man had caught her attention in any personal way.

And it scared her to death.

Two

In the kitchen, Annie set the wine on the counter and stepped back to the tray of raw vegetables she'd been preparing. "The party's right through that door." She nodded at the exit that led to the patio. "I have a few things to finish up in here."

But Dane didn't take the hint. "I really enjoyed the orientation session Wednesday night." He folded his tall frame into one of the chairs at the breakfast bar. "It was exciting to watch the trained dogs."

"Have you ever seen obedience work before?"

He shook his head. "We had a succession of mutts when I was growing up but I never saw any demonstrations of what a trained dog can do."

The way his mouth moved to form his words was fascinating. It stirred something deep in her belly—and she realized he had stopped speaking and was looking at her expectantly. What had they been talking about? Obedience. This was a topic she could manage if she just didn't think about *him*. "I remember the first time I ever saw an obedience demonstration. I was about fourteen," she said. "Patrick had just gotten his driver's license and he was itching to show off. Mom suggested we drive out to the county fairgrounds where there was a dog show being held and he leaped at the chance, even though it meant taking his younger sister along. Once we got there, I was hooked. They had to drag me away."

"Patrick mentioned that your family is from Chicago. Do your folks still live here?"

It was a personal question for such short acquaintance, a question that she might have found intrusive coming from someone else. But his blue eyes were warm on her face and she found herself answering before she thought about it. "My parents passed away while I was in college." She allowed her voice to reflect the love with which she always remembered them. "They were older when Patrick and I came along, and after mom died, my father just gave up. They were so happy together. I like to think that they're as happy now, together again."

"Was this your family home?"

She hesitated for a moment, the warmth between them forgotten under the onslaught of memory. "No. My husband and I bought this place after he established his law practice here in River Forest. As a child, I lived right in the city on Lake Shore Drive, in a high rise across from the lake."

Dane hesitated, too, and she had the impression he was weighing his words before he spoke. "Patrick told me you're a widow. Losing your husband must have been very difficult."

"It was." She bowed her head, fighting the threat of sudden tears. Just when she thought she had grief conquered, it sprang out to torment her once again. How could she still miss Nick so much and be attracted to another man? "I'll always owe Patrick a debt for the way he took over my life until I could get back on my feet. Even though I'll miss him terribly, I'm glad he's finally going to get on with his own life.''

Dane looked quizzical. "Where's he going?"

She stared at him. "Didn't he tell you why we're having the barbecue?"

He shook his head.

"This is a farewell party of sorts. Patrick's moving into his own place."

One inky eyebrow quirked. "So you'll be living here alone?"

"No." She sighed. Though she'd never let on to Patrick, his leaving was a blow. She loved the big house but there was no way she could afford it on her own. "Don't tell my brother, but I'm going to have to find something a little less costly."

"What about an apartment?"

She shook her head definitely. "I want a house of my own. It'll be hard to replace this one, though. And Ebony would hate an apartment."

"I guess she would." Dane smiled. "I've never seen a dog so well trained. How long will it take me to get Missy to do those things?"

Annie almost laughed. "Several years. Don't put the cart before the horse. First you have to complete Basic. Your challenge is to strengthen the relationship between you and your animal and have the dog paying attention to you."

His eyebrows rose in a provocative smile. "Sounds like something I'd want in a woman, too."

She dropped her gaze to the tray of vegetables. *He was flirting with her!* Panic rose. She wasn't ready for this. The moment stretched between them as she cast around for something neutral to say, something that couldn't be misconstrued...and she realized she'd let the silence drag on too long.

Conversation dwindled after that. She felt all thumbs, trying to finish peeling the carrots. Though she didn't look at him again, she knew Dane was watching her.

The idea made her even more nervous, though she didn't quite know why. He'd been nothing more than courteous and friendly and a bit flirtatious...if you didn't count the silent message those eyes were broadcasting.

Maybe she was losing her grip. Maybe it was all in her imagination. She'd been alone so long that she was beginning to—

The sudden, sonorous peal of the doorbell startled her so badly she dropped the carrot peeler onto the counter with a loud clatter.

"I'll get that," she said shakily. Almost desperately, she turned from the counter. "Patrick's barbecuing in the backyard, right through that door."

After she'd ushered in another group of enthusiastic guests, she returned to finish her preparations in the kitchen. The black knife she'd been using lay on the counter and a memory rose, of Nick slicing his thumb with the same knife in the days right after their wedding.

God, she missed him. She wished for the anger she'd felt for a long time, but all she felt was weariness. Earlier in the week, she'd visited the cemetery, as she did about once a month, to trim the grass around Nick's headstone and tidy it up so that it didn't look so...alone.

As if the losses would be intertwined for all time, she remembered that he wasn't really alone, that Honey, their prize Rottweiler, was with him. The thought squeezed her heart painfully and a lump rose in her throat.

Stop it, Anne Elizabeth. Just stop thinking about what you can't change.

Blinking with fierce resolve, she looked out the wide window above the sink to where Patrick was gesturing wildly with a meat fork. He was in the middle of a group of people, obviously telling a story and enjoying himself immensely. His red hair gleamed in the bright sunlight. She was glad to see that he, at least, appeared to be happy now. The withdrawn, silent stranger who'd flown to her bedside in the hospital had been a shock, even through her grief. It had been months before she'd pried the truth out of him, learned that his marriage had ended the same week she became a widow.

Living together had been good for them both. She sighed, willing the grief back into its box. No woman could have asked for a more supportive, more loving brother in the past few hellish years. And she was going to miss his irrepressible silliness.

The back door opened and Annie hastily swiped at a tear that had escaped and was making a quick getaway down her cheek. She turned back to the dip she was mixing as her best friend, Jeanne Krynes, came over to drape herself across the counter beside Annie.

"Holy cow! Why didn't you tell me Adonis had moved into the neighborhood?" Jeanne faked a swoon, pressing her hand to her ample bosom.

"I presume you're referring to Dane?" She was proud that her voice was calm and even.

Jeanne grinned and smoothed a hand over the gleaming coil of blond hair swept out of the way. "None other. Did you get a look at the way he fills out those fine-fitting shorts?"

"Jeanne! Have you even met him yet?"

"I don't have to meet 'em to scope 'em," Jeanne said. "And I scoped your new neighbor. As I said, Adonis."

"Dane has black hair," Annie retorted. "Adonis is usually depicted as a blonde."

"Details, details." Jeanne waved a hand in the air. "He's drop-dead gorgeous and you know it." She sank onto a chair at the table and propped her long, tanned legs on the opposite seat. "Six foot two, eyes of blue," she warbled.

"Shh! He'll hear you." Annie could think of nothing worse than having Dane hear Jeanne extolling his virtues through the screen door. Especially when she privately agreed with her friend.

"So what if he hears me?" Jeanne swung her legs down and rose to lean her elbows on the counter. "Look me in the eye and tell me you don't think he's a fine-looking specimen of Number One Grade-A American Beefcake."

Annie felt the weight of her grief lessening under Jeanne's irresistible good humor. "Do I have to say it ten times?"

Jeanne's mouth quirked. "Without laughing."

They both chuckled.

Then Annie sobered. "I'm going to miss my brother."

Jeanne's brown eyes softened sympathetically, and she reached a hand over the counter to cover Annie's. "I know. If he wasn't such a pain, I'd tell him how wonderful he's been to give up three years of his life for you. But I guess it's time you got on with your life. Nick would have wanted you to." She sighed and squeezed Annie's fingers. "Is it getting any easier?"

Annie shrugged. "I guess." She knew what Jeanne wanted to hear. But she honestly couldn't say that she was glad she had come out of that operating room alive. She dropped her gaze to stare blindly at the tray of vegetables.

How did people do it—live on for a lifetime after losing the one they loved? How did they smile and act as if they genuinely enjoyed the warmth of a spring day? How did they laugh at jokes, or keep from screaming at the memories that sprung, unexpected, from around every corner?

It was true she'd learned to live with her grief. But every day was a struggle.

Shaking off the tears that threatened, Annie dredged up a smile for Jeanne. Squaring her shoulders, she picked up the vegetable tray. "Hold the door for me?"

Dane took the platter of barbecued chicken from Patrick and headed for the glass-topped table beneath the yellow umbrella. It was heavily laden with food, far more than the several dozen people scattered around the pool could consume.

He was happy to have an excuse to get away from two of the unattached females Patrick had invited. Both were the kind of good-time party girls who pursued a man at the slightest sign of interest. He knew the type well—and avoided it like the plague. The next wife he took was going to be a one-man woman.

As he hunted for a place to set down the meat, the back door opened. Annie came out, followed by her friend, Jeanne, the statuesque blonde to whom Patrick had introduced him earlier. She was married to Joe Krynes, who was frolicking in the pool with their two toddlers.

He envied Joe those kids. He'd wanted to start a family right away when he'd married Amanda, but she'd wanted some time...which eventually turned into a flat refusal to consider having a baby. Ever. Period.

At least, not *his* baby.

As he cut off the painful memories, his determination firmed. He fully intended to find a wife again someday and have that family. But he was smarter now. He didn't have to give his heart to get what he wanted, and he promised himself he'd never let a woman take him for a ride again.

His gaze was drawn to the man coming out of the pool with a child on each arm. He'd learned from Patrick that Joe Krynes had shared a law practice in Oak Park with Annie's husband. Joe smiled at the women approaching from the house.

The contrast between the two was striking. Annie was small, with her long copper braid and big blue eyes whose wary expression shouted, "Keep away!" Jeanne was much taller, a blonde with sparkling, naughty eyes of spaniel-brown. She offered him a come-hither smile as they neared. "Gimme a hand, handsome, and we'll rearrange this table to make some space."

He smiled back, aware of the open appreciation in Jeanne's gaze. Only a happily married woman could be that cheerfully lecherous. He wished Annie would look at him like that, he thought as he moved to take the tray of vegetables from her. "Where do you want these?"

Annie gave him a small, lukewarm smile as she surrendered the tray. Her head wagged once in the direction of the second patio table that held other picnic necessities. "Right over there would be fine."

She couldn't make it any clearer if she wrote it on her forehead, he thought as everyone came to the tables and Patrick brought over the chicken he'd finished grilling. Annie Evans wasn't thrilled about having him here tonight, and she definitely wasn't interested in flirting with him. She'd cut him dead when he'd dared to tease her earlier in the kitchen. As far as she was concerned, he was just part of the furniture.

Trouble was, he was beginning to think he was going to have to satisfy this yen he'd developed for her. It was becoming a matter of pride to get her to notice him as a man.

But when his gaze sought her again, she was hurrying over to Patrick, who was beckoning. One of the male guests stood beside Patrick, and after what looked like a few hearty comments, Annie's brother went back to the grill and left her alone with the guest. Though Dane couldn't hear what they were saying, it was obvious they were exchanging pleasantries.

He thought about joining them, about making sure the guy didn't hit on her, but before he could make up his mind, she drifted away again. The man looked mildly chagrined as he watched her retreat, and Dane struggled not to let his satisfaction show. Apparently, her aversion to guests wasn't restricted to him.

When everyone had gotten a plate, Dane looked around for an empty seat. There was one beside Annie and he made for it just in time to preempt another man from achieving the same goal.

"Sorry," Dane said blandly. He turned in Annie's direction, seeking a topic he knew would draw her out. "Do you look forward to the beginning of each new class you teach, or does it get boring after a while?"

She tilted her head consideringly. As she did, her long braid slipped to the side and he had to clamp down—hard— to resist the urge to wrap his fingers around the thick rope of hair and feel its texture, heft its weight...pull her closer.

"Obedience classes never bore me," she said.

Dane jerked his attention away from her hair to focus on the blue gaze she was directing his way. "Why not?"

"Each new group of dogs is exciting to watch as they learn to follow commands. I imagine it's a lot like teaching people. No two students are alike. In my case, that's even more true since the students come in handler/dog pairs. No two handlers work a dog in the same manner. It always fascinates me to watch the developing relationship between an owner and his dog as they interact."

Dane gave her a sideways grin. "Or the lack of it."

She didn't allow her lips to tilt up at the corners. "You seem to have little faith in my ability to help you to learn to manage your dog."

He choked on a piece of Patrick's excellent chicken. "No, that's not it at all." Hell! He didn't want her thinking he was going to be a thorn in her side throughout the lessons. "It's just that my dog is so...bouncy...that I can't imagine she's going to respond very well to training."

She did smile this time, and his pulse rate accelerated as deep dimples flashed in her perfectly rounded cheeks. "You'll be surprised."

Silence fell.

What else could he talk about that might interest her? She sat beside him, looking small and fragile and deliciously cool in her pale yellow shorts and striped sleeveless top, but she appeared completely unaware of his interest. He couldn't imagine how she could be so oblivious, when he felt like a radiator on the high setting, just from sitting next to her. Her blouse was a sheer fabric and he could see a hint of lace beneath...for such a small woman, her breasts looked surprisingly full. Suddenly, he noticed that Jeanne Krynes was grinning at him from across the circle of chairs and he wrenched his gaze away, feeling guilty color come into his face. Talk. He needed to find something to talk to Annie about....

"Patrick conscripted me to help with moving day."

Annie looked at him and smiled sympathetically. "Poor you. I bet he didn't tell you about his rock collection, did he?"

He made himself smile in return. "No. And I've just moved in, so I won't need him to return the favor, either." He remembered what she said about looking for another home. "I can see why you love this place. Was the pool in when you bought the house?" The shadow that slipped into her blue eyes was the same one he'd seen earlier when she talked about her husband, and he couldn't help wondering how it would feel to have a woman love him like that. "No," she said quietly. "The pool was a later addition."

"Your idea?"

"My husband's." Her eyes were blank again, as if she'd turned inward, denying him access to the woman behind the defenses. "Nick and I bought this house seven years ago, right after he and Jeanne's husband, Joe, opened their law offices."

He wanted to question her further—hell, he wanted to know everything there was to know about her! But he was afraid that if he pushed her, she'd only retreat farther into that polite coolness she used so effectively.

"An-nie. Hold me?"

Before Annie could respond, the little Krynes girl clambered into her lap. Dane watched curiously as a spasm of—

pain?—discomfort of some kind, darkened her blue eyes for an instant before she smiled down at the tiny blonde. What went on in her head? She was an enigma, a mystery, and he wanted to solve the riddle of her reserve.

After the meal, nearly everyone sat around the pool or swam. Annie did neither. Instead, she brought her dog out of the house. Rather than rejoining the party, she wandered down to the far side of the yard, where Dane could see her examining a bright bank of summer flowers.

He grabbed his towel and dried off, then donned his T-shirt and joined her.

Ebony leaped high into the air for the Frisbee Annie tossed. As Dane approached, the dog came trotting back to her, leaning heavily against Annie's legs as she relinquished the Frisbee to her mistress.

He watched as Annie patted Ebony, irresistibly drawn by her pink cheeks and sparkling eyes. He bent and stroked the wide head, chuckling when the Rottweiler's broad backside wriggled back and forth in delight. How could he have thought this dog looked menacing? "You're a big old friendly fool," he said, fondling Ebony's ears and allowing the wide tongue to bathe his hand.

"Not always," Annie said. "She has a side you haven't seen here today."

"Is she trained to protect you?"

"I've had a temperament evaluation done on her and she passed. That means she acted aggressive in appropriate situations, and I have no doubt she'd defend me if anyone tried to harm me."

"She's not trained to attack?"

"No." She shook her head definitely. "I've never had a dog trained to attack. It's a big responsibility to have an animal that's a weapon."

Over Annie's shoulder, Dane could see Jeanne and Patrick cleaning up the remains of the meal. He would help in a moment, but he couldn't resist continuing the discussion while she was so open and receptive.

"Have you had other Rottweilers?"

Annie froze for a moment. She shook her head once, and her throat worked, but nothing came out. Tears sprang into her eyes.

What the hell had he said?

Dane felt as if his gaze were glued to hers. The horrifying sear of sadness in her eyes made him wish he could swallow his tongue; he was staggered by the depth of the pain he was witnessing. Despite what he knew of her past, he'd half suspected her reserve was deliberate, a teasing test of wills that he was expected to overcome. But he couldn't have been more wrong. The woman behind those mental walls lived in a hell he hadn't imagined.

Impulsively, he put out his hand, touching her lightly on the elbow. "I'm sorry. Don't answer if it's painful." He looked away from her to give her a chance to compose herself, and gazed across the pool where Joe was down on his hands and knees giving young Mindy a horsey ride. Beside him, he felt, sensed, her drawing in a deep breath, then letting it out in a controlled sigh.

"It's all right," she said quietly.

There was a long silence between them that he didn't try to bridge. What could he say? All he knew was that it most certainly wasn't all right. And that he hated being the cause of her pain.

Finally, he bent down one final time and ran his palm over Ebony's broad head. He risked a glance at Annie but she was staring into a past he couldn't share, reliving events at which he could only guess. The kindest thing he could do for her would be to leave.

But as he straightened and opened his mouth to thank her for the barbecue, she said, "I had another Rottweiler. Before Ebony. Honey earned titles in both conformation and obedience. We were coming home from an indoor show when a tractor-trailer jackknifed just ahead of us. Nick, my husband, couldn't avoid it.''

Dane froze for a second. Ugly, graphic pictures rose in his mind and he had to force himself not to reach out and hug her to him, to cut off the compulsive flow of words with compassion before she made him feel her pain again.

"Honey and Nick both died." She sighed and her breath caught. "I'm sorry. I rarely talk much about my loss. I feel like I've done nothing but dump on you all day.''

"I don't mind." He stroked the dog again, then surprised himself by taking her hand. "Annie, I'd like to see you again. Would you have dinner with me next Saturday evening?''

The inspiration was out of his mouth before it was fully into his head, but the moment he heard himself speak, it hit him that he wanted her to say yes more than he'd wanted anything in a long time. He kept his gaze on hers, willing her to agree.

She was silent for an interminable moment and he braced himself for rejection. Hell, that should be no big deal. He was used to it.

"I'd like that," she said slowly. "But I have to warn you, I'm out of practice at dating.''

"That's all right." Relief spread through him like a slow-moving river across a floodplain, so wide and deep that he felt limp beneath the weight of it. He knew a fierce satisfaction but quickly masked it. If she knew how badly he wanted her, she'd never set foot outside her door with him. Calmly, he said, "We'll be out of practice together.''

"I find it hard to believe that you don't date much." Her voice was high and breathless and he realized he still held her hand, stroking his thumb idly across her palm. Glancing at her face, he saw hectic color spreading across her cheeks as she discreetly tugged at her hand.

Slowly, enjoying the flustered squeak she gave, he raised her hand to his lips and pressed a lingering kiss against the soft, warm skin. ''I haven't had the urge to date much since my divorce. Until now.''

The Basic Obedience class began at six o'clock on Thursday night.

It was just like any other class, Annie lectured herself. There was no reason to have butterflies battling their way out of cocoons in her stomach, no reason at all. It was probably something she'd eaten. She'd grabbed a quick sandwich from the deli down the street after the four o'clock Puppy Kindergarten class—maybe the tuna had been on the edge of turning. There couldn't be any other cause for this jittery feeling.

As the students began filing into the room with their dogs, Annie assessed each animal as she greeted everyone at the door. The Lab puppy was going to be a handful—he was a very playful nine months. The Dalmatian was the one in charge of his master, a relationship she hoped to be able to turn around by the end of the eight-week session. The German shepherd dog was just like all others of his breed, strong-willed and tuned in to one person and the shelty was so submissive, she bet he'd make a puddle on the floor the first few times he was corrected—

And the blue eyes gazing down into hers drove every coherent thought from her head. Had Dane grown more handsome? She knew it couldn't be, but in the four days since she'd seen him last, she'd swear his jaw had gotten squarer, his eyes more commanding, his lips more firmly chiseled. A lock of black hair fell onto his forehead in an irresistible curl. Deep slashes of dimple creased his cheeks as he flashed her a grin that revealed perfect white teeth.

He was breathtaking. *And she had a date with him on Saturday.* She must be out of her mind. No woman could be immune to that charm, could she?

Of course not. She'd noticed that every woman at the barbecue had turned up the voltage on her smile when Dane arrived. They'd have been more than happy to entertain him if he'd been receptive to their cleavage and their conversation.

A short, happy bark snapped her back to her senses and she smiled a little as she reached out to pat the Doberman straining to be noticed at Dane's side.

"Hello," she offered quietly, willing her voice to be normal. He might be good to look at, but he was just a man. Just a student, whom she happened to know personally. She should be relieved that she'd finally noticed an attractive man.

"Hi." His voice was as deep as she remembered. "Missy's raring for action. This should be interesting."

"It should be *educational*," she replied. Unsure of what to say to him, she turned her attention to the dog, lavishly petting Missy before sending them in to join the rest of the group.

The class went well, despite her awareness of the black-haired man with the black dog.

As formal instruction hour ended, she moved around the circle of dogs, handing each owner an instruction review page. For a few, she made personal notes. Then she dismissed the class. Although her classes were an hour long, she always scheduled a half hour to allow for questions afterward, and tonight was no exception. Twenty minutes later, as her Novice class began to straggle in, she was just finishing with the last of the Basic students.

Dane had been standing near the back of the group during the question period. She was aware of his patient presence, aware of the blonde with the apricot miniature poodle who'd zeroed in on him as soon as the class ended. They appeared to have struck up a light and easy conversation and she could have hated the woman for that. She forced herself not to glance in his direction, to attend to the students asking earnest questions about training techniques.

Finally, there was no one else left. She offered Dane and

the blonde what she hoped was a neutral smile. "Any questions before you leave?"

"No. I'm anxious to get started." Dane shifted a step closer, keeping his Doberman on a tight lead. "I'll pick you up about seven on Saturday, if that suits you."

She could see the blonde's ears perk up as smartly as her poodle's. Her face felt as if it were about to catch fire, and she willed herself to relax. *It's just a date. Everyone does it.* "Seven would be fine," she managed to say. "What should I wear?"

A strange light flared in his eyes for an instant. Then she thought she must have been mistaken because his voice was perfectly level and normal when he spoke. "I'll be wearing a tie, if that helps."

Dressy. She nodded.

There was an awkward pause then, and he finally said, "I'll see you Saturday."

"See you Saturday," she echoed. Saturday. Only two days away. A part of her dreaded the mere thought of dating. Another part was responsible for the shaky feeling that weakened her knees every time Dane walked into a room, and it was that part of her that could barely wait until Saturday to be near him again.

Three

___

Dane parked his white sports car in the circular driveway in front of Annie and Patrick's house, admiring the long, elegant lines of the Prairie-style home. As he knocked on the door, he remembered the way she'd nearly stammered with nerves on Thursday evening. He must be crazy to be wooing a cautious, skittish beauty like Annie. Only a certified nut case would take on such an impossible task.

He'd always enjoyed a challenge.

The door opened then and he snapped to attention. He'd never seen her in a dress, and if he'd thought she was beautiful before, now she looked…well, ravishing was the only word he could come up with. And it was a fair approximation of what he would like to do with her, too. She'd worn her hair up, in an elegant twist that lent a classical beauty to her features. The dress she had chosen to wear caressed every one of her curves as if it had been painted on. Simply styled, it had a slim skirt with a wide belt topped by some kind of interesting bodice that wrapped across her breasts with no visible means of closure.

"Hi!" she said.

Her voice was animated and he was surprised by her high spirits. Then, as he looked closer, he realized the high spirits were nerves. Her smile was brittle and her eyes were too bright…she looked terrified, but trying hard to cover it.

"Hello." He kept his voice low and calm, hoping to reassure her, though his fingers itched to trace the neckline of that dress, to find out what, if anything, was holding the wrapped bodice together. "You look lovely."

"Thank you." Now her voice was a mere whisper. He wondered if she was regretting her decision to have dinner with him. He certainly didn't.

No, indeed. The dress made him long to touch. To explore that bodice, to slide his palms over the material draping her hips and thighs until he'd created a need neither one of them could resist.

And then what?

He'd very carefully avoided thinking of what might occur after he'd slaked this thirst he'd developed for Annie Evans. But now faced with that vulnerable, almost terrified look frozen on her pretty face, he knew this wasn't going to be as simple as he'd first imagined. Annie wasn't the type of woman to amuse himself with casually after he conquered. Nor was that all he wanted, if he were honest with himself.

When he'd first seen her, realized that she wasn't just another woman looking for a good time, he'd been seized by a compelling urge to overcome her reservations, an almost primitive conquest instinct that he suspected was closely tied to her seeming indifference to him. The thrill of the chase, perhaps?

Perhaps. But now he wanted more from Annie than just the challenge of getting into her bed. How much more…? Well, he wasn't sure he knew the answer to that. *Yet.*

A loud masculine clearing of the throat recalled him to

the present. He realized he'd been staring at Annie until she was blushing. Patrick, who'd just entered the room, was glaring at him like an outraged father.

Deliberately allowing his amusement to show, he said, "Calm down, Patrick. I'm not going to gobble up your sister." He never took his eyes from Annie as he said, "Even if she is the most beautiful woman in River Forest." Oops. Wrong thing to say. The compliment clearly unnerved her even more.

He smiled at her, trying to tell her with his gaze to relax and was gratified when she made an obvious effort to pull herself together.

"Would you care for a drink?" she asked him.

He made a show of checking his watch, although it was unnecessary. No way he was going to linger under Patrick's protective eye a second longer than he had to. "I think I'd better pass. Our reservations are downtown at seven-thirty."

"Where are you going?" Patrick asked.

When Dane named an exclusive restaurant that was known throughout the Chicago area for its French cuisine, Patrick whistled. Then his good humor reasserted itself. "I don't know if she's worth that much. I'd opt for fast food, myself."

Annie sniffed. "No wonder you have trouble keeping your dates around for the second outing."

"My choice." Patrick preened. "'Love 'em and leave 'em,' that's my motto."

Dane laughed as he took Annie's elbow and steered her toward the door. "Ever heard, 'The bigger they are, the harder they fall'? It applies to egos, too."

As he shut the door behind them, Annie was laughing, a sweet, silvery sound that warmed his heart.

It appeared that she had subdued her reservations as she said, "Good comeback. It's rare for somebody to best my brother once he's on a verbal roll." But her tone was affectionate.

"How long have you and Patrick lived together?" he asked.

She raised an eyebrow. "You mean this time?"

"How many times have there been?"

"Three, if you count growing up, when we had no choice." She smiled. "And believe me, growing up with Patrick was an experience no one could forget."

"I can imagine." His tone was dry. "So when were the second and third times?"

"The second time was in college. He went to the University of Wisconsin and I followed two years later. We decided to share an apartment...which also was something to remember," she added wryly. "He had so many girlfriends I felt like a secretary trying to keep his schedule straight. And the worst part was that none of them knew about the others."

Dane laughed. "I can picture Patrick juggling fifteen women. Were you the same with the men?"

"Was I—oh, no." The animation drained out of her voice. "I met Nick, my husband—only he wasn't my husband then, of course—my very first week on campus." She gave a soft, sad little laugh that touched something deep inside him he'd thought was gone forever. "We fell in love on our first date. We got married the week after I graduated."

"Fell in love?" He echoed her words, knowing his cynicism had to show. "You mean you were sexually attracted."

She looked taken aback and a blush crept up her neck to spill into her face. "Well, that, too, but the physical side of our relationship was only one of the reasons I loved Nick."

"There's no such thing as love." He beat back the momentary nostalgia her words had produced. Any memory he had of young love had been an illusion, nothing more than a sensual preoccupation he'd shared with Amanda. As always, the thought of her betrayal was more than he could deal with. "Love is a euphemism that people use to dress up sex. Especially when it's great sex."

Annie's face was red all over now and her arched eyebrows drew together. She studied him carefully, as if he were a broken-apart puzzle and she were the person determined to fit all the pieces together again. "I have to disagree," she said in a soft but inflexible tone. "Nick and I never...I was a virgin until our wedding night, so our decision to spend the rest of our lives together wasn't based on sex. It was based on love."

He was silent, noting with relief that they'd reached the car. This discussion was going to go nowhere fast. He opened her door without speaking again, closed it after she'd slipped into the passenger side and walked around to settle himself in the driver's seat. It wasn't until he'd reversed the car out of her driveway and was moving out of the neighborhood that he spoke again.

"So now you're living with Patrick for the third time. Will you be glad when he moves?" Selfishly, he wanted her to pull her attention back to him, away from the husband for whom she still seemed to care so much.

She didn't answer for a moment and he figured she was angry at his last statement. He glanced across at her, only to be struck by the beauty of her profile etched against the Indian-summer sky. "In some ways, I'll be glad," she said finally. "Patrick was living in New Mexico when I was widowed. He had just separated from his wife. He came home to pick up the pieces of me and has stayed for three years. I'll miss him, yes. But I've felt guilty for disrupting his life with my problems. He might be remarried and a father by now if it weren't for having to look after me. Each of us needs to get on with our own life again, so in that respect, I'm glad he's moving."

Thank God she'd let their moment of discord drop. "You're very lucky," he reflected loudly. "I never had any sisters or brothers. I'd kill for a close relationship like you two share." *Hell, I'd kill for a sibling even if we weren't close.*

"I've always thought growing up as an only child must be very lonely," she said.

"I wouldn't know." Now why had he said that?

"Why wouldn't you know?"

His cryptic comment clearly had confused her and he was sorry he'd said it. Over the years, he'd learned that if he had to talk about it, it was best to just say it and get it over with. "I was left on the doorsteps of a church parsonage as a newborn. The only thing I had with me was a note with my name on it. The social services people don't even know if Hamilton was intended as a last or middle name."

He'd heard her suck in a breath of dismay as he spoke. Glancing over at her, he said, "You don't have to feel sorry for me. I was raised in a series of very acceptable foster homes."

"I'm not feeling sorry for you. What I am feeling is a strong urge to get my hands around the neck of the woman who gave you away." Her normally placid voice was as fierce as he'd heard it yet, and he forced out a light laugh.

"I wouldn't expend that much energy on her. If she didn't want me, I'm probably lucky she put me where she did. I could have wound up in a trash can."

Her fists were still clenched in her lap, but she made an effort to respond to his tone. "I guess you have a point. You say you had foster parents?"

"Three sets. The families are all very special—it was simply an unfortunate series of happenings that prevented me from being raised by any one of them. For example, one of my foster fathers lost his job and had to move out of state to find work."

"Have you kept in touch with any of them?"

"Yeah, but it'll never be like having a family of my own. That's why I think you're lucky to have Patrick." He made an effort to lighten the conversation. "Even if he is...rather unique."

"Patrick may be quirky, but he's very special," she said, smiling a little. "Our parents both died while I was in college. I don't know how I could have gone on after the accident without him."

Silence filled the car then, but this time it was a comfortable silence that lasted until they were off the expressway, heading down Michigan Avenue. They spoke easily on the way into Chicago. As he drove, Annie pointed out local landmarks that he should be sure to visit someday, including Orchestra Hall, where the Chicago Symphony Orchestra played, and the Art Institute of Chicago.

It occurred to him that he could ask her to come down here and sightsee with him tomorrow, but he didn't want to press too much, too soon. She'd been reluctant to accept one date initially—she might refuse another if she felt pressured. And he wasn't prepared to take that risk.

During dinner, he entertained her with stories of the co-workers he had just met, and she told him about some of her experiences training dogs. Driving home, though, she clammed up again and he could sense the tension in the air, perched between them as solidly as a wall. He suspected he knew what was bothering her.

This was a date. And dates usually ended with a kiss. Was she dreading it? Or could she be anticipating it as much as he was? She was so quiet and still that he couldn't tell.

Taking a chance, he reached over and squeezed her hand where it lay in her lap, then let his palm lay loosely atop hers.

"Thank you for tonight. Moving to a new city has its lonely moments," he said.

Annie concentrated on his words. She was hearing him, but nothing made sense except the feel of his hard, warm hand covering her own and the intimate way his long fingers lay against her thigh. She could feel the heat searing her through the flimsy fabric of the blue dress. Swallowing to relieve a suddenly dry throat, she tried her voice, "You're welcome."

His fingers tightened briefly around hers, then he released her hand abruptly, returning his own to the steering wheel to guide the car smoothly into her driveway. Annie glanced over at him across the confines of the car's red leather interior.

Dane was...quite a man. Attractive and sexy.

Too attractive. And far too sexy.

Dane tempted her to take risks with her safe, comfortable life-style. She wasn't interested in changing it. Was she? Her heart had swelled with pity—and something more— when he spoke of his past. He'd been hurt, though he'd never admit it. And he could hurt her. She knew he was dangerous; knew it as surely as she knew that he could make her care again. And she wasn't about to do that. Not when she'd seen it all turn to ashes once before. *No way,* she silently told the huge silhouette at her side. *No way am I going to care about you.*

She wondered who she was kidding.

His voice broke into her thoughts as he escorted her across the driveway, but he halted her with a hand under her elbow before she could precede him up the walk. She hadn't left a light on and the evening shadows made the night a dark, intimate canopy filled by their presence. "If I come by tomorrow evening when I walk Missy, would you like to walk along?"

She knew what she should say. *No.* But her lips refused to form the word. She wanted to see him again, to be with him and explore whatever was growing between them.

Placing his hands on her shoulders, Dane softened his tone as he gently rubbed small circles with his palms over the silky fabric. "Tonight wasn't so bad, was it? Am I mistaken in thinking you enjoyed yourself?"

She stared at the paisley-patterned silk tie directly in her line of vision. His wide shoulders towered above her head and the huge hands masterfully caressing her wreaked havoc with her thought processes. She raised her own hands to where he massaged the softly rounded shoulder joints, intending to stop him, but he forestalled her by linking her fingers with his and holding them clasped between their bodies. Close to panic at the thought that he might kiss her, afraid more of her own treacherous responses than of Dane, she tugged her fingers free, sighing in unconscious relief when he allowed her to back away a pace.

"N-no. Tonight was...very nice. Thank you for the meal." She made a production of tucking her clutch under her arm with both hands. "I suppose tomorrow will suit. I'll see you then." Abruptly she turned and almost ran up the flagstone walk to the front porch, tossing over her shoulder. "I can let myself in. 'Night."

Dane noted her flustered reaction to his touch. She was so damn cool and collected most of the time that he wasn't even sure she returned the attraction he felt. Amused at her hasty retreat, he stood in her driveway, listening to the staccato tap of her heels on the flagstones. When the light in the entryway of the stately old home flashed on, and the porchlight winked once, he slowly folded his length into the white sports car, wondering ruefully how the hell long it had been since he hadn't gotten so much as a kiss on a first date.

Dane hadn't told her what time he would be by on Sunday evening, but she usually saw him walking his dog around six. When the doorbell rang at five forty-five, she had just finished tying her leather sneakers but her hair, which she'd washed and left down to dry, was still flowing around her body.

"Oh, rats!" she said aloud, grabbing her brush and a huge plastic clip with teeth in it to confine her heavy mane of hair. Pounding down the wide front stairs, she yanked open the door in time to see him securing Missy's lead around one of her front porch pillars.

"Hi! I'm running late. I'll only be a minute. Come on in and make yourself at home." *Shut up, Annie, you're babbling.* She moved aside so that Dane could enter. Her quick perusal revealed long, muscular legs in navy shorts paired with a knit shirt. She assured herself that her pulse was racing from flying around getting ready—*not* from ogling a man's legs. When a moment passed and he failed to move into the house, she looked at him quizzically.

"Was it something I said?"

Still standing in the open doorway, Dane slowly shook his head like a man awakening from a hundred years' sleep. His blue eyes were fixed on her unblinkingly as he ignored her query, smiling slightly. "Good evening," he said almost reverently.

Then, before she realized what he was up to, he clasped her elbow and turned her in a slow circle. "I've never seen such hair," he murmured. "Have you ever had it cut?"

"Just the occasional trim," she replied, bemused by his intense interest. At the pressure of his hand, she turned fully to face him again. Each movement made the copper strands twist and shimmer with a life of their own. Dane reached out slowly, pulling handfuls of fiery tresses forward to cascade over her breasts.

"Amazing," he said. Then, in a tone a full octave lower, he informed her gravely, "There's something we overlooked last night."

"What?"

"This." Tilting her chin up with one gentle finger, he bent his head and lightly touched his lips to hers.

Too shocked by the unexpected move to draw away, Annie stood passively as his large hands tunneled under her hair to cradle her jaw. *No!* she thought wildly. *I'm not ready for this!* When he teasingly flicked his tongue across the closed line of her lips, she gasped, unprepared for even the

light, nibbling kiss. The air seemed to thin. She couldn't
draw enough breath, couldn't even think about moving as
he invaded personal space that had been inviolate for years.

She could feel the furnace of his big, hard body crowding
closer to hers, and at the second brush of his heated tongue,
an answering spark flared in her. An unexpected frisson of
need shivered down through her body to center between her
legs and she gasped, fearful of the blatant sexual pull he
exerted so effortlessly. He brushed his mouth slowly across
her parted lips twice more before slanting his head and settling his lips more fully against hers.

His teasing tongue slipped between her lips with her second gasp, and suddenly, fear evaporated under a blazing
need to calm her fevered senses with whatever magic spell
he could provide. Unable to resist the primal demands he
called from her body, she softened, leaning forward to bring
her body into contact with his fully aroused male one.

In a moment of electric stillness, Dane withdrew his
mouth a hairbreadth and studied her upturned face. He must
have recognized her total female submission, because he slid
his hands boldly down her back, hauling her up against him
and fastening his mouth on hers.

Annie stiffened at the suddenness of the deeply intimate
move and made a choked sound. Part of her was still wary
of the sensations he aroused. She tried to turn her head
away, but he twined one hand through her loose tresses,
thrusting his tongue into the moist recesses of her mouth,
and she stopped resisting as her entire body began to move
in counterpoint to that rhythmic penetration. Her soft breasts
pushed against the rock-hard planes of his chest, and she
didn't resist when he lifted her completely off the ground,
clasping one hand to her rounded buttocks to fit her hips
against the ridge of hardened flesh at his thighs.

After the moment of instinctive fear, the sensual demands
he was making blotted out all but the need to assuage her
own desires. She began to respond mindlessly to the erotic

play of his tongue and the slow, deliberate rub of his aroused body over her woman's mound. Her nipples were hard pebbles under the chambray top, clamoring for more contact. She squirmed more fully against him, totally lost in the moment…until the door slammed resoundingly just behind them. *Her brother!*

Annie jolted, once again struggling to free herself from Dane's embrace, but he subdued her with that effortless strength, pushing her head against his chest and keeping his arms hard around her. What must Patrick be thinking? Her brother had a wide streak of protectiveness where she was concerned; she only hoped he wasn't going to feel it was his duty to—

A loud guffaw interrupted her train of thought.

"Don't look so fierce, Dane." When she turned to face her brother, Patrick's handsome face wore a broad grin. "Just because I caught my one and only baby sister—"

"Shut up, Patrick." Strands of her hair were clinging across the shoulders of Dane's short-sleeved shirt. It seemed easier to concentrate on removing them than it was to meet her brother's gaze.

"I mean, just because you two were in a clinch so tight a crowbar couldn't have pried you apart—"

"Shut up, Patrick," Annie repeated.

"What I can't figure out is how come a combustible combination like you guys hasn't gone right up in flames."

"Patrick!"

"It nearly did," Dane said, and the sound of his deep voice sent shivers chasing up her spine. She took a step away from him, and this time he let her go.

"Hey, don't let me interrupt anything." Patrick folded his arms and leaned against the doorframe as if he intended to stay and take notes.

"Out, you—you twerp." Annie advanced menacingly toward him, brandishing the brush she'd discovered she still held.

"All right, all right. I can see when I'm not wanted. I'll just slink on out to the kitchen and make my poor, lonely little self a sandwich. You two go ahead and...well, you were doing fine without my help!" He vanished through the swinging door to the kitchen as Annie's brush struck the wood where his head had been a moment earlier.

Annie pointed at an ivy-covered building with a discreet brass plaque beside the door. "Remember my friend Joe? That's his office."

They'd been walking for nearly thirty minutes and Dane figured they were well over a mile away from home, even at the leisurely pace they were keeping for the dog's sake. This was the second time they'd gone walking together in the week since The Kiss. The kiss he longed to repeat. He glanced at the place she indicated, then looked again. Closely.

The sign read, Evans and Krynes Associates, Attorneys-at-Law.

"This is the practice your husband and Joe established?" Stupid question. Of course it was.

Annie nodded. "Joe has taken on two new partners since...since Nick died. I've told him he doesn't have to keep the name, but he wants to." She smiled, and there was a sad fondness in her face. "I guess it helps him."

Dane evaluated the soft undercurrents of grief in her voice. He wanted to learn more about her marriage, about her husband. He wanted to understand her, *needed* to understand her, but he was afraid she'd clam up if he questioned her. She retreated into silence faster than anyone he'd ever known.

In as casual a tone as he could manage, he said, "How long were you—how long did you have together?"

"We knew each other for four years before the wedding. We were married about three years. And he's been gone that long already." She sighed, and the sound quivered with emotion. "Sometimes I can't remember what he looked like, the sound of his voice. Sometimes I wonder why I had to be left."

"Don't." He wanted to reach for her hand, but each of them had a dog in heel position. "You can't ask those kinds of questions. It's futile. You have to accept that this is the way it happened. You have to go on. Not forget, but go on." Damn. Why had he brought this up? It was so clearly painful for her. And he had less than no notion how to comfort someone filled with the kind of grief she appeared to have all bottled up inside.

"I know you're right. And believe it or not, it's getting easier. The memories still hurt, but they're beginning to fade. You know what I regret the most, though?"

She glanced up at him, and he was surprised to see her delicate features harden.

"We wanted children. But we wanted to wait a few years until the law practice was solid." She shook her head. "Now he's gone and I'd give anything to have a child."

"I know exactly what you mean. It's the one thing I regret about my divorce. I might miss the chance to have kids of my own because I made the wrong choice in a wife." He knew his voice reflected his bitterness and frustration.

Annie was silent for a moment. Then she said, "But you have plenty of time. You'll meet someone new one of these days."

He hoped she was right. But he didn't want to tell her he was already methodically searching for the woman who would be a perfect mother to his children. In fact, he didn't want to talk about himself at all. "The same goes for you. There might be another man out there who will give you those kids you want."

"Uh-uh." She shook her head so vehemently, tendrils of copper curls pulled out of her braid. "I'm never going to love like that again. I doubt I'll ever remarry. And that hurts. Because I'd love children of my own.''

He hadn't said anything about love. Yet he found himself resisting the picture she painted. ''You might change your mind one of these days. You're what…thirty?''

''Almost.''

''Twenty-nine years old. Ten more years could change a lot of things. You could meet someone tomorrow.'' But he hoped she wouldn't. Not until he'd figured out what it was about her that he felt so drawn to, not until they'd played out whatever scene he was sure they had to play out together.

To his surprise, his words seemed to help. She sniffed and her lips curved upward again. ''You sound like Patrick. He's always telling me Nick would have wanted me to get my life together and meet other men.''

''Would he have?''

She nodded. ''Probably. Nick didn't have a selfish bone in his body. He wouldn't have wanted me to grieve.''

''Tell me about him.'' The words startled him as much as they probably shocked her, but he found that he meant them.

She was silent and for a minute he feared he'd overstepped the boundaries of their friendship. Or whatever it was they were creating. He knew he wanted more, more than Annie was able to offer right now.

''Nick…where to start?'' she mused aloud. ''How do you take all that a person was and distill it into a few sentences?''

''Don't try,'' he said promptly. ''Just let the memories flow. Don't organize them for my sake.''

She took him literally. For the next twenty minutes, a torrent of words poured out of her. They were standing in her driveway again, finished their walk, when she closed her mouth with a snap, as if just realizing where she was.

"Wow. I can't believe I talked that whole time." She looked a little dazed. "Why didn't you tell me to shut up?"

"I didn't mind," Dane said gently. "You must have cared for him very much." It was true. Every word she'd spoken had been filled with love for her deceased husband. It reminded him of his own miserable marriage and how far short of his optimistic dreams it had fallen. All he could think was that Nick Evans had been the luckiest guy on earth, to have been loved like that.

"I did." Her voice was quiet and sober. "Sometimes I think I was very fortunate, to have had that kind of love in my life, even though it didn't last long. Some people look all their lives for it." She glanced at him. "Do you know what I mean?"

"No." He knew the stiffness that had invaded his body puzzled her from the way she was looking at him, but he couldn't prevent it. He gave a laugh that was intended to be offhand but came out sounding harsh and hurt all at the same time. "What is love, anyway? Just a fantasy. Most people settle for a lot less, even when they think they've found the real thing."

Annie's eyes were very blue, soft with sympathy. "Is that what happened to you? With your wife?"

"Amanda." He spoke through his teeth. "Her name was Amanda and I thought we loved each other. But I found out that what I called love was nothing more than pretty great sex. Isn't that what love boils down to when you take all the fancy words away?"

"Dane, I'm sorry you were hurt—"

"I wasn't hurt." He moved away from the compassionate hand she placed on his forearm. "I was *lucky*. If Amanda hadn't left, I'd still be worshiping the ground she walked on while she was looking for a better deal."

Four

She must have been temporarily insane to agree to this. How could she have forgotten how she hated this kind of thing?

Annie glanced around the crowded room at the other people attending the cocktail party. The alcoholic beverages being guzzled like water, the too-bright smiles and the too-hearty laughter made her stomach churn and quiver. Everywhere she looked, people were greeting one another with effusive hugs and kisses that looked too intimate to be on display.

And it was nobody's fault but her own that she was here. She *had* been out of her mind when Dane had asked her to come with him to this party, too dazzled by his charm to realize exactly what she was agreeing to until it was too late.

He'd been diffident, offhand, as if he was afraid she was going to refuse. And the contrast between that and his usual commanding persona had been so intriguing, she hadn't thought about what he was asking her to do.

"Annie, I've been invited to a get-acquainted cocktail party by the president of the bank's board of directors. Would you be willing to attend with me? I know it won't be a lot of fun for you, but I'd really like to have you there."

She'd actually been pleased, she recalled. He knew so much about her work. It was the perfect opportunity to find out a little more about what he did at the bank.

Now, looking around the crowded room, she saw that no serious business discussion was going to take place here today. When these people partied, they made a mission of it. Dane appeared to fit right in, though she knew he'd only worked at the bank for a few weeks. He was soon swallowed up by a boisterous group of men and she scanned the room for a corner where she could sit undisturbed.

Ah, there. She shrank into the corner, hoping that if she was quiet no one would notice her. How could she have forgotten how bad she was at making small talk? At finding something—anything—to say to people with whom she had absolutely nothing in common. It had been one of the few things she regretted about her marriage to Nick. She was terrible at The Social Thing. *Incompetent, that's what you are. A social zero.* Though she could scarcely bear to admit it, in her secret heart she felt an element of relief that now she didn't have to suffer through the endless functions that lawyers and their spouses were constantly attending.

"Hey, Millicent, who was that hunk I saw you with the other night?" A young blonde with what looked like several layers of makeup winked at several of the others as a group of women drifted over and claimed the arrangement of seats near Annie. "He was…not to be forgot." She giggled at her own wit.

Millicent looked annoyed. "Shh. Sherry, I swear you have the biggest mouth east of the Mississippi." She tossed a lock of carefully curled ebony hair over her shoulder and smiled reminiscently. "He works in my office. We just went out for a drink after work."

"And Paul doesn't mind that?"

Millicent shrugged. "What Paul doesn't know can't hurt him."

"And who are you?"

Annie realized with a start that the speaker was looking straight at her. The woman, tall with mannishly cropped hair, had just joined the group of women.

Millicent waved a hand in her general direction. "She came with the new man."

"I thought Dane wasn't married," the tall woman said again, making no effort to introduce herself.

"He's not." Annie rose and forced herself to hold out a hand. "I'm Annie Evans, Dane's neighbor."

The woman regarded Annie's hand with a slight smile, then raised a lighted cigarette to her mouth and inhaled. "We don't get formal around here. I'm Charlene Jenkins."

"Charlene wasn't expecting you," Millicent said to Annie. "She was hoping she could get a little of that action tonight."

"Or at least get a jump start on the rest of us," Sherry offered with another giggle.

"Why don't you have a drink?" Charlene took Annie's shoulder and turned her toward the bar. "It'll loosen you up."

Annie dug in her heels, realizing that her distaste must have shown, but she was past caring. "I don't care for a drink, thank you."

Charlene stopped pushing at her shoulder and eyed her in an assessing manner. "Oh God, not another bore like our sweet hostess."

There seemed to be nothing to say in response. It might not be kind of Charlene to have pointed it out, but she *was* a bore. Annie gritted her teeth and kept the social smile plastered in place. These women were vulgar and rude. They made the unendurable small talk she'd always hated seem positively irresistible in comparison.

"Annie?"

She glanced in the direction of her name. Her hostess, Lilith, was beckoning. The diminutive silver-haired matron had been by far the most genteel lady she'd met since coming through the door and Annie hastened to the woman's side.

"Have you had a glass of punch and something from the buffet?" Lilith slipped an arm through hers and steered her to the far end of the house.

"Thank you." Annie took a deep breath, realizing how tense she'd been as her shoulders relaxed from their rigid pose. "I'd like something to drink. Nonalcoholic, please," she added.

Lilith smiled. "Alcohol does amazing things to people's sense of propriety, doesn't it?"

"Amazing." Annie made an effort to smile.

"You mustn't mind those women," Lilith offered. "They're a bunch of bored housewives with too much money and too little to do. They play fast and loose with their own husbands and anyone else they can find, and they were hoping Dane was available."

Annie shot her a wry grimace. "Did I look that distressed?"

"I've tolerated them at enough parties to know when they're bothering someone." Lilith's faded eyes twinkled. "Let's speak of something more pleasant, shall we? Do you work, dear?"

Annie nodded. She was so grateful for Lilith's rescue that it was a moment before she realized the question required an answer. "Yes. I own a canine training school."

"Dog training?" Lilith's eyes lit up. "I love dogs. When the children were at home, we always had at least one golden retriever around the house, but now that it's just

Arnold and me, I've downsized. Would you like to see my new baby?''

Annie nodded, grateful for the familiar topic.

"And where do you two think you're escaping to?"

The man was tall, but his eyes twinkled with the same kindly lights that Lilith's did. Dane stood beside him, obviously waiting for the answer.

"Oh, Arnold, have you met Annie?"

As Lilith introduced her husband, Annie realized the affable-looking Arnold was Dane's boss.

"Annie's a dog trainer, Arnold. Imagine that! I'm taking her for a peek at the puppy."

Arnold chuckled. "Why don't you go along with them, Dane. That's the only way I can be sure Lilith will find her way back. She hates these get-togethers with a passion."

Lilith rolled her eyes. "Don't be rude, dear. Go and mingle with our guests."

As she led them down a hallway and into what was obviously a family room, Annie marveled over what she'd just heard. So Lilith didn't like these things, either? No one would ever guess. Maybe she could take some lessons from Lilith on the fine art of socializing. Then she wouldn't feel like a millstone around Dane's neck—

Whoa! That thought brought her up short. As Lilith showed off the Maltese puppy that weighed less than two pounds when its long white coat was soaking wet, Annie asked herself when she'd begun thinking about being around Dane long enough for her social prowess to matter?

Dane eased his big body onto a chair in Patrick's newly furnished dining room, strained muscles protesting. Annie hadn't been kidding about the rock collection.

He knew he'd be stiff tomorrow. When Patrick had asked him to help him move from Annie's to his new place, Dane hadn't known that in addition to the things at the house,

Patrick also had several rooms of furniture in storage. It was just like Patrick to forget to mention that small detail.

Annie carried two plates, one piled high with pizza, which she set before him, and one with two slices, which she put down at her own place.

She must have caught something of his mood, because she smiled and asked, "Are you wiped out?"

"Not as much as I will be tomorrow," he said with a wry grin. "Your brother forgot to explain just how much stuff he had stashed away when he suckered me into helping with this project."

She looked both mischievous and sympathetic at the same time. "Patrick's good at getting people involved before they know what hit them. Is there anything I can do for you?"

Rubbing the back of his neck, he smiled tightly. He'd like to show her exactly what she could do, and his body rose to meet the occasion. Stamping down the need for her that ran like wildfire through his blood, he shook his head and pulled out the chair next to his. "Just sit down here and keep me company."

As she slipped into the seat, the sound of metal clanging against metal jarred his ears. Joe Krynes stood at one end of the table with his toddler son, J.J., who was banging a spoon against the side of a pan with great enthusiasm.

"Hear ye, hear ye," Joe intoned as he held the pan out of J.J.'s reach and handed the child to his wife. "Jeanne and I have an announcement."

Eyebrows went up around the room.

"Do we get any hints?" Patrick asked.

"Sure." Joe grinned. "I'll answer 'yes' or 'no' questions."

Patrick drummed his fingers against the table. "You're taking a vacation."

"No."

"You're buying a new house?" someone else asked.

"Nope." Joe's eyes twinkled.

"You're expecting another baby."

Joe was silent for a moment. "No," he said, "*I'm* not, but…"

"…Jeanne is!" finished the speaker. "Congratulations. How long do we have to wait to see the newest member of the Krynes family?"

Joe and Jeanne exchanged a warm, conspiratorial look that Dane silently envied. What would it be like to have that kind of closeness with another person?

"I haven't been to the doctor yet," Jeanne said, "but we figure the baby'll be here shortly after Easter."

Dane glanced at Annie, measuring her reaction to the announcement.

Her small face looked pinched and white but she made a valiant effort to smile. "Congratulations! Another wee one for me to cuddle."

"Jeanne's incubating *again?*" Patrick sounded mildly shocked. "Man, haven't you two figured out what causes that yet?"

Joe just grinned and smiled. "We already know."

God, he was jealous. A son and a daughter, and now they were expecting a third child. Dane wondered yet again how he could have misjudged Amanda so badly that he'd lost his chance at all this. It only hardened his determination not to make a similar mistake in the future.

Beside him, Annie was talking to J.J., who had moved into her lap when Jeanne left the room. She was playing finger games with the giggling toddler. Every time she stopped, J.J. shouted, "'Gain, Ann-tie, 'gain!"

Joe chuckled. "The kids call her Aunt Annie, but J.J. hasn't figure out that it's two words yet."

Dane looked at the happy toddler. The child grinned back at him with the assurance of someone who's never met with rejection. Experimentally, Dane poked a finger into the little boy's middle. J.J. squealed and giggled, squirming in Annie's lap. Annie watched the child fondly, but the sadness Dane had glimpsed before still lurked in her eyes.

She'd lost her husband before they could start a family and he knew she minded the loss—she'd told him so. These children probably reminded her of her own loneliness every time she saw them, reminded her that she might never have any of her own to love. From the look on her face, it was obvious that she liked children. How she must regret not having her own.

She could have your child.

The thought was so unexpected that he caught his breath. He glanced at Annie again from the corner of his eye, afraid she might somehow divine what he was thinking. What *was* he thinking, anyway? Sure, he was more attracted to Annie than he'd been to any woman since...since he couldn't remember when.

Now that the treacherous seed had been planted, he couldn't keep from furtively examining it over and over again. Annie would be a wonderful mother, he thought, watching her with the chubby toddler, and he already knew she longed for children of her own, so there would be no unpleasant changes of heart after the wedding. They were compatible, they were going to be great in bed together—

J.J.'s mother entered the room again and the child lurched off Annie's lap and went wobbling across the floor to Jeanne.

Dane turned to Annie. This hadn't been a date, exactly, but he hoped she'd let him take her home. He wanted to consolidate the ground he'd won when he'd kissed her the other day. She'd seemed remote and withdrawn after attending that stupid cocktail party with him the other night, and he'd forced himself to give her only a chaste peck on the forehead. Tonight was going to be different.

"Ready to go? It's been a big day and I have to work tomorrow. I can drop you off at your house if you like."

Annie's shoulders drooped as he helped her to her feet

and she raised one hand to massage her forehead as if to ward off a headache. "That would be nice."

He couldn't stand to see her look so beaten. Stepping forward, he placed his hands at her waist and drew her to him, turning so that his back was to the rest of the room. "What's wrong?" he asked in a low voice. "Jeanne's news got you down?"

To his relief, she allowed herself to rest against his chest as he began to rub her back in small circles. She felt incredibly soft and warm beneath his hands and he was supremely conscious of the tips of her breasts brushing against him.

Her head dipped once in assent. "A little bit. It reminds me of what my life should have been like."

"It still can be." *You could marry me and have a whole houseful of babies.*

"I'm fine just as I am." But she didn't sound fine.

He could tell this wasn't the time to push her and he wasn't ready to blurt out any half-formed plans. "I couldn't agree more. You're perfect just the way you are." He'd been striving for a light, playful tone, but the words came out in a husky half whisper.

Annie slowly raised her head from his chest. Her eyes were wide, her gaze questioning. She had beautiful eyes. Tonight they were a soft, misty blue, fringed by lavish dark lashes that matched the shade of the braid trailing down her back, bumping the backs of his palms where they cradled her. What would she do if he kissed her? His gaze slid to her mouth, wide and appealing, measuring the sweet bow of the top and lingering over the full bottom lip. As he stared, her lips parted slightly and he became conscious of her breath rushing in and out, bathing him in warmth. His body stirred, pulsed, growing to fullness, and his hands tightened fractionally on her back as he fought not to pull her against him.

Behind them, someone laughed. Belatedly, he remembered that they were standing in a roomful of people. With a silent curse, he let her go. "Let's get out of here."

She seemed subdued on the short ride to her home. When he handed her out of the car, he wondered if she was going to slip away from him the way she had the first time he'd taken her out to dinner, but she allowed him to take her hand and lead her up the steps to her front door, where he turned to face her.

"Give me your key."

His voice was a low growl. It made her stomach jump in anticipation. She knew what he wanted, and she knew that tonight, if Dane kissed her, she wouldn't resist. She longed for his touch, ached for it, with every fiber of her being. She didn't understand or even like the way her body reacted to him, but just for tonight, she wasn't going to think about anything.

He took the key she dug out of her bag and unlocked her door, then handed her the key.

She slipped it into her pocket. "Thank you." The air practically quivered with tension; she wondered if he could possibly be unaware of how much she wanted to lose herself in him.

When she raised her gaze to his face, he wasn't smiling. Instead, his features looked as if they were graven in stone. Time seemed to stop for a long, breathless moment as he raised his hand, and she held her breath in suspense.

When his long fingers slid underneath the heavy fall of her hair and cupped the back of her neck, she sighed. Slowly, his gaze commanding hers, he drew her braid to one side, wrapping it around one lean palm.

Annie quivered in delight as his head slowly came down. It was always like this when he touched her; all her senses focused on the sensations aroused by his clever fingers and seeking lips.

He kissed her and kissed her, until her knees buckled and she was clinging to him. At last, he raised his head and his eyes glittered in the dark shadow of the porch. "When can I see you again?"

"I—I don't know." Her voice sounded breathless and weak, even to her. "I can't think when you're touching me."

Dane laughed, a deep, primitive sound of satisfaction. "Good." Slowly, he released her and stepped back a pace. "I'll call you tomorrow."

She nodded once, then slowly turned away to open the door. Just as she put her hand on the knob, she felt him step forward again. His warm lips touched the tender skin at her nape and she drew in a sharp breath, unprepared for the surge of longing that shot through her.

Standing perfectly still, her head bent, she closed her eyes in ecstasy as he trailed a lingering kiss around to nibble at the lobe of her ear. She swayed back against him and his large, capable hands clasped her hipbones, pulling her firmly into contact with his big, hard body. He was aroused; she could feel the telltale ridge of his manhood pressing intimately into the small of her back. As his tongue dipped into her ear before swirling in a leisurely manner around the delicate shell, she whimpered, unable to stem the small sound that rose unbidden from her throat.

The tiny noise seemed to break the spell that held them. Dane withdrew his hands from her hips. "Tell me to leave."

She expelled choked laughter. "Will it work?"

"Unless you want me in your bed tonight, you'd better hope so."

She turned to face him, suddenly unsure. Everything was happening so fast. What did she really know about Dane Hamilton? She was a widow. A woman who still compared every man she met to her husband. But she'd hardly thought of Nick since Dane had come into her life. Her thoughts were chaotic, strewn with conflicting feelings of longing and guilt, need and remorse.... "I'm not ready to ask you in," she said.

"I know." His voice was still deep and rough, but oddly soothing. "Go inside. Now. I'll call you."

He did call her, several times, although they didn't see much of each other in the next week. On Thursday night, he was the first student to arrive for class, simply because he couldn't wait any longer to see her.

"Hello." He stuck his head around the door of her office as he and Missy entered.

"Hi." The way her face lit up when she saw him was an encouraging sign. Did she want to be with him as badly as he wanted to see her again?

Unable to stop himself, though he knew anyone could walk through the door of the center at any moment, he stepped into the office and held out his hand. Without a word, she placed her much smaller palm in his and rose. Dane gathered her to him, gasping as her soft curves pressed against him. He buried his face in her hair and inhaled deeply. "You smell sweet."

He felt a little laugh that bubbled up from inside her. "It must be the 'Eau de Dog' I applied this morning."

He smiled, rubbing his chin lightly along her temple. "You're slandering my sense of smell." Then he shifted back a fraction so that he could see her face. "Have you missed me?"

She hesitated and his stomach dropped to his toes. *This shouldn't be so important,* he lectured himself. Then she nodded, and immediately he felt as if he could sprout wings and fly.

But all he said was, "Good," in a voice deep with satisfaction. He hadn't intended to come in and kiss her first thing, but as he gazed at her, he knew he had to taste her again. Slowly he lowered his head.

Annie didn't make any move away from him. In fact, she rose on tiptoe to meet his descent. The moment their mouths met, he knew he'd been wrong to do this.

Wrong. Because moving away from her without being sated was going to be hell on earth.

He forced himself to go slowly when all he wanted was to plunge his tongue into her and demand a response. But Annie reminded him of a wary doe and he was afraid if he moved too fast, she'd bolt. So instead, he stealthily increased the intensity of the kiss as they stood locked together in her office, kissing her until he couldn't remember where he was or what had come before this moment.

When he'd initiated the kiss, his hands had settled at her waist. Now he carefully, easily, slipped them beneath the hem of the loose sweatshirt she wore until his fingertips rested against flesh. His tongue continued to master her mouth and while she was so fully his, he risked flattening his palms over the bare skin of her back, savoring the silky texture of her beneath his hands. Slowly he rubbed rhythmic circles that matched the cadence of their mouthplay, and with each circle he increased the scope of his reach by millimeters, until his thumbs were brushing the sides of her full breasts with each stroke. Still she didn't protest. The next time his thumb swept across the ripe mound beneath her shirt, he spread his hand wide, whisking his thumb directly over the taut, straining peak concealed by a thin layer of satiny fabric.

Annie jerked and gasped against his mouth. "No! Dane, wait." Frantically she stepped away from him, pulling at his hands.

A hollow click preceded the opening of the outside door, heralding the arrival of other students. He uttered a silent curse, holding her by the waist when she would have put the width of the small room between them. "Annie." He stood very still until she glanced at him. "Tell me why you stopped me."

Color rose in her cheeks. She looked around the office. "Not here. It's not...private."

He felt a primitive delight leap within him. "Did you dislike what we—what I did?"

She dropped her gaze and her color rose even higher. The pause was pregnant with anticipation. "No," she said in a stifled tone.

"Good." He pressed a quick, hard kiss onto her startled lips and released her before any inquisitive students came looking for her. "The next time I touch you, it will be someplace where we won't be disturbed."

Her eyes were dark and unsure as she stared back at him for a moment. Then, apparently deciding silence was the best defense, she got Ebony out of her training crate and left the room. He stayed in the office for a moment longer to get his unruly body under control so that he didn't embarrass Annie—or himself—in front of the class.

As the lesson commenced, only part of his mind was on working his dog. The other part watched Annie, assessing every move she made, wondering how long it would be until he could touch her again. He was determined to have her now that he knew how responsive she was, and that she wanted him, too.

Once again, the speculations that had been rolling around in his brain surfaced. Was Annie the kind of woman he wanted for a wife? He knew she wanted children, so there'd be no problem there. He found her company soothing, her gentle humor healing and her sweet responses to his touch so wildly erotic that just thinking about it produced an uncomfortable surge of excitement centered in his groin. Was that enough for marriage?

He was beginning to believe that it would have to be.

It seemed fate was conspiring to keep her from making any rash decisions. He had meetings. She had classes. The following weekend he had to drive to Peoria for a wedding...two weeks crawled by and she didn't see Dane except during obedience class.

She'd never minded the odd hours before, but having a job that demanded she work evenings and Saturdays when everyone else was off seemed to be a big disadvantage all of a sudden.

Annie shook her head as she knelt in the flower bed at the front of the house on Sunday evening checking her autumn annuals. It was probably just as well she hadn't been free. She was becoming much too obsessed with Dane Hamilton. Just because he had enough sexual charisma to melt her into a puddle at his feet didn't mean she should jump into bed with the man. Annoyed at herself, she yanked hard on a particularly stubborn weed and when it easily tore loose, landed square on her backside in the dirt with an inelegant curse.

"Who won?" The amused masculine voice coming from directly behind her didn't belong to Patrick. Her heart skipped a beat and her breathing became shallow as her body reacted to the presence of the man who'd been in her thoughts.

He was clearly struggling against an outright guffaw, and reluctantly seeing the humor in the picture she must have made, she craned her head around to stick her tongue out at him before she collapsed into laughter.

"Better be nice to me. I come bearing gifts," he said. Reaching into a white paper bag, he produced a sinfully delicious-looking banana split and two spoons.

"Oh, yum!" Annie's eyes widened in delight. "My hero! I absolutely love banana splits. Where'd you get this?"

Blue eyes twinkled at her reaction as he told her the name of a local dairy. "If you can tear yourself away from your flower beds—" here his smile dissolved into a chuckle "—we can share it."

Annie leaped up. Before she allowed herself to consider her actions and chicken out, she stretched up and kissed his cheek. Then, embarrassed by her forwardness, she led the way into the house.

Dane took one spoon and dug into the sundae, holding a tempting spoonful of ice cream right in front of her lips. "Open sesame."

Annie let him feed her the bite of sundae; it was an oddly intimate sensation. Her eyes clung to his for a long moment as she savored the cool treat. "I didn't expect to see you tonight."

"I got back into town early." He paused to wolf down a huge bite of ice cream. "Do you mind my stopping by? I'm sorry I didn't call first but I came on impulse." He flashed her a grin. "It's lucky you were home or I'd have had to eat this whole thing myself."

Annie couldn't help but return the smile as they divvied up the snack. When he turned on the charm, he was irresistible.

Who was she kidding? He was irresistible even when he wasn't trying to please. His raven hair gleamed, casually disordered by impatient fingers. Thick, arched dark brows nearly met above a blade-straight nose and strong chin, a chin that Annie knew could jut into a stubborn firmness. As she watched, his tongue slid out and smoothly swept the last particle of ice cream from the spoon. She couldn't suppress the surge of desire that shot through her body at his unconsciously erotic motion.

When Dane lifted his gaze from the empty container, she knew he could read naked need in her eyes. His eyes narrowed to mere slits of blue as he dropped the forgotten plastic to the table. One lean, blunt-tipped finger lifted. Slowly, he tilted up her chin and when she didn't protest or pull away, he pulled her closer and lowered his mouth to hers.

She kept her eyes open, locked on his, until the first contact. But when his lips touched her waiting mouth, she sucked in a small gasp of air, and her eyes drifted closed.

Five

Dane surrendered himself to the sweet sensations of kissing Annie, ignoring the roaring rush of his body urging him to move faster, deeper, farther, and keeping it light and non-threatening as he knew she needed it to be. He kissed her like that for longer than he thought he could stand, until she slipped slender arms around his neck and speared her fingers through his hair in a signal that she was as involved as he was. Not wanting to scare her, he slipped his own arms around her slim waist, pulling her out of her chair sideways across his lap without breaking the kiss.

He nibbled and played with her warm, soft lips, seeking her tongue. Hesitantly, it seemed, she allowed him to part her lips and touch the tip of his tongue to hers. The erotic sensation sent an electric quickening through him and he forced himself not to rub his aroused body against her like some inexperienced teenager. When he had enticed her into meeting him halfway, he sucked at her, pulling her tongue into his own mouth to continue the erotic foreplay.

Her hands clutched at his biceps. He told himself to take it slow, to go easy. But he felt as if his willpower was made of soft clay as his fingers reached out to stroke and pet the sweet mound of her breast as he had once before. Annie whimpered at the first shock of contact but she didn't pull away and he was encouraged to make bolder forays. As he continued to knead her breast, her fingers slid across his broad back, pressing him even closer. His thumb and forefinger skillfully pinched and rolled the tip of her swelling flesh through her dress and bra and she began to shift restlessly.

Experience had taught him to read female signals. "Easy, sweetheart," he whispered against her mouth as he slid his hand down her torso and slowly, sweetly stroked the vee between her legs. "Easy," he whispered again when her thighs clamped together on his hand and she moaned. He was perilously close to the edge of his own control, his heated sex throbbing rhythmically against her hip as they strained together, seeking a better fit for their bodies. Breaking contact with her mouth, he lifted his head to measure the distance to the hallway. Annie immediately transferred her attention to his neck, nipping the corded sinews along the side. He shuddered. God, she was driving him wild. Her little noises and soft body felt so good he knew he had to have her. But not here. Concentrating fiercely to resist her long enough to get her somewhere more private, he decided to carry her upstairs. He knew the stairwell was right in the front hallway.

He rose and lifted her into his arms all in one smooth motion. Striding into the hallway, he paused at the front door and locked it with one hand. The implications of that very final-sounding click obviously reverberated in Annie's ears; her eyes grew enormous as she registered his intent to stay.

"Your back will be sore tomorrow," she said, smiling.

He paused in the hallway. "You'll just have to help me find a position that won't strain it too much."

She buried her face in his neck to hide the blush he'd seen beginning to spread. "That's not what I meant!"

His chest heaved with laughter beneath her and he stopped at the bottom of the stairs. "I know." He was silent for a moment. "I want to stay with you tonight. Am I right in thinking that's what you want, too?"

Annie raised her head from his shoulder. He read hesitation in her face for a long, agonizing moment. Then she said softly, "This is what I want." In a rare display of courage that he knew must have cost her, she ran her hands into the silky thickness of his hair, pulling his head down and finding his lips with her own. Dane groaned, afraid he'd never be able to take this as slowly as he should, given her lack of recent experience.

He climbed the stairs in silence. When he reached the top, he hesitated, wondering which one was her room. Annie lifted one hand from where it lay against his stubbled jaw and pointed to the second doorway on the left. With three measured strides, he was in her bedroom.

Standing beside the bed, he released her legs, allowing her to slide down over his taut body until she touched the floor.

"Where's a light? I want to see you."

Obediently Annie snapped on the beruffled, feminine lamp on the table beside her bed. It was a small light, and its low illumination barely reached into the darkest corners of the room.

Still, it satisfied him. He reached past her and swept the covers back to the foot of her wide bed. "Such a big bed for one little body." What he really wanted to ask her was if her husband had shared this bed with her—he didn't know why, but the idea bothered him.

As if she sensed what he really wanted to know, she said,

"Nick never slept in this bed. I didn't keep any of our furniture after he was killed."

Her tone was bleak and he was immediately sorry he'd reminded her of her past. Reaching for her, he cuddled her against him. The contact reignited fires that had been temporarily banked, and suddenly he couldn't wait any longer. Removing a small packet from his wallet, he tossed both onto the bedside table before bending to her. She lifted her chin to meet his descending mouth. The gentle pressure of his lips opened hers easily and he slid his tongue inside to explore the ridge of teeth, sucking persistently at her tongue until she followed his dancing retreat into the moist depths of his own mouth. He slid his arms down her back as he responded to the exciting foray her tongue so tentatively made. Then he boldly let his hands wander over her firmly rounded buttocks, lifting her until her feet dangled off the carpet and the hardened bulge of his arousal nestled in the vee at her thighs.

A wave of weakness swept over her and she melted bonelessly against him, assailed by intense physical sensations that she had never dreamed she could feel. Deep in her torso, an unaccustomed throbbing had her shifting against him, rubbing herself rhythmically over his hardness in a unconscious effort to alleviate the building tension within her. Dane shuddered, wildly thrusting his hips against her through the barrier of their clothing. She was more responsive than he had ever imagined in his most erotic dreams...and he'd been tormented by plenty of them since he'd met her. She had him ready as a stallion and he hadn't even gotten her clothes off yet. Sweat beaded his upper lip as he fought for control. More than he'd ever wanted anything in his life, he wanted to do this right for her. She was too fragile to be taken with anything less than the gentlest touch he could manage.

Summoning all his willpower, he released her soft curves, shuddering again as her ripe figure rubbed against him.

He smiled crookedly down at her, reading every nuance of her passion-dazed expression. "I don't want to hurry this," he told her. "We have all night." Smoothing his palms up her torso, he framed the generous weight of her breasts between his spread thumbs and forefingers. "I want to see these beautiful breasts. I've been driving myself crazy imagining what they look like."

Annie blushed and he smiled. How she could still do that after some of the erotic movements she had made was beyond him. It pointed, once again, to the extraordinary blend of innocence and sensuality that he was sure she didn't realize she possessed. He could see the rosy color spreading up her neck even in the dim light cast by the little lamp. His thumbs lifted to flick across her nipples for an instant and then he was sliding those knowing hands around to the back of her dress, smoothly releasing the zipper beneath the unbound mass of her hair. Stepping back a pace, he stood, breathing hard, just looking at her for a long moment. The strapless sundress was loose, but it had caught on the peaks of her upthrust breasts. He reached out and inserted one finger between the neckline of the dress and her silky skin, running it from the tip of one breast to the tip of its mate. Just that action made the dress fall away from her petite body, pooling around her ankles.

Dane sucked in an involuntary breath, standing as if turned to stone, staring at all her displayed beauty. She had worn no bra beneath the dress, and her sole garment now was a pair of tiny panties, which were cut so low that he could glimpse the beginnings of the copper curls covering her feminine mound. To his delight, her breasts were bigger than he had envisioned, round and full without sagging, topped by rosy-pink nipples that were tightly beaded. He already knew that she had a waist he could probably span with his hands. The one detail that his vivid imagination hadn't supplied was the creamy texture of her skin as it flared into smooth thighs kept slim and lightly muscled by hours of hard work. He could feel his heavy arousal rising to full attention, but he forced his mind off his own needs, correctly reading the embarrassment she was unable to hide.

"You have nothing to be ashamed of," he told her in a husky voice. "You are perfect."

Annie managed to find her voice, though she was conscious of the heat staining her cheeks as well as a very different type of heat curling insistently through her midsection. "No, I'm not," she objected. "I'm too small and my hair is the most awful shade—" She stopped abruptly as Dane reached out to cup the weight of one full breast in a tanned hand, reacting like a cat to the stimulating caress.

He watched her back arch as she unconsciously pushed herself against his hand. "You are not too small. Your breasts are generous and I can barely keep my hands from tearing the clips out of those glorious curls of yours when you wear your hair up. You turn me on so fast and so hard that I have trouble hiding it when we're in a public place. Now—" he took a deep breath "—will you help me undress?"

Tentatively, she moved her hands to the small buttons of his shirt. Although trembling with nerves, her slender fingers moved surely down the front of the garment, revealing an ever-widening strip of toasty skin lightly covered with silky black curls. As she neared the waistband of his pants, her hands slid inside the shirt, smoothing it off his sleekly muscled shoulders. Unable to resist, she slowly dipped her head to bury her nose in the cloud of curls, inhaling deeply. He smelled musky and excitingly masculine and she detected faint traces of his cologne. Nerves were forgotten as she was caught up in the sensual excitement he radiated. Rubbing her nose from side to side, she encountered a flat male nipple which rose to meet the gently circling tip of her pink tongue.

Eyes half-closed, awash in the sensations she was evoking, Dane watched her lightly trace his nipple with that teasing tongue for a moment before the pleasure threatened to cut short her explorations and his hands slid from bare hips to her shoulders to draw her a hairbreadth away from him. "No more," he commanded, and her eyes flew to his in confusion. Smiling in self-derision, he added, "I can't take it."

His hands left her shoulders to swiftly deal with the rest of his clothing. As he drew his slacks down over strong thighs, the evidence of his desire was clearly outlined by clinging navy briefs. Then he removed those, too, with an impatient sweep of his hand. He was bigger, more aroused, than Annie had known a man could be, and she quivered deep inside at the thought of joining with that magnificent frame in the act of total intimacy.

Dane mistook her long silence for fear. Drawing her into his arms, he feathered open-mouthed kisses along her jaw, down her neck, and finally to the crest of one sloping breast. "Don't worry, baby," he breathed against her skin. "We'll be a perfect fit."

Waves of excitement coursed through her as his lips suckled strongly at her. She could feel his satiny hardness brushing insistently against her belly, and her legs suddenly wouldn't hold her another second.

Sensing her capitulation, Dane moved to take swift advantage, scooping her up only to deposit her almost instantly on the mattress. Long fingers hooked in the tiny panties and pulled them off. The bed gave as he joined her, and Annie was conscious of the way his broad shoulders deleted her view of the room before his dark head came down and she closed her eyes. He kissed her deeply, repeatedly thrusting his tongue into the moist depths of her mouth as one skilled hand shaped the sensitive peak of her breast until she was whimpering and moving restlessly beneath him.

"What's the matter?" he crooned. "Let me make it better."

His words washed over her, but the exact meanings were

lost; *she* was lost, drowning in the magic that his hard fingers were working on her flesh. As one calloused hand slid firmly down her stomach, combing through the crisp curls between her legs, she drew in a sharp breath. It was released in a thin cry as a dexterous finger probed the soft folds of the feminine rise, dipping and rubbing the small bud hidden there, sending fiery messages to every part of her body.

Annie responded totally to that knowing hand for uncounted minutes, trusting him without question, and her hips lifted repeatedly, legs shifting and spreading to invite a more complete possession.

Dane nearly succumbed to the need screaming at him to take her when he slipped his hand between her thighs. Her eyes were closed and her bright tresses spilled across the pillow as her head thrashed from side to side. She was slick with her own moisture and he knew he wouldn't hurt her if he took her now, but he wanted more. Holding back his own desire to lose himself in her writhing excitement, he carefully slid two fingers deep into her, continuing to stimulate her center with the butt of his hand. Her back arched and she gave a muted scream which he caught with his own mouth. As she peaked, ever-spreading waves of fulfillment lapped through her body, relaxing muscles held stiff and tense with desire.

He was nearly wild with the need to be inside her. Even as her body jerked and shuddered with her spasms, he was kneeing her thighs farther apart and guiding himself into her with frantic haste. His buttocks tensed and flexed at the first touch of her dewy wetness and then he drove into her, measuring his full length once, twice, and then again. She was as tight as a true virgin, and she felt so damn good clasping him within her pulsing body, so hot and wet...he had wanted this to last, but he was too far gone to wait. He could feel tiny fingers of fulfillment dancing up his spine, and then he was groaning out his own completion as his hard body slammed into her again and again, releasing his pent-up needs in jetting succession.

Annie lay quiescent beneath his greater weight for long moments in the dim room as his harsh, gasping breaths gradually resumed a more normal respiratory pattern. Her arms and legs were still wrapped tightly around him and she savored the intimacy of lying like this, still holding him within her. Tears trailed from the corners of her eyes as she relived the beauty of their lovemaking in her mind. Dane's head lay heavily on her breasts; she tenderly passed one hand through the wavy tumult of black silk locks.

As her movement registered on his sated senses, he lazily lifted his head, propping himself on his elbows above her without separating himself from her body. An inky eyebrow quirked in concern as he saw the tracks of tears slowly disappearing into the moist russet curls at her temples.

Dane groaned. "Did I hurt you?" He had thought she was aroused enough to accommodate him comfortably; he would never forgive himself if he had so crucially misjudged her physical readiness. He heaved his big body up onto his forearms, preparing to disengage himself, but she only tightened her limbs around him, the deceptively fragile-looking legs exerting pressure to keep him deeply inside her.

She linked her arms behind his head and pulled him down for a slow, sweet kiss that reassured him before she even opened her mouth to speak and he relaxed his tensed muscles again. "No, you didn't hurt me, you silly man." She smiled up at him through the tears. "I just didn't know…I've never…it was never that good for me." She settled on the evasive terminology with a small shrug.

Awareness flared in Dane's intense blue gaze. He understood what she hadn't explicitly stated. It explained the curious air of innocence he had sensed in her repeatedly, despite the fact that he knew she'd been married. "That makes me very happy," he said gently.

It was true. Knowing that she had reached ultimate satisfaction for the first time in his arms made him feel manly and proud and possessive in a manner he'd never felt before. It also made him feel like doing the same thing again, he reflected in amazement. He glanced down to see her blue eyes round in surprise, then he could almost read the anticipatory expression on her face as she wriggled experimentally underneath him. He chuckled, feeling a heady pleasure in his unexpected ability to renew their lovemaking. The chuckle died abruptly as another surge of arousal swept through him, tightening his body in a rush of desire. He bent his dark head to her breast and her fingers rose to clench convulsively in the thick strands of his hair. Together they moved again in a silent dance of love punctuated only by the creak of the bedsprings and the slide of body on body.

She woke from a dreamless sleep in the middle of the night. For an instant, she was confused by the hard weight pinning her middle. Then, as she grasped an arm and felt crisp curling hair overlying warm skin and sinew, memory came flooding back.

Dane. They'd made love. She felt…she felt guilty, as thoughts of Nick replaced the contented languor with which she had awoken.

But why should she allow herself to be ruled by guilt for the rest of her life? Nick wasn't here. She had loved him, had never wished him gone. But he was.

And now she had Dane. He'd overwhelmed her at first. If she was honest, he still did. But she was drawn to him in a way she'd never experienced before, not even with Nick. Her mind shied away from labeling what she felt for him—it was too soon for grand pronouncements. But she knew that her life had been altered completely and unchangeably by what had passed between them tonight. She was his now, if he wanted her.

She found herself avoiding any thought of how she'd feel if he didn't.

The warm weight of him against her distracted her from deeper thought. He had merely shifted his considerable weight to one side and pulled her into the curve of his naked frame to sleep after the second time they made love. He still had one leg thrown across her. Her head was pillowed on a bulging bicep and the other large hand cupped a breast possessively. She smiled quietly.

Then her thoughts turned to more mundane concerns. Mother Nature's call could no longer be ignored and she carefully slid from his arms to the side of the bed. He stretched and rolled over onto his stomach, burying his head under a pillow. Shaking her head in amusement, she walked silently across the floor to the bathroom.

Returning to the bed a moment later, she began to slide back in as stealthily as she had gotten out. When a large hand yanked her suddenly over to sprawl across his chest, she gave a startled squeak.

"I thought you were still sleeping," she said breathlessly.

"I couldn't sleep without you in my arms." He rubbed his chin against the top of her head.

She kissed his collarbone, wondering what to say, opting for a light reply. "Guess you'll have to keep me around so you can get your beauty rest."

"You bet, baby. Now that I've finally got you, I'm not planning to let you go. You're stuck with me for good."

A warm glow spread through her. He did want to be with her! What did he mean by, "for good?" She couldn't think of anything to say that wouldn't reveal how much his words meant to her, so she said nothing, choosing instead to lay her head on his shoulder.

A pregnant silence followed his words. Hell, he thought. He hadn't meant to rush her; those words had just slipped out. He guessed it was a good sign that she hadn't pulled away, but had instead settled herself against him like a small cat. But what was she thinking? Cautiously, he asked, "No response?"

She lifted her head from where she'd been cuddled against him and made eye contact for the first time. He could just barely see her eyes, wide and serious, in the darkness. "Define 'for good.'"

He measured her face. "As in 'til death do us part."

Another silence descended and he could feel the fine tension that had invaded her limbs. Then, when he was about to turn on the light so that he could gauge her expression to see how badly he had handled this, she responded once more. "You've obviously forgotten a few crucial details. Why don't I explain how a marriage proposal should be tendered?"

Letting out a deep breath he hadn't realized he was holding, he laughed and rolled her beneath him, settling himself familiarly between her legs. "I think I can take it from here. Do you mind if I forego the part where I get down on one knee?" To emphasize his words, he lifted his hips slightly. The blunt flesh of his newly revived arousal probed at the hidden entrance to her and she willingly lifted her bottom to receive the evidence of his need for her. They both gasped as he slid slowly, deliciously into her, not stopping until he was fully sheathed in her moist depths.

"I haven't been able to get you out of my mind for weeks," he growled against her lips. "I know this is sudden, but I know what I want, and I want you to marry me."

He still hadn't actually *asked*, she noted, and he hadn't said he loved her.

Apparently he read her hesitation as refusal, because he said, "Think before you decide. We'd be perfect for each other. You want children, so do I. You love this house, so do I. If you marry me, you can have both those things. I don't mind your career. We turn each other on so totally, no one else is ever going to be able to compare."

"I know." Her voice was a thin thread. "But what about…love?"

For the first time, she felt his big shoulders stiffen where she'd laid her hands against them. "Love doesn't exist," he said, and his tone was harsher than any she'd ever heard him use. "We're compatible in all the ways that count. Isn't that a lot more important than an emotion that could change tomorrow?"

In the darkness, he could feel her withdrawing from him mentally, though his flesh still claimed hers. "I don't know," she whispered.

A surge of panic crashed over his head. She couldn't refuse him—he needed her. Nobody else would do. Dropping his head, he sought her mouth with single-minded determination. "Let me convince you," he whispered against her lips.

Morning light was streaming into the bedroom when Dane opened his eyes again. He gave a cursory glance around the quietly tasteful room before turning his attention to the woman still sleeping in his arms.

Nothing would bring him more pleasure than to come home to her at the end of every day. He had to restrain himself from clutching her in a fiercely possessive hug as the memory of their lovemaking reverberated in his head.

She slept deeply as he watched her, deriving immense pleasure from simply holding her. That glorious hair was spread wildly out across the pillow, trailing over her shoulders and fanning across his own chest in fiery disarray. The sweet bow of her mobile lips was slightly parted and he could see the serrated edges of pearly teeth that he recalled had nipped in abandon at his neck last night. The sheets were tangled low at their hips and her upper torso was bared to his gaze. She had the creamiest skin he had ever encountered. He could trace the delicate network of veins beneath the fine-grained flesh and his eyes followed those life-giving vessels to the crest of one breast. Her nipples were a deep shade of rose-pink, capping the ripe mounds like cherries on an ice-cream sundae. Idly his thoughts wandered to the future and he imagined how those beautiful breasts would look full of milk for an infant. A baby...made by the same act of intimacy they had shared last night. He pictured a strapping son with his mother's blue eyes and hair of flame.

The smile froze on his face as he suddenly realized what his driving desire to possess her had led him to forget last night. Hell! Raising his head slightly, his eyes confirmed what his brain had just remembered. The incriminating foil packet lay undisturbed on the nightstand right where he had dropped it beside his wallet. He had had the presence of mind to put protection within easy reach but he had been so caught up in the responsive movements of the perfect little figure nestled next to him that all thought of birth control had gone right out of his head.

A telling statement, he reflected without amusement. He had always been scrupulously careful about such things for his own protection as well as his partner's. The very fact that he could forget necessary measures like that showed him how very deeply this woman had gotten under his skin.

Beside him, Annie stirred, perhaps sensing his disquiet. Blue eyes snapped open as her body protested movement and she recalled the events of last night. A red tide of color swept up her neck and tinged her cheeks as she forced herself to meet his gaze. "Good morning."

"Good morning," he returned, squeezing her gently. "I can't believe you can still blush like that after the things we did last night. Do you remember when you—"

"Dane!"

He laughed and she smiled tentatively. That smile relaxed nerves he hadn't even realized were strung tight. She didn't look like a woman who was going to turn down his proposal. And if she was a little less delighted about it than he'd hoped, he figured she'd been taken by surprise. Well, that would soon pass.

"If I tell you how beautiful you look with your hair all mussed, will you kiss me?"

In answer, she turned in his embrace to press her lips as high along his jaw as she could reach. Shifting her to her back, he leaned over her and leisurely explored her mouth in a potent kiss that had her breath coming faster when he finally lifted his head.

"Much as I would love to keep you in bed all day, I know it's not practical," he informed her. "Especially if you want to be able to walk tomorrow!"

Annie smiled shyly. "I have to be able to walk," she reminded him. "I have classes tomorrow."

"And we have plans to make."

"Dane…" Her eyes shifted away from his.

"Annie…" He took her chin in one hand and raised her face to his. "I want you more than any woman I've ever met. I want a life with you. Marry me."

"I can't make that decision right now," she said, and he was surprised by the strength of her objection. It shook him more than he wanted to admit. "I have to have time to think about this." She smiled at him. "If I let you railroad me into this, you'll think you can get away with it for the rest of our lives."

It wasn't what he wanted to hear, but her final sentence gave him hope. He decided to give her one last gentle nudge. "I won't promise not to try to influence your decision, but I'll respect your need to think it through. I know what I'm asking is a big step for both of us. But don't make me wait too long—we may have a need for haste."

When she raised uncomprehending eyes to his again, he smiled wryly and gestured sheepishly to the bedside table. As she turned her head to see what he meant, he went on. "You got me in such a dither last night that I completely forgot to take any precautions. Although we hadn't discussed starting a family right away, it doesn't bother me in the least." His hand slid tenderly down to rest just above where he knew their child could already be forming. "As a matter of fact, I can't think of anything that would make me happier than to see your body carrying my child."

She was silent again and he could almost see her counting in her head, though he couldn't tell how she felt about his words. Finally, she said, "No, it's the wrong time."

"That's just as well. I'd like to be married before we start a family."

"Dane..." Her voice trailed away helplessly. "I might not be able to have children as easily as you imagine." Reaching for his hand, she placed it over her abdomen. "Feel that?"

He did. For the first time, he noticed the distinctive ridge of scar tissue beneath his fingers. Pulling back, he looked down at the long, ugly scar that marred her smooth skin.

"It's from the accident," she said. "Everything was repaired to the surgeon's satisfaction, but afterward I contracted some kind of infection that invaded one of my fallopian tubes. I've been told that although I can still bear children, my chances of conception are about fifty percent now."

He only half understood what she was saying. His mind was reeling. He hadn't realized that she'd been injured in the accident that had claimed her husband's and dog's lives, hadn't realized that she must have been a hairbreadth from death herself.

"My God," he said, and his voice was hoarse with shock. "You could have died, too."

Annie nodded. "But—"

"Hey! Sweet sister of mine! Could I con you into making me an early breakfast this morning?"

"What the hell is he doing here?" Dane growled, reaching for his pants.

Annie scrambled out of bed and he caught a flash of

sleek, pale skin before she struggled into a flannel robe. "I'll get rid of him," she said.

Dane finished dressing slowly, listening to Annie's footsteps receding down the steps. The shock of what she'd just told him was still reverberating in his head. For the first time, he acknowledged to himself that he didn't want to live without Annie for the rest of his life. Somehow, she'd become more important to him than any woman since Amanda—hell, she was more important than that! He'd wanted Amanda physically, fiercely in the early days of their marriage. But he couldn't remember ever *caring* about her the way he cared about Annie. Knowing that she'd nearly died was a horrifying thought.

The sound of voices downstairs prompted him to open the door and start down the hall. He realized Patrick probably hadn't seen his car, parked behind the house as it was. He wasn't entirely sure he liked the way Annie had leaped to head off her brother. To him, the sooner they told people, the better. It would give him one more way to bind Annie to him.

Six

"Sorry, I'm not going to have time for breakfast this morning," Annie told her brother firmly.

Patrick was already busy pouring water into the coffeemaker he'd just filled. "Aw, come on," he said. "It's only seven-thirty. What have you got to do so early?" He turned and gave her an angelic smile. "I was afraid you couldn't make breakfast without me."

Annie snorted. "Fat chance. More likely you didn't have any food of your own so you decided to come mooch from me." But she smiled at him. Breakfast together had been a part of their routine when they'd shared the house. This was Patrick's way of checking up on her, making sure she was doing all right on her own, and she couldn't be mad at him for caring.

But she really had to get rid of him!

Patrick was opening the refrigerator. "How about if I make some scrambled eggs since you're in such a hurry? You can run and get dressed and we can eat together."

"Patrick, I really don't have time." Annie crossed to him and put a hand on his elbow. "How about tomorrow? You can come over, and I'll make you the biggest breakfast you've ever had."

"You might as well let him stay. I'll make western omelets. Bet you didn't know I'm a mean hand with a skillet."

The deep voice froze Patrick in his turn from the refrigerator. He clutched the carton of eggs he was holding with both hands.

Annie's hand fell away from her brother's arm. She'd been so worried about getting Patrick to leave that she hadn't heard Dane come into the kitchen behind her.

Slowly, Patrick set down the eggs and turned to face Dane. Annie did the same, taking in Dane's proprietary air and the fact that he was acting as if his presence in her house this early in the morning were an ordinary occurrence.

He was lounging against the doorframe with one foot crossed over the other, looking supremely relaxed. But she read the silent challenge in the blue eyes he leveled on her brother.

Patrick cleared his throat. "Good morning, Hamilton. Fancy meeting you here."

Annie closed her eyes. Dear heaven. Her normally easy-going brother had a protective streak a mile wide and she could tell from his flat, almost deadly tone of voice that he was bent on protecting her now. Patrick might deceive other people with the laid-back, humorous front he presented to the world, but she knew that beneath the surface was an unwavering implacability that sprang into action whenever he perceived a threat to someone he loved. And right now, that someone was her.

"I could say the same. Don't you have a home of your own?" Dane's tone was equally cool.

She opened her eyes again to see him smile, but it wasn't a warm, friendly expression. No, it was more a baring of the teeth. And Patrick reacted accordingly. She was used to reading signs of aggression in dogs and these two weren't acting much differently—she could almost see each man bristling his fur and trying to outstare the other.

"I may have a home of my own, but I still consider my sister my responsibility," Patrick said. He took a step forward and Annie hastily grabbed his arm. "I won't let her be taken advantage of."

"Your sister is an adult. She can make her own decisions." It was almost as if Dane were deliberately goading Patrick into a fight.

"Stop it, Dane." Her tone was sharp and irritated. From the back porch, Ebony barked sharply, responding to the sound of distress in her mistress's voice. "And you stop it, too, Patrick." Again she tried to take Patrick's arm and pull him away, but her brother's feet were planted in an aggressive stance and her tug on his arm had less effect than a gnat landing on it.

The room was silent except for the breathing of the two men. Then Dane turned away and pulled out a stool at the breakfast bar, taking one opposite for himself. "Have a seat, Murphy. We need to talk."

"I'll say we do," Patrick growled. He went toward the stool, but Annie could tell he was still on the offensive. She held her breath, wondering what Dane would do next.

When he looked across at her and held out a hand, she stood for a moment, confused. But the silent command focused on her overrode her objections and she crossed to him, allowing him to take her hand in his and pull her to his side.

"I've asked your sister to be my wife." Dane switched his gaze back to Patrick, and a note of humor replaced the tone he'd used earlier. "Granted, it means I'll be related to you, but I thought it over and decided she was worth it."

If she'd been in the mood to laugh, the classic look of shock on Patrick's face would have been just what she needed. His mouth actually dropped open and his blue eyes widened. After a moment, he looked at her.

"Is that true?" he demanded. "Are you going to marry him?"

"Well," she hedged, "I haven't agreed yet, but the topic is under discussion." To Dane, she said, "If you think just because you've announced this to my brother that you can rush my decision, you can think again. I told you I wouldn't be hurried into anything."

When she glanced back at Patrick, for the first time his face held a hint of its usual lightness. "Isn't this kind of quick?" he asked.

"Yes," she said.

"No," said Dane simultaneously. "Not quick enough by a long shot."

Patrick looked from one to the other of them, and his gaze was dancing with humor. "You're going to have your hands full," he said to Dane.

"I know."

Annie huffed out a breath of disgust and pulled herself away from his side. "You two are ridiculous. Two minutes ago, you were ready to tear into each other, now you're the best of buddies again."

"I can't fight with my future brother-in-law," Patrick said reasonably.

"What happened to the Great Protector?"

"You don't need to be protected from the man if you're going to marry him."

"We haven't made any decisions," she said through her teeth.

Patrick didn't even hear her. "I knew you were perfect for each other."

"You did not." Annie flicked the end of a dish towel at him.

"Oh, yes, I did. Why do you think I invited him to that barbecue?" He dodged the dish towel when she flung it at him and held up three fingers. "If we're having omelets, I'd like a three-egg platter."

As if in agreement, they all dropped the subject of marriage after that and conversation was general over the meal. As soon as breakfast ended, Patrick excused himself and headed for work.

"Thanks for letting me intrude on you two lovebirds," he said cheerily as he banged out the back door.

Annie shifted uneasily, wondering if Dane intended to announce that there was no love involved in his decision to marry her. But he acted as if he hadn't absorbed what Patrick said.

Instead, he looked at his watch. "I have to go home and shower and change," he grumbled. "I'd rather stay here with you all day. Can we have dinner tonight?"

Annie nodded. "I don't have classes on Monday nights." She gasped as he pulled her into his arms. "But the rest of the week will be kind of hectic," she added. He lifted her until she fit snugly against him and she closed her eyes, her thoughts scattering.

He nuzzled her neck. "I'll bring clothes with me tonight. And my dog. Then I won't have to rush off and leave you tomorrow morning." He dropped his head and kissed her possessively. "Is that okay with you?"

Annie nodded, too dazed to protest. At his request, she even gave him a key in case she was still at the training center when he arrived after work. When the front door closed behind him, she walked slowly back to feed Ebony and clean up the kitchen.

What was she going to do? Dane was aggravating, exciting, compelling. She couldn't resist him. In her heart, she knew she'd said a fond goodbye to her memories of Nick the first time Dane kissed her...because she was falling in love with him.

She should be happy. She should be ecstatic! He wanted to marry her. He desired her.

But he didn't love her, didn't believe in love. He'd been clear about that. And worse yet, he didn't want her love.

On the other hand, he was offering her a second chance at children of her own. She had no doubt he'd be a devoted family man. But could she live without love?

She had three private lessons scheduled that afternoon and the first one ran late. That backed up the other two and she got home later than she'd planned. She was dirty and she smelled like dog, so she opted for a quick shower before Dane arrived.

She was toweling herself dry when the phone rang. Heading into the bedroom, she flopped across the bed to reach the receiver.

It was a potential client calling for information and she had to dig in the drawer of the bedside table for a pencil and pad to take down the lady's address.

"I'll be happy to send you our brochure," she told the woman. "It has a list of classes and times in it and you can come observe a few times before you make any decisions about enrolling your dog." She was just hanging up the receiver when the bedroom door swung open behind her.

Annie jumped. Twisting her head around, she saw Dane framed in the doorway. She felt horribly self-conscious, wrapped only in the bath towel she'd thrown around herself when the telephone rang, but at the same time she was aware of her near nakedness in a deeply feminine way.

When her gaze met Dane's she saw that he was equally aware of what she wasn't wearing. A thrill of excitement flashed through her, tightening her nipples into hard pebbles. His face flushed and his nostrils flared slightly, as if scenting her arousal. She felt a heavy, throbbing sensation deep in her abdomen and she simply lay waiting, unable to make herself move as he strode to the edge of the bed in three long strides.

He'd looked in the kitchen and all through the downstairs before coming up to the bedroom. When he had opened the door, he had been stunned to find Annie lying on her stomach across the bed with only a small towel for cover. He could see the rounded swell of her satiny bottom and the enticing shadows of feminine folds between her legs. Instantly, he was so hard he ached and when she squirmed slightly, he knew he had to have her. Approaching the bed, he held her blue gaze as he deliberately unzipped his pants and popped the snap at the waistband.

The small sounds echoed in the silence of the sunny room. Her eyes rounded even more as he pushed his pants and his briefs down in one motion and reached for her. She drew in a sobbing breath as his hands closed around her ankles and then he was pulling her back over the bed, separating her legs on either side of his lean hips until the pulsing life of his manhood was eagerly nudging the soft curling hair inside her thighs. He bent over her, pulling the towel away and dropping it on the floor, sliding both hands under her to gently rub and squeeze her nipples and palming the generous weight of her breasts in satisfaction.

Annie cried out and her back arched as she clenched fistfuls of the quilt. He slid one big hand down her stomach, burrowing underneath her shifting hips to circle the tiny bud of flesh he found with a sure, intimate touch that had her gasping. She bucked wildly beneath him and he groaned, unable to control his body a minute longer as the clasp of her flexing buttocks held and released him rhythmically.

Frantically, he tore open the small packet still lying untouched on the nightstand and donned its contents. He had intended to turn her over, to suck at those pretty breasts and kiss the full lip that he could see caught between her teeth as she turned her head from side to side, but instead he grasped her thighs, pressing his aroused length into the slick moisture of her depths, inexorably filling her as she continued to rub her soft bottom against the black hair that bloomed at the juncture of his legs. He withdrew frantically and began a driving rhythm that quickly brought him to the edge, but he wanted her to be with him, so again he found

the tight button below the triangle of copper curls and stim-
ulated her.

She was so wildly sensitive that at the first touch of his
finger the storm broke and her body jerked in ecstasy. Feeling the inner clenching that signaled her release was all he
needed and his own body followed her to a pulsing fulfillment that drove him more deeply into her with each forceful
spasm.

Gradually the world stopped spinning and Annie became
aware of her surroundings again. Her cheek was pressed into
the quilt that covered the bed. Dane had collapsed on her
and he groaned as she purposely tightened her inner muscles
in an unseen caress.

"Don't you ever know when to quit?" he teased. Gently
withdrawing from her, he found his feet just long enough
to flop onto the bed beside her and pull her across his chest.
Her long hair clung to the sweat-dampened muscles of his
stomach as she angled her head to look up at him.

"Apparently not," she answered his joking query. Then
she looked at him again, shaking her head and smiling,
though her cheeks were pink. "Do you realize you're still
wearing a tie?"

He laughed. "A few minutes ago, I had more important
things on my mind than my attire." Then he rolled to a
sitting position, effortlessly righting her to sit beside him on
the edge of the rumpled bed and she could almost feel the
restless energy radiating from him. "Let's get dressed and
go hunting for engagement rings. I'd like to have one on
your finger as soon as possible. We could look at wedding
rings, as well. I've decided I'd like to wear one, too."

Annie glanced at him from beneath her lashes. He
sounded as confident and self-assured as usual, but he was
watching her with a surprisingly vulnerable look in his blue
eyes...almost as if he was afraid she would say no.

She took a deep breath. There was no point in making
him wait for her answer. She might have reservations about

the wisdom of marriage to Dane, but she loved him…so much that she'd take him with no love if that was the only way she could have him.

"All right," she said. "I'll marry you. Let's go look for rings."

The following fortnight was a whirlwind of activity. Once he'd talked her into marrying him, Dane seemed determined to mesh their lives as quickly as possible. Each evening when Annie returned from her night classes, he'd moved a few more of his possessions into the house they'd decided to keep. His dog's crate was installed next to Ebony's and Dane and Annie spent several evenings catching the late news with the two black dogs stretched out on the floor at their feet. And when the news ended, he carried her to their bed and made passionate love to her every single night, worshiping her body with a single-minded intensity that reassured her that this decision was right for them both.

He produced a marriage license and set up a time for the civil ceremony they'd agreed on at Oak Park Courthouse. Joe, Jeanne and Patrick would be their only witnesses and it was Dane's suggestion to postpone honeymoon plans until the Christmas holidays so that Annie's classes wouldn't be disrupted.

On the day of the wedding, they dressed together in the big bedroom they were sharing now.

Dane fumbled with the hook and eye at the back of her pale yellow silk suit for several seconds before he finally succeeded in maneuvering the tiny catch into place. "There." He dropped a kiss onto the back of her neck beneath the coil into which she'd pinned her hair. "Are you ready to go?"

Annie turned to face him, loving the way he'd brushed his dark curls down and the serious blue eyes he turned on her.

"I'm ready." She picked up her matching purse, then

something else caught her eye, a final detail she'd over-looked in the mad rush of the past few weeks. Walking back to her dresser, she picked up the picture of Nick that stood there in a small silver frame.

Gently, she touched the smiling features, so hard to recall with clarity anymore. She'd loved him with all her heart, would always carry the memories with her, but now her heart belonged to Dane. Silently, she said goodbye as she opened a drawer and placed the frame facedown inside. Dane was watching her as she turned to him once more. "I'm ready," she said again.

He nodded, coming across the room to place both hands lightly on her shoulders. "You won't regret this marriage," he said in a deep tone. "I promise you that I'll take care of you and our family."

And he would, she was sure. He'd be a wonderful hus-band and father. And if he couldn't love her as she'd once been loved, at least she'd have the pleasure of giving him children they could share. As surely as she knew her love for him would never die, she knew he would love their children with every fiber of his soul.

On a Saturday one week after their wedding, Dane met her at the training center at noon. She had a class at ten and another at eleven on Saturday, but they'd arranged to go into Chicago after her second class ended.

He walked into the big room where she held classes just as the last few students were leaving.

"See you next week, Mrs. Hamilton," called one of the students. A primitive surge of satisfaction ran through him at the name—he still had trouble believing she was really his except when she lay beside him in the big bed at night. They were going to Peoria tomorrow to have dinner with some of his best friends. They'd been a little miffed that he hadn't told them he was getting married until after the fact, but he'd been afraid, in some part of his mind that he barely dared to acknowledge, that she might change her mind at the last minute. A woman had made a fool of him once—never again.

"I'm almost ready." Annie gave him an intimate smile that warmed him and turned him on at the same time. He'd forgotten how satisfying being married could be. Or perhaps he'd never really known it before, with Amanda. He couldn't recall ever feeling the inner glow that Annie's smile produced, the sense of well-being that merely holding her in the night or kissing her at the door gave him. He could barely remember Amanda anymore, but he knew that most of what had driven their relationship had been based, purely and simply, on sex. And when that had worn off, they hadn't had much in common. They hadn't even really liked each other all that well, if he were honest.

He couldn't imagine ever tiring of Annie in any way.

Of course, tiring of her would entail seeing a lot more of her than he currently did, he thought, only half-amused. In the month since he'd moved in with her, into the house they referred to now as "theirs," he'd realized just how much of Annie's time was consumed by her business.

A lot. She taught classes Tuesday through Friday evenings as well as several more during those days, and these two on Saturday morning. Although Sunday and Monday were technically her days off, he knew she often set up private lessons on Monday. It was a bad combination with his typical day, which ran from early morning until four-thirty in the afternoon with occasional evening meetings.

Oh, well. He'd known what he was getting into when he'd married her. Children would complicate things, but when kids came along, they'd find a good nanny and work out the details when the need arose.

Annie came out of the office then with her jacket and a purse. She usually wore jeans to teach, but today she'd dressed up a little since he'd offered to take her out to lunch.

She looked pretty, if a little tired, in her pink sweater and gray slacks.

They drove down to South Chicago first, to a renovated warehouse that sold salvaged grillwork and decorative embellishments. Wandering through the place was fascinating. There were literally thousands of pieces of grillwork, none matching and only a few large enough to fence a very small yard. Annie finally chose a piece with cherubs welded into the grill to have fashioned into a gate to hang between the stone pillars that led to the enclosed backyard. On the way out, a stone urn caught his eye and Annie was easily convinced that it would look wonderful on the front steps.

As they headed for the car, staggering under the weight of their purchases, someone hailed him.

"Hey, Dane! Doing a little shopping?"

Dane recognized William Machlowski, the head of computer operations at the bank. He headed toward them, towing his wife...Cheryl or something like that. He vaguely remembered meeting her at a cocktail party weeks ago.

William bustled over and Dane set down the urn and the grillwork in time to have his hand pumped enthusiastically. "See you made some purchases. We're down here to look at a griffin Sherry insists we have to have. You do remember my wife?" He indicated the blonde at his side.

Dane nodded politely. "Nice to see you again. I believe you've met my wife, Annie."

Annie smiled. "Hello."

"Hel-*lo!* And congratulations on snaring this hunk! Charlene was absolutely livid when she heard." The blonde giggled.

"Actually," Dane said, "it was the other way around. I had to beg her to marry me."

"Oh, you." Sherry slapped his forearm playfully. "Isn't he silly, Will?" Then she looked back at Annie again. "This is just perfect timing. I was going to call you this week. We have an opening in our weekly girls' bridge club and we decided you'd be the perfect one to fill it.''

There was an awkward pause, then Annie said, "I'm so sorry, but I don't play bridge.''

"You don't play...*everyone* plays bridge. Well, no matter, I suppose we can teach you.'' Sherry sounded truly perplexed by such a problem. "Where *have* you been living, dear?''

He wanted to laugh aloud at the expression on Annie's face. She clearly couldn't figure out how to extricate herself from the woman's insistence. He couldn't imagine being condemned to play bridge with Sherry and her friends every week.

"She doesn't have the time for card games." Dane wrapped his free arm around Annie. "My wife owns a business that takes up most of her days, and I'm afraid I want all of her free time to be devoted to me.''

William laughed too heartily. "Sounds good to me.''

Dane felt a little sorry for the man. He couldn't see Sherry Machlowski devoting time to anyone other than herself.

"Well, if you're sure...'' William's wife clearly thought Annie was missing a great opportunity.

"Dane's right. I am too busy. But it was thoughtful of you to think of me.''

Annie's voice rang with sincerity but he knew relief was just beneath the surface.

"We have to be going,'' Dane said. "Good seeing you both.''

"You, too,'' Sherry echoed. As her husband led her away, she said to Annie, "Just be sure you don't let your business interfere with your wifely duties, dear.''

As soon as the other couple were out of earshot, he turned to Annie with a big grin. "Let's have lunch. Then we'll go home and you can brush up on your 'wifely duties.''"

They drove down to the Art Institute for lunch in the enclosed garden room. The weather was tricky at this time of year, but the day was warm for autumn and the restaurant was open. The classical notes of a piano sonata floated across the air as they were seated.

Beautiful fall flowers had been planted in the tubs and beds near the tables, but Annie barely noticed her surroundings. She ordered absently and sat silently as Dane did the same.

She thought he was enjoying the atmosphere and the music, when he abruptly reached across the table and clasped her hand.

"What's wrong?"

Startled, she looked up. He was looking at her expectantly and she knew if she tried to dodge the issue, he'd worry her until she gave in, anyway.

She sighed. "Seeing Sherry again got me thinking about things I've managed to ignore since we got married. But I can't forget them forever. Sooner or later, you're going to be sorry you married me."

Dane looked dumbfounded and uncomprehending. "What do you think you've done that's going to make me change the way I feel about our marriage?"

"It's not what I've done...." She sighed again. He really didn't get it. "It's more like what I don't do."

"What you don't do?"

"Yes." She leaned forward. "That conversation earlier reminded me of how inept I am socially. I was never good at the stuff lawyers' wives are supposed to do and now I'm married to a banker and I'm even worse!"

Dane looked perplexed. When she would have pulled her hand away, he held on with a grip she couldn't break. "What kind of stuff are lawyers' and bankers' wives supposed to do?"

"You know." How could he be so obtuse? "Entertaining. Chitchat." Misery swamped her. "I'm terrible at talking to people I don't know. I don't want to embarrass you.

And what if your bosses are looking for a man with a wife who can handle all those social functions when they're trying to decide who to promote?''

Dane was looking at her as if she'd just flown in from another planet. He let her hand slide from his this time when she tugged. "Let me get this straight. You're afraid that you could hurt my chances for advancement if you don't play the games that the other wives do?''

That was it in a nutshell, though he'd missed a few points. She nodded.

"Annie..." Dane lifted his shoulders in a gesture of total male frustration. "That's the craziest thing I have ever heard. I don't think you have to worry about affecting my job. Besides, you socialized just fine with Lilith at the cocktail party, if I recall correctly.''

"Only because she liked to talk about dogs.''

"So what? You talked to her, didn't you?" Then his blue eyes sharpened. "You think I want you to play cards with William's wife and her friends?" He waved a hand dismissively. "Forget it. You might come home with that manic giggle.''

Annie almost laughed but she was still too upset. "I'm afraid I might embarrass you,'' she mumbled.

"Sweetheart—'' Dane reached across the table again and took both of her hands "—you'll never embarrass me. Every man we meet is too busy noticing how beautiful you are, and the wives are too busy noticing their husbands noticing to be thinking about what you are or aren't saying.''

"I'm not beautiful,'' she said automatically.

"You are to me,'' he responded. "Now quit worrying about something so trivial. I don't care if you hate to socialize. I'm not wild about it, either. We'll just make sure we do as little of it as possible.''

Their meal arrived then and she let the conversation drop. His words had reassured her, but she still worried that she might be a burden to his career. Then another thought struck her, less palatable even than those that were worrying her.

Dane hadn't married her for her social prowess. He'd married her for her reproductive capabilities and for that alone. She knew he wanted children as soon as possible. Glancing across the table, she watched him tearing into the double-decker sandwich he'd ordered. Just then, he looked up, and catching her staring, he shot her a wink and a grin.

Her heart squeezed in pain. She loved him so much. When had he come to be her whole world? And was there any chance that he would ever come to love her?

On the way out of the Art Institute, they walked through a room displaying a medieval collection. Dane seemed to want to linger as they examined suits of mail, lances for jousting and horribly heavy-looking shields of decorated metal.

"This one might fit you," he told her as they marveled over one suit of armor.

"Men certainly were much smaller a century ago," she said.

"Funny the things you learn as an adult that destroy the romance," he responded.

"Such as?"

"Just what you said about men being smaller. When I was a kid, I was fascinated by the Arthurian legends. One of my foster mothers was always reading me stories about the Knights of the Round Table and their chivalrous deeds."

"Camelot."

"The perfect court for the perfect king."

Annie smiled at him. "I used to think of my marriage to Nick as Camelot. I haven't thought about that in a long time."

He shook his head, gazing absently at the armor. "You can't imagine how I envy you those memories."

"Well," she said, shrugging, ill at ease and sorry she'd

brought up the topic of first marriages. "Nick and I never really fought. I don't know why."

"My ex-wife and I fought enough for two lifetimes."

She was painfully aware that he'd told her next to nothing about his past with the first woman he'd married. She'd been curious but the opportunity for such a discussion had never presented itself before. "What kind of things did you fight about?"

No answer.

She glanced at his face and was immediately chilled by the closed look he wore. Dane was usually so open and even-tempered—

"We fought about a lot of things." His tone was mild and his face, when she looked again, was composed into its normal expression. But something final in his tone warned her that this particular line of inquiry was finished.

She wondered what he'd suffered at the hands of his first wife that could make him look like that.

Seven

Annie's schedule was unchanged during the next week, except that she was a little busier than usual. It was the first week to register students for the winter-session classes and she had dozens of applications to check, organize into the proper session and file.

In addition to that, she had a touch of the flu.

It wasn't a severe case, because she was able to function. But all week long, she suffered through nausea that at times made her feel she might have to dash for a bathroom. The funny thing was, she felt pretty good every morning. But by the time her classes began in the evening, she felt distinctly queasy, so much so that she couldn't eat dinner for three nights running. The other nights, she managed to get down some soup that she'd made over the weekend and reheated when she was too busy to cook.

On Thursday, she had a Puppy Kindergarten class at four o'clock. Dane had gotten in the habit of bringing in sandwiches from the nearby deli about five-fifteen and they shared a meal and a few private moments before the Basic students from the class he was taking began to straggle in just before six.

This particular Thursday, Dane came breezing in as the last of the puppies was leaving.

"Hi." He greeted her with a quick kiss, which turned to concern when he got a look at her face. "You still aren't feeling well, are you?"

"No." She sank into her office chair. "Is it that obvious?"

"Other than the fact that your face is green, no."

She cast him a small smile. "Very funny. I hope I shake this soon. How was your day?"

Dane drew the sandwiches from the bag. "My day was interesting. We're considering a loan to a guy who owns a pretzel factory and I got a personal tour." He stuck two straws in the lemonade he'd brought and unwrapped the sandwiches. "Do you want pastrami or—Annie!"

The sight of the sandwich had done it. Her stomach, which hadn't been happy at all since about three o'clock, decided to rebel. Bolting out of her chair, she raced for the bathroom.

She barely made it. As she knelt on the floor in front of the toilet, Dane came in behind her. Silently he took a paper towel from the dispenser, wet it and handed it to her, then flushed the toilet.

"Thanks." She felt too ill to be embarrassed as she accepted the hand he extended to help her to her feet.

"Have you considered that you might be pregnant?"

She stared at him, openmouthed, calculating in her head. "I sincerely doubt it...oh!" She *had* missed a period, come to think of it, but she hadn't even thought about it in the turmoil of adjusting to married life. "I'm a little late," she admitted. "But it's way too early to tell."

"Not for a blood test it isn't."

Hope and excitement blossomed within her. "Yes," she said slowly. "I guess you're right."

She called the doctor's office first thing the next morning and the receptionist told her she could come in right away before she ate any breakfast.

As the woman at the doctor's office had instructed, Annie dutifully collected a urine sample. But right after Dane left for work, a disappointingly familiar sensation warned her that she was beginning her menstrual cycle. The light spotting she felt was only the beginning.

Her disappointment was intense as she changed her panties, more so than the occasion warranted. If she had been pregnant, it would have been from the one time before they were married—nearly five weeks ago now, wouldn't it? They had plenty of time to start a family.

If only Dane wasn't waiting to hear some news…she almost canceled the doctor's appointment, but she decided to go, anyway. Just to be sure.

The receptionist slid back the glass panel above the counter with a cheerful smile when Annie approached the desk in the obstetrician's office. "Hello. May I help you?"

Annie held up her little glass jar with a sheepish smile. "My name is Anne Elizabeth Hamilton. I'm here for a pregnancy test."

The receptionist took the jar and in a few moments, Annie was given a blood test. She explained to the nurse who was attending her that she had started her period, but when the nurse heard how late she was, she said, "Well, it can't hurt to be sure."

Annie fidgeted nervously when the woman left the room. On the wall was a chart showing a cross section of a pregnant woman with a fetus curled in her womb. Amazing. Another chart detailed how the tiny life grew, at what week a given body part budded on the tiny torso, when the baby's eyes opened and when it began to swallow. Yet a third chart listed types of birth control—not something she foresaw needing in the near future, she thought with a warm glow. It was nice not to have to worry about—

The door opened. The nurse had a slight smile on her face.

"Congratulations, Mrs. Hamilton. Your body might not have figured it out quite yet, but you are definitely pregnant."

"I am? That's wonderful!" Annie closed her eyes, feeling a thrill rush through her. Then her eyes popped open again. "But what about the bleeding?"

"Some women have a little spotting early on," the nurse told her as she set up a prenatal conference for the following month. "It's nothing to worry about unless it persists or you have a heavy flow. If that happens, call us right away. Otherwise—" she patted Annie's hand and smiled "—we'll see you in about a month."

At nine-twenty she was walking out of the doctor's office in a daze, clutching a fistful of booklets and handouts on prenatal care.

Dane was in his office dictating a letter when he saw Annie coming down the hall. She had only been to the bank one time since they'd married. This time, the smile on her pretty face told him everything he needed to know.

Completely forgetting the secretary, he leaped to his feet and met her in the hall, sweeping her into his arms.

"Good news?"

"Good news," she confirmed.

He threw back his head and laughed aloud, spinning her around. "I can't believe it! I'm going to be a father! We're going to be parents!"

Several of his co-workers had stuck their heads out of their office doors in response to the commotion; over Annie's head he could almost see one or two of them doing a fast mental count. Who cared? His wife was going to have a baby!

"Congratulations," said his secretary, rising as he reentered his office with his arm around Annie. She grinned. "We'll finish this later."

He nodded, his attention on his wife. *His pregnant wife!* Delight streaked through him, followed immediately by concern for Annie. "How are you feeling? What did the doctor say? When is the baby due?"

"Whoa!" She held up a hand in self-defense, ticking off her answers on her fingers. "I feel okay...for the moment. I didn't see the doctor, but I did speak with a nurse who made an appointment for my first checkup in four weeks. And—" she looked momentarily bewildered "—I don't know when the baby is due!"

Dane laughed again. "Well, I can probably give you a rough estimate, seeing as how I was in on the creation of this little miracle." He kissed her, then kissed her again more deeply when she responded to him the way she always did, her body curling into his, the fine electricity they generated together zipping through him, stirring male instincts and male flesh in unmistakable signs of desire.

He damn near forgot where he was when she did that. Letting her go, he hooked his foot around a chair. "Here, sit down. You shouldn't be on your feet any more than you have to be."

Annie's eyes slowly focused and sharpened with amusement. "Don't tell me you're going to be a worrywart. Women have been having babies for centuries and a lot of them worked harder than I ever will." She dropped a sheaf of papers and pamphlets on his desk. "This is all about early nutrition and fetal development and exercise and birthing class options—you name it, I have it. Here."

She handed him a little cardboard square with a movable wheel attached to it. "You wanted to know our due date. That'll tell us."

Intrigued, he flipped the little gadget over and read the directions on the back, then looked over it at her. "Okay.

When was your last…oh." He felt rather foolish. "You haven't had…since…it was that first time, wasn't it?"

She nodded, blushing only faintly. "I think so."

He knelt beside the chair. "That means we're going to be parents in—" he consulted the little wheel "—July."

"July." She whispered the word as if it were a prayer.

He looked at her shining eyes. "You are the most marvelous woman in the world," he said, putting his arms around her again. "I can't believe I found you."

Annie floated through the next few days on a cloud of happiness heightened by Dane's delight in her condition. The spotting had stopped just as the nurse had indicated it would and she didn't tell him about it at all.

Jeanne called and they hashed over physical symptoms, baby names and labor and delivery information. Annie started a list, at Jeanne's urging, of all the things she and Dane would need for the baby.

She continued to feel queasy in the evenings. She discovered that if she ate like a horse in the morning and didn't eat anything after about two p.m., the nausea was mild enough for her to get through her early-evening classes. She enlisted one of her most experienced dog handlers to oversee the three late classes on Tuesday, Wednesday and Friday and temporarily stopped attending the Thursday-night meetings of the canine club. Fortunately, her eight-week Basic classes had just graduated and wouldn't resume until January.

One evening after she came home from her late class, Dane came into the den where she was lying on the couch watching an early edition of the news.

"How are you feeling?" he asked, settling himself on the edge of the cushions, against her hip.

"Pretty good. Maybe my hormones are adjusting at last." She smiled at him, loving the solicitous manner with which he treated her. It might only be because she was carrying his child, but it allowed her to pretend that she was special to him, that he cared about *her* rather than simply about her condition.

"I have an ulterior motive," he warned her.

"Oh?" Her expression was full of coy innocence. She placed her hand over his where it rested lightly on her abdomen. He'd made love to her often since they'd learned about the baby, but he'd been as careful and gentle as if she were made of the most fragile porcelain. She found she missed the rough, urgent mastery with which he'd taken her before he learned about the baby.

"Not that," he said indulgently. "Though I'm not saying the idea doesn't have merit."

She grinned, feeling sassy. "I thought it was a pretty good idea, myself. But what's your 'ulterior motive'?"

Dane's face lost its contentment. "I have to go out for dinner next Tuesday evening. Business meeting I couldn't wriggle out of."

Since he'd learned of her pregnancy, he'd rarely gone out in the evening.

"That's okay." And it was. She'd miss spending time with him, but she didn't want to interfere with his job.

"Trouble is, the guy's bringing his wife. I told him you worked on Tuesday evenings, but I think he was expecting me to try to get you to join us."

She was silent. What did he want her to say? Was he expecting her to cancel her classes or get a substitute? Guilt rose. She had known when she married him that she wasn't the kind of wife he needed. "I'm sorry I can't join you," she said in a near whisper.

"Annie, look at me." Dane's voice was firm and she realized she'd been avoiding his gaze. "Don't be sorry. I wouldn't have told you at all but I didn't want you to worry about where I was or who I was with." He turned his hand over beneath hers and squeezed it. "Actually, I wish I had your excuse. The guy's a crotchety old geezer and I'd have begged off if he weren't on the board of directors.''

On the board of directors! She felt worse than ever, but he was clearly trying to make her feel better and she didn't want him to worry. ''Sounds like I'm getting off lucky.'' She took his hand and carried it to her breast. ''Now that that's out of the way, what were we discussing?''

''I don't remember.'' But his hand moved to shape her breast as if he couldn't help himself.

She stretched, enjoying the beginnings of arousal produced by the warmth and nearness of him and the stroking sensation at her breast, putting her fears into the back of her mind. ''Is it coming back to you yet?''

''It is. Are you sure it's okay?'' At her nod, his blue eyes grew intense and heavy-lidded. ''Hold that thought.'' In one quick, smooth motion, he was on his feet, calling the dogs. They staggered up from their relaxed positions on the floor near Annie and he called them to their crates on the enclosed porch.

''Sorry, girls,'' she heard him say to them. ''There are just some times when a cold, wet nose isn't lovable.''

He turned around after he closed the back door, planning to retrace his steps through the darkened kitchen to rejoin Annie in the den. But as he moved, he bumped squarely into her standing right behind him. He automatically thrust out his hands to catch her and she stepped into his arms, pressing herself against him and lifting her face for his kiss.

He was more than willing to oblige. His body responded immediately to the feel of her warm curves and he slipped his hands under her bottom and lifted her, fitting her more intimately against him. He thrust his tongue into her mouth, kissing her deeply for long minutes, then he trailed his lips across her cheek and lifted his head to inspect her face in the shadows.

If she knew what it did to him when she got that dreamy, absorbed expression on her face, she'd have an incredibly powerful weapon at her disposal. He was impatient to touch her, too impatient to carry her all the way upstairs. Pivoting, he set her down on the edge of the counter, freeing his hands to deal with the tiny buttons that ran down the front of her blouse. He couldn't wait to touch those beautiful breasts. As the blouse parted beneath his fingers, he realized she had pulled it free from her skirt and started working the buttons open from the bottom. That aroused him even more and he became supremely aware of his hardened flesh pressing against her through the barriers of their clothing. He was standing between her legs, which she had wrapped around his hips when he set her on the counter. He surged once against her, a temporary cure for what ailed him, and then she was yanking her blouse and bra off and pulling his head down toward the tempting mounds of creamy flesh, tipped with hard buttons which were little more than darker-colored shadows in the dim room.

She was driving him crazy! Although Annie never failed to excite him beyond reason, she had been a fairly passive lover throughout the recent weeks of their passion, letting him take the lead. She was so beautifully responsive that he hadn't realized until now that she had never displayed any aggression in their lovemaking. Her frantic need to have him touching her breasts inflamed him even more and he groaned as he palmed the cool slopes, lifting one ivory mound to suck strongly at its peak.

She gasped and arched toward him, damp hands tunneling through his hair to pull him even closer. He continued to suckle her and the ache in his loins grew to an enormous throbbing. Rocking her buttocks from side to side, she shifted repeatedly over his stiffened shaft. Her hands moved from his hair to tear in haste at the buttons of his shirt, tugging it out of the way and pulling his undershirt up underneath his arms so that she could touch the muscled planes of skin covered with whorls of black curls. She found his nipples and brushed her thumbs over them until they were as hard and tight as her own.

He hadn't intended for it to go this far this fast but the need that rose to claw at him like a living thing wouldn't be appeased. Forgetting their surroundings, he lifted handfuls of her cotton skirt out of his way until all that remained between her legs was a swatch of lacy panties. He tugged them swiftly down, moving away only long enough to remove them altogether and then he was back, the tender skin of her inner thighs deliciously hot and exciting against the exposed flesh of his belly.

Unable to resist the lure of her satin heat, he trailed his fingers down over her warm, soft belly, not yet swollen with the evidence of his child growing within her. Soft flesh gave way to a cloud of silky curls shielding the very heart of her desire; with a groan, he curled his fingers farther down, tracing her repeatedly until moisture slicked the humid flesh beneath his questing fingertips.

She was like an untamed mare in his arms, twisting and plunging as he entered her with nothing more than his fingers and he caught her sobs of breath in his own hungry mouth. Her hands slipped down between them and he felt her ripping at his belt and the fastenings of his pants...then glorious freedom as his erect manhood burst free of the confining cloth. She surrounded him with hot, silken fingers before he could draw in enough oxygen to protest, to halt her before she sent him over the edge of the chasm on which his self-control was precariously perched—and then it was too late. He could only groan deep in his throat as she caressed him at a steadily increasing pace, throwing his head back and clenching his teeth as her thumb slicked over the tip of his straining flesh, spreading the moisture that she found there.

Like someone demented, he quickly tore her hands away, feeling the end overtaking him in great bursts of thrusting power. He was out of control as he grasped her slim hips and lifted her onto him, exhaling in relief as he felt her warm, tight depths accept him totally, taking his pent-up pulsations as he spilled his seed. At the same time, he pushed her body to a quivering crescendo that had her screaming before she arched repeatedly into his big body in her own shivering, pulsing climax.

As his body relaxed, occasional frissons of aftershock quaked through him. His legs abruptly felt like jelly and he slid to the floor, still holding her against him. He collapsed flat on his back and she fell forward, using his massive proportions as a pillow.

Neither of them stirred for a long moment. Finally, Annie drew in a deep breath and exhaled. "Shall we sleep here?"

He snorted. "Easy for you to say. I'm the one lying on the floor." He raised a large hand and caressed her bottom gently. "Let's go to bed."

Dane had gone downstairs to let the dogs out when she awoke the next morning. She turned on her side and hugged his pillow to her. Until recently, she'd been an early riser. Now Dane made breakfast for her instead of the other way around. The exhaustion she'd heard so much about was taking its toll on her and she often went back to sleep again after he left in the morning. Her bladder also was letting her know that her body was changing, she thought in resigned amusement as she threw back the covers.

It wasn't until she went into the bathroom that she discovered she was spotting again. And the blood was a bright, frightening red this time.

Terror seized her. Jeanne had never mentioned anything like this, so it couldn't be normal. She wanted this baby so much—was she losing it? And Dane. He would be devastated.

Coming back out of the bathroom, she threw on her clothing. The doctor's office opened at eight and she intended to be there.

Dane came in as she was slipping on her shoes. "Wow! She stirs." Then he caught sight of her face. "Honey, what's the matter?"

She read in his eyes all the fear she was feeling as she told him about the spotting.

"Do you think we...what we did...hurt it?"

"I don't know," she answered miserably. "It shouldn't have. The nurse told me intercourse was fine."

"I'm coming to the doctor's with you."

It was a little thing, but having him with her made her feel so much better. They arrived at the office promptly at eight and when Annie explained the problem, they were shown directly into an examining room. After the examination, the doctor, whom she'd used since she was married to Nick, was matter-of-fact.

"I don't feel much enlargement in the uterus but that's not unusual this early in a pregnancy, especially if we've miscalculated the due date and you're not as far along as we think."

"But is the bleeding normal?" Dane cut right to what was worrying her, as well.

The doctor hesitated. "It's not necessarily *abnormal,* although continued spotting wouldn't be a good sign." He pulled Annie's sweater down gently and helped her to sit up on the examining table. "Right now there isn't much we can do except wait. The first trimester is the time when the embryo is establishing itself in the womb. If there is any reason for that not to happen, this is when it occurs. It's simply Nature's way of ensuring that most babies born are healthy and normal."

"So we should just wait?"

The doctor smiled. "I said there's little we can do, not nothing. I want you—" he turned to Annie "—to stay off your feet as much as possible. Rest until you think you can't stand to stay in bed another minute, lie on a couch if you can. If you have to get up, find a chair as soon as possible. And no exercise. No walking, even.''

Annie was stunned. What about her business...? But she wouldn't take even the smallest chance if it might endanger the baby. ''All right.''

The doctor nodded approvingly. ''Let's hope a little extra rest will set everything right. But if you have any more spotting, even a tiny bit, contact me immediately. We'll set up an ultrasound to see what's going on in there.''

She felt much better after talking to the doctor, although her head was whirling with the arrangements she'd have to make with the canine center. Dane drove her home and settled her on the couch. He'd called in to the bank to tell them he was taking the morning off.

As he returned from the kitchen with a large glass of water and a plate of grapes and vegetables he'd prepared for her, she said, ''This will speed up my timetable for scaling back the business, but the more I think about it, the more comfortable I feel with it.''

''Scaling back the business...?'' he echoed.

''Yes.'' She smiled and shrugged. ''I'd have had to do it when the baby was born, anyway.''

Dane set the glass on a coaster and settled himself on the edge of the sofa. ''Annie, are you sure you want to do this?'' His eyes were very blue and his handsome features were set in serious lines. ''I don't expect you to give up anything you don't want to. I know we haven't talked about it, but I assumed we might hire someone to care for the baby when both of us were working, maybe even a live-in nanny. For that matter, we could hire someone who would go with you to work so the baby could be near you.'' He placed his hands on her shoulders. ''I want you to be happy.''

How can I be happy without your love? It was the first thought that flashed through her mind and she immediately dropped her gaze from his, afraid he might read the naked longing there. She shouldn't be discontented, she lectured herself. Dane might not love her but he cared about her. They had a good, solid marriage and this baby was something that delighted them both.

"I am happy," she said softly. "This baby means so much to me. I don't want to be one of those career mothers who barely sees her infant. I want to be there for all those firsts." She placed her hands on his strong forearms. "I enjoy what I've created with the canine center, but I'm going to enjoy being a mother more."

Dane's expression relaxed. "You sound like you mean it."

"I do!"

"I know that now. I didn't want you to think I expected you to give up something you loved."

Inside her, a wall gave way. The insecurities that had plagued her since the earliest days of her first marriage, the fears that she wasn't the right kind of wife for a man whose business included an ability to socialize, were swept away on a rising tide of understanding.

Dane truly didn't consider her to be a social negative. He wanted her to be happy. He didn't care what kind of work she did or if she even worked at all. And he was sure that she wouldn't be a burden to his career, or he wouldn't be so insistent in his determination to be sure she was making the right decision with her canine center.

On Tuesday of next week, she was lying on the couch with her feet up when Dane came through the door.

"Hello." She barely got the greeting out before he leaned down to kiss her. Immediately, she forgot all about anything else she'd planned to say as his lips molded hers in sweet demand. It was going to be a long four weeks, she thought, until the next checkup. One of the additional things the doctor had recommended they do was suspend their lovemaking until her next checkup.

"Hello." He pulled his head back a fraction. "I missed you today."

Her heart leaped at the husky words. "I missed you, too." She knew he was frustrated by their circumstances from the hungry kisses he gave her every evening, but for the first time, she allowed herself to hope for something more. Could it be possible that he was beginning to love her the way she loved him?

As he slipped an arm under her back and another under her knees, she circled his neck with her arms. "It's not time for bed yet. Where are you taking me?"

"I have something to show you." He carried her effortlessly through the kitchen, onto the back porch and out to the driveway.

"Where's your car?" She was confused. In the driveway, where he usually parked the little white sports car, was a burgundy sedan. The metallic finish gleamed and she saw that it was so new the price sheet was still tacked to the window. "What's this?"

He laughed. "A car. Our car, to be precise. Like it?"

"But..." She still didn't get it. "What happened to the Jaguar?"

"I traded it in," he said promptly.

"What?" She twisted in his arms to stare at him. "But, Dane, you loved that car! Why did you trade it for this?"

He laughed and kissed her forehead. "Don't worry on my account, sweetheart. I did enjoy owning the Jag, but it was just a car. We need a family car now in addition to the van." He walked toward the pretty vehicle. "Want to sit in the driver's seat and check it out?"

As he set her gently on the burgundy leather seat, he kissed her again, lingering for a moment to nuzzle her cheek.

Regret seeped through her. "I'm sorry we can't—I can't—would you like me to...? Oh, forget it!"

"It's okay," he said softly, smiling at her embarrassment.

"I enjoy kissing and touching you. It doesn't mean we have to make love each time I do. I can wait until you're with me again."

The hope grew a little stronger within her breast. Even though they'd married for reasons that had nothing to do with love, there was a chance that their marriage could lead to love. The words nearly charged out of her mouth then, *I love you*. But she held them back. She didn't want to make him feel uncomfortable. And they had the rest of their lives to share their love.

Eight

Another week passed. She hired additional help at the dog center and planned to cut back the courses offered in the winter session. She already rented the building to the Dog Guide Puppy Club and a local cat fanciers club on a monthly basis, but she ran an ad in the paper to attract other groups who might be hunting for a meeting place. Although the classes she was keeping would still cover her expenses, she hated to see the building stand empty much of the time.

The following Saturday, Dane carried her down to the couch, which had become her regular resting place. He allowed her to sit up for a while in the morning since she'd been lying flat all night and she propped her feet up as the doctor had requested. Dane immediately left the room, and she assumed he'd gone to make breakfast. But he returned with a folder, which he dropped in her lap. "Here. Look through these while I get us some breakfast." He grinned and winked at her as he turned to leave.

Wondering what had produced his high spirits, she

opened the folder. Several catalogs spilled out. Catalogs? Curious now, she picked up one and noticed immediately that the corners of several pages were turned down. Flipping to one, she discovered that it was the beginning of a section on cribs and nursery furniture. Another displayed a new product that automatically sealed dirty diapers in a small plastic package. And a third page contained descriptions of accent pieces in nursery motifs, lamps, switch plates and bookends that all matched a theme.

She laughed aloud and began to study the pages with real interest. Had there ever been a more excited father-to-be?

"See anything you like?" Dane came into the room again, carrying a tray set with breakfast for two. Placing it on the coffee table, he carefully sank down next to her and placed his arm around her.

She snuggled closer, feeling cherished. "Lots. How about you?"

"I haven't looked too much," he admitted. "But I thought that since you can't go shopping, we could decide what we wanted this way and order it."

They debated and decided, argued and agreed during the next two hours. Annie was shocked at the amount of baby equipment and furniture Dane seemed prepared to buy without batting an eyelash.

"I don't want this baby to lack anything," was all he said when she protested.

"Babies have been raised all over the world with far less than this," she responded with stubborn reason. "Children need love and attention, not *things*."

He only shrugged, refusing to rise to her bait. "Then this kid will have it all, because we already know he's going to be cuddled every waking moment of our time, anyway."

"But...I really think *this* is an unnecessary expense," she said, pointing to the three infant seats he'd selected. "One is plenty. I don't need one for downstairs, one for upstairs and one for the dog center. I'll probably forget they're there and carry one from place to place, anyway.''

He eyed her, clearly measuring her determination. Then he sighed. ''I guess I am going a little overboard, aren't I?''

''A little?'' She gave him a dry look.

''I'm sorry, but this is important to me.'' His tone was defensive. ''You don't know what it's like to grow up as a child watching other kids get all kinds of things from their parents. My kid isn't going to learn to ride a bike on an old secondhand that's already been through two families.''

Annie bit her lip, deciding not to point out that babies couldn't tell if something wasn't brand-spanking new. Dane rarely talked about himself. In fact, he retreated from the subject when she tried to introduce it. This opportunity was too welcome to miss. ''I know it's important to you,'' she said, and waited.

''Damned right it is.'' He got up from the couch in a single, restless movement and began to pace around the room. ''My kids are never going to wonder what it would be like to be loved.''

Her heart ached for him. She understood now. This buying spree wasn't about making sure his child had the biggest and the best on the block. It was simply overcompensation—Dane's answer to blocking any chance of his child's feeling the neglect that had stung him throughout his own formative years. In some way, creating this family and doing all the things he'd longed for as a child would give him a measure of peace from his past.

How could she deny him that? In retrospect, her concerns about spending seemed small. ''All right,'' she said. ''As long as our checkbook doesn't whimper when we open it, you can get whatever you like.''

He looked at her strangely. ''But I don't want to get whatever I like. I want you to be involved in this, to help me make decisions.'' His face hardened. ''I already had one wife who didn't care about half the decisions I made, I don't need another.''

She didn't speak. This time she didn't know what to say. After a moment, it was as if he couldn't stand the expectant silence.

''Amanda only bothered to argue with me when she was directly affected by whatever I wanted to do. Like have a child.''

''She didn't want children?''

The corners of his mouth turned down. ''Not mine. Oh, she said she did when we got married. But when I started to press the issue, she balked.'' His eyes narrowed and Annie was glad she wasn't the one of whom he spoke. ''She stalled me for months, for over two years. We finally had it out one night and she admitted she didn't want to be tied down with a child. Ever.''

There was a short silence.

She couldn't imagine any woman crazy enough not to want Dane's baby. ''And so you got divorced,'' she said with soft sympathy.

He snorted and it was full of an ugly self-mockery. His voice was bitter as he said, ''I left her for a few months. To think things through. But I'm not a quitter and I decided to try again, to give her more time and see if we couldn't work things out.'' He raised his gaze to hers and she almost recoiled at the rage banked behind his eyes. ''But when I went home, she had already found a replacement for me. And she was pregnant with his child.''

Annie gasped. She closed her eyes against the bleak pain in his gaze. She wanted to reach for him, to offer comfort but she knew from the rigid set of his shoulders that he wouldn't accept it from her.

His story explained so much. And as his words sank in, her heart shriveled into a small ball of pain. She'd been so sure that eventually she could win his love. But Dane wasn't about to allow himself to love her, or anyone. He wouldn't even accept her comfort.

And why should he? She wasn't someone he loved. After what he'd been through, he wasn't going to open himself up to that kind of hurt again. Understanding didn't make it any easier to realize that her dream of being loved by him was no more than that—a dream.

With her heart a leaden weight in her chest, she turned to the next item on their list.

Another disquieting thought wormed its way into her mind, but she didn't have the courage to ask him if her primary qualification for becoming his wife had been her willingness to bear children. Actually, she knew she didn't have the courage to hear the answer.

They decided on nursery furnishings and he set the information aside. He would order everything on Monday. Right now, he wanted to concentrate on Annie. She'd been even quieter than usual throughout the afternoon and evening and she'd pleaded fatigue at an early hour.

When he carried her to bed, he could feel the resistance in her small body and he realized with a shock that whatever was eating at her had something to do with him. But a mental review of his behavior, of their recent conversations gave him no clue as to why she might be upset with him.

"Is something the matter?" he asked once she was tucked into her side of their big bed for the night.

"What could be the matter?" But she wouldn't meet his eyes.

A chill invaded his system. He'd never realized how much he needed Annie's unquestioning warmth and approval, her silent support and sweet caring. Until now, when she seemed to be withholding it.

Didn't she realize how much he needed her? Determined not to let her create distance between them, he bent forward and set his lips to hers. She didn't resist him, but she didn't respond, either. Softly he molded the contours of her mouth until she allowed him to part her lips and seek the sweetness inside. He increased the intensity of the kiss gradually, pulling her up against his chest and kissing her deeply until she grasped his biceps and moaned in protest.

Almost immediately, he remembered her condition. "I'm sorry, sweetheart," he murmured gently, placing his lips against her forehead for a last caress. "I miss making love to you. I can't wait until this baby is born."

"I can't, either," she said, and he was relieved to see the trusting warmth back in her gaze again.

He went downstairs to let the dogs in and crate them for the night, and when he came back to bed, she was already asleep, curled on her side with one hand under her cheek, palm up. Warm feeling surged through him as he crawled into bed beside her and curled protectively around her.

His wife. Mother of his child. He'd take care of her.

It was still dark when the groaning woke him. The bedside clock read five-twenty a.m. Disoriented, he sat up and switched on the light. His confusion turned quickly to panic as he realized what he'd heard was Annie crying.

She was still on her side, but now she was doubled up, with her knees drawn up. As he bent over her, she moaned.

"Annie! Sweetheart, what's wrong?" His heart leaped into his throat.

"Dane." Tears leaked from the corners of her eyes. "Something's wrong. I...hurt. Call the doctor."

He threw two blankets over her as he punched the buttons of the telephone. The answering service had to locate the doctor and have him return the call, and he sweated out the minutes that seemed like hours passing, letting her squeeze his hand when pain rolled through her, fear turning his big body into a shaking frame of flesh.

When the telephone rang, he pounced on it. Annie's doctor listened to Dane's stumbling explanation, then asked him to bring her to the hospital. Daylight was just beginning to touch the night sky with streaks of rose and ivory as he carried her slight weight in his arms through the doors of the emergency entrance.

In an examining room, the doctor palpated her stomach, then raised sober eyes to Dane. "I want to do an ultrasound immediately. She doesn't seem to be developing as she should be for a woman who is about nine weeks along."

"What do you think the trouble is?" Dane felt frantic, his attention divided between the doctor and Annie, who was grinding her teeth in pain now.

But the doctor refused to speculate. "Let's see what the ultrasound shows us."

Things moved rapidly after that. Paperwork had to be completed and orderlies came in to help Annie out of her clothes and into a regulation hospital gown. They brought her liquids to drink and asked her to drink as much as she could. Before Dane knew it, they were placing Annie on a stretcher and carrying her to another part of the hospital.

"Will I be allowed to stay with her?" He kept pace with Annie on the stretcher as the orderlies moved down the hall, still holding her hand.

"Sure." The technician who met them again outside the door of the room where the test would occur, took a moment to pat him on the shoulder. "The calmer you are, the more you can help your wife, Mr. Hamilton."

Calm! As they positioned Annie on the table and set the machine in place, he wanted to scream aloud. This was his wife in pain and they wanted him to be calm. Belatedly, it occurred to him that she could be losing the baby, but he refused to allow himself to dwell on that fear. If this didn't work out, they could always try again. The important thing was that they help Annie.

The test seemed to take forever. He watched the screen that displayed the contents of Annie's insides, but none of it was identifiable. He helped Annie to the bathroom as soon as the ultrasound was finished and waited anxiously outside the door until she came out, still in the grip of the pain that seemed to be clawing at her abdomen.

"It doesn't feel like labor," she panted as they helped her back onto the table and she lay down. "I always imagined labor to come in waves. This—just hurts."

He could hear the technician and the doctor conferring in low tones and then the doctor came into the room.

"Mr. and Mrs. Hamilton, the ultrasound shows an ectopic pregnancy." He must have read their blank expressions correctly because he continued. "What that means is that the fertilized egg attached to the inside of one fallopian tube rather than traveling on into the womb where it needs to be to grow to term. Mrs. Hamilton will need immediate surgery to remove the embryo. As it grows, it becomes too large for the tube until the tube ruptures. The pain you're having is probably a warning of that very thing. If the tube ruptures, the condition can be fatal to the mother as well as the baby."

"So we're going to lose the baby?" It was his own voice, Dane knew, but it sounded like some weary stranger's.

The doctor nodded, his eyes full of grave sympathy. "I'm afraid so."

"But Dr. Milner—" Annie's tones were full of choked urgency. "What will this do to our chances of having more children?"

The doctor hesitated. "I can't really address that just yet, Mrs. Hamilton. If we are able to save the tube, the possibility exists that future pregnancies could occur, but scar tissue often forms in these situations. We just don't know. I have to warn you that the prognosis for keeping the tube intact in these cases is usually very poor."

The prognosis is very poor. The words battered themselves against his brain, slowly sorting themselves into an awful truth. Because of the accident, this was the only functioning fallopian tube Annie possessed. If this one was dam aged or destroyed by the misplaced pregnancy, she wouldn't be able to conceive his child.

Too late he realized he'd been silent for too long. He looked down into Annie's eyes and saw instantly that she was realizing the death of their dreams, as well. Her small face was pinched and gray and in her eyes welled the tears of a bleak defeat that broke his heart.

Leaning down, he slipped his arms around her slender shoulders, hugging her to him while his own eyes stung. Not for the first time, it hit him how tiny and fragile she really was. His protective instincts kicked into gear. Reassuring Annie was his first and most important task. Later, when he was alone, he could examine how this would affect him.

"The doctor's going to take care of you," he said against her hair. "I'm sorry about the baby, but it isn't the end of the world." Two orderlies approached then, to take her away in preparation for the surgery. He bent down to kiss her lips. They were cold, and up close he could read the anguish in her eyes so clearly that he wanted to cry. "I'll be waiting for you," he said, though he could hardly get the words out for the tears that threatened to choke off his voice.

He called Patrick immediately, and Joe and Jeanne Krynes, as well. Within an hour, all of them descended on the waiting room where he was sitting in a state of numb anxiety.

When he told them the doctor's bleak assessment, Jeanne turned her face into Joe's shoulder in tears. One hand went to her own abdomen and Dane knew she was sharing their loss. Joe clasped Dane's shoulder briefly and Dane saw the glimmer of moisture in the other man's eyes.

Patrick turned away, staring out the window for long minutes until Dane joined him. He felt raw and sick inside with grief, but Patrick was Annie's brother, someone she loved, and he knew he had to try to comfort him.

Patrick's hands were clenched on the protruding edge of the windowsill when Dane stepped to his side. He was staring out the window with narrowed eyes, but Dane doubted he could have told anyone what was outside. He slung an arm around Patrick's broad shoulders. "You doing all right?"

The shoulders beneath his arm slumped. "It just isn't fair." Patrick's voice was dull with pain. "She's had enough rotten lumps in her life. I've felt so good lately, so damned good because she seemed happy again—" He stopped, turning to Dane with an appalled expression. "God, Dane, I'm sorry. I should be the one listening to you."

Dane shrugged. "It's okay. You've been a rock of strength for her for a lot of years. It makes sense that this would be hard to take."

Patrick's eyes, as blue and deep as Annie's, searched his face. "I know you two were really excited about the baby." His face changed to sorrow. "And to find out at the same time that there may not be any more…that's tough. How are you doing?"

Dane hesitated. He did feel grief for the little life that wasn't to be. But he was more concerned about Annie. "I'm okay," he said roughly. "Or I will be as soon as somebody tells me Annie came through all right."

Just then someone pushed the double doors from the surgery wing, interrupting their conversation. When Dane recognized the doctor who'd operated on Annie, he moved across the room like a shot from a cannon. "How's my wife?"

The doctor nodded. "She's stable and doing pretty well. Right now she's in the recovery room. As soon as she can be moved back to her room, you can see her."

"What are her chances of having more children?" This

time Patrick spoke. He put an arm around Dane's shoulder as if to brace him.

The doctor switched his gaze to Dane, and he read the answer there before the man spoke. "I'm sorry, Mr. Hamilton, we couldn't save the tube. It had sustained significant damage. Your wife still has one intact ovary, but she won't be able to conceive the conventional way."

Behind him, Jeanne began to sob. The doctor looked both helpless and defeated. "I'm sorry," he said again. "If you check at the desk, they'll direct you to the recovery room. You should be able to see her soon."

Annie was going to be all right. Dane started down the hallway, oblivious to the presence of the others behind him. He hoped they would let him see her soon because he thought he might tear the place apart otherwise. He had a lot to tell her.

Regretfully, he thought of the children they might have had together, girls with blue eyes and their mother's mahogany tresses, boys... It didn't matter any more. His dream of children could never be realized. And he didn't even care.

He loved her. He'd loved her for months and he hadn't even told her. Thank God she was going to be all right. Thank God he'd have the chance to tell her how much she meant to him.

He was waiting in her room when they wheeled her in, and as soon as all the hovering attendants had left, he stepped forward and took her hand. "Hi, sweetheart."

She rolled her head toward him. "Hi."

He was shocked by the lifeless quality of her voice. Maybe it was the result of the anesthesia. Though he'd planned to tell her how he felt right away, he just couldn't tell her now. He leaned forward to kiss her forehead.

She rolled her head away again and his kiss landed somewhere near her temple. Tears seeped from the corners of her eyes.

"Honey, don't. Please, don't." He felt helpless and panicky as he gently blotted the tears with the corner of the sheet. "Try to rest and we'll talk when you wake up."

She did drift off into a restless sleep. Three times the nurses came in to check her vital signs and she allowed them to poke and prod, then closed her eyes and slipped back into whatever dream world she was inhabiting. Several times she woke, nauseated, but a few sips of carbonated soda seemed to help. The nurses told him it was probably the effects of the anesthesia and that she'd feel better tomorrow.

Around four o'clock a meal came. Annie was in no shape to eat it and he suddenly realized he hadn't had a meal since dinner the night before. As he finished wolfing down the cardboard hospital food, he realized Annie had awakened and was watching him.

He smiled at her. "Welcome back. I thought you were going to sleep around the clock."

"I wish I hadn't woken up at all. I lost the baby, didn't I?"

He hesitated, then nodded. The sorrow in her eyes broke his heart anew. "Sweetheart, I'm sorry. I feel badly about our baby, too. But you're going to be fine."

"Am I?" Her voice was dull. "Will I be able to have more children?"

He hesitated again.

The slight pause was fatal. Her shoulders shook as she turned her head away again.

"Annie..." He sank on to the side of the bed, mindful of not jolting her incision, and stroked his hand from the ball of her shoulder down her arm and back again in a comforting gesture. "Children would have been nice...but that's not what's most important to me." He picked up her limp hand and squeezed it. "You're what I care most about. If we don't have children...we'll be all right."

She went still but she didn't turn to face him.

What had he expected? He knew he'd phrased it badly, but he'd thought she'd at least acknowledge his words. He opened his mouth, then shut it again. Maybe his timing was just lousy.

But old hurts rose to taunt him. If she loved him, wouldn't she have responded when he tried to reassure her?

If she loved him... The great vein of insecurity that had been buried in his heart since Amanda had refused to have his baby lay exposed, clogging his thought with its poisonous residue. Annie had never said she loved him, even though he'd thought she did, had *hoped* she did. All his life he'd looked for love, had longed for someone to whom he was the first light in the sky and the last ray at sunset. He'd stood on the outside all through his childhood, longing for a love like that.

When he'd met Amanda, he'd wanted it so much that in his mind he'd made their relationship something deeper, more meaningful than it ever was in reality. And when she'd shattered his heart, he'd thought he would never recover. But Annie had stolen into his life and his heart—

And he'd thought she loved him. It looked as if he'd been wrong again.

He studied her pale profile for a moment longer, but still she didn't acknowledge his presence or his words in any way. Slowly, he took his hands from her and got to his feet. As he made his way from the room, the remains of his heart slid to the floor and shattered into a thousand shards.

Five days later, Annie was released from the hospital. Simply walking from the car into the living room exhausted her and she sank into a chair in the den and accepted Ebony's and Missy's exuberant licks. Their unquestioning joy cheered her a little, but only for a short time.

"Can I get you something?" Dane paused in the doorway after taking her suitcase upstairs. He looked handsome and worried, self-contained and...unapproachable. As he had since the first day after surgery.

"No, thank you. I'll be fine. Jeanne said she'd check in at lunchtime so you won't have to come home."

He hesitated. "All right. If you're sure you don't need me...."

"I'll be fine." *If only you knew how much I need you!* But he'd already vanished from the doorway and she heard the back door close quietly as he left for work. She heard the engine of the new family sedan he'd bought a week earlier purr to life and then he was gone.

And she dropped her head and let the tears fall.

She hadn't cried in the hospital since that first day, when she'd realized how much she'd lost. Too little privacy. And she hadn't wanted Dane to walk in and see her crying. It wasn't his fault this had happened.

It wasn't her fault, either. But she knew the loss of this baby and the impossibility of conceiving again spelled the loss of her dreams of love and the end of her marriage.

The tears fell faster as she thought of how noble he'd been the day of the surgery. *You're what I care most about....* But he hadn't said he loved her. The omission was telling.

It had broken her heart to realize his words had been prompted by nothing more than pity. She'd been too busy trying not to sob aloud to tell him he didn't have to pretend. And she hadn't been able to look at his beloved face knowing that he didn't really love her as she loved him.

Nine

Jeanne came over close to lunchtime. She had an oddly hesitant manner about her and to Annie's surprise, she lingered on the back doorstep until Annie invited her in.

"What's the matter with you?" Annie asked. "Any other day you'd barge right in. You don't have to act different just because I'm married."

Jeanne tried a smile that wobbled around the edges. "It isn't that. I was afraid—I mean, if you can't bear to see me, I'll go away."

It was true that Annie had been trying to pretend she didn't notice the bulge of early pregnancy under Jeanne's loose shirt. The baby was due in May, just weeks before her own baby would have arrived.

She sighed, reaching for Jeanne's hand even as her eyes filled. "Get in here, you fool."

Jeanne came forward with her arms outstretched and Annie stepped into her embrace. They stayed like that for a long moment until the tears were under control. Feeling the hard mound of Jeanne's abdomen pressed against her was a bittersweet sorrow but Annie forced herself not to think about it. Stepping back, she said, "I'm not going to be able to avoid seeing pregnant women and babies for the rest of my life, you know."

"I know." Jeanne wiped her own tears before slinging her coat and purse across one of the kitchen chairs. "I wasn't sure you were ready to be confronted with someone else's pregnancy just yet."

Annie nodded, unable to deny it as she turned away to make tea.

Jeanne pulled out a chair. She placed a tea bag in the mug Annie offered her and propped her feet on a chair opposite the one in which she sat. Changing the topic, she regaled Annie with the latest news from around the community.

By the time they'd finished the tea, it was lunchtime.

"Don't get up," Jeanne warned Annie as she rose. "You're supposed to be recuperating, remember? I brought lunch along." She opened the picnic hamper she'd brought with her and began to set out the meal she'd put together.

They ate while they continued to talk, though Annie noticed Jeanne studiously skirted any talk of child rearing or childbearing. Maybe by the next time Jeanne visited, Annie would feel up to asking the normal questions and discussing babies, but today she was grateful for the omission.

As Jeanne repacked her things in the basket, though, she gazed across the table at Annie seriously and her hands stilled. "How's Dane taking this?"

The question caught her flat-footed. To her horror, Annie felt the tears well again. "All right," she managed to say, swallowing. "He'll be fi—" But the dam broke and more of the tears that she'd suppressed in the hospital sprang up, swamping her in the misery that was breaking her heart.

Jeanne's face registered distress. In a flash, she was around the table and pulling a chair close so she could cradle Annie in her arms. "Oh, honey, I could tell by the way he watched J.J. and Mindy—as if he could just cuddle them to bits—that he longed for kids of his own. Has he been terribly upset?"

Annie only shook her head.

Jeanne rocked her, snagging a napkin from the table and drying Annie's tears herself.

This was what she needed, Annie thought bleakly. But instead of receiving comfort from her husband, she was dependent on the charity of others. With a final sniff, she forced herself to sit up and stop leaning on Jeanne. Quietly, she said, "I don't know if Dane's been upset or not. We're not communicating well these days."

Jeanne said nothing but her expression held dismay.

Annie continued before she lost her nerve. "Dane only married me because we both wanted children and this was a convenient solution. Now that I can't conceive, I imagine he'll want out of the marriage." Her voice quavered on the last two words but she bit down on the inside of her lip until the pain was stronger than the agony tearing at her heart.

Jeanne snorted. "That's nonsense. Dane loves you. He's not going to leave you just because you've had a rotten break."

"No, you don't understand." Annie shook her head emphatically. "I knew when we got married that the most important thing in his life was becoming a father."

"Are you trying to tell me there was no love involved in your marriage?" Jeanne sounded wary and disbelieving.

"Not on his part." She gave the pregnant woman a weary smile. "I'm sure my feelings for him are no secret, but he doesn't—"

"Bull."

Annie stared at her. "What?"

Jeanne smiled. "I've watched Dane. The way he looks at you." She paused and rolled her eyes heavenward. "It makes my engine purr."

"I didn't say he wasn't...attracted to me," Annie said awkwardly.

"You'd be lying through your teeth if you did!"

Annie blushed.

"So you think he's just...wild about your body?" Jeanne's tone grew softer. "You might not think he cares for you, but I'm sure he does. You should have seen him in the waiting room while you were in surgery. He was sick with worry."

"Perhaps, but I'm sure losing the baby and learning that I couldn't give him more was what he was thinking of."

"What makes you think Dane doesn't love you?" Jeanne took Annie's hand. "Some men aren't good with words, but it doesn't mean they don't care."

Annie regarded her silently for a moment. In a few succinct sentences, she told Jeanne the story of Dane's first marriage. Then she said, "When he proposed to me, he as good as told me that he didn't want to love me, and that he wanted a relationship that didn't include love."

"So you've never told him you love him, either?"

Annie shook her head. "I can't burden him with that, not after...after what happened. He hasn't touched me since the first day in the hospital. I'm sure he wants out of this marriage so he can find a whole woman who can give him children, but he's simply too noble to tell me."

And it was true. He hadn't kissed her, hadn't held her, hadn't touched her in any way except for the most impersonal touches when he had no choice. Like the hand he'd extended to help her into the car from the wheelchair this morning. To her, craving his touch as she did, the mere clasp of his hand had been the most welcome sensation in the world and she'd found it difficult to hide her reaction. He hadn't appeared even to notice.

For once, Jeanne didn't have a ready answer. Her pretty face was troubled as they cleaned up the remains of the lunch she'd brought and after a few more words, she went home while Annie dragged herself upstairs for a nap.

The next six weeks were more of the same. Dane treated her like a convalescent guest in a nursing home. He was unfailingly polite and concerned for her welfare, but he never touched her willingly. He couldn't have made it clearer that he wanted out of the marriage.

They never discussed the baby they'd made together and lost.

It was like the worst sort of torture ever devised, to have to live with him, loving him as she did, and know that someday soon he'd leave.

As her strength returned, she began to walk the dogs again and to visit her canine center, to make plans to return to work full-time. It wasn't what she would have chosen. But Dane didn't want her and the rest of her lonely life would be unbearable if she didn't keep busy.

He knew he couldn't stand the pressure much longer. They were like two strangers, politely touching on the surfaces of each other's lives, backing away before any deeper interchange could occur. Living with her, seeing her pain every day and knowing that she didn't want his comfort was more than he could take.

One evening, he came home from work to see her sitting in the kitchen, staring sightlessly at nothing. When he walked into the room, she made an effort, getting to her feet and walking to the refrigerator. "Hello. I have a roast in for dinner. Would you like a salad with it?"

"Annie."

"What?" She didn't turn to face him.

He shook his head in frustration. It was like talking to a wall. "Is there some way I can help you?"

She took him literally. "No, thank you. All I have to do is chop some lettuce."

"I didn't mean that." He made an impatient motion with his hand. "Ever since you came home from the hospital, you've barely spoken."

She was silent for a minute more. Then she turned to face him and when her gaze met his, he was seared by the sadness she exuded. "I don't have much to say right now."

As she slipped by him and left the room, he stood with his hands curled into fists of impotence. He was afraid to try to approach her further, when his every overture seemed to only heighten her pain.

He'd hoped that her depression would abate as the weeks passed. But with each new day that dawned, Annie seemed more mired in a private world of stoic grief that he couldn't penetrate. Her fortress was so solidly defended that he didn't dare approach her for even the simplest touch. The infrequent times that she asked him for help or that he was able to assist her left him battling a painful desire so fierce that he had to walk away before he grabbed her and dragged her to him for the embrace he could almost feel.

He found himself more jealous now of her dead husband than he'd ever been in the past, merely because the man had known what it was like to be loved by Annie.

He supposed her withdrawal was understandable. She'd lost so much in her life. Losing the baby had been one blow too many. The glow that always had lit her blue eyes with an inner warmth was gone now, a casualty of her miscarriage and one loss more than she could handle. He'd thought he could refocus her life, bind her to him and create a family and a love that would endure for the rest of their lives.

But he'd been wrong. His love hadn't been enough.

* * *

In her room, Annie sat on the edge of the bed, her arms protectively curled over her barren womb. Living with Dane, knowing he was longing for children, was the worst kind of torment she'd ever envisioned. It felt as if she'd lost a husband all over again, though he was still living here in the same house with her.

She was going to have to offer him his freedom.

Until now, she hadn't been able to entertain the idea of Dane leaving. Until now, she'd lacked the strength to let him go, even though she knew it would be the right thing to do.

He'd never initiate it, she was positive. He'd married her and even though things had gone sour, he wouldn't back out unless she convinced him that she would be fine alone.

Over breakfast on the day of her six-week checkup, he said, "I've arranged to go in late today."

"Oh?" She glanced at him, but her gaze bounced away without meeting his.

"You need someone to drive you to the doctor."

She flushed slightly. "I was planning on driving myself. I'm sure I'm well enough. You don't have to take time off."

"It's no big deal." She clearly didn't want him to accompany her. But for some reason, he wasn't feeling particularly sensitive today. "What time's your appointment?"

"Ten, but you don't—"

"I said I'd drive you." His tone of voice left no room for argument.

But at ten o'clock, Annie gathered the keys to her van from the hook in the kitchen. "Why don't you follow me? I'm sure I'll get the 'A-okay' to drive again and you won't have to take extra time away from work to bring me home."

He studied her for a moment, realizing that she wasn't going to yield. "All right."

The drive to the doctor's office was short, as was the wait.

In what seemed like no time, he was standing in the familiar examining room watching the doctor check Annie.

"Everything looks good, Mrs. Hamilton. You've healed nicely. You can resume normal activity now, including driving and walking. And intercourse." The physician closed his chart and crossed his arms over it. "Have you two considered whether you'd like to try again to have a baby?"

Annie stared at the doctor. "But...I can't."

He smiled at her. "You may not be able to conceive in the normal fashion, but you still have a healthy ovary, presumably healthy eggs and a perfectly usable uterus. And a track record of conception. If you're interested, I'll refer you to a fertility specialist who can evaluate you as candidates for an in vitro fertilization program."

"We're not interested," Annie said.

"We're interested." Dane spoke at the same moment. Hope leaped within his breast. He'd resigned himself to a life without children, but he realized that if there was a chance that he and Annie could still have a family, he'd jump at it in a heartbeat, if only to take the shades of sorrow from Annie's eyes.

The doctor was silent for a moment. His eyebrows rose. He and Dane both looked at Annie. She was gazing at the floor and her chin quivered as if she was trying to hold back tears.

"Perhaps you two should discuss this before we make any decisions," the doctor said quietly. "I know losing this baby was difficult. And it's created some challenges, but it doesn't mean your chance to become parents is gone. Think about it and call me." He shook Dane's hand and slipped out of the room.

When the door had closed behind him with a soft whoosh, Dane stepped to Annie's side. She didn't look at him until he placed a gentle forefinger beneath her chin, lifting her face for his inspection.

"Could we please go somewhere and talk? It's important to me," he added, afraid she might shut him out again.

Her shoulders seemed to slump a bit and a tear escaped and went slipping down her cheek. Then she nodded. "All right."

They dropped her van off at the house and he called his secretary to say he wouldn't be coming in. Then he helped Annie into the new sedan and came around to the driver's side. She didn't say a word, not even when he left River Forest and got on the Eisenhower Expressway into Chicago. The silence in the car was thick and oppressive through the entire ride.

Driving around the bottom of the Loop, he passed Grant Park and turned north on Lake Shore Drive, putting the vast, gray expanse of Lake Michigan's Chicago Harbor on their right. The lake looked dark and choppy and cold today, in keeping with the sullen skies that threatened rain. It matched the way he felt inside.

The silence inside the car was absolute. He drove on and on, past Lincoln Park and finally swung the car into a parking spot facing a deserted stretch of beachfront. In the summer, there would be people all over the place, but in late November, the bitter breezes off the lake kept all but the most hardy water-lovers away.

He switched off the engine. They'd be warm enough for a while in the car. Slowly, he pivoted in his seat to face her. "We need to talk."

"I know." Her voice was stifled.

He hesitated, choosing his words with care. "Losing the baby was a big disappointment for you—"

"And an even bigger one for you." He could hear the sorrow in her voice and tears glinted in her eyes as she turned toward him. "Oh, Dane, I'm sorry."

"Annie, you don't have anything to be sorry for." Could

she possibly believe he blamed her for something that was no more than rotten biological luck?

"But I do," she whispered, and she looked so stricken he didn't speak, waiting for her to explain. "You were very clear from the beginning that you wanted children, that you were marrying me for one reason...to bear your babies. And now you're stuck with a wife who may not be able to give them to you. I know how important it is to you to be able to have children."

"Annie—"

"No, wait." Slowly she drew off the wedding ring and the beautiful sapphire engagement ring he'd given her. "Take these. You need to be free to find a woman who can help you fulfill your dreams."

Dane stared at her, feeling his heart being torn in two as she pressed the rings into his hand.

With a muffled sob, she fumbled for the handle of her door and flung herself out of the car. Before he could react, she was walking away from him, out onto the desolate beach. Her head was down and her shoulders heaved.

The evidence of the grief she was carrying smote him like a blow from a hammer. In that moment, he knew he couldn't bind her to him, force her to acknowledge his presence in her life, when it so clearly brought her painful memories. He should let her go. Blindly, he opened his own door and followed her out onto the sand. "Annie!"

The wind whipped around him. She was far enough ahead of him that the gusts of air snatched his words away and she didn't hear him. He sprinted after her, heedless of the sand shifting beneath his feet, filling his shoes.

Grabbing her elbow, he pulled her to a halt. "Annie, wait."

She tried to turn away but he held her in place with relentless pressure, seeing the tracks of her tears staining her face, feeling each one as an arrow in his heart.

"You can start divorce proceedings tomorrow." His words dropped like stones between them.

If it were possible, her eyes dimmed even more. "Is that what you want me to do?" she asked in a lifeless tone.

The moment was frozen between them, her question echoing with implications. His heart shouted, "Hell, no, that's not what I want!" His brain overruled it, however, and he heard himself cautiously throwing the ball back into her court. "I want you to be happy. Whatever it takes to accomplish that is what I want."

She hesitated.

So did he. He sensed that they were balanced on a knife-edge of change, that his next response could shape his life for the rest of his days. Quietly, shedding his pride and risking his heart, he asked, "Do you want a divorce, Annie?"

The wind howled around them, slapping her braid against her shoulder. She raised her gaze to his face, but for once he couldn't read anything in her expressive eyes. "I want you to be happy," she said. "If you're free, you can look for another woman to have your babies." Her voice quavered at the end, but she didn't look away.

"What if I don't want to be free?"

Annie threw him a pain-filled, incredulous look. "Why wouldn't you?"

"I meant what I said in the hospital, you know." He tried to keep his voice as light and casual as possible. "I don't want any other woman. Children aren't as important to me as keeping you in my life."

She smiled a little then, dislodging a tear, which ran down her cheek and dripped onto the collar of her shirt. "Dane, you want children. I can't give them to you. I appreciate your willingness to be noble, but it isn't necessary."

"I know it's not necessary!" Patience had never been one of his virtues and he was getting sick and tired of trying to make his point. "Dammit, Annie, I'm not being noble. I love you. If you love me, too, we can overcome anything, even not having children of our own."

Her eyes were wide and shocked and he couldn't for the life of him tell what she was thinking. It was too late for graceful exits, he decided. He might as well jump in and say it all. More calmly, he said, "Will you put my rings back on your finger and please answer me?"

Deep down in the depths of her eyes, a tiny blue flame sparked. And in that moment, he dared to hope again. Her lips curved up the tiniest bit in the first real smile he'd seen on her face in weeks. "Could you repeat the question?"

He stared at her for a moment, gauging the slow, deliberate words. He held out the rings, taking her hand in his. "Annie Hamilton, I love you. I want to keep you for my wife, with or without kids. Children would be a great bonus, but they could never replace you. Do you love me?"

Her face grew serious. "Yes," she whispered. Then her voice grew stronger and her eyes began to shine. "Oh, Dane, I thought you only wanted me for...for..."

"For your reproductive organs?" He couldn't suppress the chuckle that wanted to burst free as he gently slipped her rings back on her finger.

"Something like that." She took his face between her hands. "I love you. All I want is a life with you." She laid her head against his chest. "And children, if we can have them."

Dane stroked the length of her braid, reveling in the softness of her body, the silky hair beneath his hand, the warmth of her pressed against him. "The doctor said we haven't run out of options yet. But I don't want to press you into anything you're not willing to do. All I need to make my life complete is you."

Annie pulled back a fraction and looked up at him. "Of course I'm willing to try anything we can to have children."

Her smile wilted a bit around the edges, but she continued to gaze into his eyes. "I'll always be sorry our first pregnancy didn't work out. But if the doctors think we stand a chance of trying some alternative methods, I'm all for it."

She shivered as she finished the last words and he hugged her to him. "Let's get out of this wind."

As one, they turned and began walking back toward the car. He kept an arm possessively around her, some part of him fearing that if he didn't hold on to her, all they'd just said might disappear.

Annie laughed, pointing at his feet. "You're going to have to go home and change."

He looked down. His shoes and socks were covered with sand and his gray wool trousers had grains of sand clinging to them, as well. He tightened his arm around her. "Maybe I won't go in to the office at all today."

"Is that an invitation I hear in there?" Her face was glowing, her eyes as warm as he'd wanted to see them for weeks.

"It is." He expanded on the idea that was coming to him. "We owe ourselves some courtship time. Time to be romantic." Stopping just short of the car, he turned to face her, slipping his hands inside her coat and under the long sweater that she wore until his fingers registered the hot, silky texture of woman beneath his hands.

She sighed, snuggling closer to him, slipping her own hands around his back and down to palm his buttocks through his pants. He gasped as her hips tilted into his and he felt the immediate leap of passion rising between them. Annie tilted her face in invitation and he accepted, covering her mouth with his own, tasting the sweet heat he'd been denied for weeks. As he delved deeper into her mouth, his hand slid up to shape and mold her breast.

Annie moaned into his mouth and shivered.

Shivered?

Dane pulled his head back and laughed, straightening her sweater and turning her toward the car again. "How romantic—you're freezing to death."

"But all for a good cause." Annie snuggled closer, kissing the side of his neck as high as she could reach. "Let's go home. I bet a big, strong guy like you has some hot ideas on how to warm me."

Epilogue

Annie shifted the toddler on her hip as she stood on tiptoe to peer out the kitchen window. "Look, Lizzie, Daddy's home. When Daddy comes in, you can show him the card you made for him today."

The dark-haired tot made a futile lunge at the window as Annie caught her. "Dad-dee! I see Dad-dee!"

Annie set her on the floor. "Run into the den and get your card for Daddy, okay, princess?"

"O-tay!" At twenty-one months, Lizzie didn't know the meaning of the word *walk*. She zipped off toward the den, her little legs pumping as fast as they could go. Annie watched her fondly. *Our little miracle*, Dane called her. And that was exactly how they'd felt when she'd been born nine months after Annie had undergone the process of in vitro fertilization. They'd held their breaths nearly every day of her pregnancy, affected more than either of them cared to admit by the loss of the first baby they'd made together.

Lizzie came screeching back into the kitchen then, and five-year-old Stephen barreled in behind her. Today he was pretending to be a fireman and the red plastic hat he'd gotten during Fire Prevention Week in kindergarten was mashed firmly down atop his unruly white-blond curls.

"Where are your glasses, young man?" Annie asked her son.

"In my room. I'll get 'em, Mommy," he answered, making an abrupt pivot and racing off toward the stairs, the sound of a fire siren trailing behind him. Ebony and Missy, who were his constant companions, loped after him.

They'd made the decision to adopt just last year, though they'd been on a waiting list since shortly after they'd lost the first baby, when they'd gone through the initial paperwork in case their chances for having biological children failed. Stephen, legally blind in one eye as the result of an infection he'd had as an infant, had been overlooked by dozens of adoptive parents, but the moment Dane had seen the little boy, he'd been interested. Lizzie had been less than a year old when they'd first begun to consider adopting additional children and though Annie had assumed they'd be looking for another infant, the four-year-old Stephen had captured her heart the day she'd first seen him in the foster home where they'd gone to see two infants.

"Would you take me home?" he'd asked Dane, climbing into his lap without reservation. "I need a daddy and a mommy."

She'd been touched to tears, she recalled, and Dane had been nearly unable to respond to the hopeful child. They'd gone home that night and discussed it.

"The placement officer says the babies are much easier to place, and that she has a waiting list," Annie had said tentatively to Dane. "That dear little Stephen was certainly a character, wasn't he?"

Dane had nodded. "I imagine with his vision problems,

he won't be first on anyone's list." Then he'd turned to her and his gaze had been hopeful. "Except maybe ours. How would you feel about adopting a child that's older?"

They'd applied to adopt Stephen the very next day and he'd come home with them a short month later for a trial period. Adjusting to having a very lively little boy in addition to a baby had been…interesting, she recalled with a smile, but they'd never been sorry. And she knew that Dane would always feel especially happy to have made a difference in another lonely child's life.

Her only regret was that they hadn't had Stephen from the day he'd been given up. All she had from the first four years of his life were a few pictures that had been taken for adoption portfolios over the years and a tattered teddy bear that he'd only recently felt secure enough to sleep without.

As Lizzie came rushing back into the kitchen with a grubby piece of paper clutched in her fist, Dane opened the back door.

"Dad-dee!" shrieked the little girl, hurling herself at him.

Dane stooped just in time to catch her, setting his briefcase aside and rising with Lizzie in his arms.

"How's my princess today?" he asked her. "Were you Mommy's helper?"

Lizzie nodded solemnly. "Made din-ner. 'Tephen he'p."

Dane pretended amazement. "You and Stephen made dinner? Wow. I can't wait to taste it." He took the paper that Lizzie was shoving at him. "What's this?"

"Card. Mom-mee he'p 'Izzie."

Dane looked at the scribbled crayon marks covering the dog-eared sheet. "I love you, Daddy," he solemnly read aloud. "This is a beautiful card, Lizzie. You did a good job."

He looked over her head at Annie. "Hi, Mommy. Thank you for helping Lizzie with her card."

The little girl squirmed to be set down and he complied,

coming over to link his arms around Annie's waist and pull her into his arms. "How's my number one princess?" he asked softly.

She smiled up into his eyes, still as blue as the day they'd met, though he was getting a few silver strands in the dark hair near his temples. "Just fine," she said.

"Busy day?"

She smiled wryly. "If changing diapers, building with blocks, carpooling three kindergarteners to school and back, picking up the party invitations from the printers and teaching two Basic classes while Stephen was in school and Lizzie was at the baby-sitter's counts, yes, you could say I was busy."

"How do the invitations look?"

"Very nice." She leaned into him. "If you'll help me address them this weekend, we'll be in pretty good shape. I already have a tentative menu planned for our annual spring cocktail party."

Dane pressed a leisurely kiss onto her mouth, lingering to taste the sweetness inside. "What a hostess. All that work, and you even have dinner ready. Is that why I love you?"

"No." She leaned into him and deliberately brushed her hips back and forth against him, over and over again. "Maybe later I'll remind you."

A clatter of little feet accompanied by the tick-tack of dog toenails on the tiled floor warned them that Stephen and the dogs were about to descend for their own greetings. "I'm going to count on that reminder," he said in a husky voice, "even though that's only one of the reasons I love you."

And he released her to greet his son.

* * * * *

Dear Reader,

I started to write *An Unexpected Addition* ten years before I had a story for it. All I had was the vague premise of a couple of characters named Kate and Hank, a lot of kids, llamas (well, actually, a somewhat curious pushmi-pullyu J), a Christmas tree farm and the house where they all lived. Needing a lot more in order to do the characters justice, I back-burnered the story for a while.

While I wrote other books, Kate and Hank's story percolated in the back of my mind. I began to know who Hank was, who his daughter was, what his conflict was with Kate—and the fact that she was formerly a nun. The book started to take real shape. Then I visited my sister in Denver—and everything fell into place. I went to the VA hospital and learned about the prosthetics one of Kate's kids needed, got out to a llama ranch to meet the llamas in person, did the rest of the research I hadn't completed in Michigan.... It was true serendipity.

An Unexpected Addition is one of the best and hardest books I've had the opportunity to write. Working with Hank's daughter—the teenager with the bipolar chemical imbalance, manic depression—was one of the most difficult things I've ever done. It was also rewarding, knowing I could wave my keyboard at the end of the book and say, "Hank will get her some help. Maybe she'll make it." It was also a joy to let him reach out and find Kate, to bring him into her life, as well, and to create a family—problems and all—where there'd been nothing but blank pages and thin air. Enjoy!

Cheerfully,

Terese Ramin

AN UNEXPECTED ADDITION
Terese Ramin

For Sean, because he is.
And for Damaris, who said,
"Write the book you want to write." Thanks.

To Jeanne,
who took the pictures, made suggestions,
worried and always lets me take her for granted.
Thanks for keeping the Complaints Department open.

Acknowledgments

My thanks to Sheila Davis and Tom Pettipren,
who talked with me about their own and others' experiences
with foster children and foreign adoptions. You taught me a
great deal. Blessings on you and all of your children. Thanks
also to Kathleen Daly, med tech, Denver V.A.M.C., for
putting me in touch with live llamas and their people, and
with the V.A.M.C. prosthetics service. Thanks and
appreciation to Bob Riley of Boulder Ridge Ranch, Boulder,
Colorado, for spending so much time answering my
questions and introducing me to his llamas, indulging my
curiosity, and for his patience and humor when I induced
his normally mellow friends to spit when they usually don't—
at people, that is—ever. Special thanks to Dennis Luse,
Certified Prosthetist, of the Denver V.A.M.C.
prosthetics lab, for his time and patience in answering
my questions about juvenile amputees, prosthetic limbs and
for showing me practical solutions to impractical problems.
I would also like to acknowledge a research debt to the work
Motherless Daughters: The Legacy of Loss, by
Hope Edelman, Addison-Wesley Publishing, 1994.
Any mistakes, stretches of reality and leaps of faith
are entirely my own.

Prelude

Tuesday after Mother's Day

Evening sun slanted harsh and red through the low-slung windows, cutting a brilliant swath across the living room to catch in the miniature glass panes of the Victorian dollhouse that leaned half overturned against the couch toward the middle of the carpeted floor.

For an instant, when he saw the apparent chaos through the watery glass panels of the door in his vestibule, Hank Mathison's heart stopped. *Megan,* he thought. The voiceless mental whisper was filled with all the terror, panic and paranoia of a former undercover agent for the Drug Enforcement Administration who was also a parent and whose home didn't look the way he remembered leaving it this morning, *and* whose teenage daughter had failed to meet him when and where she was supposed to.

With an effort he forced himself to breathe slow and even, to remember that he hadn't worked deep cover in almost five years or done any undercover work at all in the past thirteen months. He was involved in nothing at the office that should cause his family to be the target of conspiracy. Panic, as he had firsthand reason to know, was a killer; composure was the only thing that would get you through a crisis. Especially if, as often happened, the crisis turned out to be imaginary.

On the other hand, no matter how foolish he might feel afterward, it never hurt to be careful. Especially where Megan was concerned.

Turning sideways to the door to make himself the narrowest target possible, Hank reached under his jacket for the weapon holstered at the small of his back, then stretched to turn the old glass doorknob. A gentle shove creaked the cantankerous portal open. He stepped into the house.

Silence lay about him, sharp and caustic, accusing. Dust motes, settled since the Molly Maids had been through the previous week, startled in the sudden soft swirl of air and fizzed against the sunlight. The stale scent of burned toast hung limp in the stillness, laced with the memory of this morning's loud generation-gap conflict and—

Muscles he'd long ago forgotten existed slumped gratefully. As quickly as panic had risen it stilled; the calm underside of his brain recognized "situation normal" as recall stirred. Megan, yesterday morning; him reminding her he'd leave work early to pick her up for their family counseling session after school; her cutting her last class and blowing him off, then not coming home until well after dinner last night.

She'd been much too giggly high to benefit from the where-the-hell-have-you-been, you-scared-me-to-death tongue hiding he'd needed to give her after an evening spent making frantic phone calls and calling in markers from his local law-enforcement buddies trying to find her. Worried as he'd been about her, and rebellious and hell-bent as she'd seemed the past couple of years, it was the first time he'd ever seen her come home high. And that had frightened him more than anything else she'd ever done.

Her behavior always peaked for the worst near and during the holidays. Mother's Day had never been meaner.

Disbelief, denial, anger—three of the five stages of grief. Even after five years, she had never bargained—with him or God—over her mother's life, and was nowhere near acceptance. Her anger seemed resolute. It was the world she lived in—at least at home with him—and dragged him into daily. As she reminded him often, *he* was the one with the sudden-death job, but Gen was the one who'd died suddenly. Damn him.

"Why couldn't it have been you?" She was passionate, filled with an anguish that refused to abate with time. *"Why wasn't it you?"*

He'd taken in her dilated pupils, the strained, pouchy softness beneath her eyes, the drugged lassitude of her movements and forced himself not to react to her bait, deliberately leaning over to smell her breath.

She'd shoved him away with a disgusted, "What do you think I am, Hank, stupid? I had to drive Zevo's car. I'm not drunk."

"You're high on something, Meg. What is it?"

"Oh, Daddy, you are such a narc." She'd rolled her eyes and given him "The Look," which proclaimed him stupid, naive and too damned old to get it. Her skin seemed unnaturally chalky against the artificial jet of her hair and the blackness of her clothes. The diamond stud piercing her left nostril flashed in the light when she moved her head. It was one of a pair Hank had given Gen on their tenth anniversary; he'd passed them on to Megan as Gen had intended to for her sixteenth birthday. He doubted that Gen had meant for Megan to wear one of them through her nose. "Lighten up and remember what it was like to be sixteen, would you?"

"Damn it, Megan, I remember perfectly well what it is

to be your age, and this isn't it. Now what the hell are you on?''

She'd turned her back on him with a flutter of her fingers, pale against the dark leather of her fingerless gloves. The collection of earrings around the lobe of each ear bounced and clinked lightly against each other. ''Don't get your boxers in a twist, Pop, it's nothing illegal.'' Then she'd added, airy, scornful, ''It's not even prescription.''

''Then what the hell is it and why are you high on it?''

''You call this high?'' She'd laughed at him, shrill, delighted, and flounced off toward her bedroom, her calves a white flash between her short black socks and ankle boots and the hiked-to-the-knee wrinkles of her tight black spandex workout pants.

So far as he knew, she didn't work out.

''This isn't high, Dad, this is endorphins. This is just exercise trippin'.''

He was shaking, angry, impotent, scared beyond belief for her. She looked more fragile to him than usual, more…vulnerable. Her face looked pouchy and shadowed, almost mottled, beyond what she did to herself with cosmetics.

Too late to gain her trust, he wondered if she'd been crying. Her eyes were bright, shining with liquid and hidden pain, pupils swallowing irises, the whites around them lined with red. She was hiding stubborn secrets behind bravura, but he knew she was scared. He wanted to grab her and rattle her senseless and force her to trust him, to tell him what had happened, what was wrong—besides the obvious.

But he wouldn't touch her while either his anger or his fear could hurt her.

Disbelief, denial, anger.

''Tell me, damn it, in case I have to take you to the hospital in the middle of the night to get your stomach pumped.''

Another mocking giggle, filled with the knowledge that

there was nothing he could do—short of physical violence—to force her confidence. And the sword she wielded was the recognition that he loved her too much to come near her in anger.

"Megan—" he'd begun, softer and steadier this time, his ire, if not worry, controlled.

"Sorry, Dad." She'd yawned big and stretched. "Can't talk, gotta catch some *Z's*. School tomorrow."

Then she'd left him standing helpless and distraught, staring after her when she sashayed carelessly down the hall to her bedroom and shut him out of her life. Her Nirvana CDs played quietly deep into the night.

He'd gone to his own room and tried to sleep, but climbing the Matterhorn on his hands would have been easier. Hell was knowing that in her eyes his most grievous offense was that he wasn't Gen.

You're the one who should have died, damn you, not Mom.

Their conflict was old, charged with the moldering pain of them both still needing the woman who'd loved them and run interference between them; the wife and mother who'd died without warning and left them alone—strangers within their own skins—to cope with each other five years earlier.

Disbelief, denial, anger…bargaining…acceptance. God, he wished Megan could. That she *would*.

Instead, Megan told him constantly, one way or another, that the choices she made had to be her own for better or worse and he had no right to raise hell because of them. Of course, he knew all he really wanted was to prevent her making mistakes that would cost her more than her inexperience would allow her to imagine.

This morning he'd tried to talk with her—not *at* her, as she'd accused him; as he'd once accused his own parents—but sleeplessness and disquiet had taken their toll on calmness. Instead he wound up doing exactly what his parents had done: preaching and lecturing, while she grew more and more sullen and withdrawn.

He'd told her to be home tonight, that she was grounded for a week. She responded better to requests than commands; he tried to remember that, but didn't always—especially when she seemed to deliberately try to force his patience beyond bearing.

She'd told him to take his grounding and go to hell; he might be her keeper, but he couldn't force her to stay in his jail.

They'd had a rip-roaring argument about the previous night, other nights, other days that ended with Megan storming down to her room, grabbing up the dollhouse he'd made her for Christmas when she was five and storming back to dump it at his feet—a symbol, she'd said, of her returning all the love he'd attempted to buy and coerce out of her over the years instead of simply being there for her, the same as he'd never been there for Mom. She'd accused him, as she had often through the intervening years, of being the reason Gen was gone. She'd denied his right to censure her conduct, impugned his parental responsibility to monitor and teach—or attempt to—however badly he might do it, and rejected his right to be concerned for her.

Then she ran from him again, darting out the door to the car of a waiting friend in her omnipresent black uniform: Oversize T-shirt and too tight pants, black socks and scuffed half boots. Her punk-spiked, ebony-dyed hair and eyebrows, eyelashes, eyes and lips lined with obsidian kohl...only the almost vampire whiteness of her skin contrasted the unrelieved stygian mourning of her look. He hurt for her and for himself, but for all his years and experience with the world it seemed there was nothing he could do to relieve either of them.

How much do you love her? How badly do you want her back? Do you love her enough to...?

The questions wafted, too often asked, too often unanswered. Unanswerable.

To what? he wondered, not for the first time. To give her up, let her go, give in, get tough, request an intervention, walk away? To put a constant monitor on her behavior by quitting his job completely, living in her pocket twenty-four hours a day, seven days a week?

The last thought was neither realistic nor practical. He had to earn a living for them somehow, keep up with the mortgage, insurance and groceries, see to the needs of the living; she had to have some independence. Regardless of how irresponsibly she spent it, achieving some autonomy from her father was integral to Megan's growth, her future well-being and self-respect. Mistakes were part of the process. He just hoped neither she nor anyone else got hurt or worse while she went about sorting herself out.

Not to mention that short of nailing her into a barrel and feeding her through the bunghole until she was thirty, there wasn't a chance in hell he could make her do anything she didn't choose to do.

She was old enough to defy him, to demand his respect for her *right* to do what she chose with her own body. But she wasn't emotionally mature enough to understand that respect was a two-way street, that it must be given to be received. That she had to respect herself before she'd ever be able to comprehend respect accorded her by anyone else.

Especially her father.

Sighing, he clicked on the safety of his .38 and snapped it back into its holster, then righted the dollhouse. Spindled on a roof spire, a sheet of paper fluttered and crackled, catching his eye. He should be grateful, he supposed, that she'd at least left him a note this time.

He turned the bit of paper right side up, though he could read the cryptic message upside down. *At Li's.* Damn, he should have figured. She always ran to the Andens' house after they'd fought, took refuge with Li and her mother and siblings whenever she was frightened or unsure. Had ever since Gen died.

She wanted to move out there, live with Li and her family, leave him behind.

She'd first started asking if she could within a month of Gen's death. He'd tried to gently point out that they had a house, had a place to live together. She'd screamed at him that she didn't want to live with him; she wanted to live with Li and Tai and David and Bele and Kate-who-loved-and-understood-her and who had room for lots of kids and liked lots of kids and was always fostering some, and *not* with him, because he was never home anyway and she didn't know him because he was always working and never home the way Mom had always been home and she didn't want to live with a stranger.

Disbelief, denial, anger.

At the time he'd put it down to her being distraught over losing not only Gen but her unborn sister. Even five years ago, at eleven, Megan had understood enough of what the doctors at the hospital said to realize that if Gen hadn't been pregnant, she probably wouldn't have died when she did. Instinct let her blame Hank for killing her mother, let her run from him, refusing to hear anything further; it was safer than learning only Gen's own selfishness had caused the aneurysm that killed her. And Hank found he couldn't burden Megan with the truth so soon after. Later he hadn't had the heart to tell her that if Gen hadn't wanted another child so badly, if she hadn't been so opposed to adoption, if she hadn't lied to him about her doctor's warnings not to become pregnant, if she'd told him how likely it was she wouldn't survive to term, then he never would have…

Never would have slept with her again if he'd known, if she'd told him, if that was what it took.

But she hadn't and he had and that was what the present boiled down to: *if.*

If.

Disbelief, denial, anger.

Now he had a sixteen-year-old daughter in constant and escalating trouble, a child-woman who hated him on her best days and whom he couldn't reach even on his best; a career he'd gradually whittled back to nothing in order to be home with—and for—Megan as much as possible; and the desperate sense that he'd not only run out of ideas but options; that the next step he and Megan would take, no matter how badly he—and, who knew, maybe even she—wanted to avert it, would be juvenile detention, jail, drug rehab or worse.

And God help him, blind and naive as it might make him seem, he wanted to believe they needn't go that far, that she would come out of this…phase the better for having been through it. Trust that under all Megan's teenage angst, defiance and hell was a terrific, responsible kid he was too close to see.

His colleagues, most of whom had seen similar stories played out over and again, called him an idiot; the psychiatric counselor who worked with him and Megan— or just him when Megan didn't show up for sessions—fed him the say-nothing pap that all parents wanted to believe the best of their children.

He'd laughed in the counselor's face, suggested their time was short and within it she'd better tell him something he freaking well didn't know. Only he hadn't been quite so polite.

He gave her credit for keeping her cool, for simply stiffening and asking him if he'd ever been a hostage negotiator.

"I know the drill," he'd said. *"Feed 'em lip service, but create trust. Stall for time, but don't lie. Request a show of faith, gain ground, find out what they want and use it to take 'em."*

She'd nodded. *"Exactly,"* she said, and waited for him to put it together with Megan, with discussions in past sessions, with the dawning knowledge of what he'd refused for far too long to see: he was his daughter's hostage, as she was his. Negotiating the path to their future as a family was the only hope they had.

Bargaining.

As the therapist suggested, in his fear of losing her—Judas H. Priest, what a laugh, huh? In his fear of losing her he'd lost her long ago—he'd flat out avoided giving Megan what she'd spent the past five years asking for: sanctuary with Li's family. It seemed wrong to him to involve anyone else in his travails, but God help him, he was at the point with Megan where if it would help get her back, he'd get down on his knees and beg the universe.

Acceptance.

She was his daughter. From the moment she'd been conceived, she'd owned his heart. But maybe she didn't know that anymore, couldn't know it. Maybe he'd forgotten how to tell her.

And maybe if he learned to stop isolating himself from her, to accept the terrible thing that had happened to them, she could, too.

In defeat he reached for the phone and tapped out the number for the most irritating and opinionated goody-two-shoes he'd ever met in his life: Li's mother, Kate Anden.

Acceptance.

Chapter 1

A pushmi-pullyu shoved at the screen window beside his bed, with both noses trying to get a better look at him.

Groggy and disoriented, Hank shook his head and blinked at the beast, wondering what a fictional creature from the pages of one of Megan's old Dr. Dolittle books was doing in his dream.

Nothing constructive apparently.

Shaped like a llama, but with a head at both ends—myth was a creative business, after all—Hank watched one delicate black nose find a weak spot at the side of the screen, then push hard enough for the lightweight mesh to tear. Immediately the nose on the head at the other end of the body enlarged the opening and shoved inside; the first head hummed inquisitively at the second head, which hummed conversationally back. As though reassured, the black head joined its red counterpart underneath the mesh. Two pairs of intelligent long-lashed liquid brown eyes studied him curiously; two sets of long banana-shaped ears twitched. Then the split reddish-brown lip below the blackish-roan-colored nose *lupped* up the cotton sheet covering his legs, pulling it off him.

"Hey," Hank muttered and yanked the sheet back over himself. Dream or not, no mythical creature—especially not one out of a child's book—was going to see him nude. He turned over and covered his head with his pillow, hoping that ignoring it would make the dream go away.

It didn't.

Instead the pushmi-pullyu's nearer nose flipped the pillow off his head and whuffled warmly in his ear.

"Hey!"

Startled, Hank jerked and rolled instinctively away, banging his hip hard on the bed frame before he hit the floor. So much for the hope that he was dreaming.

"Maizie, Clarence, get out of there," a sharp, youthful male voice called from somewhere just beyond Hank's window. "You're not supposed to be out here."

Guiltily, the pushmi-pullyu withdrew from the window, then apparently folded itself neatly in half and departed swiftly, both heads facing in the same direction. Which meant either he'd seriously gone round the bend imagining the two heads belonged to one animal, or there was one seriously double-jointed two-headed beast running around out there. In a moment the curious beast faces were replaced by the face and body of a slight-built Asian-American youth in his early twenties.

"Sorry for the intrusion, Mr. Mathison," this new apparition said, "but the *crias* didn't get to meet you last night when you and Megan moved in. They think they're supposed to meet everybody, so they decided to introduce themselves." Fine-boned hands reached through the torn screen to pull the levers that released the screen's frame from the window. "I'll fix this and have it back in a jiff."

Without another word he disappeared, leaving Hank almost more perplexed and unenlightened than he'd felt when the pushmi-pullyu heads first appeared in his window. Before he could gather himself back together sufficiently to either sort out his confusion over where he was or get off the floor, the youth who'd taken his screen reappeared as suddenly as he'd gone.

"I'm sorry. We didn't have a chance to meet yesterday, either, so you don't know who I am, do you?" He extended a friendly hand through the screenless window. "I'm Tai, Li's oldest brother."

Hank stared blankly at Tai's hand, desperately attempting to orient himself. He always knew where he was, *always*. He never got taken by surprise, never forgot himself, ever. It was too dangerous, one of an undercover agent's worst nightmares. But damned if he could figure out where he was or what was going on here. Tai? Li? Pushmi-pullyus and *crias*? Wasn't *cria* what llama babies were called?

He was pretty certain he hadn't been to Peru, Bolivia or anywhere else in South America where they used llamas for at least two years now. In which case, where the *hell* was he and how the devil had he gotten here?

As though reading Hank's mind, Tai turned his hand sideways and used it for punctuation when he prompted patiently, "Stone House Christmas Tree Farm, Stone House Originals? The Andens? Your daughter's my sister's best friend since kindergarten? You talked to my mother about some problems you were having with Megan, then rented our guesthouse and moved in last night—"

Light dawned—no mean feat in a cabin thickly surrounded by oaks, maples and towering pines.

"I remember." Wincing at the twinge in his bruised hip, Hank pushed himself back up onto the narrow bunk and extended his hand toward the window. "Tai, yeah. Hi. Heard a lot about you from Megan and Li. Nice to finally put a face on you. Excuse the, uh…'' He gestured at the sheet. "I usually wear pants to meet Meg's friends."

Tai grinned. "No prob. We're not much for ceremony around here."

Hank grimaced. "I noticed. Meg didn't tell me you keep llamas."

"Llamas, alpacas, a couple of vicuñas we managed to find and import…" Tai shrugged. "They make a great security patrol, but mostly we raise them for the fiber, er, the wool. As to who keeps whom…that's a toss-up."

"Hmm," Hank commented, noncommittal, aware that some observation seemed necessary, but unsure what might be appropriate. "That's…interesting."

"No, it's not." Tai's frank grin widened, his dark eyes amused and wise to Hank's ploy. Almost automatically Hank filed away the knowledge that to underestimate this man on the basis of his youth and appearance of innocence would be a mistake he'd be well advised not to make—if he valued what remained of his ego, that is. "It's a fact you'd rather learn later when you're more awake, if at all."

"Mmm," Hank agreed before he caught himself, then shrugged, sheepish, and shoved unruly hair off his forehead. "You always do this to people you don't know?" he asked.

Tai nodded. "Pretty much. Ma says it saves time and establishes the ground rules without a lot of fuss."

Ma, Hank reflected darkly. The unsettling, wild-strawberry-haired, stubborn, tact-is-a-four-letter-word-so-I-leave-it-home Kate. He should have guessed. "Does *Ma* have a lot of ground rules?"

"One or two." Tai straightened away from the windowsill and collected the screen again. "Well, better get to work." He started to leave, then turned back, snapping his fingers. "Oh, yeah, I almost forgot. Ma said to tell you Megan snuck up to the house and spent the night in Li's room, and since you probably haven't had time to stock your pantry, if you want breakfast it's almost on the table, so you better come on up before everybody with hollow legs gets there and grabs the choice bits first—I'm quoting.''

Hank yawned, at once covering unreasonable annoyance and sleepiness with the back of his hand. Of course Kate Anden had ground rules all the kids around here—including Megan, blast it—followed and repeated. He only need remember the list she'd handed him when he'd asked to rent this place: nice, neat and straightforward, positive, clear and concise, every ''don't'' preceded by a ''please'' and followed by a ''thank you,'' and every ''do'' preceded by a warm ''be our guest and…'' Damned ornery woman would probably hand a list of ground rules to the Almighty on judgment day and expect them to be followed.

Damn it, what made Kate always appear to be so much more competent a single parent than he was?

She chose to be a single parent from the get-go, fool, that's what.

And Megan wanting to be here with Li, her siblings and Kate—Megan willing to follow Kate's rules *enthusiastically,* damn it!—was the reason he'd shut up their house, *Gen's* house, and moved out here for the summer after all. It wouldn't accomplish anything if he didn't start out by making the best he could of a situation he didn't want to be in.

He knew it was fear that lay behind this unfamiliar sense of pettiness, fear of a future devoid of Megan. His daughter was old enough to make choices, and by her actions she found Kate the perfect antidote to life with him. But he couldn't lose her. Megan was his life, his last connection to the wife he'd loved to distraction but had never understood.

Quashing dissonance with effort, he nodded at Tai. ''Yeah, okay, appreciate it. Let me get dressed and I'll be along. Thanks.''

Maybe later he would mean it.

Kate Anden stuck out her lower lip and puffed air at her perspiring forehead. Glued into the sweat, strands of loose hair fluttered about her eyes, refusing to give ground.

Irritably she let go of her spade and swiped the back of her forearm across her face. Blasted stuff, always in the way. Where she'd ever gotten the idea it might be *fun* to grow her hair out she'd never know. An un-nunly vanity, no doubt, after years of wearing it tight cropped around her ears for the sake of practicality and health during the time she'd spent working in refugee camps in South America, Vietnam, Cambodia and Nigeria. But enough was enough already. She really was going to cut the blasted stuff this time, the very *instant* she had more than five minutes in a row and a pair of scissors.

Finding more than five minutes in a row and a pair of scissors in the same place at the same time was something of a family joke, however. Between Christmas-tree farming and llama ranching, custom handcrafting and parenting, 4-H sponsoring and a little of thising, a little of thating, the requisite items never did seem to quite get the hang of meeting.

'Course, it probably would help if she'd at least braided it this morning, like she usually did, instead of leaving it loose. What had possessed her to commit the rash act, she hadn't a clue—or rather, she *told* herself she didn't.

Believing herself was another matter entirely.

She'd *told* herself it was a cool morning and let it hang around her shoulders and back to her waist—she'd grown it out for a lot of years now—for the warmth it provided. But she didn't believe that, either. It was that *man* she'd rented the guesthouse to, Hank Mathison, who had her behaving like an irrational middle schooler or some female peacock spreading her feathers to show off for whichever male peacock happened to be in the area.

The fact that it was generally the male who preened for the female didn't help in the slightest. Heaven help her, she'd never behaved like this in her *life*. What the dickens was wrong with her now? Especially since she was pretty certain she and Hank Mathison didn't even *like* each other. At all.

Sighing, she spread gloved hands over the backs of her hips and stretched her back. In front of her lay an acre of freshly mulched and cultivated Douglas fir transplants; to her left and right, the fifteen acres of five- to ten-year-old spruce, firs, cedars and pines Tai and the boys would mow and cultivate over the next week for spraying in the following week; behind lay the house, llama sheds, toolsheds, workshop and recently-planted kitchen garden where she could see her two youngest sons playing with the hose. Mike and Bele, her eight-year-olds. From separate gene pools and different parts of the world entirely, but two of a kind nevertheless. She grinned and stretched forward, unkinking muscles from another direction.

A hawk screamed overhead, circling the empty field across from the house in search of prey. Around him the sky was clear and blue, sans even a wisp of cloud fluff. It had been on such a day nearly a decade and a half ago that she'd left the convent for the last time to take up life in an unsettling, unsheltering world. The clarity of a blue sky on a beautiful morning had not prevented it from being a scary day, however. Not because she'd been forced to desert the life she thought she'd been called to, but because she'd chosen to leave it, known in her heart she had to. Realized— with some regret—that her true place in life was outside the contentment and cloister a religious order had to offer.

But where she'd been headed, she hadn't a clue.

And now there was here, right now, this morning: three kids successfully adopted; one adoption in the works, nearing completion; two Ukrainian foster sons here indefinitely; one Finnish exchange student who would leave at the end of the summer; a dozen 4-H members here to work with the llamas and the trees; and one bent-on-self-destruction teenage girl who happened to be her only daughter's best friend.

And the teenager's widower father: a too-pretty-to-have-a-brain, arrogant, brutish—according to Megan—know-it-all, pain-in-the-butt sonofagun who'd been too busy risking his life cowboying after bad guys to be around his daughter much when she was still young enough to learn to trust him. A cretin with the sensitivity of a gnat when it came to women—and particularly adolescent women who were really still little girls in "hot babe" bodies; who was unable to appreciate good sense when Kate was willing to give it to him. And willing to give it to him *free* at that.

She glanced toward the narrow, dark tree-cluttered drive that veered off behind the equipment sheds en route to the guesthouse and grinned suddenly, laughing at herself. Well, maybe Hank Mathison was right after all when he called her a self-righteous goody-two-shoes. She wasn't certain how goody-two-shoes she was, but he *did* have a point when it came to her bouts of self-righteousness. It had never been any secret that she and the absolute conviction that she knew what was best for everybody—especially everybody *else*—were on excellent terms.

No wonder she'd done so badly in the convent.

But she still didn't have a great deal of use for Hank Mathison. No matter how belatedly concerned with his daughter's welfare he was.

No matter how unglued merely shaking hands with him over the rental contract had made her feel.

No matter how often she'd had to shove him out of her sleeping dreams since.

She'd never in her life met a man who'd ever made her feel unglued or even a tiny bit flustered, who'd ever had anything remotely to do with her dreams. She didn't think she'd ever in her life since she was a moony sixteen even experienced *that* kind of dream. And she could do very well without them now, thank you just the same.

Still, he had the softest, coolest, firmest right hand of any man she'd ever met.

A pair of young llamas bolted through Kate's patch of new transplants, interrupting her reverie, their soft-padded, two-toed feet neatly missing the unfledged trees. A pair of recently turned teenage boys followed close on their heels.

"Ma, hey, Mom!"

"Kate, Kate!"

Not nearly so graceful or surefooted as young llamas— size twelve feet on a fast growing thirteen-year-old body made grace a thing of the future, if it arrived at all—Ilya, the younger of Kate's foster sons, came to a halt in front of her. He wobbled precariously between transplants for a moment before unintentionally planting one oversize, unmanageable foot squarely on the fragile fir at her feet. She heaved an exaggerated sigh and made a face at him.

"Thanks," she said dryly. "That should firm the soil nicely. Where's the fire?"

"Excuse." Carefully he removed his foot, bent and straightened the squashed bit of green. It listed hard to port. He eyed Kate, guilty and hopeful at once, falling back on accented English and foreign ingenuousness in self-defense. The fact he hadn't possessed much of either since the start of his second school year here the previous fall didn't faze him in the slightest. "It will grow?" A question and a statement.

Kate leaned over to right the mashed seedling for him. "Is it broken?"

Ilya inspected the fir's twiggy shaft. "No?" Doubtful.

Kate swallowed a grin. Amazing how convenient his lapses of English were. "Yes, you mean?"

"Oh."

Crestfallen, the youth dragged a line in the dirt with the toe of his shoe. Beside him his best friend, Jamal, regarded Kate with a combination of fear and defiance—almost as though he expected her to strike Ilya for accidentally mushing a transplant.

That was ridiculous, of course. The baby trees were quite

literally about a dime a dozen; she and Tai always over-planted, knowing they were bound to lose a few seedlings to any number of things: llamas, deer, rabbits, insects, kids' feet...

With an inward sigh Kate plucked the ruined tree from the earth and set it aside, then pulled a replacement from the bunch left to plant. This wasn't the first time she'd wondered about Jamal's home life. Unfortunately without either an invitation to butt in or Jamal trusting her enough to confide in her—*if* indeed there was anything to confide—her overly righteous nature and bad experience had taught her there were a few lines better left uncrossed.

Even though she would willingly, and had for other kids in the past. Wanna see the scars?

With a silent snort of *yeah, right,* she got to her feet, handed the new transplant to Ilya, collected her spade and made a slit in the dirt. "So," she said, "what are you two flying blind about?"

"Huh?" Caught off guard by the lack of dire consequences, Jamal watched her, puzzled, skittishly poised for flight. Waiting for retribution to sneak up and cuff him none too gently on the back of the head, Kate guessed.

Thoroughly unconcerned by contrast, Ilya knelt and fiddled the tree roots into the dirt gash. "We came to tell you the *crias* are loose." All but a trace of accent had disappeared.

"I noticed." Kate stamped the earth around the roots, stepped the square blade of the spade in a few inches away, then leaned it forward to pack the dirt tighter around the base of the tree. A few feet the other side of the transplant line Maizie and Clarence regarded her with interest, undoubtedly storing information for future use. The saw among llama owners and breeders was: "Llamas are the second most intelligent creature after dolphins, which probably makes them smarter than people. They will change your life." Absolutely true, all of it. Especially that last.

She made a face at them, then looked at Ilya. "Anything else?"

Ilya grinned. "Tai said to tell you they tore the screen out of Mr. Mathison's bedroom window and woke him up. He wasn't very happy about it and he didn't know we kept llamas. Tai thinks you'll hear about it at breakfast."

Another face, this one an exact replica of Ilya's older brother's *oh man, do I hafta?* She sighed, this time aloud. "Put Maizie and Clarence back with their mothers and get in to breakfast. I'll deal with Mr. Mathison."

Now if only she could figure out why she anticipated that prospect with such relish...

There was something decidedly...bewitching about the place.

He could feel it even through the fog in which he'd woken, could understand a little of what drew Megan here time and again, to hide in the shadows of Kate Anden's always green trees. Pagan beliefs, he'd told Megan a long time ago, explaining the origin of the Christmas tree to her, held that trees that stayed green all winter had magical powers. Maybe it was his own fault she ran here from him. It was the stories he'd told her when she was a child.

She was still his child.

The scent of dew-laden pine, balsam, cedar and spruce, of fusty earth and trampled ferns and wintergreen leaves, sifted into his nostrils when he stepped out of the cabin onto the front porch. The trill of red-winged blackbirds warning each other of his passing, the songs of finches, bluebirds and swallows, the constant chant of the spring peepers and the other frogs that filled the woods and marshy areas deeper in—the chaos of sound blended and caught at his ears, filtered through his nervous system to settle a soul jangled raw by too much civilization, paperwork, politics, news...by too much Megan in crisis.

The slur-sound of vegetation to his left made him start.

Three deer shied and leaped away from the sough of his feet on the roadbed; he stared after them, lungs shuddering, heart pounding. It had been five years since he'd spent any time in the jungles of Colombia and Bolivia chasing cocaine farmers and their lords, and still his subconscious couldn't feel safe surrounded by trees.

With an effort, he stood still and breathed, letting scent and sound, the cool touch of shadow on exposed skin become an instant of peace he'd forgotten he'd been missing. Sweet solitude with no place he had to be, no responsibilities he had to face, no decisions he had to make that would affect anyone else's life. Two blessed minutes to himself— a lifetime it almost seemed.

If only he could figure out how to make it be enough.

He moved forward, walking the rutted quarter-mile trail from the cabin to the house that he and Megan and their luggage had jounced down the night before in the car, trying to take in everything around him at once. He wanted, he realized with a sudden disquieting start, he *needed* something from this place not only for Megan but for himself.

For *him*.

The kitchen was huge and warm, richly scented with sizzling meat, coffee and carbohydrates, a true farm kitchen.

Aromas dragging at his senses and making his insides gurgle in anticipation, Hank walked across the stone-floored mud room and rapped on the wooden screen door. When no one answered, he let himself in.

Immediately to his left, a long, dark green-painted wooden table with matching benches sat before a bank of open windows framed by filmy-looking lace curtains. Around the table a boisterous group of boys of varying sizes, colors and ages straddled the benches helping themselves to platters of pancakes, toast and sausages; plastic gallons of milk and juice passed hand to hand to fill mismatched plastic movie and superhero glasses from sundry local fast-food restaurants.

At the stove-top griddle on the far side of the kitchen stood two teenage girls in bright T-shirts and jeans with their hair ponytailed in vivid neon scrunchies. Without difficulty he recognized Li's long black hair and creamy Asian skin, her slim, graceful hands shoveling pepper-speckled scrambled eggs into a bowl. She looked the way she always looked to him: pretty, healthy, mature beyond her years, sure of herself and her place in the world, clear-eyed, knowing and…innocent as opposed to naive. Beside her, the girl with the laugh-curved mouth, soft brown hair and natural-glow skin wielding the pancake spatula also appeared fit and uncomplicated, young, and if not yet entirely certain of her direction, then at least convinced that she would eventually find one.

It took him a full thirty seconds and a startled heartbeat to realize the girl beside Li was Megan.

Talk, laughter and an astonishing variety of gross mouth sounds floated around Hank, yet he heard nothing. Stunned, he stared at his daughter, wondering who she was, how she'd gotten the black dye out of her hair so fast, what she'd done to liven up her skin tone from the ghastly paleness she normally sported and why she never looked like this at home.

Multiple personalities, his mind whispered, turning over possibilities in psychiatric jargon, searching for a pigeonhole. *Schizophrenia. Manic depression and this is the manic part.*

"Morning, Mr. Mathison."

Brisk and breezy, Kate Anden strolled in to Hank's astonishment, her flyaway, sun-kissed red-gold hair crossing his line of vision before the rest of her had a chance to. He looked at her.

"That's my daughter," he said, adequate response lagging well behind the event.

Kate nodded. "Different, isn't she?"

His mouth flattened, his wary gaze returned to his daughter. "I'm not sure that's the word I'd choose."

"No," Kate agreed without thinking. "It's probably not. You probably chose schizophrenic."

Attention arrested, Hank turned to her. Not a pretty woman by any stretch of the imagination; she was hardly what he could call plain, either. She had a quality, a beauty—honesty forced him to call it that—that was almost feral: big teeth in a slight overbite in a mouth that was overly generous, both literally and figuratively; eyes of a pale tourmaline blue with dark rings around the irises and in the left a rust-colored freckle next to the pupil; skin both freckled and flushed from a life spent largely outdoors; hair that was thick and riotous with a blend of autumn colors, fuzzy and unruly and playful—at present, an unbound rufous chaos that whirled about her waist; a body both slim and overly lavish, seductive but demure because she gave her attributes not one second of regard, didn't...play them up or take advantage of them or acknowledge them at all.

She also had a smile that could halt a hungry tiger in its tracks, a throaty, infectious laugh and a voice that would soothe the most cantankerous drug lord he'd ever met. Which was why he'd never been able to deny Megan permission to come here and get lost and found among the hordes of Kate's adopted children, foster children, exchange students and the multitudes of extras that drifted to her shores. When they'd shaken hands over the rental agreement on the guesthouse three days ago, he'd felt a shock from the center of his palm to the bottom of his toes—almost as if she'd hidden a practical joker's buzzer in her hand.

There'd been only skin between them, however. Hers hard and dry and impersonal, moisturized soft, but used to work. He shouldn't have felt anything, but she'd made his hormones snap, crackle and fizz awake.

Damn it.

He had a daughter to worry about; he didn't need to have his sleepy libido roused just now, and particularly not by a woman who couldn't have been further from his type—hell, who couldn't be further from any man's type, hc'd guess—than the saintly and pushy Kate Anden.

He cast a glance at Megan, then back to Kate.

"Be nice if things were really this simple, wouldn't it?" Kate asked quietly.

Caught off guard, Hank nodded, his eyes once again on Megan, his thoughts focused on her and far away at once. "Yeah, it would. But nothin' ever is."

"You sound like you've got personal knowledge of that." Crisp and doubtful. Unexpectedly...gentle.

Drawn back from haunted places, Hank turned his head and stared at her. She viewed him, eyes frank and unwinking, blunt and psychic as she'd been four-and-a-half years earlier when she'd called him at his office to announce that he'd better stop on his way home and get some maxi-pads for Megan who'd started her monthlies a week after Gen's death and had been borrowing pads from Li regularly for the five months since. And to inform him that Li, then barely twelve, was the one who'd had to instruct Megan in the whys and wherefores of a woman's cycles and bodily functions and did Hank maybe want her, Kate, to pull Megan aside and correct any misinformation his daughter might have been given, since his daughter obviously needed someone to talk to and he, apparently, wasn't it?

He didn't like Kate any better now than he had then, despite the fact she seemed to hold the keys to his daughter's psyche—and probably because of it.

The center of his right palm itched with memory anyway.

He reminded himself that smoke didn't have to mean fire. That gentleness didn't necessarily equate with *like,* as in "I like you." That desire didn't have to be acted upon.

Still, in the interest of even footing he ignored the sensation of being singed and went on the attack instead.

''I knew you had a lot of kids, but these can't all be yours.''

As though she'd expected the move, Kate grinned at him. There was something faintly mischievous in the curve of her mouth, imperceptibly mocking, subtly inviting. A sense of humor he'd been unaware she possessed. A you've-changed-the-subject-but-it-doesn't-matter-we-can-go-back-to-it-later.

A dare-ya.

He'd rented her guesthouse for how long?

''They're ours this morning,'' she said.

Chapter 2

She viewed him deadpan. Serenely serious.

It took him a minute to register the *ours*. Too late. Irritating and enigmatic as he'd ever found her, she sashayed across to the spitting coffee maker before he could call her back without alerting the mob at the table, collected a mug from the hooks underneath a cupboard and offered it to him.

"Coffee, Mr. Mathison?"

"Sure." Hank eyed her, out of his element, knots of ulceration forming in his stomach. A curious jigger of anticipation—not unlike the buzz of making a successful first connection on an undercover—doodled down his spine.

Up until Gen's death he'd been of the daredevil undercover DEA breed—necessary to the cause, but heavily monitored nonetheless—a risk taker, a cowboy who'd gotten juiced on bandying words, deeds and attitudes with the worst the world had to offer. A flea on the back of the drug-cartel elephant, he'd thought of himself: incessant and irritating; unable to stop the elephant, but occasionally causing an itch serious enough to bring it to its knees.

Still, none of that had prepared him for this.

Of course, he thought wryly, none of that had prepared him to be Megan's father alone on his own, either, and look how successful he was at that.

He saw Kate set down the coffeepot and crossed to her while watching the impostor Megan laughingly pass a platter of pancakes and sausages to the boys at the table.

She turned to him, clear-eyed and beautiful, the way he always wanted to see her. "Pancakes, Dad?"

"Who are you and what have you done with my daughter?" Kidding. Suspicious. Putting his foot in it.

She laughed, "Da-ad," and returned to help Li at the griddle.

Maybe he hadn't stepped in too deep. And if they'd made this much progress overnight, maybe they wouldn't have to even stay the whole summer.

"How do you take it?" Kate asked.

"An inch at a time," he said honestly.

She gave him a straight face. "Your coffee?"

"What?"

He looked at her; chagrin caught up with him at the same time the conversation did. He'd stepped into that one, all right. This woman had a mean sense of humor; he'd have to stand on his toes in order not to get caught in it again. "Oh. No, I mean milk, no sugar." He inhaled, consciously bringing himself back into the moment. It had been that conspiratorial *ours,* the intimation of *you-and-me,* when he was absolutely certain there wasn't.

Despite the return of the phantom fizz to the center of his right palm.

"Thanks." He accepted the mug she handed him and sipped, feeling awkward at the silence she didn't appear to notice. He broke it. Idly. "What exactly does *ours* mean?"

She grinned. "I wondered when that'd catch up with you."

"Not soon enough, apparently."

"You said you wanted this to be a working vacation." Silent laughter was bright in her eyes. She enjoyed poking and prodding him. Relished spooning the previous week's desperate pledges back at him with a shovel. "You said you wanted to get your hands dirty and be reintroduced to Megan and get to know her and forget about being a paper pusher with the DEA."

He gave her narrow-eyed scrutiny. "What, did you write our conversation down verbatim?"

She offered him glib. "Photographic memory."

"For everything, or only what it suits you to photograph?"

She looked at him, surprised by the question, the observation. She adjusted her view. Guarded.

Thoughtful.

"Touché," she said and saluted him with her mug.

He chalked a mental point in the air. Direct hit, score one. And he hadn't even intended to.

He also hadn't realized that bandying words with the enemy would return so naturally—or feel so good—any place outside a sting operation. It had been a long time since he'd worked a sting.

Being an assistant director for the midwest DEA, Detroit office, meant spending half his time trying to halt the offloaders of drugs within American borders. The other half was spent trying to train educators, families and the local police in ways to prevent drug dealers from permeating an area—often a depressing and thankless task. He'd had to develop skills for the job that were unlike any he'd used on the front lines, to learn to play office politics and budgetary tunes, to control his enthusiasm for any single operation by ever bearing in mind the big picture. To play party pooper—often not so different from parenting a teenager, he'd discovered—when *he'd* always hated the guy who put the damper on *his* party, when he'd been the one working the street.

But now, here he was again, lips working automatically to a tune somebody else had written, his sense of humor rusty with disuse but kicking in nonetheless, his brain improvising instantly in enemy territory. It felt *good*.

He hadn't even realized he'd missed it.

"Here you go, Dad, Kate."

Megan stepped into the middle of the eye duel he fought with Kate, plates at the ready. Knowledge and calculation glimmered almost perceptibly behind her eyes and inside the faint smugness of the smile settling her features, he noted. Whether deliberately or not, for the first time since Gen's death Megan had found one of the things she'd been looking for: a woman to play him against. A gender ally.

"Pancakes, eggs, sausage patties," she said. "Enjoy."

"Meg—" Hank began, but she evaded his voice and was back across the kitchen with Li, the table and the wall of vociferous boys placed neatly between them again.

Kate eyed Megan speculatively, recognizing the transparent ploy for what it was. And not liking it.

She'd been played against other adults by other kids in the past, but never more adroitly than it appeared she'd been played this time. It meant she might have to ally herself with Megan's father in the crunch, and she wasn't sure she'd want to.

Her jaw tugged tight, eyes puckered around the thought. "Cute trick," she said.

Hank nodded. "Yeah," he agreed, thoughtful himself. He looked at Kate, tracking the direction of her reflections by her expressions. "It is, isn't it?"

"She do this with you often?"

"Often as she can."

The corners of her mouth tucked a little. "Mom's a saint in heaven, but you're alive so you're the bad guy?"

He nodded. "That's the part of it I can figure out."

They viewed each other again, perspective canting. Communication on a wavelength only parents can hear—in a sort of parental shorthand instinctively improvised to maintain private communication in a world filled with big-eared kids—made him eye her hard, suspicious. This was not what he'd expected—*she* was not what he expected: a self-righteous goody-two-shoes, perhaps, but she wasn't blind. He might never be able to like her, but with a little judicious footwork he'd be able to work with her.

The same rapport made Kate look at him, too, a third time, and shake loose a fallacy she'd known better than to believe but had believed anyway: he was not who Megan—or even Li—said he was. There was something more to Hank Mathison than the self-involved DEA cowboy, hard-nosed pain-in-the-butt paper pusher she'd been told he was.

She consoled herself with the fact that she had no idea what "something more" was—and had no intention of finding out.

As often happens in a house filled with preteen and adolescent boys and two mid-teenage girls, a sudden shriek cut loose. As one, Kate and Hank turned toward the source of the cry, to find Li standing at the kitchen sink with one arm outstretched, a sealed Ziploc bag dangling from her fingers as far away from her as she could get it. Next to her, Megan hid her face in her hands and shuddered.

Hank started toward his daughter, all comforting, protective parent, then stopped short when he realized she wasn't upset by whatever it was in Li's hand. She was laughing so hard she could barely stand.

It had been years since he'd seen Megan laugh for pleasure instead of to cause pain.

"Who—left—the—stoat—in—the—sink?" Li asked, teeth locked hard together, every word glacially enunciated.

Grisha, Ilya's fourteen-year-old brother, started away from the table and grabbed the bag from Li. "It must thaw."

"Thaw?" she asked. "*Thaw?*"

"To make the..." he hesitated. "The taxidermy."

"Thaw?" Li said again, outraged. "This was in the *freezer?*"

Grisha nodded, eminently reasonable. "In the big meat freezer in the mud room. I found it last Thursday, freshly dead." He held up the bag so the tableful of boys could admire it. "I was most careful. I made sure it is very clean and the bag is closed very tight so you can see the green line like they show on TV to be certain, then I put the bag in Tupperware in the bottom bin where nothing was and washed my hands up to my elbows with that betadine scrub Dr. Chmiel says he uses between patients and before surgery. Bele and Mike have never seen a weasel. It is for science and education I brought it home. I told them we could skin it and stuff it like a taxidermist for their 4-H group. I could not leave it out to rot waiting for today."

Li stared at him, speechless. "That's…that's *gross.*"

Surprised, Grisha stared at her. "You have never dissected frogs or sheep's eyes or worms or anything for your biology class?"

"That's different."

"How?"

"Well, for one thing they aren't road kill—"

Hank glanced at Kate, looking for reaction cues.

She shrugged. "Don't listen," she advised. "It's the only way."

Lips pursing around a reluctant grin, Hank nodded. He'd had a feeling the way back to track would be drastic, but this…

He glanced once more at his daughter. On the other side of Li, Megan sagged against the counter and howled. Witnessing her enjoyment, deep inside him an ember stirred and began to glow. He swallowed, leery.

He'd been told that oftentimes grief ran in cycles, receding and returning in stages, that hope returned after the grieving process was complete, after you got through the denial and isolation, the bargaining and anger, the depression and finally the acceptance. As recently as yesterday it had still seemed that in five years he and Megan had hardly gotten through the initial round of anger, and were still a long way from hope. Today, within the space of twenty minutes and regardless of his wariness, hope kindled and a few skittish cinders took fragile flame.

Maybe, despite the table and the boys she'd put between them, the multitude of distractions, the woman Kate and her extensive brood, maybe out here surrounded by the magic of trees that stayed green even in the winter he and Megan could get to there from here yet.

After breakfast Kate showed Hank around.

It was a nervewracking job, but somebody had to do it.

"The sheds on this side—" she pointed left "—are for the mother llamas—we call them the 'girls'—and their *crias*. The 'boys' are on the other side of the workshop. Now over here—"

She was pretty sure she wasn't, but she *felt* as if she was babbling. She'd given this tour a thousand times to people who should have been far more daunting, but she'd never in her life felt so uncomfortable and awkward around anyone as she did around Hank Mathison.

"The workshop started out as a way for Tai and Li to earn extra pocket money, maybe pick up a little for college. They did dried flower and herb arrangements, some simple wood stuff—crèches, birdhouses, you know. We took 'em around to some of the local farm markets and things sort of escalated from there. By the time the other kids came along, we were running—"

It was a good thing she'd given this tour to other parents so many times before that she didn't have to think about what she was saying. Simply walking along beside him left her skin with the prickly, irritated sensation of an allergic rash and made her feel short of breath, restless, fevered and wishing to be elsewhere. Sort of. She also sort of didn't want to be elsewhere.

Mostly, and for no apparent reason, she wanted to scream. And giggle hysterically. And slap herself silly, so this obnoxious fluttery-prickly-stilted-feeling idiot would get out of her psyche now, at once, immediately.

Or sooner.

"And we sort of inherited the alpacas from a family who was moving to New York. My brother left me a llama with Mike when he died, and well, we found we liked 'em so much we took on a couple more and things sort of escalated from there. Now we work with a couple of the 4-H clubs, do parades, fairs, things like that, teach the kids how to train the llamas for packing or guarding sheep herds or whatever. We've just started taking a couple of the 'boys' around to the local nursing homes, doing a little, um, llama therapy. People who don't respond to anything else just sort of seem to take to the llamas. The llamas seem to have a kind of…empathy, sympathy, with people who are hurting. Li took Harvey in to one of the homes last week. There was a hundred-and-one-year-old lady who'd been basically catatonic since her husband died. Harvey sniffed her nose and she looked up at him and started crying, latched onto his chest wool and wouldn't let go. Harvey just took it." She grinned. "'Course Li paid for it later. Llamas remember things. When she took him out to put him in the van, he switched his hindquarters around, thunked her into the wheel well and gave her a look Li swears said, 'If you *ever* do that to me again—'"

She looked at Hank, watching his face—for what, she wasn't sure. She reminded herself of Li at thirteen, when her daughter had won backstage passes to a Bush concert: thoroughly and totally adolescent. And *why* she felt this way as thoroughly and totally escaped *her* now as it had Li then.

Fortunately, it didn't seem to show—much. Also, fortunately, becoming everybody's mother had taught Kate the value of laughing at herself and, for the most part, how to ignore adolescent side effects.

She concentrated on what she was saying, instead of on things over which she apparently had no control.

"And this is where we build the miniatures and do most of the other woodworking." She waved a hand at the long tables and tools set up in the heated pole barn behind the three-car garage.

Hank nodded, head on automatic pilot; he swept the room a restless glance. "Looks great." His impatience to move on was undisguised.

Kate shook her head and withheld a sigh.

It had been a long morning showing the distracted and therefore taciturn Hank around; wherever she pointed, his thoughts and gaze were elsewhere—looking, she presumed, for Megan, who'd disappeared with Li and Tai as soon as the breakfast dishes were cleared and loaded into the dishwasher. He had not, she was pretty certain, heard a word she'd said since breakfast. Or noticed anything "funny" or...or...*artificial* about her, either.

Or noticed her at all.

Darn it.

She rolled her eyes and shuddered at that inadvertent internal comment. How old was she, anyway?

Oh, just about *that* old. Or young. Or immature, as the case might be.

Grow up, she told herself rudely. *What on earth is the matter with you?*

She took a sideways peek at the almost too neatly trimmed honey-wheat hair, the time-chiseled features that flirted with a beauty not unlike that accorded the gods by sculptors, the unusual mead-colored eyes... Yep, she was right. Hank Mathison was simply too blessed pretty for her good.

He was the first man she'd ever found so, too. Which brought into the chaos of the moment a whole set of complications she'd never even considered possible, because she'd never thought them hers to contemplate. She had, after all and once upon a time, planned to spend her life in a convent where recognizing the existence of…of…cute guys, as Li would put it, and *libido,* as Tai had so succinctly phrased it when he'd discovered the existence of his, was frowned upon. And she'd never found cause to change that outlook since then simply because she was no longer, as it were, "married to God."

So why now? she asked heaven with some exasperation. *Why give me thirty-some-too-many years of no fireworks and no missin' 'em, then suddenly dump this into my life?*

Because there's no time like the present, heaven or her guardian angel whispered back.

Kate would have sworn there was laughter in the response.

She was glad at least someone found humor in the situation. She, herself, could see the potential for comedy, but it was the kind of comedy where tragedy lurked around the corner ready to pounce the minute it found an opening.

Megan Mathison was a cataclysm biding its moment. Never had that been more clear to Kate than this morning. Megan was also a child who'd lost her mother at one of the most crucial stages of her life, a young woman whose emotional psyche and ego were often still only eleven in a sixteen-year-old's body. She wanted all the things other children wanted—happiness, love, attention and a fairy-tale future—but her ability to achieve her ends by nondestructive means was seriously skewed.

Instinct had brought her to Stone House time and again; reflex made her behave like a kid with a split personality, acting to suit the moment and her own untempered perception of it, causing her to do whatever she had to in order to snow whoever she wanted on her side at the moment. In this instance, Kate. And if Kate managed to get to know and stop…discounting or disliking or something…Hank, if *she* started to act like a teenage girl with her first crush, who knew what Megan's unconsciously manipulative instincts would lead the real teen in this situation to try.

No, Kate sighed. This was definitely not the time to wind up infatuated, for the first time in her life, simply because her suddenly confused and unreliable hormones found Hank Mathison attractive.

"So what goes on in here?" Hank asked.

Kate snapped out of her reverie. She had no idea how long she'd kept Hank standing in the double-width workshop doorway, and it was clear from the look on his face that he had no idea they'd already toured the place.

She'd often thought from the way her late sister-in-law had handled her late brother—Mike's parents—that men as men and not as brothers or fathers or platonic friends must be exasperating beasts. Now she was sure of it.

Canting her head she looked up at him, shading her eyes against the sun haloing out behind him. The same irreverent imp that had been largely responsible for her getting asked to leave the convent reared its cockeyed sense of humor and made her gesture again at the tables, tools, the oversized supply locker along the back wall and say, "This is where we hide the bodies."

That brought him back from wherever he'd been. Fast. "What? What bodies?"

Kate grinned. "I wondered what it took to get your attention."

Hank viewed her irritably. "You've had my undivided attention all morning."

"Yeah, right." Kate snorted and shouldered by him, into the sunlight. "Your undivided attention. If this is an example of your 'undivided attention', it's no wonder Meg feels shorted."

"What the hell are you talking about?" Stung, Hank grabbed her arm, swung her about. A mistake. Especially since he'd already spent the too-long morning trying to curtail his body's awareness of this woman he wanted only to see as a rival for his daughter's affections, or as a means of getting Megan back and not as a *Woman*.

But *Woman* she was. And a hell of a lot of one, at that.

There was a spark in her he hadn't counted on seeing, an electricity in the tourmaline eyes that leaped and crackled, potent when it struck him like a physical blow square in the chest. His lungs grabbed for air as though he were suffocating; his pulse missed first one beat, then two, then caught and charged like the leader in an ice-skating game of crack-the-whip where he was the tail hanging on for dear life so he wouldn't fly off into a tree or a snowbank and come up full of bruises, disgracing himself.

He let go of her arm at the same moment her hand came up to pick his fingers off. Her hands were as strong as they looked, as magnetic as he remembered. Their physical link lasted an instant longer than necessary.

Too long.

He swallowed and put space between them, then completed his thought. "I don't short Meg any attention. My entire life revolves around her—"

"Your mistake," Kate interrupted flatly. It took everything she had in her to simply fold up the fingers that had touched his and not look to see if they were as blistered as they felt. "Not mine."

"So where the devil do you get off accusing me of ignoring my daughter, when you're the one making things so stinking easy for her here she'd rather not come home?"

"You think she comes here because life is *easy?* When she's here, I expect the same things from her that I expect from my own kids and every other kid that comes through here, and let me tell you, buster, that ain't *easy.*"

"I mean," Hank continued as though she hadn't spoken, "the least you could do—" Damn, why couldn't he stop smelling her, tasting the sunshine emanating from her, let go of the sensation tingling through the nerves of his hand…of the imprint of steel strength and vitality encased in the silken skin of her arm sheathed in a clean cotton T-shirt ''—is make it less attractive for her to be here and—''

''Oh, and just how do you suggest I do that?'' Heat shifted and rose through her system: irritation and something else. Something sharp and clinging, tenacious and beguiling, dangerous. Sweet heaven, she wanted to get away from here, from him, from the sizzle and pop of a passion she couldn't understand and that had little to do with the disagreement they were having. That had everything to do with a *want* she'd never before experienced and didn't wish to experience now. Not for him. Not for anyone. She found scorn and let it filter into her voice. Anything to keep whatever this was at arm's length. ''You think I ought to start beating them or something—''

''Mom, Mom!''

''What?'' Kate snapped more sharply than she intended. Immediately guilty, she looked down at Mike and Bele who, oblivious to her tone, danced like excited puppies at her elbow. ''What's up?'' The grin her two ''babies'' almost always provoked was a shadow in her voice this time.

''You gotta come see what we found in the dig!'' Mike tugged at her arm, willing her attention with his enthusiasm.

''It's huge!'' Bele bounced, one-legged, at her other elbow, equally enthusiastic, his hands holding his crutches spread wide to demonstrate dimension. ''A bone this long at least. You have to call the University of Michigan—''

''Nuh-unh,'' Mike objected. ''Michigan State.''

''U of M,'' Bele repeated firmly, pale palms flashing wide for emphasis against the darkness of the rest of his skin, as remarkably single-minded in this as he was in all things. ''We found a really real dinosaur this time, not just some old cow bone and—''

''And Risto says,'' Mike interrupted, referring to the Finnish exchange student who'd spent the past ten months living with them while taking classes with Li at the high school, "that if it's not a dinosaur, then it might be from a woolly mammoth or a saber-toothed tiger or maybe even an eohippus that migrated all the way up here from New Mexico, but Bele 'n' I think it's too big for that—"

"And even if it's not an eohippus or anything except something regular like a murder victim," Bele picked up the thread of the conversation from Mike, almost physically yanking it back to himself, "you still have to come see, cuz it's super important and we've never dug up anything like this before."

"Something regular like…?" Speechless, Hank stared at the youngsters, one fair and the other dark, too far removed from his own boyhood to remember the gruesomely delightful turns of a young boy's mind. The long-time cop in him keened instantly at the word murder; it took real effort to get him to back off this time and remember these were not his everyday bad guys he was dealing with here. But this *was* the second time in less than ten minutes he'd been caught by this family casually mentioning something about dead bodies. Hell of a good thing he didn't work homicide then. And thank *God* Megan's mind had never wandered down such macabre corridors when she was eight—so far as he knew.

But then he probably wouldn't know, gone as often and as long as he'd been, would he?

"Of course I'll come see," he heard Kate say. "But dead body or dinosaur bones, manners first." She turned to him. "Mr. Mathison, have you met my sons Mike and Bele? Boys—" She turned back to them. "This is Megan's father, Mr. Mathiso—" Arrested in mid-word, her focus sharpened on Bele's crutches, sank to his left leg, which Hank noted with shock ended a few inches below his knee. "Where's your leg, Bele? You haven't lost it again, have you?"

Bele made a face at her. "Mo-om. I only did that once and it wasn't my fault. Mike hid it."

"I did not," Mike said indignant. "It was right inside the window seat where I put it. And anyway, you wouldn't give me back my baseball glove and I needed it."

"I didn't take your old glove and it wasn't yours, it was Li's old one and they were going to play *me,* not *you* if you hadn't taken my foot and—"

"Boys." Exasperated, Kate stepped in and brought them back to the point she'd sidetracked them onto. Much as she loved them, there were moments when she wanted to squash them both like tomato slugs. *Insects by day, angels only in sleep,* she'd laughingly told one of the other nuns at the Red Cross hospital they'd set up in El Salvador, observing a pair of scruffy but angelic looking noninnocents con yet another journalist into the purchase of something the "angels" had undoubtedly just swiped from the reporter's pack. "We found the prosthesis, you both got your own baseball gloves, we're done with it, but it doesn't explain where your leg is now—"

"I have a sore on my stump," Bele said matter-of-factly. "I need a new leg."

"A new one?" Kate asked dismayed. "It hasn't even been four months yet, has it? Did you try a lighter stump sock?"

Bele nodded. "It's still too tight, and it's too short, too. I'm growing."

"And to think we once thought too much coffee would stunt your growth." Kate sighed.

"I don't drink coffee," Bele said, affronted.

"Maybe you should start."

"No way! It's disgusting."

"My tennis shoes are too small for me, too," Mike put in, not to be outdone—and because it was the truth. His feet had been triple-E width since birth. "And Bele's old ones are too skinny for my feet, even if his foot *is* longer than mine. I tried them on."

Arms akimbo, Kate eyed them with mock exasperation.

"Weeds," she pronounced, then grinned and ruffled Mike's straight white-blond hair and brushed a hand over Bele's short-shaved wiry black curls. "Feed 'em, water 'em and ignore 'em and they grow like brush fire."

"Mom." Mike rolled his eyes and leaned away, after first reaching up to tap her face with annoyed affection.

"Mo-om." Bele looked up at her with *don't do that* in his voice and love in his eyes.

Back of her wrist to her forehead, Kate moaned with melodramatic sadness, "They don't need me anymore. Sigh, sob." They laughed and she grinned. "Okay. I'll call Dennis and make an appointment to get you fitted for a new socket and pylon, Bele, then while we're in Ann Arbor we'll do shoe shopping. Right, Mike?"

"And lunch at Arby's?" Both boys, in near unison, grinned at each other over this neatly laid trap.

"We'll see," Kate agreed dryly. She jerked a thumb toward the house. "C'mon, Bele, I want to take a look at your leg, make sure it's clean 'n' all. You'll have to use your crutches till it heals—"

Agile on his crutches as any other child on two legs, Bele danced out of reach, shaking his head. "Nuh-unh, you don't have to. Meg already washed it and put stuff on it. Come *on*, Ma," he said, impatient and imploring. "Before Grisha finds our bone—"

"And steals it to figure out how to test for *age* or something," Mike finished.

Unmatched sets of white teeth flashed first at each other, then at Kate, the grins of young boys filled with the possibilities of an entire summer stretched out before them. Eagerly they awaited Kate's laughing nod, then swooped away, looking back only once to make sure she followed.

It might have been his imagination, but Hank thought he discerned Bele moving a little faster to keep up with Mike, saw Mike unconsciously measuring his steps to match the sweep of his brother's leg; crutches and feet hit the ground in perfect time, matching the unbidden plummeting of Hank's heart to his stomach. What, how, who, when—questions he couldn't keep up with zipped past the back of his throat without touching his tongue; only one held any clarity amid the numbness in his brain: how could they...he was only a little boy and they were so...how could they just...

Accept?

Wait a minute. His mind did an unexpected double take. *Megan* took care of Bele's stump sore? *Megan? His* Megan? Willingly?

Four steps across the drive in front of him Kate turned and looked back, pale eyes clear as the sky, full of a knowledge and understanding he still didn't grasp and had never wanted to possess. But all she said was, "Coming, Mr. Mathison?"

Incredulous and...curious as he was, he couldn't bring himself to do anything less. Hank went.

Chapter 3

"It happened not long before he came to us," Kate said without preamble when Hank caught up with her. "He's from a tiny village in southwest Zaire. His family walked three hours to the river for water. He was very young, maybe four. A water skin got away from him. He walked into the river to catch it and a crocodile took his leg."

Hank's heart twisted, sinking in his gut. He'd seen worse things happen to children during his time in Colombia and Bolivia; the only way to deal with horrors he couldn't stop or control had been to look past them, harden himself, not get involved. Here, because of Megan, he was involved by default—even before he'd known there was a Bele. He couldn't—didn't want to—look away. He had to say something, but what? No matter how badly you wanted them to be, words were never adequate to tragedy. "That's terrible."

Kate shrugged, matter-of-fact. "At the time, yes. Now it's inconvenient sometimes, not terrible. Ask him. He's got the coolest left foot in the third grade and he can do anything on it the other kids can do on the ones they were born with and more things on one foot than they'll ever be able to do. The croc could have killed him. Instead it made him special.''

"But—" Hank began and subsided. He was way out of his depth, his element and the range of his control here. "But Megan?" he asked finally, painfully, hating himself for needing to question his daughter's abilities. Hating himself for not knowing as well as he wanted to what her capabilities were. "She...took care of Bele's leg and you don't need to..." He hesitated, neither wanting to belittle his daughter nor indicate the depth of his inability to trust her to do the right thing on her own. "She's only a kid," he said lamely. "What if she... You don't need to...check on her work?"

Kate looked up at him, surprised. She didn't intend to sound sanctimonious; Lord knew, with all the mistakes she made with her kids—past and present—she had as little right to sanctimony as anyone. A trace of it crept into her voice anyway. "Every kid's got a story she wants somebody to listen to, Mr. Mathison."

"You think I don't know that, Ms. Anden?" Hank snapped. Nothing stung worse than truth. "I haven't exactly spent my life with my head in the sand when it comes to—"

"Mr. Mathison, please." Kate held up a hand and Hank chewed his anger into silence. "I didn't mean to imply..." She hesitated. No, that wasn't quite true. She probably *had* meant to imply exactly that. "I shouldn't have said..." Another pause. No, that wasn't true either. *Somebody* had to speak out of turn sometimes; if it had to be her, well... "I'm sorry. I can be rather, er..." She made a face. Confession might be good for the soul, but that didn't mean she enjoyed it. "I'm a little, um, self-righteous sometimes. It's not an attractive feature. I'm working on it, but I still have a tendency to react first and think later sometimes. I do apologize."

Astonished not only by her directness but by her willingness to recognize and accept her own flaws, Hank stared down at her. "That must have hurt."

Kate nodded and made another face. "You'll never know."

His anger faded abruptly. Caught off guard he grinned. "You might be surprised."

"Probably not as much as you'd like me to be," she returned.

Hank laughed. "Touché."

They stopped in the grass a hundred feet shy of the mound of earth Kate and Tai regularly salted with broken clay pots and sharks' teeth and had long ago christened the Stone House Burial Mound and Archaeological Dig and exchanged wary grins. Common ground stood between them, ready to be claimed. Years of conflict peered over their shoulders, whispering caution in their ears. They looked at each other through curious eyes, and the fizz neither wanted to feel or recognize—that neither wanted reciprocated—tingled dully in the nerves of their right palms, hung like an itch out of reach between Kate's shoulder blades, sank like a hungry growl in Hank's belly without cause or reason.

Too busy gently brushing clay from the bone in the dig to be aware of adults in the midst of adult hankerings, no children appeared to rescue them from each other, nor from awareness and uncertainty.

A man who'd always had a knack for not wanting what he couldn't have and for taking what he wanted without regrets, it unnerved Hank to find himself desiring something—some*one*—he didn't plan to take. To find himself aching, drawn to step closer to Kate. To be near enough that loose strands of her long apricot hair reached out in the trace breeze to wrap around his fingers and cling to his hand seemingly to invite him nearer still. He threaded the web of coarse silk between his fingers and watched Kate's face through eyes hooded with self-loathing and desire.

Nervously Kate ran her suddenly dry tongue over her lips and watched him back. This sinking, quavering, butterflies-in-her-stomach, no-holds-barred, this-is-*it* thud of her pulse was beyond her ken, a sensation she'd never before experienced. She didn't *want* this, didn't know what to do with it, could read the *be careful* plainly printed on Hank's face and had no idea how. She also experienced a surge of heat and feminine power, a feline urge to stretch and taunt—a soul-deep fear that if she did, she'd suddenly find herself hip deep in a quagmire and sinking fast with no anchor rope to haul her back.

She flicked a skittish glance toward Mike and Bele, too far away and too up to their elbows in muck to be of any use, then returned her gaze to Hank. She shut her eyes and tried not to feel the primitive thing emanating from him. Felt his fist tighten in her hair.

A modern woman to the soles of her toes, Kate realized that if she wanted to be rescued before the unknown closed around her, she'd have to do what she always did and rescue herself.

She sucked in a deep breath and did so. "You don't like me, do you, Mr. Mathison?" she asked. It might do them both good to be reminded of where they'd always stood with each other.

Knocked unceremoniously out of the moment, Hank loosed her hair and blinked at her. The bile of self-disgust rose in his throat, mingled with the irritation and restlessness of an unwanted craving left unsatisfied. How did she do that? he wondered. Take a moment and twist it out of reach so easily. And why did he care that she had?

He swallowed and raised his guard, refusing to let the tightness in his shorts govern him. He'd come here to save his daughter, not to assuage his own loneliness with an ex-nun mother of seven. "This isn't about *you*, Ms. Anden, it's about Megan. Period. For what it's worth, I don't feel I know you well enough to either like or dislike—"

"I didn't invite you to dance, Mr. Mathison," Kate interrupted with some asperity. "I asked you a question. You came to me because of your daughter. The sooner you and I get things clear between us, the sooner we can get past them and help Megan."

Hank's mouth thinned without humor, his eyes hardened. "No, Ms. Anden," he agreed with contempt—whether for her or for himself, Kate couldn't tell. "I don't like you. But I'll work with you. For Megan."

"Why?" Her mother had often rebuked her over how easily Kate's tongue raised blisters on other people's hides. Chided her about goading a person with her *why's* until she'd managed to rub the blisters raw.

But she had to go on, had to press until the other person gave her the answers she needed. Whether she wanted to hear them or not.

She repeated the question. "Why, Mr. Mathison?"

Hank's mouth twisted at her stupidity. "She's my daughter. I love her."

"No." Kate shook her head, impatient. There was an answer here someplace, she could feel it. An answer about Megan. "Don't get me wrong. You loving Megan is great, but it's not what I meant. What I meant was, why don't you like me? Is it just *me* the concept, *me* the blunt goody-two-shoes ex-missionary-ex-nun and you've got a thing about ex-missionary-ex-nuns, or is it because of something Megan said—maybe an idea she planted. A point of view she has that's maybe a little…" She hesitated. This was the man's daughter she was talking about, after all. "A little *skewed?*"

Light dawned slowly. This wasn't, as he'd assumed, about Kate, but about Megan. And about how Megan reported and interpreted things. About Megan doing her damnedest to…what? Play him against Kate since a long time before he'd had his first chance to witness her doing so at breakfast this morning.

His first reaction was anger at Kate, to choose not to believe ill of his daughter.

His second reaction was to understand that this was the sort of thing he'd suspected all along but chosen to ignore in the face of other drains on his energies where Megan was concerned. Another symptom of the dysfunction that existed between him and his daughter.

He sighed. "I don't know. Maybe. Probably. It's been so long the specifics escape me."

Kate nodded thoughtfully, and hands in the pockets of her jeans, turned and moved once more toward Mike and Bele's dig. "And a lot of the reason I've never particularly cared for you has to do with things Meg's told Li and Li's told me, with stray comments Meg's made when she's here—the fact that she's always sneaking over here. I mean, teenagers are pretty territorial, so why would a kid prefer to have somebody else's stuff around her instead of her own, if nothing's wrong at home? And you didn't know—she didn't tell you—about Bele and she's pretty much been his mother hen since the day he arrived."

"I see." He had nothing else to say. Nothing to feel but the same sense of deadness he'd felt the day Megan had called, hysterical, and he'd arrived home to find Gen lying near death in the shower with the hot water running cold around her. The two most important people in his life were also the two he'd always known least well.

"In all this time has Megan ever told you *anything* about what she does when she's here?" Delicacy wasn't her forte, but she could try.

Hank shook his head. Admission hurt. "No. She's always been a...private kid. And she's been coming here so long, maybe I forgot to ask, or she didn't answer or I didn't *want* to ask because I knew we were a long way apart, but never realized how far. I wish..." He shook his head. "No, it's too late for wishing on what's been. Here and now is where we start from. So...." Grimacing, he hunched into his shoulders, then straightened and puffed out an uncomfortable breath, grabbing the bull by the horns. "So," he said again, decisive this time. "What can you tell me about my daughter?"

They reached the boys before Kate could fill him in on more than Megan's history with Bele, beginning less than eighteen months after the death of her own mother. It was both too little and almost too much.

She told him how his daughter had been there when she'd taken the call from the nuns in Kinshasa, relaying the message that Bele's mother had died in childbirth the year before, that his father was dying and had requested the sisters contact Kate—who'd worked at the mission years before and knew the family well—and ask her to adopt Bele.

About Megan pleading to be allowed to go with her to collect the motherless boy—even though Kate was not taking Tai, Li or Mike with her. Megan pacing anxiously on the wide front porch the day Kate and Bele arrived home. Megan hiding in a corner where Bele wouldn't see her, weeping over the little boy's losing his parents, his probable fears about coming to a place so far from his home, her empathy over his injuries. Megan fierce and protective while the Anden family doctor tried to check Bele over and treat him; Megan coaxing and gentle, luring Bele into his first bath when he'd been too afraid of possible crocodiles in the open water to go in on his own.

Megan insisting on going with the rest of the family on Bele's first trip to the prosthetist who'd fitted his leg. Megan asking questions and demanding to be taught how to care for Bele's leg—then supervising to make sure Kate would do the job properly whenever Megan wasn't there to see to it personally.

Megan needy, giving, sheltering, loving.

Megan being all the things she refused to let Hank see.

It was a lot for a father who'd long been given only a

view of the punk-haired-rebel side of his daughter to digest all at once.

It also made him even more afraid every time he wondered what must have happened the night she'd driven Zevo's car home and come into the house high. What his instincts told him had to be true: she'd been protecting someone, but he couldn't begin to imagine who or why.

When they arrived to admire Bele's and Mike's bone, he was reeling and ready for distraction.

After ascertaining that the bone was not from anything human, Hank surprised himself by letting his guard drop and getting into the spirit of the thing, delicately turning the bone over in his hands, brushing off the remaining dirt, using his brief stint in forensics to offer scientific speculation on what it was. It was almost certainly from a long dead cow or deer, but the boys were happier with other potential explanations: coyote, wolf, miniature horse or, of course, eohippus.

Ignored in the face of more learned counsel—pure bull, Hank assured her later—Kate watched him and the boys with interest. This was a side of Hank Mathison she'd doubted existed and could not have anticipated. The boys' reaction to him, their eagerness to drink up his attention, was something else for which she was not prepared.

She'd considered the necessity of an adult male example in the lives of her children, and especially her boys, only fleetingly. When she'd first adopted Tai and Li, her brother was still alive. Since he and his wife had died and left Mike to her when he was barely fifteen months old, she hadn't had time to doubt her abilities to be father as well as mother. The other boys had arrived in rapid succession and *voilà!* Here they all were.

Oh, there were men around Stone House during every tree-cutting and shipping season—hardworking and friendly, surly and sour, itinerants as well as family men— but she'd never noticed any of the children behaving then the way Mike and Bele hung onto Mathison's attention now. Curious. Maybe she'd simply been too busy with each harvesting season's madness to notice a difference in the kids. And maybe Megan's father was simply as different from other men where her kids were concerned as he seemed— *felt*—to Kate herself.

The vague flavor of jealousy on her tongue that Hank should so easily win their regard and the more powerful surge of pleasure she found in their excitement to hold his attention also took her off guard. Mr. Mathison was not the only one getting an education here. Her own private education hadn't even been *on* the list of things she'd imagined happening this summer, because *she,* unlike Hank, already knew everything she needed to know about raising kids.

Sort of.

She glanced at her boys, then to their intriguingly open and unforeseen teacher. But the unexpected was okay— within bounds.

Maybe.

Again she felt that curious flash of something she couldn't identify low in her belly, the fluttery, flirty tightening in her lungs. It was, she'd decided the moment he'd called, her job to unbalance Hank Mathison this summer, to be the one to make him sit up and take notice of his daughter. His unbalancing *her* was not part of the bargain she'd made either with Hank or herself.

And yet…the foreign sensations trickling through her bloodstream were not unpleasant. Anxious, yes, but not awful. Not even bad. Just restless. Like being a kid and waiting for something wonderful-dreadful to happen that might just be so good you'll get sick to your stomach if it doesn't turn out the way you're afraid to want it to. Similar to, but not quite the same as the way she'd felt waiting for the courts to decide she would be a suitable adoptive parent even without a husband.

She was pretty sure the anticipation of impending motherhood had made her feel as nauseated and expectant as any pregnant woman in her first trimester. But this, although she had no way of actually knowing *personally,* didn't feel like that at all. This felt a lot more like…

Well, probably a lot more like pregnant women might feel just *before* they got pregnant.

Oops.

Kate's jaw dropped; she stared at Hank, confirming the fizzle in her pulse, the constriction in her lungs, the sensation of…*quickening* that ran through her at the mere sight of him with Bele and Mike.

The mere sight of him anywhere.

Horrified at herself, she turned her back and covered her mouth. Jiminy Pete, of all the stupid, disgusting— Llamas were more civilized. Independent creatures that the girls were, *they* didn't get hot simply because some studly boy with the right length wool or the cutest little patch on his nose walked by unless they wanted to.

If her llamas could be adult about how they felt and when they felt it, it was ridiculous to think she couldn't.

But she couldn't.

Stunned by the suddenly duplicitous nature of a body that had never—as far as she recalled—betrayed her before, she turned to find some other distraction to think about. Instead she found Hank striding toward her, looking younger than she'd ever seen him, smiling back over his shoulder at something Bele was excitedly telling Mike.

Not that she'd seen him a lot before this morning, but still—

"Fly catching, Ms. Anden?" Hank asked, eyeing the mud on the end of her nose. So scrupulously clean as she always was around him, he found the mud both oddly comforting and mightily amusing.

Kate stared askance, too aware of him and the hamster running its squeaky wheel through her veins and arteries to comprehend his pointed glance.

A laughter he'd not experienced in years rumbled silently through him. A wicked grin tipped his mouth.

Hands on her hips, Kate glared at him. "Is something wrong, Mr. Mathison?"

"Not at all, Ms. Anden."

Hank's lips compressed; he glanced skyward trying not to laugh. He'd no idea what had happened to him in the few minutes he'd spent in the dig with Mike and Bele, but he hadn't felt so much himself in, well, an incredibly too long time.

A wayward sputter of humor escaped Hank. He took a deep breath and did his best to stifle it.

Kate's glare grew solicitous, mildly wary. "Are you certain you're all right, Mr. Mathison? You look like you're about to explode."

"Never felt better, Ms. Anden," he assured her, then bent double and howled when she rubbed her cheek and another streak of mud appeared.

"Mr. Mathison, what *is* the problem?"

There was an element of *schoolteacher getting pissed* in her voice that made Hank laugh harder. He couldn't help himself. He'd finally met someone on whom he'd have said there were truly no flies, a parent with seemingly perfect children to whom he'd often felt somewhat inferior. And the first time he spent longer than five minutes in her company, his competition wore mud on her face.

Competition. The word sobered him the instant it formed. Was that really what he felt? That this was a contest, a winner-take-all battle—and *all* was Megan?

He straightened. He'd never seen his attitude toward Kate in such sere light before. It wasn't a pretty picture.

"Hank?" Concerned. Not stilted with formality.

Real.

It was the first time she'd used the familiar form of his name. It sounded odd coming from her mouth. As if it didn't belong there.

Or as if it belonged there a lot. Breathy. Breathless. Against his mouth. Close to his ear.

His jaw tightened, his gaze slid over her face. Pale freckles and sun glow; laugh lines beside her eyes; small mouth, full lips.

Kissable.

Damn, he didn't want her. Couldn't.

Wouldn't.

Did.

The mud was no longer funny, a mar on the landscape. He moved a deceptively lazy hand, brushed her face suddenly and the smudge was gone.

He'd always had fast hands—except where he wanted to make them slow.

Shocked, Kate gaped at him. "Mr. Mathison!" The outraged schoolteacher was back in her voice full force.

Hank grinned, but there was flint in it this time. This was neither the time nor the place to resurrect his hormones. They were, after all, *his* hormones. He was their boss; he controlled them, not vice versa.

Yeah, right. Who was he kidding? "Relax, Ms. Anden." He shoved her chin up with the tip of one forefinger, closing her mouth, and showed her the mud in his other hand. "It's dirt, not an assault."

Then he dusted off his hands and stalked away.

Too dumbfounded for a moment to react, Kate stared after him, then at the muddy dust on her left boot, then once more at his receding back. Not a bad view, she decided without meaning to. He exuded power and grace in every loose-hipped movement, the impression of muscles bunching and smoothing even through the relaxed fit of his clothes. The phrase *nice tush* floated through her mind; her lips twitched. For a woman who'd felt totally furious less than two and a half minutes ago, it was not exactly the most outraged thought she'd ever had.

So, then, shut ma mouth, she told herself derisively.

Laughter bubbled in her throat. He certainly had. Right after he'd taken the filth she'd never even realized was on her off her nose.

There'd been mud on her nose.

Because she'd been too busy staring at Hank Mathison's mead-amber eyes, tawny blond hair, pretty face and musculature to notice it.

And Tai's favorite sarcastic adolescent phrase—the one that was now the family's favorite complaint—had always been, *"Gee, Mom, no flies on you, are there?"*

The laughter in her throat broke free on a whoop. No wonder Mathison nearly rolled in mirth. She, who all too often thought—smugly, yes, be honest—of herself as far too smart to be caught unaware had been caught unaware. By the mud she was always telling her kids to wash off *their* faces.

She doubled over and laughed until her sides hurt and the tears ran. God always did find a way to give her a poke when she was being too smarty-pantsed for her own good.

"Mum, are you all right?"

Mike and Bele bounded up beside her, full of concern—and curiosity.

"Fine," she wheezed, trying to contain the chuckles, but failing.

"What's so funny?"

"Mr. Mathison—" She snorted laughter, swiped a hand across her face on a chuckling sigh. "Mr. Mathison told me a joke."

"Tell us," they begged. "Tell us."

"I can't—" A chortle got in the way. She cleared it out of her throat. "I can't." She shook her head, grinning. "It— you had to be there. It doesn't translate."

They were at an age where bad jokes and magic tricks were a major part of life. "Aw, Mom. Please?"

She shook her head again. Such a lot to have learned— mostly about herself, only some about Hank—in a morning and gee, wouldn't you know, the summer's dance had barely begun. "Sorry, guys, you know how bad I am with jokes."

Bele gave her a disgusted look. "Yeah, you always get the punch line in the wrong place."

"Sorry." She shrugged an unrepentant apology. "Nobody's perfect."

"Yeah, yeah, yeah," Bele agreed, still disgusted.

He was, Kate reflected with amusement, a long way from the frightened child she'd brought home from Zaire.

"Hey, I know!" Mike of the big ideas. "We can get Hank to tell us."

"Hank?" Kate asked, surprised. He hadn't invited *her* to call him Hank. 'Course now that she thought about it, she hadn't invited *him* to call her Kate, either. Probably ought to remedy that. Especially if she was going to have a crush on the man. And it appeared, she discovered with amusement and consternation, that she had one whether she wanted to or not. It'd make the daydreaming she didn't have time for so much easier, if they called each other by their first names.

"He said to call him that," Bele yelled, already starting away. "C'mon, Mike, let's go find him before he forgets the joke."

"Yeah, old guys, bad memories," Mike agreed, dashing after him.

Kate's lips compressed painfully on a snort, holding back guffaws. A thought occurred to her. "Hey, wait a minute. You guys know where Meg is? I need to talk to her." Needed to confront her—gently, of course—and ask her just what the dickens she thought this morning was about. Tell her to at least mention where she was going to her father before she snuck up to Li's room in the middle of the night, to make sure Li didn't mind the intrusion on her privacy and to quit yanking her and *Hank's* chains.

"Upstairs, cleaning out the shower."

"Thanks." Grinning she turned and headed for the house.

If she couldn't straighten out the father without total distraction setting in, she'd go to the child. It was high time
somebody quit walking on eggs and got a few things straight
with Megan.

Bottle of glass cleaner in one hand, used paper towels in
the other, Megan peered out the newly spotless octagonal
window of the upstairs bathroom and watched Kate arrive.

Even if the windows hadn't been open and she hadn't
overheard Kate ask the little boys about her whereabouts,
she'd been around long enough to recognize the look on her
favorite mentor's face, to diagnose the purpose in her stride.
Someone was in for what was known around the Anden
household as a "chat."

Chats weren't necessarily *bad* things, but they were often
a bit more revealing to the person on the receiving end than
the chat-ee might prefer. In the eleven years she'd been
hanging around with Li, Megan had been chatted with on
more than one occasion. As uncomfortable as it might feel
at the time, she didn't mind Kate's chats. Kate never chatted
with anyone she didn't care about, rarely chatted without a
reason and almost always expected and accepted back chat.
She also always treated everybody the same, and unlike
some of Megan's other friends' parents, and especially unlike Megan's own dad, neither Megan nor anyone else ever
had to wonder where they stood with Kate. There was a
certain comfort and security in that.

Still...

Quickly she gave the back of the toilet a final swipe,
dumped the paper towels in the basket and put the glass
cleaner under the sink. Now all she needed was someplace
to hide. Because even if she hadn't heard Kate ask where
she was, Megan knew with the dread of a guilty conscience
that she was the one in for it. And security or no, it didn't
mean she particularly *wanted* to be chatted with today. Particularly since she couldn't see where she'd really done any-

thing to warrant one. And even if she had, she felt too mixed up inside to really want to discuss it now. Not until she figured out what exactly she'd done, why she'd done it and how to defend herself from it.

She'd hoped coming to live with Kate and Li and the llamas—sometimes especially the llamas, whose constant expression of stoicism and serenity, whose five-thousand-year connection with humans often made them appear wiser and more connected to people than their human partners could ever be—would just magically make all this insanity running around inside her head come clear and go away. It scared her some that so far it wasn't, but it was early hours yet and she still hoped.

She was also still afraid.

Because, damn it, she couldn't even tell Li this, but it was really getting just so freaking hard some days to keep track of who she was.

Chapter 4

So she had a crush on Hank Mathison. After all these years of judging him...well, not one of God's greater creations, who woulda thunk it?

Not her, that was sure. She was way too old for this nonsense. She hadn't had a crush on a boy since...oh, probably Steve Heckerling in the tenth grade. And she'd gotten over that quick—crushed, yeah, but over it—the minute he'd told her to quit dreaming that the star of the track team would ever want to go out with a red-haired, bucktoothed, goody-two-shoes like her who wasn't going to put out.

Her braces had been off for six months at the time, her mouth not nearly as horsy as it had been. But the boys she'd gone to high school with were stupid about things like that. She'd called him a hormonal jerk who wasn't even strong enough to be in charge of his own mind. The insult had gone over his head and made her wonder how she could ever have been attracted to him in the first place. But the youthful heart made the eyes see what it wanted them to see: sensitivity, smarts and strength, where there wasn't any.

Within the next year she'd felt the call to join the convent and that had been that for boys.

She hadn't missed feeling giddy and stupid and tongue-tied at all. Even if the mature part of her brain thought it *was* funny as all get out.

"*Phweet!* Hey-up! Come on, boys, granola time!"

Whistling and clapping, Kate leaned on a four-by-four fence post and called the studs and geldings in from the west pasture. Fanned out along the length of woven wire fencing designed to prevent stray dogs from bothering the herd rather than to keep the herd in, Ilya, Mike, Bele, Jamal and some of the 4-H-ers rattled Ziploc bags full of llama treats, adding encouragement. The three-legged rottweiler, Taz, ran up and down the fence line, slobbering and grinning. When the cloven footed got cookies, so did she. Part of her training, Ilya said.

Yeah, right. Kate rolled her eyes at the thought. Training, my left big toe. Spoiled-rotten dog.

It didn't take long for the llamas to respond. They enjoyed treat time. Humming and clacking they trotted over the rolling hills from their pasture, ears alert, noses twitching. Their leather-padded, two-toed feet made soft thuds on the bare earth as they approached.

Off to the north from the direction of the tree fields, came the rough roar of a tractor jouncing up a rutted track. Tai, Risto, Grisha and the 4-H tree team were on their way in.

Across the drive, Li, Megan and another group of 4-H-ers emerged from the catch yard—a pen small enough so the llamas couldn't run when you had to catch them for shearing, toenail trimming or other unwanted attention, but large enough so they could circle off their nervousness—near the females' corral and headed for the workshop. After an afternoon spent shearing the moms' bellies, sides and backs to ready them for the coming summer's heat, they were laden with bags full of llama, alpaca and vicuña wool.

Tomorrow they'd shear the boys and begin to brush and card the fiber, cleaning it for spinning.

Hank strode behind them, carrying the sheep clippers and the granola-bribe bucket. Distance and the sun hid the expression on his tanned face, but from the way he walked Kate guessed he was not a happy camper. An afternoon spent listening to teenage and preteen girls could do that to any man, but particularly to a father. Kate would, no doubt, hear about it after dinner. They could trade insights and information just like real adults. And if he didn't volunteer the information, she'd ask—if she could keep herself from giggling like an eleven-year-old in his presence long enough to do so, that is.

Sheesh, what a horrible thing to contemplate. She didn't particularly remember wanting to be eleven when she was eleven. Twenty had seemed the perfect age to her then. Once she'd gotten there, twenty had been interesting, but now was better. Lots better. Mega, stupendously, infinitely better. It was also beside the point. Which being, that at least Hank had found his daughter today—and hopefully spoken with her—which was better than Kate had managed to do.

It was the first time in memory she'd suspected Megan of avoiding her. She'd have to quiz Li about that.

The first llama face hove into range, inquisitive nose thrust out to bump hers. Along the fence line llama necks stretched, noses reached for granola bags. 4-H-ers called to their favorites, offering goodies with one hand while they scratched hard, woolly necks with the other.

It was late afternoon after a hard working day. Time to feed the camelids, put the farm equipment to bed and send all non-Andens home to supper.

Except, of course, Kate allowed, for *him*.

Without invitation her gaze ran to Hank, who was emerging from the workshop. Dusty black jeans rode low on his hips, a stained gray T-shirt adorned with endangered rainforest inhabitants clung to an irregular vee of sweat on his chest. Nice, very nice, one side of her brain murmured.

The other side wondered why sweat made him look even more appealing than clean had, then the two split into debate teams to analyze the issue. A free-for-all ensued over the topic of fairness—how unfair it was that men always seemed to come out looking better when they were filthy than women did—so Kate sighed and did the only thing she could think to do: told her brain to cut the comedy and concentrate on other things.

It would have been fine if her brain listened. But since she so rarely took her own advice, it didn't.

When he leaned into the fence next to her, she started, cheeks reddened. Either he didn't notice the blush or he ignored it. Point for him.

"They seem so serene," he said quietly.

"Mmm." Kate nodded. "They are, usually. Almost..." She hesitated. People who didn't know llamas often misunderstood mention of the seemingly telepathic or sometimes spiritual connection between the animals and their humans. Hank looked at her, waiting. She shrugged. In for a penny and all that rot. "Almost mystical," she finished.

He rested his chin on a closed fist. "Mystical?" Curious, not disbelieving.

"It's hard to explain. Most of the time they just seem to...understand things that people don't." She pointed at a pure white male in the middle of the herd; head lifted, ears forward as if probing the air, he scanned the perimeter of the yard, obviously looking for something or someone in particular. "There. That's Harvey—I told you about him this morning."

"Llama therapy, the old woman at the nursing home." Hank nodded, grinning when Kate slanted him a sideways glance. "I heard. It only looked like I wasn't paying attention."

"Ah." She nodded wisely. "I see."

He snorted. "I bet."

She ignored him. "Anyway, as I attempted to tell you then, Harve…picks up on what people are feeling and…I don't know, *calms* them is the simplest way to put it. People in need gravitate to him, he finds them. He's particularly good with the kids we get out here. He's a…special friend of Meg's."

"He is." Flat and unemotional, tentative and…wistful.

Afraid to believe.

For a long moment Hank stared at her, then switched the intensity to the white llama leaning into his daughter's embrace. Was this where she came when she skipped their appointments with the department's psychologist? Had she instinctively sought and found her own treatment? Could he hope…no, he didn't even want to name the wish for fear of destroying it.

He'd never heard of llamas being used in this particular capacity, but he was familiar with the concept of pet therapy and its uses with Alzheimer's patients and the elderly, with chronic fatigue syndrome and psychiatric hospital patients, with dying children and adults. It had something to do, perhaps, with nonverbal communication, the psychic link between humans and animals and the will to live. Or, as with the Alzheimer's victims, psych patients and those with chronic fatigue, the will to remain within the moment. Maybe…

Naw. He swallowed, looked everywhere but at Megan and Harvey. He wouldn't think it. It was too easy to want to believe in what amounted to an experimental theory out of desperation. Sort of like believing in magic.

"So," he said with feigned lightness. "Is Harvey named after Jimmy Stewart's six-foot rabbit?"

Kate eyed him thoughtfully. Long experience with people who needed to doubt before they hoped made her scan his features in swift appraisal, let her see the almost masked fear, the desire to believe, the not quite hidden plea for time to digest, sort through. Empathy made it easy for her to give him what he sought.

"Very good, Mr. Mathison." Cheeky voice, exaggerated applause, she responded in turn to the flippancy of the question. "You're a classic-movie buff?"

"Hank. When I have a chance. You?"

"Kate." There, that took care of the Mr., Ms. nonsense. And about time, too. "I enjoy movies, period. Good, bad, classic, whatever, as long as it's escapism. We watched whatever we got hold of at the missions and in the camps. Funny how good even a bad movie seems after hours or weeks of trying to hold back other people's misery."

His expression was suddenly hooded and faraway. "I can imagine," he said quietly.

Kate studied him, drawn to something in his voice, behind his eyes—things he'd done because he had to, things he'd seen because of things he'd done. Almost an expectation of...judgment. "Can you?"

It was his turn to look at her. There was no presumption on her face or in her voice, only genuine interest, intense curiosity and...a quality of mercy he could almost touch. Odd. Mercy was hardly a commodity he equated with this day and age, with her, but there it was written in those iceberg-blue eyes. Not quite what he expected. But then, so little about her was. He nodded. "Yeah."

In the llama yard Harvey's ears pricked sideways, forward. The llama cast a glance toward Kate and Hank, then touched noses with the girl. She hugged him tighter, burying her face in the long wool. He stood quietly, allowing the invasion of his space without demur; after a moment he turned his head, his calm gaze settled once more on Hank, a speaking look. Uncomfortable as it made him, Hank stared back.

"What?" he asked Kate.

She shrugged. "He knows," she said simply.

"Knows what?"

"About you and Megan."

Hank turned sharply, but before the *"What?!"* could pass his lips, the first of the parent-collecting-kid vehicles pulled up behind the house and Kate was gone.

He turned back to the yard. Harvey stood a few feet from him, gaze calm and steady, studying him hard; the intelligence in the liquid brown eyes was palpable, undeniable.

Uneasy with the all too perceptive nonhuman scrutiny, Hank looked past the llama. Alone nearby, Megan waited, arms slack at her sides, watching them as if she hoped... what, he couldn't tell. Not sure what was expected, Hank looked to one, then the other. The whole thing felt absurd, but he'd witnessed too many unexplainable things—both bad and good—in his life to simply dismiss this one. Whatever this one was.

A sensation shuddered through him: warmth, comfort, compassion, understanding. A thought that wasn't his entered his mind unbidden: *Don't worry, Hank, we'll work it out. She wants to figure it out.*

Startled, he peered at Harvey; the llama blinked at him. Then its long throat made a regurgitating movement and Harvey turned away and resumed chewing his cud. Swallowing uncertainty, Hank let his gaze slide back to his daughter. For the first time in he didn't remember when, there naked on her face, Megan's vulnerabilities showed.

Evening crept in on shadowed feet, heavy with a symphony of tree frogs and crickets, the whisper of night birds taking wing. Light that would have seemed warm and inviting on a winter's eve showed through sheer curtains, an unreal electric yellow-pink that seemed almost garish against the soft pink-blue-violet shades of approaching night.

Voices hovered behind the light, youthful laughter stroked the shadows, mingled with the clatter of pans in the kitchen sink, the harsh, watery *shurr* of the elderly dishwasher. Normal life, alive and well in the countryside of mid-Michigan.

Caught by the instant, Hank leaned against the lumpy fieldstone side wall of Stone House, listening, half wishing this life belonged to him. That it *didn't* was and always had been his choice, he knew. To join the DEA, to be a part of some alternate reality was a decision he'd made long ago—Gen and Megan notwithstanding. But even they had never made him quite want to be part of *this,* the softness of daily moments, the slow and steady progress of a life that didn't chronically exist on the underbelly of violent death.

He understood with regret that even now a part of him resented being here, blamed Gen for leaving him here, forced to deal with day-to-day realities instead of living on extremes the way he'd done working the streets or under-cover. Understood that another piece of his dissatisfaction lay in the fact that what he and Megan did could hardly be called *living* by any definition—often seemed hardly more than existing—was, in its own way, as extreme as any life he'd lived undercover, but without the adrenaline rush.

Without the momentary euphoria of a case closed, a job accomplished.

Living on the constant edge of a rush was easier, after a fashion, than living daily life. It was simpler—more black-and-white. You trusted yourself, your control of a situation, or that was all she wrote. You kept your eyes open, your ears sharp and slept ready for flight or whatever else might overtake you at a moment's notice.

Here was more complicated, less distinct, grayer, harder to control. Here there wasn't just himself to face, or be concerned about; here was Megan. He still trusted himself, his decisions, but too often that wasn't enough; *she* didn't trust him, his decisions; she made her own. And too much of the time they turned out bad.

For both of them.

He shut his eyes and again felt the strange weight of the

llama's gaze on him, the bulk of Megan's unvoiced questions and vulnerabilities, the physical presence of compassion that flowed from Kate. The prayer inside his head remained the same as always: *Bless my daughter, Megan Genevieve, take care of her. Keep her safe, well, healthy, alive, breathing and happy. Help me to understand...*

"Dad. Hey, Dad, you out here?"

Hank started, as surprised by what she'd called him as he was by being hailed at all. *Whoopee!* zinged through his starved parent system. *Dad,* she'd called him Dad. Without sarcasm or ridicule, simply matter-of-fact, kid to parent, his name. It was ridiculous to revel so in the sound of a three-letter word.

He reveled all the same. Take what you can get, when you can get it, and enjoy it, he told himself. Rule number one for dealing with teenagers. "Here, Meg."

Megan's hair swung loose over her shoulder when she leaned over the side of the front porch to see him. "I'm going to the movies with Li and Risto, okay? We won't be late."

"That was a question?" Wary surprise and unintentional irony hovered in his voice. "You're asking me?"

Something fleeting flashed across her face: anger, rebellion, resentment, animosity...pieces of the Megan who'd lived with him the past five years. Reminders that however much her personality seemed to have flip-flopped since they'd arrived at the Andens', the problems that had brought them here were far from gone. Then her features smoothed and she was the Megan of this morning once again: disgusted teenager with the rolled-eye, let's-humor-the-poor-benighted-parent attitude.

"*Tcht,* Da-ad." Translation: say "fine" and don't embarrass me. "Okay?"

"Who's driving?" She let him parent her so infrequently he was almost out of practice. He had to keep his hand in while he could.

"Tai's gonna drop us off on his way to pick up his girlfriend and take Grisha and Ilya to the Comic Pit and the little guys for ice cream—"

"Hey, who you callin' little, shorty?" Mike asked, towering above her on the porch wall.

Megan didn't blink. "And he'll pick us up when the movie's over. Okay?" She grabbed Mike's legs and hoisted him down. "I'm callin' you little, wise guy, now get off there before you kill yourself." Then she turned back to her father, the epitome of an impatient, normal, well-adjusted kid living a normal, well-adjusted life. "Okay? Dad?"

"Okay."

"Thanks, Dad." She blew him a kiss. "See ya."

A kiss? A *kiss?* He hadn't gotten one of those from her, blown or otherwise, in longer than he wanted to recall. "Don't be late," he said, for the sake of saying something.

Again there was a flash of hostility quickly covered, another lurking reminder of her apparent ability to dissemble at will. But all she said was "Da-ad," in two syllables drawn out through tight teeth, annoyed. Then she was flying off the porch with the rest of the kids, piling into the van, and they were gone in a sputter of gravel and dust.

Thoughtful and more than a little unnerved by his daughter's mercurial moods, Hank jammed his hands in the pockets of his jeans and watched them go. Was this Megan a fluke, a mirage, or had he done something almost right for a change? Maybe? Possibly? Naw, probably didn't have anything to do with him. Right? Jeez, what was wrong with a guy holding out hope?

What was wrong with a guy pleading to see only the best for his child?

The aluminum screen door onto the porch whined open, soughed shut. Kate stepped onto the porch.

"Is it safe?" she asked warily. "Are they gone?"

"Is it *safe?*" Eyebrows cocked in mock astonishment, Hank stepped around the edge of the porch and looked up at her, the fuzzy apricot-gold halo of hair that framed her face caped out around her shoulders and arms. Sensation, recognition churned in his belly; he tamped it down. *Not the time, not the place, not the woman,* echoed hollowly through the halls of his psyche like some unfriendly specter on a rampage. He did his best to listen. "You, oh great queen of all mothers, slayer of dragons, font of all wisdom, are asking me, the devil dad from hell, if it's safe? As opposed to what?"

"Don't be sarcastic," Kate advised him. "I deal with sarcasm all day. It doesn't impress me and I'm too tired for it tonight."

"Sorry." Grinning, Hank mounted the steps to slouch against a support pillar. *Stupid to go closer,* his conscience whispered when scent coiled in his nostrils, slunk into the back of his throat; salt, musk and woman. *She'll bewitch you. Better to stay clear.* "You're the one with the endless patience, a gazillion kids and all the answers. I couldn't resist."

"Try," Kate suggested. "And it's strictly blind luck, you know." She slumped onto the porch swing on a sigh and pulled her feet up, trying to ignore the unfamiliar warmth that constricted her chest, curled into her toes when he smiled. "Man, that feels good. You know, I love that bunch of hooligans and I wouldn't trade them for anything, but they're exhausting and it's a relief to have them *gone* sometimes."

"You wouldn't say that if they were gone all the time." A statement flat and quiet, full of the conviction of experience.

"Nope." She shook her head, watching him while her pulse fizzed and jigged restlessly in her veins. Seemed she'd spent a lot of time watching him today. But what else did you do with an untamed, uncaged, exciting but potentially dangerous beast with which you were not familiar? She'd watched the communist soldiers who came through the refugee camps with a similar degree of wariness. 'Course, the only tattoo that had beaten in her chest when she'd seen *them* was fear, not this...nervy anticipation and...*crush.* "You're probably right. But they're not gone all the time, so I can say it and mean it."

"Lucky you."

She nodded complacently, choosing sincerity over irony. "You betcha."

Disbelieving laughter chuckled through him. "Jeez Louise, woman, you'd be easy to hate."

"Mmm." Kate stretched her neck and settled more comfortably into the swing, observing him. Enjoying the view. No harm in looking, right? "So I hear."

Hank grinned, then unslouched to move over and sit on the wall closer to the swing. *Dumb move,* his tightening gut assured him. *Dumb, dumber, dumbest.* "What, you mean I'm not the only parent who has a problem with you?"

She snorted. "Hardly. Most parents find out I'm an ex-nun, figure I must be perfect and use me as a measuring stick to decide what they will or won't let their kids do—"

"You mean like, 'Is Li's mother letting her go?'"

Kate nodded and finished the thought. "That or they remember the nuns they had in school and imagine me ten times worse."

Hank's turn to snort. "Yeah, I know that one. The neighborhood moms used to pull some of that with Gen, too. It's easier to point at someone else than have convictions of your own."

"What do they do with you?" she asked, idly curious.

"The single ones throw themselves at me, the married ones bake macaroni-and-cheese and flirt." He heaved a regretful sigh. "Not one of them thinks of me as a role model."

Kate chuckled. "Poor baby."

"Yeah, right." He propped a foot on the wall and draped

an arm over his raised knee. "So, what about the parents who don't think you're perfect?"

"They do like you," she said, squiggling her back to scratch it on the swing. "Call me *Ms.* Goody-Two-Shoes and take me in avid dislike."

Laughter shouted out of Hank, long and delighted, cleansing. "So," he said when he could speak, "I'm in good company, then."

Kate made a rude noise. "If you want to call it that."

"I do," Hank assured her, chuckling. "It happens so seldom."

"I'll bet."

"Ah-ah-ah. Don't be that way. Doesn't sound like Saint Mom to me."

"That's Ms. Goody-Two-Shoes to you."

"And that makes me who?" He grinned, his teeth a snowy gleam in the half-light, all wolfish charm. "The filthy beast?"

"If you like," Kate agreed equably, amazingly coherent for all that her pinging pulse kept shouting, *He's better looking than Cary Grant, hugely better, best!* "But I never said it. *Thought* it a thousand and a half times—"

"But never said it," Hank finished for her. "Right."

"You asked."

"My mistake." He settled back against the roof support beside him. "You ever see that movie?"

"The one with goody-two-shoes and the filthy beast?"

"*Father Goose,* yeah."

"Maybe fifteen, eighteen times." Kate dangled a leg off the swing and shoved her foot against the floor to set it rocking. "I think between that, *Life with Father, Cheaper by the Dozen, The Sound of Music, With Six You Get Egg Roll, Yours, Mine and Ours,* and all the rest of that insane-parents, fifty-zillion-kids genre I was pretty much brainwashed into this kid thing from the start. Looked like fun, you know?"

Hank studied her silhouette in the yard light, suddenly curious about her beyond the unwelcome call of his libido. "It's not?"

"Mmm, a lot of the time, sure. It's also nerve-racking, painful and never boring, and Lord—" she sat up, sounding rueful "—what I wouldn't give for a little boring sometimes."

"Unh-huh, and I'll bet you were dragged into this non-boring life kicking and screaming."

"No." She shook her head. "I left the convent kicking and screaming—figuratively, that is. My choice, their suggestion—mutual decision—but it scared the bejeebers out of me. If I wasn't a nun, who was I? What was I going to do? All that rot. I mean, I could still be a missionary, work the food trains, volunteer with the International Red Cross, but that didn't answer the big question I thought I had the answer to when I took my vows. When I found Tai—or he found me—in that refugee camp it was like—" Her hands popped wide in enthusiastic demonstration. *"Wow! Light bulb! Major revelation!* I didn't have a husband, so going forward wasn't a piece of cake, but the nun thing on my résumé has its uses. We didn't look back."

"Yeah." Hank nodded, understanding. "That's the way I felt when I first joined drug enforcement. Like a big sponge to be used to mop up the bad guys, make the streets clean for kids like Meg."

"But it's not the way you feel now." It was a statement, not a question.

"No," he answered, an ounce of bitterness surrounded by contempt. "It's the sort of work that no matter which side of the desk you're on, it uses you up. No matter how many battles you win, the war goes on. If you're not battling bad guys, you're fighting your own higher-ups to let you get at the bad guys. I moved up in the ranks hoping to change some of that, but it makes no difference. Now I'm a bureaucrat. That might be up some guys' alleys, but it's not up mine. At least," he amended wryly, appalled by his own vehemence, "not with this attitude."

"I'm glad you said that." Kate laughed gently. "Saves me from having to point it out."

"Gee thanks. I knew if nothing else, I could count on you to be tactless about my early mid-life crisis."

She shrugged. "Hey, what are ex-nuns for, if not a little verbal knuckle wrapping now and then?"

Hank chuckled, amusement edged in irony. "I'll keep that in mind."

They sat quietly for a bit, digesting evening songs and revelations, companionable.

Or as companionable as the intermittent flickerings of adult hungers allowed.

Hank recognized the difference immediately. Looking at her—the overly lush curves and summer hair, the wide open, innocent without innocence features; smelling her, remembering the touch of her hand in his brought the burn, without question. But it was no longer a burn without apparent reason, without liking. It was more. Harder, hotter, more insistent. More disturbing. More comfortable—God, when had it gotten comfortable to be with her?

More dangerous.

He couldn't get distracted from the reason he was here: Megan and only Megan.

Megan.

"She looked pretty tonight, didn't she?" he asked suddenly, wistful.

Kate nodded, without having to ask to whom he referred. "Megan's a beautiful girl, Hank." She slid down the swing, close to where he sat on the wall, and touched his jeaned ankle, then repeated with conviction, "Beautiful."

He stared at the spot where he could feel Kate's fingers on his leg, willing himself not to feel the spread of heat upward. An edge of tension ran down his spine. Undercover experience had taught him to ignore a potential problem at his own risk; to avoid the temptation to create one at all costs. If she kept touching him, they would have a problem of major proportions—instead of one that was just bigger than a bread box. He didn't move. "I wish she wasn't so..." He huffed a breath and hesitated, choosing his words. "So damned confused. So blasted confusing."

"Yes." She was silent a moment, then. "Did you talk with her about this morning?"

"No." He shook his head, shifting erect on the wall, sliding his ankle out from underneath her hand. Enough already. "She kept someone or something between us all day. I didn't have a chance."

"Me, either." Kate rose and moved to stand at the wall beside him, leaning into the top rail. Closer to him than she'd intended. Closer than she had a feeling she should be, than it was safe to be. But she didn't back up. Couldn't. It was a rule: go forward. Always. No matter what. "She's avoiding me, too. She's never done that before."

Hank released the breath he'd held without realizing it. It seemed childish and petty to be glad, but he was. It meant he wasn't the only one. It meant he wasn't alone, as he often felt.

It meant she was too damn close.

He could feel her warmth adding to the heat of his own skin—near enough to touch, but far enough away so he shouldn't feel anything from her at all. Or as if he wanted to feel more.

He already felt too much.

It was a little like waiting to close a long prepared sting, or loitering around until the other shoe—one that was maybe a size ninety—dropped. Adrenaline in his veins, fever in his blood. Exciting, stimulating, challenging. Could he or couldn't he get out of the way in time? Did he want to? How close could he get to that icy fire before getting burned? How close did he want to get?

Real close, his pulse told him.

Soon.

He swallowed, tasting desire on the back of his tongue. Whoa, he thought. Not acceptable, not appropriate. Not here, now or ever.

But he wanted. Bad.

God help him.

He slid off the wall onto the porch, intending to put distance between them; decreasing it instead.

"Hank?"

A question he couldn't answer, so he didn't try, simply slipped a hand into the heavy cape of her hair and let it wash through his fingers. She backed away. He pursued her; he couldn't stop himself.

"Hank...please. I don't understand."

As though he did.

Her eyes were silver-white pools in the fading dusk and yellow glow of the yard light. Wary, not quite afraid. She looked at him the way she might if caught in a corner, as though he were, somehow, either predator or contagion. As though it would not be wise to turn her back even to run.

He viewed her as he might either human prey or something toxic: carefully, from all angles, with every sense open to danger. Knowing he was the taller, heavier, stronger, but that small size wouldn't necessarily make her less lethal. He backed her into a corner of the porch, trapped her between the pillar and his body. Surrounded her with his arms, hands cramped around the pillar to either side of her head.

"Kate."

Desire roughened her name in a way she'd never heard it, never imagined hearing. Mesmerizing. The sound sent tongues of flame licking down her spine; heat made her shiver without understanding, wanting to hear him call her that way again. Instinct made her afraid of what she wanted.

"Please, Hank, I—"

He heard nothing but his name, the plea that lay underneath fear, the seductive whisper of invitation. His head lowered the nine inches separating his mouth from hers. "Kate…"

She made a soft sound of uncertainty, "No, I—" but the hand she placed on his chest to hold him away betrayed her, drew him closer. Before she could press her lips shut against him, he took her mouth.

Chapter 5

Soft.

Her mind registered the texture of his mouth with surprise. So very soft.

So very exotic.

It had been twenty years since the last boy kissed her. He'd been a friend, the kiss a shared moment sitting in the dark on theater steps waiting for the curtain to rise on the last play of their high-school career, more goodbye than hello. Nice, soft, yes.

Nothing like this.

For all its gentleness there was demand in Hank's kiss, a hunger and passion that claimed her response before she was aware of giving it. Before she was aware of her own need to give it and take his.

Drugging.

Breathless murmurs, the quiet whimper of a plea without words. Amazement slid through her when she felt the sounds coming from her own throat.

Her fingers were on his chest, kneading his chambray

shirt, trying to bring him closer. Astonishment and fire laced through her when the length of his body accepted her invitation, and pressed hers hard into the pillar. Consternation made her gasp and stiffen when his hands moved to her face, thumbs pressed her jaw, urging her mouth wider; when his tongue caressed her lips, seduced its way by them to brush over the sharpness of her teeth, made an intoxicating sweep of her mouth. She didn't know how to kiss like this; that old friend on the theater steps had never taught her. Hank would find her lacking and stop and she didn't want him to and—

But he didn't. He anchored a fist in her hair, slid his other hand down her back, over her rump and deepened the kiss, coaxing her tongue to play. She melted and came to him because she couldn't resist him. Because she didn't want to.

Her hands, uncertain what to do with themselves, clung to his waist, slipped restlessly up his sides and chest, found his face and opened wide to touch him, to hold him.

So sweet.

She tasted like nothing he'd experienced before, like nothing he'd known existed. Innocence without naïveté. Passion without the darkness he was used to having accompany it. Power without corruption. Tender, hot, luscious, welcome…welcoming.

Rare.

He filled his hands with her softness, feasted on her rarity, gorged on her welcome. Shivered when her hands claimed his face, drew him into her. Went willingly where he knew he would drown.

Craven. Depraved.

He moved his tongue from her mouth to her jaw, her throat, her ear, back to her mouth. This was not how a man kissed a woman the first time; in some rational part of himself he knew the beast in him had crossed a line, but he couldn't care. Didn't want to. Wanted only to go on tasting and sampling until he'd fed on all of her, licked and suckled her head-to-toe and back again until she was boneless. Until he could make her part of him.

Like Gen, for all her loving him, had never been.

Shock bit him; panic, pain and horror—like ice water and acid fire in one—shriveled all his cravenness and passion in the stillness of a missed heartbeat. What was he doing, where was he going?

God, what had he done.

"No."

Hands clamped around her upper arms, he levered himself away from Kate. Shuddered and caught her hands, backing out of reach when she moaned and would have drawn him back. He wanted to go back.

He wanted to go back into her arms and her kiss and more.

More…

He shut his eyes and breathed great gulps of air while his lungs burned, his gut twisted and his body called him a dictionary full of unprintable names.

Kate's fingers curled in his, uncertain. "Hank?" Soft and bewildered. A plea to understand.

"No, Kate. God, don't." He let go of her and wheeled violently away, shoved his hands through his hair, bunched them into fists and jammed them into his back pockets where they couldn't get loose and reach for her again, do to her all the things he couldn't let them do. "I didn't want this. I *don't* want this. We can't do this, what are we doing?"

"I don't know." She was shaky and disoriented. Smoothing her hair behind her ears, she tried to regain order. "You kissed me first, so you tell me."

"You kissed me back."

"Yeah." She nodded, disbelieving. "I did." She touched her swollen mouth uneasily, made an inadequate gesture. It had never occurred to her to think she would ever kiss a man—*could* ever kiss a man, any man, but especially *this* man—like that. Feel compassion for him, yes, but this... "I guess...I don't know, maybe you took me by surprise." An understatement, if ever she'd made one. She'd taken herself without warning, too.

"I took you—? What...you mean you'd respond like that to anyone who surprised you that way?"

Kate swallowed. "I don't know," she told him truthfully. "You're the first person who's ever ambushed me successfully. I don't know how I'd respond to somebody else. If I would."

"You don't know how you'd...because nobody's ever...?" Incredulous, Hank rubbed a hand across his face and stared at her. Who the hell was she, anyway?

When it came right down to it, he knew nothing about Kate Anden except that she had a lot of kids and had once been a nun, yet somehow by default he'd trusted his daughter in her keeping for years. Assumption—as they'd already discussed—stated that because she'd been a nun, then a lay missionary, she must be the perfect saintly person, the holy, wholesome influence so many people—parents besides himself—thought her. Reality, as so often happened, was something else entirely. No matter how real the tapestry of kindness and generosity, the illusion of perfection that Megan and others verbally wove around Kate was merely that, illusion.

The real Kate, the woman behind that single, scorching kiss, was a thief who could steal him blind, a heart-and-soul looter with the potential to leave him wanting her to swipe him deaf and mute as well. Succumbing to the temptation of her lavish body, the compassion with which she treated his daughter would do neither him nor Megan any good. Could, instinct told him, damage his relationship with his daughter beyond repair—especially if things between him and Kate didn't go well.

Or went so well that the only thing he'd want to do for the rest of the summer was jump Kate Anden's bones. Went so well he wound up ignoring Megan, the way she'd accused him and Gen of forgetting her when they got wrapped up in each other every time he came home after an extended absence. And as drum tight as he felt right now, not to mention how many years he'd been celibate, forgetting why he was here in favor of a hot summer affair was a frightening possibility.

"Look," he told Kate evenly, emphatically, "This can't happen, I'm not here for this."

Something in his tone made Kate still and straighten. "Not here for *what?*" she asked carefully.

"This." He made a harsh gesture indicating the two of them. "Here. Now. A minute ago. Things are complicated enough without…" He hesitated.

"Without what, Hank?" She felt wooden, numb. Betrayed by a body she thought she'd known well—hers. It didn't matter. She'd functioned just fine feeling like a stick of wood in the refugee camp on the border between Burma and Thailand where she'd found Li, betrayed there by a calling she'd thought her own. She'd reevaluated and rebuilt who she was then; if necessary she would do the same now. "Us kissing?"

"Without us going where that particular kiss would have gone in another three minutes."

"I live with teenagers and eight-year-olds, Hank." She held control in a tight fist. Well, at least sort of. She lifted her chin, pretended he was the Burmese colonel who'd tried to intimidate her out of his way so he could get at a student protester, and kept her voice level. "We don't do subtlety here. There's too much opportunity for misunderstanding when things aren't spelled out."

Jaw taut, he stared at her. She knew nothing about him, but because he was Megan's father she'd offered him her guesthouse and in a backhanded way entrusted him with her children's lives. He had to make her understand—as bluntly as possible—that although he was hardly the beast his daughter's exaggerations had made him out to be, it still wouldn't be wise to get comfortable with him. The way he felt right now, he could easily turn into the wolf who'd destroy them all.

"Sex, Kate," he said, harshly, crudely. "I'm not here to get my rocks off with you."

She didn't flinch. Teenage foster kids often arrived bearing trunks full of emotional baggage and used their verbal skills to shock and rock, to keep her a good stiff arm's length away. She'd heard worse. None of it hurt like this, of course, but he didn't need to see that. "I didn't think you were," she told him calmly. "I know you're here because of Megan and only Megan. I know I agreed to rent the guesthouse to you because of Megan alone. I know we've never been particularly fond of each other. I'm not sure I understand why it happened, but that kiss had to be a momentary aberration. It'll never happen again."

Hank snorted. "Don't try to kid yourself or me about that, Kate," he said tersely. "You looked at me moon eyed most of the day and my shorts have been too tight thinkin' about you since we shook hands over the rental agreement, so don't pretend 'it'll never' because you say so. Even Mike and Bele could tell you different."

"Could they." Flat and careful, more challenge than question. A muscle ticked in her cheek.

"You bet." Hank nodded. "And if they couldn't, the older kids sure as hell can."

She eyed him oddly in the half-light, flabbergasted. Of all the arrogant, conceited, I-am-God's-gift baloney she'd ever heard, this had to be the biggest crock.

"Let me get this straight." She squared herself to him, arms akimbo, foot tapping. *Be afraid,* the stance warned him, *be very afraid.* "Because I've developed some sort of high-school crush on you and you're wearing too tight skivvies and we shared one boffo kiss, you're telling me I should run screaming any time you get within six feet of me unchaperoned because if I don't our hormones will turn into rampaging elephants we can't control, even though you think I'm a goody-two-shoes and I've often considered you a pain-in-the-butt sonofagun?''

Hank swallowed an unwilling grin. Put like that, his assessment of the situation did sound a smidgen melodramatic. Still... He shrugged and let the excruciating throb behind his zipper be his guide. "If the situation arises, it won't matter what we think of each other, Kate," he assured her quietly. "Moon eyes and tight shorts are a lethal combination any time, but right now...you need to know—I have to tell you—that kiss didn't do anything for me except make keeping my pants zipped around you a lot more painful."

Her lungs tightened, her heart pounded high in her throat. She couldn't catch her breath. "It does?"

"Yeah."

Something unidentifiable jittered up her spine. Nervousness, maybe excitement, probably fear...and something else. "Really? You've, um, been thinking about *me?*" She'd misheard him. Her ears were full of wax. That had to be it. She probably ought to make an appointment with Dr. Moody to get 'em washed out. Until then, maybe if she rephrased her original question she'd understand the answer better. "You lust after *me?*"

"Not by choice," he said ruefully, running his hands through his hair and wishing she'd shut up and quit doing whatever she was doing, which instead of relieving the itch in his pants, was steadily making it worse, "but yeah. I lust after you. You find that so hard to believe?"

"Yes...no...it's just, um...it's never, ah...*Me?*" she repeated, more to herself than him. She looked at him. "Are you *sure?*"

"Oh, absolutely." Hank nodded, amused by her astonishment in spite of the tension coiled inside him. You'd think she'd never heard it before. And the places she'd been, nun or not, body like hers, she had to have heard it plenty.

Of course, maybe that was the problem. She'd heard it too often, under questionable circumstances with her hair tucked into a wimple. Maybe she'd never had to believe it in quite the same way before. "I'm sure. And I'm getting more sure by the minute."

"Oh," Kate murmured. Then, flustered again, she realized what he'd actually said. *"Oh!"* She viewed him wide-eyed and swallowed. "Well, then." She swallowed again and jammed a hand in a pocket, came out with something she used to whisk her hair back and tie it out of the way, the nun disappearing into her cowl. She took a deep breath, blew it out and repeated briskly, "Well, then. I guess we've spent enough time together for one day, then, haven't we?"

"Yeah," Hank agreed dryly, "I'd say we have."

"Oh. Okay." She edged a few steps toward the door. "I guess all that's left, then, is to say good-night."

"Mmm."

"Well, then." She nodded at him, then opened the door. "Good-night, Mr. Mathison."

"Good-night, Kate."

For a moment they stared at each other through the screen—Kate wary, Hank hungry—then she scooted into the interior of the hallway, out of the light, and Hank was alone with the fireflies and the unquiet knowledge that neither he nor Kate was as tame as they wanted the world to believe.

Nor as tame as they'd believed themselves.

With a grimace and a sigh he descended the porch steps. Such a lot to have learned in a day, and gee, wouldn't you know, the summer's dance had barely begun.

Chapter 6

July

Time passed, dragging one moment, like lightning the next.

Minutes, hours, days winked by, painful on two fronts: the one where Megan continued to do her best to be where Hank wasn't; and the one where he found it next to impossible to avoid Kate.

He didn't want to avoid her.

Being near her was torture.

She was a taste on the back of his tongue he couldn't get rid of, a drum in his veins, a curse calling to the beast within him the way wolves were drawn to howl at the moon. Within the civilized veneer he wore to make pretense look like reality at the office, he could almost feel himself unraveling.

There was infinitely more to her than he'd ever wanted to imagine.

She was wry, dry and sarcastic, funny, human and vulnerable. Like him she recognized and abhorred—and too often tried to ignore—her weaknesses, did not deny but reveled joyously in her strengths.

Something about her fed the part of him that used to get high on drug raids, fueled the adrenaline junkie in him: an element of danger, an undercurrent of risk, a genuine quality of mercy—a serenity and an innocence that underlay the knowing-but-refusing-to-be-cynical exterior; a threat and a promise of passion unexplored and therefore untapped, which beckoned even as it warned him away.

Unfortunately, he'd never been able to walk away from a puzzle until he solved it.

Living on a working tree farm and llama ranch meant, of course, exactly that: working. Dawn to dusk. What time the trees, garden, workshop and quadrupeds didn't require, the kids did.

They had music lessons, ball games, part-time jobs and early morning twice-weekly trips in to the local farmers' market to supplement their college funds. They had 4-H club, which meant local, county, then—with luck—the state-fair competitions to prepare projects for, parades to be in and costumes to create. They had dental appointments and doctors' appointments and prosthetist's appointments. Fortunately besides Kate, Tai, Hank and car pools, Li and Megan both drove—and did so willingly.

Before the day ended, Kate and Tai had office work to attend to: records to keep, wholesale tree buyers to line up for fall, calls to return and would-be llama owners to talk with. A city boy, despite his many treks to and through the jungles of drug-trafficking countries, the amount of work to be done between sunrise and sunset staggered Hank. And Megan's eagerness to participate in any and all aspects of Stone House's enterprises positively floored him.

For himself, he liked feeling physically bushed at the end of the day, liked the sense of accomplishment, the fact that he could literally see what progress the farm made day-today. Liked the grit under his fingernails and the appetite being outside gave him. And he got a kick out of seeing Megan, and sometimes Li, sometimes Bele and Mike, at least once or twice a day when they loaded lunch or a mid-afternoon snack onto a couple of the llamas and packed it out to the tree fields. Loved seeing so much less of the angry side of Megan, glimpsing so much more of the beautiful child she'd been at five—even though she continued to go out of her way to avoid him. He even enjoyed the calluses forming on his hands and the daily muscle aches of physical labor, because stripping down and showering it all away at the end of the day felt like heaven.

Liked very much not having to deal with kiss-ass office politics, agency jurisdictions, cowboy special agents and the constant barrage of walking-a-tightrope paranoia.

Instead of the daily office routine, the work he did varied by the day; when one job finished, the next began. One day he and Risto restrung electric fencing, the next he was pruning and shearing trees or whacking weeds or learning from Grisha how to use a hand lens to check Christmas tree needles for blight and insect infestation or getting Megan to—grudgingly—teach him to handle llamas. Spare time he spent in the woodshop reacquainting himself with his carpentry skills or sorting out the kids: getting Bele and Ilya to teach him to carve; talking insects and fungus with Grisha-the-budding-naturalist; learning how to train dogs from Mike; clandestinely salting the archaeological dig with Tai; learning that Ilya's friend Jamal spent almost as much time running away to Stone House as Megan used to; and keeping an eye on Risto.

He couldn't name why or how he knew—call it cop's instinct—but he knew something wasn't entirely right with the youth. There seemed to be something between the Andens' exchange student and Megan, an undercurrent of furtiveness and secrets known and kept—unwillingly. But exactly which of them kept whose secrets he couldn't tell. So he did what he'd learned at Quantico and managed, from experience, to be good at: he watched.

He also worried.

But none of what he did to occupy him elsewhere kept him from dreaming about and wanting Kate.

Tough age, he decided wryly. Both his and Megan's.

He knew without doubt that if he were simply here to play a role, was merely here to be Special Agent Mathison undercover, dealing with the escalating complexities of the situation would be easier. The man he became undercover was a straightforward two-dimensional individual who lived by simple rules.

Don't trust anyone; don't break cover for any reason.

You've only got yourself in there, so look out for number one.

Don't get close; don't get sentimental. Use people, but don't make friends.

Never consider the other guy; especially when he's probably the bad guy.

Tuxedo rules, he thought of them; basic black-and-white, custom designed to keep him sane and intact, return him home with the fewest scars possible when the job was done.

But this was not his job, this was his life, his daughter's life; no set of tuxedo rules, however frilled the shirt or fancy the studs, had ever been designed to guide him through that. And the hungrier being near Kate made him, the harder it was to concentrate on finding the path that would lead him to Megan.

Not that his losing sight of the path could ever really be Kate's fault—no matter how badly he might like to make her the scapegoat.

He thought of the picture of him and Megan in his wallet. Taken early the previous fall at a department barbecue, it showed him with his arm around his daughter's shoulders while she laughed at something off camera, her arm linked about his waist. Funny how much a liar a camera could be, how nothing ever looked wrong in snapshots from company picnics, but only seemed to go wrong when the camera was turned away.

No, *he* was the one who'd lost sight of the best ways to reach Megan. The simple ways that had brought them together easily when she was a child and he'd return from assignments had long ceased to apply: a quick hug and a toss in the air; a special because-you-had-to-stay-home-while-I-was-gone gift and a tickle contest; an hour or two spent examining and identifying the bugs on the sidewalk and in the sandbox that Mommy was too squeamish to look at. It was enough, Gen used to tell them both flatly, that she no longer killed spiders in the house because Megan had begged her not to after they'd read *Charlotte's Web.*

He remembered that family "discussion" with particular fondness. Megan had giggled over Gen's arachnid pronouncement and shot her father a conspiratorial glance; Hank had winked at her and congratulated Gen on her forbearance, since having spiders in the house was not only good luck but controlled the presence of less desirable insects as well and was, thereby, a boon to their environment. Then he and Megan had gone off and laughed themselves silly over "Mommy's little insect problem."

But Megan had been five then, Gen was still alive and "Father Magic" was a kiss that could equally mend a scraped knee or a broken heart.

By the time she was eight the hug, the gift and the tickling were still in, but the toss in the air was out and the insect hour had become a couple of hours spent at the roller rink, the batting cage or taking her and her friends to the movies or shopping at the mall while Hank felt guilty about leaving Gen to handle most of the things that required parent participation at school or about not being able to volunteer to coach Megan's T-ball team or even to make most of her gymnastics meets.

By the time she hit ten the gift was taken for granted, the

hug was accepted if she had time, tickling was a Dad-I'm-not-in-the-mood thing and the one-on-one father-daughter moments were getting hard to come by. Friends and phone calls took precedence; school and extracurricular activities had increased. When he had time for her, her time for him was gone.

By the time Gen died he and Megan were nearly strangers, and lost time was a commodity Hank wished he'd invested in when the moments had been available and the price had been closer to his grasp. He missed her company, missed her innocence and cursed himself for the cynicism too often printed on a face that mirrored his—except that Megan had her mother's eyes. In all the years he'd known her, never once had he seen cynicism in Gen's eyes.

No, stubborn, constant optimism and never accepting *no* for an answer had been Gen's forte. It was also the sword by which she'd died.

He missed Gen and Megan most, avoided Kate most, in the evenings when his resistance was down and his druthers were closest to the surface.

"Morning, boys."

Kate's cheerful voice carried clearly through the open kitchen windows and Hank made a wry face. Kate, on the other hand, refused to avoid anything at all, regardless of what it was. If she had a problem she could identify—or one she couldn't, for that matter—she didn't hesitate to confront it. None of this if-we-ignore-it-it'll-go-away nonsense for her, no, sir. She went at a problem head on, pedal to the metal. He didn't think he'd ever met anyone as willing to face down what bothered her as Kate Anden. And since he was what currently bothered her...

"Appreciate the offer, but I've been handling this sort of thing by myself for a lot of years. Besides, it's not safe for you to be around me, remember," she'd told him yesterday when he'd come up on her in the middle of the driveway struggling to remove a stripped fitting from the mower and

stopped to help. *"You get too close and I might lose my head because you just make me too crazy inside, Mr. Mathison. It's hard to think around you."*

The day before it had been something else in a long line of what he could only think of as confrontational flirting. Whatever she said, it was always exasperated—with herself more than him, she'd confessed two days ago—always honest and most often at her own expense rather than his. Unfortunately, instead of making her less desirable, her distracted comments only made her more so. There was nothing more attractive to a man—or at least nothing more enticing to *him*—than a woman with a sense of humor, who tartly told him to go away every time she saw him, because "you twiddle my buttons just by looking at me." He'd gone away wondering what she'd do if he reminded her it wasn't his buttons she twiddled with her glance.

He knew it was playing with fire, but in some perverse corner of his mind—if he couldn't spend the day with Megan—he was half tempted to spend the day with Kate just to see what she might verbally have in store for him today. He wouldn't, but he was tempted.

Sighing over lust's abominable timing, he stepped through the open mud-room door and walked into the kitchen.

It wasn't a 4-H morning, so only Kate, Bele, Mike and Jamal were in the room. Kate was at the stove humming something jazzy and making what appeared to be French toast, Jamal was setting the breakfast table and Mike and Bele poured milk and juice and played with the refrigerator door. Intensely curious to know what they were trying to do, Hank stood quietly in the outer kitchen doorway and watched. While one practically stuck his nose against the rubber seal and went cross-eyed, the other slowly shut the refrigerator door. They repeated the process, slow and fast, switching places until Kate finally rolled her eyes and looked at them.

"It goes out when you shut it," she said.

Two pairs of little-boy eyes—one pair brown, the other pair black—and one pair of warm mead adult male eyes turned to her. The little-boy eyes were dubious and suspicious, the adult's curious to know what they might be talking about, but also amused underneath arched brows.

"How do you know the light in the fridge goes out when you shut the door?" Mike asked. "You can't see it."

"I know because I replace the light bulb if it's not on when I open the door."

"Yes, but," Bele argued, all reason, "maybe you have to replace the light bulb because it's on all the time and never *goes* out until it *burns* out."

"It goes out when the door is closed," Kate assured him firmly. "Trust me."

"Yes, but *how* do you *know?*"

"Yes," Mike echoed. "How?"

Kate eyed them thoughtfully for an instant, shrugged, and went to pull open the refrigerator door. She leaned over to point out the heavy round sliding peg on the door's inside frame. "See this button?"

They nodded.

"Watch." She pushed the button in and the light went out, then she looked at the boys' disappointed faces and sighed. Another piece of magic exposed for the charlatanism it was. "That's how I know."

"Oh."

Deflated, Mike and Bele each pushed the button several times, swung the door in and out to make sure that it would indeed push the peg in as it closed, then dragged off in search of more interesting mysteries to solve. Swallowing a grin, Hank crossed the kitchen to help himself to coffee; offered a cup to Kate. She declined.

"Do you always pop their balloons like that?" he asked.

"What?" Puzzlement cleared. "Oh, you mean the door?"

He nodded.

She shrugged. "Yeah. I hate to do it, but with two of 'em

the same age with the same curiosities at the same time..."
Another shrug accompanied by a grimace. "It's the two-puppy theory. What trouble one doesn't think of to get into on his own, the other will. Better I should puncture a few balloons than let them figure stuff like that out the other way."

Hank lifted a brow, an unspoken question.

"You know," Kate said, gesturing with the French-toast turner, "One of 'em gets inside the fridge, the other one shuts the door..."

A grateful fizzle of tragedy averted ran down Hank's spine. "Ah," he muttered, mentally shuddering at the unwelcome picture imagination painted. Thank God he hadn't had to think about that particular accident, trying to raise Meg by himself. "Preventive parenting."

Kate nodded wryly. "Only kind there is. Jamal—" She turned to the lanky youth who put down his last piece of flatware and looked at her—almost painfully eager, Hank thought. "You wanna call everybody in? Breakfast's about ready."

"Sure, Kate."

Jamal went out through the mud room and onto the porch to jangle the bell beside the door. Kate listened for a moment before going back to the stove, tapping her toes and humming the way she'd been before Hank came in. Sipping his coffee, Hank watched her, fascinated by her lack of inhibition, disturbed by how...simple...it had become in two short weeks to stand in the Anden kitchen every morning while Kate cooked or did whatever else came to hand and just...*be*.

It was hard to remember a time in his life when things hadn't been complicated, complex. And it wasn't as if they weren't now, but somehow...he couldn't define it even to himself. The hard stuff just seemed to feel like *less* here, the better stuff like *more*.

Quit trying to analyze it to death and enjoy it while you can, he cautioned himself.

He straightened and did his best to follow good advice. A sudden snatch of the lyrics Kate sang penetrated his consciousness, making him nearly choke on something between astonished laughter and an unexpected surge of heat when he realized what she was singing.

"Oh, I wish that I could wiggle like my sister Kate," Kate sang, doing a two-step twirl with the spatula, over to get a box of eggs out of the refrigerator. She returned with an exaggerated set of shoulder-arm jiggle-shimmies that set her entire upper body asway accompanied by an ain't-misbehavin', throaty-voiced, *"shimmy, shimmy like jelly on a plate..."*

There was more, but all at once Hank found himself laughing too hard to understand the verse. Personally, Kate's wriggles didn't so much remind him of a plate full of jelly as they did the gentler sway of a thick, rich pudding. Chocolate mousse with fine chocolate shavings was his personal favorite. Eaten slowly, flavor savored, spoon licked...

But it wasn't a spoon and chocolate mousse his wayward imagination put into his mouth, let alone made him envision.

Already warm, fever lit him without warning from the inside out. Unprepared for the quick, harsh wrench of desire, he inhaled too sharply and swallowed coffee wrong. Abruptly he found himself coughing and choking instead of laughing. Jamal left the bell clanging and was beside him in an instant, pounding on his back.

"Hank—Mr. Mathison—you okay?" he asked anxiously. "You need some water or somethin'? Bele—" He gestured to the child who'd returned to the kitchen in response to the meal bell. "Get him some water."

"Dad." The mud-room door banged and Megan came in, put a hand on his shoulder. "Are you all right, Dad?"

"Fine," Hank wheezed. "Just give me a min—"

Kate's hand was on his, pressing a glass into it. "Here's

some water.'' The coolness of her fingers burned into his; he jerked away. The glass dropped to the floor in a clatter of plastic and splashing liquid.

Their eyes met; heat scorched between them, unbearable and provocative, seething and undeniable.

''No,'' Hank said hoarsely. Then he pushed by his daughter, through the herd of Andens coming in for breakfast and slammed out of the house.

Intent only on restraining physical urges that threatened to overwhelm him, Hank didn't feel the hand that reached for his shirtsleeve, nor see the wounded, little-girl-lost look Megan sent after him; didn't hear the soft, frightened, ''Dad?''

Couldn't see, then, that for convoluted reasons she'd never been able—and wasn't able even now—to articulate, Megan thought he was running from her....

In a small pocket of quiet surrounded by chaos, Kate, Megan and Jamal stood trying to sort it out.

''Man, I'm starvin','' Ilya said in his exaggerated American accent. ''What's for breakfast?''

''No apple juice?'' Grisha asked, head in the refrigerator. ''I think I would rather have apple juice this morning than orange juice.''

''Mom, did you make bacon?'' Mike rummaged in the meat keeper in front of Grisha. ''Hey, Bele, look what I found.''

Bele jammed himself into the open refrigerator beside his brother. ''Huh, so that's where it's been. What's my baseball doing in the fridge?''

''Don't know,'' Mike said. ''Maybe you forgot it was in your hand when you got an orange or somethin'—''

''Ilya, keep that blasted dog away from the girls. She's been teasing 'em again.'' Li, sounding disgusted, came in slapping a pair of goatskin gloves on her jeaned thighs. ''She's covered in llama spit and now it's all over me, too.''

"Phew." Ilya pinched his nose shut. "Get away from me. You stink."

"Oh, I do not. It's dry already, but if you don't teach that animal some manners I *will* make you stink—"

"What's up with Hank?" Tai removed his yellow-and-green John Deere tractor cap and stuffed it into his back pocket as he stepped into the kitchen. No hats at the table. It was a rule. "He looks like somebody's set the hounds of hell after him." He eyed Kate. "What'd you do to him, Ma?"

Too distracted to answer, Kate simply gave him a look. She couldn't be sure what was going on with Hank, but she could venture a guess—something similar to the toe-curling, jelly-for-knees shock she'd received when their fingers collided.

Jamal, deciding what he'd seen, said, "He inhaled his coffee. I think he went to be sick."

"You do?" Megan asked, painfully hopeful, agonizingly tentative. "Do you think maybe I should go see—"

"No, I'll go," Kate volunteered quickly. Yes, it might be good for both father and daughter if Hank really was sick and Megan went. On the other hand, if he wasn't, if it was something else...

A swift glance at Megan confirmed all Kate needed to know: insecure, bewildered child reliving some real or imagined parental slight from the past, mistakenly superimposing it on today.

Geez Lou-eeze, she thought. *Like there isn't something smarter I could do than go anywhere near Hank Mathison with jello knees and kiss-me-senseless soup for brains.*

Still, since somebody had to do it, it was undoubtedly better if she went than Megan. And truth be known, she was more than a little curious about what had caused Hank's reaction.

"Didn't anyone ever tell you about curiosity and cats?"

Sister Viveca had asked her once, reprimanding Kate over some mischief she'd caused while still a postulant.

"Sure." Kate had nodded intemperately, too wise, too young and too inexperienced for her own good. *"Curiosity killed it. But, Sister, it also teaches. When I was little I had to get singed before I really understood that fire burns."* And so it seemed she would have to go get singed to understand now.

Sighing, she offered Megan the pancake turner. "You do breakfast," she suggested. "I'll see about your dad."

"Would you?" Relief was evident in the way Megan snatched the spatula.

"Yeah." Kate headed for the door, tossing directions over her shoulder as she went. "Mike, get a rag and mop the floor, please. Bele, help Meg. Don't wait breakfast."

Then, leaving order behind, she went in pursuit of chaos and the discombobulating Hank Mathison.

She found him in the shadows behind the equipment barn, soaking his head under the cold spray from the hose they used to fill the llamas' water troughs.

Tongue tucked between her left molars, Kate watched Hank drench himself, torn between amusement and disbelief. There had been times when her brother was a teenager that their mother had told him to go soak his head and wash whatever immoral notions he was entertaining about his girlfriend—later his wife and Mike's mother—right out of his mind, but she'd never known Mike senior to actually do it. She'd never known anyone to do it.

"Does it help?" she asked.

"What?" Startled, Hank straightened and swung about; icy water splashed over his shoulders, down his bare back and chest, soaked his fly. He cursed. "Damn, woman. I should've known you'd never leave well enough alone."

"I *am* much better at interfering," Kate agreed modestly. Hank snorted something impolite. Kate would have laughed, too, but for some reason her throat refused to produce the sound.

It seemed silly for a woman who couldn't understand why other women got so hot and bothered hunk watching at the beach to have to admit, but she couldn't quite seem to take her gaze off Hank's sculpted chest. Muscular without being overdone, his smooth pecs and abs held her attention to an indecent degree.

Made her wonder what they'd feel like to touch.

Air twisted, got fouled up in her throat at the mere thought. She couldn't seem to breathe right—no doubt the reason she couldn't find the breath to laugh. You'd think she'd never seen a half-naked man before, the way it felt as if her tongue was hanging out of her mouth, but of course she had. It was just that none of *them* looked like *him*. Had ever kissed her like he had.

Bad enough she couldn't sleep without dreaming about that kiss, him, without having to deal with how the memory of it, the sight of him, made her feel when she was awake—particularly when he was around. Hot and bothered didn't *begin* to cover it.

"So," she said, forcing her gaze and her thoughts away from the tiny furl of heat igniting deep inside her. Her eyes lit on the towel hanging from a ring screwed into the side of the barn and she whisked it out of the ring and tossed it to Hank. "I take it you didn't rush out because you're sick?"

He caught the towel, began to wipe himself off. "Oh, I'm sick all right," he assured her, "just not in the way you mean."

Kate swallowed against sudden dry mouth. "I'm sorry to hear that," she whispered.

He quit toweling himself, arrested by the sound in her voice. "Why?"

"Because..." She cleared her throat, moistened her

mouth, suddenly uncertain how to proceed. Stunned by her unaccustomed hesitation, the desire to quibble.

She hated being at a loss for words, hated getting caught in inadequacy. Hated feeling that for Megan's sake as well as her own she should ignore rather than address this silent struggle going on between them. She'd never been very good at pretending something didn't exist when it did. In her experience ignoring a potential problem usually only made it bigger, instead of making it go away. Still, for perhaps the first time in her life, politeness won out over the desire to speak her mind.

"Jamal—" Another pause. Second-guessing herself. She hadn't wasted time on second guesses since the last time she'd blown a true-false multiple-choice test in high school. Didn't know why she was now. If this was what having a crush—or whatever it was adult women got—on a guy was like for a grown-up girl, no wonder so many teenage girls wound up in the kind of troubled relationships they did. "Maybe I should ask what you mean about how you're sick or not first." An uncomfortable two-breath lull. "For the, um, sake of, um…clarity. You know?"

He viewed her as if he didn't know who she was. "Clarity," he said carefully, making sure he'd heard her right.

She nodded, looking at the toe of her right shoe, ducking his gaze.

Hank studied her. The gently mocking, always serene sense of self-confidence that usually radiated from her irritated the hell out of him, but this was far worse. Timidity didn't become her. He didn't want her wearing it, not for him. Not because of him.

Odd.

He'd thought the only thing he wanted was her to quit messing with his hormones so he could concentrate on Megan. When had how Kate Anden felt become important to him?

Oh, probably about the night he'd kissed her and she'd sent him reeling by kissing him back.

Funny how that worked. Where the body wanted to go, the mind followed.

So where did that leave the heart?

Lagging to the rear, making sure nobody got left behind. Waiting to see if it was safe to catch up...

Eyes thoughtful on Kate, Hank rubbed the towel through his hair, which was shaggier now than he'd worn it since he'd accepted the assistant directorship. He wondered briefly if Kate liked it better shorter or longer. "You sure you want me to *clarify* for you what happened?"

"No." She shook her head, didn't pretend to misunderstand him. Raised her chin and looked at him. Shrugged her mouth and grimaced. "Do it anyway. Because if it's me, we have to talk about it."

He couldn't resist. "And if it's not you?"

"It's not?" Relief and disappointment vied for position. She wanted to believe relief won, but it didn't. "Then you need to let Meg know you ran out so fast because you had to be sick, that you're all right now."

"What?"

"She's afraid she did something to make you leave."

His expletive was harsh and self-directed. "She didn't."

"I know that. You know that. Jamal told her he thought you were feeling sick. She believed him enough to want to come after you. I figured that might be a bad idea if..." Her voice trailed off uncertainly.

"If it was you and not something else," Hank finished.

Kate nodded. "But it wasn't, so—"

"Yes it was," he interrupted quietly. His eyes were dark, dangerously deep, his look as intense and intimate as a touch. "It is. You. I couldn't stay in the same room with you, I wanted you so badly. Want you still."

Stunned, Kate swallowed a ragged breath. No one had

ever looked at her the way Hank Mathison saw her now,
had ever told her...desired her...made her feel...

Like walking into him and drowning. Like turning forever
into a moment. With him.

"Oh, spit," she whispered.

"Yeah." He nodded, troubled. "You could say that."

"But we can't— I don't— It wouldn't— It's not..." She
pressed her lips together, staring up at him, lost. This wasn't
her area of expertise. She knew everything she was supposed to say to the kids, to Tai, to Li, the limits she'd put
on Risto for his stay with them. But that was them. This
was her. This was her feeling things, both physical and emotional, she'd never felt before, that she'd never thought
about feeling. That there had seemed no point to feel.
Things that the wisdom of inexperience didn't cover.

One kiss more than a week ago... It was something that
filled out night's restless dreams, that intimated a hundred
things she understood only intellectually. Still, the roil of
emotions, the sense of intimacy, produced by one kiss—
even a kiss as hot as that one—should have subsided by
now.

Shouldn't it?

She'd know how to handle this, know what to say, if it
had to do with one of the kids. She'd managed a lot of
situations doing relief work in military zones, dealt with
threats of rape and worse things. But this was different. She
didn't know what to say to herself, had no idea how to
handle—or discourage—Hank's desire for her.

Or her desire for him.

"The thing about being an adult," her mother had once
told her, *"is that it means not having to act on all your
desires. It means being able to choose the way you want to
go, not just the way that gratifies the moment."*

Kate had believed her. But she'd never before in her life
been presented with a choice or an admission like this.

"I don't know what to say," she told him baldly. "I've

been in a lot of situations, but this is the first..." She stopped, shook her head. No, don't tell him that. Keep it simple. He didn't need her to tell him this tension between them was getting to be as hard for her as for him. "Isn't there something you can do about..." A helpless pause. "Can't you... I mean isn't there some way for you to..." Another lapse while she hunted for evasive words. "*deal* with it...that doesn't involve me?"

An almost bruised amusement flickered across Hank's face; he nearly laughed. "I take it you weren't one of those nuns who rapped boys' knuckles then sent them to confession and told them they'd go blind if they *dealt* with it that way."

It took her a moment to decipher her unintentional double entendre and his response to it. When she did, embarrassment stained the pale skin of her neck, bled upward with its attendant heat into her cheeks. "I'm sorry," she mumbled, flustered. "I didn't mean to suggest..." She stopped, deliberating. Embarrassment drained slowly, replaced by perception. "On the other hand," she said thoughtfully, and Hank nearly choked, "That might be the practical solution, don't you think?"

Chapter 7

It was his turn to flush, to squirm, to chuckle with discomfort. He, who, because of his many years in drug enforcement, thought he'd seen and heard everything.

"Practical, maybe," he agreed, sounding somewhat strangled, "but hardly a solution." Of all the conversations he could ever imagine having with anyone—particularly with a woman who was an ex-nun—this wasn't one. So how had it gotten to this point, anyway? *Oh, just lucky, I guess.* "Certainly not satisfying. Definitely not long-term."

"Oh." She seemed wistful. Disappointed. Glad. Torn among emotions.

"Yes," he agreed gently. "Oh." He looked down at her, watching the pale eyes with the navy rings around the irises, seeking he wasn't sure what. Answers, strength, respite from the thing between the two of them that he knew was inevitable. And irreversible. "And not only that, but it wouldn't do anything for you."

"Oh, but I'm used to being celi—"

She broke off, biting her tongue on what she'd been about

to say. It sounded too much like an accusation. He finished it for her.

"You're used to being celibate."

She nodded.

"So am I." He smiled thinly, draped the towel back through its ring to dry. "And it doesn't make a damn bit of difference."

"I wouldn't know."

"Wouldn't you?" A challenge. A dare to deny the truth.

Self-conscious in her desire to lie, she looked at the ground. "You must have dealt with this sort of thing before."

"No."

Surprised, she raised her head. "But you're a man."

The corner of his mouth lifted with scorn. He'd expected better of her. "And you're a sexist."

She laughed at that, a dry, humor-filled, self-deprecating sound. "Sometimes. But that's not what I meant here. I just meant you're a man, you've been married, you aren't a monk, you've been around, you must've had to…manage… desires you don't intend to act on."

"Yeah, I have. It's called not wanting what you can't have."

"I know that one," Kate said softly. "I use that one. It's not working this time."

Something in him leaped at her admission; he wasn't alone. In the next instant he quashed elation and regarded her steadily. "No. It's not."

Silence passed between them while they digested revelation, shied from it. Faced hunger, avarice, want. And discarded them as inappropriate to the moment.

"So what do we do?" she asked.

He shrugged. "Follow the rules. Remain focused on Meg, because I don't want to risk losing her. Don't wind up alone together. Never touch. And you've got to quit telling me how scrambled your brain gets when you look at me. For one thing, it's not dignified. For another, it's not dishonest to keep something like that to yourself. And third—'' He grinned wryly. ''Third, hearing how I make you feel makes me crazy. So far, it's only your timing and the number of kids who've been around that've kept me this side of the line we keep drawing in the dirt.''

''Don't forget fourth,'' Kate said quietly. He looked at her. She hunched a shoulder and told Hank the same lie she told herself. ''I don't know about you, but I think…I think I'd only be in it for the sex and that's not enough.''

''Good point.'' But he looked almost as unconvinced as Kate felt. ''So.'' He pulled his shirt off the shelf where he'd left it, next to the stiff brush they used to scrub out the llama troughs every day. Gathered it together in his hands and slid it over his head, aware in every fiber of Kate watching him. Of the fact that what he'd rather be doing was taking her shirt off her, putting his hands on her and feeling hers on him. Knowing damn well that, despite what Kate said, if she were to lay down with him the result would be far more than sex, but still less than either of them was entitled to. ''We're agreed.''

Kate sketched a line between them with the toe of her boot. ''You stay on your side of the fence, I stay on mine.''

He stuck out his hand. ''Shake on it?''

Kate snorted. ''After what we just talked about? Not likely.''

Hank grinned. ''You're learning.''

''Yeah.'' She watched him finish pulling his shirt down over his chest and sighed regretfully. ''And ain't education a bitch.''

Then she picked up the hose he'd discarded, and to the sound of Hank's laughter, she turned it on herself.

Establishing the rules of their relationship didn't make it easier for Kate. If anything, seeing Hank on a daily basis— even from a distance—got harder.

She couldn't relieve her own tension simply by tossing some comment at him, because now she understood that as far as Hank was concerned such commentary was merely a tease that made self-control more difficult. Also, the more she saw him, the more she liked him.

He was hardly the pasteboard character his looks and his daughter had proclaimed him to be. He was as multidimensional as people come, as vulnerable as his daughter. And a man capable of emotions he could neither control nor let anyone else share.

She didn't know who he'd been when he'd worked undercover, but the man who sprayed and fertilized trees with her sons, who invited his daughter to help him raid their collections of South American souvenirs and Indian artifacts in order to keep Mike and Bele in "dig fossils," and who squeezed Li's shoulder when she was nervous before her audition for the county symphony, simply grinned and hugged her afterward when Li won her chair hands-down-going-away was a man Kate had never expected to meet. Never even considered might be out there.

Had never let herself dream of finding.

Besides being sexy as all get-out, the Hank she saw daily was decent, honorable, honest and able to laugh at himself—all things she'd recognized before but had half decided would diminish as the summer wore on. Instead of diminishing, however, Hank's talents only seemed to increase as time wore by until Kate uncovered the secret he hid deepest: he was a man capable of loving without reservation or restraint, without conditions.

No matter what game Megan played, he stayed within range, refused to walk away even in those moments when she treated him to her worst. That his daughter couldn't see past her own pain well enough to see how much her father loved her was something Kate recognized, as well. Understood that as much as Megan needed to hear the word, needed him to tell her rather than try to show her how he felt, Hank could hardly voice his love for her in any way Megan could hear. And it made Kate ache for them both.

Love them both.

It also made it harder for her to stay away from him. But she understood that he couldn't afford to let her near even to offer comfort—or perhaps that was especially to offer comfort—because she had a feeling she knew where *comfort* could easily lead. Passion was a sneak thief and a con artist that could gull and dupe its way through the noblest emotions, leave them stripped and tattered all over the floor. So instead of even allowing herself to do something as simple as offering to pour Hank coffee, she stayed on her side of the breakfast table and let him pour it for himself. Instead of enjoying a few minutes of purely adult conversation on the front porch after supper, she adhered to the rules and kept kids or llamas or bolted doors or an electric fence between them.

But she couldn't stop herself from seeking him out across a distance, meeting his eyes, reading the same sense of urgency, of need, in him as she felt in herself. Couldn't stop the want.

And July got older, bolder, hotter, greener, the sky stayed blue and streaked with jet streams and the sun burned....

The tenuous peace fell apart early on a brooding, muggy and torpid Michigan evening tasting of storms that refused to come.

It was the fifteenth of July, the thirty-eighth anniversary of Genevieve Mathison's birth. Hank never thought about the date. Megan did.

They were alone at the guesthouse—a rarity, what with Megan spending most nights in the extra bed in Li's room and with them both taking meals up at the main house with the family. As Kate put it when Hank had stiffly suggested he wouldn't want to intrude on the Andens more than he and Megan were already, since Hank was paying for his and Megan's beds but they were also putting in long days working for Stone House, the least the Andens could do was provide the board. Except that Hank was never quite sure what headway he and Megan were making as father and daughter, the arrangement worked well. But tonight when he came in to clean up before supper, Megan was there ahead of him, dressed to the nines and carelessly expectant.

Maybe he should have had a premonition or figured it out, then, but he had other things on his mind: Kate swimming in the pond with Mike and Bele, modestly attired in a skirted one-piece bathing suit that teased his imagination no end, for instance.

"Wow." He made a circling motion with his finger, whistled appreciatively when Megan turned slowly to give him the full effect. She was dressed in a slim-cut, sleeveless white button-front dress and white strappy sandals. There were small pearl studs in her ears, a pearl cocktail ring on her right hand and a slim gold watch on her left wrist. Her hair was soft, pulled gently away from her face by a comb in a style he'd always particularly liked on Gen. He didn't think he'd ever seen his daughter look more grown-up or more beautiful. "You're a knockout. Is that dress new?"

She shook her head shyly. "No. You've seen it before, but it's been a while."

"No-o-o," he said, light and teasing, drawn out with disbelief. "I'd remember if I'd seen you in that outfit before."

She flushed, suddenly all gawky teen. "Thanks. But you didn't see it on me. It's Mom's. She wore it to Aunt Sara's wedding. It finally fits me. I always wanted to wear it."

"Mom's." The foreboding that hadn't prickled through him earlier sifted along the edge of Hank's nerves. He'd thought he got rid of all Gen's clothes—or rather had asked her sister Sara to do it within months of her death. The jewelry he'd put aside for Meg himself, presented the pearls to her six months ago when she'd turned sixteen. Knowing what was inside it because he'd told her, she'd tossed the box aside without opening it. Apparently things had changed since then.

He took another long, hard look at his daughter. God, she did remind him of Gen. Not so much physically as something in her demeanor: hair, makeup, attitude...almost as if he was looking at a photograph. Almost as though Megan had taken a picture of Gen into the bathroom with her, set it up in front of her and copied the image onto herself.

Nope, he decided uneasily, this didn't feel right at all.

Things had been going misleadingly well of late, he knew, and he felt he should have been prepared for *something*. But dressing like Gen, to *be* Gen... Even given Meg's repertoire of creative ways to act out, this was a new one. He didn't like it.

But then, like many parents, he knew he was prone to not liking things he couldn't understand.

Still, this did seem awfully morbid and unhealthy. He also didn't know how to handle it. Or why it was manifesting now. It wasn't Christmas, Mother's Day, Thanksgiving, the anniversary of Gen's death or even the Fourth of July, so why...

Try to stay cool, he advised himself. *Keep it light. See where it goes. Maybe she's just got a...a special date.*

"Did Aunt Sara give the dress to you?" he asked idly.

"Un-unh." Megan smoothed tanned hands down the length of white. "She let me choose whatever I wanted to keep, when she was sorting through Mom's stuff. I kept most of it. We're the same size now."

Not *I'm the same size she was,* but *We're the same size now.*

He kept his voice neutral. "You mean you're the same size Mom was, don't you?"

"What?" Megan looked at him, distracted. Not sensitive to the comment the way Hank thought she'd be. Not actually seeming to notice it at all. "Oh, yeah, sure. Was."

Agreement, simple as that. So why couldn't he accept her concession without suspicion?

Without concern.

"So what are you up to tonight, all dressed up?" he asked.

Mistake. He knew that the moment the question left his mouth.

Her head came up, all of her attention captured; hurt crossed her face. "You know."

Oh, hell. Either she'd told him something he'd forgotten, left him a note he'd never read, or this was one of those read-her-mind-psychic things, where no matter what he did or how carefully he proceeded he screwed up. He was already screwed.

"Uh, I don't think so, honey." Women who got hurt at the drop of a hat and who made him walk on eggshells so he wouldn't hurt them more were a pain in the butt. And yes, she was his daughter, she owned his heart, she'd inherited many of her emotions from her mother, but right now she was hurt, he was tiptoeing on eggs and, damn it, when she was like this she was still a pain in the butt. "I'm sorry if I've forgotten something, but maybe if you tell me what it is we can fix it—"

"Fix it?" She was offended, incensed; Hank knew he'd fix nothing tonight. "We shouldn't have to fix anything. I'm not your secretary, I shouldn't have to remind you, you should just know, you should be able to look at a calendar sometimes and remember on your own. Instead, you always have to ruin it—"

Sweet heaven. Hank stared at his daughter, pale and appalled. Memories tumbled backward five years to Gen's last birthday three months before she died, two months before she told him she was five months pregnant. Hindsight and hormones had explained the way Gen lashed out at him that night—in words and emotions Megan repeated, now, almost verbatim.

He hadn't known their daughter had been near enough to hear, let alone that she would remember.

She was ranting at him now, nearly shrieking. Had worked herself up well past the ability to hear anything, but especially reason. Stamping around, tearing off the ring, watch and earrings, pitching them onto a table, she was well beyond Gen's hormone-driven but justifiable—he *had* forgotten her birthday that year, many years, after all—anger.

Had forgotten many things important to his wife, in pursuit of his job.

But this wasn't Gen screaming at him now, it was Megan, and this anger was more like the temper tantrums she'd suffered from when she was three and four and didn't want to do something. Then he, when he was home, or Gen would literally have to lie on top of Megan while she screamed uncontrollably—often for nearly an hour—simply to prevent her from throwing herself into something or off of something in her rage and doing herself serious damage.

Small and young as she'd been, adrenaline had made her strong and frightening, able to nearly lift him off of her. And despite the time or two Gen had mentioned something about Megan giving in to moody rages since then—probably, now that he thought about it, about the time Megan might have been headed into puberty, like a pre-PMS sort of thing—Gen and Hank had both thought their daughter had pretty much outgrown her tantrums by the time she started kindergarten at five.

Now, however, it didn't appear as if Meg had outgrown anything. Her uncontrolled rage scared Hank more than anything he'd seen his daughter do since Gen died—including Mother's Day, when she'd come in high and thrown the dollhouse at him.

This was beyond his knowledge and ability to manage; beyond, he was very much afraid, even the department psychologist's expertise. For himself, Hank couldn't very well simply lie down on top of his sixteen-year-old daughter and let her scream and flail at him until she exhausted herself, the way he'd been able to cushion and protect her from herself at four. As for the department's psychologist... helpful as the woman wanted to be, her primary training was in test giving and dealing with adult agents who were as adept at disguising their anxieties and appearing normal in her presence as they were at dissolving in a crisis. She'd never been exposed to this side of Megan, felt that Hank was dealing only with adolescent rebellion complicated by the death of a same-sex parent. Clearly this was more than that.

Or maybe it wasn't. Maybe he was overreacting and this was normal sixteen-year-old behavior under this very specific set of circumstances. Sexist as it might sound, maybe this was merely a not-so-simple case of PMS and she'd be fine in a couple of days. Or maybe when this tantrum played itself out, everything would be fine. Maybe this was merely another form of release, like hysteria or crying.

And maybe he was a terrified parent grasping at straws of rationalization and hope.

Helpless, he reached out to touch Megan's shoulder, wondering how an expert would handle this; tried to gather her into his arms to quiet and reassure. She screamed and struck at him, scratching his arm with sharp polished nails and pushing him away, and he could only stand powerless, watching her remove herself to the bedroom she'd been assigned but rarely used. The door banged shut behind her, the lock snicked into place. Silence was abrupt and complete, as hard on his ears and psyche as Megan's rage had been.

Not sure what he intended, he walked to the door of her room, wanting to be near her, somehow. Inside the room he could hear her sobs—more like paroxysms of unintelligible wrath at first—and slumped to the floor beside her door, worn and alone, his back to the wall.

He didn't know how long he waited with his head leaned

back, eyes shut, listening to her. Knew only that the time and voice of her pain, grief, rage, whatever, seemed interminable and costly. Gradually relaxed only when Megan's emotional frenzy took on the quieting tones of real tears. Then he wrapped an arm around one upraised knee, let his other leg slacken sideways and awaited Megan's return.

Kate wondered about Megan and Hank when they didn't appear for dinner, stopped when Li mentioned she thought father and daughter had some sort of special evening planned—dinner out or something, Meg had said. The announcement made Kate curious, but busy with supper preparations and mildly concerned about Risto's latest unannounced disappearance, she merely wished Hank a mental *godspeed* and hoped that the thaw between parent and child had finally begun.

It was a relatively mild evening—ninety degrees with a modest eighty-five percent humidity relative to the day's one-hundred-and-two degrees with its accompanying thick and cloying ninety-five percent humidity. They ate a cold meal outside in the shade of a spreading oak at the two long picnic tables set up for the purpose; citronella torches posted a perimeter around the tables to keep the flies and mosquitoes at bay.

With a lot of kids, the family's evening meal was lively and entertaining, occasionally informative and never boring. Outside on a hot July night, it was also a little raucous, prone to bad jokes, snickers and the sporadic flinging of macaroni or peas—supposedly behind Kate's back. The dog, Taz, who was not allowed to beg from the table in the house, snuck underneath whichever table Kate was not at outside and cleaned up whatever Mike or Ilya didn't like. Born in a place where food was often scarce, Bele ate whatever was put in front of him—although he no longer had a tendency to gorge himself sick, not knowing when he'd have his next meal. Outside, Kate turned her back on minor infractions of the Dinner Table Rules and Manners unless the violations got out of hand.

After dinner the family's resident firebugs, Li and Grisha, tepeed the broken-up wood from old pallets—Tai brought them home regularly, free, from a local warehouse—in the nearby fire pit. Mike, Bele and Ilya cleared paper plates and cups from the table to add to the evening fire effort; Tai, his girlfriend, Carly, and Kate covered leftover perishables and removed them to the house, returning with roasting forks, bags of marshmallows, packages of Hershey bars and graham crackers.

Hot as it was, the younger boys urged swimming before dessert.

Kate eyed them, then her oldest son's girlfriend and asked, "Carly, will you lifeguard these hellions? I need to talk with Tai and Li a minute."

The younger woman cast her a curious glance, swiftly masked. She'd been with Tai four years now, considered his family hers, and there was very little Kate said to Tai but hesitated to share with her. Which meant she had a reason this time. "Sure."

"Thanks." Kate waited until Carly shepherded her appointed troops off to the pond before turning again to Tai and Li. Without preamble she asked, "Is Risto drinking again?"

They stared at her, surprised, then thoughtful.

There had been a problem with alcohol early in the exchange student's tenure with them, only partially excused by ignorance, cultural differences, and an ofttimes more lenient spirits policy in Risto's native country. He'd have been expelled and sent home by the exchange program on the spot had Kate not intervened on his behalf.

She knew from personal experience how difficult it was to be far from home, speaking a language you were familiar with but which was not your native tongue; understood the temptation to want to fit in whatever the cost. She also understood that Risto was the only child of a wealthy family and used to living by a different set of standards than she exercised. But after the first few turbulent months, he'd seemed to settle in nicely—primarily, Kate suspected, because he hadn't wanted to be sent home early. Or to return home to Finland at all.

Since school let out for the summer, though, and Risto had once more started disappearing without word, Kate wondered if she'd done the right thing in lobbying the exchange program to let him stay. Wondered if she shouldn't have let Risto be sent home, where he could return to being his parents' problem instead of hers.

Undoubtedly a selfish thought, but there it was.

Life's tough, get a helmet, she cautioned herself with an inward grimace, silently repeating Mike's and Bele's latest favorite cartoon advice.

And at least when she was worrying about what Risto might be up to—or *in* to—she wasn't thinking about Hank.

Now Kate looked at Li, who looked doubtfully back and said, "Drinking? I don't—I'm not sure, but I don't think…" She turned to Tai.

He shook his head. "He comes out pretty groggy some mornings, but I haven't smelled anything on him. He sleeps in with Grisha and Ilya and they haven't said anything—and Grisha's got the nose of a bloodhound."

"Do either of you have any idea where he is? Or when he left?"

Tai and Li eyed each other and shrugged.

"He left," Tai said, "probably around four, when he came in from the fields to do something and didn't come back. As for where he went…" He lifted a shoulder, let it drop. "Far as Risto's concerned, I'm an egghead plowboy, so how would I know?"

"Yeah," Li put in, "and I'm a nerd-geek-spook-egghead-goody-two-shoes-milkmaid-freaky-animal-lover, and guys like Risto don't tell girls like me squat because he knows if you ask me and I know and it's for his own good, I'll tell you."

Kate swallowed a smile at her daughter's offhandedness. In her day—gee, did that make her sound old, or what?—being called anything on Li's list was tantamount to being ostracized for life from all polite society. Li, on the other hand, considered such name-calling a compliment. *"Nerds are the world's billionaires,"* was her prosaic response—and had been since grade school.

"I see," she said, amused. Then she sighed. "Okay, so nobody thinks he's drinking or knows where he went, but he probably left around four. It's seven-thirty now. He didn't drive, he didn't take a bike, so—"

"I might know where he is."

Stuffed gym bag in hand, Jamal stood off to one side shifting from foot to foot, ill at ease. Kate regarded him, taking in both the picture and the implication behind it in a glance.

"Your mother out of town again?" she asked.

Jamal nodded once without looking up. "I think she be gone a while this time. She wondered, could I stay here like we been doin'." He lifted his head, face strained, not quite pleading. "It's time you need extra help an' all, an' I'll help out with everything—"

"I know you will, Jamal," Kate assured him quietly. "You always help, you work hard. We're lucky you can be here. That's why we keep Ilya's top bunk empty when you're not here. It's yours."

"Thanks." Jamal grinned shyly, giving Kate the impression that praise and simple acceptance were rare commodities in his life. She could change that. Other things she couldn't change.

She waved gratitude away and cautioned gently, "If this'll be an extended stay, you'll have to tell me what and why so we can make...temporary legal guardianship arrangements if they're necessary."

Jamal took a deep breath and swallowed hard. "Okay." He eyed her. "Y-you want we should do that now?"

Kate shook her head. "Later'll be soon enough. First tell me what you think about Risto...."

His legs and back were stiff, and he had to go to the bathroom.

Wrinkling his nose, Hank sniffed the air around him. He also needed a shower. Bad.

Stifling a groan, he shoved himself up the wall, stood a moment stretching. Behind Megan's door all was quiet; Hank wondered if she'd fallen asleep. He pressed an ear to the wood, listening, tapped gently and said, "Meg?"

No response.

Figured. Still, he hadn't really expected one. He knocked again, tried the knob. Again no response; the door was locked.

Sighing, he wiped a hand tiredly across his face and spoke to the door, hoping his daughter was listening. "I'm going to shower. You need anything before I do?"

Silence.

Defeated, he stared at the door, his shoulders drooping. The temptation to say *"Screw it,"* and leave Megan to whatever hell she chose to inhabit was strong tonight, as hard and bright as the light from the descending sun crowding into the living room through a minuscule break in the trees outside. The impulse was momentary and would pass, it always did; it was only the thought's guilty aftertaste that lingered.

His lips compressed; he puffed out his cheeks on a breath and let the air out slowly. Enough, for the moment, with letting his child rule both his every action and his psyche. He needed a shower, damn it, and he was going to take one.

Tramping firmly on doubt by telling himself he'd only be in the shower five minutes, that even parents with infants sometimes had to leave them alone in their cribs that long,

Hank stalked through the kitchen, stripped off his clothes and stepped into the shower.

"You think he's where?" Kate asked incredulously—for the second time. *"Where?"* With all the legal bars that abounded, including some that served alcohol to minors, why would anyone need to run an *illegal* bar in this day and age?

"Blind pig couple miles up the road," Jamal repeated. "I heard him talking with Meg about it. I think they mighta been there before."

"A blind pig?" Kate mouthed the words as though they were foreign. "A blind *pig?* I thought they went out with prohibition."

Jamal shrugged. "Meanin' no disrespect, Kate, but if you think that, you don't know nothin'. There's a market, people gonna sell liquor without a license, you got prohibition or not. That's what my grandpa used to say."

"Yes, but a blind pig?" She felt like a broken record, but disbelief was like that. "And they serve *children* there?"

Jamal nodded. "Kids ten, eleven years old go if they want to drink, smoke, gamble. Parents even drop 'em off thinkin' maybe they just goin' to a battle of the bands at a teen club with their friends or whatever. Adults got no need for a blind pig anymore 'less they want to hold secret meetings or gamble or something."

"Secret meetings?" Kate stared at him. This just got worse and worse, and she felt stupider and stupider. Had she ever been a teenager? Had she ever known *anything* like the things her kids already knew? "What kind of secret meetings?"

"I dunno. Could be anything, I guess. Things like maybe—"

"Hate groups," Carly interjected quietly.

Hank swiped soap from his face and reached up to switch the shower head to "massage." He would take an extra minute, damn it, Megan or no, because he needed it.

Cool water chattered over the back of his neck, drowning tight muscles. Sighing, he let his head drop forward, forcing himself to relax. God, he'd needed this. There was nothing like washing crisis away with dirt in a cold shower—even when the reprieve was only temporary.

He enjoyed the peace as long as he dared, then shut off the water and toweled quickly, slid into a pair of running shorts and reluctantly let himself out of the bathroom. Time to rebeard the lioness in her den.

He was halfway across the kitchen when the receding sound of a car motor caught his attention. His head whipped around. He knew that motor. That was his car.

With a furious oath he glanced at the top of the refrigerator where he normally tossed his keys when he came in. Missing.

"Damn."

Six long strides took him to Megan's open door. Gen's dress and the strappy sandals lay in a heap on the floor.

Megan was gone.

The boys had finished their swim and come rampaging back only moments before to burn their fingers and make s'mores; Carly had slipped over to stand beside Tai and join the discussion.

Torn between the desire to make himself some dessert and also to separate himself from the littler guys in favor of being included with the older guys—even Jamal was younger than him, after all—Grisha smashed a couple of cold marshmallows between a pair of chocolate bars and hung at the fringes of the group, listening. Ilya, on the other hand, quickly burned half a dozen marshmallows, built a handful of sticky treats and brought them with him—and generously handed half of them to Jamal, who made a distracted *oh, gross* face and passed them back.

For their part, Kate, Tai, Li and Jamal turned to Carly, appalled.

"Hate groups?"

Clearly Carly's suggested reason for secrecy hadn't occurred to any of them—including the urbanwise Jamal. Or perhaps that was particularly the urbanwise Jamal.

The corners of Carly's mouth tucked wryly, her shoulders hunched an apology. "I'm a waitress, I hear things. I don't know how much I can believe most of the time, but that's something I heard in a way I couldn't *not* believe it."

Kate stared at her, not wanting to take it in. The fact that she had to sat poorly with her. "Risto might be at a blind pig run by a hate group?" Not only streetwise but worldwise, she'd thought there were few surprises any of the kids who came through her doors could throw at her. Apparently she was wrong.

Carly shook her head. "I don't know for sure, that's not what I meant. You were wondering, I heard about maybe one that exists like that where these…this *society* can print pamphlets and make plans and find recruits. It's not like I know where it is, so it's probably not the same one and that's not where he is, you hear what I'm saying? I mean, if some people can run one blind pig for one purpose, other people can run another one just to…just to…make easy money."

"I suppose," Kate agreed, hardly comforted. Risto was in her care, her responsibility—until he went home next month. Of course, if she found he'd been sneaking off to an illegal liquor joint—of any kind—she'd personally see to it he was shipped home under the exchange program's chaperonage by the end of this week. Risto's staying here was not a necessity but a privilege, and one he'd managed to abuse already, at that. She believed in giving a kid a second chance and even a third, but in this instance she had to think of her own kids and the effect Risto's activities would have—were already having—on them, too.

Especially if the police were involved.

And they would, of course, have to be. For the first time her mind turned to Hank—not as the subject of her errant daydreams, but as a cop who'd know how to handle the problem. Know who to call and how to bust the blind pig— if indeed there was one—and how to proceed with Risto afterward. Hank would probably even appreciate having the tables turned on her for a change, as in *her* needing his help to avert a crisis instead of vice versa. And this was one crisis she wanted to prevent *now*.

"Li—" She turned to her daughter. "Did you say Hank and Meg were going out to dinner tonight?"

"I thought that's what Meg told me. I didn't see their car leave—"

"It was parked at their house when we came back from the pond," Grisha volunteered.

"Good," Kate said. "Then I'll ask Hank to help—"

She turned at the sudden rumble of a car motor nearby. Behind her the Mathisons' dusty white Chevy four-door bounced up the back drive and out the front without slowing, Megan behind the wheel.

Chapter 8

The house was a big, dirty yellow clapboard thing with enclosed steps mounting the outside to the second floor.

Sprawling with additions appended at haphazard angles through the years, it had once been a legal combination of business and residence. Situated on a rural section of the main highway almost halfway between the affluent small town Hank and Megan called home and the slightly larger county seat, it was a perfect hide-in-plain-sight location for a teen-geared blind-pig gambling parlor. Run by a pair of twenty-something ex-cons, it was a lively place whose posted intent was to provide a venue for middle- and high-school-age garage bands to prove themselves.

In actuality, it provided what it advertised and more.

At the main-level entrance, it was strictly an unlicensed teen-to-twenty club that served nothing more stimulating than cherry cola. If a few ten-, eleven- and twelve-year-olds filtered through the cracks to mingle with a crowd that was primarily aged thirteen to eighteen, with a few immature twenty-year-olds thrown in, oh well. It was the bar that lay below the main level that provided much of the attraction, coupled with the poker, blackjack and roulette tables hidden in the attic above the second-floor living quarters. The first-floor club acted as a screening base for the other two.

Palms sweaty, Megan slid Hank's car into a spot hidden behind a pair of Dumpsters located at the rear of the gourmet deli-party shop about five hundred feet from her destination. Too many law-enforcement people in the area knew Hank's vehicle for her to risk parking any closer.

If he'd just remembered…

But no. She stiffened her jaw, felt the skin around her eyes tighten, her mouth harden with the movement. She was over that little parental screwup and on to better things.

Adrenaline, already pumping, spurted with renewed vigor through her veins as she alighted from the car and leaned the door shut. She breathed deep, savoring the rush. She'd been to the club plenty of times, but she'd never before stolen and driven her father's car, never come alone. And it was his own freaking fault that she did it tonight.

First time for everything, she thought, angling the sideview mirror and bending to check her appearance by the light of the setting sun. She fiddled a few stiffened spikes of heavily gelled bangs across her forehead, then tilted her head critically to eye the eight rings and studs in her left ear, the six danglies in her right ear; flicked the ring in her right nostril before glancing quickly about. Spotting no one, she slid a hand down the front of her tight-fitting bustier-style zippered leather vest to plump and adjust her sweating breasts. A humid ninety degrees and climbing was hardly the weather for leather anything, but Danny and Earl kept the air-conditioning up and the fans on, so she'd be comfortable enough inside. Also, the motorcycle-bad-girl look advertised exactly the wares she intended it to advertise and suited her mood down to the ground. Now all she needed was a dose of *ma huang* and a tequila shooter or two, and she'd be chilled just fine.

She slipped an arm through the thin strap of her tiny rivet-studded purse and carried the strap over her head. Then twitching her slim leather miniskirt into place and shining the metal toes of her boots on the backs of each other, she headed for the club.

Hank reached the house at the same time Kate was stepping into the van to go looking for Risto. She regarded him with surprise.

"I thought you went out with Meg."

"You saw her?" he asked grimly.

She nodded, taking in his disheveled appearance, the fury and fear that seethed beneath a facade of rigid control. "Fifteen, twenty minutes ago, maybe less. In your car." Her concern showed. "We assumed you were with her."

"No." Short and succinct, the single word stated volumes.

"She bolted?"

"That's one way to put it."

"What's another?" she asked softly.

Arrested by her tone, he looked at her, then away. "It's Gen's birthday. I guess she thought… No—" He shook his head, confused and angry. "I don't know what she thought. Anyway, she was all dressed up when I came in, made up to look like Gen. I said the wrong thing. She pitched a long tantrum, then waited until I got in the shower to steal my keys and the car."

His jaw worked. He gazed at Kate without seeing her, his eyes haunted. "She's never gone this far before, Kate. When she was little she had rages, but this…this one was worse than the one she had the morning before I called you. I don't know where she went, how much money she's got or if she's coming back. I hoped maybe she'd taken the car for spite and cooled off by the time she got up here. I guess not."

"You want to call the police?"

"I don't want to involve them unless it's necessary."

"It might be," she said.

Then she filled him in on Risto's disappearance and what the kids had told her about him, Megan and the alleged blind pig.

The basement was dark and hazy, raucous with laughter from voices that had yet to change, loud with music.

Just inside the doorway, Megan filled her lungs with the taste of secondhand tobacco and looked around, letting her eyes adjust. Kids milled everywhere: at the makeshift bar, the jukebox, congregated thickly around the two pool tables, piled together on vinyl makeout couches and chairs in the corners and along the walls. She scanned the crowd quickly, spotted her quarry slouched forward at the bar, one booted foot propped on the rail that ran its squared-off bottom length. Hand on hip, she put on a full-lipped pout and swayed over to drape a possessive wrist over his shoulder and blow in his ear.

"Hey, Zevo."

Zevo took a negligent pull on a squat-necked Pabst, threw back a shot of something cheap and vile-smelling before acknowledging her. "Hey, Megan." He shrugged out from underneath her wrist, deliberately turned to inspect the room, appearing to ignore her. "Long time."

"Been out of town." She ran an idle hand up his chest, playing the scene from old movies. She knew the difference; Zevo didn't. "I missed you, baby."

"Yeah," he said sarcastically, still refusing to look at her, "That's why you spending the summer hangin' with the brainiacs and llamas out at the Christmas-tree castle, cuz you miss me."

Megan's hand flexed on his chest, nails digging in sharply, suddenly, startling his attention her way. "Wrong," she said flatly. "I'm spending the summer with the geeks and the llamas because I want to, and you don't tell me what to do." Her voice changed timbre, softening to a purr. "But that doesn't mean I haven't missed you, too, babe."

"Yeah, okay, all right." Verbally backing off, Zevo rubbed his chest where the marks from her nails stung. "I missed you, too, Meg. A lot." He wrapped a diffident arm about her waist, no longer sure where they stood physically. Megan hung back for an instant, making sure he knew who held the power, then pressed into his embrace, caressing the line of his jaw with her cheek. He smirked out at the room at large and slid his hand possessively down her hip, turned his head to take her mouth in a boy's sloppy, greedy kiss. "Yeah, we back," he murmured. "Whataya want, doll?"

Megan's response was a sizzle of breath against his mouth. "Dose of herbal ecstasy and the usual."

Zevo grinned and hauled her more snugly against him. "Mmm," he muttered. "I like it when you get tight." He kissed her, with a lot of tongue, then tapped money on the bar. "Hey, Earl. Packet of *ma huang* 'n' a tequila shooter, lime, no salt."

Within moments a labeled plastic packet containing ten little blue editions of legal herbal speed, a shot of tequila and a piece of lime appeared beside Zevo's fist; the money disappeared. Zevo picked up the packet and handed it to Megan.

"Here ya go, doll."

"Thanks, Zevo."

Carefully she slit the packet open, collected five of the blue pills, and handed the rest to Zevo. He accepted them with a grin, offered her the tequila, watched her wash her dose down. She shut her eyes and shivered slightly when the liquor hit her throat, then quickly bit the lime, chasing tart squirts of juice after the tequila. A sigh of anticipated artificial well-being escaped; hazy eyed and calm she leaned out of Zevo's arms and peered through the atmospheric murk at him.

"You seen Risto?" she asked.

*   *   *

The feel of Kate's fingers in his hair in the fading daylight might have been immensely gratifying—if not for the circumstances and the number of other people watching her fluff and consider the strands. Unfortunately Hank's rebellious body didn't see it that way and he was having great difficulty paying attention to particulars, namely the unmarked sheriffs' and state policemen's cars sitting in the shadows off Kate's front drive and the reason her fingers were playing with his hair in the first place.

"So buzz it and carve your initials in it," he snapped, feeling the heaviness of Kate's breasts against his upper arm, much too near his face. All he had to do was turn his head to find that damp, inviting cleavage at mouth level. What his body wanted was nothing more than to drop her on her back and bed her on the spot. What he was getting instead was flak. He was tired of the ongoing argument over whether or not he'd be of any assistance setting up the blind pig for a raid—and delivering Megan and Risto from it, assuming they were inside, before it occurred. "I don't give a—" He bit back an obscenity, controlling his temper with an effort. "I don't care what it looks like in the polite world, as long as it does what it's supposed to for the moment. If there's a chance Meg's inside, I'm goin' in."

"I could give you a mohawk and paint the number of the beast on your face and you'd still look like somebody's narc-enforcement parent in jeans and a T-shirt," Kate snapped back. She was finding Hank's proximity equally distracting.

She'd never before found the scent of hot male particularly alluring, never had so much trouble giving an adult a haircut. No matter what she did to stay out of the way, every time he moved some part of his arm came in contact with her nipples, irritating, teasing and stimulating. She could barely think under the influence of that unintentional friction, let alone skin his head to resemble something—oh, for cryin' out loud, who knew what he needed to resemble. Something extremely neat and military probably, but with him distracting her by living, she couldn't guarantee the result without worrying about lopping off his ears in the bargain. And she rather liked his ears exactly where they were. Lord, maybe she should have gone parking with Steve Heckerling the single time he'd invited her back in tenth grade. Then at least maybe she'd have a little experience to fall back on in dealing with whatever this was she was feeling and Hank wasn't doing to her here.

She yanked his head firmly in the direction she wanted it and tightened her hand on his chin to hold him in place, the same way she had to with Bele and Mike. Perhaps she'd have better luck ignoring her body's importune announcements if she thought of Hank as just another one of the boys. *Yeah, right,* her mind snorted. *As if.* "And if you don't sit still, I'll be carving scalp with these clippers in a minute instead of hair."

"If you want my opinion," Tai said, not for the first time, "Hair or no hair, if this joint's teen geared you're gonna be too old to get in."

"Yeah, but," Carly argued, repeating her own theme for the evening, "if it's a recruiting point, buzz him, dress him right, give him the language and he'll fit right in."

"I don't give a fig what you do to him," the local sheriff muttered peevishly to the commander in charge of the local state-police post standing beside him. "I don't want a civilian screwin' up my operation—"

"I'm not a civilian," Hank pointed out for the hundred and fifteenth time. "I'm a—"

"Even if," the sheriff continued emphatically, glaring at Hank, "he is some sort of glorified used-to-be-undercover desk-jockey fed. Civilians and any kind of feds always confuse the issue and muck things up, cuz they don't understand local sensitivities."

"Not to mention the amounta paperwork ya gotta file and

the Infernal Repairs malarkey ya gotta deal with if anything happens to 'em," the statie concurred mournfully, deliberately referring to the department's IAD team by one of its more repeatable aliases. "And they're so outta touch with the bottom line that somethin' always happens to 'em."

The sheriff scratched his thinning pate and chuckled morbidly. "You got that right," he agreed. "And the worst of it is, they always find a way to put themselves in charge and drag you down with 'em."

Hank eyed them without rising to the bait. He wasn't dragging anybody anywhere. He was going after his daughter and leaving them the rest, that was all. Then they could be up to their eyeballs in jurisdictional squabbles over disposition of seized booty with the ATF—Alcohol, Tobacco and Firearms—and the FBI to their hearts' content and leave him out of it.

His own opinion of the state, city and county cops represented here—unvoiced from necessity since Kate still had his mouth and chin squinched between her fingers, holding his head in place while the hair clippers buzzed beside his ear—was that the locals were the ones who had a tendency to drop the ball in joint operations, which was why he was a fed in the first place. Feds, or at least the DEA anyway, simply did it—

Kate's fingers brushed the sensitive skin at the side of his throat, interrupting the completion of his thought; reaction was quick, a straight fizzle of heat to points south, all senses wrenching awake and alive with the adrenaline rush preparing an undercover brought. Hank shut his eyes and his jaw clenched against bad timing; his mind wryly rejoined the thought in progress. As far as he was concerned, the DEA simply did *everything* better. Period.

And some things even better than others. He caught Kate's eye. Reaction and recognition were physical, mutual, immediately denied. But that was an assertion best pursued some other time, if at all.

If.

He shut himself off from the sudden tang of wistfulness on the back of his tongue, forced himself to feel only the itchy drift of hair down his cheeks and neck. Megan liked Kate. Maybe that would make it okay, someday when he and Megan got done with this insanity, to entertain the unchaste thoughts and daydreams of this autumn-haired former nun that he could no longer avoid.

Never depend on someday, his father's voice whispered at his mother's funeral. *All you can ever be sure of is now.*

But *now* was impossible, and both he and Kate knew it.

The clipper's drone ceased; his shorn head felt almost cool in the heat.

Kate released his chin and stepped back, cocking her head to regard him critically. "I dunno." She handed him a mirror, picked up a second and angled it so he could see the back of his head. "I can take more off the top if you want, but that's about all I can do with the back and sides."

Tai shook his head. "I don't know," he told Hank dubiously. "Seems like a heck of a lot of hair to leave to the birds for five minutes' work, *if* you can even get into the pig."

"Oh, I don't think it looks so bad." Carly leaned her chin on Tai's shoulder and combed her fingers playfully through his straight, collar-length black hair. "Looks cool and comfortable." She grinned into Tai's neck. "Maybe you should try it, Tai. Be cute on you."

Tai's response was an impolite snort.

The waiting cops' observations were both ribald and largely unprintable. Kate glanced back at the house, but if any preteens or adolescents with big pitchers had escaped Li's watchful eyes to eavesdrop on adult conversations, they weren't visible. *Good,* she thought. Ilya's and Grisha's American vocabularies were quite unprintably large enough as it was.

For his part, Hank didn't bother with the mirrors, disregarded the comments. Instead he ran a hand over his head, closed his eyes and *felt*.

Yes, there it was, the soft bristly sensation of a military buzz cut with enough left over on top to satisfy vanity. He dug a little deeper, getting into character. And there, hiding in the corners of his psyche, was the clean-shaven military washout with the off-kilter smile and the axe to grind against the world. He was a not-quite-scary sort of guy who never wholly fit in anywhere. He'd been different from his classmates in grade school and the two years of high school he'd managed. Not terribly intelligent, but narrowly read and lately liking to think himself an intellectual. He was a loner who gravitated to the edge of trouble without quite participating in it. He wanted to, though. That was why the marines had appealed to him. Tough guys, ready for trouble, willing to take it to the limit. But they'd rejected him. Psychologically unfit. The reasons were nonspecific. He knew he was marine material—special-forces quality—even if they didn't. One day he would prove it. Maybe soon. But not tonight. Tonight he just needed a few beers in an out-of-the-way place. Maybe lay out a few feelers because he'd heard maybe somebody with a special project in mind was recruiting guys like him.

Guys who were ready to do anything.

The corners of Hank's mouth lifted slightly, part of the rough contours of the character he was creating and becoming. The keen edge of a familiar rush, more potent than any drug, teased at his system, promising more to come. He opened his eyes and looked at Kate.

The change was subtle but distinct, a trifle frightening. Her eyes widened; she stepped back.

"Hank?" she asked uncertainly.

He nodded, looked at the cops. Ready to chuckle some more, their laughter died aborning.

"Judas-stinking-Priest," the statie muttered—respectfully. His hand swept in the direction of his weapon, paused, suspended like his laughter somewhere between incredulity at what he was seeing and what he knew to be true.

The sheriff merely shook his head, disbelieving, a testament to Hank's "talent."

Tai's comment was succinct and to the point, a word he rarely used. "I guess this is why you worked undercover, huh?"

"Guess that means I don't remind anybody of somebody's narc-enforcement dad anymore," Hank responded quietly.

Kate shook her head. "If this was how I first saw you, I'd warn the neighbors and not let my kids anywhere near you."

"Good," Hank said. He turned to the locals. "So, we ready to do it?" he asked.

Risto was playing poker at a rickety round trestle table in the center of the attic casino. His normally ruddy-complexioned Scandinavian features were pale; the pile of chips in front of him was sparse. He acknowledged Megan's approach by pulling his handful of blue-backed cards tighter to his chest and ignoring her. She laid a hand on his shoulder.

"Time to go, Speedy," she said, calling him by the nickname he preferred.

He shook his head, impatient. "Not yet."

"Risto—"

"Do you have money?" he asked without looking up.

"Not for you," she said, short and irritated. They'd had this conversation before and she understood compulsion too well. She wouldn't give him away to Kate or Tai, but she also had worries enough of her own without feeding Risto's addictions, too.

"Meg—"

"How much you down?" Brutal and direct was the only way she knew how to deal with a friend who'd lost control of his limits. It was the way Li dealt with her, the way she'd learned from Kate.

"It does not matter." Risto smiled crookedly up at her. "I will win it back this hand."

Megan peeled his cards away from his chest, viewed them scornfully and let them slap back into place. "Not with these cards."

The other poker players grinned; the one to Risto's left made a big show of tossing a pile of chips into the pot, which the exchange student couldn't match. Risto threw his cards face down on the table, swearing vehemently at Megan in Finnish.

"I'm out," he said, shoving back his chair to rise.

One of the other players, older than the rest, stayed him, holding out his hand, rubbing thumb over fingers in the universal symbol for money.

Risto shook his head. "You know I don't have the money with me."

"Make sure we get it—with interest—within seventy-two hours." The man's voice and face were avid with threat and anticipation, a reminder that an opportunity for violence would be almost as welcome as cash.

Risto nodded, looking only at the fist around his arm. "You hold my…" He hesitated, searching nervously for the term momentarily lost from his English. "You have my IOU."

"Let him go, Danny." Megan stepped forward to take Risto's arm. "You've got his marker and his word, you hear what I'm saying? He's never welshed before, so give it a rest."

"He's never been down over a grand before." Danny's voice was lazy, his features were anything but. "That's serious green, so you hear what I'm sayin', little girl. Speedy comes through, or we work out a payment plan that could include you."

Megan's lip curled with contempt. "You'd like to be

tough, wouldn't you, Danny?'' she asked. "But bein' tough's hard when you keep wearin' a little boy's name.''

She turned to go, but Danny released Risto and grabbed her wrist, jerking her back. "You better watch your mouth, babe, 'fore it winds you in a world of trouble.''

Megan smiled, eyes hard and amused at once—the look, if she'd but known it, a carbon copy of Hank's scary don't-corner-me-or-we'll-find-out-who's-tough challenge. A bead of sweat appeared on Danny's upper lip, his eyes skittered over her face. Megan didn't congratulate herself; she'd inherited a certain reputation as Zevo's on-again, off-again girlfriend, but it didn't take a whole lot of chutzpah to weird Danny out. Without visible effort, she twisted her wrist out of his grasp.

"Go bite yourself, Danny,'' she advised him evenly. Then she took Risto's hand, turned on her heel and walked away.

The sun was below the horizon, but the sky was still rippled with color: orange-gold-pink along the lip of the world, going up to almost white, fading into mauve and indigo above that; below, the earth burned with faintly retained daylight, fading quickly to dusk's hard-to-see-through gray and black.

Watching the sky, Hank pulled the scuffed S-10 pickup he'd borrowed from Tai into the small lot beside the yellow clapboard house and shut it off. The engine knocked with post-ignition noise, hiccupped, sputtered, then whirred to silence. An almost nauseating eagerness thrummed his veins, sent cocaine-like clarity rushing to his brain while his heart picked up speed and the bottom fell out of his stomach with the electric pulse of adrenaline. For the first time in five years he felt wired, alive, hyperfocused, fearless; wondered how the hell he could ever have given up this sensation, this arrogant, all-consuming knowledge that tonight he'd once again found his zone and could do no wrong.

That tonight, every shot he took at the basket would swish through unencumbered and unquestioned.

Then he remembered Megan and the electricity turned up a notch, took on subtly different overtones: fear, worry, doubt, anger.

He wrapped his hands around the steering wheel and squeezed, channeling all his energy into a simple isometric reach for unfettered awareness and calm. He was a DEA agent in an assistant director's suit, but he was not an agent tonight, he reminded himself. He was a parent. This was not a branch of a South American drug cartel he was after here, but his daughter, his child—and other people's children. He was not a rodeo rider charged up to take on a killer brahma tonight; he had to gear down, keep it low-key, remember that he had an entire tricounty area's narcotics-enforcement team waiting on his signal to do cleanup. He was not out here alone, and though he would enter the house by himself, he didn't think he'd come out alone. He was here to collect Megan—he hoped to hell she wasn't inside—period.

He was also here because of Kate—to protect Risto.

At the mere thought of her, a dull, thick ache centered low in his loins, brought pain with the tightening of his jeans. He could almost feel the rub of her nipples through her loose T-shirt and modest brassiere when she stood behind him clipping his hair; sense the swell of her breasts much too close to his cheek—the memory and sensation enhanced, he knew, because like any addict, he was high right now on his own drug of choice, one created by his own body. Nothing like a good rush to bring the noblest intentions to their knees.

Megan, he reminded himself grimly, *you're in this for Megan. Sex with Kate is not part of the program. Wanting to have sex with Kate is not part of the program. And even imagining making love and not just having sex with Kate is way too complicated and absolutely stupid. Idiotic. Out of the question.*

Torture.

And not only that, but he wanted, with all his heart, to make love with Kate Anden and to hell with the consequences.

Needed to make love with Kate, explore every facet of her body and her person, without worrying—or even thinking—about Megan.

The timing of his needs, wants, desires had never been more inconvenient.

Damn. He released the steering wheel and stepped out of the truck, easing his pants away from the uncomfortable stiffness in his crotch. He didn't need this.

He did *not* need this.

So he slammed the truck door, reminded himself of the names he'd been given to get himself inside the blind pig and strode purposefully toward the entrance, concentrating only on the task of the moment.

And not thinking about Kate.

"I don't believe you did that," Risto exploded when he and Megan reached the steps down to the main floor. "You are *crazy.*"

Megan grinned, exhilarated. "Yeah, but it worked, didn't it? C'mon, let's go downstairs, I'll buy ya a drink."

"*Ei kiitos.*" Risto shook his head. "No, thanks. I don't drink anymore in America. I promised Kate."

Megan peered at him. "You won't drink, but you'll gamble?"

Risto looked away, guilty as questioned. "I didn't promise about gambling."

"That's splitting hairs, Speedy." Thoroughly righteous, thoroughly hypocritical. "This is illegal, too. And you're addicted to gambling, even if you aren't to alcohol."

To his credit the youth didn't deny the truth. "Oh, I'm a black pot, but you are a clean kettle, right?"

Megan straightened, deliberately offended. "I don't know what you mean."

"Yes you do." His lip curled disdainfully. "You cannot have it two ways, Megan-*terttu*." His nickname for her, the word meant "cluster," referred, in his use, to the number of different people she seemed to pack into her singular personality. "You do *not* ask me to confess about me what you…" He paused, locating the word. "What you…*nix* about you."

"Nix?" she asked, mocking him and his command of her language. Avoiding a truth she recognized but refused to admit. "Don't you mean *deny?*"

Risto's jaw tightened under her derision. "You are a bitch."

She grinned, accepting complaint as compliment. Moistening the tip of her index finger, she made a mark in the air.

He flushed but continued, "I like the rush winning cards gives me, but you like danger. You didn't stand up to Danny for me, you did it because making dangerous men look ridiculous in front of their friends gets you high."

She sniffed. "Danny's not dangerous, he's a coward."

"*Ja,*" Risto agreed seriously. "He is a coward. Being a coward is what makes him dangerous. He would stab you between the shoulders and you would never see it coming."

"He'd stab me between the shoulders, if I turned my back on him—if we were alone," Megan corrected. "But I won't turn my back and we'll never be alone, so he can't. Anyway, it's not me he's after right now, it's you. How the hell did you lose a thousand dollars to him and how you going to get back your marker?"

"I don't know." Worried, he shrugged his entire body. "And I think the cards are marked."

Megan tapped her upper lip thoughtfully. "Are they," she said. Her eyes gleamed.

Risto eyed her warily. "No," he said emphatically. "Don't help."

"But I want to." She smiled. "It'll be fun."

"No."

"Sure it will." She caught his arm, tugged him down the steps. "C'mon, you can buy *me* a drink and we'll talk about it."

"*Nej*, no, *nyet, non, ei*, absotively not." Vigorously Risto shook his head, dragging away from Megan's hold. "You will *not* help. You will—"

He stopped short, eyes wide. A single Finnish expletive hit the air. Loosely translated, the word meant "pig manure."

"What're you bitchin' about hogs for—" Megan began, turning back to him, then saw what he'd seen: Hank crossing the main floor toward the basement steps in company with Earl. She swallowed. "Oh, damn," she whispered. Then anger hit. "Well isn't that just kick-you-in-the-crotch-and-spit-down-your-neck fantastic. The bastard doesn't trust me."

"I could guess why," Risto offered helpfully.

Megan quelled him with a glance, then hesitated, suddenly unsure which direction to go.

Risto caught her hand. "You have a car?"

She nodded.

"Out the side," he suggested.

They went.

She wasn't there.

Neither was Risto.

Hank didn't know whether to be glad or concerned; the rush in his system dropped off briefly, then returned at a more intense level as the pure cop in him took over from the cop-parent. Not having to think about Megan being here, it was a high he could savor and fiercely enjoy. It wasn't quite the same as kicking down doors and facing possible death on a supercharged DEA raid, but it was far superior to desk work. He wandered through the hazy rooms with one of the men whom the police were outside awaiting his say-so to arrest, noting the apparent ages of the participants, counting heads, taking it all in.

The air was of one big party; the party goers of all ages and not, as Jamal thought, strictly teens to twenties. The youngest kid in the place appeared to be about thirteen, the oldest about forty-two. High-school students—many of them with beers in hand, not a few of them blitzed beyond the ability to know what they were doing or that they were doing it in public—did, indeed, appear to make up the bulk of the underground nightclub's patronage to the tune of about one hundred seventy-five partiers in all.

Pulse rat-a-tatting to the beat of a variety of emotions, Hank observed several liquor and drug-paraphernalia sales, bought a beer out of a pop machine and a bag of marijuana and some cigarette papers from Earl before making one last sweep of the interior on his own. When it became indisputably apparent that Megan and Risto were nowhere on the premises, Hank went outside and turned his purchases over to the officer in charge who gave the signal to commence the strike.

Among other items confiscated, the raid netted twenty-three thousand dollars in cash, controlled substances, narcotics paraphernalia, the pop machine filled with beer, twenty-seven bags of marijuana, pagers, gaming tables, a roulette wheel, computers and computer files pertaining to controlled-substance trafficking, alcohol sales and gambling activities.

Of the 183 persons present, over a hundred were minors under the age of twenty-one. Forty-three under seventeen were ticketed for drinking under the zero-tolerance law; twenty were released to their parents and the remainder were eighteen or older.

The bust gave Hank a grim buzz of satisfaction, the

knowledge that, because the area was rural instead of urban and consequently less populated, he'd helped to put a real crimp—however brief—in the local narcotics pipeline. He felt for the unsuspecting parents called to collect youngsters from the scene, but at least they now knew where their children were. Which was a helluva lot more than he could say for himself.

Damn.

Megan dropped Risto off half a mile from Stone House so he could pick and choose his own route home while she went in another direction.

She was flying high after their unwitnessed escape, talkative and jittery, buzzed on the *ma huang*—also known as ephedra, a major source of ephedrine—and faintly intoxicated from the tequila she'd had with Zevo. In other words, in no shape to encounter Kate, her father, Tai or even Li.

It was too bad, really, because the way she felt at the moment she could deal with anything. Sometimes the inside of her head was like a bad neighborhood she shouldn't go into by herself, an isolated village with no way out—unless she...medicated herself. And then she all too often paid for the indulgence in so-called sanity...later.

At the moment, however, all the little pieces of herself that had earlier seemed as if they were going to fly off every which way and get lost so she'd never be able to gather them together again were now firmly cemented in place. The trouble, as always, was that she didn't know how long the pieces would *stay* together. They had a bad habit of ripping to bits every time she turned her back on them. Right now she didn't trust them farther than she could throw them— which wasn't far. Nope, someplace else would be better than going back to Kate's just yet.

Mind elsewhere, she gripped the steering wheel and casually veered her father's car out of the path of oncoming headlights. The wail of a horn followed the other vehicle's retreat. Megan shrugged, waggled a hand at the back window and giggled, giddy.

"Don't get your jockeys in a twist, buddy," she yelled out the open window. "All's well and all that rot, you know."

God, it felt *good* driving tonight. She threw back her head and whooped loud and long. Yeah, *damn* good. Probably didn't have anything to do with driving a car she'd stolen from her father, either. Or leaving Hank hanging back at Danny's and Earl's with his thumb up his butt wondering where she was.

"Whoo-hoo!" Laughing, she whooped again, enjoying the crudity, wishing Zevo were here to share it with. Adolescent male that he was, he appreciated a good laugh at her narco dad's expense. And, God, the look on Hank's face when he stood there lookin' around and didn't spot her— *priceless!* Totally stellar.

She sobered for half a second, recalling how her father had looked with his head shaved, in his seen-better-days clothing...the expression on his face standing beside Earl. There had been a slow moment where she almost hadn't recognized him. If she hadn't seen him dressed to go undercover once when she was a little girl and supposedly in bed long asleep, she might not have. He "didn't bring his work home with him," he'd always told her when she'd asked. Home was for family, not what he did to maintain the family.

In fact, she wasn't supposed to know he'd ever been a cop undercover—and might not have if her mother hadn't told her once when Gen had been in one of her "moods." It was after this revelation she'd started spying on Hank whenever she could, trying to learn why he left them, what "undercover" looked like.

Why he'd left her alone with a mother who often hadn't been quite able to...maintain her balance in the world...when he wasn't around. And how he could possibly not have known what his own wife was like.

No. She shook her head. She wasn't supposed to think about that. Her mother had been beautiful, perfect, exciting. Her mother had loved her to distraction when Hank wasn't around, had told her secrets bigger than herself. And she'd been good to her promise and her mother's memory and kept those secrets from her father, because who could talk to a man whose first wife was his work? Nope, Hank was the fly in the ointment, then as now.

Now...

Already wide, her eyes suddenly widened further as realization struck. Ohmigod, *undercover.* Security at Danny's and Earl's was slim to nonexistent, limited to keeping parents and other questionables on the main floor near the outer doors where there was little to see, but Hank had come in *undercover* to start the raid—and find her. Laughter perked and bubbled, burst in near hysterical giggles and guffaws that made her feel as if she had to wet her pants. Undercover, God. The big hotshot narc who'd gotten a busload of commendations for plying his talents and she'd beaten him at his own game! Damn, whoa, *yes!* She'd beaten him, yeah! What a picture. She was better at his game than he was. Not bad for a kid who felt as if she was flying apart inside her head half the time.

Not bad at all.

High from the punch of achievement as well as the liquor and herbs, she pushed the accelerator to the floor. She swerved the steering wheel again, this time around a deer leaping over a ditch and onto the edge of the road. Smooth. Damn, this felt righteous. She could drive like this all night, pushing the car to the limit, playing chicken with herself. Maybe that was what she'd do—at least until she sobered up enough to go back to Kate's, and until enough time had passed that nobody would guess she and Risto had been out together. Had to keep them guessing...

Of course—

A little of the wind went out of her sails when the qualifier slipped into her mind. Of course, there was always the chance her father would get the police to issue an all-points for his car. And for her. It wouldn't be cool to get caught by the cops in her current state. That might be worse than simply trying to duck Kate and company back at Stone House. She thought about it a moment. Yeah, that could be tons worse. She could lose her license and her freedom and...

And any respect Kate might have for her, any of the trust she'd come to value at the Andens', any time with Bele or the llamas, her friendship with Li...

"Damn."

Swearing, Megan pulled the car to the side of the road and rested her forehead on the plastic wheel. Intermittent traffic whooshed and rushed past her, kicking bits of sand and gravel through her window to sting her arm and cheek. She was seriously screwed up right now, beyond anything she wanted anyone to see, but the possible consequences of just driving on were more than she wanted to face. She didn't care what Hank thought— She hesitated. At least she didn't *think* she cared what her father thought about what she was doing tonight. But Kate's and Tai's and Li's and Mike's and Bele's and Grisha's and Ilya's opinions meant something to her. More than something. A lot.

"Okay." She shrugged her mouth and swallowed. "Think, girlfriend. Use your brain. Get it in gear." She thought for a bit, alternately folding her lips around her teeth and gnawing on a fingernail. "Okay, all right, here's what you'll do. Drive in to Speedway, put gas in the car, buy a toothbrush and toothpaste, use 'em, get a large espresso with ice, drink it and go home."

Hell. She grinned suddenly, enjoying the conjured picture. If Hank and the cops were as busy bustin' Danny and Earl and roundin' up everybody at the club as it looked like they'd be, it might even be she could get back to Kate's before he did with a full tank of gas. And that oughta really keep him guessing.

"All right." Even white teeth flashed back at her when she eyed herself conspiratorially in the rearview mirror. "Let's do it."

In a spitting shower of gravel and dust, Megan wheeled the car back onto the highway and headed for Speedway.

Chapter 9

Twilight was hot and restless, coated with clouds whipped around by hot breezes.

Kate sat on a stool inside the female llamas' night enclosure, eyes closed, meditating, while the hot and humid wind prickled her skin, drying sweat and replacing it almost simultaneously. The taste of brewing storms teased her mouth, sent unease skittering like ants underneath the sweetness of the silence she drew around herself, troubled her silent vespers.

Behind her the house was dark, all the chicks in residence and tucked up beneath the quiet roar of the attic fan pulling cool dehumidified air out of the basement.

Risto had returned before dark and apologized, shamefaced, for not letting someone know he was taking off to see friends. There had been a quality of evasion to the admission. The fact that he'd assumed mistrust and offered to let her smell his breath, give him whatever drunk test she wanted, made her feel oddly uncomfortable and not the least bit reassured.

Megan had spun into the driveway and parked behind the house about forty-five minutes after Risto's arrival. She'd alighted from the car dressed like a suburbanite's idea of a biker chick, and without explaining her absence hesitantly asked if her father was around. Informed that he was out looking for her, her face had taken on a strange tightness; when she kissed Kate good-night her breath was mouthwash sweet, her eyes were iris-less and wild.

Unable to judge simply from Megan's behavior, Kate couldn't be sure if the all-pupil look had to do with something the teen had ingested or with the diminishing light level. When Megan had asked if it was okay to spend the night with Li, then asked Kate to tell Hank where she was when he came in, Kate had assented out of uncertainty rather than kindness.

Uncertainty was why she was out in the llama pen communing with the girls and her thoughts.

Sitting with the llamas was calming, somehow gave clarity to fuzzy situations, made thought easier and enhanced meditation. She didn't do uncertainty well, had been confronted with indecision only rarely in her life. Not even Tai's adolescence had thrown her—and he'd been her first. Li, too, was more mature than her age. Dubiously Kate supposed—having heard it suggested by other families who'd adopted children of Asian descent with a similar lack of problems—that ethnic and genetic heritage might be the difference. But it didn't explain Grisha, Ilya and Jamal, with their entirely different backgrounds.

Of course, Grisha and Ilya weren't sixteen yet, and Jamal, while he'd spent an awful lot of time with Kate's family, had just started living with them tonight. For all Kate knew, things would be different once Jamal got used to being here all the time. She hoped they wouldn't—and even went so far as to doubt they would—but anything was possible.

No, although Tai, Li, Grisha, Ilya, Jamal, Bele and Mike all had their little quirks, Kate had only rarely experienced disquiet over anything to do with them. And even then the disquiet hadn't lasted more than a moment or two. Nope, it was merely Risto and Megan who left her feeling she didn't know what to do, or how to handle their...uniquenesses.

Of course, maybe she just didn't know as much about her kids as she thought she did. For instance, did Tai sleep with Carly? He and Carly were both twenty-one and she supposed whether they did or didn't was no longer any of her business. But she'd also never wondered before, either. As complete in and of themselves as the couple seemed, Kate imagined the two of them sleeping together was likely, but...yes, thinking about it was awkward for her, made her squirm.

Probably the same reason she'd never wondered... uncomfortable parent things...about Li—other than the fact that Kate always knew where Li was and couldn't imagine when Li would find the time to do sex, drugs or other harmful things.

She sighed. A parent had to let go of a child sometime, and if Tai hadn't learned where care and caution were needed, where love was necessary before now, Kate could no longer teach him. And anyway, now besides being her son, he was the senior half of their Christmas-tree partnership and her friend. She trusted him.

Perhaps, she consoled herself—grasping at straws, yes, but every parent was entitled to a little straw grasping now and then, weren't they?—her lack of conviction in dealing with Risto and Megan lay in the fact that they weren't really *hers* to deal with.

So then how, she asked herself dryly, do you account for how uninhibited you are if Jamal needs to be corrected when he's here, hmm?

That was different, she assured herself—earnestly. He came with Ilya, they were a pair. If one got in trouble, the other was usually there with him. Same as Bele and Mike.

But, the devil's advocate in her brain argued, Megan

came with Li. You've never had a problem dealing with her before, so why now?

The answer rose unwillingly. *Hank.* It wasn't Megan who made her unsure; it was having Hank here with his daughter. It was a sudden caution about stepping on parental toes that were not her own. It was...

Hank himself.

It was standing behind him clipping his hair and brushing up against him and not being sure if she was brushing up against him on purpose because she liked the way he felt, craved the physical sensations that ignited with any unexpected touch. It was the memory of a kiss and a conversation. It was the powerful knowledge he'd given her when he'd told her how much he wanted her. She didn't remember any man ever wanting her because she was herself and not because she was healthy and buxom and had big breasts.

Not that she had a lot of experience to fall back on there.

It was also because she liked him, Hank the father, Hank the man. Hank, who made her blood boil. Hank, whom she'd discovered it was easy to love on the friendship level and whom she didn't think she'd mind loving on whatever other levels were left.

Emotionally.

Physically.

Head and heart, soul and body, all the facets that made up her person. And his.

The truth of the matter was that until Hank Mathison had set foot on the farm, she hadn't known she could feel...

Like this.

Craven. Alone. Lost. Alive. Blossoming.

True, she also hadn't known until she'd left the convent that she could be anything besides a nun and a missionary; hadn't known until she'd found Tai and Li that she could be a mother or a tree farmer or raise llamas or run a miniatures business. From experience, she'd always assumed that need begot ability. But ability had nothing to do with Hank.

She'd found Stone House because when she left the convent she'd needed someplace to go; the crafts had started as something to do with her hands and as a way to help make ends meet. The tree farm had happened as a means to put college money aside for the kids, when she'd adopted Tai and Li. The llamas had arrived accidentally with Mike, inherited from her brother with his son. She'd meant to sell them and never gotten round to it—and now they were a major part of her family's life as well as income. For better or worse, her life was a series of accidental discoveries that grew out of each other and taught her things she'd never known before. And that was Hank: an accident with unforeseen consequences; an education she'd never expected to have.

She'd always known she was a woman, always appreciated the uniqueness of her gender, but until Hank Mathison she'd never known what it was like to feel...

Like a woman.

To want to be a woman in every sense of the word.

Intensely.

To need to understand the physical subtleties of her body, to covet a knowledge she didn't possess.

Unconditionally.

To quite simply and emphatically crave Hank and everything he was, everything he would be.

Passionately, unequivocally, irrevocably.

To understand that for more than thirty-five years she'd been missing a piece of herself that she hadn't even realized existed, and that piece had a name, and its name was Hank.

When in doubt, she thought moodily, take 'em by surprise. Including yourself. It was the motto she lived by.

Lord, why did she have to pick the very moment Megan was in crisis to figure this out and admit it to herself, and who on earth had put Murphy's law in charge of timing?

Probably some masochist, the imp in her head said.

It was one of those rare occasions Kate agreed with the imp.

A llama's sudden warning *clack* brought her alert from reverie. The whinnying, crowing call echoed from the females' pen to the males' loafing shed. The twenty males and geldings lined their fence, the twenty-five females and their young bunched together, curious and watchful, ears alert. Their attention seemed concentrated toward the front of the house. Sure enough, within moments Kate heard Tai's truck rattle down the drive. Mind full of cautions, heart full of care, she let herself out of the pen and went to greet Hank.

He was out of the truck by the time she reached it, leaning over his car with his hands flat on the hood. Trying to feel how long it had been there, Kate guessed, whether it was just arrived or had sat a while.

"She came back about an hour after you left," she volunteered. "Risto got here before she did."

Hank started, jerked around looking for her. She moved around the truck into his line of vision, and stood against the car's driver-side door. He relaxed slightly, took his hands off the hood, then hooked them into his back pockets.

"She all right?" The question was tight, controlled. Worried.

"She's fine. Dressed like a biker babe and lookin' for you—sort of. A little…spooked looking, but none the worse for wear, I guess."

"Was she—" He swallowed, chasing a dry mouth, hating the question. "Was she…high?"

"I don't know, Hank." Kate gave him an unhappy one-shoulder shrug. "Her eyes were all pupil, but the light was bright. She was lucid, she wasn't wobbly. A little wound up maybe, but not high the way I remember seeing kids hopped up when I was in school—or even when I was working the missions."

He ran a hand across his face and through what was left

of his hair, then nodded tiredly. Gentleness ran through Kate.

"You okay?" she asked.

"I dunno, Kate. She's here, she wasn't picked up in the raid, but the kid she dates when she wants to make me crazy was. He said he hasn't seen her for weeks, but I dunno. I just don't know."

"Anything I can do?"

"Nah." He shrugged, lost. "I don't think so. Where is she?"

"Upstairs in bed. Asked me if I'd invite you to have breakfast with her. So I am."

"I should go up, tell her I will." He looked like he didn't want to.

"And quiz her?" she queried softly.

"Yeah." Hank laughed without humor. "How'd you guess?"

"Predictable Parent Response number five seventy-four," Kate intoned pompously. "When a kid flies off the handle and takes off, question her about it no matter what time it is."

Hank's jaw tightened, his mouth forming a hard line. He took a step toward her. "You think I should wait?" There was a hint of challenge and ugliness in his voice, a note of *back off, babe, you're crossing a line.*

Kate heard the unspoken message and ignored it. "For what it's worth."

"Not much."

The snap of anger surfaced, aggressive, threatening. His eyes were an occasional glitter in stray moments of light.

A frisson of anticipation ran through Kate, fierce and almost joyous, consolidating the murk of her uncertainties over Risto and Megan, focusing thought, word and action on Hank. On the immediate pleasures of offered battle.

Never formally a soldier, she was nonetheless all warrior at heart.

She inhaled, drawing herself up, taking her own step closer to him, planting her feet. Ready.

"You don't want to do this," she warned.

He shifted, wary, but not backing off. "Why not?"

"Because I'm not the person you're angry with. And I'm on your side. And you're too smart to alienate an ally."

His stance relaxed without losing any of the tension. "You sure?"

"I'm sure."

He regarded her for a long moment, his jaw working. Something in the shadows of his expression altered; intensity and tension proceeded from anger to some other, rawer, less controllable emotion.

He moved another pace toward her and raised a hand... then stopped, his fingers closing tight around a handful of humid night as though to grip something sliding through the sweat of his grasp.

Excitement fingered Kate's skin, trickled with perspiration through the fine sensory hairs standing alert on her arms. With an effort Hank drew a harsh breath, then sighed it away.

"Okay," he agreed abruptly, pivoted and left.

Almost before Kate realized he was going, he was gone, long strides taking him past the llama yards, the workshop and equipment barn, and out beyond the wolf oak that dominated the grassy knoll separating house grounds from the male llamas' knobby day fields. When surprise abated, resolve firmed and she followed him without thinking.

Caution told her to let him go.

Neither instinct nor her heart was familiar with caution.

"Hank," she called softly. "Hank."

"For the love of God, woman, stay away from me." His voice was rough with strain, ragged with invisible exertion. "I can't let you near me right now. Do you understand that? I can't."

"And I can't let you go off alone like this."

He lengthened his stride, outdistancing her again. "Go away, Kate." It was both plea and demand. "It'd be better for both of us if you did."

"Why is it only better for both of us when you decide it is, not when I do?" she wondered aloud, hustling to stay in easy earshot.

"Because I'm bigger'n you and the mood I'm in I could hurt you and I doubt you could do me any real damage."

"Wanna bet? I've been around a lot more dangerous people than you, Hank Mathison, and nobody's managed to maim me yet. I may have been a nun, but that doesn't mean I'm a pacifist or that I don't know how to take care of myself."

"Oh, man." Hank stopped short among the trees at the west edge of the llamas' meadow and spun to face her. "Lady, that is such a crock. You don't know jack about takin' care of yourself in a situation like this. If you did, you'd be on the other side of a door with a deadbolt right now, not out here challenging me, away from anyone who could help you."

"I'm not here to challenge you, Hank." She came to a stop in front of him, put out a hand. "I'm here to help, if I can."

"You can't—" Her fingers touched his arm; he jerked violently away. *"Don't."*

Her hand stayed where it was, poised where he'd left it in the air. She moved toward him again. He watched her come, his breathing unsteady.

"Don't what?" she asked.

"Don't touch…" Air hissed savagely between his teeth, sucked hard into his lungs when she laid her hand on his. His muscles were hard and knotted with restraint; he twitched backward a step, but didn't pull away. "Judas, woman." Each word was an explosion, contained only by force of will. "I'm hanging onto sanity by my fingernails here. Do you know what you're doin'?"

She shook her head and worked her fingers into the fist he made. She didn't know for sure what she was doing, but she wanted to.

Real bad.

Eyes intent on the shadows that were his face, she stepped forward, reclaiming the space he'd put between them. "What am I doing?"

His fingers clenched around hers, drew her hand toward him. "Making it hard to breathe." He swallowed. She was too close; he could almost taste the texture of her skin on his breath. He couldn't think. Couldn't do anything but want. Her. Need her. "Making it hard, period." He exhaled, a rough sound. "Everything." He looked down at her, drew a fast breath of courage and opened her hand, flattened it against the bulge in his fly. Fought himself to simply hold her fingers there when she flinched in surprise and tried to draw away. *"Every*thing," he repeated.

Gulping air, Kate stared down at where she could see the outline of her hand, pancaked under his like a child's game of hand-on-hand, light against the darkness of his jeans. Sensation was intense, detail clear and mesmerizing.

The denim was soft and worn from a thousand washings, the ridge beneath it fascinatingly bone-like. Of their own volition her fingers flexed along that stiff outcropping, causing it to pulse tauter, eliciting a painful hiss from Hank. His fist clamped with crushing force around the contours of her hand and it was as though a savage had replaced what was left of this civilized man. She raised her face to see him, understanding with sudden clarity how important it was to take advantage of time rather than letting time take more advantage of her than it already had.

"You follow me now?" he asked tightly.

"I think so."

She spoke so softly, he couldn't tell if there was loathing or something else in her voice. She didn't try to take back her hand and he didn't think he could let her go to save his life. It had been so long.

So *long*… and nobody else he wanted to share this with. Only Kate.

The wind chose this moment to shove aside the clouds and loose the moon. Light slanted in to join them beneath the trees, revealing what shadows concealed. Hank saw not loathing on Kate's face but curiosity and gentleness, passion and empathy in almost equal measures. Her free hand lifted; the side of her forefinger defined the shape of his cheek and jaw, chin and throat. He stood very still, feeling the pulse in her fingertips, the willingness and longing in her touch, and forgot everything he was, including his name, in the fullness of her.

"Kate." A single breath, that was all he could catch.

Looking at him, *seeing* him in a way she hadn't before, Kate felt something inside her clutch and give way. Lungs tight, she touched the side of his face with the flat of her palm. He shuddered. Power flowed through her, innately feminine; knowledge uniquely female made her smile. Her palm relaxed against his face, traced down to cup his jaw, drew him within reach. She leaned forward and his breath murmured roughly across her lips.

"Kate." He was floundering. Fumbling to hold onto the boundaries he'd set around them for reasons he could no longer remember.

Trembling.

Her mouth grazed his briefly and withdrew, blew a soft sigh across his dampened lips and nuzzled them again. Boundaries ignited and crumbled, burned to cinders and blew away. When her mouth opened on his, he was there ahead of her, taking as he gave, sucking her breath into himself, feeding his back to her, sharing life.

The kiss consumed like rage, but infinitely sweeter, relentlessly hotter. His hands were everywhere, touching, kneading, holding. In her hair and sliding low down the small of her back, anchoring her to him twice; she wrapped her arms underneath his and held onto his shoulders, pulling him to her with all her strength.

They didn't kiss so much as feed like starving people who'd had food set before them, then been forced to see, to smell, to imagine, but not eat. Finally released, they had no time for amenities, to ask permission, to be polite. There was only time to touch, to feel—to frame each other's faces between their hands, to slide fingers down chests or tunnel them through hair. To pull at clothing that was in the way and discard it as quickly as possible without losing contact the way they'd already lost control.

Tongues dueled and clashed, laved and suckled salty skin; already feverish, their bodies slickened with sweat and would not cool even in the gathering wind. Their hands were as desperate and needy as their mouths, sliding through perspiration to places heavy and aching for relief. When Hank's fingers tangled in the red curls at the apex of her thighs, teasingly low but not low enough, Kate gasped and squirmed, finally brought her own hand down to place his where she wanted it. Hank's laughter at her impatience was rich and touchable, brushed her eager skin like a thousand extra fingertips.

His fingers made her body burn and weep, drew sobbing pleas from her throat. She clutched his shoulders and ground herself against him, bringing her belly tight to his loins and rocking. He gasped, but continued to let his fingers stroke and torture until Kate slipped a hand between them. When she cupped him and rubbed the pad of her thumb over the head of his moistening sex he jerked and went rigid. Then before she knew what was happening, he kicked her heels out from under her and laid her back on the pile of clothes they'd shed.

He didn't need to part her thighs, she did it for him. When the tip of his sex breached the flesh guarding hers, nudged the damp bud just above her opening, she whimpered and arched, pursuing him, luring him. When he leaned forward and brushed his length heavily against her a second time, she unraveled a little and cried out; her pleasure flamed with her ragged breath in his ears, so he held himself above her and pushed against her a third time. Her hips bucked hard upward, rubbing his length, begging for him. Her throat called him, her body wept harder, pleading.

He thrust at her entrance; tiny tremors surrounded him, clasping and milking his flesh as though in welcome for the missing prodigal. His ears filled with Kate's *oh-oh-oohs* of culminating pleasure.

Exerting what little control he had left, he pressed into the small shocks that coursed through her, withdrew slowly, slid forward again a little further. The gasping *oh*s became inarticulate murmurs, then shocked, breathless pants of intensifying rapture that called to him to join her even as they urged him to drive her higher still. Her body felt like heaven, tight and wet and lushly extravagant. He pushed deeper, thrusting with each contraction, his own looming ecstasy increasing with hers. So tight, so slick.

Too tight.

In the moment of lucidity before madness he felt it: no barrier, but the path had never been used, was wild and precarious, a passage he forged for himself. With the last of his strength he braced himself to look down at her, her face abandoned, her hair a wild carpet spread around them. He didn't know if he could stop if she asked him to, but the gift she presented him was too precious to accept without trying.

"Kate."

Her throat arched, breasts plumped against his chest, engorged nipples pouted with invitation. He tried not to look at them. To remember how they tasted.

"Kate, listen to me."

"Hank," she said breathlessly, her back bowed, belly undulating against his, hips pumping and rotating frantically, raveling his resolve. "Please, Hank, please."

"Kate." He was desperate. Every time she moved, a bit of the ledge he was poised on crumbled, drew him toward frenzied completion. He couldn't keep her still.

He didn't want to keep her still.

"Kate, look at me."

Her head moved back and forth, arms tried to draw him down into her. He wanted to slam into her and into her until they were both screaming. Instead he caught a fistful of her hair, forcing her attention. Eyes dark with desire stared up at him. It was a hell of a time for an attack of conscience, he knew, understanding the pleasures her body was only beginning to experience for the first time, understanding that rational thought—under the circumstances—would probably be even more difficult for her than him, but he had to make the offer. Hell, it was already too late to go back in one sense. He hadn't climaxed, but his body had begun to leak for her the moment she'd touched him. Still, he had to be willing to stop if she came to her senses and told him to.

Even if it killed him.

"Kate." Judas, he didn't even know what to say. *Please don't say no, please don't say no.* "Are you sure you want this—want me? Are you sure—" He hesitated. She lay almost still looking up at him, eyes heavy lidded, mouth curved in a come-hither smile. The muscles around her pelvis clasped at him, shuddering a little. His mouth went dry and he shifted slightly, realizing the mistake even as he made it. Fought himself for control when she shut her eyes, tipped back her head and moaned, letting the shimmy of current take her, bring him further inside. "Kate, damn it. Please—" He swore when she moved to pull him deeper still. Grimly tightened his grip in her hair.

The grin she gave him was impudent and knowing, fully female. He swore again. She laughed, husky and seductive, and that ripple of movement nearly undid him. He struggled physically to hold himself back.

"I want you, Hank," she assured him. "I choose you. I give you what's left of my…" The grin became a low, thick, tempting chuckle; languid hands caressed his chest, trailed dilatorily down between them to touch the beginnings of their joining. Her heart filled her voice, even as he felt himself growing thicker and more rigid, stretching to fill her, to touch the deepest part of her and himself. "What's left of my virginity…because you're the only man I've ever wanted to have it and could ever imagine wanting to give it to. Now would you please shut up, and like the songs say, rock my cradle, because I'm damn close to something that feels like it might be spectacular and I want to know what it is and you're the only man I intend to let show me."

"I am." A groan that was almost a question.

She nodded. "Yes. You are. Now tell me, teach…" She dug her heels into his back and undulated her hips, causing him to rock forward off balance. To slip in their shared sweat and lunge deeper into her slick sheath. "Does it do anything for you if I move like this? Does it help—"

She wasn't able to complete the question around the tongue that suddenly stopped her mouth, could as abruptly form no more words even in her head when he stole them with her breath by pulling back and thrusting hard to embed himself fully inside her.

Could only gasp when each succeeding thrust drove a little deeper, pulled a little more from her. Could only cry out when the contractions took her, scream her pleasure when he sucked the crest of one breast into his mouth and pumped hard into each small earthquake to create a monumental one.

Stabbed harder and faster until there was nothing left of her alone and she was a shouting, sobbing, sighing part of him.

And in the humid earth of her body, Hank spilled potent seed into her unprotected womb.

Chapter 10

All in all, it was quite a night.

Once found, they were loathe to leave each other—though they tried often enough. More than once, one last kiss turned into more; clothing, reclaimed, was discarded before they had a chance to put it on.

Out of sight of the house, they played like reckless children set free of the watchful eye of parents after dark for the first time, laughing and chasing, splashing and wrestling in the pond to cool off—children, that is, until wrestling gentled and intensified, leading to adult pursuits.

They took and gave and shared, exploring each other until Hank would have thought they were so familiar with each other's bodies that there was nothing more to discover. But there always was. There was this mole or that scar, this spot touched just so that turned her body into a molten flow of lava shuddering beneath him, that spot caressed, which made him stiffen and bow and scrabble to hold onto the earth while he begged her to stop-don't-stop-oh-God-Kate-*please*.

Even when they finally forced themselves to remember who they were and headed back toward the house barely three hours before dawn, they were still too new with each other to stop kissing and touching.

When Kate's enthusiasm knocked him on his butt on the bench around the old wolf oak at the juncture of yard, field and driveway, Hank was already hard again, had one hand up her shirt, the other down her shorts. Somewhere at the back of his mind, he'd no doubt they'd both be sore in the morning, but just now couldn't bring himself to care.

She was his only avocation at present, his preoccupation, and this was the time they had, with no future guarantees. He didn't want it to end. Hands on her hips, he leaned back against the tree when she straddled his lap and watched her face while she rode him, close enough in the shadows so he could read her expression, intoxicated with concentration and desire and euphoria. When she opened hot eyes and looked at him as she reached her peak, he shattered.

The contractions of release pulsed through them long after she slumped forward in his arms and wrapped him up in hers.

It shouldn't have been possible, he knew even if she didn't. He should have been...drained dry...long before now. But so should she. Should have been raw and at least uncomfortable if not in actual pain. Should have been exhausted and temporarily sated. But they weren't. And no celibacy, however long lasting, nor blind-pig-raid-adrenaline-high could explain why, not more than twenty minutes later, Hank found himself once more in such desperate need that he backed Kate up against the rear of the equipment barn and took her where they stood—twice...although the second time he was too wobbly kneed to stand for the entire experience and wound up on his back in the dirt with his hands fisted in Kate's hair and her mouth sealed tight to his while they both bucked and cried out in release.

And he knew damned well that *that* time should have definitely been enough to last him…for however long it had to last him. And it *was*—sort of, at least for the moment— but it also wasn't. Because now that they really were finally both panting and tired and relaxed and giddy and full of each other, they still held onto each other, shared a single space, walking as close together as two people could without falling.

He didn't want to let her go, however briefly, to spend what was left of the night alone in his narrow bed. He wanted to be in hers, have her in his—it didn't matter which—as long as they slept together. As long as they were together.

For her part, Kate was well beyond the ability or the desire to think. What thinking she chose to do had been done early in the evening while she'd waited for news, for Risto and Megan, for Hank.

When he'd arrived she'd simply followed instinct and gone to surrender her body where her heart already lay. She could not give one without the other—at least not this piece of her heart or this part of her body. Her heart was an easy captive, ensnared without reservation—particularly by children—elastic and more durable than anything else created by God or man. But the piece she gave to Hank was different, had been cached forever, forgotten like the smallest jewel at the bottom of a dragon's hoard until the very moment she'd snatched it up and handed it to him. And it didn't matter whether or not he realized how dear the gift was to her. It was his now to cherish or lose, keep, return, put away or give away as he chose. A true gift was given and forgotten, did not have conditions placed upon it, should not have to be worn or displayed simply because the giver came to call.

She recognized, too, the gift Hank gave her in return. Whether his heart was fully involved or not, he'd given her his body, too, shared his passion, rendered to her all he had

to give anyone at the moment. The knowledge that he did
not waste fleshly desires anywhere and anytime the urge
struck him was a powerful aphrodisiac, a priceless treasure.
She could no more have withheld from him whatever he
asked than she could have held back a comet by its tail.

When they reached the back porch where she'd earlier—
forever ago, it seemed—clipped his hair, they stood in the
semidarkness before sunrise, holding each other with gentle,
reverent hands, and kissed softly. Laughed painfully, conspiratorially at the discovery of swollen mouths and bitten
lips; kissed again, anyway, in spite of the bruises.

Hank buried his face in her neck. "You smell like me,"
he whispered.

"Funny," she murmured into the hollow of his, "I was
just thinking the same thing about you."

He shoved her hair aside and pressed a kiss below her
ear. "Yeah, I know, I stink. Ain't it grand?"

Kate chuckled, rubbed the backs of her fingers over his
stubbled cheek. "Don't think I've ever smelled anything
sweeter in my life than you right now."

"Mmmh." He ran his hands the length of her back, over
her rump and back up again. "Me neither, you."

Quiet closed around them, thick with humidity and the
singing of frogs. Hank roused himself to lean back and look
down at Kate.

"You should go in and get some sleep while you can."

She brushed a smile across his throat. "So should you."

"I'm not ready to go in yet."

"Mmm." Kate folded herself back into his arms, snuggled her cheek against his chest. "Neither am I."

"Good," Hank murmured into her hair, gathering her
close. "Good."

Down the road at the neighboring melon farm a rooster
crowed; Harvey pricked his ears and ran the perimeter of
the boys' pen humming and calling. Daylight, rife with
heavy clouds pierced by searing sun, touched the horizon:

nearly time to rise. Reluctantly Kate pulled away from Hank.

"I should go in and put the coffee on, get breakfast started."

He shook his head. "I'll do coffee and breakfast. You go in and take a hot bath before your muscles stiffen up. You're going to be sore."

She didn't, he noted with amusement, argue. "What about you?"

Gentle fingers traced her cheek. Hank smiled. "I have never," he said truthfully, "felt better in my life." He dipped his head to place a light, lingering kiss on her mouth, then repeated for emphasis, "ever." Then he turned her and guided her firmly up the steps, through the mud room and into the kitchen. "Now, go soak and clean up," he commanded, "before we both find out how depraved I really am and I attack you again."

"Not if I ambush you first," Kate muttered agreeably.

Hank grinned. "We'll experiment with ambushing later," he promised. "Now, go."

Tai passed Kate on her way through the living room to the back bedroom hallway and the first-floor bathroom.

"You're up early," she said, surprised—and guilty. He could have walked in on her and Hank in the kitchen—not that they were doing anything much, just sort of wrapped up in each other, but...

But, she admonished herself practically, it would have been a little embarrassing for all of us, yes. Still, Tai was a big boy, old enough to handle his mother "gettin' some" without the very idea damaging his psyche. Not to mention that—given his rather droll sense of humor—he probably would have found Kate mooning over Hank in the kitchen pretty funny.

"So what's up?" she asked.

Tai shook his head. "Not much. Gotta meet Gus Krahn

out at his farm in Cohoctah in an hour. Got the ag agent comin' out to look at some sort of blight in his trees he's never seen before. I want to hear what Shiner's got to say about Gus's trees and get back before it storms, but other than that it's B-A-U.''

Kate raised her eyebrows. She'd just figured out what the phrase *24-7* which Li and Megan tossed around, meant— twenty-four hours a day, seven days a week—and now here was another one. "B-A-U?" she asked.

Tai grinned. "Business as usual," he told her.

She rolled her eyes. Of course. "I should have guessed."

"You're gettin' slow in your old age, Ma." Tai bussed her cheek and headed for the kitchen. "There coffee?"

Kate sniffed the air, rich with the aroma of the Jamaican Blue Mountain roast. Her mother had brought the beans back from her latest jaunt with Habitat for Humanity to rebuild homes near Kingston destroyed during a hurricane. "You can't smell it?"

Tai shook his head. "Hay fever's got my nose in a snit."

"So take your medication and breathe deep," Kate admonished and shut the bathroom door behind her.

For a moment Tai stared thoughtfully at the closed white six-panel door. Just a second there, he would have sworn his mother glowed...not unlike the way Carly did after they'd spent a long *hot* evening at her apartment. But no, he dismissed the idea as ludicrous. That couldn't be. Kate was his mother, for God's sake.

He shook his head. Nope, not possible. Mothers did not, at any time, act like some horn dog's girlfriend. Although he'd often thought she should, his mother didn't even date, so how and when could she...

Still, her mouth *had* looked a bit swollen, also like Carly's last night after...

No. No, nope, hun-unh. He shuddered, slapped himself on the forehead and told himself to get his brain out of the Dumpster. She was his mother, and unlike Tai where Carly was concerned, his mother had self-control. He was out of his mind to even consider anything else.

Spurning the notion for good, Tai hiked up his jeans, stepped into the kitchen and startled Hank.

She hated his haircut and he looked like sex.

Eying her father with calculation, Megan set a tray of coffee, juice, bagels and strawberry cream cheese on the large electrical spool Tai had found and Li had cleaned up and painted for use as a table on the front porch.

Peering guardedly back, Hank poured himself his sixth cup of coffee of the morning and wordlessly offered to pour Megan a cup. She shook her head and poured herself some juice instead, offered Hank the plate of bagels and cream cheese. He selected a pair of bagel halves, glopped cream cheese onto each and withdrew. Megan made her own selection, smeared a dainty layer of the pinkish cheese over it and sat in the bamboo chair near her father, the spool table between them.

The air was still and sticky, the sky gray-green with the possibility of tornadoes. Already south-central Michigan was under a six-hour watch with a severe thunderstorm warning in effect. So far this summer, however, the weather had been full of threats without follow-through. Oh, some medium to heavy squalls, but nothing as destructive as the meteorologists predicted. The weather was more like building tension, layer on layer, that petered out just when you thought it would either explode and have done or blow over altogether.

A lot like his relationship with Megan.

"This is nice," Hank said, although he wasn't sure whether it was or not. He wanted to ask Megan where she'd been the previous night, but she typically did not respond well to questioning, preferring to volunteer information—if she was going to inform at all, that is.

Watching him, Megan nibbled at her bagel and nodded.

She couldn't, for the life of her, remember why she'd invited him to breakfast-for-just-the-two-of-them this morning. Spending time alone with him was always so awkward since her mother had died. She suspected that a large part of the problem was that she and Hank didn't particularly like each other, although she was aware he loved her. She wasn't real sure sometimes how she felt about him, but he was what she had.

And damn it to hell and back, this morning when he should have been fit to be tied over her disappearance and the raid from the night before, he looked like freaking *sex,* sorta the way Zevo did when they'd been doin' some heavy makin' out and he'd been tryin' to get inside her pants and got carried away. Like Zevo's, her father's lips were swollen and there was a love-bite bruise at the right corner of his mouth and *damned* if he didn't have a *hickey* on his throat. And for a man who seemed like he wanted to either question his daughter or throttle her for scaring him half to death he looked too pretty stinking *satisfied* with himself for belief.

He was too *old* to look so...so...like he'd gotten *plenty* last night, when common knowledge was that men hit their sexual peak when they were still boys of eighteen and it only went downhill for them from there.

God, it was just entirely too gross to contemplate.

Not to mention that, if he'd really loved her mother he shouldn't be gettin' any *anything* from anywhere but his wife. And dead didn't matter, loyalty did, and he was her *parent* for spit's sake and his betrayal set a bad example for *her,* didn't he realize that? He was her father, and fathers—even widowed ones—weren't supposed to need or want or act dishonorably and they weren't supposed to...

What they "weren't supposed to" got a little muddled in Megan's head from there, but she was pretty certain it made sense—if only she could straighten it out enough to bang that sense into Hank's head.

Or even her own.

Instead, because confusion, disappointment and pique made her forget anything she might have said that was remotely civilized, she swallowed the bite of bagel she was chewing, swigged a mouthful of juice and said conversationally, "Gee, Dad, you look like you've been in a whorehouse, and maybe you shoulda showered before breakfast. Who'd you screw last night, anyway?"

The bite of bagel Hank was about to take fell out of his mouth and into his hand. His eyes narrowed, his mouth thinned. "Pardon?" he asked softly.

Megan shrugged, enjoying the shock on his face—life would hardly be worth living if she couldn't knock Hank on his heels at least several times a week—and simplified the already coarse language for him. "Was it anyone I know, and did you at least wear a fun bag to the party so I don't wind up an orphan in a few years?"

She'd made love with Hank Mathison.

And not just once, but several times.

Kate tried to hold it back, but the grin came anyway, uninvited, wide and naughty and joyous. Wow. Double and triple *wow*. So *that* was what the fuss was about. No wonder. It was *amazing*, incredible.

And Hank, himself, was more than she had words to describe.

She'd realized that long before she'd known she would lay with him, but now...she understood more, knew everything she'd already known about him in some deeper part of herself—inside her heart, inside her soul and inside her body as well as inside her mind. He was decent and honorable, funny and wry, possessed of an able-to-laugh-at-himself sense of humor. He was passionate and uninhibited, unrestrained and capable of giving wholly, unconditionally of himself. He was a man of strength, as capable of violence as he was of love, but a man who knew himself well enough to hold violence in check...even as he could not say love.

And that was the thing she knew about him now that she hadn't realized before. That he had seen and heard important words used too lightly to convey things they didn't mean. He meant what he said when he said it, but he preferred to "show, not tell," because the fewer words used, the fewer lies that could be told. He'd seen and done enough lying in his career to know.

She climbed out of the bathtub—tepid to cool water in the morning's already stifling heat, instead of the hot water Hank had prescribed—and sloughed condensation off the mirror, wondering if the imprint he'd made on her heart showed as plainly on her face as it felt like it did. There was her mouth, plumped out from kisses as though she'd had collagen injections; below her left ear, the sucking print bestowed by teeth and tongue, and there, in the fleshy mound above her right breast a similar but darker brand that named her as his.

Looking down at herself, Kate fingered the symbol of Hank's claim, noted the softened but still distended pout of her breasts and nipples. Even now they ached as much for his touch as they did from it—and that ache was as sweet as the sting between her legs, the awareness that if he asked she would gladly welcome him there again, this instant.

Whether he knew it yet or not, he was hers.

And that was the difference she saw in the mirror when she looked this time: a softening around her mouth, the glow in her eyes that proclaimed her not only a woman who'd taken a lover, but a woman who'd chosen a mate, a woman who loved.

"Was it anyone I know, and did you at least wear a fun bag to the party so I don't wind up an orphan in a few years?"

Two hours later, still reeling from his daughter's verbal punch in the face, Hank sat in the shade near the equipment shed and stared at the bits of llama halter in his fingers. It hadn't occurred to him until Megan's…ill mannered, to say the least…question that he and Kate hadn't been the least bit careful.

Startled he might be, but Hank couldn't regret not using protection when he did realize it—well, he *could* but it wouldn't do any good now—because, well…regret wasn't his way. Not to mention that it wasn't possible for him to regret anything he'd shared with Kate the previous night. Not no way, no how, as Gen's granddad used to say.

Blood tests wouldn't be out of the question, of course, but he'd been clean as of his last physical, and sitting behind a desk for the past five years rarely, if ever, put him at risk of accidental exposure to anything except whatever flu was going around the office at any given time. And as for Kate, well…he'd gone with her when she took Bele into the prosthetics unit at University of Michigan Medical for his fitting. While Bele and the prosthetist had gone about deciding whether the boy needed only a new pylon or both pylon and suspension, Kate had gone off to the lab to donate a pint of blood—a regular routine, according to what Dennis had told him. From the health standpoint, Hank figured they were as safe as conservative, nonrisk behavior could make them.

Which didn't make Megan's question any easier to answer.

It wasn't her crudity that bothered him so much as her attitude. Crudity he understood, had on occasion used himself as a cover for emotions he needed to hold at bay, or to disguise realities that were too vulgar to deal with in any given moment. Crudity buried insecurity, fear, forced attention away from an instant, substituted for boldness, acted as an anchor to peers in the rough seas of adolescence—and, as often as not, adulthood.

No, although it was hardly attractive and certainly didn't make his daughter more likable, and while he hated both hearing it come out of her mouth too easily and finding himself shocked when it did, the gritty-to-obscene language she used to voice her observations wasn't the problem. It was the whole way she seemed to look at sex, love and everything else.

He *could* say, "You won't be an orphan because of my carelessness." Or he could go on the offensive and ask her—God, what a thought—what *she* used.

Or he could sit where he was and feel as if she'd ripped out his heart with her callousness, then jammed her thumb in his eye for good measure.

None of those responses were acceptable when what he had before him was a prime opportunity to talk with his daughter about the differences between love and sex, peer pressure and choice, reckless behavior and commitment.

Still, it was difficult for a father to describe the difference between having sex and making love to his hard-as-nails sixteen-year-old daughter when he wasn't ready to admit the possibility of *love* to himself. Harder, yet, to explain the differences between the willingness to make a commitment and a casual fling, emotional experience and inexperience, choice and the acceptance of accountability, whatever the outcome, to someone who was still going out of her way to avoid certain responsibilities and who, because of her lack of years, thought she knew it all. So he didn't try.

Besides, at this juncture, it was none of Megan's damned business anyway, and Kate hadn't said, "Hey, go ahead, spread the news, tell the kids we made love last night and that we're probably going to again and see how they deal with it."

He also wasn't ready to share his new…relationship—for want of a better word—with Kate with anyone else yet, and especially not with Megan.

Despite how…permanent…being with Kate had felt the previous night, they were still way too new to be sure of each other. Whatever he'd felt, she'd felt, might all have been an accident of time, place and circumstance, rather than something lasting. He didn't think that was the case, but it had been a long time since he'd shared intimacies with a woman and it had been a "never before" for Kate with a man, so what did he know?

Not much sometimes, judging by Megan, that was sure.

Which brought him down to the thing that troubled him, sitting alone in the doorway of the equipment barn repairing a llama halter and watching the ominous sky: what he'd actually said in response to Megan's provoking question.

"Honey—" He'd risen to lay his palms flat on the table, then leaned forward until he was nose to nose with her; his tone had been scalding. *"If I even considered doing anything like you suggest last night or ever, you don't have the language to describe it. I do not now, did not last night, nor will I ever screw anyone. The only time or way to have sex is when it's more than sex, when you're ready to make a commitment to another person and make love, with love. Until you've got that figured out you're not anywhere near old enough to even consider it for yourself, let alone question me about my alleged activities. You got that?"*

Then he'd left and Megan had been the one with the fallen bite of bagel in her hand and the shock on her face.

Shocking her for a change felt good, but Hank wasn't certain he'd handled...the details...as well as he might have. Wasn't sure he'd said all there was to say and was pretty convinced he should have stayed where he was instead of leaving.

Was sure he could have put things in a little more positive light, left room for further discussion instead of closing off potential dialogue quite so...effectively.

Still, whether he let her know it or not, she'd had quite an effect on him. Within thirty minutes of leaving Megan, he'd showered, dressed and taken a run into a pharmacy for condoms. It might be a bit like closing the barn door after the llamas got loose, but the flip view was: better late than never.

Or so he hoped.

Chapter 11

The day progressed in dregs and bits, cranky with humidity and crowded with emotional portent.

With the sky as threatening as the weather report, everyone stayed out of the fields and near the house. As the heat rose, Kate had the older kids rig awnings to extend the cooler areas around the loafing sheds and the surrounding trees. Bele and Mike also helped Li run hoses and set up sprinklers and wading pools in the open pens to keep the llamas cool.

The bandanna Kate wore to hide the hickey on her neck did double duty when she wrapped a tube of crushed ice in it and once again tied it under her hair. The chill was heaven amid the temperatures of hell. Hank made sure no one was around to see, then dropped a kiss on her temple when she brought a similar ice-filled bandanna to him. She smiled up at him and drew her finger along his jaw in a gesture of intimacy and familiarity that spoke volumes.

He had trouble letting her go after that, but anything further was inappropriate to the moment so he did—reluctantly.

Time was a commodity they both needed and neither could afford, stretched as it was to accommodate more than possible already. Maybe he thought, watching Kate stride across to the house, they could squeeze in dinner together one night, a movie or something.

It was the "or something" that lay closest to the surface of his heart.

Troubled eyes following her father whenever he was in sight, Megan stood in the shade with Harvey and, hardly aware that she was doing it, brushed the patient llama in the same spot until he trod gently on her toe in an attempt to get her to quit or move on. When that failed, he switched his hindquarters around and bumped her into the maple they stood beneath. When she rocked sideways into the tree and eyed him with surprise, Harvey stretched out his neck to sniff noses with her before swinging his head and butting the brush out of her hand. The message was as plain as the body language, "Enough already, knock it off." Then he touched his nose to hers again, looked around at where her father helped Belc reposition a wading pool, and turned back to her. Harvey's communication this time was equally—if disconcertingly—clear inside Megan's head. *"It's been a long time, little one, and he's not like llamas. All life cycles forward, it doesn't stop for death. Your father is a lonely man, and a lonely man needs a life mate. Time to grow up, little friend, and get over it. Time to respect your father's humanness the way you want him to respect yours."*

Having experienced this inexplicable sort of...telepathic communication with Harvey before, Megan was hardly surprised by the gentle rebuke. Kate had long ago matter-of-factly told her that five thousand years of interaction with humans made some sort of communication between their two species probable. She'd suggested Megan consider the contact she shared with Harvey as a bridge to understanding, a far more advanced and enhanced version of the type of communication that existed between humans and house pets such as dogs or cats.

Accepting whatever kind of special rapport existed between herself and the llama, however, didn't mean Megan was also willing to buy Harvey's...*observations* as gospel.

No matter how right he might be.

Hank jumping down her throat this morning when she'd accused him of having indiscriminate sex had been both eye-opening and disturbing. It had never even occurred to her he might fall in love again—nor that, being a man and a seemingly rather obtuse man at that, he would have such romantic notions of what sex should be. If he wasn't her father, she might find his attitude cute, but archaic.

Nearby Harvey tossed his head and made hawking and spitting sounds in her general direction. Megan ignored him, refusing to believe the camelid might actually be commenting on her thoughts.

Tai arrived back from his discussion with the extension agent at Krahn's tree farm, thoughtful and determined. Although the new strain of blight that was attacking Gus's trees and turning them brown before killing them seemed to be confined to the specific genus of firs he grew and apparently wasn't spreading to his pines and spruces, Tai knew better than to be complacent simply because Stone House didn't grow the firs.

Against Kate's admonishings and in spite of the storm warnings and rising winds, he collected his hand magnifier and headed for the fields on the tractor. He would, he assured his partner—and he stressed the word, separating Kate from her maternal instincts as effectively as possible—take Risto with him and do a fast check of the trees and come back in and, oh, by the way, her bandanna was slipping and she had a bruise on her neck that looked like a hickey and she might just want to cover that up before Ilya and his rampant imagination concocted a story about it....

* * *

Tai wasn't the only one who had comments to make Kate think twice about…well, *things*. Li also had a few things to say—although none of them was directed at Kate per se. But they did strike home.

Hard.

It was early afternoon in a quiet kitchen. Kate was boiling macaroni and preparing raw vegetables for a macaroni-salad supper; Li and Megan were at the table separating the day's mail. Amid the pile of envelopes were two that were identical, one addressed to each of them. Li quickly slit hers open, while Megan paused first to read the return address.

"Baby shower," she pronounced scornfully before Li could pull her card loose and tossed the envelope aside unopened.

Li nodded, regarding Megan thoughtfully. "Lynn Deering's. She must have decided to keep the baby after all."

"Or she let her parents decide she was going to keep it."

Trying to appear as if she wasn't, Kate moved quietly about the kitchen, ears hard pricked, listening.

"You don't think she should?" Li asked.

"I told her I thought she was a fool for screwin' around with Barry at all, let alone without protection. She said they were in love—" Megan exaggerated the word "—and Barry doesn't like condoms cuz they 'don't feel natural,' and it didn't matter if she got pregnant, anyway, because creating a baby would show their *love* to the world. I tried to tell her to open her eyes, that Barry's puttin' it to Kiki Sorensen and Ellie Dane and God only knows who else, too, and everybody *knows* they're not exactly *discreet* about where they spread their legs, so she better get down to the clinic and find out if she's got anything ugly and she tells me to stuff it in my bra and pretend I've got boobs. But she goes to the clinic anyway, and everything but her pregnancy test comes back negative, so they give her a bunch of literature on her options.

"So then she goes and tells Barry and he smacks her in

the eye and calls her a liar and a bunch of other things—
like slut—and dumps her and goes off and knocks up Mar-
cia Glass and does the whole routine again because 'they're
wrong,' and Lynn figures she's been an idiot and decides
it'd be better for her and the baby if she gives it up and
finishes school so much the wiser. But now she's not because her parents think that 'doing the right thing' means
she should keep a baby she's not ready for because 'she
made her bed and now she's got to lie in it,' an' it just
cheeses me that when there are so many people out there
who can't have kids the natural way and are dying to adopt
babies that her parents can't see that 'doing the right thing'
could mean so much more than keeping a baby nobody
wants because it's your flesh and blood. So no.'' Megan
shook her head, all self-righteous I-told-her-so. "I'm *not*
goin' to her baby shower and look like I approve of what
she's doin', when I think she's just a damned weak-bellied
idiot."

The stamped foot and *so there* were absent, but loudly
implied.

"Megan!" Shocked, Kate—who wasn't supposed to be
eavesdropping, even though the girls were sitting not ten
feet from her and hadn't lowered their voices so she
couldn't—swung about to say something suitably appalled
and hopefully wise, but Li waved her mother aside and beat
her to it.

"She's your *friend*," Kate's daughter said tightly.

"Friendship has limits," Megan observed, unperturbed,
rising to stack the mail in piles at the end of the table.

Li stiffened, then worked her neck and made herself relax.
"Does it," she said mildly. It was hardly a question. Her
eyes sparked, but instead of clenching, her hands spread
open before her, almost in offering. "And what limits do
you put on our friendship?"

Megan viewed her, surprised. "None, of course."

"Why not?"

"Because I don't."

Li's jaw jutted. "Wrong answer," she said softly.

For the first time since Kate had known her, she saw Megan squirm uncomfortably. "Li..."

"Why not?" Li repeated. A thread of strong emotion ran like tensioned wire between the two words.

"Because..." Unease settled in Megan's features. "Because...I can count on you no matter what."

"And you've never been able to count on Lynn?"

"Lynn's always in my face about stuff," she said defiantly. "You're not."

"I get in your face all the time," Li pointed out. "Especially when you're hangin' out with Zevo and that bunch of scags."

"Yeah, well, I've known you forever," Megan said with asperity, "and you don't screw around or date guys like Barry."

"And I always let you in, no matter what you've done lately, and Lynn's mother won't let her."

"Yeah, well..."

"So what do *I* get out of this relationship? I mean, do I have to worry about you deciding you don't like who I'm seeing or something and dumping me because it's too hard to cart the friendship around anymore, even though I lend you my mother anytime you need one?"

Megan's lips pinched and her eyes clouded, vulnerable. "Li, I know how it seems sometimes, but you know that's not the only reason I come here. You're like my sister. We fight, but it doesn't change anything."

"Yet," Li supplied.

"Ever," Megan shouted.

"Yeah, well, that's the way Lynn thought you were with her, too. She's as much there for you as she can be, when some guy isn't messin' with her head. You've known her since diapers. That's longer'n you've known me. Now she needs you to buy her some."

Megan's mouth opened, then closed for lack of retort. Her shoulders slumped; she looked at Li. "Sometimes I hate you."

"Yeah, well, get over it," Li responded dryly. Then, prodding Megan with her elbow, "You want to go shopping?"

Megan rolled her eyes and grimaced. "Do I have a choice?" she asked.

Grinning, Li shook her head. "No."

"Oh, fine, then," Megan agreed—ungraciously. "But I'm not buying diapers."

Li bent to drag her purse out of the pot cupboard. "You don't find the symbolism appropriate?"

"What?"

Li eyed her, all innocence. "You don't think she should have stuck rubber pants on Barry before—"

Laughter hiccuped out of Megan, cutting Li off. "Geez, Li. And we all thought you were the nice one."

"I am," Li said firmly and turned to Kate. "Okay if we take the van and run into town?"

"How does the sky look?" Kate countered.

Li shrugged. "Not worse. Don't worry, we'll keep the radio on and hit a ditch if we have to—and we won't be gone long."

Kate looked from her daughter to Megan and back. "Okay." She nodded, then added, "Take the grocery list?"

Li eyed Megan who shrugged. "Sure," they agreed.

Kate went into the office and came back with an envelope containing the grocery list and money, handed them to her daughter with a couple extra bills and a quick hug. "Get Lynnie a baby bathtub from me, okay?"

"I will, Mum." Li returned the hug with a swift peck on Kate's cheek. "Thanks."

They left.

Lips pressed tight together against the foreboding she'd hidden in front of the girls, Kate collapsed on one of the long benches and rested her elbows on the table. She gnawed her thumbnail and swallowed hard. Rubber pants. Oh, crumb.

She hadn't even thought about condoms the night before. Or anything much else, for that matter, except having Hank as deeply inside her as possible, as often as possible. And she couldn't even claim being a teenager for an excuse since she hadn't been one for close to twenty years. And it wasn't as if she'd never considered birth control. She had been on the pill during her years in refugee camps set up at the edge of border or civil wars. Her decision had come in the wake of the rape and murder of mission nuns in Central America and Africa. It was, she felt, better under the circumstances to prevent the possibility of pregnancy by rape than to bear a child condemned by the violence of its conception.

But she wasn't on the pill anymore, and the rest was neither here nor there at the moment.

Worrying the inside of her cheek between her teeth, she rose and went to pull the appointment calendar out of the kitchen's telephone drawer. Counted backward to the date of her last period. Bit her lip at the number: fifteen days today. Mid-cycle.

Possible.

Hand clutching her stomach, she shut the drawer and breathed. Stared thoughtfully into the middle distance trying to think. Possible. Having had an irregular monthly before she went on the pill and an extremely regular one ever since, Kate knew too much about the rhythms of her own body, had participated in too much emergency midwifery and family counseling to deny likelihood when it stared her in the face.

She sucked air, blew it out. Pregnant. Maybe. And Bele's adoption wouldn't be final for another two months. If she was, and family services found out, would it mess things up? But maybe she wasn't. Better not to obsess over it then, and maybe appear guilty and nervous, in case the adoption rep picked up on something that wasn't even there to worry about. And what about Megan…and Hank?

She felt herself pale. Oh, Lord. What had she done? She didn't really know Hank all that well. She'd let emotion get away from her because, well, he just…

Felt *right*.

Bad excuse, she knew, but there it was. Wars and marriages had both been started over less. And if it was just himself, he'd probably be all right with…whatever. But Megan… Oh, Lord, *Megan*. She barely accepted her father as he was, let alone…

Oh, gosh. Oh, blast. Oh, stupid, bloody *hell*.

But maybe she wasn't. Maybe…

She huffed another breath and straightened. Maybe she ought to go find Hank right now and apprise him of the possibility so he'd—no, *they'd*—have plenty of time to figure out how to handle all the potential situations if a consequence of thoughtless loving came to call.

The sky was black with clouds when Kate crossed the drive in search of Hank.

In the southwest thunder growled; heavy wind from the same direction spit dirt and light gravel at her, pushed her hair into her mouth and eyes. In the llama yards, the shade awnings alternately snapped taut in the wind and sagged toward collapse on keeling poles. Around the yard and fields, trees swayed and bent, branches swung like wild arms tangling and parting.

Kate gathered her hair together, and with a quick glance to gauge the storm's nearness and a worried one down the track to see if Tai, Risto and the tractor were on their way in, changed course for the pens to drop the awnings before the wind took them down atop the milling llamas.

On the other side of the drive, Hank emerged from the woodshop with the five younger kids and their constant canine companion. When he saw Kate struggling with the canvas, he jerked a thumb, sending the boys toward the house, then ducked his head and ran to help her.

"Where're the kids?" she yelled over the wind when she saw him.

"House, basement," he shouted back. "Girls?"

"Shopping. Hopefully they'll stay put till this blows past."

Dragging canvas into a quick, transportable bundle, Hank nodded. It was ten miles to the department store-strip mall complex, far enough in Michigan for a completely different set of weather to exist. "What about Tai and Risto?"

Kate collapsed the last of the awning poles and cast a worried look toward the tree fields. Overhead the wind grew wilder and the sky roiled black with clouds. The first fat drops of rain splatted her face and hair. "Still out. I hate it when Tai does this."

"You want me to run out and drag 'em in?"

"No." She shook her head. "Either he's on his way in or—"

The sudden crack of lightning and a prolonged crash of thunder cut her off. The wind gathered breath and roared, severing a branch from one of the trees above the picnic tables and pelting them with hail. Hank grabbed Kate's arm.

"Come on!" he shouted.

Together they ran for the nearest shelter: the barn.

"Where's Mum, isn't she coming in?" Bele asked, frightened.

Standing on a chair so he could see out one of the tiny basement windows, Jamal shook his head. "She's okay. She 'n' Hank got to the barn. They'll go down in the pit."

"Is there a tornado here yet?" Mike asked, interested. "The radio says one's coming."

"I can't see anything," Grisha announced from his post at the west side window. "Too much rain an' stuff. But I hear a train."

Ilya shoved his brother off the wooden box he was standing on. "We don't have a train here."

They looked at each other, then at the rest of the boys.

"Tornado!" they all shouted at once—or perhaps crowed would be a more accurate description, and *Adventure!* a more accurate shout. Grinning at each other in half-delighted terror, they dashed to a corner farthest from the windows, huddled around the radio and held onto the dog's collar, clutched their flashlights and waited.

Whatever the new blight that was decimating Gus Krahn's Fraser firs, it hadn't come near Stone House's Douglas firs.

With a sigh of relief, Tai allowed the wind to tear the last branch he'd chosen to examine out of his hand and let the hand magnifier he wore on a strap around his neck swing free against his chest. It swayed lazily with the ripple of his T-shirt; he faced southwest, gauging the sky, letting the strengthening wind whip his hair out of his face. Thunder sounded close overhead, green-black clouds raced toward him, leaving a muted gray swath peppered by lightning gashes at the horizon. Behind him he heard a fizzle and *crack,* turned in time to see the storm fold and break one of the birch trees clumped at the north edge of the field.

He ran for the tractor, tagging Risto on his way. It was way past time to head in. Instead of following, the Finn grabbed Tai's arm and gestured wildly at the dark funnel forming in the western sky. Without a word the two turned and dashed to throw themselves facedown with their arms covering their heads in the shallow gully on the opposite edge of the field.

Loitering under the shopping-center overhang, smoking and waiting out the weather so he could continue skateboarding illegally with his buds, Zevo spotted Megan and Li when they parked outside of the mall.

"How 'bout I go to Hallmark and get the wrapping paper and cards for Lynn and you get the groceries," Megan suggested.

Eyeing the sky, Li nodded. "Good idea, save time." She checked the number of items on Kate's shopping list. "Meet you at the car in, um, half an hour?"

"You got it."

They parted. Mood as black as his jacket, Zevo waited until Li was inside the grocery store before taking a last long drag then pitching the stub of his cigarette into a puddle near the curb. Hands tucked into the pockets of his sagging baggies, he sauntered forward and barred Megan's path.

"Hey, babe," he said. There was nothing friendly in the greeting.

Megan attempted to step around him. "I don't have time right now, Zevo. I'll talk to you later, okay?"

"No." Zevo shook his head. Faster than Megan would have thought possible a hand came out of a pocket and fisted around her wrist, pulled her roughly forward. "Now."

"Zevo, stop it," Megan said sharply, twisting her arm, trying to free it. Without success. She looked up at him, saw the something in his eyes that told her this was not "business as usual" between them, that he'd unwrapped himself from around her little finger and figuratively taken the ring she'd always led him around by out of his nose.

That he and only he, not she, would be in charge of this conversation's beginning, middle and end.

For the first time in their relationship, she tasted fear. "You're hurting me," she told him in the cool, scathing tone that had so easily kept him in his place in the past.

He smiled. "How 'bout that?" Once again Megan tried to wrest her arm from him. His grip tightened, he wrenched her back. "You know how tight handcuffs get, Meg?" he asked softly, shaking her wrist. "Just like this."

"I don't know what you're talking about and I have to

go, Zevo," she said. Alarm showed. She swallowed it. "Really."

"Your cop pop put me in handcuffs last night, Meg." He spun her around and caught her other wrist, fit it into his hand with the first. She struggled to no avail; he shoved her face first into the wide expanse of brick between store windows and held her there with his free hand between her shoulders. "Like this. Then he dragged me out to a car and locked me to the seat and made me sit like that. It wasn't comfortable."

"I don't know what you're talking about, Zevo." The brick beneath her cheek was damp and rough, scraping whenever Zevo pulled up on her wrists to make sure he retained her attention. Beyond the overhang, rain poured down in sheets. Zevo's smoking buddies grouped around him, hiding him and Megan from chance gazes. "I wasn't there. I told you I came in last night to find Risto. I had to take him home."

"Who tipped the cops to the club?"

Puzzled, she tried to look at him. Yeah, so Hank was the law, big deal. It had never made a difference before, what of it now? "What?"

"Your pop, Meg. There's a raid and he's the first cop in, but you're gone. Him and me, we meet once, but first guy he picks up is me. Who told him about the party, Meg?"

"Not me—ow! Damn it, Zevo. I didn't know he'd come lookin' for me. Ease off."

"Not till you tell me—*Geez*—" He broke off swearing when a van skidded up to the curb behind him and sent a wave of rain splashing up his back. "What the—" He turned and the splash of rain flung by fast-moving windshield wipers hit him in the face. His friends scattered.

Li slid half out of the van and yelled over the downpour. "Hey, Meg, quit screwin' around, would ya? We gotta go."

Zevo stabbed an angry finger at her. "Back off, Anden. Meg an' me got business to finish."

"Yeah, yeah." Li nodded. "I see *you* got business, but I don't think Meg does, and if you don't let her go before the sheriff gets here—" A dull wail rose over the thunder. Li cocked her head. "Oh, great, listen, there they are. I think I hear sirens."

Zevo's head snapped around, his grip loosened. Megan yanked free and scooted into the van at the same time Li ducked back inside, put it in gear and backed up. Then she shifted into drive, roared forward and splashed Zevo once again.

Megan viewed her rescuer with astonishment. The deliberateness with which the even-tempered-to-a-fault-Li had gone about drenching Zevo was a side of her friend she'd never seen. Usually Li simply scorned him. "Li?" she asked, not sure if it was.

Li ran a hand down her wet hair and snapped the cool water into Megan's face like a wake-up message. "Yeah?"

Euuw, Megan thought. *P.O.'d for sure.* "Nothing," she said carefully. "Just checking."

They were silent for a moment.

"I thought you were done with that jerk," Li said—although "exploded" might be more accurate.

"He's not that bad."

Li veered right out of the parking lot. "He jams you into a wall and you defend him? What have you got, Meg, rocks for brains?"

"Back off, Li, it's my business, not yours."

"You mess with him on my time and you make it my business," Li shot back. "What would he have done if I hadn't come up then?"

"Nothin'. Somebody would've seen him and called the cops, same way you did."

"I didn't call the cops, you dolt, I bluffed. The phones are down and the electricity's out. That's the civil-defense siren blowing. They've spotted tornadoes west of town. I was comin' to get you to get inside somewhere, but I think we're better off out of Zevo's reach. What was he threatening you about anyway?''

Threatening her? Megan glanced sharply at Li, recognized the truth and paled. God, he had, hadn't he? Because of her nosy, Dudley Do Right father. Threatened and tried to intimidate and...

Physically hurt her. Or at least might have. In broad daylight—well, murky rain light, anyway—with people around and everything. And she couldn't have done anything to stop him. For all her would-be toughness, she didn't know how. Oh, damn. She was stupider than Lynn by a long shot. At least Lynnie never let Whatshisjerk get violent—or anything that came close. At least Lynnie knew where to call a halt and when to make a choice. But she didn't. She only knew the choices all seemed to get made for her, or by accident or default or something. That she didn't really have anything to do with them.

Except, somehow, to precipitate them.

No. She shook the thought away. It wasn't her fault, it wasn't. None of it. She wasn't to blame. Her mother didn't get pregnant and die because Megan wasn't the perfect child; she got pregnant because Hank couldn't keep his hands to himself, then wouldn't let her have the abortion the doctor thought she should have. And she died alone because Hank was too busy to be there, got there too late to be of any use, even though Megan called begging him to come, to hurry, to fly.

At least that was what Megan thought she remembered. But suddenly it all seemed awfully fuzzy and she wasn't sure...her memory didn't seem quite...accurate.

In fact, it seemed dead wrong. She was scrambling events, mixing things her mother said with things Gen had done, and they didn't make sense. But they were supposed to. They had to. Otherwise, what did she have left?

Nothing.

Oh, God. Barricading her face behind her hands, she

swallowed the taste of bile. No, she was right the first time. She had to be. It was Hank's fault, this problem with Zevo, her mother, all of it.

Hank's fault.

Without warning her stomach churned and rolled, as muddled as her thoughts. Clutching her middle to hold her insides in place, she grasped at Li's arm.

"Pull in somewhere," she said tersely. "I think I gotta be sick."

The pit was a narrow cement rectangle cut into the floor of the equipment barn, which the tractor or other vehicles could be driven over so that someone could stand underneath and work on them. When not in use it had a heavy plywood cover that rolled into place to prevent accidents. Kate and Hank sat inside the pit, backs to the concrete, with the cover pulled partially over them to protect their heads.

Between the storm and the clouds, the pit was lightless and cooler than the surrounding barn, clean but faintly redolent of gas and oil coupled with the scent of a man and woman who were attracted to each other in close proximity. It was a short step from nearness to the age-old means of seeing by touch in the darkness; from touch to the wordless communication and comfort of fingertips and lips on each other's skin.

Exploration went no farther than a few gentle kisses and enough touching to reassure themselves that they were each the same people they'd been the night before. *Want* was a companion here, but not ruler. Rather they held each other close while their minds strayed to other concerns... The children—all of them—and whether or not they were safe; each other—and what to do about this thing that groped for footing between them; last night and how to approach each other about their recklessness.

Outside the wind howled, the rain pounded, thunder deafened, lightning flashed.

Hank's hand drifted idly over Kate's hair while his arm held her pillowed against his chest. One leg thrown across his lap, she listened to his heart beat, his lungs fill and empty. Conversation and courage had never seemed so evasive. Finally, though, Kate lifted her face to confront issues, at the same time that Hank's free hand cupped her chin and raised it.

"It's the middle of my cycle and—" she began at the same time he said, "We were pretty damned careless last night and—"

"What?" they chorused together, then chuckled, self-conscious.

"You first," Hank offered.

"No, it's okay. You go ahead."

"Sure?"

Kate kissed his wrist and nodded, uncertain. "Yeah."

"Okay." He drew a breath, touched the pad of his thumb to her lips wishing he could see her. "I wasn't too careful with you last night. I should have protected you. I'm sorry. I bought condoms this morning, but if…" Damn, how did he say "if you're pregnant, I'll do whatever you want, but I don't know what *I* want?

"But if…whatever…"

She stopped his mouth with her hand. "I understand, I think," she said. "You need to know, it's the middle of my month and the condoms might be too late, but I wasn't thinking either, and maybe I should have protected you." She felt amusement stretch his mouth beneath her fingers. "I'm sorry, but I'm not, you know? And if I'm pregnant…well, it never occurred to me before that I ever might be, and I certainly never planned on it, but if I am…" She hesitated searching for words.

"I'll be here no matter what you decide," Hank said firmly, then repeated sadly, "No matter what."

Another woman might have taken offense. Kate grinned.

"Will you," she said dryly. "That'll be handy since all I planned to do was say, 'Thank you.'"

He caught her face between his hands. "What?" Now he really wished he could see her. It might help his hearing if he could, because he didn't think she could possibly have said what it sounded like she'd said.

Kate raised herself to brush a kiss across his lips. "Thank you," she whispered against his mouth and he felt drugged, all powerful, joyously male. "Thank you, thank you, thank you." Her fingers played about his waist and a smug grin plastered itself to his face. "And I mean that. Thank you for the possibility, for the…the…unexpected maybe. I just never thought…I mean, *me* having a baby of my own. Wow. That's…that's…"

"Intimidating," Hank supplied.

"Incredible," she corrected. Then she added honestly, "And scary. And maybe not as well timed as it could be, what with Megan and Risto, and Bele's adoption not being final and—"

"And maybe not anything at all," he reminded her. He'd spent the past five years with the serenity prayer as his dearest and most oft ignored companion, but not today.

Kate touched his face, a gentle benediction, almost as if she'd heard his thoughts. "And maybe not," she agreed softly. "But it was a pretty exciting minute wondering, wasn't it?"

Hank laughed. It was a pretty exciting everything with Kate around. "Your middle name wouldn't be Pollyanna, would it?"

"Nope, sorry, it's Mary. Same idea, though. Find the best part of a situation and make the most of it."

He huffed something that was more irony than amusement. "Not every situation has a best part," he said.

"No," she agreed quietly. "But we can worry about the bad parts later. If there is a *later* to worry about. *Lord, grant me the serenity* and all, you know? Right now I'd rather make the most of the time we've got right here.''

"How should we do that?" he asked—warily.

"I don't suppose," she mused, running her fingers lazily up the center of his chest, "that you happen to have those condoms with you?"

He shut his eyes and felt *want* constrict his lungs, pool with the blood in his loins, distracting him from the moment's worries. In less time than it took to expel a breath she became the fever in his pulse, his only need, his all. It might be a little soon to discuss it, but if she was pregnant, he would do more than merely be here for her. He would be here, there and everywhere for her as long as she would have him. As permanently as possible. Rings, licenses, witnesses and everything.

And if she wasn't pregnant he still wanted the permanence, the commitment—her days and nights and forevers— as soon as possible.

And Megan would just have to accept it.

His fingers stole across Kate's breast unhindered by restraint. "As it happens, I'm sitting on a couple of rubbers right now. Why? You interested in a lesson in their use?"

She shrugged, grinning. "As long as we're stuck here and it's for the sake of my education... If you feel up to it, it might help keep our minds off the kids."

"If I feel up to it?" In an instant Hank had her flat on her back, and loomed over her in mock outrage. Laughing, she held her arms open to him.

When the sound of wind traveling by freight train passed overhead, he was deep into demonstrating exactly how very up to furthering her education he felt.

The outer barn door slid open and gray light intruded, almost blinding despite its dimness.

"Mom?"

Engaged in disarranging clothing they'd each just finished *re*arranging, Kate and Hank came guiltily apart, gulping air. "I'm here, Mike."

Kate pushed herself to her knees in the pit, hastily reaching to hook her bra. Naturally, inanimate object though it was, because she was in a hurry it had no intention of cooperating. Getting behind her, Hank brushed her impatient fingers aside and smoothed the hooks into place. His hands lingered underneath her T-shirt for a moment, smoothed the contours of her breasts in farewell; he dipped his head to nudge the wealth of her hair aside, his lips brushing a gentle brand at the back of her neck. Leaning into him, she reached back and touched gentle fingers to his face. Then he released her and reached up to push back the pit cover, boosted her out, hoisted himself out after her.

She got to her feet and dusted herself off, carefully not turning to offer Hank a hand up even though she wanted to. Wishing, briefly, that she had enough experience to know how to make reaching for him a natural part of her life instead of the stolen moments it had so suddenly become— and, in a family this size, could not remain. But she'd never particularly cared for dating the few times she'd gone out in high school—too awkward—and she'd never had a lover, so there was an awful lot she had to learn. Besides how to make condoms a pleasurable part of lovemaking. She smiled to herself.

Like how to go about having a…a…more than a friendship with a man in front of the kids.

Full of their basement adventure, Mike and Bele rushed forward to greet her and Hank; Ilya, Jamal and Grisha followed more…nonchalantly, as if the storm hadn't bothered them at all. As eager as the younger boys, the dog mooned anxiously around Kate's knees, licking at her hands.

"Is the storm over?" she asked, hugging rain-damp sons and patting Taz.

"Yeah." There were excited nods. "The radio says so. It's only raining a little now."

"Yeah, an' the house is okay," Bele said, "cuz we looked, but there's branches down and trees and—"

"We don't have 'lectricity or phones—"

"I, um…started the…*generator,*" Grisha volunteered.

"An' one of the loafing sheds is sorta sagging," Mike continued as though there'd been no interruption, "but the llamas are okay."

Hank came up behind Kate. Without thinking, she stepped closer and settled into place half a step in front of him. Sharing space. Of its own volition, his hand strayed to the small of Kate's back, slid up to her shoulder. He pulled it away, tucked it safely into a pocket. It just felt so much more natural to have her in the crook of his arm. He had to watch that.

Had to figure out how to make being with her an acceptable part of their kids' lives.

"Are the girls back?" he asked.

Jamal eyed him oddly but didn't comment, merely shook his head. "Not yet. But the radio said only one tornado touched down and it wasn't in town, so—"

The sound of motors and gravel under tires cut him off and took them all to the barn doors. From behind the barn, the tractor bearing Tai and Risto—wet, but apparently none the worse for wear—jounced up the track and into the yard. At the same time, Li pulled the van up behind the house, a county sheriff's car close behind. The deputy drove straight back to the barn, parked and got out, putting on her hat.

Recognizing the young woman as one of the officers involved in the previous night's raid, Hank moved forward to meet her. They shook hands.

"Director Mathison," the deputy greeted him formally.

Official, Hank thought. *Bad news for somebody.*

He nodded at the law-enforcement officer, becoming in the instant the formidable shirt-and-tie DEA AD he was at the office. That he was more than a little grimy and wore jeans and a T-shirt didn't matter. The deputy sheriff squirmed almost visibly and straightened.

"Deputy Schulhauser," Hank acknowledged coolly. The tone commanded respect; Schulhauser's demeanor gave it. "What news?"

Deputy Schulhauser glanced at Tai, who moved up to join the group in the shelter of the barn door, and Risto who swallowed and hung back, then over her shoulder at the scuff of sandals on gravel that signaled Megan and Li's approach. She looked at Hank, then apologetically at Kate.

"Are you Kate Anden?" she asked.

Kate nodded. "Yes."

Schulhauser eyed the number of children regarding her with interest and gritted her teeth. "Perhaps you'd like to send the kids in the house out of the rain, ma'am?"

Kate glanced at the boys and Li, took in Megan's defiant stance and cocked an eyebrow at Hank. He lifted a shoulder, then let it drop. *Your call,* his expression said. Kate turned back to the sheriff. "Is this about last night?"

Schulhauser nodded.

"Then I think," Kate said judiciously, "we'll go ahead and just consider this today's classroom and you the visiting speaker." She eyed her crew. "Pay attention, guys."

Yeah, right. As if they wouldn't.

Schulhauser pulled a notebook out of her hip pocket and glanced at it. "We understand you have a Risto Pal—" She struggled with the pronunciation a moment, then gave it a creditable go. "Palmunen staying with you?"

Kate nodded, looked over her shoulder to catch Risto edging away and crooked a no-nonsense finger at him. "Yes, I do." She moved to stand beside the pale exchange student. "This is Risto."

Schulhauser snapped her notebook closed and viewed the youth and his American family. "I'm afraid, ma'am, that we found his name next to quite a substantial sum in the gambling files we collected last night.'' Her stance changed subtly, squared as if in readiness for either fight or flight. ''I have to take him in for questioning.''

Chapter 12

Late August

The stick had a plus.

Swallowing, Kate stared at the pink cross on the end of the third home pregnancy test she'd taken that morning.

Correction. The third *positive* home pregnancy test she'd taken this morning. And since they were all different brands, really the only thing left now was for her doctor to confirm it.

And, of course, telling Hank and the kids.

Sightless, she stared at the bathroom mirror. Physically she'd never felt better in her life, had the feeling that pregnancy as a condition would thoroughly agree with her. She had no morning sickness, wasn't tired, nothing. Her breasts were maybe a little tender and her emotions seemed closer to the surface than usual, but she could live with that. Still, the moment five weeks ago when she'd told Hank that all she could say about the possibility of being pregnant was

Thank you! seemed a long time gone. A lot had happened since the day of the storm.

A lot.

She and Hank had, for one thing, started dating—much to Tai's amusement, Li's shy pleasure, Megan's consternation and the younger boys' enthusiastic encouragement—and she'd gotten to know him a lot better. Enough to know that loving him would be both the easiest thing she'd ever do in her life and the hardest. It would be for keeps. He was a man with whom she could not only share a child but a life, if a few intrinsic pieces of their previous lives—like their personalities and Megan—didn't keep getting in the way.

Megan had been moody and strange ever since the day of the storm and kept more and more to herself, avoiding even Li. Perhaps part of her behavior had to do with Risto being returned to Finland as soon as the police were through questioning him after the raid. Certainly some of it had to do with her father allying himself romantically with Kate and therefore establishing a place for himself within a family Megan had always considered her own private haven. And no doubt some of it was related to the tree that had split in the tornado and gone through the roof of the guest-house, bringing Hank to live in the main house.

Although he, himself, was the one doing the primary repairs, Megan had been rather vocal in suggesting that her father would do better moving back to their own house for the rest of the summer. *She,* of course, would stay with the Andens as planned. She didn't, she said, like the idea of putting Kate and Tai out of their office by moving a bed in there for her father. The fact that Hank was up as early as or earlier than everyone else and didn't need the office during the day was of little import, as far as his daughter was concerned.

She'd also said that what with him and Kate *dating*—the very word was twisted with a wealth of emotion and confusion—and all, him sleeping in the house hardly seemed appropriate.

Kate warmed a little with the thought. Megan might have a point there. It *was* awfully difficult to simply say goodnight and watch Hank go off to bed by himself. The fact that Kate and Hank had both done some careful after-hours sneaking around and had gotten very little sleep—whether together or apart—in the weeks since Hank had moved into the house seemed only to confirm his daughter's concerns. No matter what she told herself, Kate couldn't seem to stay put where Hank was concerned. He was equally bad when it came to her.

And it wasn't just the physical stuff—although that was pretty *Wow!* to say the least. It was being together rather than separate. It was having a best friend for the first time in heaven knew when, learning that sharing anything with Hank was infinitely more intoxicating than keeping it to herself. It was having him *there,* close enough to reach for, to laugh with.

It was also watching him with the boys, watching them blossom because of him—even Tai, grown, graduated and his own man though he was—and seeing Li turn to him as she'd never had a chance to turn to a father for seemingly inconsequential things that Kate hadn't realized Li cared about. Like how her daughter looked before she went out on a date. When Hank told her she was beautiful, Li glowed. When Kate said the same thing, Li accepted the compliment, but it was a compliment that carried less weight for being expected.

As for Megan...

Certainly there was jealousy on Megan's part when Hank paid compliments to Li, or gave his attention to the boys, but there was more to Hank's daughter's moodiness than the green-eyed monster accounted for. Kate could feel it. Megan wanted Kate to be there for her, the same as always, but she didn't seem to want Kate near her father. Or her father near Kate. But whether that was a divide-and-conquer sort of tactic or more jealousy, it was impossible to know.

The girl also seemed to have developed a rather... *eclectic*...sense of reality.

To say the least.

Megan's perceptions of what was going on around her were skewed—often in the extreme—frequently paranoid and more than a little unpredictable, even where Bele was concerned. Where seven other people—Anden kids, in this instance—saw a thing happen one way, Megan was certain to interpret it another, and most often in terms of how it affected her personally. Kate didn't even want to *think* about what might have gone on in Megan's mind the one time Megan had caught Hank kissing Kate. His daughter's verbal reaction had been quite astonishingly loud—and incoherent. And the kiss hadn't even been one of the mind-numbing kind Hank excelled at, but a gentle buss of the kind Kate found melted her heart and soul into a quivery puddle at his feet.

It was that almost chaste intimacy between Kate and her father that seemed to incense Megan most.

She'd also begun to disappear at odd hours, pretty much stopped working with Harvey and dumped what she referred to as her "goody-two-shoes clothes" into the trash. She still spoke to Bele, appeared to want to do things with him, but even where he was concerned she was reserved and...not exactly tense, but something close to it. She was frequently up, then very down, sometimes almost giddy, sometimes afraid. She was also disruptive and all too often angry enough that even the boys—besides Ilya and Jamal—who were usually oblivious to the moods of the people around them, walked carefully.

In short, living with Megan was a stunning illustration of how easily one person could affect both the tone and quality of the lives of those around her.

Drugs were, of course, the first thing they considered, but

neither snooping nor a watchful eye nor a—on the face of it—routine back-to-school physical complete with urinalysis and bloodwork turned up anything untoward. She refused, even at Kate's, then Li's request, to participate in a psychiatric evaluation, making that course impossible to pursue.

Li's response, when asked about her friend, had been a firm albeit unhappy and guilty apology and an anxious, "I couldn't say."

Wouldn't say was more like it, Kate guessed, but since she'd never had reason to distrust her daughter before, she wasn't entirely certain how to go about doing so now.

That Kate *wanted* to trust Li no doubt played a big part in it, too.

And now Kate was pregnant. Not doctor-officially yet, but as officially as a missed period, three positive home pregnancy tests and the absolute knowledge of a woman who knew her own body extremely well could make it.

She tapped a fingernail against her front teeth, considering. How was she going to break this to the kids? Especially after all the lectures she'd given them on the dangers of unsafe sex and the value of abstinence until marriage. And now here she was, twenty-some-odd years older than any of them, and she'd managed to, well, bluntly put, screw up once and get caught. Some example she set, huh?

For almost thirty seconds she considered attempting to sell them on the idea of another immaculate conception. Unfortunately, llama breeders that they were, they were far too well versed in the how's, where's and why's of procreation to believe even briefly. Even Bele and Mike had seen Mike's maternal aunt's birthing-room video and could quote chapters from *The First Nine Months of Life* at her, so...

She wasn't terribly concerned about her own kids—oh, they'd have questions and certainly comments, but in the end a good time would be had by all—in particular the doted-on-by-its-siblings and soon-to-be-spoiled-rotten baby. Especially given that it was Mom who'd messed up, not one of them. But there was no telling how Megan would handle this news. She seemed to be having a difficult enough time being Hank's only child, and now that he and Kate had managed to complicate the situation with a very unplanned number two…

Kate grimaced. Maybe she should make a doctor's appointment, confirm her condition and get a prescription for prenatal vitamins, but then wait until Hank and Megan moved back to their own house to make the announcement. Why that would necessarily make a difference Kate didn't know, but it was an option. Still, they'd be here only another ten days or so, and what was another week and a half out of nine months?

Better than one third of her first trimester, that was what.

On the other hand, it didn't seem particularly fair to keep Hank hanging for even another day, let alone another week. It might be *her* body, but he'd made it perfectly clear her body could contain *his* child and that meant he had as many decisions and choices to make, as many parental rights, privileges and responsibilities, as Kate did.

Which might, now that she thought of it, actually be a good reason to keep the news from him a while longer. He was already plenty darned arrogant as it was. Add a baby on top of it and…

She sighed. And nothing. And he was also restless.

He didn't talk about it, but she'd felt his mood more and more clearly since the night of the raid. It affected everything he did. He missed the action of undercover, she was certain, craved the kick, was balking at the mere thought of returning to his desk in less than three weeks. She didn't want to be one more chain binding him to a life he didn't want but couldn't, out of his own sense of duty, commitment and obligation leave.

Not that she wasn't considering this a little late in the game. If she didn't want to…tie Hank down, what had possessed her to make love with him in the first place?

Thoughtlessness, that was what. And greed. And lust. And need and desire and liking him and....

And a sense of caring that easily translated to love.

In short, although it was certainly no excuse, he was the right man—even if it was the wrong time—and she couldn't help herself.

She didn't want to.

So, where did that leave her? Tell him now or tell him later, she was still going to tell him.

Sighing, she drummed her fingers on her neck. Decisions, decisions...

He couldn't sleep.

Restless, Hank prowled the house, checking doors and windows, peeking into rooms, looking at the kids. It was easy to move silently. After only five weeks, he knew every squeaky board in every floor, had done what he could to shim or lubricate or reattach most of them. The simple labor, the ability to seek out the problem, give it some thought and fiddle with it until he'd corrected—or at least improved—it was probably one of the most satisfying things he'd ever done. Brains and brawn working in cooperation at *his* command, not someone else's.

He liked that, enjoyed being his own man for the first time in who knew how long, owning his principles instead of having to...manipulate and rationalize them to accommodate someone else's bidding. Here at Stone House no one was second-guessing him, changing the rules, rewriting the script, straining his resolve. Or at least, when they did, there were reasons for the second-guessing, changing, rewriting that he not only understood but could applaud—life reasons, not political nuances.

At the office, even as assistant director, he had his higher-ups to answer to; they wanted results from him now as badly as they had when he'd been merely an agent, but they also expected him to *get* results from his agents and underlings without telling them everything they might need to know to resolve their cases, let alone what they sometimes needed to know to stay alive. He hated it, but it was a job he knew and could do while he tried to let Megan grow up. And like it or not, that was bureaucracy; everything was "need to know." He was told no more than someone in the upper echelons deemed needful, was allowed to pass on even less.

Until this summer he hadn't fully realized how poorly he'd slept since becoming AD, but Megan had always been his bottom line, his reason enough. Now he knew that sleep either hadn't come out of constant fear for someone else, or when it had it was like the restless sleep of the haunted dead, without repose. He wouldn't trade Megan for the world, but he half thought he'd sell his soul not to have to go back to office politics and the uncertainties of life in a suit. He didn't want to go back to deep cover or anything close to it, either.

The truth was he finally accepted what he'd been seeking for the past five years—and maybe longer. Life with Kate and the kids and the farm was plenty complicated, but it was also simple, basic. He worked hard not simply to make a buck, to feed some nebulous adrenaline addiction, but because he wanted to, because here he was part of a whole, something infinitely larger than himself and Megan. Here, he made a difference.

Here also made a difference in him. And for the first time in more years than he wanted to remember, it was a difference he could like.

If only he could somehow make it permanent.

He cat footed across the open second-floor landing to an open doorway. There were the boys, Bele and Mike, asleep in their bunks on the north side of the upstairs. Their floor was coated with debris: fallen Lego pirates and knights, a stormed castle to be repaired before the next invasion, Bele's prosthesis—still wearing its shoe—the peg leg Hank had made for Mike and a tumble of shared clothing both clean and dirty. They were a constant ad for the concept of "what's his is ours," no matter which *his* was whose at the time. And that included Bele's leg. Occasionally pirate kings needed a peg leg, so why not use the ready-made one?

No amount of pleading, commanding or reasoning on Kate's part could convince them that Mike shoving his folded knee into the socket of Bele's prosthesis was hard on both it and him. It was a problem easily solved in the woodshop, though. Kate had called him a show-off for thinking of making Mike a peg leg, but Hank had been plenty pleased with himself for doing so.

Grinning at the memory, he left Bele and Mike's room and poked his head into the one next door. In variously contorted stages of deep slumber, Grisha, Ilya and Jamal snored, their personalities evident even in their sleep. At the foot of Ilya's bunk, clothes lay where and how they'd fallen; at the head of Jamal's, everything was neat and precise, draped or folded right side out. On the other side of the room, Grisha's makeshift desk—two sawhorses with a solid-core security door stretched across them—was cluttered with his microscope and slides, notebooks and specimens. The star theater Kate's mother had given him for his birthday stood beside his bed, turned on and forgotten, casting the print of constellations over walls and ceilings. Smiling, Hank stepped carefully over and pulled the plug to turn it off, then paused with his hand on the foot rail of the lower bunk. Something like regret slid against his conscience when he looked at the bed Risto used to occupy.

Though she'd dealt with it openly, Kate had been devastated by the questioning the youth had undergone, the spate of scrutiny and questioning she'd been forced to undergo because of Risto's activities, and his eventual removal from Stone House. And during it all, there had been the other kids to deal with, their questions, their hurt and the youngest boys' inability to understand why one of their favorite people had to be summarily withdrawn from their lives before he was supposed to be. Then they'd recovered relatively quickly and left Kate with her own demons to deal with, the sense of failure that she hadn't prevented what she knew she really couldn't have prevented.

The feeling that she should have known, should have seen what was happening. He could hold her, make love to her, try to tell her passionately that there was nothing she could have done because that was what he believed, but he couldn't make what she felt change overnight. And he couldn't change his part in the revelations.

He moved on to Li's room.

The moonlight revealed both girls asleep, lightly snoring. It pained him to know that if he didn't actually see Megan's head, or her arm and one leg trailing outside the sheet, he'd have gone in to make sure she hadn't stuffed her bed with pillows and snuck out. Being unable to trust his child hurt more than anything he could remember—except Gen's suicidal betrayal of his trust.

He moved on, not pausing when he passed the third-floor staircase on his way back downstairs. Tai hadn't yet returned from Carly's. With amusement and empathy, Hank wondered how long Tai would be able to live with the nightly trips to and from his lady's apartment, how soon it would get too difficult to leave Carly before morning—and how Kate would deal with the situation when it arose. It was one show he definitely wanted to be around to see.

The thought of Kate brought him to her door, his ultimate destination when he'd begun this restive prowl.

Hank smiled softly to himself. He didn't think he'd ever seen anyone more beautiful in sleep. Nor more beautiful awake, either, for that matter. It was just harder to enjoy when she was awake. Kate rarely stayed in one place long enough for him to savor simply looking at her.

He'd made the complaint one evening, wishing she'd be still so he could gaze at her. When he'd called her beautiful, she'd been insulted, reacting as though he'd accused her of something odious. She was, she'd snapped, much too busy to stand still like some mannequin and be beautiful for his benefit. In almost the same breath she'd accused him of being obnoxiously handsome and requested he "do something" about his appearance so she could quit staring at him and get something done. Like what? he'd asked, laughing at her. Like clean up, she'd responded tartly, since it was when he was filthy that she had the hardest time keeping her hands to herself.

He'd made a quick check for prying eyes at that and hauled her into an empty closet in the woodshop and urged her to demonstrate what she wanted to do with her hands instead. The result had been immensely rewarding for them both.

The memory of that half hour made him hard and aching. Her willingness to drop everything for a momentary exploration, her ability to pull from him more than he'd ever thought possible in every capacity, the way she could become part of him, share intimacy with a glance no matter who was around, never ceased to amaze him. To sleep without her was to lie awake wanting her, or to fall into the hottest dreams he'd ever had. In either instance, thoroughly dissatisfying. He wouldn't wake her, but it was better to stand in her doorway and watch her a while, let the sough of her repose lull him than to fall into a slumber her spirit or his latest falling out with Megan would interrupt.

When long enough had passed, he turned to go. The light shifting of her mattress stopped him.

She jacked herself up on an arm. "Hank?" Her voice was soft and drowsy, a sound he didn't get to hear often.

"It's me." He padded noiselessly to her bedside, touched gentle fingers to her cheek. "I didn't mean to wake you. Go back to sleep."

She drew his hand under her cheek like a pillow and snuggled into it. "I will as soon as you lock the door and come to bed."

God, exactly what he wanted, needed. Had for weeks. Exactly what he didn't dare do. "Tai's not in yet."

"I know. He's at Carly's. He'll be home before the kids get up." She yawned and shifted, reaching to pull him closer onto the bed. "You can get up then, too."

An invitation, a temptation and an insight all in one. Amazing. Even half asleep she could cover the bases without missing a beat.

"I shouldn't," he whispered. "What if Megan...the kids—"

"Lock the door," she murmured, a suggestion, a command. "If they knock, you can go out the window and come in through the back."

"Sneak around?" he asked, chuckling. "I'm not seventeen anymore."

"Neither am I," she said softly. "I'm an adult and that means I get to choose where I sleep and with whom. If I was seventeen I wouldn't need the sleep, but I'm not and I do and so do you, so shut up, lock the door and come to sleep before I wake all the way up and keep you awake for the rest of the night, too."

It was difficult to argue with illogic when he didn't want to, so he did as he was told. She butted contentedly up against his erection and went back to sleep while he lay awake in exquisite pain wryly cursing himself.

The dream was a pleasure so intense he didn't want to wake.

He was in Kate's bed, his hands filled with her hair. Her mouth was on him everywhere, her tongue running in long, slow torture over his chest, his nipples, down his stomach, tickling his belly. Gliding wetly through the furl of hair on his abdomen, into the nest of his thighs. She flicked the tip of her tongue up his jutting length, then took a slower, heavier taste, finally taking him into her mouth.

He didn't know if he made a sound, but he couldn't lie

still. His heels and shoulders dug into the mattress, bowing his body taut. His lungs sobbed for air.

He tried to pull her off, to tell her he couldn't hold on, but didn't know if he succeeded. Then he felt the rub of her nipples up his chest, tasted himself on her tongue when she kissed him and straddled him. He thought he held her away, pleaded with her to wait until he could protect her. Thought he heard her gentle his protests with the promise that she didn't need or want protection from him, that caution of that nature wasn't necessary any longer, so please, Hank, let me love you.

Then, because neither his body nor his heart could say no to that, he found himself suddenly taking charge, turning her so he could touch and taste and taste and touch...driving her as she'd driven him until he couldn't hold back anymore, until all he could do was enter her, fill her. Slide and pump, strain and gasp and meet her until they were no longer two hearts beating in syncopation but one pulsing to a single rhythm. Until they were a stormy jumble in the center of her bed, mouths fused to catch and hold each other's cries, bodies joined so tightly, so smoothly it was impossible to tell where his ended and hers began.

Shaking in the aftermath, he thought he heard her say it, words he badly wanted to hear but couldn't say for fear of cheapening them, "I love you."

But it was only a dream and dreams often lied, so he couldn't be sure and didn't ask the dream Kate to repeat it. Then the dream faded and he slept the sleep of the dead with Kate wrapped around him.

It was late dawn before the whine of the back screen door opening and closing woke him. Groggy and disoriented, he rolled out of bed and stood swaying in the morning light, trying to get his bearings.

He was on the east side of the house, not the west as he should be. He blinked and looked at the filmy half curtains and valances, the short, wide rocking chair with its green flowered cushions, the mirrored dresser and small antique writing desk. Kate's room. And he was naked, alone.

Confusion and a kind of startled amusement pulsed through him in equal measures. What the hell had he done? And wasn't not knowing where he was or how he'd gotten here exactly where he'd come into this thing with Megan and Stone House and Kate two months ago?

He had a vague memory of falling asleep with Kate, but the rest of it…he had no memory of shedding his clothes, even in his dream, no memory of anything except the incredible intensity of passion and the most profound sense of completion and peace he'd ever felt in his life.

Except judging from his current state of undress, it probably hadn't been a dream.

He shut his eyes and breathed. Memory woke. God, no, not a dream. Certainly not the fact that he'd crossed a line and slept the night in her bed. Certainly not the physical part. As for the rest… He couldn't be sure about the rest, but he had to find Kate. They had a lot to discuss.

His gym shorts were on the floor beside the bed; he picked them up and slid into them, stepped to the door and slipped into the hall.

And ran into Tai.

Shoes in hand, Kate's eldest son stopped dead at the foot of the stairs and gaped at Hank. Hank stared back. Between them flared an awkward silence. Hank broke it first.

"Morning, Tai."

"You slept with my mother last night," Tai responded. Straight to the point, every bit his mother's son.

Hank grimaced. So much for the assumption of innocence until proven guilty.

"Yep." He nodded, surprised by how easy the admission proved. "I did." He crossed his arms and propped his shoulder comfortably against the wall, a man on a mission that had yet to be revealed. "You just getting in from Carly's?"

Tai's turn to look uncomfortable—briefly. "Not that it's your business."

A smile ghosted Hank's features and retreated. "Nor this yours," he agreed.

"She's my mother," Tai pointed out. "I got a sister and younger brothers to look out for."

Hank nodded, not the least offended. "Yes, you do, you're right. But your mother's a grown-up and my intentions are...honorable."

Tai flattened an unruly grin. "I kinda thought so, but I had to check."

Flabbergasted, Hank stared at him.

Tai shrugged, didn't bother hiding the smile this time. "You guys were on the porch swing when I got home one night a couple weeks ago. You were too...busy...to hear me when I hit the porch. I turned around and came in the back way."

For the first time in twenty years, embarrassment climbed Hank's neck. Great, just great. He was farther gone on Kate than even he had realized if he couldn't even hear one of her kids approaching when he was kissing her. Or whatevering her. Especially whatevering her.

Mortification climbed higher, into his cheeks. Geez Louise. Caught necking and petting—and he hadn't even known he'd been caught—by a twenty-one-year-old with a sense of humor. Exactly what he needed. Who else had seen them that he didn't know about?

The question must have been written on his face because Tai's grin broadened. "Li saw the two of you come back from the pond one night pretty late, too. Frankly, I'm surprised you didn't try the bed sooner. The ground must be pretty tough on older bones and—"

"Tai!" Kate exclaimed, dumbfounded, coming out of the living room behind him. Tai reddened at the sight of her. "I can't believe—what do you think you—you're talking about me—who—" At a loss for words, she closed her mouth and looked at Hank. This was her bed they were talking—*laughing*—about here. When she wanted Tai to know Hank was sharing it, she'd tell him herself. "And you! I can't believe you're standing here encouraging him to speculate about—"

"It's a guy thing," Hank assured her—and recognized the mistake too late to call it back. She'd been a little more sensitive than usual of late. A symptom of guilt over last night or...

"A what?" Kate asked carefully, calling him back from speculation before any further ideas had a chance to form. He viewed her, guilty but unrepentant. She was pretty sure he wasn't smirking—quite—but he might as well be.

The flush started in her belly and crept upward, flashing heat through her chest, sent fire climbing up her throat and neck, into her cheeks. Anger, sweet and pure and clarifying. Egotistical, provincial, sexist *pig*.

Oops, Hank thought, noting her rising color with interest and anticipation. He grinned. It had been a long time since he'd been within range of good old-fashioned female fireworks. Kate's reaction bore all the markings of the killer queen of female fireworks. He could hardly wait.

Just as well, since he didn't wait long.

Her eyes flicked from him to Tai and back, then to the top of the steps where the grunts and groans of rising boys filtered down the stairwell.

She set her jaw, jabbed a finger at Tai. "We'll talk about you, Carly and the guesthouse later. You—" she turned and grabbed Hank's wrist, yanking him away from the wall "—come with me. I want to talk to you."

"My sentiments precisely," he agreed and yanked her back, startling her.

Tai gave him a *What do you have, a death wish?* face and headed up the stairs two at a time, getting out of the line of fire. Hank stopped him with a word, silenced the fuming Kate with a glance and a gentle finger to her lips.

"Tai."

Tai turned.

"We okay with this?"

Kate's son inclined his head, shrugged his mouth. "I got questions and concerns, but adult to adult, you're right. It's not my business. Just don't let it hurt the kids." He glanced at Kate. "Or Ma, either."

"*Ma* can take care of herself," Kate snapped.

Hank nodded at Tai. "Do my best."

Tai ascended the stairs. Hank looked down at Kate who stuck her nose in the air, turned her back and crossed her arms. He sighed, turned her forcibly around and rested his hands on her shoulders.

"Kate…"

She glared at him, ducked out from under his hands. Men could be such high-handed idiots sometimes. "Not here," she said firmly and, head high, back stiff, stalked off through the kitchen and into the office.

Hank followed to the percussion thump of boys barging halfway down the stairs, then grabbing the railings like parallel bars and swinging the rest of the way. The thud at the foot of the steps shook the house. Given the force of their landing and how many of them there were, no wonder it felt as if there was a slight dip in the floorboards at the foot of the staircase or that there were constant black handprints on the wall beside the front door from when they flew too hard and had to catch themselves.

"Knock it off," he automatically called over his shoulder—just like any real parent. "You'll break the banister." *You'll hurt yourself* was a mother's admonition, not a dad's.

If they heard they ignored him. Just like real kids.

Mentally reminding himself to check for a loose newel post or rails, Hank stopped in the kitchen long enough to collect a cup of coffee and say a strangled "Good morning" to Li, whom he hadn't expected to see. Then he stepped into the office, shut the door and faced Kate.

She sat cross-legged in the middle of the desk waiting for him, face set, pale eyes darkened with intensity. Her hair was pinned here and there about her head in a futile attempt to control it.

He wanted to step forward and abet its escape, but a glance from her stopped him.

Irritably she collected an unruly bunch off the back of her neck, twisted it up and plucked a plastic pin from the nest atop her head and skewered it into place. More rebellious wisps fell into her eyes and she glared at them, stuck out her lower lip and puffed them aside. Hank did his best to keep his smile to himself. The situation before them seemed to call for decorum—or at least restraint—but she did make him want to laugh more than anyone he'd ever known.

It wasn't merely that she was often funny—though she was. It was the sheer sensation of release and relief he found in her company, a quality of joy, an effortlessness of being. The welcome that greeted him no matter what or where, no matter when.

The same qualities that made control impossible when he touched her.

The same reasons he wanted to touch her now.

He kept his hands to himself.

"About last night," he said quietly, and let it hang, watching for her reaction.

Her eyes lit, her mouth softened. "Last night was lovely," she said.

"I shouldn't have stayed. I'm sorry if I...embarrassed or..." He hesitated over the old-fashioned word, but couldn't find another that seemed to fit as well. "Compromised you in front of Tai—"

"Tai and Carly are getting married," Kate interrupted.

Hank stopped. Grinned. "That's great," he said. "Carly's terrific. She'll be good for him."

Kate shrugged, troubled. "They're young," she said, surprising him.

He cocked his head, watching her. He'd never been able to guess what went on in Gen's head—besides frequent contradictions—but Kate was different. Not predictable, different. He'd have thought she'd be excited by the prospect of having Carly as a daughter-in-law.

"They're young," he offered slowly, feeling his way, "but they're mature. They know who they are, what they want and where they're going. They've known each other ten years and they've been dating for five. I wasn't even twenty-one when I married Gen. Tai's got a whole year on where I was. Young marriages can work, Kate."

"I know."

"Then what?"

She wrinkled her nose and shrugged, chagrined. "Well," she hedged. Very unlike herself, she knew. But with Tai suddenly engaged and planning his wedding, things had grown far more complicated in the past half hour than she'd anticipated. From where she was standing, thinking about Megan and Bele and last night and any number of other things, they didn't look to get less tangled any time soon. She looked at Hank, then quickly away. "Well…"

"A very deep subject," he agreed, "but I don't think your well is the reason—"

An excited clamor of whoops and yells rose in the kitchen, cutting him off before Kate had a chance to.

Exasperated, she swiveled and scooted off the desk, headed for the door to find out what was going on. "I'm not *punning*."

"I know you're not." Hank caught her before she'd gotten six steps and made her face him, ran his hands up her arms.

She tried to ease away. "I should go see what's up before they—"

"Kate." He hushed her with her name and a look. "Tell me," he urged.

"Well…" She made a wry face, eyed him sideways when he groaned and grimaced. "Sorry. It's just that, well—I mean *um*—I don't know, ah, Tai and Carly want to get married in March and I don't know. I mean her parents…hmm." She puffed out a breath, glanced up at Hank and gathered air back into her lungs, then let it out on a *whoosh*. "I don't know how well they'll handle the groom's single, ex-nun mother showing up eight months pregnant for the wedding, especially since they can't hide me because Tai's asked me to walk him in and give him away, too, and I said sure, why not? Now, he might change his mind after I tell him—"

The tumult in the kitchen now pounded on the office door. "Mom, Ma!"

Hank swallowed a wealth of emotions he could neither name nor separate. Delight, chagrin, worry, doubt, Megan—who had an entire battlefield of emotions of her own. Disappointment when he decided that was what last night must have been about. Kate was pregnant, they were both healthy, love could be as careless and spontaneous as they wanted to make it. Somehow, he'd figured there would be more to the moment, if it arose, than that.

Disbelief because somehow, despite the odds, he'd probably figured that maybe this moment wouldn't arise at all.

"You're preg—"

The door burst inward in the middle of the word, spilling Mike, Bele and an attempting-to-hold-them-back Ilya into the office. "Ma, Ma! Tai and Carly are—"

"nant?"

The three boys stared at Hank and Kate in utter fascination, their excitement over Tai's announcement lost in the possibility of more intriguing news. Kate closed her eyes and let her face thump forward into her hand. Geez-oh-pete-oh-man. This wasn't how she'd planned to tell any of them,

Hank included, but well, that was the reason you had to be fast on your feet, wasn't it, because how often did life adhere to plans?

With a sigh and a glance of apology at Hank she eyed Mike and waited, knowing what was coming.

But she was wrong. Oh, Mike's mouth was open, the words were formed, but it wasn't he who stepped into the room and put the question to Hank like an accusation. It was Megan.

"Who'd you knock up?" she asked.

Chapter 13

Pandemonium reigned.

"What is 'knock up?'" Grisha and Ilya wanted to know, their English lacking a certain amount of slang.

Quick on the draw, Jamal looked at Kate. "Who's knocked up? And why does Meg think Hank did it?"

"Is one of the llamas pregnant and we didn't plan it?" Bele asked.

"I thought Hank said somebody was going to be an aunt," Mike said, puzzled.

"Tai, is Carly pregnant? Is that why you're getting married?" Li poked her older brother.

"What?" Tai, whose head was elsewhere, eyed Li as if she'd not only lost her marbles but had deliberately buried them somewhere, then forgotten where "somewhere" was. "No, Carly's not pregnant. What are you talking about?"

"Hank said someone was pregnant."

"Oh, and you just assumed—"

"Hank didn't *say* someone was pregnant," Megan interrupted tightly, "he *asked* if someone was."

Li eyed her, amazed. "Who did he ask, you?"

Megan looked at her. Li misinterpreted the look.

"Oh, Meg, you're not, are you? I mean, not Zevo—"

"God, Li, as if! Would I do that to a kid? Besides, I know how to use a condom and anyway, what I asked was who *he* knocked up. He didn't ask *me* anything."

"Who *he* knocked up? But I thought you said he was the one asking somebody—"

Mike tugged at Kate's arm. "Is 'pregnant' like when we let Harvey in with one of the girls an' she lets him mount her an' we call it breeding her, then if it takes, in eleven months there's a *cria?*"

"Michael Anthony Anden, you know darn well what pregnant is."

"I know," Mike agreed. "But everybody's talking 'bout different things at once, so I thought I'd just check an' make sure we're all on the same page."

"Make sure we're all on the same page?" Kate pulled in her chin and looked down at him. "Who've you been talking to lately?"

"Nobody. Jus' Bele."

"Yeah." Bele nodded. "But we been listenin' to lotsa people an' that's what they say."

"So," Grisha said to Hank, "'Knock up' means make pregnant?"

"That doesn't sound very good," Ilya observed. "Knocking on somebody sounds like it would hurt and I don't think getting pregnant is supposed to hurt until the baby is born. Now if you said—"

What Ilya might consider more plainly descriptive than the term "knock up" was something Hank had no desire to contemplate, let alone hear. "Enough!" he roared, unable to stand the lunatic speculation any longer.

Surprised, everybody looked at him—even Megan. He looked only at Kate. She hadn't yet answered his question, and while the answer might embarrass him briefly in front of all these ears, he did rather want to know he'd heard her right, that he was about to become a father for the second time. And since it appeared he didn't have a choice, he'd worry about how Megan would accept or reject the idea later. Himself, he didn't plan on rejecting anything, especially not a baby or Kate.

"Kate?" he asked quietly.

She glanced at the kids, shrugged her face, turned to him and nodded. "Yes, I'm expecting a baby."

The silence went from surprised to stunned. The kids looked bug-eyed at each other, at Hank, at her. Their mouths opened, closed; questions formed visibly on their faces, got lost before they could be voiced. The translation process from disbelief to reality hit them each differently.

Mike viewed her with abstract interest; if there were undercurrents of impropriety in her announcement, it didn't occur to him to recognize it. Babies, schmabies. Lots of kids had come to live with them in his short life, what was one more? A big family was fun, and besides he always got to give and get some sort of present when they came, so hurrah for them.

That none of them had been infants delivered from Kate when they'd arrived was neither here nor there, as far as he was concerned.

Bele, who knew his adoption was not yet complete and whose eight-year-old misperceptions understood only that part of the reason he'd come to live with Kate was because his birth mother had died while delivering a baby sister who'd also died, looked apprehensive. He neither wanted anything to happen to Kate, nor did he want to have to leave this home and family, too.

Grisha appeared ready to discuss the event as it related to his naturalist's mind and his somewhat vague memories of when his mother had been pregnant with Ilya. He also shot a look at Jamal and Ilya that said something to the effect of *All right, it's not us in trouble this time.*

Ilya missed the significance of the event altogether, because it didn't apply to him specifically and didn't look as if it would in the immediate future. Long-term affect was not yet up his alley. On the other hand he did eye Hank with speculation, as though forming an opinion.

Jamal's face took on a look of pinched concern; unwed pregnancy was not new to his life; he'd seen it happen a multitude of times, but didn't know how to react in this specific instance. He was looking to Kate for his cues on whether or not to congratulate or console or protect. He also shot her a somewhat judgmental look that stated louder than words that she was no better than anyone else he knew if she couldn't follow the very rules she'd blathered on about regularly to every kid in earshot.

Staring at his mother, Tai sat down in the nearest chair looking as if someone had punched the air out of his gut and stolen the one sacred relic of his existence.

Li darted shocked glances from Kate to Hank to Megan and back; her mouth worked, forming expressions and discarding them, settling finally into an ambivalent but hopeful half smile. As in, maybe she wasn't really here at all and had heard Kate wrong, to boot.

Megan's jaw clenched and relaxed in concert with her fists; a single word slid out with the softness of expelled breath, hung in the air unheard. Her expression remained hooded, her gaze focused at a point near her left toe. Fury, terror, revulsion and excitement quarreled among themselves, supersized emotions competing for position. He just couldn't leave well enough alone, couldn't let her be happy, could he? He always had to get in her way, no matter what it was she wanted, he always had to ruin things. How could he do it, how could he?

It wasn't enough he'd always been able to take her mother away from her by walking through the door, now he had to do the same thing with Kate. Why did he have to come here with her for the summer? Why couldn't he have just let her come to Stone House by herself? If she'd just run away and complained to somebody he was...oh, hell, she didn't know, abusive and neglectful and oh, God, *anything,* maybe he'd never be here at all, never have been able to pull his damned Mr. Charm act, walk through the Andens' door and steal Kate away when *she'd* found her first.

And it wouldn't even be so bad if he'd only taken Kate away from her by dating Li's mother and turning her into one more adult on his side against her, but he had to go and do what he'd done to her mother, too. He'd taken Gen away forever by getting her pregnant and leaving her to die, now he had to make a baby with Kate and maybe kill her, too.

She couldn't let him do this to Li and Bele and everybody, take away the only constant any of them had ever had in their lives, but preventing the act was beyond her control. It was already done.

Oh, God, she'd wanted the baby sister the doctors had said Gen would have borne if she'd survived; she *wanted* the sibling inside Kate, wanted the family she only had here with the Andens, but in her head the pain and commotion were too much, memory flaunting her ability to contain it. All the why's she didn't know; the wherefores no one had ever explained to her about Gen and Gen's death—and she knew there had to be some excuse for some of her mother's behaviors, her mother's...*ways,* for everything her father had done then, did now...

Damn, oh damn, oh damn. She couldn't hold on to the rush of thoughts, the worry, the fear that somehow it wasn't all Hank's fault, it was hers for not being good enough, for being too troublesome, too erratic the way her mother had sometimes been erratic—for making her mother want another baby badly enough to die to try to get one. *Please, God, please, don't let anything bad happen to Kate, God, please.* Oh, *God,* she couldn't be here, she couldn't do this. She had to drown the agony, numb it, kill it for once and all. Her mother was gone and she couldn't just stand here and watch it happen because of *him* again, not to Kate, she couldn't. She had to get out of here *now* because if anything happened to Kate before the baby was born it wouldn't only be Hank's fault for not being able to keep his hands to himself like grown-ups were supposed to be able to, it'd be hers for letting her father get anywhere near Kate at all. And, God help her, she would do her damnedest to punish him for that.

Watching her father, she sidestepped an inch, then a pace, then another toward the door. Hank didn't take his gaze off Kate.

Eyes full of Hank, Kate, too, missed Megan's move.

Hand unconsciously guarding her belly, Kate searched his face, soaking up expression and nuance, both uncomfortable under his scrutiny and hoping their baby would get Hank's honey-mead eyes, wheat-brown hair and beautiful, tempestuous mouth.

Well, maybe not the tempestuous part, at least not right away.

She couldn't be sure how he felt, but she thought he might be...pleased. Also a wee bit apprehensive. She saw his glance flicker over Megan and Tai, alight briefly on Li, then Jamal, flit over Grisha and Ilya, linger on Bele then Mike, to return, furrow browed, to Bele.

She took her own quick tour of the kids' reactions, found a multitude of expressions that would have to be sorted and dealt with individually. The apprehension on Bele's face, however, was her most immediate concern. She opened her mouth to ask him about it, but Li broke the silence first.

"When is the baby due?"

Releasing a sigh she hadn't known she was holding, Kate turned to Li. "The middle of April."

"*April?*" Tai repeated, indignant. "As in a month after Carly's planning the wedding, so you'll be built like a house at it?"

Half laughing, Kate shrugged apologetically and nodded. "Timing's lousy for you, I know."

"April. Geez-oh-*man*." Tai rolled his eyes and slumped in his chair, resigned. "Great, just great. Thanks, Ma. What, you couldn't listen when you explained to us where babies come from and why we *plan* when the llamas will have theirs, so it's best for the *crias* and the girls, as well as convenient for us? I mean, for pete's sake, you never heard of condoms?"

"Yes," Kate responded tartly, "I have. And I believe I also suggested to you that condoms—a man-made item, if you'll remember—can leak and are therefore not foolproof, in which case, the only sure prevention is abstinence."

"Abstinence?" Tai eyed her pointedly. "Since you're the one telling us you're pregnant, I don't get your point."

"Tai—" Hank started, anger rising, but Kate held up a hand stopping him.

"Gee," she said levelly, viewing her son pointedly back, "I guess now you'll understand that if you don't practice what I preach it *can* happen to you."

Tai's grin was instinctive, reluctant and appreciative. "That's good, Ma, I didn't see that one coming. And, yeah, I guess it does prove what you preach—in a backward sort of way."

Grisha nodded. "Examples are much easier to remember," he agreed seriously and Hank choked. "Like when they show you a picture of what a word in English means, instead of only telling you in Russian." He cocked his head and studied Kate innocently, speculatively, the nosy mind of the naturalist-philosopher who read everything that crossed his path ready to ask embarrassing questions simply because he truly wanted to understand the answers. Hank saw the fact they'd be mortifying coming but, totally miscalculating the direction they'd take, failed to step forward in time to prevent them. "For example," Grisha wondered, his accent thickening with thought, "are you get...*knock up* on purpose from a...sperm bank? Or are you get—"

"Grisha!" Li gasped.

Tai slid out of his chair onto the floor from laughing too hard. Li kicked her brother. He rolled out of range but couldn't stop snickering.

Hank could only stare at all three of them in amazement, laughter startled out of him. What the hell had he gotten himself into?

As indignant and huffy as Hank had ever seen her, Li turned her back on Tai, poked Grisha in the chest. "That's not the kind of thing you say," she told her foster brother flatly.

"Why?" Grisha asked, genuinely puzzled. "You don't want to know who the...sire...are—*is* so you know what comes in the baby? You know, like we only keep a few of the boy llamas...*intact* because they're the only ones who will make good fathers and breed the right long fiber or something?"

Incensed, Li sputtered, "Llamas are *not* people. You don't *breed* people for the right kind of baby—"

"Hitler did," Jamal began, eyes alight.

"I'm the father," Hank said firmly before that discussion could get started.

"Well, of course you are," Grisha, Ilya and Jamal agreed, surprised he felt the need to announce a paternity they'd assumed by his presence.

Tai stopped laughing and rolled to his feet. Li stood beside him, accusations softer and torn printed on her face.

"I thought," Tai said somberly to Hank, "you told me you wouldn't hurt her."

Hank looked at Kate, then back at her eldest son, who held his gaze steadily; a muscle ticked in Hank's cheek. What to say, when so much needed to be said and he hadn't enough words to say anything? How could he explain without appearing to make excuses, reassure without seeming to patronize or sugar coat?

"What do you want me to say?" he asked, holding out his hands. "That I didn't intend—"

Mike tugged at Kate's arm, pulling her attention away from her elder children and Hank.

"Bele's scared," he said, concern showing. "He thinks you could die from having a baby like—"

Kate dropped to her knees and reached for Bele before Mike could finish. "Oh, Bele, your mama—"

"I'm *not* afraid of anything." Unhearing, frantic to shut Mike up and not be seen as a scaredy-cat, Bele socked him in the arm. "An' anyway I said don't tell, everybody always worries when you tell."

Mike socked him back. "You always tell for me and besides, Ma says we don't hafta face everything we're scared of alone until we're older'n Tai at least, and you are *too* afraid she'll die and never finish adopting you an' you'll hafta leave, you just tol' me you were."

"Bele." Gently Kate took his chin in her hand. "Is that true?"

Bele looked at the floor. "Sorta."

"Which part of 'sorta'?"

Bele's mouth twisted as he viewed Kate sideways. "Sorta all."

"Oh, sweetheart!" Kate pulled him into her arms. "Your birth mother was sick from the ebola virus when she died. Your father was afraid you'd get sick, too, and asked me to take you home with me and adopt you when he found out he was dying, too. I'm not sick from anything and I'm not going to die from being pregnant."

"Are you sure?" Mike asked, checking the facts for his too-anxious-to-ask-himself brother.

Kate swallowed a smile. "Very sure."

"And Bele won't have to leave, ever?"

"Why would he have to leave?"

"If you don't finish adopting him cuz of the baby."

"The baby?" Kate asked, astonished. "What does the baby have to do with anything? Of course I'm finishing adopting Bele, what are you twits talking about?" She hugged both boys fiercely. "Nothing could make me not adopt you, Bele. I love you, you're my son just like Mike. You're ours. We see the judge the day after Labor Day and take the day off school and have a cake to celebrate, the same as we did for this guy—" she grinned at Bele and squeezed Mike "—and he's a lot more trouble than you'll ever be."

Bele sucked air, tremulous but relieved, and slouched against Kate. "He is a lot of trouble, isn't he?"

"Not more'n you," Mike told him indignantly. "You get in the same trouble *I* get in." He relaxed, tapped Kate on the head. "But it's still good he doesn't hafta go away like Risto, cuz I didn't want to hafta leave like I told Bele I would if he couldn't stay."

Kate groaned in mock exasperation, covering stronger and more maternal emotion. "What did I tell you about Risto? He was never staying in the first place, he was only visiting for a year. And second..." She tickled both boys, who squirmed but not hard enough to leave the circle of her embrace. "What would I do for entertainment if you guys left, huh? I'd be bored to *death* and you wouldn't want that on your consciences, would you?"

"Well, we *are* pretty interesting," Mike agreed.

"And we'll never bore you," Bele promised. "We'll always find something to keep you busy."

Kate cringed. "Don't work too hard at that, okay? For a mother, a little boredom sometimes can be a wonderful thing. But I will need you to entertain the baby. She or he will worship the ground you walk on and feel so lucky to have two such terrific big brothers."

The boys looked at each other, pleased. Something passed

between them, an unspoken, apparently telepathic understanding that Kate had long since learned to be wary of.

"What?" she asked with misgiving.

Mike looked at Bele who looked at Kate. "Could we have a girl?" her dark-haired son asked.

"Yeah, a sister," the blond agreed.

She eyed them strangely. So far as she knew, they both thought girls one of God's less useful inventions, especially when they were your sister. "You don't want a little brother?"

"No." They shook their heads and shuddered.

"Nathan Leung has a new baby brother," Mike informed her, "and he said it pees straight up in the air on him when anybody has to change its diaper."

"Yeah." Bele nodded. "And we're not changing poopy diapers, either."

"I see." Kate choked back a laugh. "Not that you've ever changed poopy diapers before, but I suppose that's beside the point. Anything else?"

Before they could put together a list and get back to her, she was distracted by voices raised on the other side of the room. She caught the tail end of Tai's vehement tirade, something about Hank's responsibilities to his mother and the baby, interrupted by an exasperated, frustrated Hank who sounded as if he'd had enough of being verbally castigated and had already attempted to tell Tai the same thing he told him now in six other ways.

"Damn it, Tai, shut up and listen and quit being your mother. I am not, *N-O-T*, going anywhere, I don't want to go anywhere, this baby is *mine* as well as your mother's and I damn well intend to be as much a part of its life as she is and more, if necessary, because I want this baby as much as I wanted Megan. Can you get that through that pigheaded skull of yours? *I'm staying*. Period, no arguments, got it?"

"Oh, I hear that part," Tai said evenly. "It's the rest of it I wonder about."

"What rest of it?" Kate got to her feet and came to stand protectively beside Hank. "There is no 'rest' of it."

"Yeah, there is," Tai responded flatly, eyes on Hank. "There's a *lot* more."

"Like?"

"Like..." Li hesitated, looked from Hank to Kate to her own feet, then squared her shoulders and faced them both. "Like is he going to do the right thing and marry you?"

"What?" Kate asked, dumbfounded. The idea of marriage had never occurred to her once while she'd been holding her breath wondering if she was pregnant, nor when she and Hank had continued to be lovers.

Li swallowed and repeated herself. "Is he going to do the right thing—"

"Yes," Hank interrupted quietly, firmly, "I am going to marry your mother," while at the same instant Kate asked flatly, "Right for whom?"

Astonished by their opposing reactions, Kate and Hank stared at each other.

Houston, Tai thought with resignation, *we have a problem.*

Chapter 14

"Out!"

Kate cast one infuriated look at Hank and waggled a thumb between the kids and the door, ushering them quickly out. She spun on Hank the moment the door closed behind them.

"What do you mean, 'of course' you'll marry me? Did you even intend to ask or were you just going to tie me up and haul me off to the nearest Vows-R-Us wedding chapel or whatever it's called and file my 'I do' at gunpoint?"

Hank winced. He'd known the moment the words started to leave his mouth he'd made a mess of his intentions. "I spoke out of turn, I'm sorry, and yes I intended to ask you—"

"I mean," she interrupted, too incensed to acknowledge the apology, "it's not like we've ever even talked about marriage or anything, or like I ever planned on it in my life, or like I haven't done just swell raising God knows how many kids on my own and Risto doesn't count, I didn't have

him long enough or young enough to do anything with him
and—''

"And what the hell did *you* mean, 'right for whom?'"
Hank's voice rode over hers, completing his diverted
thought. "For the love of Mike, right for the baby, of
course, right for the kids, right for me, right for you—''

"Right for the baby, the kids, for me *and* for you?" Interrupting her own tirade, Kate stalked the room, eying him
as she might any other lunatic who confronted her. "That's
a pretty darned arrogant assumption, don't you think? Who
the dickens died and put you in charge of knowing what's
right for everybody, anyway? 'Cause I don't see six feet of
dirt over *my* face and I *am* legally responsible for seven of
the eight kids we're talking about here, and that doesn't
include the one inside me—''

"Which I put there," Hank pointed out.

"And very nicely, I might add," Kate agreed, not missing
a beat, "and that's another thing—''

On the other side of the office door the kitchen buzzed
with whispers and silence.

"D'you think she'll marry him?" Li asked, stirring waffle
batter for breakfast.

Tai snorted. "Because she's pregnant? Sister Kate?
You're joking, right?"

Li shook her head wistfully. She might always have had
the mother Megan envied, but Megan was the one with the
dad. "I didn't think so," she said.

"What is?" Hank asked, diverted by Kate's *and very
nicely.*

Suddenly distracted, she paused, mouth open, and looked
at him. "What is what?"

"What is the other thing *that* is?"

Was he laughing at her? Kate viewed him suspiciously.

His eyes gleamed, more amber than mead, but his face was merely curious. "What other thing?"

"*That* other thing?"

"Hank." Kate controlled her temper with effort. "If you don't speak plainly I am going to rattle you senseless."

"You've already rattled me senseless by letting me wake up in your bed this morning and announcing you're pregnant," he pointed out. "I can't imagine what more you plan to do."

Kate raised her brows and looked at him.

He grinned, waved her away. "I know, I know, give you six seconds, you'll think of something."

She snorted, and turned to shuffle something on her desk. "You're cute, but I'm still not marrying you."

"Why not?" Hank caught her arm, pulled her around and forced her to look at him. "I want my child, Kate."

"I know you do, Hank." She offered him a sad smile, touched his face. "I won't keep the baby from you. We don't have to marry, just so you can be its dad as well as its father."

"Damn it, Kate." He slammed away from her in frustration. "I'm not going to do a weekend-hobby thing with another kid. It didn't work for Megan and I was married to Gen. I also don't want a six-months split. Or even joint custody. Joint custody doesn't give me the first year of 2:00 a.m. feedings and silly baby or crabby baby and colic and teething. Even if Meg and I keep living in the cottage after the repairs are finished, I don't get that because I'd be in a separate residence." He tossed a hand in a gesture of helplessness. "I want to be *here*, Kate. Not just for the baby or for myself but for you, too. To take up the slack when you need to sleep. To be part of all of it. Your kids' lives, the farm, all of it."

"You said it yourself, Hank." It was her turn to pursue him, make him look at her. "You were married to Gen and it didn't work for Megan because you were married to your job, too. I'm not going to be your wife so you can go back to deep cover knowing you've got a safe place to leave Meg.''

''Go back?'' He stared at her, appalled. ''I'm not going back. I don't want to go back, I want to go forward. You think me going back to undercover is what this is about? Job convenience? Adrenaline highs?'' He ran a hand through his lengthening hair. ''Damn, I don't even want to go back to the office next week. I mean, hell, Kate, think about it—''

''Can you hear anything?'' Bele asked, ear smashed tight against the keyhole.

Beside him, antenna ears angling for best advantage against the door, Mike shook his head. ''Nope, nuthin'. We need Grisha's stethoscope.''

''Or a microphone to slide under the door,'' Bele suggested.

They eyed each other, consideringly.

Li crossed the room to pull milk glasses out of the cupboard near them. Sun flashed in the glass and figurative light bulbs lit simultaneously over Bele and Mike's heads. Glasses! They could use glasses to magnify the sound.

Or they might have if Li hadn't noticed them and said, ''Get away from the door, you guys. If Ma wanted you to hear what they're saying in there, she'd've invited us all to stay.''

Rats. They looked at each other. So close and yet foiled again. Sighing they moved toward the mud room, feet dragging. But not for long.

Mike brightened first. He grabbed Bele's arm, dragged him out of the kitchen. ''Window!'' he whispered excitedly.

His brother's eyes lit. ''It's open,'' he agreed.

Casting a quick glance behind them to make sure their goody-two-shoes sister hadn't overheard, they slipped out the mud-room door and dashed around the side of the house to stand underneath the office window.

"Hell, Kate, think about it…" Hank laughed without humor. "If I wanted to go back undercover that badly I could have dumped Meg in foster care or on Gen's sister a long time ago. Cripe, I probably could have found some woman willing to marry me and mother Meg for the price of an absentee husband and a signed-over paycheck, not to mention my insurance policy. So if that's what you think, if that's the holdup, just tell me what I gotta do to convince you I want to be here, nowhere else, and I'll do it."

"You know there's more to it, Hank."

"Then don't dance with me, Kate, spell it out."

"There's Megan, Hank, there's love."

"Love." Face carefully blank, he skipped the issue of his daughter as too much to deal with in a word and moved on to bolder things. "You need a word, you want a declaration?"

"Don't you?" she asked gently.

He shook his head. "Words don't cut it for me, Kate, they never have. I need pictures. It takes more to hold a family together than words."

"Yes, you're right," Kate agreed. "But I thought you were talking marriage here, too, not just family. And that's meant to last longer than the kids, so it's got to start someplace besides great sex and an accidental baby."

"It's more than sex, damn it—"

She held up a hand to halt his automatic protest. "I'm glad." She smiled briefly. "Very glad. But you have to remember, I don't have a frame of reference for that the way you do, and marriage has never been on my agenda, not even once in my life, Hank. And now you want me to consider not only having…" she laughed, uncomfortable with the inadequate concept "…a boyfriend for the first time ever, but to think about two weddings, our baby, Bele's adoption and what's best for *all* the kids, all on the same day at the same moment.'' She raised an open hand, let it drop closed at her side, asking for understanding. ''I can't. I shouldn't. Neither should you. Not all at once. Geez Louise, I mean—'' She shrugged, looked at him. ''Don't you at least want to get used to the concept first? Let the kids get used to it? Let Megan...I don't know...I just can't think it's wise or even fair to...'' She hesitated.

''Dump a baby, a wife, seven siblings and a whole new life-style on her all at the same time?'' Hank supplied bitterly.

Kate nodded. ''Yes,'' she said softly.

''She's always wanted to be part of your family, Kate. She's begged me for years to leave her here and go away. When she runs away from me, I've always known where to find her. She's always here.''

''She's run here because it's safe and to get your attention.'' She hated pointing it out, reminding him. ''She's run here because—'' she snapped her fingers ''—my doors are open and it only takes me that long to decide to take on a kid. But since you and I started...dating...she's run from here, too.''

The pain was deep, an ache with a sting beneath it. ''She always comes back.''

''So far,'' Kate agreed. ''But who's to say what she'd do or where she'd go if she couldn't get your attention because you were too busy giving it to me or the baby or one of the other kids. She used to tell Li how much she hated you for the way you'd come home from work and she felt like she'd stop having a mother because Gen paid all her attention to you.''

''Yeah,'' Hank said tightly, ''and I used to get it from Gen for how much time I spent paying attention to Megan. God.'' He pinched the bridge of his nose between two fingers, smeared unexpected emotion away. ''I didn't even know I remembered that.''

He hunched his shoulders, turned to look out the window. "I used to feel like a toy they fought over, like it wasn't up to me how to divide my attention, but them. It didn't happen all the time, just sometimes, family junk, you know? Like I'd walk into some battle I didn't know they were having because I was out of the loop so much. Meg'd tell me one thing, Gen'd tell me another. She was my wife—who was I supposed to believe? That's why I want to be here for this one, because I don't want to be out of the loop again."

"I'm not arguing that, Hank. I only want to do what's best for the kids. And I don't know how best for any of them it'd be to bring Megan, you, a baby and an uncertain marriage into their lives full-time all at once. I mean, Li's already started covering up something for Meg, I can feel it. She's never done that before. The way Megan behaves affects them, affects you and me—and all she has to do is walk into a room. If she's happy, great. If she's in a mood..." She grimaced, let Hank draw his own conclusions.

"There's a lot of lives we've got to consider here, Hank, and if you and I can't start out—" She grinned lopsidedly, using Mike's phrase. "If we can't start out on the same page, where're we going to end up? I mean, I didn't go into being a nun to quit, or because I thought I was making a mistake, I thought I was pursuing my life's vocation. I was wrong. Being a mom, that's right. Being a wife...I don't know if I could do that, Hank. And marrying for the sake of convenience... What would that say to the kids? Life's a throwaway as long as it's convenient? That's not fair to any of us, and how good is it going to be for Meg, when we're not even sure about it?"

"I'm sure," Hank said quietly. "I lie awake nights thinking how sure I am. I want you in my bed, in my life, in Meg's life. I want to be in yours and the baby's and your kids'. I never make promises lightly. I will be here because absentee parenting is a crock."

* * *

Bele looked at Mike. "A father," he breathed.

"He could really be our dad." Mike fairly trembled with excitement. "And he *wants* to!"

"An' if they got married *today*," Bele suggested, "he could 'dopt me 'fficially with Ma next Tuesday. Then I'd be a Mathison like Meg and the baby, not an Anden."

"No," Mike objected. "You can't be a Mathison if I'm an Anden, then we wouldn't be brothers."

"Yes we would, you dork." Bele punched him. "Cuz we'd make him 'dopt you, too, as part of the deal."

"Ooh," Mike said, drawing it out clownishly, making a show of light dawning. He pursed his lips. "What about Li?"

"I dunno." Bele shrugged. "Maybe we should ask her."

They dashed back around the house in pursuit of Li and the dream they'd just begun to have.

"But again you're talking about *parenting,* Hank," Kate said flatly. "Not marriage."

"Damn it, Kate." Tired of arguing, Hank swiped a hand across his face and through his hair. "Parenting is what this is about right now."

"Like hell it is," Kate shot back. "Be honest. Is that what you're going to tell Meg? Tell her it's okay to walk into marriage, whether you love someone or not, because there's a baby on the way? Then will you also tell her why Gen really died?"

He regarded her mutely, an answer without voice. "What's Gen got to do with this?"

"Maybe a lot. Did you see Meg's face when I told everybody about the baby? You have to tell her, Hank. It might not make—"

"Tell her what, Kate? That the mother she idolized wanted another child so badly she lied to me about how it would affect her, then told me not to worry about it she was on the pill, anyway, then she went ahead and let me get her pregnant? That I trusted Gen, but she was so stubborn and so selfish that the only thing she could see or hear was what she wanted, and that she didn't think twice about what she might do to Megan or me? I can't trash her mother's memory. Even if I wanted to, why would she believe me now?"

"She needs to know so she can make her own decisions about it, Hank. Whether she believes you at first or not, you have to treat her like a grown-up and tell her, now that she's old enough to understand it. She needs to know you got hurt, too, and she needs to mourn the real reasons her mother died so maybe she can move forward to something new. She needs to learn to trust you and herself, but mostly she needs to see you trust *her* emotionally with a truth you've hogged to yourself since you found out Gen was pregnant."

He studied her, torn between humorless laughter and disbelief. God, what pap. How had she ever survived the life she'd led, being so naive? The way he'd been raised, a man did *not* dump his personal pain, his marital problems on his child, no matter what the provocation. He didn't ask his *child* to shore him up, when what he was supposed to be doing was taking care of her.

Ruthlessly he ignored the little voice inside his head reminding him that not so long ago, the staff psychologist had told him much the same thing. Of course, five years ago, she'd told him the opposite. But that was then. Five years, for him, in terms of growth and maturation was very little time. Five years for Megan had taken her from childhood to adolescence to being a sometimes mature, sometimes immature, young adult. Kate and the psychologist were probably right about what he should tell her. Trouble was the how and when.

God, it was hard trying to grow up with your children. Trying to know when to treat them like adults and how to do it...

"Life's not as simple as telling anybody anything, if they can't or don't want to see it for themselves, Kate."

"Maybe not," Kate agreed softly. "But people—especially kids—need to be told things anyway and—"

Tai stepped into the kitchen wiping his hands on a towel from the mud room, where he'd washed up after turning the llamas into their fields for the day. "They still at it?"

Li placed a pitcher of juice on the table. "You mean you weren't outside listening under the window like Bele and Mike?"

"Fat chance," Tai returned. "I'm older'n that." He waited half a beat, then couldn't help himself. "They hear anything interesting?"

Li grinned. "I thought you were too old."

"Spill it, small fry, or I'll give you a noogie."

"Real mature, Tai. Carly's going to marry you?"

He made a gesture of mock threat.

She laughed. "Okay. All they heard was Hank say he wants to be out here with *all* of us, which they translated to mean him adopting them and being their dad, too."

Tai's brows raised. "Wow. I never thought of that."

"Me neither. I'm still trying to get used to her actually dating. You think Hank has? Or Megan?"

"You got me." Tai shrugged. "But you can bet Ma's thought of it. Talk about your blended families."

They were silent a moment. Then Li said cautiously, "I wouldn't mind if he wanted to adopt us. He's not at all like Meg said. I think he'd be a good dad."

"Yeah." Tai nodded. "But it's not up to us." He shook away his own vague wistfulness. "Anyway, speaking of dads, you seen Meg? I need her to help me with Harvey. He looks a little lame this morning."

"No, and she was supposed to help me with breakfast."

They looked at each other. This wasn't the first time in

the past several weeks that Megan hadn't been where she'd told them she'd be.

"You think we should worry?" Li asked.

Tai puffed up his cheeks, blew out a shrugging breath. "Got me. You know her better than I do. Maybe she's just off someplace trying to…I don't know, put it all together or something. It's sorta a lot to take in at once."

"I dunno," Li said doubtfully. "She usually takes Harvey for a walk when she's tryin' to figure something out."

"Maybe she's helping Ilya and Jamal in the woodshop?"

"You didn't look?"

"Why would I do that?" Tai asked, and went, chuckling, when Li picked a spoon off the table and threw it at him.

"Turkey," she muttered, disgusted. Then she ran to the door to yell after her brother. "Tell 'em all to come in. Breakfast's ready."

Hank cut off Kate's lecture on the merits of people telling other people things. "Why did you invite me into your bed last night?" Speaking of things people—he, personally—wanted to be told…

Caught off guard, she had the grace to blush and look guiltily away. "I wanted to know what it felt like to sleep next to you all night."

His grin was almost smug, torn out of him in spite of his best efforts to contain it. "We could sleep together every night, if we were married."

She wanted to smack him. She settled instead for pointing out the norm. "We sleep together a good part of almost every night even though we're not."

His grin slipped. "You mean it's okay to sleep with me, but not marry me? You used to be a nun."

"Used to be, Hank," she said flatly. "Important distinction. And even when I was, it didn't mean I was asexual. If I had any impulses, I ignored them because they weren't part of what I was. And to be perfectly frank, if you didn't ring my chimes I'd be fine, but you do and just because I *want* to sleep with you, because I want…to be with you any time I can doesn't mean I think it's right, it just means I make the choice every time. I'm a grown-up, I can do that.''

She held up a hand to stop him when he would have interrupted. "If I wasn't pregnant the answer might be different, but also if I wasn't I don't think the question would be on the table right now. But the fact of the matter is that I am and it colors everything. The way I was taught, the first priority in a marriage should be the marriage, darn it, meaning we have to kind of be able to separate the two. I mean, marriage is a lot of work and so are kids. To go into both at once…" She hunched her shoulders, looked pleadingly at him. "Wouldn't it be best if we were sure what's between us first? Not to mention that in this day and age, a woman does *not* have to be married simply because she's with child.''

"True enough," Hank agreed softly. "But wasn't that the point of Noah's Ark? Two by two? Two to make them, two to bring them up?''

"Ah, geez, don't get going on the two-by-two routine, Hank. In the nonhuman animal kingdom the father rarely does any of the child-rearing. Primates, maybe some, but mostly it's the mother there, too.''

The truth stung. "You don't believe in Hillary Clinton's axiom that it takes a village to raise a child? That they become better people the more care and love they have around them? The more people share in their growing?''

"Sure, but…" She hugged the slight thickening that her tummy had become and turned away. He wanted what he wanted, she knew. He wanted her and the baby and all of them. And he would care for them all, she knew that, too. But marriage was not a windfall, an accident of circumstance, a commitment to take lightly. She couldn't give him what he asked, not like this. Not without time.

She shook her head, certain of her own arguments. Certain she loved him, but not certain if she loved him enough—or even, quite that way. Not certain that he loved her as well as he liked her—if at all.

"We're not talking about a village here, Hank. It's more and less than that. You don't marry a village. You marry one other human being and you do it on the premise that it'll last for life. And the fact is, you don't have to marry me to be part of our child both legally and emotionally. Bottom line, I may never have borne a child before, but I've filled out a lot of birth certificates and I can give this baby any last name I choose, whether it's yours, mine or the man in the moon's. But I'll give it yours, and you'll sign the papers as the baby's father with all the legal rights that implies and we'll go on from there. Simple."

"In your dreams," Hank said flatly, and stalked out.

Troubled, Kate watched him go. For the first time in the almost eight weeks of her pregnancy, she felt queasy.

Chapter 15

The day did not get shorter from that point.

After he left Kate, Hank avoided Anden stares and speculation and went looking for Megan. His mind was on damage control, his heart was troubled. Along the fringes of conscious thought ran a faint desire to chuck it all and let whatever would be run away with him if he couldn't run away with it.

When he found his daughter, Megan took one look at him and ran. He didn't want to let her go, but she was too old to chase down, toss over his shoulder and tickle until she was ready to listen. She'd been too old for that for a long time.

So, with communication with Megan stifled by years of restraining the truth and communication with Kate at an impasse, Hank set his back teeth and stubbornly did what he was best at: gathered up all the pieces of the puzzle around him and tucked them away for later perusal, moved forward as best he could.

He didn't want to win Megan's confidence by destroying

her image of Gen; as he'd told Kate, it would be almost the same thing as taking Gen away from her a second time. Not to mention it was probably too late for that anyway. Even if Meg decided to believe him, who was to say that she wouldn't simply hate him all the more for being the bearer of bad tidings, however true?

No, life, as he'd spent most of his learning, was not as simple as "telling" anybody anything. You had to bring a lot more evidence to any revelation than mere words—the justice system that employed him was ample illustration of that. And even when you had it in spades, evidence often lied or could be doctored, witnesses could be coerced or lose their memories, testimony—like statistics—could be manipulated and shaded to reflect what the defense, the prosecution or the coached witness chose it to reflect.

Or appear to reflect.

In a world where Kodak commercials sang about pictures being worth a thousand words, where video-camera enthusiasts intruded everywhere, running rampant in order to capture and "show" everything, and where the axioms "actions speak louder than words" and "show, don't tell" were preached to children by parents and English teachers, but where most people preferred—and thrived on and lusted after—the "tell all," Hank was a man who lived the axioms. Words were items that too often got in his way—the way they had with Kate this morning. Words were not the things that had kept his parents together for what would be forty-three years come November. Words alone had not seen his grandparents through almost seventy years, were only a very little of what bound him to Gen.

Words could be harsh or loving, argumentative, destructive or empty. The things he'd witnessed with his parents, grandparents, his life with Gen were the emotions on the other side of the words: the loving touch, the unworded apology, the welcome in the eyes, the light left burning all night for the absent, after everyone had gone to bed.

So, since he couldn't give Kate the words she seemed to want, couldn't find Megan to tell her what she apparently didn't want to hear, he did what he could: went on with the work at hand, the work he'd grown to appreciate and even love. The trees, the llamas, the kids…while he watched Kate. He knew gut deep and without words that a life with Kate, their baby, her children and Megan was what *he* wanted; knew it was the first and only thing he'd wanted for himself in years. Both because of and despite Kate's too-blunt opinions and self-righteous, goody-two-shoes exterior. He was, after all, hardly perfect himself, what right had he to expect her to be? Not to mention that the woman underneath the sometimes imperfect exterior was warm and genuine and had a heart as big as the universe and an ability to love that was like bedrock. All he needed to view for evidence was her children, her farm, Megan…and himself. Without his willing it to happen, she'd become part of his blood, his peace…

His heart.

He didn't know how to tell her that, the same way he wasn't yet sure how to tell Megan everything she needed to hear, but in his soul he knew these things. And all he could do while his mouth sought the means to form the words his heart wanted to release was go on as he'd begun.

And try to woo Kate without words by leaving wildflowers on her desk, fresh-picked wild berries in the fridge and keeping pints of the hard-to-come-by chocolate-raspberry truffle ice cream she'd lately begun to crave in the freezer.

He also allowed himself the painful luxury of hope.

With the exception of a few questions—like where would the baby sleep, who would have to change its diapers and could they dress it up and stick it on a backboard and sling it from a llama for authenticity in next summer's parades the way some of the South American Indians used to do—the younger boys were much as they usually were.

The older boys, particularly Jamal, had questions they couldn't quite frame about her and Hank, about living arrangements and the chores Kate normally did. But for the most part, they, too, got over the news quickly and went about being who they normally were.

Aside from going overboard about not letting her do anything she normally did, especially if it was heavy, Hank maintained a thoughtful distance.

Li's expression went back and forth between concern and romantic ideals, wistfulness and curiosity. She wanted to know everything from what sex felt like to what love felt like—and she assumed Kate and Hank must be "in love" or the pregnancy would never have happened—to how excited her mother must be about the prospect of the infant Li could hardly wait to hold. Not knowing quite how to voice her questions tactfully, she asked nothing, merely watched Kate from a strict distance and behaved awkwardly when they were near.

Late in the day when she'd had time to work herself up to it, while they were alone together husking corn for supper, she did let one opinion fly. And it was the one Kate least expected and would far rather she'd kept to herself.

"You know, Mom, it's hard enough living with a mother who's such a saint that everybody expects me to be one, too, and who everybody else's mother says—" Her voice went high and unflatteringly mimicky and Kate winced. "*If Li's mother says it's okay for Li, then go ahead, you can do it, too.*'" Her tone returned to normal—if a tad self-righteous. And painfully truthful. "But now I'm gonna have to live with a mother nobody's gonna want to leave their kids around because she's fallen from grace so far as to get pregnant by a guy she never used to like and won't even marry to make things right."

Carefully Kate put down the ear of corn she'd stripped and looked at Li. Li flinched but didn't look away, letting her mother know this was important to her. Kate worked her jaw, straining for composure.

"Look, Li," she said quietly, evenly, "I'm not going to tell you that the way I got pregnant is right, but what's past is done and it's how we go on with it that counts. Second, you don't marry someone just to 'make things right' because a make-things-right marriage rarely works. *If* I ever marry it will be—I hope—for the right reasons, not just because I'm pregnant or because you think I should. And if you or anyone else can't deal with that, tough. Third, I like Hank Mathison more than I'm going to tell you, but he and I each have more on our plates than we can easily manage right now and neither of us needs to add a hasty wedding to the pot. Whether he knows it or not, he needs time and I never planned on bearing a child or getting married ever in my life and that means I need time, too. Now." She collected the big pot of corn and rose. "I'm going inside to start supper. If you want to talk about the baby, fine, let's. But back off marriage, Li, because much as I love you, it's not your opinion that's going to make me decide."

Then, heart striking painfully inside her chest, she turned and headed smartly for the mud-room door.

Usually almost as forthright as his mother, Tai avoided Kate as long as he could, which was most of the day, since he was out inventorying their salable trees while she was busy ordering wreath rings, wire, tree tags, flagging ribbon and advertising. Determined to get rid of the awkwardness between them, Kate shooed the other kids out the back and joined her oldest son on the front porch after supper.

"C'mon, Tai," she prodded. "I know you've got some judgment to pass, so dump it and let's move on."

He looked at her, pursed his lips over a comment, then let them relax and shook his head regretfully. "I can't. Sorry, Ma, but I really don't know what to say. You've never been pregnant before."

Kate nodded, deciding frankness was the best policy. "I never had sex before, either, Tai."

"Is that what it was?" Disillusion colored Tai's voice. "Sex, curiosity, not love? After all the things you told me?"

Kate sighed. "Tai, when I started talking to you about sex, I was parroting the things I was supposed to say, the things I believed, not speaking from experience. I still believe most of the things I told you, but...I wouldn't say this to the younger kids, but even brief experience offers insight. There were things I didn't understand when I talked to you."

"Like what?" He was both vulnerable and curious.

"Like..." Kate shrugged. She'd gone this far, she might as well go all the way. "Like—and I'm sure you've already found this out with Carly—how difficult it is to stop when the right person touches you."

Tai made a sound of wry disgust, avoiding the back-handed invite to reveal the extent of the relationship she suspected and he knew he had with his lady. "Geez, Ma. You used to be a nun. I think of *me* that way, not you."

"Yeah, I know." Kate puffed a breath of laughter. "And I prefer not to think of you that way, either. Guess that's the growing-up part for both of us."

"Yeah, but for pity's sake, Ma, a baby? Now?" Tai canted a quick glance her way, grinned wickedly when his mother raised her brows in question. "I mean, you're old enough to be its grandmother."

Startled laughter worked its way out of Kate's throat. "Oh, well, thank you very much, Mr. Smarty-pants. I'm barely what, sixteen years older than you? And my body tells me I'm plenty young enough."

There was a crunch of gravel as Carly's car came down the drive and parked beside the house. Grinning, Tai moved toward the steps to welcome her.

"Yeah, but," he said over his shoulder to Kate, "you've

got to think about chasing a toddler around when you're forty.''

"Go suck an egg," Kate advised him tartly. "If I'm too old to chase a toddler when I'm forty, I'll let you know, and you and Carly can come do it for me."

"Do what for you?" Carly asked, coming up the steps.

"Chase toddlers for me when I'm forty," Kate said—uncomfortably.

Carly eyed her curiously. "What, did you find another kid to adopt? Hi, love." She leaned into Tai for a kiss, then murmured, "Did you tell 'em?"

"Oh, yeah." Tai nodded, sounding aggrieved. "Now wait'll you hear what they've got to tell you."

"Who's got to tell me?"

"Ma and Hank."

"They're getting married, too?" Carly guessed, teasing. "They've only been dating a couple of weeks."

"Yeah, but they've known *of* each other for eleven years," Tai pointed out, thunking his mother with an elbow to her ribs.

"It's not the same thing," Carly said flatly.

"My point exactly," Kate agreed, poking Tai in the chest.

"Yeah, well." Tai crossed his arms and stared at her. "Now tell her why the question came up at all."

"The question came up? Really?"

"Well, I suppose it would," Kate said, forestalling any comment Tai might make. She settled a hand on her stomach, already a habit, she was surprised to note. "I'm pregnant."

"And the baby's due less than a month after our wedding," Tai added.

Speechless, Carly blinked at him, then turned to Kate. For maybe half a heartbeat she viewed her prospective mother-in-law with amazement then she started to chortle, then to laugh so hard the tears ran. Tai watched her with concern, fearing hysteria when she kept trying to say something her mirth kept choking off. But all she said when she could finally pull herself together enough to wipe her eyes and say anything was, ''And I was afraid the wedding would just be pomp and dull.''

Kate rolled her eyes. She should have known this was how Carly would react. Even as a teen, the young woman had been the cheeriest, least flappable person Kate had ever met.

''You don't think your parents are gonna freak?'' Tai asked. ''They're having a pretty hard time with this, as it is.''

''They freak over everything,'' Carly reminded him, still chuckling. ''So tough Tootsie Rolls. It's not their wedding, it's mine.'' She toasted Kate with a glass of iced tea. ''Congratulations, Ma. How's Hank feel about it?''

Kate shrugged. ''He's not talking to me because I won't marry him.''

Carly laughed again. ''Sounds committed to me.''

''Or like he should be,'' Kate muttered and, to the sound of their chuckles, left her son and almost daughter-in-law to spark alone on the front porch swing.

Megan kept her distance by simply staying out of sight, keeping solely to herself, ignoring everyone and basically not showing up until her ten-thirty curfew. And then she came in obviously wired and obnoxiously loud. At that point Kate, up to her eyeballs with worrying about Hank's daughter, pulled Megan into the main-floor den, shut the door in Hank's face and reamed the teen up one side and down the other about the example she was setting for the younger kids and about living by the house rules if she wanted to continue to be welcome at Stone House. Megan blinked at her in some astonishment over the choiceness and quality of a lecture she'd never before gotten from Kate, but aside from one or two surly comments about hypocritical adults presuming to tell her what to do, she kept her mouth shut.

Affronted and royally peeved by Kate's chutzpah in taking on his child without a by-your-leave or at least inviting him to be present, Hank set his back teeth and crashed the reaming out.

"Back off my daughter, Kate. If she needs to be cussed out, I'll do it."

Kate swung on him as though ready for the confrontation. "This is what it'd be like if we got married, Hank. Equal partners in the kids and their discipline. And she's high in *my* home right now, she's sleeping under my roof, she's interfering with my kids, I'm going to say what I've got to say and if you don't like it, think hard about what you asked me this morning."

Well and truly flummoxed by a truth he'd spent nearly three months accepting—that Kate had tiptoed pretty carefully but had nevertheless called Megan out whenever necessary, the same way he'd chided her kids, if less often—but had ignored this morning, Hank shut up long enough for Kate to return her attention to Megan.

Intent on each other, neither of them saw Megan pale and clutch for something to hold herself erect when Kate mentioned the word "married."

What Hank *did* see, however, was that the same parts of Kate's chidings that struck home with him also bull's-eyed with his daughter. Kate yelled at a child because she cared about the child, and somehow that concern and affection came across. Not because of anything she said, although she said plenty, but in the tone of her voice, in her refusal to lay guilt, in her request for Megan to take responsibility for her actions and choices, in the way she reached for Megan when she talked. Touching Megan's shoulder, earnestly taking her hands, speaking not only to her but *with* her both physically and emotionally on several levels at the same time. Showing disappointment but accepting responsibility for the fact that Megan might also have reason to be disappointed in her.

Chewing Megan out the way a mother chewed out an almost grown-up daughter.

The vision gave him pause. But it was the fear and accusation staring at him when Megan briefly caught his eye that made the iron band form around his heart and start to squeeze.

Life moved forward.

In spite of the children's best efforts to drag summer on forever, August twenty-sixth arrived and with it, a new school year.

The repairs to the guest cottage were finished, and with a mother's blessing and misgiving, Kate watched Tai and Carly move into it together. It was, she knew, probably the best solution all around, allowing Tai to remain on the farm while giving him the distance and privacy he and Carly wanted and needed at this stage of their relationship. But she couldn't help but wish they'd kept the "living together" part of things for after their wedding.

Funny how upbringing always seemed to meddle in your druthers, no matter how liberal you thought you'd become.

Hank did not move himself and Megan back to their house in town with the start of the school year as planned, but instead coerced, then charmed Kate into letting them stay with the simple promise—or was that threat?—that he'd move into Tai's vacated room on the third floor, but he intended to live in her pocket until their baby was twenty-seven, so she'd damn well better just get used to it. He *did* return to work with the DEA, but he went back unwillingly and against his better judgment.

Against the wishes of both his heart and body, he did not set foot in Kate's bedroom. He stole a kiss from time to time, but went no further. Giving her room. Giving them room was often the better part of valor, especially when he didn't want to make things worse. Still, not touching her was one of the hardest things he'd ever asked of himself—

pregnancy gave her a glow and a scent he could neither ignore nor resist—but he knew that the more often he was with her, the more difficult it would be to leave her. Until she understood her own heart for the long term, he wasn't willing to settle for the short.

Kate missed his physical presence badly, but discovered it was the simple sharing, the emotional closeness that had begun to grow out of their physical intimacy that she craved most.

With her father back to the regimen eight-, ten- or twelve-hour days away from home, Megan once again began to dress in unrelieved mourning, stopped communicating with anyone at Stone House and though no one knew it spent much of her time in a furtive search for chemical and herbal relief for the ache in her heart. When she was around, she watched Kate relentlessly. More often than not, however, she made up school-related excuses to be gone.

Kate and Hank suspected, but only Li knew for sure that Megan was lying.

The thing that Kate came to realize with a heavy heart was that it was impossible to know your teenager by living with her.

Chapter 16

September 18—11:53 p.m.
Fifth anniversary of Gen's death.

Sweating in the late-night heat, Megan leaned against the still-warm brick on the south side of Stephen Gorley's house at the back of her old neighborhood, shivering. She was dizzy, weak and her heart felt funny, pinging, then pounding in irregular cadence, and she couldn't seem to breathe properly.

Beside her Zevo rolled his cheek along the bricks seeking a cool spot to chill the fever in his brain.

"Man," he whispered, "I don't feel so good. Can't get the right stuff since the cops closed down Danny's. Maybe we shouldn'ta messed with a different brand of ecstasy. Never know how it's mixed."

"Ya think?" Meg muttered.

Through the open windows and doors of the Gorleys' house the illicit parents-out-of-town-back-to-school party raged. A little louder and the neighbors across the road and six acres away would call the police. There weren't enough trees to block the sound.

"How many'd we take anyway?" Zevo asked.

"Nine," Meg said. "Salesgirl said the best buzz came with twelve."

"Nuts," Zevo whispered. Hand reaching toward Meg, he slid laxly against the wall. "I think I took more'n you."

She looked at him. By the light from the garage he looked pale and gray, his eyes too bright and wide. *Bad*.

She hadn't seen him much since the day outside the Hallmark store. Funny thing, she'd always assumed she'd only ever gone out with him to annoy Hank, but when Zevo wasn't around, she missed him. Even after he'd banged her into the wall. Stupid and sick, she knew, but she'd read somewhere that even soldiers on leave occasionally missed the abuses and uncertainties of war. It was all in what you got used to; anything new was scary.

Kind of like her and adrenaline rushes and better the devil you understood instead of the angel you were afraid—for reasons you couldn't quite define—to trust.

Like Kate staying healthy and happy while she was pregnant, and Hank not leaving Megan to fend for herself because he had a new and easier child to raise. God knew, she was having a hard enough time holding onto herself.

"Meg?"

Next to her, Zevo slid along the wall, his hand fumbling at her breast. She slapped it lethargically away. She might have missed him, but she hadn't missed him that much.

"Meg."

His voice was a breath exhaled and lost on a syllable. His fingers groped for her once more. In something like slow motion, she turned her head a half a degree at a time, watched without comprehension while Zevo sagged unseeing toward her, skidded roughly down the brick and collapsed against her legs.

* * *

Unable to sleep, Kate flopped from one side of her bed to the other, restless in the heat. Flat as it still was, her abdomen felt tight and swollen—even her forgiving cotton underwear seemed confining tonight—and her breasts ached.

For and because of Hank.

A board creaked somewhere in the house and she jacked up on an elbow wondering if he was up. Everything made her think of him lately. Of course, everything had made her think of him fairly constantly for the past three months, so that was nothing new. It was the *way* she thought about him, of him, of late that was different.

She rested her chin on her folded hands and stared at the lightly billowing lace that lent an aura of privacy to her room. Moonlight spilled through the filigree with the scent of mown grass. She'd been taught from birth that people were to be loved, that love was the thing you gave with an open heart to anyone who crossed your path—and everyone who didn't—irrespective of how they treated you. She'd been taught, and learned to believe, that love could move mountains, change attitudes, devour hatred. That you didn't have to *like* a person in order to love them. That love was a simple willingness to accept people as they were, to treat them as you hoped to be treated. And in that way, she'd loved Hank easily from the beginning, even while she didn't like him and was hard put to accept the person she'd been told he was.

In spite of how she'd seen her parents together, her brother Mike and his wife, the thing she'd never really been taught was that love had degrees, could confuse and be tangled with emotions previously foreign to her.

She'd long understood, of course, how the fierce quality of protective love she felt toward her children, toward the infant growing inside her, differed from the unexpectant ''love'' she kept open for other people. But the way she felt about Hank...lost, insecure, anxious, greedy, aching, lusting, found, full—as if a bubble was expanding inside her chest, buoyant and tight to bursting all at once.

As if she needed to hear how he felt about her before she could spill her heart to him.

As if she shouldn't need to hear how he felt in words, should be able to read and accept it in the illustrations he left for her every day.

She pouched her lips into a self-derisive knot and rolled onto her back. He'd stunned her when he sat her and Tai down earlier this evening and asked if they couldn't use him full time around the farm. He'd been thinking about it for a while, he'd said, especially the past few weeks back at work, returning only to watch Megan getting further away not only from him but from all of them.

He needed, he'd said, to be around to keep better track of Megan until she didn't need him anymore. Told them that by returning to the bureaucracy at his level of law enforcement he'd rediscovered how much he hated it. Told them that he needed to make a change in his life, wanted to try another direction and that *here* was the direction he wanted to go.

He'd pointed out what he could do and where—between the llamas, the Christmas trees and the workshop—they could use him most effectively, reminded them how useful they'd found having him around over the summer. Offered to buy into the farm as a partner, take some of the weight off Tai. A new baby, he'd told them—mostly told Kate—would take up more time than any of the kids she'd raised so far, including Mike who hadn't been quite two when his parents died.

Life was risk, he'd told them, but there were some risks he'd lately learned were worth more than others. Stone House was one of them.

Tai, of course, had been willing to shake hands and make a deal then and there. He'd never made a secret of how much he liked Hank, but Kate hadn't realized before how heavily the weight of the farm sat on her son's shoulders, nor how much the burden had eased for him with Hank around.

It was difficult to accept—heck, it was nearly impossible to even *contemplate*—that after the many years she'd spent almost believing she knew it all, that she truly knew next to nothing. Knew nothing about Tai, nothing about Li and less than nothing about Megan.

Knew nothing about Hank, or even about herself.

He'd come to her to learn how to deal with his daughter, but Kate was the one who'd received the education.

That Hank would so willingly humble himself to come to her—and not only her, but Tai—in search of a job, a new life...she couldn't think. He floored her, flabbergasted and crushed. She'd decided he was one kind of man—terrific and sexy and great with the boys and all that rot—and here he showed her he was somebody else, too. What kind of a man was strong enough to come to a pigheaded woman and a kid half his age with his hat in hand and, in the same breath he asked for help, arrogantly describe why they needed him around, anyway? To change the direction of his life on a moment and a prayer.

A wry half smile tilted her mouth, chased the answer out of the cobwebs where it had hidden for more than a month and made her admit it. A man on whom it might be worthwhile risking the unexplored areas of her heart, that was who. A man who should be told how she felt about him, confusion or no, no matter what he did or didn't say to her aloud in return.

Whether they married or not. And in the past couple of weeks she'd come to find she wasn't nearly as opposed to the idea as she'd once been. Or else she was beginning to at least get used to the thought.

The desire for it.

She rolled onto her side and shut her eyes, pursuing rest

if not actual sleep. In the morning she would talk with Tai about accepting Hank's offer, then she would find the man in his room or at his office and make him one of her own.

"Kate?"

Her name and the light tap on the door brought her quickly around, heart pounding with anticipation. "Hank?" Speak of the devil.

Or was that speak of the would-be guardian of her angels?

"Yeah." He eased through the partially open doorway, careful not to nudge it to the creak.

She sat up and the sleeveless cotton shirt she wore to bed gapped open. "What's up?"

Hank let himself look once, then shut his eyes. The vision played inside his lids, disruptive and enticing: the disarray of her hair straggling out of the unruly bun atop her head; the soft glow of her skin and eyes in the peekaboo moonlight; the invitation in the hand she splayed open to indicate the bed beside her. God, what kind of woman mothered seven kids, got pregnant, turned down marriage but willingly, lovingly invited the father of her unborn child into her bed without conditions whenever he wanted to come?

Only Kate Anden, the keeper of his heart.

Not now, he cautioned himself. *Not yet. Someday...*

"You seen Meg?" he asked, hauling himself forcibly away from the brink of forgetting why he was here in favor of remembering how it felt to love Kate. To be with Kate.

"She's not in bed? I thought she had a past-curfew date she cleared with you, but I thought I heard her come in already."

"No. The note she left me made me assume she was spending the evening with Carly and Tai." The shortest route to hell, he'd learned long ago, was through assumptions. He'd allowed himself the shortcut, anyway. "She's not there, either."

Kate compressed her lips against the discouraged slump

in his voice, then twisted to find her clock. "What time is it?"

"Little after midnight. She should have been in an hour and a half ago."

She swung her feet out of bed. "Did you check with Li?"

Hank nodded. "Li thought Lynn came by to pick her up and she went into Brighton to pick up some stuff from the house. I called both Lynn and the neighbor who has a key to the back door. Whoever picked Meg up, it wasn't Lynn. She's not at the house, doesn't appear to have been there and nobody's seen her."

"Zevo?"

Shaking both with apprehension and her own weakness and unsteady heartbeat, Megan slid carefully down the wall to jiggle Zevo's shoulder.

"Hey, Zevo. You okay? You all right?"

The youth lay atop her legs, a dead, unmoving weight. She wasn't sure she could feel his breath.

"Oh, *sh*—Zevo!"

Feebly she tried pushing him off her, away, but the weakness was almost a kind of numbness now, affecting her hands. They seemed separate somehow, not part of her and she could hardly use them. In some part of her brain, it didn't seem to matter anyway. She almost wasn't part of her body anymore and, somehow, that didn't seem too bad a thing. If she couldn't feel, she couldn't get hurt again, the ache would be gone.

Off to one side the light was suddenly brilliant, blinding. A dark figure in what looked like a dress stood inside it. Megan relaxed.

"Mom?" she whispered, lifting leaden fingers toward the figure. "Mom?"

Restive and uncertain, Hank paced the kitchen while Kate puttered about for something calming to do, finally settling on folding laundry at the kitchen table.

The silence went long until at last Hank slammed the flat of his hand into the wall in frustration.

"I hate this," he exploded. "Where the hell is she? Why the hell can't I do something?"

"What could you do?" Kate asked quietly.

"I don't know. Look for her. Find her. Wake people up until I know where she is and if she's all right."

"Run around like a chicken with your head cut off," Kate supplied seriously. "Tie up the phone so she can't get through if she's in trouble and remembers to call—"

The phone rang. Arrested by coincidence on the far side of the kitchen, Hank swallowed and looked at the instrument. Automatically noting the name Frank Gillespie on the caller ID display, Kate picked it up.

"Megan?"

"Mom?" a teenage male voice said.

Kate shook her head at Hank, who closed his eyes on displaced hope and did not relax.

"Who is this?" she asked, instinct causing her to mentally count heads upstairs despite the fact that she didn't recognize the voice and could come up with a full in-house complement to boot.

The voice on the phone said something in gibberish.

"Who?" Kate asked again. Something in the youth's cranked-up tone put her on reflexive parental alert. She pointed at Hank, at the caller ID display, jerked a finger to tell him to come check it out. He came immediately and without question.

"Brandon," the voice managed.

She yanked the phone book out of the phone-table drawer and handed it forcibly to Hank, once again indicating the ID display, then the phone book. "Brandon who?"

More gibberish cluttered by party noises in the background, then *"Mom, I've smoked too much crack and I don't think I can do this life anymore."*

A wrong-number suicide call? Damn, damn, damn! *Keep him on the phone,* she told herself. *Keep him talking.*

"Brandon, where are you?"

More gibberish followed by a sobbing giggle, then the click of a broken connection. Breathing hard and swearing in a manner she normally didn't employ, Kate replaced the receiver and whirled on Hank.

"Did you get it?"

He nodded. "It's an address in Brighton. What's up?"

"Suicide call from a party," Kate said and grabbed the phone as it rang again. The same caller name crossed the display. "Brandon?"

There was the sound of the party, an instant of babble and another click. Replacing the receiver once more, Kate shoved a hand through her hair and covered her mouth.

"Think," she muttered to herself, "What do I do? Call the police."

She reached for the phone. Hank stopped her.

"Tell me first," he suggested calmly. He hated being at loose ends, but a crisis he could handle.

Kate looked at him, took a deep, tranquilizing breath and repeated the call verbatim.

"Okay." Hank considered the situation for half an instant. "Call the number back. If you can get through ask for Brandon. If not, call the police." He pulled his car keys out of his pants pocket. "I don't know the people, but the address is in the neighborhood adjacent to mine and I can get from here to there as fast as the police or paramedics can."

"What about Meg?"

Hank blew out his cheeks on a breath. "I dunno, Kate, but this is something I can do. I can see about somebody else's kid and after that, since it's a party not far from the house, chances are it's got friends of Meg's at it. Maybe they can help me find her. Hell, maybe she's there. I've got the cell phone in the car, you can call me if anything comes up here.''

''Hank—''

He shushed her with a quick brush of his lips across hers. ''I'm sorry, Kate, I can't just sit, I have to act. I'll be back.''

Then he was gone.

Eyes narrowed, Kate stared at the seemingly almost vibrating space he'd vacated and wondered if this was the reason history had titled some women as ladies-in-waiting.

Kate called back the Gillespie phone number. The line was busy or the phone was off the hook, so she called the police, explained the phone call she'd received, her concerns, told them Hank was on his way and gave them the address. Then she waited.

She sat. She stood. She finished folding clothes and scrounged together a load of dark clothes for the washer—not difficult in a household their size.

She tried to read, but it was a ridiculous waste of effort because she couldn't concentrate.

She pinched her chin and tapped ragged fingernails against her teeth, squinted down her nose at them and went to get a file and Li's creams and gave herself a manicure. It wasn't a very good one, given she wasn't used to paying that kind of attention to herself, but the effort was both frustrating and mildly distracting.

She dusted the living room and moved the load of laundry from the washer to the dryer.

She got out the heavy rosary her mother had given her the day she'd taken her vows and entered the convent, and she prayed. She'd gotten as far as the fourth Sorrowful Mystery when the phone rang. Hank.

''I'm at McPherson emergency,'' he said hoarsely and without preamble, naming the local hospital. ''Come.''

Her jaw tightened, but she kept the fear and the questions out of her voice. "On my way," she told him.

Then she called the guest cottage and woke Tai, got Li up to come downstairs nearer the phone until Tai could get to the house, crumpled the unfinished rosary in her hand to finish in the car and went.

It didn't even occur to her to realize that he trusted her enough to call her to him with a single word, without wondering if she would.

He sat in a waiting-room chair looking tense and haggard, older than his years, defeated. He didn't even look up when Kate approached and perched on the edge of the chair beside him, slid warm fingers into the crook of his near hand.

"Is it Megan?" she asked.

He nodded, eyes blind on some spot in the near distance only he could pinpoint. "She was at a different party a couple streets behind ours with that kid she dates sometimes—Zevo. Call came in right after the police broke up the party at the Gillespies'. Brandon was in the owner's study fiddling with a gun. He's okay, wired to beat the band, but alive. They called his parents and took him upstairs to psych for observation. Zevo's dead. Meg was collapsed next to him. They don't know what she took, but they found a bag of pot and a couple vials of crack on her, no used equipment. Her heart's not working right. They're getting ready to transfer her up to cardiac intensive care. They think she'll be okay, but it's still iffy. If she pulls through, she's looking at charges of possession and drinking under the teen zero-tolerance law."

His mouth trembled; he stiffened his jaw and canted his head to Kate. "I saw her, Kate. They've got her on oxygen and she's hardly with it, but she opened her eyes and took one look at me and said, 'You're not Mom. God, I'm still alive, aren't I?'" His mouth twisted and stretched tight, his eyes filled, shiny with tears he refused to shed; his fingers closed painfully around Kate's. "I don't want to lose her, Kate, but I don't know how to keep her alive if she doesn't want to be."

There was nothing she could say to make it better, to make it go away, so she said nothing, simply touched his chest to let him know she was there to hold onto if he needed an anchor in the storm and sat with him and waited through a parent's worst nightmare.

September 19—4:22 a.m.
CICU waiting room

"Mr. and Mrs. Mathison?"

Hank turned at the sound of the male nurse's voice without noticing the assumption of Kate's identity. She opened her mouth to correct the mistake, then closed it again. In the face of other things, who she was or wasn't hardly seemed important.

"How is she?" Hank asked.

"Stable." The nurse shrugged. "Comfortable. She's sedated right now, but you can sit with her for a while if you want." He turned at the squeak of rubber-soled shoes behind him, nodded toward the tiny Malaysian woman in pink scrubs who approached. "Doctor Yanga would like a word with you first. Dr. Yanga." He motioned at Hank and Kate. "These are Megan's parents."

The intern on night call acknowledged them with a look, indicated with a question-mark face and a flick of her eyes that she'd like to collect a cup of coffee before joining them. Eyes glued to her, Hank swallowed and shrugged. Couldn't be too bad if the physician thought there was time for coffee before speaking to him, could it?

Either that or else this was going to take some time and Dr. Yanga was fortifying herself for the ordeal.

Kate touched his shoulder, her voice low, "Do you want me to go?"

He folded a hand tightly around hers, moved his head a fraction of an inch to the negative. "No. Stay, please. I need you here."

Dr. Yanga finished filling a disposable cup, then crossed to perch on the edge of the coffee table in front of them. "I think your daughter will be okay." Her voice was thin and heavily accented, difficult to understand. "We'll keep her for observation two or three days to be sure." She paused, consulted the chart in her hand. "She has some alcohol in her system, but the main problem is the *ma huang*. You know it?"

Hank eyed Kate askance, shook his head. It wasn't a substance on his drug-war lists—at least not by that name.

The doctor nodded as though the answer was to be expected. "We see it sometimes lately, not so much, but more often than before. It is a Chinese herb also called ephedra, used to make the ephedrine that goes into asthma inhalers. It's not illegal, but very dangerous for many people if it is not carefully used. It made your daughter's heart go like so—" She fluttered her fingers to illustrate an irregular pattern. "Too fast, then too slow, no rhythm. Also the blood pressure goes too high. That is what happened to your daughter. The other boy died from it, but he took more. She took too much, she almost died, but help came in time. Very fortunate. You have questions?"

"Where did she get the *ma huang?*" Kate asked.

Dr. Yanga shrugged. "Hard to say. Could be..." She struggled for the word. "New Age head shop, I think it is called. Come in packages like so..." She formed her thumbs and forefingers into a triangle. "...maybe ten to twelve pills in a box. There's no regulation, so it's hard to say if all pills are made exactly the same. Shops can claim they're all natural, give energy, but nobody knows how much *ma huang* is in each pill."

"But she'll be all right?" Hank pressed. In his experience

"stable" could mean anything and intensive care units of any sort were not kind to the emotions.

"Maybe so," the intern agreed. She waved a hand toward the door. "You can see."

Without letting go of Kate, Hank rose, pulled her up, and followed the doctor to Megan's bed.

Chapter 17

By the second day, Megan was pretty much her old self
once more: surly, uncommunicative, full of At-Ti-Tude...
and self-satisfied.

Although initially frightened by her experience, she
seemed to view both her father's and Kate's concern for her
with smugness and indifference—a combination of "gee,
look how fast I made you jump" and "boy, I can do anything and you'll pick me up and I won't have to pay for
it." The latter attitude was particularly prevalent when the
local law extended Hank the professional courtesy of not
arresting Megan on the spot, accepted his guarantee that she
would turn herself in as soon as she was released from the
hospital.

Her demeanor did not sit well with Hank.

Even when he told her about Zevo, tried to impress on
her how lucky she'd been, her only visible emotion was in
the muscle that jumped along her jaw and a bored, stony
stare.

As a DEA agent, his entire adult life had been spent attempting to correct a balance between the terrible choices people made and controlling the availability of illicit substances that too often turned choice and experimentation into addiction. He'd long believed in imposing certain restrictions and responsibilities on choice, in safeguarding those stipulations with his life if need be. He was having a difficult enough time accepting that for the most part there was likely nothing he could have done to prevent Megan from choosing to be where she was right now. It was devastating that she chose to defy him by flaunting his work and beliefs the way she'd done. That she needed and wanted to escape her life—or enhance it or a hundred other words and justifications he couldn't understand—so badly she'd been willing to risk her life to do it.

That despite the fact she'd been caught "holding" and had any alcohol at all in her underage system, the thing that had almost killed her was a herb he'd never heard of and whose sale to minors or anybody else he couldn't regulate.

When he'd looked at her attached to heart monitors and tubes, saw Zevo's body, all he wanted to do was pick Megan up and hold her tight, bring her home, yell at her and lock her in her room until she was thirty. Mostly he wanted her to tell him, to make him understand, what the *hell* she could possibly have been thinking when she swallowed the *ma huang* with its liquor wash-me-down?

Kate, too, was disturbed by what she saw in Hank's daughter, but instead of bewildering her, all Megan's attitude did was grind—and cause her to narrow her eyes, pull Hank aside and suggest he say thanks, but no thanks to the local law's offered professional courtesy. She also suggested he talk to the would-be arresting officers, cop parent to cop, about posting a showy guard outside her hospital door— Megan had, in the past, posed some flight risk after all— and letting them cuff her and take her into custody on her release.

A night or two in jail or juvenile detention might, she

pointed out, stopping Hank before he could protest, prove to be just what the doctor ordered. Because, while this might be the worst time—so far—that Megan had figured Hank would rescue her from the consequences of her irresponsibility, it wasn't the first. And if he continued to rescue and protect his daughter, it undoubtedly wouldn't be the last time.

"I mean, for pity's sake, Hank," she said, pounding the point home, "think about it. Meg nearly died this time. The guy standing next to her did. Maybe it's time you draw the line, toss out a little tough love and find out if she's really as tough and as far gone as she acts. Worst case, you find out you really got your work cut out for you. Best case..." She offered him a one-shoulder shrug. "Maybe you find she's really just a scared kid looking for some kind of attention she doesn't know how to ask for and you don't know she needs."

"Butt out, Kate," he told her tersely, angrily, not for the first time. She might be right, but now was not the moment he could bring himself to step back, take a breath and separate his love for his daughter from his need to hover and protect her by lashing back at Kate. "Back off. You've interfered enough. What the hell do you know about tough love? If you hadn't always let Meg run to you and stay, instead of sending her back to me when she was younger, maybe we could have sorted out what's ailing us a long time ago and this wouldn't've happened."

He stooped, nose to nose with her, fighting himself and her, warring with his heart. "You're so damned certain you know it all where kids are concerned, but, lady, maybe all you've been is lucky. And whatever you know, it sure as hell didn't do you any good with Risto and it hasn't made much difference with Megan lately."

Kate stepped back, stung by the verbal slap. He'd asked for her help, all she'd done was try to give it to him. Saint Kate, at your service. Right?

Oh, yeah, sure. She blew herself a mental raspberry. *Get off your high horse, martyr.*

On the other hand, he was also right. She never had done much to discourage Megan from running away to Stone House, the same way she'd never done much to discourage the other teens who straggled into and out of her life over the years. She was, as her mother had often tried to tell her, a big-time buttinsky. Maybe, as that woman had frequently attempted to suggest, the better part of valor in some situations was to back off, not bulldoze forward, to step aside so someone else could pass.

To not assume she was the only one who could right a problem simply because she was good at it.

There was no real way to do it gracefully, to say it without appearing piqued, but she had to say it, "I'm sorry, Hank. You're right. I do overstep. She's your daughter. You have to deal with this from the inside, and all I have to do is peek in your window and think I know it all, tell you this is what I see. I don't have to live with the decision like you will."

He eyed her incredulously. For reasons he knew exactly how to define, her apology incensed him more than any self-righteous preaching she'd ever done. "Stuff it, Kate," he told her flatly and stalked out.

The hospital hallway seemed too bright and artificial, too confined for the collection of emotions spreading roots and trailing vines through his chest. He pushed his hands through his hair, tried to suck air too deeply into constricting lungs. Had to pinch the bridge of his nose, shut his eyes and concentrate before the sentient overflow got away from him. It was too much all at once, that was it. Megan, a baby, a family, a woman he wanted, needed, almost more than he needed his soul…and Megan wanted to do without him, and the baby and the family had Kate who'd proven over and over through the years that she was capable of doing whatever she set her mind to, whether it was raising children or maintaining her flourishing farm and businesses, without a man to help her.

Without him.

And he needed them all, loved them all—the children equally with each other and Kate...Oh, God, and Kate! He loved Kate more than anything. More than anyone.

More, period.

Everyday, all the parts of her, the impossible and the saintly, the opinionated and the imperfect. Her luscious body and lavish mind and generous heart. Kate. Damn her, she *would* have to live with whatever he decided to do about Megan. The child they shared between them was part of Megan, too, a flesh-and-blood sibling. No way they could change that, no way he wanted to. And that meant Kate would share Megan's life, share *his,* damn it, whether she put her name beside his on a marriage license or not.

His name on the baby's birth certificate wasn't what would make him its father, only his presence in its life would do that. Same way only Kate's presence could make her its mother.

Rationally he knew that her not being around for Megan after Gen died probably wouldn't have made things better but worse. He knew her kids weren't perfect, that she'd made her mistakes with them, but their...learning experiences...had simply, thankfully, taken place on the right side of the law, and had been less dangerous than Megan's blunders and explorations. But rationalization had nothing to do with how he felt at the moment. Passion, fierce and undeniable, was the word most aptly suited to the here and now, encompassed all the other emotions: anger, futility, desire, love. But passion like this was not the way to approach either Megan or Kate.

Or was it?

He stopped short in the hall, staring blindly ahead, causing an EKG tech to swerve abruptly to avoid running her cart into his heel. Losing his head to passion could mean death both literally and figuratively on the DEA playing fields, but he was not working either undercover or behind a desk for the DEA here. Could attaining the future he sought truly be as simple as a word he could illustrate with toughness or a lifetime of care after he said it?

Maybe not always, but in this one instance...he'd tried everything else, entrusting Kate and Megan with not only his silent heart but the word *love* as well...

If it backfired on him, he was pretty certain he was the only one who could be hurt.

With Kate beside him, Hank called the police from the pay phone in the waiting room. When they arrived he did the hardest thing he'd ever done in his life: walked into Megan's room and told her he loved her, that she owned his heart, but that he had no idea how to impress upon her the things she needed to know to survive the course she'd set for herself. Then he stepped back out of the way and stood by while the police read Megan her rights and officially took her into custody.

He could have requested privilege, to stay with her, but when the officers told him to go since Megan was now out of danger, he went.

Megan's eyes shot daggers in his direction, and were looks deadly, he'd have been on the floor, no question. He felt as if he was down there, dying anyway, but though comfort was elusive, he hoped one day to be able to find it in today's act. She had to find her own way through this experience; he couldn't shield her from the repercussions of every choice she made for the rest of her life, had to let her go—a thing much easier to do in theory than in practice. Had to let her separate herself from him if she must, but expect her to take adult responsibility for her adult mistakes.

Had to let her go through the system unless and until, he'd decided, she agreed to go into a halfway house for runaways and make a real effort to help herself by accepting and participating in counseling and therapy both on her own and with him.

And Kate.

Because married or not, Hank told his daughter, Kate was in their lives, a part of them—a part of *him*—with or without Megan's approval.

Heart in her throat, Kate studied him while he said it, when he turned to hold her gaze and wordlessly hand himself into her keeping. Her throat burned and stung with emotion it was the wrong time to voice. But she held onto him, his hand, his arm, tucked herself under his shoulder and hugged his waist one armed when he led her out of Megan's room.

Outraged, Megan screamed defiant epithets after them, demanding Hank's return—then, when he didn't, shouting that he was just like Gen, that he hated her the way he must have hated her mother because he was always leaving them, that he was deserting her the same as always.

That he was killing her the same way he'd killed Gen, by not being around when he was needed.

He stiffened at that but didn't stop, shutting Megan's hospital door behind him.

Staring wide-eyed at the solid wood panel, Megan felt her first flicker of fear. He really wasn't going to make what she'd done okay, wasn't going to stop. She'd gone too far this time and he didn't care, wouldn't let her punch his buttons anymore.

She was on her own.

"You all right?" Kate asked, a short time later when he put her in the van and told her to go home. He planned to stay at the hospital until Megan was released, then follow her through booking. She might not see it as much—certainly not what she thought she wanted from him—but it was what he could do.

For what that was worth.

"No." He shook his head. "But I'll survive."

"Hank..." She hesitated, lifted gentle fingers to his face, smoothed them over the stubble along his jaw. "I didn't mean—"

"No." He shushed her with his mouth on hers in a heartfelt but undemanding kiss that accepted as it gave. "Not now. If it's important, you can tell me later. I've got things to tell you, too."

She cupped his chin, brushed her lips along his jaw. Not to stimulate, but to love. "I could stay with you."

He shook his head and eased her hands away, then stepped back. "No. We've got more kids than Megan who need some attention and I have to do this one by myself."

"Okay." She reached up to kiss him once more. "But if you want me—"

"I'll call," he assured her.

Kate believed him.

It didn't occur to her until she was pulling into the driveway at home that Hank had used the *we,* claiming her kids at the same time that he accepted her suggestion on how to handle Megan.

A slow, wry smile curved her mouth. On the other side of darkness and indecision lay light.

It was easily one of the longest nights of his life.

He prowled the hospital corridors never far from Megan's door, exchanging nods with the cop on guard there as if she was some big-time criminal posing a flight risk. But then, that was what he'd asked for, all the show they could give him.

Give her.

She looked scared—still mouthy and defiant, but with fear setting in—when she was released in the morning, wheeled out of the hospital, handcuffed and put in the back of the squad car for transport. Dry mouthed, Hank watched her with his hands fisted tight at the bottom of his pockets to prevent himself from trying to take her away from the police. This was for her own good, he reminded himself, a drastic response to Megan's drastic behavior.

No justification made the vision of his daughter in handcuffs easier to bear.

He followed the squad car to the station, requested courtesy and walked through Megan's booking with her—fingerprints, photos, questioning, the works. She lifted her chin and kept her eyes on him the entire time, accusing and somehow amused, as though she'd decided that the show was boring, she knew he'd never leave her to spend any kind of time locked up. And the truth was he'd hoped he wouldn't have to. But he was wrong.

So was she.

She spent the long weekend waiting for her Monday-morning arraignment in juvie. He spent the weekend in hell.

He asked to see her Saturday morning. She refused to see him. By Saturday evening she agreed to the visit, then cursed him roundly when he wouldn't agree to spring her. Cursing didn't work, so she tried tears. The tears nearly undid him, but he swallowed the ache in his chest and stood firm. After the tears her mercurial emotions went from sly, to derisive, to abusively hateful, to one of her unnerving rages. He steeled himself, moved table and chairs in the interview room out of her way so she couldn't hurt herself, requested a counselor but flashed his badge and refused to let any of the detention staff into the room or to remove the hysterical Megan from his company.

When she'd played herself out enough to be coherent, she accused Hank of a multitude of things, including attempting to kill Kate by getting her pregnant the same way he'd killed Gen.

It was at that point he lost it.

In front of the youth psychologist who'd sat through the end of her rage with him, Hank hauled Megan bodily into a chair and made her stay there while he told her he'd had more than enough, that it was about damn time she got what had really happened to Gen through her head.

Then while Megan tried hard not to listen, he told her.

Then he left.

He didn't see her at all on Sunday.

On Monday morning, a much quieter and more reasonable Megan asked to see him with the psychologist before her court appearance.

Although moderately repentant, she offered no apologies for what had gone before and Hank expected none—offered none of his own. Locked up with no place to escape herself or her thoughts, she'd been forced to confront five years' worth of feelings she'd been avoiding. About her mother, her father, herself. Found herself recognizing the misinterpretations she'd long put on some of the things Gen had once said to her, understood the justifications she'd made for her mother to live with some of Gen's more bizarre behaviors—behaviors Hank had rarely if ever witnessed.

With no one but herself to verbally abuse, she'd remained in the interview room with the psychologist long after Hank had gone, cycling through the stages of grief, crying and disbelieving at first, then denying, then angry again. She'd gone from anger to a bargaining of the if-you'll-just-let-me-go-I'll-be-good-from-now-on type. Acceptance was harder to come by. She was sixteen years old and acceptance wasn't yet part of her make-up—was, in fact, genetically lacking in her personality. Gen had never accepted less than what she wanted out of life and Hank himself was not good at accepting what he didn't like. Megan did, however, accept and recognize her own need to do things differently, to change her negative point of view—to undergo not only counseling but therapy to help make herself whole.

There were no guarantees, but Hank sat and listened to her, watched the psychologist nod and felt the roots of hope wedge open a closed place inside him.

Megan also asked for alternatives to juvenile detention—
no matter how tough.

So, instead of winding up in the courtroom, they wound
up in judge's chambers. The judge, a father with teenage
daughters of his own, reviewed the case and Megan's history, the psychologist's suggestions, spoke briefly with
Hank alone, talked individually with Megan, then called everybody back in and suggested a stiffer solution than he was
inclined toward: one month in a halfway house for troubled
teens, two years of court-monitored probation, the loss of
Megan's driver's license until she was eighteen and individual, family and group therapy.

Face pale and knuckles white with the strain of physically
holding onto her nerves, Megan gulped, glanced once at
Hank beside her and nodded agreement. The attorneys accepted the bargain and the sentence was set to begin immediately. Megan was released to her father's temporary
custody and admonished to report to the halfway house by
the end of the school day with a small bag and all the
schoolwork she'd missed over the past week.

Kate and company—from Tai and Carly to Bele, Mike
and the dog—met Megan and Hank outside in the courthouse gardens. Megan reddened, embarrassed, when she
saw them, ready to flee but for Hank's arm about her shoulder. Still, when Mike, Bele and Taz launched themselves at
her, she hesitated only a moment before stooping to hug
them tightly.

"We were worried about you," Bele said, disengaging
himself from her stranglehold.

"Yeah," Mike agreed. "We didn't want you to die from
doing something stupid."

"Especially not until we could tell you Harvey got a baby
on Annabeth and Mum says if it's built right we can train
for a marathon llama like those ones that run in the llama-
thons, but we have to ask you first cuz you trained Harvey
to run with you and know how to do it."

The middle boys were more awkward but nearly as welcoming.

Grisha—bless his tactlessly curious mind—skipped the welcome and went straight to the questions, wanting to know what being arrested in America was like.

Li was standoffish, worried about Megan and afraid to trust her.

Tai uncustomarily held his tongue instead of saying what he thought of what Megan had put his mother and her father through.

Carly gave Megan a quick hug and told her to pay no attention to what Tai was thinking.

Kate smiled a welcome but stood back, letting Megan make the first move. The teen hesitated a moment, glancing at the younger kids then at Li, Carly and Tai. Carly got the message first.

"Come on, guys," she urged. "Meg needs to talk to Ma. Let's go exercise the dog."

When they were gone, Megan moistened her mouth and looked at Kate. "I need to apologize for what I did and the way I behaved," she said tentatively. Looking as if she hoped somehow Kate would disagree.

Kate didn't. In fact, all she did was regard Megan steadily and wait.

Megan licked her lips again, compressed them, gathering courage. "The judge said I have to do a bunch of things like go to a halfway house and lose my license till I'm eighteen and have therapy." She glanced at Hank. Swallowed. "Some of it's family therapy, and I was just wondering—" Another uncomfortable peek at her father. "I don't like the way things—" She shook her head, impatient with the half truth. "I don't like the way *I've* been lately and I know you don't have much reason to want me around anymore but I...I was wondering if you could maybe come to some of the family stuff with me an-and D-dad because you've kind of been part of my family for a long time and

now you're having my little brother or sister and maybe…
maybe…'' Suddenly she pleaded, ''I mean it couldn't hurt,
could it?''

Stunned by the request, Kate studied Megan for a moment
before raising a questioning brow at Hank. He blew out a
breath of his own surprise, gave her a barely perceptible
nod. In his bed or out, she'd be a part of him and Megan
one way or the other.

And more importantly, they'd be part of her and hers.

Reading more in Hank's face than she was prepared to
see at the moment, Kate slid her gaze quickly back to Megan. ''Sure,'' she agreed. Breathlessly. Smiling. Not quite
comfortable, but more willing than she'd expected to be.
''Just let me know when.''

She was waiting on the front porch for Hank when he
returned from taking Megan to the halfway house.

They hadn't had a chance to say more than a few words
to each other in days—and those words had been within
range of radar-eared children, so even then they hadn't said
much. She came to greet him when he tiredly mounted the
steps, slipping her arms around his waist in a full-body hug.
Her tummy felt snug and full against his belly, and she had,
he could feel, undone the top button of her pants under her
T-shirt to accommodate the baby.

He stroked a hand through her loose hair, set her away
from him and splayed the other across her abdomen. ''Getting big already, is he?''

Kate shrugged. ''I've gained five pounds in the past
month. She must be.''

He bent and kissed her. ''He, she, the only thing I care
is that it's healthy and has your eyes and hair.''

''And your mouth,'' Kate added, tracing a pinky around
his.

''And an easier time getting through adolescence than

Meg,'' Hank said softly. He kissed her little finger. ''But you'll be there from the start, so it probably will.''

Kate stroked his face. ''So will you.''

''I'm not sure my presence'll be as necessary as yours.''

She pulled back, viewing him with surprise. ''Doubts, Hank? That's not like you.''

He shook his head and grinned wryly. ''Not doubts, self-pity more likely. I just put my only daughter in a halfway home, you know. You've never had to do that with any of yours.''

''Strictly prayer and luck,'' Kate assured him, half laughing. ''That and twenty-four hours a day spent in their shadows will get you a lot.''

''Like an abbreviated vocabulary and a nervous breakdown?''

She grinned. ''Exactly.''

For a moment they shared silence, then turned as one and moved to sit together on the swing.

''How was the house?'' Kate asked.

''Oh, you know.'' Hank shrugged. ''Noisy. Chaotic. Lots of kids, but it seems to be pretty well run. Good house parents, psychiatrist in residence, strict rules—it's not here but what is? I think—I hope—it'll do her some good until they let me bring her home.''

Kate nodded, then rested her head in the hollow of Hank's shoulder. She shoved a foot against the porch floor to rock the swing. ''Speaking of home…'' she said tentatively.

He shifted to rest his head on hers. ''Were we?''

''If we weren't, we're about to.'' She pushed herself up on his chest, close to his face. ''Hank, if I said *yes* would you remember the question?''

He stared at her uncomprehending for a moment, then with gradually dawning hope. ''Kate…are you saying yes?''

''I think so.''

''God, lady, you'd better know, because this isn't going to be easy. Meg's started to come around, but they warn you about backsliding and you and the kids might be better off if you could just walk away, no attachments—"

"Too late," she said softly.

"What's too late?"

"The no-attachments part. I'm already attached to you and so are the kids."

"It'll be rough," he warned, doing his best to talk her out of it, praying he wouldn't succeed.

Kate laughed. "*Rough* was never in question, Hank. Good grief, we've got eight kids between us at the moment and one on the way and by definition that's not easy, but you know, a united front, an us-against-them has a certain appeal. Not to mention…" She looked down at the buttons on his shirt. "I love you and I love Megan. Mostly I love you."

"You do." Not a question.

"Yeah." She nodded. "And I think I said no before because I was half worried about not hearing the words from you—which was stupid, when I thought about it, because everything you do, you do with love and, really, words like *I love you* and *I'm sorry* don't mean anything without the feeling behind them and—"

Hank cupped her head in a hand and bent toward her. "Shut up, Kate," he said thickly and kissed her.

Long and hard and again. Then he said what had been on his mind for quite some time. Hotly. Against her mouth. "I love you, lady, now and for the rest of my life. Tell me again that you'll marry me."

She did.

Postlude

The bathtub drain was clogged again and he was standing in water to his ankles.

Sighing, Hank shut off the shower's sibilant spray, bent and unscrewed the drain, reached into the well and pulled out clumps of long sunset-colored hair. His wife had forgotten to empty the drain again.

"Kate!"

"In here, Hank."

Annoyed, Hank wrapped a towel about his hips and padded, dripping, into the sitting-room-cum-nursery he'd added onto their bedroom just after their daughter was born. October dusk crowded the nursery, carried him back the long hard year it had taken to get them here.

They'd married last All Hallows' Eve while Megan had been in the midst of a major backslide. But it had been that backslide and the psychiatrist who'd been able to observe her at the halfway house that had pinpointed the root of Megan's violent mood swings: a big-time chemical imbalance called manic-depression.

A daily dose of lithium and a lot of family and individual therapy had helped tremendously. All was not perfect, but it was a damn sight closer than Hank had ever expected.

Of the other kids…

Tai and Carly were blissfully, happily married and still living in the guesthouse. Tai in fact had taken out a few trees to make room for the sizable addition they'd need when their triplets were born next February. He and Carly had been more than a little stunned to learn about the multiple babies, but were now taking it in stride—and simply planning in threes. Excited aunts, Li and Megan, had already volunteered for nanny duty, while uncles Mike and Bele had once again reiterated their refusal to mess with poopy diapers or boy babies until they were potty trained.

Always brighter than her peers, Li was graduating from high school a year early and looking at a full ride to Chicago's Northwestern University, courtesy of their music department.

Megan was both envious of and ecstatic for her. Her own high-school career was a bit more up again, down again, but after a session of summer school she was caught up and passing her junior classes.

Grisha had won a scholarship to a private high school that specialized in science and went around with his head in the clouds and his feet catching in every rut and raised up bit of carpeting he passed.

Ilya was happy with life and doing well, which was everything that could be wished and more.

Sadly, Jamal was once more back with them—permanently this time. He was a joy in their lives, but they had all hoped that the last time his mother had gone for help to beat her crack habit she'd had it licked. Unfortunately the crack had other ideas. She lived day to day now in a group home, her mind gone. Jamal visited her often, but it was hard on the fourteen-year-old. Sometimes she knew him, but usually she didn't. He went anyway—and almost always Ilya and some of the other kids went with him.

No matter what you did, there was always something, wasn't there?

Reflecting, Hank pitched the hunk of hair into the basket and looked once more at his wife. Kate stroked a finger down Halla's arm, looked up at him and smiled. The infant's name meant "unexpected gift" and she certainly was. Annoyance fled. Hank touched the baby's cheek where she suckled at her mother's breast. Even after six months he couldn't get over how beautiful she was.

She was also a handful, her personality developing by the day. As though to illustrate precisely how much individuality she'd gained today, she grinned slyly up at her father, letting milk dribble out the corner of her mouth while she pretended to consider being finished with her meal. Hank made a move to take her from Kate and the baby laughed at him, then latched firmly onto her mother's breast once more. The game lasted a couple more rounds until Kate, not Halla, decided she was done playing it and hoisted the silly infant to her shoulder for a burp. Halla noisily obliged, then promptly fell asleep before Kate could get the spit diaper out from under the baby's chin. She sighed and rolled her eyes when some of the baby spit dripped off the diaper before it could be absorbed and onto her nightshirt.

Hank chuckled and felt his hair-in-the-drain irritation fade, suitably avenged by the shortest member of the family. He lifted the plump infant into his arms and cradled her a moment before placing her on her stomach in the crib. He couldn't say marriage with Kate was the most *convenient* thing he'd ever done, but living without her had definitely been *in*convenient. And living with her did have its advantages.

Like the one displayed before him now.

Breast exposed, Kate scrubbed at her shirt. "Remind me to order rubber clothes the next time we have a baby," she said, exasperated.

"*Are* we having another baby?" he asked, mightily interested.

Kate glared at him. "Bite your tongue." She thought about it for a moment. "Although, I don't think I'd mind in, oh, say a year?"

Hank leered at her, eyes lingering on her milk-plush breasts. "I think that could be arranged."

Kate saw where he was looking and huffed at him in mock indignation, covering up. He squatted next to her and drew the shirt away from her breasts.

"Don't hide," he said softly. "I like looking at you."

"I know," she agreed, running her fingers lightly down his chest to find the towel's tuck. She flicked the terry cloth aside. "You like the body very much."

"Oh, and you don't?"

"Well," Kate hedged. "I like your mind, too." She glanced up at him and grinned. "Well, no, I take that back. Actually I love your mind—and everything else—but your mind…is just as devious as mine."

He grinned back at her. "I'll take that as a compliment since that's exactly what I like best about yours, my love." He leaned in toward her, forcing her backward in her chair. "Yes, indeed, no doubt about it. Your mind and what you do with it to make me crazy in the middle of the night is definitely one of my favorite things."

"Flatterer," she whispered. Then he slid a palm up her thigh, took her mouth and stole her breath and she said nothing at all.

And for the foreseeable future, that was exactly what they both wanted.

Because after all, happily ever after was merely a matter of moments and expressions, more than the words at the end of a fairy tale. It was the unconditional love that allowed two people to create a family and to weave the joys and sorrows, the angers and fears into fabric to last a lifetime.

* * * * *

Beloved author
JOAN ELLIOTT PICKART
introduces the next generation of MacAllisters in

The Baby Bet:
MACALLISTER'S GIFTS

with the following heartwarming romances:

On sale July 2002

THE ROYAL MACALLISTER
Silhouette Special Edition #1477
As the MacAllisters prepare for a royal wedding,
Alice "Trip" MacAllister meets her own Prince Charming.

On sale September 2002

PLAIN JANE MACALLISTER
Silhouette Desire #1462
A secret child stirs up trouble—and long-buried
passions—for Emily MacAllister when she is reunited
with her son's father, Dr. Mark Maxwell.

And look for the next exciting installment of
the MacAllister family saga, coming only to
Silhouette Special Edition in December 2002.

*Don't miss these unforgettable romances...
available at your favorite retail outlet.*

Where love comes alive™

Silhouette Books is proud to present:

Going to the Chapel

**Three brand-new stories
about getting that special man to the altar!**

featuring

USA Today bestselling author

SHARON SALA

It Happened One Night...that Georgia society belle
Harley June Beaumont went to Vegas—and woke up married!
How could she explain her hunk of a husband to
her family back home?

Award-winning author

DIXIE BROWNING

Marrying a Millionaire...was exactly what Grace McCall was
trying to keep her baby sister from doing. Not that Grace had
anything against the groom—it was the groom's arrogant
millionaire uncle who got Grace all hot and bothered!

National bestselling author

STELLA BAGWELL

The Bride's Big Adventure...was escaping her handpicked
fiancé in the arms of a hot-blooded cowboy! And from the
moment Gloria Rhodes said "I do" to her rugged groom, she
dreamed their wedded bliss would never end!

Available in July at your favorite retail outlets!

Silhouette®

Where love comes alive™

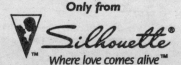

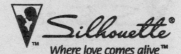